I0745595

The Justicar Jhee Mysteries

-Anchor Trilogy-

by Trevol Swift

THE JUSTICAR JHEE MYSTERIES: ANCHOR TRILOGY Copyright © 2020 by Trevol Swift. All Rights Reserved.

All rights reserved. No part of this book may be reproduced in any form or by any electronic or mechanical means including information storage and retrieval systems, without permission in writing from the author. The only exception is by a reviewer, who may quote short excerpts in a review.

Cover designed by 100Covers.com
Edited by Matt Turano and Trevol Swift

This book is a work of fiction. Names, characters, places, and incidents either are products of the author's imagination or are used fictitiously. Any resemblance to actual persons, living or dead, events, or locales is entirely coincidental.

Trevol Swift
Visit my website at swiftnesse.com

First Printing: May 2020

JOIN THE SWIFTNESSE COMMUNITY

~

Join the Swiftnesse Readers' Club to get a free copy of **Justicar Jhee and the Spectral Armada**, receive special offers, and hear about future books!
swiftnesse.com/spectral/

Justicar Jhee
and the
Cursed Abbey

-The Justicar Jhee Mysteries Book 1-

by Trevol Swift

To my grandmother who taught my family to love reading.
To my Cousin Snoopy who helped make me the nerd I am today.
Rest in power.

1

———

THE YACHT

~

Accommodations

"Taking vows at Tranquility Bridge Abbey may be hazardous to one's health. At least if you are male."

A constituent had sent the message to Jhee's official justicar account via the anonymous crime reporting system. Jhee had queried the area's death records some time ago. While she awaited the results, her junior husband, Kanto, practiced his lute behind her in the stateroom. The Storm Shield's interference left her no other way to address the report mid-voyage.

Lightning drew Jhee's gaze away from the message on her digital conch and to the large, squared portholes of her stateroom. The ensuing crack drowned out Kanto's notes. Beyond the polymer glass of the portholes, stormy skies beckoned. The yacht Jhee and her household had chartered to the capital heaved along the storm-riled seas. Jhee forced her attention away from the storm and the message. Her focus should have been spending time with her second husband, who had just ended another tune.

"Thank you for your patience," Jhee said.

"If your mind was going to be elsewhere the whole time, then you aren't really here with me, are you?" Kanto said.

Jhee pushed her seat back from the desk to face the oh-so-very-young Kanto. "Please, play for me. You'll have my complete attention."

Kanto plucked a note on the strings and played beautifully as he always did. It lifted her spirits. Lighter and happier of mood now, she found her foot tapping along as his bright notes filled the stateroom. His expression slipped

3

from smiling to pure absorption in the music. She imagined this is how she looked when she worked on legal decisions or arcana.

The luminosity of his golden eyes intensified, adding a vibrant glow to his deep-brown skin. Kanto's music resonated throughout the room. The extra slick look of his build and blue-black cast to his body hair and braids commanded the eye. No doubt the result of his meticulous grooming and exercise routine. If only their relationship were not so new and awkward. Inland, he would be the toast of the Imperial Isles. There he would find a more suitable household than hers—both him and Mirrei.

Despite her promise, Jhee's thoughts drifted to Mirrei. She played with the edge of a parchment. Both so young. Too young for her. She pinched the bridge of her nose.

Before Jhee could apologize to Kanto for getting distracted again, her conch chimed. A flashing notice announced the data analysis of the death records around the abbey had completed. The lure of the potential case and the arcane-infused storm vied with her youthful husband for her interest. The unsigned message had arrived just before Jhee and her marriage cohort's departure. She skimmed through several results that the analysis had flagged. Most seemed routine. She hovered her thumb over disable search.

The date on the latest deaths caught her eye. Three deaths in rapid succession, less than a long-moon or extended lunar month apart?

Kanto's lute playing intensified as he segued into another selection. Prior to her additional marriages and her reassignment to the capital, Jhee would not have hesitated to follow-up. She closed the search results.

Did Jhee dare work on another design or healing derivation? Soon, Kanto would conclude the musical piece he practiced. With the music's end, Jhee lost another means to politely deflect his romantic overtures. She tidied the digital, seaweed skin parchments then jotted down the last bit of a healing derivation she had previously begun.

In the capital, Jhee would have no time to run down cryptic complaints about crime from unknown folk in the Outer Reaches. Jurisprudence and teaching would replace investigation and legal proceedings. A wave pitched the yacht enough for the seaweed-and-polymer parchments on her desk to slide. She steadied herself then, tucked her hands into her robe sleeves to hide her white knuckles. Assuming the First Makers allowed them to arrive at the capital intact.

The music swelled as Kanto reached the tricky crescendo sequence. Jhee triple-checked her part designs for her Mechanist's ritual objects, then sneaked a peek at the music box schematics.

The yacht lurched. Jhee's parchments scattered along with the tallies from her fishing lanes and the massive ledger of legal findings. Kanto missed a few notes. She gathered her fallen work, then glanced at the clock. That would be all. She had already spent more time working than she said she would.

The musical composition ended. As per their unspoken understanding, Jhee set her work aside once he finished practicing. She stacked the derivations, music box plans, and part designs for her orrery together neatly with the tallies before using them to mark her place in the ledger.

He joined her at the desk and handed her a parchment. "Missed one."

Jhee snatched up the sheet, worried it might be the music box schematics. She wanted that to be a surprise. It turned out to be healing sequences. The handwriting did not match hers, yet the work was excellent. The penmanship on the derivations showed a notable decline the further down the page she read. It brought to mind heavy thoughts of Mirrei resting in the next stateroom under Shep's care. Kanto's time, she admonished. She hastily tucked the sheet into the ledger with the others.

"Arcana?" Kanto asked. "Don't worry. I will shield my poor delicate male eyes."

"Not for these. Healing sequences."

The golden light of his eyes dimmed. He laid his hand with its impeccably manicured and lacquered nail claws on Jhee's shoulder. "How far along are you? Did you need a few more minutes?"

"I think I have some promising avenues. I need to take some time to think about them, though."

"Talk me through them?"

"Which would no doubt bore you to brackishness. This is your time, of which I have already stolen too much for others."

"*Our* time."

Her conch chirped. Jhee winced. Kanto sighed and motioned for her to address it. She made an apologetic gesture to him and picked her conch up. A notice indicated her last attempt to upload to the judicial archives had failed. Miserable weather and interference from the storm zone had made her transfers slow when they worked at all. She checked her conch's holding capacity. It was running low. She restarted the transfer. She brandished and silenced the conch for him to see, then set it aside. He inclined his head in approval.

Kanto laid his lute across his knees. "We should retire."

Jhee's stomach sank at the prospect. She became all too aware of the pitching and yawing of the yacht. "No. Your playing was helping."

"I think that's enough for now."

"If that is your wish, this is your night."

"*Our* night."

As Kanto packed up his lute, Jhee's gaze fell upon the robe he had laid out on the bed when he arrived. He rushed over with a smile. He held it up proudly for her to see.

"Try it on. Mirrei and I finished the last bit of tailoring. I want to ensure the extra pockets didn't ruin the lines."

Jhee undid her sash.

"Let me," he said in a silky voice. He stepped closer and switched the robes Jhee wore. She and Kanto caught each other's gaze. "Perfect fit."

His eyes sparkled and took on a deep golden hue. A smoldering shade she hoped hers matched. They touched their foreheads together. A tingle corruscated through her as he gently brushed his *esca*, the illuminated golden star in the center of his forehead, against hers. He caressed the small of her back. A moan escaped her. He bent in, and she pulled his mouth against hers.

A knock sounded at the stateroom door. Kanto's posture sagged. His eyes pleaded with her, "No."

Jhee, however, refastened her sash with the new robes. Such a smooth, handsome face. Many older women in her position took husbands much more disparate in age. She wanted to make him as happy as he tried to make her. That would be enough to make this arrangement work until the capital. She stepped away from him and affected her most official stance.

"Enter."

~

The Dispute

The first mate stepped in and doffed her cap to Jhee.

"Sorry to disturb, Justicar. We've had a dispute arise amongst the crew."

"Details." Jhee snatched her conch from the desk. The transfer to the archives had failed again. She found and deleted some non-critical files from the spare and sparse, then set it up to record the trial. She still got a critical space warning.

Kanto plopped down on the bed and folded his arms. "More work. Lovely."

She faced him. "I ask your indulgence, husband."

"Go."

"I'll hear their case here. First mate?"

"Yes, Justicar?"

"Have the disputants bring any evidence they wish to present here in fifteen minutes, and I will do my best to render them justice in the Grand Empress and Emperor's name."

The first mate excused herself.

"I'll go next door with Mirrei and Shep."

"Yet, I require your assistance as witness and scribe."

His ears perked up. "You want my help with a case?"

"Unless you don't feel you are up to the task?"

"No, no. What do I need to do?"

The spotty connection did not allow them to do a proper set up of the judicial code base on Kanto's conch. Instead, they painstakingly copied over and adjusted access rights from Jhee's. By the time the follow-up knock came, they had cobbled something together that would work.

"Now, fetch me my stones and tabard from that case over there."

The first mate brought in two crew women. They doffed their caps and seated themselves respectably like two fine and stalwart women. Their extended time above decks had given them denser body hair and flattened noses, which had shifted their appearance towards otters. The rain had caused everyone to take on sleeker aspects gradually enough one might forget. They looked sheepishly at Jhee but stared daggers at each other.

"Now, state your names and what seems to be the nature of your dispute."

Both talked over each other.

"Enough. One at a time. You"—Jhee gestured at one—"go first."

Apparently, the plaintiff had purchased an ice chest full of oysters, clams, and cockles from the defendant. The plaintiff claimed the delivery was light and wanted a refund. Jhee took possession of the evidence they brought with them, namely the chest of sea meat and the payment. She pulled a luggage scale from her arcana toolbox. The defendant turned her cap round via the brim, and the plaintiff appeared smug while Jhee weighed the chest and its contents. Kanto tapped his sketch pencil against the bag of shell coins in dispute. The plaintiff shifted her weight back and forth, coughed, straightened the objects on the table.

Not content to stop there, Jhee called for a mug and a bowl. She doled out portions until she emptied the ice chest. As she did so, the defendant wrung her hat in her hands.

The defendant let out a breath and smiled. "You see, just as I said. One full container of sea meat. She just wants to get out of paying."

"I counted how many mug fulls. I know how many eight quarts of sea meat is and that won't enough," the plaintiff said.

Jhee picked up the empty chest. Too heavy. She placed her hand in the carton and noticed it ended two finger joints higher than the table. More than Jhee could account for with the thickness of the insulation. After motioning for Kanto to stop tapping, she shook the chest. A rattle came from the presumably empty container, and the heft shifted from side to side.

"But wait, what's this?"

Jhee popped open a false bottom containing rocks and sand. The defendant went bug-eyed.

"I knew it! You're a cheat."

The crew members had a brief scuffle over the sack of shell currency.

"Enough," Jhee said, using her siren module to enhance the command.

They stopped fighting immediately. Jhee seized the currency purse and dropped it on the table. She paused. Kanto also perked up. He had heard it too. Too flat.

Jhee dropped the purse on the table again. She hefted the bag a few times. A quick appraisal with cypher-enhanced senses proved some shells gilded fakes. Jhee curtailed a second altercation.

"I'm ready to render my judgment. Are you ready to accept it?"

"Yes, Justicar," they both said.

"I find, in this matter of the first crew woman against the second crew woman, against the defendant. I sentence you to issue a partial refund equivalent to one-quarter the agreed payment. In the countersuit, I further find that the plaintiff was also in breach, and she is to return approximately one-quarter of the sea meat, the amount she shorted her payment. Given that these appear to be what you have already done, I judge the matter settled. Should either of you wish an appeal and review of this finding, you can file with the royal archives for one at your expense."

The disputants left.

~

A Lesson

Kanto took the kettle and poured them each a cup of tea.

"A chance to see you work up close. You sounded so official and commanding." Kanto handed her pencil sketches along with his notes. "I hope you don't mind. The conch was doing most of the work, so I made these."

"Multi-talented. You shall overwhelm them at the capital."

"Your praise honors me. I enjoyed watching you work, *denbe*."

"I was afraid you'd found it terribly boring."

"Not at all. It gives me insight into how your mind works."

Jhee played with the teacup. "I enjoy the citrus flavor of this tea we're drinking. Tell me about this blend."

"Orange blossom and passionflower from off the Ylush Archipelago's southernmost tip. In the latest dispatches from the capital, all the influencers are drinking it. It's renowned for its properties as an aphrodisiac and fertility aid."

Jhee swallowed the tea hard. She reminded herself she agreed to this marriage and its terms. The dispute, while a fortuitous diversion, had also diffused their romantic momentum. Shep's advice fluttered through her mind.

"He doesn't know you. Don't expect him to yet. If anything he does pleases you, from romance to gifts, don't make him guess."

"I never thanked you for my lovely robe. Thank you."

"I'm glad it pleased you."

"It's subtle how you worked in the house colors via the coral and turtle shell motifs."

"Precisely. I'm glad you noticed."

"I may not always behave like it, but I notice."

"Not as impressive as cyphering equations, but to each their talents." Jhee fiddled with her saucer. Kanto took another sip of his tea. "Did you mean what you said at dinner about getting me arcana training?"

"With the bans lifted, Tihalmec Imperial Academy at the capital has been accepting and teaching male students, even in the cyphering program. I think you would take to it quite well."

"Teach me yourself like you do with Mirrei. Or you could align me so I could be a subject like Shep."

Jhee winced at that characterization of Shep. She steered the conversation away from crosstalk. "I might teach you element drawing. For cyphering, though, the latest research shows the process is different enough for males to warrant special instruction."

"How?"

"Well, I'm glad you asked that question." Jhee gushed about data and articles she had read. Kanto smiled and nodded. She lapsed into a professorial tone. She went silent once his brow had developed a permanent furrow. "Listen to me drone on. You asked for a lesson, not a lecture."

"If anyone can figure it out, you can. It's a puzzle then. A puzzle I could help you unravel. We can start now."

"I'll get you training at the capital."

"Isn't tonight the night you humor my whims?"

Jhee fidgeted. "I want to give you the best. I don't want to limit your potential."

"You will make an excellent instructor, both with me and in your new position. Do you think you'll miss being a Justicar?"

"I'll still be a Justicar, an academic one."

"Teach me then. It will be great practice for both of us."

"Meditation first. Though the situation may make it difficult. Like this." She shook out her arms and planted her feet wide on the deck. The yacht rose and fell again with the rough seas. She curled her toenail claws into the deck boards. She pressed the bridge of her nose. "Clear and center," she said.

Once Kanto matched her stance, she talked him through a visualization of the celestial clockworks of the universe. With it fixed in their mind's eye, they moved hands and body to mimic its celestial motions. Rains driven by the perpetual storm system lashed against the glass in gusts too irregular to match its timing.

The giant mass of supernatural power imbued in the storm outside pressed against her inner essence. She braced herself and deep-breathed.

"The storm's not outside," he said. "It's within."

"Exercise care. Don't let it draw you in. Use the porthole as a buffer. In its current state, it's a muddle where the arcane finds little purchase. Too many have cut, heated, bent, and performed any other innumerable manufacturing processes to shape it into what it is now. Those same traces should buffer us."

The yacht sailed on through the rolling seas. In calmer times, she might have found it anchoring. Now, her stomach roiled. She indicated they kneel. She stilled herself until her stomach settled.

"What next?"

"Unfortunately, it gets much more boring from here. Formulations and schematics."

She awakened her conch to find more notifications. She hesitated on the death irregularities again.

"What was it?"

"Mm?"

"The message on your conch that troubled you."

"Some curious deaths at a cloister of celibates."

"A cloister of celibates. No doubt they killed themselves from being denied one of the Makers' greatest gifts?"

She took the humor as well-meaning, talismanic, and chose not to admonish him for it. "No doubt. This must be so distressing for you. Tell me about the latest fashion trends from the capital."

He folded his hands and looked at her sideways. "Do you really want to know about fashion? I thought we would be poring over charts."

"Tonight is about doing what you enjoy."

"Tonight is about doing what we both enjoy, denbe. It should not be one-sided."

"We do what I want on most other nights. I wish to be more considerate and take an interest in your interests, especially with how neglectful and rude I've been this evening."

"We're still finding common ground. It won't always go smoothly. What bothers me most is how you don't relax with me and let all your other worries go, if only for a few moments."

She touched his hand and gave him an exaggerated once over with her gaze. He pecked her on the nose. Then another tentative one. He gained confidence for a firmer kiss. She squeezed his hand for encouragement. He ended the kiss with a wide grin.

Thunder crashed overhead. Jhee stepped back. "Not exactly the pleasure cruise I promised you. I'm sorry we've had to travel so near the storm zone. The major routes are congested and in disarray. Hopefully, the course the captain has plotted near the edge of the buffer zone will save us time. Don't worry. We'll rejoin high society for festival season."

"I'm not worried. If you say we will be there in time, we will." Kanto indicated Jhee sit. Once she had, he massaged her shoulders. "I want us to attend all the shows when we reach the capital. You can show me off to all the blue-skinned elites."

"We will see."

Few pursuits disinterested her more. Perhaps Kanto's age did not concern her so much, but that they were so ill-matched.

"Those death notices aren't the only matters which have you preoccupied."

"The pirate attacks in the outlands are getting more frequent."

"The location of some of your most lucrative seabeds. Your investments in sustainable aquaculture almost went under because of the shield. Yours was among the few farms to survive."

"Um," Jhee acknowledged, surprised he knew that much about her investments. "I'm hiring extra security, displaced locals. Hopefully, it will be enough to keep them from turning pirate."

"Be mindful of them aiding the pirates from the inside."

She quirked her mouth at him. "What a thoughtful observation."

"I'll try not to feel insulted."

"You gave me a gift. It's only fair I give you one."

Jhee rose and rummaged through the bottom drawer of the dresser. First, she pulled out an unadorned, cracked music box wrapped in a cloth bundle. She rethought and chose the top drawer. She set a jeweled candy dish wrought of smoky polymer glass on the tea table. The amethyst and citrine stones matched the tones of Kanto's robes.

"In my preferred color palette, no less. I think my excellent fashion sense is rubbing off on you." He lifted the lid. "Wait! Are those?"

"Lace root melon taffies."

"My favorites. How did you know?"

"It's what I do. I learn things."

"Grandmamere gave me these when I told her something new about her guests. Sometimes I even received little cherry, citrus cakes."

"Lady Kaydence. This weather has its upsides."

"That she can't contact you regularly."

They grinned. Kanto bristled up his body hair and snuggled against her. It made a noticeable difference with his wiry, slim frame. Jhee enjoyed a nice and full build to wrap her arms around. Her young, virile husband was impressionable and eager to please. Had Jhee done him a disservice by bedding him when she intended not to make him a permanent part of her household? As soon as they reached the capital, if not before, she meant to seek new arrangements for Kanto and Mirrei. Then it would be her and Shep again.

Jhee let her fingers play in his fluffed body hair. "You're quite the cuddler and the least fitful sleeper."

Kanto touched the small of her back like he had earlier. She molded against him. Her mouth set in a thin line when it sunk in the only way he could have known where to touch her to get that response.

Shep. The questions about arcane techniques and historical trivia she knew he cared nothing for. She saw, now, the orchestrated appeals to her vanity. Shep must have coached him. With their night underway and she had already flouted its rules several times, she dared not call Kanto on it.

He cast his gaze down, then looked back up at her. "Don't be mad. Mirrei and I must take our clues from *denme*, senior spouse, on how best to serve our denbe."

"Serve not service."

Kanto had planned on not being called to account. While the premeditation irked Jhee, she had been in the wrong. She mustered the graciousness not to withdraw from him. He continued to stroke the small of her back, and she stroked his ears. The tension and the awkwardness seeped away. All forgiven.

Their travel yacht lurched to a sudden stop. They tumbled into a heap.

2

ARRIVAL

~

Tiles and Tunes

In the stateroom next door to Jhee's, Shep and Mirrei played tiles. Shep fingered his eye scar while he planned how to defend his matriarch tile against Mirrei's onslaught. He had considered getting the facial scar removed, but he wanted the reminder.

The yacht lurched. The tiles scattered in all directions. Shep checked Mirrei, who nodded to show she was fine. He paused to listen.

Yelling came down from above deck. Crew members barreled by their door. Something banged against the door. Mirrei jumped. The doorknob rattled, then turned. Shep flung it open, ready. Jhee and Kanto stood there.

"You can't seriously be going out there?" Kanto was saying.

"They may need an artificer," Jhee answered. "Stay with Shep and Mirrei until I return."

Shep harried them in from the passageway. "Wife?"

"Everyone here fine?" Jhee asked.

Shep gave a quick nod.

"How is Mirrei doing?"

"About the same. What's happened?"

Bax, Jhee's head servant, poked his head in a moment later. "Sorry to disturb you, Justicar."

Bax led Dari, their family's shark dog, on a leash. The hound perked her ears up and whined at the sight of Shep. He and Jhee petted her.

13

"There, there, old girl. Bax, assessment?" Jhee asked. Bax and Dari were as much a part of their family as anyone in the stateroom.

"Forgiveness, Justicar, the wild wave drove the ship into a reef. The crew's working to free us."

Jhee took the leash. "See what you can do to help. I'll be up there soon."

Bax's wizened face creased with concern. "Aye."

Jhee led Dari into their stateroom. Kanto took the hound from her. "At least change your robes."

Jhee gathered a warm outer robe and deck shoes from her stateroom before she returned to the passageway.

Shep met her, frowning. "*Denye* is right. The world can turn without you for one crisis."

Jhee lowered her voice, "It is nothing to trouble yourself about, dear one. Stay here. I'll assess the situation. Keep everyone reassured."

"As you wish, dear wife."

"Wait, your robes," Kanto said as Jhee headed above deck.

Shep regarded his two *dendes*, junior spouses, and affected a smile. He retrieved the tiles and set up the board again.

"Who wants to play?" Shep asked. Neither responded. He tried again, addressing them by their gaming names to keep the mood light. "Tunes? Sprite?"

"Pass," Kanto said and went to the porthole to sulk. Shep and Mirrei resumed their places at the tile board.

"Will denbe be fine?" Mirrei asked.

"She always returns safe and sound." Shep mixed the tiles and made the first play. "Try that, Sprite."

"You're lucky our last game got interrupted, Pup." Mirrei smiled and countered. Her laughter was interspersed with coughing fits. Kanto gave her his usual sidelong glance then took up his lute. "Could it be pirates?"

Kanto made a musical flourish and switched to a more somber selection. "My thoughts exactly."

Mirrei's eyes went wide, and she leaned forward. Kanto now played a harrowing tune with a sense of urgency.

Shep hoped Kanto caught the rebuke in his expression. Pirates would have found the primary routes as inconvenient as they. They may have made the same calculation their captain did to brave the storm zone instead. "Doubtful. They're finding it far more lucrative to loot sunken homes."

The last thing Shep needed was Kanto's wild stories and drama frightening Mirrei. Although, the youthful woman appeared more intrigued than scared.

"'Don't be another crisis she has to manage,'" Kanto said. He bowed his head and played something light. "We shall take our cues from you on how to respond."

"While you're watching out for us, who's watching out for her?" Mirrei asked.

A question Shep had grown tired of asking. Hopefully, increased familial duties might succeed where he had failed.

~

The Reef

On deck, rain pelted Jhee's face, and the wind howled as if the Wave Witch herself hailed them. Her sleeves snapped in the maelstrom like pennants. What did it say about her she preferred a deadly storm to more time alone in her stateroom with Kanto?

Sailors equipped with long, hooked poles crowded the left side of the deck. The entire crew, like those earlier, also resembled otters more than when their journey had started.

"Careful, ladies. Steady. This is a protected reef," the captain yelled.

Jhee ran to the side. She breathed deep then glanced over. Water, deep blue-black, darker even than the high imperials' skin, gave away nothing. Her throat tightened. She braced, like always expecting to see something slither beneath the surface or catch glimpse of an enormous, scaly, glowing eye. When she saw nothing of the sort, she exhaled. Followed up as always by cursing herself for foolish fancies. She faced away from the sea to address the crew. "Spotlight."

To draw the sea. Almost as daunting a prospect as testing the storm. Jhee rolled up her sleeves and cleared her mind. She engaged the gears of transmutation within herself. The liquid essence of the waves and the fiery source of the spotlight's incandescence became clockworks in her mind. Within her, the Divine Mechanism used her as a conduit to bridge the two. Her esca tingled. The tingling grew as did the spotlight's glow. The deepest blue water lightened as if the water itself illuminated. Not bad for a Water tertiary. She doubted a Water dominant drawer could have done better.

The famed and magnificent sapphire and ruby coral of Bibsbebe's Reef had hooked itself to one railing on the yacht. What an inauspicious omen. She would not conclude their journey and arrive for her new duties at the capital as one who had destroyed the thousand-year-old reef.

Jhee paused. Unless the crew were shipwrights, they should not draw the yacht. It had to be the reef. The contradiction coral was, both flesh and bone. Earth drawer work: the element she had the least expertise with. She looked at the all-female crew. That meant they were less likely to expert Earth drawers.

"Do you have Earth drawers?" Jhee yelled.

A sailor hesitated a moment then at a signal from the captain joined Jhee. "I can do both aspects but as subsidiaries."

"Good enough."

Jhee communicated with hand gestures how she wanted the sailor to manipulate the coral. She steeled herself to look over the side again. She reached out through the universal mechanisms to the water, winding and guiding it away from the reefs so as not to dampen the sailor's watch work.

"You." The captain gestured to another sailor. "Put your hook there. If we get under it, we might dislodge from the reef without damaging it."

The captain looked over and nodded. She waved for the sailors to do as Jhee suggested.

The sailors wedged their billhooks in. With a mighty crack, the yacht shuddered and drifted away from the reef. Sapphire and ruby-colored fragments floated away and sank beneath sight. Nowhere near as disastrous as it could have been. The tingling in her esca ceased as she stopped her concentration on her spell sequence and water drawing. She leaned heavily against the yacht's side, careful not to look back at the water. The winds died down, and the seas calmed, but the rain continued strong as ever. The Storm Child had not done having its fun with them.

Bax came over.

"Assessment," she said.

"We've cleared the reef, Justicar. It damaged the ship. We're taking on water. We must put aground to affect repairs."

"Makers' whim, if it's not one problem, it's another with this journey."

"Aye, Justicar. The pumps should keep us afloat until the squall passes."

"Where precisely are we?"

"Northern edge of District Sixteen."

Jhee stroked her nose. "What's that glow over there in the distance? There's an abbey around here, isn't there? Could that be it?"

"Aye, the storm light from the Drakists on Torilsisle. They have a bay and a dry dock large enough for a yacht such as this."

The death record irregularity searches. "Ask the captain to contact them. Have the monks and nuns dispatch tow skiffs once it's safe. Use my official title if necessary."

"At once, Justicar. Now, please, get below."

The lightning lured her attention again. The storm, the beautiful Storm Shield, had its own slight glow. Thermals and winds and lightning made to behave as mortals willed. Truly, it was the marvel of all marvels. Those who created the storm system used the same methods as she did in her daily works. The scale and sheer number of artificers and elementalists made for a fascinating complexity. One an artificer could be forgiven for wanting to test herself against.

When might it be clear enough for a rescue? The Storm Child had cost her family much in the past. Not today. She thrust her divine-granted will beyond the yacht into the forces of the storm.

The storm yanked at her. Despite her earlier warning to Kanto, she had no buffer to dull the onslaught. She lowered herself into her stance and seized a piece of the storm. She fought to impose an order on it, to reveal its workings like any other device. Residuals of the hundred and thousands of elementalists who had shaped the perpetual storm system bombarded her. Snatches of sound and fury shattered the visualization of the clockworks. She released the storm and let it keep its secrets for now.

Her sleeves no longer whipped back and forth with as much ferocity as before. She heard Bax's voice much clearer now.

"You've done enough, Justicar. Let's get you back inside, or Mr. Shep will have my pouch."

Bax saw her safely below decks. Jhee blanked her expression and counted in her head, both to shed the features she gained via weather adaptation and to present a composed demeanor. She knocked on her cohort's stateroom door, and Shep swept her inside. Mirrei and Kanto sat beside the porthole. She embroidered while he brushed her hair and hummed.

Jhee shook herself off. Shep took a towel and brusquely wiped the moisture from the hair she had developed as her body adapted to the rain. "Let's get you out of these wet things."

"You forgot to change your robes," Kanto said.

She glanced at the pile of clothing, and the new robe was mixed amongst her wet things. Kanto made an exasperated sound. She rubbed the bridge of her nose. Her headache had reasserted itself now the excitement had passed. A sneeze rocked her balance and made her sinuses feel as if they would explode. "I think I may have caught cold."

"Serves you right."

She placed her hands upon his shoulders. Steady voice. Without panic. Without worry. His shoulders relaxed under her grasp. "I know, I know."

Mirrei stifled a cough. Jhee turned her attention to her. Kanto gave up his seat for Jhee.

"Have you no admonishment for me, *dende*?" Jhee asked.

Mirrei hid a weak smile behind her hand. "None that has not already been given, denbe."

"You'll be happy to know we'll be leaving these dreadful waves and cramped cabins for a brief stay on land."

"Where?"

"An abbey nearby."

Kanto narrowed his eyes. "One with a cloister of celibates?"

"Um, yes."

"For how long?"

"Not long. There are some minor repairs we need to do."

"Us too." Kanto held up her robe and shook his head. Jhee jerked her head at Mirrei. He took a position next to Mirrei and squeezed her shoulder. "We'll be in time for festival season. Once we reach the capital, we'll see the Grand Court in all its finery. Catch the biggest shows. Shop in all the finest shops. Won't that be fun? We might even meet the Grand Regents themselves or glimpse the Wave Wanderers. Jhee promised."

Mirrei nodded then was overtaken by a coughing fit. Shep laid a towel on Jhee's shoulders. Everyone exchanged worried glances over Mirrei's head.

~

The Landing

Four deaths not three in half as many moons, Jhee thought.

The Storm Child had returned to hir mischief though with not as much vigor by the time their yacht came within sight of the abbey at Tranquility Bridge. The imposing structure loomed on a large outcropping of rock set apart from the nearby isle. Its storm light swept around in a circle from the highest shell spire with the elongated-conic shape. Three additional spires, each shaped like a different gastropod shell, spiraled up into the sky silhouetted against the ever-present glow of the Storm Shield.

The yacht's crew proved to expert water drawers and had not needed Jhee's arcane skills. Jhee had not spent the time idle as their damaged craft limped towards the aforementioned abbey. With their visit to the abbey inevitable, she had instead trained her faculties on the matter of the abbey's high death toll. A closer inspection of its death notices had revealed the previous abbess had also died unexpectedly.

A cement slab big enough to host a ferryboat projected from the mountainside surrounded by smaller, natural rocks. The skiffs towed the yacht into position where lay brothers and sisters caught their mooring ropes then looped them around mooring posts. A few smaller boats for emergencies and supply runs bobbed upon the waves. Those working the lines paid no attention to crashing waves or sea spray. Within the sleeves of her robes, Jhee dug her nails into her palms every time a storm-driven surge struck the slab or strained the ropes. Her mind filled with the image of them overwhelmed and swept away. What would be worse? Screams or silence.

The dock workers' hails brought Jhee back to the present. Mirrei and Kanto huddled against Jhee as they approached the slab. Shep's reassuring hand on her shoulder blade gave her the support she needed.

Stalwart, Jhee forced her attention to the abbey itself. A different question needed answering. The incongruity of the abbey's deaths dragged Jhee's thoughts further away from images she'd rather forget. Four deaths at the abbey in such a brief span would have been more understandable if they all had happened at once or under similar circumstances.

Antenna arrays mounted to the central spire wobbled in the high winds. Lightning flashed off the sun arrays on its roofs and those in the fields beside it. The brightness gave glimpses of the newly built, glass-domed hothouse modules. Full-sized, life-like figures made of brilliant coral lined the eaves and facade. Preservatives and arcane protections stopped the statues and famed, blood-ruby red walls and emerald green roof from bleaching over the years in the onslaught of sun and rain. Constructions hewed from similar coral to that which had scuttled their yacht. She could not help but think the First Makers wanted her here.

"What a ghastly place," Mirrei said.

"Certainly not what I'd call tranquil. Precisely the sort of austere place I'd expect of ascetics," Kanto said.

Jhee swallowed hard, her stomach churning, as they sailed past the breakers. "This place boasts empire-renowned mineral springs. Very good for the health."

"Is it truly made of coral, denbe?"

"No doubt some form of mineral encrustation subject to rapid fossilization, thus keeping its color. It becomes its own natural coral rag or coral concrete."

Shep moved his hands to Jhee's shoulders. "I think I rather preferred the yacht."

Jhee raised an eyebrow. Had she been alone, she might have kissed the solid ground once they disembarked.

A stern-faced woman about Jhee's age met them at the dock entrance. They exchanged formal gestures of greeting. "Greetings, my Lady Justicar. Welcome to Tranquility Bridge's Redoubt of the Drakists. I am the prioress. I see to the grounds and provisions. Please, pardon our delayed response. We had a tremor here. The second in as many long-months."

Servants, laypeople, and a spattering of shabbier laborers bustled by them with produce and fresh-caught sea meat.

Jhee used her siren module to make herself heard over the din, "Thank you. I must admit to wanting to visit for some time. I corresponded with your abbess, Saheli, about acquiring some of your famous nectar wine. Is she around so I might pay my respects?"

"Saheli passed into the Makers' sphere some months ago."

While Jhee's query had not flagged Abbess Saheli's death, the minimal details and maximal allegory had aroused her curiosity nonetheless. "My deepest regrets. Who may I ask is in charge now?"

"Pyrmo is our current abbess."

"You seem beset by tragedies lately," Jhee intimated, offering her a chance to elaborate.

The prioress frowned at all the baggage Jhee's servants unloaded. "You took all this on a pleasure cruise and in a storm no less."

"I've been reassigned to the capital. I thought we might make an excursion of it. A tremor explains the wild wave that disabled our ship and the collapse I heard about here. The Shell Drake and the Storm Child must be restless."

The prioress grunted. Lay brothers and sisters poured out the gate on the aperture that opened out from the bottom of the crag. They helped Jhee's servants unload their belongings, including a litter for her marriage cohort. Fishing vessels and fisherfolk continued about their daily business with no great urgency. Few spared their entourage a glance. Not all seemed as practiced at their work. Even more lay brothers and sisters transported bundles of kelp and lettuces, sacks of grain, and crates of shore meat-producing animals such as chickens and pigs.

The milled symbol above the gate, a sword piercing a bridge, creaked and groaned in the powerful winds. While Jhee waited until everyone in her charge passed beneath it to safety, she studied the significant number of idle people with lean, hungry looks who watched their entourage pass. The gate swung closed behind her with a definitive rattle, sealing them inside. Or the world outside.

What circumstance caused an abbey named Tranquility Bridge to have a sword as its symbol? The spotty connection only allowed her to do minimal background research beyond what she already knew about the place. When her interest in healing picked up because of Mirrei's condition, she learned of their honey nectar wine. She had always meant to attend their seminars or visit their reliquary, yet she never found the time. Since it was in her district, she always delayed it until later. Later had arrived. The First Makers' Design be done.

"If I may, I'd like to pay my respects to your current abbess."

"This way."

The prioress led her to stone steps while the litter with her cohort disappeared through a passage under it. Jhee motioned for Bax to shadow her and the prioress. The moment she saw the precipitous height of the abbey, she had feared for Mirrei. She insisted all three use the litter because she did not want to single her out. "Is it your order's normal custom to see husbands and wives parted during their stay?"

"This route is far too precarious for a litter. You'll be reunited with them in the dormitory level after your audience with the abbess. She can explain to you more fully the rules by which we ask guests to abide."

The prioress led the way up an interminable number of stairs with a bioluminescent glowtorch. How Jhee wished she had joined her cohort in the litter. She wheezed. "Such a wealth of stairs. They may do me in before that."

"Aside from the mechanical lifts and cranes for moving cargo, we don't use most modern conveniences. Anything other would be a drain on our limited resources. Most non-essential devices have been shut down to conserve power until the storm passes."

"I saw your sun arrays."

"They are our sole means of power."

"I noticed you also possess an antenna array. I can't seem to access anything with my conch beyond the local area. Might I be able to use your communications to contact the Central Authority to inform them of my delayed arrival and the damaged reef?"

"Reception follows the weather's whims. We almost missed your captain's distress call while dealing with the quake aftermath. The broadcast transmitter's power requirements, though, are prohibitive with the overcast skies."

"The limited power and communication must make it difficult to seek aid in a crisis."

"We are a self-sufficient order. The transmitter's usage is reserved for the direst of emergencies."

"Fortunate, you've had none of those lately."

Jhee waited for the prioress to take the opening she offered.

The prioress frowned. "Indeed. You may, however, petition the abbess to use the transmitter."

Jhee sighed. "Please, lead the way."

3

———

ECHOES

~

Reception with the Abbess

The prioress knocked upon the door to the abbess's quarters. Jhee took a moment to compose herself and catch her breath while Bax hung back. The abbess welcomed Jhee by touching their *escae* as if they were old friends. She gave off an odor of smudging sticks and sacral wine. If she were not so winded, Jhee might have been scandalized by such familiarity.

"I am Pyrmo, the Mother of Rites for Tranquility Bridge's."

"Thank you for your hospitality, Abbess."

Jhee noted the dual nature of the chambers. A cat dish despite vanishing evidence of a cat. The sounding bowl, striker, and meditation rugs she expected of such a pious individual. A low altar for burning incenses. In fact, the room emanated smudge as heavily as the occupant. A hutch desk and simple glow lamp full of parchments. Half-painted easels which had not seen use in months. Shelves of seeds and elixirs gathering dust. It bore the earmarks of the previous owner as much as the current. Pyrmo must not have felt comfortable in her position yet.

"You are most welcome, my Lady Justicar. Please, call me Pyrmo."

"Please, I prefer simply Justicar."

Jhee brushed at the cat hairs on her robes and sniffed a few times. She already felt her eyes watering and nose itching. Did she put her allergy medication in the items they brought from the yacht?

"Is something wrong, Justicar?"

"I wondered if there was a cat about? Mild allergy."

23

"Cat? Ah, not anymore. Saheli's cat meant very much to her. She used to feed it from her plate and let it drink from her bowl. She painted it and rendered it in many sculptures and reliefs. It died shortly after her. They say it refused to eat out of grief. She was a true artist with a heart as much of an aesthete as an ascetic."

"Very interesting. Died of grief, did you say?"

"Ah, very tragic as many of us loved that cat almost as much as we loved Saheli. Losing them both so closely thoroughly demoralized us. We have endeavored to carry on, though. It pained me to have taken on the position of abbess as she was so respected, and I had enormous shoes to fill."

"I'm sure the Chief Abbess would not have assigned you if she didn't think you were ready."

Pyrmo adjusted her sash of office. "My assignment was a bit of a shock, but I did my best to make the most of it. Ah, you know you are not our only Imperial official and noble hosted here. The imperial vizier, Bathsheba of Toho and Wilobeia, retired to our abbey a few years ago."

"Bathsheba of Toho. Oh, yes." Pyrmo clearly expected Jhee to know who that was. Jhee touched her chin to give herself a moment to wrack her brain. When she came up empty, she improvised, "She was the..."

"The respected sage and former Imperial music tutor."

"Yes, yes. I know someone who may be so delighted to hear that. I must admit having wanted to visit here for some time. Between your seminars and empire-renowned reliquary and wines."

"The vizier works closely with our Mistress of Relics."

"Splendid. I may have corresponded with them regarding access to your archives. I was most saddened to hear of the passing of Saheli, not the only tragedy you have had of late."

Pyrmo frowned and tucked her hands inside her robes. "Yes, it has been unfortunate times. However, today you have arrived on an auspicious day. It's the hundredth anniversary of our residence here long after its sack by barbarian hordes. The abbey is celebrating our founding with a feast."

"The feast explains the commotion I've seen. I'd hate to have thought you went through such trouble for me."

"It's always our honor to welcome a noble servant of the Empire. Would that the weather was better."

"Once the storm zone stabilizes, many issues are liable to address themselves. They say peace will return to the Blessed Isles once more. We will have nothing to fear from the barbarians."

"As the Makers will, so shall it be."

"I've heard you've had communications problems due to the storms."

Pyrmo adjusted her sash of office again. "Low power communications are effectively nullified by the weather."

"That must explain why our initial hails were ignored."

"Ignored? The Justicar's pardon for the discourtesy. Must have been one of our more inexperienced operators. The rest of us were dealing with the aftermath of the second tremor."

"I hoped to use your transmitter to establish communication with the Central Authority. The prioress told me it requires a lot of power."

"Power? Just so. Under the current conditions, we minimize its use, and even then, not until the twin suns are at their maximum height in the skies. Unless you have a pressing need, your best chance of getting a message out is to wait for a storm break."

Jhee thought of her conch full of case files. They kept this long. They could keep longer. Despite her reasoning to the prioress, she had no urgency in telling Central Authority about the damage her vessel did to an imperial treasure. "No pressing need as of yet. Mostly routine work."

"The tremors knocked a few of our systems off-line and misaligned some solar sheets. I'll inquire with the power management and facilities teams to see where we are with power storage and repairs. Perhaps we have enough to power it for a few minutes at full-sun."

"Thank you, Abbess."

"My honor, Justicar."

"As our most gracious host, please pardon my ignorance of what I and my household must do to be most gracious guests."

"We are a chaste order and ask guests to refrain from fraternization with the Prospectives and the Professed. We reserve land meat for the sick or others with heavy protein requirements."

"Shore meat shall suffice. My household avoids raw land meat. Trace amounts are fine if cooked."

"Philosophical or health-related?"

"Both. No need to enact protocols, though."

"Our kitchen complies with Pascoe protocols and Blue Waters guidelines already. We prohibit a few areas to males, namely the mineral springs nearest the temple sanctuary and sections of the archives."

"No doubt to protect them from arcane knowledge."

"We are not only a chaste order. Many of us eschew all arcana."

Did Jhee detect a sneer? A religious order founded by former combatants like Drakist Adepts to her mind would have been more accepting of cyphering or at least the healing arts. "Your restrictions on arcana surprise me. I thought the magnificent preservation of your coral edifice must result from arcane arts. How do you maintain its brilliant appearance without it?"

"A secret, lost art of those who originally built the abbey. We bring in workers now and then to maintain it. More recently, the refugees have been doing the work in exchange for food."

"I did notice many idle people on your docks."

Pyrmo frowned. "Refugees."

"A question about the stricture against the use of arcana here at Tranquility Bridge's, if I may? I have been instructing my youngest consort in its use. As I am unsure of how long we will be here, I wanted to know if there were provisions I could make to continue her instruction."

The abbess looked thoughtful. "There are several fields on the bluff."

"My consort's health is not the best. An arduous trek to the bluffs may be too much. I also worry about such an open location."

"Ah, yes, I see your point and worry about the same within the walls. It is a vow. Many, especially the veterans, employed it in our secular life. We have dedicated ourselves to a life without it, which is sometimes easier in an environment without its constant use. It lessens the temptation. If you need privacy, there is a courtyard on the beach side. We control access. Only one gate and walls are high enough with sharp spikes to discourage idle curiosity. Inform me of your practice times in advance. I'll make additional arrangements to keep the area clear."

"Thank you, Abbess, that would be most ideal. A whole courtyard. I am honored."

"The honor is mine. We are doing some renovations, and it goes largely unused except for a guest who exercises his bull hound there. We'll be starting the feast soon. You and your household simply must attend. You shall be hosted at my table. Then you can have an opportunity to speak to Lady Bathsheba and the Mistress of Relics about access to the archives in person."

A headache pounded fierce behind Jhee's eyes. Her knees screamed in agony. She craved nothing more than to soak her aching muscles in a warm, mineral spring. "Again, your hospitality overwhelms me. As you wish."

Jhee forced a smile and clasped forearms with Pyrmo. Pyrmo flinched. She held up her hands, which had severe burn scars. She applied a bitter-smelling salve from a tin on her desk. "My apologies, Justicar. I sometimes forget."

"I have some small experience with healing. May I take a look?"

"No need. You must be tired from your travels, and the last thing I should do is put you to work before you have rested and enjoyed our hospitality. You should rest before the feast. I'll have you taken to your quarters so you may refresh yourself."

Jhee nodded politely and left. The prioress led her and Bax to another corridor. Her knees and muscles felt sore.

"Does your abbey have mineral springs underneath it?"

"Unfortunately, they are under the stars and exposed to the elements. Underneath us are only crypts."

"What of baths?"

"Only communal showers."

Jhee sighed. "Whelm."

"I can have a purification and rehab tub brought to you and your cohort's room."

"Splendid. Room singular?"

"Interest in taking holy orders is on the rise. Many have also been stranded here by the beastly storms, among them a troupe of itinerant performers. In fact, they shall be performing at the feast tonight. We've housed you in the dormitories instead of the hostelry with the more common guests."

"What a delight. Although a whole marriage cohort in one room. I shall not have a moment to myself to think, let alone meditate." Both the prioress and Abbess Pyrmo barely acknowledged the young men's deaths. Jhee decided to put this separation from her cohort to another use and seek elsewhere for the message sender and further details. "Best to show me to your shrine immediately," Jhee said.

"This way."

"A moment, please. I want to send my servant ahead." Jhee pulled Bax aside. "Begin making inquiries. Discretely."

"Yes, Justicar."

~

The Curious Courtyard Shrine

The prioress brought Jhee down a spiral tower to the courtyard. They emerged from the aperture door onto an exposed rain-soaked grotto. Broad First Makers architraves stood in the center without a bit of shelter for anyone who might use the pillars and basins under them for offerings. Though, the perpetual flame and water feature were protected from the Wind Witch, who howled with as much ferocity as her Sea Sister. The rest of the grotto housed many and numerous representations of the Makers and Lesser Makers. At one point, everyone claimed every ancestor or nature spirit to be a Maker.

One death flagged as unusual by Jhee's query mentioned an accident in a courtyard. Might it be this one?

"This way," the prioress yelled. "Here we are, the shrine. Please, take as much time here as you need."

"I will. Thank you."

The prioress directed her to a small, covered shrine off the main courtyard. This shrine did not contain quite so many effigies. Four nooks separated by columns housed a basin and a pedestal. Being Drakists, one held a physical carving of the Double Shell Drakes wound about the Blessed Isles consuming the other's tails. The sky pillar and basin on the left had an ever-burning candle. It provided the only light to the shrine; light which danced and leaped in partnership with the shadows it cast. The alcove on the right had a water feature on top of the earth pillar. A thin layer of gray-green algae lined the basin. Moss had been allowed to grow on the water feature itself.

A pitcher of water, a striker, and incense were already present in the alcove. Rather than use those, Jhee gave of herself. She knelt before the shrine then breathed on the ever-burning candle. Breath and warmth. She pricked her finger and let one drop of blood fall into the water-filled basin. She also used a nail file on the tip of one of her claws over the bowl. Flesh and blood. The last hollow, dark and full of stricken out totems, venerated the Unknown Maker. She said a few quick prayers and touched her esca to the ground in supplication. Best not to draw too much attention from that one.

While Jhee sought out alcoves for the Lesser Makers whose favor she did court, she took her time, scanning the courtyard for anything amiss. Rain veiled most of the yard from notice. She came upon a crumbling niche housing a rusted Mechanist wheel and axle. The basic device which represented complexity from simplicity required some effort on Jhee's part to turn. Not much call for Mechanist devotions here it would seem despite the overlap with the abbey's asceticism.

At an early age, Jhee had declared herself a follower of Mechanism. However, her duties as Justicar rarely left her time enough to perform even the minimal devotions required of an avowed Mechanist such as the construction of the devotional items. Her preferred method to honor the First Makers was through applying the force of her faculties to imbalances of justice.

Jhee looked at the message on her conch again. Her work, also, seemed never to leave her sufficient time to manage a family which had practically doubled overnight. With her new position in the capital, though, time would no longer be a problem. First of all, she must find some accommodation with Kanto. The situation as is could not stand. This move to the capital had everything strained to the breaking, least of all her tenuous relationship with Kanto. She jingled a few geld coins before the drum-beating effigy of Futou, Maker of music and freshwater, then bounced a few off his signature drumhead.

At the back of the grotto was a defaced wall carving of Toril, the War Maker. The Toril which lent this isle its name. Most of the body had gone with only the implements left to identify it. Scourge, quoit, dented shield, broken sword. Not all the Makers were equally loved.

Jhee hoped the nectar of Tranquility Bridge's and the time off the boat would do Mirrei some good. That would be at least one pressure taken off her. She prayed to her ancestors and the spirit of Miramar, Mirrei's mother. She placed her hand over the inner pocket where she kept her letter. So many remembrances: the last sight as Miramar and her daughter sailed away after their semi-reconciliation; Mirrei's tale of her standing defiantly on the beach with their sinking home behind her; the final message Mirrei delivered to Jhee. *"Protect and honor my daughter."*

"I will, old friend. I will."

Jhee thought of poor Mirrei so ill and tired all the time. Hopefully, some time on land and the abbey's miraculous nectar would do the trick. The doctors had initially diagnosed her condition as Fresh Lung Sickness. This, however, did not seem to be typical Fresh Lung Disease. Fresh Lung occurred when those from the saltier Outer Reaches moved to water with less salinity. Most recovered from it relatively quickly like Jhee and the rest of her household. Mirrei seemed to get worse the longer they sailed, though. Jhee performed the last of her devotions to Pascoe and Lashae for Mirrei's health.

Jhee performed a few abeyances to other Lesser Makers then turned back to the main grotto. So many eyes upon her. She must make them proud. Once she made a determination about the recent deaths here, she intended to focus on arcane teaching and research. This matter may well be her last field case. Perhaps her efforts were best spent inside where it was warm and dry. Meanwhile, she might also uncover whoever sent her the message.

The prioress led her towards a different aperture to exit the courtyard.

A powerful gust of wind tore the door from Jhee's grasp before she could close it after her. Jhee held onto her cloak and reached for the door. Just then, a lightning strike flashed. A silhouette wearing an elaborate mask embraced a naked, one-armed man from behind. Jhee pulled the door closed. She thought better of what she had seen and opened it again. Jhee raised an eyebrow. So much for the celibate life. She always assumed such a vow was much easier said than done.

"Allow me." The prioress tugged the door from Jhee's grasp before she could object.

"The abbess informed me of your rules against fraternization. They apply amongst the clergy, yes?"

"We are a celibate order."

"Do you impose a penalty for breaking that vow?"

The prioress eyed Jhee and stepped back. "The vow is to the Makers and one's self. One who breaks the vow has already shamed themselves. Who are we to impose additional sanction? The only distinctions we make are fraternization and seduction. One who induces another to break their vows or one who uses their position of authority to tempt the laity. These carry harsh penalty. I do hope the Justicar is not worried for the virtue of herself or her cohort."

"When I was closing the door, I thought perhaps I saw lovers at play. A naked man and another figure locked in an embrace."

"The Justicar is tired."

Jhee went back out into the courtyard and examined where she had seen the figures. The wall appeared solid except for a carving of the sword and bridge. She hurried back to where the prioress waited.

"The building across the way is a storeroom with a blind wall. You must have seen the cloister ghosts."

"Ghosts? Nonsense."

"You would not be the first."

"I prefer your original assessment. I am overtired and a little ill."

"As you have it."

"Please, have the tub for a mineral bath brought to my room as soon as possible."

Jhee needed to clear her head. She had inquiries to perform, and she had no time for nonsense, such as ghosts. "I hope our use of the Zodiac Courtyard won't cause too much disruption. Does that courtyard have the same layout as this?"

The prioress stumbled. "That courtyard has been off-limits as of late. Why do you ask?"

"The abbess said my cohort and I could use it for meditation and arcane study because it was under renovation."

"I see. If you have no truck with ghosts, I should think that would be the last place you'd dally with arcane forces."

"Because a young novice fell to his death there?"

"The young novice died there during the first tremor. Even before that, there have been reports of strange voices, tiny footsteps, the laughter of children, music and whispering in the walls. No one goes there anymore except Mr. Anshu, the animal handler."

They emerged on a residential hallway more warmly lit with glow globes than anything Jhee had seen in this place thus far.

"This is yours. We gave you the biggest, most comfortable rooms we could manage in the circumstances. No insult to your station."

"No insult taken."

4
____

THE FEAST I

~

The Two Deaconesses

Jhee collapsed in a chair, favoring the bridge of her nose. Her sinuses had now become stopped up. Ghosts. Stuff and nonsense. Shep removed her shoes and massaged her feet while Kanto brushed her hair. The rooms, though plain, had an antechamber and a tea nook with tea service. She eyed it, wishing for nothing more than a hot cup and her conch. She had nearly drifted to sleep when the mineral bath arrived.

Dari whined from a small bed by the bookcase and writing desk, as Jhee lowered herself into the tub. She reached over and gave her a reassuring pat. A little lamp and communication device supplemented the bare overhead glow lights. Kanto and Mirrei had already set up stools near the small window to work on their crafts. The bed, while a decent size, would not be comfortable for four.

Jhee yawned. "This many people in a bed. It's simply uncivilized."

She opened her eyes at the silence. Her spouses had fixed her with expressions fit to kill. She remembered the conditions they had to sleep under on the yacht. She hunkered down in the tub.

"I'll take the floor," Shep said. "You all thrash about too much, anyway."

He dug out their nightclothes and a bedroll.

Jhee shook her head and yawned. "Evening robes, if you will. We've been invited to a hundred-year-feast in the main hall."

Kanto set down his lute and pushed Shep aside. "Let me. Why didn't you tell us sooner? We could have been preparing."

"In the confusion, it slipped my mind. I must attend. The rest of you are free to refuse if you are not up to it. Bring me something more formal."

"Formal wear for ascetics?"

"This cloister boasts Lady Bathsheba as a court official in residence."

"An Imperial tutor?" Kanto touched his hand to his chin in thought. "No. No. No. Our most formal attire is with the rest of our things on the way to the capital. Our more formal attire buried in the luggage."

Kanto whipped out the robe he and Mirrei had made. "Yes, yes. Dry enough. This will have to do. I'll patch and clean it as best I can. We'll do that. A former member of the court, attire should still be simpler. As befits a humble official, such as yourself in a setting such as this. Your breaking it in the other night will only serve to make them seem more modest and humbler."

Jhee offered no input and let him and Mirrei work while she soaked as best she could in the tiny tub. Soon after, Kanto and Mirrei splashed each other with water, depriving her of the blessed silence she craved. She pinched the bridge of her nose.

"I made this sweet-smelling mint poultice to clear your head, denbe. I swear by it."

Mirrei knelt and presented her the poultice.

"A fair sight she'd be meeting the vizier with that on her head, denye," Kanto said.

"Scrape barnacles."

"Lick glass."

"Enough. Both of you," Jhee said. She regretted her sharp tone when Mirrei looked away abashed. Kanto gave Mirrei an accusing glance.

"Put it under a head wrap," Shep said. "No one will even notice."

Jhee took the poultice and let her hand linger on Mirrei's, who smiled. Mirrei faced Kanto self-satisfied. He proceeded to do up Jhee's head wrap and robe unbothered. He punctuated the finishing touches with a smug expression of his own. The feast felt more inviting all the time.

The poultice did, indeed, make Jhee's head feel clearer. She reflected on what she had seen earlier. She slipped away to summon Bax via conch. Outside the rooms, she confided what she had seen.

"One arm, but no blood, Justicar? Distressing indeed."

"It would not be a fresh injury. I've seen few enough monks here. A man missing an arm should not be too difficult to notice."

"Is your ladyship sure it's not ghosts? The servants and the laity say evil forces are at work here."

"Likely of a much more mundane cause. Investigate the storeroom then contact me after the banquet."

Jhee joined Pyrmo and the senior clergy at the high table above the other clerics in the banquet hall. In accordance with sacred geometry, six hallways radiated off the principal, vaulted room. Two exits featured barred doors. The lesser clergy ate separated by gender at long tables and benches surrounding a central stage. A Professed read scripture aloud from the pulpit. Gallery boxes flanked the main eating floor. All save for one was empty. Two men in merchant dress, one younger, one older with a goatee, watched the performance unaccompanied.

No sign of her household, whom Jhee had left to quibble over what to wear and whether to attend. She intended only to stay long enough to meet the vizier and put her mind at ease about the recent deaths.

"Justicar, I hope you had time to reflect and refresh yourself," Pyrmo said.

"Again, Abbess, I must thank you for your hospitality. My household is a bit unsettled and may make their way here shortly. We've had a trying journey." A quick glance at the table revealed nothing but clerics. The Lost Makers' place at the table had a setting but no chair. Abbesses sometimes invited anyone who called the abbey home from the highest deaconess to the lowliest servant to fill the seat and to share the abbey's inner workings with them. A custom households such as her family also followed when she was younger. "Will the vizier be dining with us tonight?"

"She sends her regards. She has chosen to spend the evening convalescing from injuries received in the quake. She asks that I pass along an invitation for tea in her quarters after the banquet."

"I would be most honored." As lovely as tea sounded, the invitation doused Jhee's notions of a short evening. "I chanced a visit to your most impressive courtyard and shrine. Would that I could have seen it in the full light of the sources."

"Bah, this weather," Sister Serra, the traditional figured cleric to Jhee's left, said. She drained the contents of her mg then thumped the cup on the table. "It stunts the plants. If we don't get enough dry time and strong light soon, the Tranquility Blossoms won't produce enough nectar for this season's demand, let alone next."

A Prospective put a fresh pitcher of wine in a central location. Sister Serra reached for the pitcher only to have the gaunt cleric to Pyrmo's right, Sister Elkanah, remove it.

"Then perhaps you should partake less of it," said Sister Elkanah. "Seminar attendance is down too. With all this disruption, we are also not making enough from cafeteria and visitors' fees to pay the upkeep on the reliquary."

"Or the greens houses," Sister Serra added.

The abbess took command of the pitcher and placed it in front of her, sloshing some on the table. Jhee considered the pinkish tinged elixir. Tranquility Bridge's healing nectar wine: one reason she had been so keen to visit.

"May I?"

Jhee pointed her cup at the pitcher. The abbess filled Jhee's cup herself. "Be my guest."

As wine connoisseurs past had instructed her, Jhee held the cup in front of her nose and swirled it to allow the bouquet to tease the palate before she drank. She tipped the cup to her lips. Delightfully sweet and flowery with the slightest peach tang. She made a satisfied sound. "The famed Golden Tranquility wine. I read of its refreshing and curative properties during my study of healing draughts. The descriptions do not do it justice."

The abbess winced. "And now the wine argument."

"Our Select blend," Sister Serra said with pride. "Named after the golden span connecting this structure to the main isle."

"To give such flattery is almost as much of a sin, as to receive it," Sister Elkanah said.

"Netherwise, the Justicar is most welcome," the abbess said.

Jhee imagined her face bore a similar expression when the dispute over the poultice broke out.

The fare they ate was a good deal more elaborate than Jhee would have expected of a cloistered order. A circumstance owed either to the occasion or Sister Serra's evident joy and delight as an epicure. Rosemary mutton with roasted vegetables met everyone's approval, save Sister Elkanah. She eschewed more sumptuous dishes opting instead for boiled potatoes, scrod, and a bowl of thin leek soup.

From what Jhee gathered, Sister Serra ran the farming operations. A horticulturist with a traditional figure, reddened cheeks, and bloodshot eyes, she laughed easily and frequently. While, the slimmer, more severe Sister Elkanah presided over the archives and reliquary. If the prioress's look was one of permanent dissatisfaction, hers was its complement, somewhere between disinterest and disgust. Fresh scratches graced her wrists. She pulled down her sleeves at Jhee's notice.

"I question the need for this banquet anyway and its taste. Our founding coming as it does so near the anniversary of the massacre.... No wonder the spirits are roiled," Sister Elkanah said.

"I should rather think it's the Mist World in retrograde. The current trines of the moons with the fourth planet. The last time they were in this position was on the eve of the massacre. We know this configuration unleashes malevolent energies upon the worlds. More than enough to account for our recent tragedies," Sister Serra said.

"Speaking of tragedy... Abbess, about the arrangements for my pupil and me, might we change them to another courtyard? I heard a Prospective died in the courtyard you've been so gracious to lend us. His ghost may not be the only one that haunts this place."

"Someone's already been telling you tales of our infamous cloister ghosts, have they?"

"The prioress mentioned it after I saw a strange sight in the courtyard. I thought perhaps it might be a residual or echo. The spirits perhaps of the more recently dead. You've had more than your fair share of suffering, both distant and not. I'm not the superstitious sort myself, but it may do well not to chance the whirlpool of fate by cyphering there."

"I'll see what we can do."

A small choir took the pulpit to perform a religious hymn. After which, Sister Elkanah read a selection from Dallighere's Descent to the Trench. The lower clergy and Professed alike sat fish-eyed and gape-mouthed from its elaborate depictions of the torments of the wicked on their way to the Irreparable Place.

"Are you, also, a practitioner of the healing arts, Justicar?" Sister Serra asked.

Jhee's marriage cohort made their entrance dressed modestly. A Prospective showed them to gallery boxes nearest the high table without separating men from women; a courtesy of the abbess no doubt. They seated Mirrei first, who curtsied then finger waved at Jhee. Kanto and Shep gave polite bows to the high table. Shep's bow was perfunctory and straightforward. Kanto's had an extra demure flourish. Their box faced that of the merchants.

"A dabbler. It's become an obsession of late. My wife has the real talent for it."

"Then we must give you a cask of Tranquility Gold for your journey, so you can have a proper sample to study."

"Much obliged, Sister Serra. I couldn't accept such a gift, especially if, as you say, you may not have enough to meet demand."

"I insist."

Jhee licked her lips. If the fruits of her investigations or future study of the wine did not yield harvest, this made the stay worth it. Healing properties or no, sips of this guaranteed a more pleasant remainder to their journey. "Very well, then. Allow me to offer a gift in exchange. Consider my skills in jurisprudence and investigation at your disposal for the length of our stay. We'll also pay the standard rental and materials fees along with a donation equivalent to the market value of say two casks to your repair fund."

The abbess's eyes brightened, while the prioress and Sister Elkanah leaned in. It reminded her of feeding time at the aquarium.

"Your patronage will be greatly appreciated. Saheli's generous heart outmatched the abbey's resources. She had instituted increased alms for the refugees. Unfortunately, we don't have the resources to continue it."

"Thank you, Abbess."

"Nonsense," Sister Serra said. "Have it with our compliments."

The prioress frowned. Jhee decided not to argue the point further here. She began a mental tally anyway and would check the market value of the casks later.

"Don't be daft, Sister Serra. As if Saheli's misplaced kindness hadn't already imperiled us. And save your 'generosity.' Justicar ethics prohibits her from accepting such a valuable gift. She's humoring you," Sister Elkanah said.

Jhee turned to the mistress of relics. "I corresponded with your previous abbess not only about the nectar but about access to your archives. We discussed a donation and archival fees."

The abbess dipped her head, which Jhee took as affirmation she had tacked correctly.

Sister Elkanah sniffed. "Your name does seem familiar. I may recall her passing those along. Our greatest religious texts in their earliest, most fragile forms are there. Their access is usually reserved for the most devout and dedicated of scholars. Your requests were very professional and thought out. I had yet to make my decision. I'll discuss the matter with Pyrmo and our librarian."

Jhee had sent those requests months, if not more ago. If the Sister were inclined to grant them, she might have done so by now. Abbess Pyrmo took the pulpit to talk about the abbey's founding and history of the island.

The feast's tone shifted more toward somber. Jhee only found intermittent enjoyment in the meal, company, or entertainment, anyway. Throughout, her thoughts lingered on the sight from the grotto and the recent deaths. An array of smells bombarded her from incense censers and licorices to spike leaf ointment and other peculiar sharp tangs in the air. Death stalked this abbey. Had she seen a new tragedy or an old as the prioress would have her believe?

"Quite the blood-soaked history Torilsisle has."

"How many Makers do you subscribe to, Justicar?" Sister Elkanah asked.

"Mechanism posits a reasonable case for as many as five, three plus a Prime Maker and an Unknown Maker, with possibly an innumerable number of Lesser Makers."

"What case do you posit? There comes the point when the worship of the various Lesser Makers becomes akin to paganism. Everyone's up-jumped ancestor can't be a Maker."

Sister Serra dipped her finger in her wine cup and then tasted her fingertip. "Mm, I'd argue by definition everyone's ancestor is a Maker, or else none of us would be here."

"Obscene. You mock too much, Sister Serra."

"Idolater."

It would seem Jhee had traded one bickering pair for another. A group including Sister Serra livened attitudes up with dancing and a few bawdy songs.

Jhee swept her cup at the cramped benches. "Quite the full house."

"Supplicants used to be rare. Now we turn them away," the prioress said.

"Ah, yes, the refugees. Many come at our doors to beg. Can you imagine?" Sister Elkanah said.

"More come each day like an enormous unwashed wave, a tsunami that can't be stopped," Pyrmo replied.

"Which is why you sought to turn my messenger away," Jhee stated.

"The Justicar's pardon, again, for the misunderstanding between your messenger and the gate staff," the prioress said.

"Not very hospitable," a woman in noble dress said. "Yes, the gall to ask charity at an abbey."

The carob-brown woman stumbled to the high table. Jhee estimated her too young to be the vizier. The woman supported herself with the table while sloshing various discarded cups to see if they were empty.

"They likely fancied you more beggars or refugees. How long did you leave the esteemed Justicar and her vessel stranded?"

"Rescuing overburdened ships in ill weather can be quite dangerous."

Jhee sipped her wine. After the woman flung aside one last cup, she flailed for a nearby chair. Once she had hold to the chair, she dragged it to the Lost Makers' place with a drawn-out, ear-piercing scrape. Everyone winced. It appears she had found a topic upon which the clerics agreed.

~

A Recitation

A female announcer came out and spoke. "My gracious hosts, I present you the spinner stylings of Mr. Zane."

A young man took the stage with a series of sticks and staffs and hoops. After a few masterful displays of staff spinning and tricks with the small hoops and the sticks, he switched to larger body hoops. He swirled and undulated his body to rotate the circles about his torso, hips, and at one point, a single shoulder.

The performer's outfit matched neither that of the figure in the mask nor the one missing an arm. Nonetheless, Jhee admired Mr. Zane's skill.

"Mr. Zane is in exquisite form tonight," Sister Serra said. "His *talent* truly is a treat for deprived eyes."

Sister Elkanah replied, "The Sister would do best to at least pretend some restraint."

"Chaste doesn't equal dead. What is the design intent to put such beauties and pleasures in the world if not to enjoy them?"

"Temptation away from the true path. It is a terrible distraction to have so many unmarried men about."

"Terrible for you, maybe. Chastity is a Drakist tenet. Hard to have one without the other."

"Precisely my point. Men should not be here."

"What do you think, Justicar?"

Jhee ruminated on her experience in the grotto, the couple, the effigies. "Does this order not believe any of the Makers males?"

"We do."

"The Design teaches us one of the many joys on the route to release is the marrying and fostering of children. Without household aid, how do they hope to gain their place in the Prime Maker's showcase? Their spirits shall be doomed to wander. Celibacy and paganism negate a societal need. No wonder your cloister is said to be haunted by ghosts. The widowed life mates of these unfortunate men and women."

"Well said," Sister Serra declared. "Then I'd say we have the contradiction backward. I'd argued such for years."

Sister Elkanah's icy stare made Jhee realize she had blundered again.

"The Justicar must then have scores of children. Or else one has to wonder what compliance with the Makers' Design marriage bestowed in lieu of chastity."

From their segregation by gender to their veneration of astrological superstition, Jhee felt as if she had stepped back in time an age. "We may never know anything else of the First Makers' Design. What we do know is they gave us intellect, sensation, and curiosity; tools with which we can know the world and ultimately the Design. Why would they not want us to use them?"

"Do you smell mint?" Sister Serra asked.

Abbess Pyrmo reddened.

Sister Elkanah snorted. "Further proof of the Unraveler's presence."

"Mint?" Serra asked.

"They say curious smells are one of the signs Unmakers are present."

"I thought it was ozone. Everything is a sign of the Unmakers according to you."

"The Unmakers' portents are many and varied."

"Like the Makers.'"

"With as much smudge and incense as you douse yourself with, it's no wonder you can't detect foul beings."

"Going back to the matter of the courtyard," Jhee started.

"What true philosophers I dine with," Pyrmo interrupted. "This light occasion is not the proper time for such heavy topics. A later time, yes?"

Finding out which one of them had contacted Jhee might also waiter for a later time, too. Mr. Zane's act concluded to much applause. Jhee chose strategic silence. She adjusted her mint poultice and wrap once their conversation turned to lighter subjects. Finding out which one of them had contacted Jhee might also wait for a later time, too.

The announcer returned. "In honor of our gracious hosts, we present a reenactment of Freytag's and Ziza's duel before the Last Redoubt of the Shell Knights. As performed by Mr. Anshu and Ms. Hethyr."

"Hethyr. A barbarian name," Jhee said.

"Ah, you are right," the abbess said.

Another man came to the stage in elaborate war gear, including two unlit fire fans. His body fur bore no trace of barbarian stipples or dapples. The mask he wore prevented a proper view of his esca. An assistant lit the tips of the fans then crouched at the foot of the stage with a bucket of water. Beside them, the announcer waited with a large blanket. The hall went silent save for the crackling of the flames as he swirled them in arcs and figure drakes.

A female figure in battle dress joined the first, this one bearing two fiery orbs on leashes. The woman's fur also was a proper, solid brown with no trace of barbarian striping. Jhee sat up straighter. The armor, though, reminded her of what she had seen in the courtyard. Both figures were in full possession of their limbs.

The two battled with their fire props. Their flickering lights swept over and around the faces of the crowd trailing wisps of smoke. Even from the high table, Jhee felt the ambient heat ebb and flow, a tide made of warmth as if the breathing of a deep drake. The pace of the scene picked up. The two darted their flaming weapons at each other. One of the fire orbs clipped Mr. Anshu's headdress in a manner Jhee was not entirely sure was planned. A gasp came from the seclusion boxes. The younger merchant had moved right up against the low wall. His two hands gripped the rail. From then on out, he flinched with each close call. The announcer and assistant's faces remained concerned until the two broke apart and went to opposite ends of the stage; Mr. Anshu nearer the seclusion boxes.

The announcer gestured excitedly at the assistant, who quickly doused their weapons. The warriors removed their headgear. Mr. Anshu glared at Ms. Hethyr. Now that Jhee saw both their escae, it confirmed neither were of barbarian descent. Though, with Mr. Anshu and the younger merchant in her field of vision at once, she could not help but notice a similarity to their eye coloring and ears.

The announcer took center stage with a little laugh. "Such a spirited performance. Now, Mr. Anshu and Itzil shall perform a reenactment of the Taming of the Shell Drake and the Storm Child's Lullaby."

Ms. Hethyr smiled at Mr. Anshu, gave an exaggerated bow to the audience, and left the stage. Now alone on stage, Mr. Anshu had switched to glow fans, which had small glow orbs instead of live fire. A growl came from the performers' entrance.

A Zicarian bull hound, a tusked canine the size of its titular bovine, burst onto the stage. Jhee gasped. She drew on the prime forces within, and her hand went to the sigil that bound her to Shep. He had already sprung from his seat and placed himself between the beast and Mirrei and Kanto.

No one at the high table or audience had made a move. Jhee turned her attention back to the stage. The bull hound came to a full stop at Mr. Anshu's command. He stomped and shouted another command. The bull hound rose up and towered over him, its paws nearly the size of his head.

Jhee slumped in her chair. "Whelm and waves."

"Forgive my lapse, Justicar. The bull hound is Mr. Anshu's companion."

Mr. Anshu and the beast performed a dance full of gentle, rhythmic movements where he appeared to lull the animal to sleep with the fans. He tucked his fans under his arm and bowed to the head table. The hall erupted into applause.

Mr. Anshu petted the bull hound then fed it some land meat from a nearby bucket. Jhee drew in a breath. Her attention snapped back to her cohort in the boxes. Shep sat rigid in his seat; his eyes firmly fixed on the pair on stage. Her conch pulsed. She jumped in her chair. He turned to her, his ordinarily amber eyes a duller shade. He forced himself to relax. The sigil on her arm had gone cold and still.

The fear, having already shaken her wits and sharpened her senses, clarified her resolve. The more she thought, the more Ms. Hethyr's mask focused her on the scene from the courtyard. She excused herself from the table to check her conch.

Found storeroom, my lady. Storage for troupe's costumes and props. Nothing else, Bax's message read.

Inquire about troupe member Hethyr.

Jhee returned to her seat. She did a double-take when she realized the other gallery box had now emptied. "Who were the other guests in the boxes?"

"Mr. Pol, a pious widower and his son, Akesheem. The young man is thinking of taking vows. Displaced or wealthy families seek the honor joining our prestigious abbey confers. And to divest themselves of surplus males." A chair scraped across the floor. The woman from earlier staggered to the pulpit. The abbess narrowed her eyes and took a long drink from her cup. "Or mere surplus. Case in point."

"Two, two by Chance, a recitation by yours truly Raigen," the drunken woman said, her words loud and slurred. "Two mothers by chance, by rites. One bears the day, and one bears the crypts by nights. Two warring duchesses dance an extended caper. Abstinence. Humility. Hospitality. Three vows as binding as vapor. Four elements: air, fire, water, earth. The drakes' eyes shall witness their rebirth."

Drunken ranting described the recital better than word-smithing. No one applauded. The banquet hall began to empty. Raigen stumbled back to her seat beside the prioress.

The golden hue to the abbess's eyes had gone fifty fathoms deeper. "Shameful."

"Truly," Jhee agreed. She glanced at her cohort. Shep still sat stiff-backed.

"Raigen seeks to take vows at the deathbed request of her mother, the former governess of the district. A request I'd deny had she not once been amongst our strongest supporters. In life, she gifted us many relics, she bequeathed us more should her daughter become Professed, which I do not see happening. If you'll forgive me, I need to properly thank and provide homage to our true entertainers."

"Excuse me, as well. I would like to check in with my household."

The abbess swayed slightly as she got up from the table. "Of course."

Jhee's conch sounded again for a live message. "Speak."

"Hethyr was not with the other performers. No one seems to know where she went."

"Whelm. Meet me outside the banquet hall."

5

THE FEAST II

~

The Poetess

Jhee joined her cohort at their box. "Alas, my dear cohort, I'm glad everyone got to see the feast performances."

"That Mr. Zane was quite handsome and skilled," Mirrei said.

Kanto folded his arms. "If you are into such unsophisticated fare. Could you believe that poetess, denye? So embarrassing."

"I was embarrassed for her," Mirrei said then shrugged. "A welcome diversion after the bull hound. I near died of fright here on the spot when Shep leaped up. Do you think they'll be animals like that at court?"

"I hear the Imperial families keep pygmy shell drakes as pets," Kanto said.

"No."

"Oh, yes."

They continued to giggle and gossip while Shep kept watchful eyes on the entrances and tugged on his forearm hairs. As Jhee approached, she heard him talking to himself, "Walls to our back good. Walls to the side. If cornered, the only way out is through, though. Confined space. No room to maneuver."

"Shep," she whispered so she would not startle him. He turned to her and smiled as if nothing was amiss. "What of you, dear heart? How are you faring?"

"Much better now that you're within arm's reach."

Jhee stroked the ridges of his ears with her thumbs. "I was in no danger."

43

He brought her hand to his eye scar briefly before standing. "Best to be cautious."

They returned to the younger spouses. "Did you have a chance to try the Tranquility Gold? I'm sure it must have met with even your high standard, Shep."

"It was decent. I don't get the fuss."

"Who convinced whom to attend the feast?"

"We wanted to," Mirrei said.

She and Kanto locked arms. "We said Shep could stay if he wished."

Shep pursed his lips. "You could very well not attend the feast unaccompanied yet alone go about the halls by yourself, denyes. Hence, we all attended."

"We would have been fine," Mirrei said. "Perish the thought of any of us having time to ourselves."

"Indeed," Kanto said.

Jhee sighed. "Shep did the right thing. We are guests here. It's perhaps best if we stick together in this unfamiliar place."

Shep and Jhee made pointed eye contact. She tucked her hands into her robes and touched the sigil. He glanced at the exits. "Fine, then we should all retire to our quarters. Yav-yav."

Bax entered the hall. Jhee remained in place in contravention of Shep's attempt to herd the lot of them towards the door. He caught her eye again.

"I have an invitation to tea with the vizier. Return to the room. Hopefully, I won't be long."

Shep folded his arms. Mirrei degenerated into a coughing fit. Kanto provided her a steadying arm. Shep cast a stern glance at Bax then escorted the other spouses out. Jhee's heart tightened as she watched them leave. They passed the poetess, Raigen, who grabbed a wine pitcher from the tray of a Prospective clearing the high table.

Bax came over. "What now, Justicar?"

"All the men of the Abbey appear to be accounted for."

"There is a population of refugees nearby."

"So. With buildings such as this, there may be a multitude of hidden ways in and out. A small matter to find one and bring young men in and out."

"These are professed Drakists, Justicar!"

"One of the eternal dichotomies of celibacy. Make further inquiries into Hethyr. See what you can learn from the performers and Mr. Pol and his son."

"Aye, Justicar."

Jhee paused about to say something else when she noticed the proximity of the poetess. She sat at one of the seats at the high table, checking the cups for dregs. "We'll speak more later."

Bax excused himself. Jhee glanced the way her cohort had gone and thought about Mirrei. She did not like the cast to her pallor. She had hoped some time off the yacht would do her good. Jhee should have joined them, but this was apt to be her last case as a field Justicar. There would be time enough for nesting later after she fulfilled her promise to their dames. She would see Kanto and Mirrei safely to the capital where they can decide for themselves what it is they want.

Raigen, who did not possess a fraction of the grace or poise Mirrei had in her littlest finger, continued to hover and scavenge the high table. How different the poetess was to her late mother, the governess. How different this drunken wastrel was to her Kanto and Mirrei. The poetess was about their age. She thought them a credit to the younger generation. They sought to better themselves despite the hard turns the sea had sent them while this embarrassment drank away her future and a possible cure to Mirrei's ailment. The wine being slurped by this wastrel could well hold the key to Mirrei's recovery.

That Raigen could so flagrantly disregard the rules of not only polite behavior but basic health and yet remain standing, defied Design. Her squandered potential stole momentum from the Divine Mechanism, where it might better serve those who needed it more. While Mirrei struggled to do even the minutest activities, this scoundrel wasted twice the energy stumbling about in drunken idleness. At the poetess's age, Jhee's oldest, surviving sisters had already begun to distinguish themselves in the navy. When Jhee reached that age, she had dreamed of following in their footsteps.

Jhee marched up to Raigen, who had produced a flask. The area around the table still smelled of incense, licorice, and burn cream. Given Raigen's state of drunkenness, she expected it to reek of a still. The poetess tipped the pitcher to her flask. "What you are doing is not only unseemly but unsanitary."

"What exactly is it am I doing, Justicar?"

Her words were clear and articulate. The poetess's hands were rock steady. She did not so much as spill a drop.

"You're not drunk."

The poetess put the flask inside her robes. "No."

"It was my proud pleasure to have met the governess. Why such a disgraceful ruse? Your mother's eyes are still upon you."

"It is because of her, I'm here. Fools can go about nearly invisible and inquire where others can't. Much like Justicars."

"So, there is more method than madness to your poem as well. If you have some proof of a crime, I'll hear it and render fair judgment."

"Proof. Therein lies the problem. I like my tongue and my head precisely where they are."

"I've made it my mission to ensure such harsh penalties are no longer imposed in the district. For slander or libel penalties to apply, a false charge would have to be leveled. However, gossip amongst bored residents is simply uncorroborated evidence, not an accusation." Jhee took the pitcher from the poetess. She squared her shoulders and added sternly, "Nor proof."

Raigen nodded. "Saheli and my mother served together, and they corresponded often. She was concerned about odd happenings at the abbey. Whisperings in the walls. Weird lights. Odd behavior amongst the staff and novices. She sent a communique where she stated another authority was undermining her. I questioned some of the staff and novices. A name continued to come up: The Mist Abbess. Saheli died soon thereafter. My mother succumbed to illness before she could inquire into it herself. Fresh Lung Sickness. I promised on her deathbed to investigate."

Jhee flinched. Her gaze flicked to where her family had left. "Most admirable. What have you found so far?"

"Taking vows here may become hazardous to one's health. At least if you're male."

"Someone may have taken it upon themselves to correct the surplus male problem."

"Three so far that I know of. All since the first quake. Who knows how many more there may be? I don't have the skills to investigate thoroughly alone. I am a simple poet. You have legal backing and Imperial authority at your disposal."

"Which also carries a decidedly higher profile and standard of conduct," Jhee stated.

"I implore you. If not for my sake, then for Akesheem."

"You sent in the complaint."

"I'm sorry I left it unsigned. Reliable off-isle communications went down around then."

"By accident or design?"

"I suspect the latter. But to be candid, it wasn't stellar before then."

That mystery solved, Jhee declared, "Leave it to me from here out."

~

A Simple Request

Before Jhee could inquire further, Pyrmo reentered the banquet hall. Raigen knocked over a cup and snatched the pitcher Jhee held.

"Justicar, you are still here." The abbess gave Raigen a look of utter contempt. "Is this wretched creature bothering you?"

Raigen uprighted the cup. Jhee took the pitcher back. "Just discussing proper conduct with our young poetess here and the vagaries of poetry."

Raigen's formerly alert gaze was now glazed over and unfocused. "It's nice to meet, meet a learned woman sophisticated enough to nuance my poetry unlike you rest of, the rest of your bores. Perhaps I'll go share my poems with the Honored Dead in the Coral Cloister. Perhaps they'll appreciate it more."

Raigen staggered away.

The abbess relieved Jhee of the pitcher. "My forgiveness for your being subjected to her."

"None needed. It was most illuminating. The poetess's carrying on has been most shameful. There are a great many young men and women here, and it's for those of certain stature to set the example."

"I shudder to think how the governess would have reacted if she were alive to see what has become of her only heir."

"No doubt she would have been most distressed. Perhaps the allure of your delicious wine overwhelmed her."

"With the exception of those who work the vats, Professed and Prospective alike are only permitted one tankard of our house wines a week or a thimbleful daily for health except on certain occasions. They may also partake of small amounts of kolal during services, but no other stimulant drinks. She appears to have found a way around our restrictions. I'll have to tell the staff to be more mindful. This is not the first time I've found her such. You know I even found going through my things and the wine cellar the other day."

"Truly. Truly distressing when such a compulsion drives you to such lengths."

Pyrmo studied the pitcher she held for a moment then placed it on the table. "I had hoped to teach her self-discipline, and in some small measure, our teachings would have a benevolent impact on her. In that, I am failing. Perhaps you may have more luck in straightening the young priss out."

"Is that all that troubles you, abbess? The deacons mentioned recent deaths."

"I appreciate how you were able to navigate the waters between those two."

When Pyrmo said nothing more, Jhee attempted a different approach, "During my stay, I was hoping to get a tour of the abbey. In addition to the archives and ingenious hothouses, I heard of your famous Coral Cloister and Crypts. For now, I'm afraid this beautiful abbey has me a bit turned around. Where might I find the vizier's room?"

"I can escort you if you wish. The vizier currently occupies our hermitage."

"My thanks. Such an intriguing design to your central hall."

The abbess walked her out an entrance different than the one which led to the main dormitories. "The abbey's layout follows the principles of sacred geometry. Six entrances from six halls to represent the six pillars of society."

Jhee jutted her chin at the chained door nearest them. "Where does that door lead?"

"The Corrections Hall."

"What of the other?"

"The other? The crypts. Both are off-limits. They sustained some damage during the recent quakes."

"I hope no one was hurt. That isn't where the young man died, is it?"

"Not there. Both had already been closed by then, the hall due to Saheli's order. She took a different view of discipline than past abbesses. As for the crypts, the risk of flooding has put them off-limits during the storms. The extreme moisture also interferes during the first few years of the preservation process we use on our honored dead, such as my predecessor."

"May I inquire as to how your predecessor died? Disease? Disaster?"

"Transfiguration. Her spirit ascended in light directly to the Maker Sphere, while several of us watched. A transcendent sight I might have questioned had I and the high clergy not witnessed it ourselves."

"Remarkable. What events preceded this extraordinary occurrence?"

"Saheli and I had spoken just that morning about abbey business. She pursued several crafting and artistic pursuits in the gardens. The weather that day was sunny, not wet and black like now. Professed as well as the visiting scholar, Sister Niza, also there for contemplation, later heard her performing alignment chants. Then the sound of her engaged in dialogue with the Makers."

"How can you be sure it was the Makers?"

"Those who saw her said no one else was there, and she sat alone on the bench, but she had completed the most exquisite sketch of her cat. No doubt, via the Makers' inspiration. She announced her intentions to take advantage of the clear weather and spend the rest of the afternoon in contemplation via construction in her favorite place, the Bridge tower. Some time later, she summoned me, the prioress, the deacons, and a visiting scholar, Niza. She delivered an hour-long sermon about the nature of cyphering and drawing with respect to the pillars of society. The Imperial Theological Department is even considering adopting it as a primary text."

"Impressive. To qualify for consideration means an independent account exists. Where might I view a copy?"

"The archives. Saheli preached with transcendent power and full of the most inspired and eloquent language the great thinker, Yrisa, upon reading Sister Niza's account, wrote a ten-paged annotated commentary of its allusions and symbolism. Those of us present felt the strength and power of the words in our bones. Her spirit became visible. A great beam of light appeared. She spoke her last words and passed out dead on the spot. With a great blinding flash of light, her spirit ascended the beam to the Divine Spheres. Before it disappeared, I touched it and was left with these burns."

The abbess displayed her hands, then tucked them away.

"I know you already think us backward and superstitious, but Niza witnessed it too. The recent deaths have quite upset the residents of Tranquility Bridge. Justicar, were you sincere about offering us your services?"

"Of course, Abbess."

"Being a woman of law and letters, I thought if you were to reassure everyone and find a more natural mundane cause, it would put many minds at ease."

"As a holy woman yourself, you see no work of Unmakers in this."

"I know Unmakers, especially the Unmaker, prefers to use mortal faces to hide hir true intent. Here we are. The vizier's chambers. Some of Saheli's artwork and writings were put in the archives. The rest of her belongings are interred with her in the crypts. Her remains and belongings may someday be counted as relics themselves on par with our other Honored dead. This right here is one of Saheli's works."

An etching hung beside a door illuminated by a glow orb. Jhee admired the workmanship.

"Superb. What became of the cat?"

"The cat? Oh, yes. We buried it in the garden under her favorite tree."

"I would very much like to read that account and the sermon if I may, but it seems as if Sister Elkanah has taken a dislike to me."

"Ask the vizier. Sister Elkanah holds her in high regard. Perhaps if she were to speak on your behalf, she might be more inclined to grant you access."

"Many thanks. Is there any opportunity for me to autopsy Saheli's remains? My duties require some training in forensic and mortuary sciences. My first husband and wife also have some medical training. I'd be interested in what the act of transfiguration does to our mortal form."

"Autopsy? The preservation process may prevent that, and as I said, the crypts are sealed right now. I'm also afraid I cannot allow a male to examine such a holy personage as our abbess or near our most sacred spaces. I shall consult with the prioress. I must leave you now and attend to other matters."

Once Pyrmo left, Jhee examined the etching once more. Exceptional work. The tiny pop of grit ground underfoot drew her attention. She paused to listen, then stared into the darkness beyond the orb. She waited for her eyes to adjust but saw no one. A whiff of the air proved equally fruitless. Because of the drenched poultice, all she smelled was mint.

6

THE AUDIENCE

∼

Teatime

On the other side of the door from the etching, the wall bore a panel with a placard pad. Jhee placed her conch against it and transmitted her social credentials. Pyrmo had not delivered her a formal invitation, so she defaulted to social protocol. The panel displayed the lady's seal, then the door opened. Jhee's position relative to hers did not require that.

Jhee entered and waited by the open door to be acknowledged. Every piece of furniture was black lacquer. No doubt brought with her from the capital. Nothing in the room was simple and utilitarian, as Jhee might have expected of someone who had retired to such an austere place. The vizier's chambers were adorned in antique instruments and battle regalia. Feathered animal headdresses. War aprons with the sea bat or silver fox. Obsidian spears with hardwood throwing shuttles. The gold and green tabards of the ancient warrior societies. Battle flutes. War drums. The trace of high-grade incense hung in the air. Along the walls, shelves stacked with books and seaweed parchments alternated with others containing chests and other curios.

Lady Bathsheba acknowledged Jhee's presence with a look and gestured to a small table set up in the middle of the room on an exquisitely woven rug. Jhee closed the door and seated herself properly. A gilded tea service crowned the table while the carpet ringed it with curved and repeating pattern borders popular with the great houses of the capital. The tea had a heavy, earthy smell more similar to kolal, likely a blend of the two. The lady hummed a little passage of music then finished a last bit of writing with her fingernail quill. She considered the page then smiled.

At last, she joined Jhee. As for the lady herself, she was an imperiously postured woman with high cheekbones who dressed in robes a step or two in finery above anything Jhee might have worn. Her hair showed the silvering of age, but just barely. Her esca appeared bright as ever. "Allow me to pour, Justicar."

The vizier poured the steaming kolal into the cup in front of Jhee. Jhee waited for the vizier to fill her own cup. She slipped the insulated sleeve over her cup then turned it thrice before picking it up in both hands. "Honors, Vizier."

The vizier turned her cup twice. "Honors to you as well, Justicar."

Jhee drank a moment after the vizier. "It's good to see the injuries you received in the quake haven't slowed you down."

"Thank you for your concern. You are familiar with high etiquette."

"I have been to the extended court in the Outer Reaches and the capital."

"Never long enough for it to sink in its claws, I'll wager. The politics takes its toll. Although it can be dull at times, and I had to seek my own amusement. Clever girl to stay out of depths you may not be prepared to handle. Keep above the waves as long as you can, I say."

Jhee smirked. She attributed the slight she felt to being called 'girl.' Some time had passed since anyone had dared. Vizier Bathsheba was likely to have been an adolescent when Jhee was born. "The storm shield has changed much. Alas, Vizier, as storm and sea reclaim the Reaches, it is my fate to be reassigned to the capital. It is now my honor to serve at court."

"And you stopped at our humble abbey along the way. Poor dear, allow me to put something stronger in that cup of yours."

"No need, my lady. I think I would like to keep a clear head after the day's events." Everywhere Jhee turned in the room, she found more treasures. She did her best not to marvel. "Vizier, I must admit to being in awe of your fine possessions. Especially the lute. My second husband also plays one and is an admirer of your work."

"A member of the Imperial family gave me that. May I ask what brings you to Tranquility Bridge?"

"Our vessel required repairs. Although I have heard some disturbing tales."

"Oh? Of what sort?"

"The prioress told me of the cloister ghosts while the deacons speak about malign forces and Unmakers, especially in the Zodiac Courtyard where the young man died."

"Worried you've seen some?"

"A place of such history must surely have its share. Of secrets as well. Then there is the abbess's remarkable account of the death of her predecessor."

"I too heard something of Pyrmo's account and read Niza's record. Your credentials. During my tenure, they still spoke of an Imperial wedding stormed by adherents of the monogamist school. Your grand dame preached with them for a time. She surely would have some words over your cohort."

"Grandmamere rejoined the Makers some years ago. I'm told all the most prestigious residents of the abbey witnessed the miraculous event. What's your recollection?"

"To be honest, I'm not sure. I'm not as religious or zealous as some. I do know we sat in a room for two to three hours with little in the way of food or drink under less than ideal conditions. Who knows what phantoms devout minds might conjure up?"

"You believe no transcendence took place?"

"Who am I to say? It is a matter of faith for each one present."

"But not you."

"I have become something of a hermit. I am here to meditate and reflect. My goal was never oneness with the Makers as some others. Nor did I seek refuge from the war mind. I contemplated service, you see. I wanted to participate in the effort to defend our lands and way of life as they tell us so often we should. In the end, I always chose not to commit. Yourself?"

"I, for the most part, saw no combat."

"But not for the whole part? Sounds like a story there."

"One I won't bore you with."

"As you desire. You're only in your position a few years I take it. Judging by accent and the style of robes from the Far Reaches and no doubt ambitious. I understand the desire to leave simple country ways behind. What are the lives of simple country folk compared to the thrill of court? Yet you remain humble and remember from whence you came. Hand-made robes and an unsophisticated head wrap. A traditional, provincial marriage cohort, two men, one woman. I'm surprised one so unestablished took on a full complement before you reached the capital where more opportunities for strategic marriages awaited. I don't envy you having to balance those responsibilities."

Jhee's fingers twitched. "Duty sometimes demands a different path."

"You are ambitious, looking to move up. Difficult to do with something like that hanging over you. New marriages hastily put together. I suppose to show up to court with only one consort would have made the wrong impression. A full cohort shows a break with your grandmere's monogamist beliefs."

"I am but a simple servant to the office."

"Forgive me. I did not mean to imply."

The urge to touch her head wrap or Kanto's repairs to her robe made Jhee focus all the more on holding her cup. She had been relieved to wear the simple, elegant gowns when she expected to be dealing with a hermit-like public tutor. She had not wanted to put on airs. Faced with the sophisticated, urbane Bathsheba of Toho, instead, she felt more a backward, country rustic. Fine. If the vizier thought her a backwater, she would use it.

Jhee pinched the bridge of her nose. "I did see something odd when performing devotions at the main shrine: a figure embracing a naked, one-armed man. This dreadful weather has given me the most egregious headache and possibly a cold. My eyes may not have been as reliable as they once were. Maybe enough to imagine that."

"Do you partake of a lot of kreel?"

"It's a staple of the signature dish of our district."

"It's been my experience that an abundance of kreel, in addition to sometimes turning you pink, can hamper mental functioning. In conjunction with tiredness or poor health, I'd say you have a recipe for hallucination."

"You sound like my wife with her dietetic beliefs."

"She sounds like a wise woman."

"Perhaps, indeed, you are both right. I rather prefer that to the alternative: vengeful spirits drawn by an abundance of death or unwed souls."

"I found a draught part Tranquility Bridge's orange cider, part signature nectar, part black orchid tea, very detoxifying and good for the constitution." The vizier hesitated and leaned forward. "Did your ship really need repairs?"

Jhee opted for caution in the event she had misread the woman. "Have I given you cause to think otherwise?" Jhee asked.

"An abundance of death. What an interesting choice of words. You've never seen fit to visit our abbey before. Three dead Prospectives would have certainly drawn the attention of an involved justicar. I would have thought rather than chasing after phantoms of the mind. You had instead come to seek my counsel on the deaths of those poor, unfortunate souls. I do admit I had an ulterior motive in inviting you here. To see if some word of our plight, and the fates of those three Prospectives, had made it beyond these walls."

Jhee sipped her kolal and tried not to take umbrage. The vizier at least confirmed Raigen's findings. The dead men were not refuge-seekers or lay brothers, but men who had committed to the Drakist way. "My office had no reports of three Prospective deaths."

"Yet here you sit. True, there is no reason the deaths should have been reported. One boy, attended by the abbey physician and myself, appeared to have died of sickness. The other two were likely accidents or suicide. One died in a cave-in. The other fell while walking along the bluffs. All autopsied by the prioress. The passing of poor rural boys of consequence to no none, even their officials."

Jhee's grip on her cup tightened. "What a lovely finger maze. Does the vizier indulge in the art of sequence and gesture puzzles?"

"A recent find from the archives. One piece of a larger set. I had been working on identifying it, though parts are missing."

"I've dabbled. May I?"

The vizier nodded. "I'd be interested in the assistance of someone so studied as yourself."

"This one appears to be missing the key, which tells you how to start."

"Would you care to try, anyway?"

Jhee weighed her desire to rest and extricate herself from the vizier's high-handedness against the opportunity to match wits with an early cyphering enthusiast. "I've taken up too much of your time, Vizier."

The vizier pushed the puzzle closer.

Jhee performed a few gestures and solved a few levels in before tripping up. "My that was a tricky one."

"Ah, delightful. Might I make a suggestion? Having finally seen it used by someone as skilled as yourself, I see it has something of musicality to it. Keep in mind rhythm and flow, and you should be able to progress further."

"How clever of them! To incorporate musical timing rather than geometric or trigonometric principles. Two simultaneous left-hand sequences. I think it may require more than one participant. Oh, I see you pass it along like a relay or rounds. This might require some time and assistance from my wife to unravel. I have to return to my cohort else they'll think I've gotten lost."

The vizier poured them another cup of tea. Jhee turned the cup then lifted it with both hands.

"I thank the vizier again for her invitation. Honors to your house and health."

The vizier raised her cup one-handed without turnings. "No need for such ceremony, and please, call me Bathsheba. I left court to get away from such formality. An acutely pleasant change. You'll have to walk me through how to use the finger maze before you leave the abbey."

Once Jhee matched her, they drank at the same time.

Jhee set down her cup. The vizier escorted her to the door. Jhee hesitated when she glimpsed the edge of Saheli's etching.

"Was there something else, Justicar?"

"I hesitate to impose more on you, Lady Bathsheba. This etching. What do you think of Pyrmo's account of the death of her predecessor? Is there anything you care to add?"

"I spoke to her as normal, and then we parted company before her noon meal." The vizier glanced about her again. "I hesitate to relay gossip. Saheli was prone to taking psychedelics around the time she took her images for the day. It wasn't unusual to hear her speaking with the Makers during her vision quests. Prospectives near her thought nothing of the conversation. As she frequently had them. What she was not in the habit of doing was giving impromptu sermons. The abbey is about personal reflection and inner peace. It came then as a shock when this one day she called upon the senior clerics to hear her preach. She gave the sermon and died. You should read

Sister Niza's account as it is most illuminating. We have a copy in our archives."

"I would like to, but Sister Elkanah doesn't seem inclined to grant me access."

"Sister Serra used you to show her up, didn't she?"

"Afraid so."

"The pitching-and-yawing between those two. The previous abbess had to do an intricate balancing act to keep them from tearing the abbey apart. They are very protective of their respective fiefdoms. If you desire access to the archives, I might be able to arrange it with the archivist. Consider it done. On one condition."

"If it is in my humble power to do so, I shall."

"You simply must consent to be my guest for tea again soon, along with your lovely household. It is rare I get to converse with such learned and higher-class individuals as yourself. I also welcome the opportunity to meet a fan."

Jhee was loathed to expose her cohort to the woman's snobbery. Yet, an outright refusal would be an insult. Not only would it hamper her investigation and prevent her from examining the archives, but it might also follow them to court. "We had a hard journey. I will see if they are up to it."

"Splendid."

Jhee affected a meek air. "The abbey appears to have been constructed in accordance with sacred geometry tenets, overly elaborate and confusing as if designed by building over serpent trails. That's ascetics for you. Celibacy. A natural crime if you ask me."

Lady Bathsheba laughed. "A natural crime, indeed. My secret. I use maps. One perk of my position as librarian is access to the old building records. I'll ether you a copy."

Jhee's still too full conch refused the transfer.

"Allow me to get you a hand map and a torch." The lady rolled out a digital parchment and transcriber. "A physical copy will serve you better in this weather, anyway. Though it won't have live position tracking. Your recognition of the sacred design of the abbey is correct. We are here now at the Bridge wing off the Prime axis. These are your quarters in the opposite wing. You'll have to cross the central hall again to reach them."

Jhee touched two of the marked openings. "I saw these barred doors in the banquet hall."

"The Corrections Hall. Part museum, part throwback to a stricter time in the Drakists' history where they kept misbehaving Prospectives and Professed. Quite lurid tales of what transpired there exist in the archives. Forbidden orgies, naïve juveniles forced to perform blasphemous rites. Imprints left from the previous residents or maybe even your ghosts. The other leads to the crypts."

Jhee laid a finger on the side of her nose. The abbess had told her the truth. Jhee rolled up the map. "I thank you for this, Lady Bathsheba."

"You'll need a provision card for the storehouse. It also includes an invitation key for your next visit. Remember, orange cider is the key."

Outside in the hall, Jhee adjusted her head wrap and consulted the map; sacred geometry indeed. A quick count and some reasoning revealed the square and hexagon layout of the abbey's original structure to be an unfolded, truncated octahedron. She traced the route to the lady's note marking the guest quarters. Then she traced another to the wing running beside the courtyard. She had no quarrel with Bax's thoroughness, but she wanted to see this windowless storeroom for herself. Her duty demanded she investigate these matters thoroughly for the good of her constituents.

Jhee set off down the hall. A noise swished after her. She whirled. Again, she found no one there.

~

The Storeroom

Jhee expelled a satisfied sigh at seeing the storeroom entrance. Not bad for a provincial magistrate. She strode boldly into the storeroom, On the way in, she bumped a shelf. A mask of Cheiropthys, the bat-faced Exemplar, fell from the shelf to the ground. She yelped but took a deep breath, so she did not flee the storeroom as boldly as she entered it.

Racks of robes and costumes lined the room. Masks and props hung from any fixture that would hold them. A quick examination of the accessories, hoods, and capes turned up nothing which matched what Jhee saw in the courtyard.

Jhee thought for a moment. She moved aside a chest stored against the outer wall made of coral cement blocks. A good solid thud met everywhere she rapped the pale blocks with her knuckles. She tapped a few more areas and pushed against every visible join, testing for voids and weaknesses. She even ran her fingers along the tiniest cracks and crevices.

The vizier's remarks had hit upon a concern Jhee had tried to suppress: her preoccupation with the capital and personal matters had caused her to fail her constituents. Jhee was hard-pressed to think who had been more self-righteous this evening: her, Lady Bathsheba, or the clergy. She needed to moderate her behavior and remember she was a guest in their place of worship.

A pebble skittered. Jhee reached into the sleeve of her robe for her knife then formed a defensive cyphering gesture. "I warn you I am versed in the combat forms. Best you show yourself now."

Jhee heard movement and whirled around. Bax held up his hands in a placating manner. "Please, ma'am, it's me. Stay your fury."

She slipped her knife back into her robes. "What?"

"Try as I might, I didn't find Hethyr herself. This." Bax pointed at a rack. He held up a pelt and tabard like the one in which Ms. Hethyr had performed. "This, though, was not here when I first checked."

"Without her make-up and costume, Ms. Hethyr may have been hiding in plain sight this whole time. She must have returned here while I tarried with bullies and fools."

Bax frowned.

"Not you, Bax."

"If I may, Justicar, your reaction seems to be extreme?"

Jhee was glad he had the courtesy not to say angry or even shaken. "Feh, this evening had tried every component of my patience. I have a constant feeling of eyes upon me other than my ancestors. To the more immediate matter, other than her costume, what else have you to report of the woman?"

"Ms. Hethyr is, at best, an irregular member of the performance troupe. A vagrant who joins up from time to time, sometimes in the familiar company of Mr. Zane."

"Odd comings and goings. Without other identifiers, we cannot be assured of her identity. The entertainer persona makes a perfect guise for an individual to come and go as she pleases to whatever purpose."

"You think she may be disguised as clergy or a lay sister? You suspect her in the killings of those young boys?"

"Yes." Jhee paused and realized she had not told Bax about that.

"The staff, Justicar. Always talk to them first. Cooks, maids, footmen, and the like will know all the gossip."

"Good to know." Jhee massaged her brow. "Do you know where the performers are staying?"

"Yes, Justicar. Permit me, ma'am. You've had a long and trying day. I pray you to return to Mr. Shep's ministrations."

"I fear he will have cross words for us either way. I cannot rest with my mind bedeviled by so many questions. And if these young men are the victims of some foul play, they've waited for justice long enough."

"You owe them the full power of your faculties, Justicar."

Bax played with the pouch on his belt as if deciding whether to push the matter. Short temper often meant short sight. She decided to rest. "Continue your inquiries with the staff then get some rest too."

He expelled a breath. "Yes, Justicar."

To Jhee's surprise, Kanto awaited her, not Shep. He had moved the glow lamp to the space by the window where he lounged in a dressing robe curled up with his conch on a salon chair, which had replaced one of the stools. With his brow furrowed as he perused his screen, and in the unassuming, dressed-down attire, he looked less the dandy and more the scholar. Mirrei stirred fitfully in the bed, while Shep snored lightly from a billet on the floor. Kanto looked up when she entered the bedchamber.

"Reading a juicy scroller, husband?"

"It's a copy of the Education Bureau report. It got copied over with the judicial archives."

"What might you be doing with your eyes glued to that?"

"I'll have you know I'm interested in cultural things such as ballet, opera, and education. I rather fancied once we reached the capital I could be appointed to an Arts or Education Council."

She quirked her head at the last. "Why stop there? Why not Education Vizier?"

"Why not, indeed?" He set the conch in his lap with a crisp snap and gave a disdainful stare down his snout at her. "Arts and their appreciation are underfunded in our educational programs, especially in places like the Far Reaches. Not everyone can devote as much time to following them as I can. If you're going to make fun, I'd just as soon you direct it elsewhere. We should have Mirrei fix whatever we did to our conchs. Some of your updates keep getting mirrored to mine."

Jhee lowered her head. She sat beside him and touched his forearm. "I'm sorry for being glib and presumptuous. It was disrespectful."

"You're in a foul mood. What has you troubled?"

"Feh, almost too much to list. To start, it seems as though I received a preview of what awaits me at court. A lesson I intend to take to heart."

"How was your tea with the vizier?"

Who do you think gave me the lesson? Jhee bit her tongue before she read statute on the vizier and her elitism. "It went well enough. I did my best not to embarrass you."

She removed her robe and put it on the chair. Kanto held up the dusty, stained clothes. He wrinkled his nose. "Ugh. Really, denbe? Again?"

"My apologies. I pursued a theory *after* tea."

"Fruitful?"

"I don't know yet."

Kanto sidled closer. He gestured at the robe. "Would you like to make this up to me?"

"If I can."

He played with the neckline of her undershirt. "Speak to the vizier about education funding. Find a way to fix it. Being a tutor herself and one of music no less, surely, she can put you in contact with the right people. At the capital, you can impress upon them its importance."

"If I can."

"You could ask her the next time you see her."

She still regretted her dismissive words to him. He was such an admirer of the vizier. His more substantial ask had such a long term, she owed him more immediate amends. "Would you like to ask her yourself?"

"Me?"

"I told her of your respect for her work and your skill with the lute. She asked if our household would like to attend her later."

She handed him the invitation key. His eyes lit up. "I'll start composing a reply immediately. And locating appropriate attire."

"Hold until the morning after we've had a proper tuck away."

7

———

THE SPIRES

~

The High Spires

"We have tea with the vizier tonight, don't forget," Kanto reminded her in the morning.

"Dinner with a vizier and famous music tutor," Mirrei said. She popped a saline pill. "How exciting."

"Tonight?" Shep asked.

"Yes, it's a family night," Kanto said.

"Jhee swapped days so she could deal with yacht repairs."

"No one told me. It'd be an insult to cancel now that we've confirmed."

Jhee covered her esca. Yesterday had been Shep's day. They had swapped it with her open day, which should have been today so she could attend to the yacht repairs. She often spent the free days with him anyway. She had only glanced at the invite key since she had not intended to accept. She took Shep's hand. "Are you up to this?" she whispered.

He glanced at Kanto and Mirrei discussing outfits. "You don't suppose he did it deliberately?"

"Regardless, I will respect your wishes. Insult or not."

"Mirrei's perked up. They're both so looking forward to it. I've had years with you all by my lonesome, I can spare some of it for them."

"You know, I hadn't wanted to do this at all. One tea was enough, but I erred with Kanto and thought this would smooth it over."

"Shall I draft marriage contracts and bring quills?"

"For the vizier? I should hope not. Besides, do you want to be the one to

61

explain to Lady Kaydence how we married her precious jewel to a cloistered hermit?"

Shep grimaced. "Good point."

"Fancy some investigating together like we used to?"

"I wouldn't feel comfortable leaving them unguarded. See to your duties, Jhee."

Shep patted her hand and joined the others in picking out clothes.

Once Jhee and company had eaten a light morning meal, they took advantage of the Maker Shrine in the designated courtyard to do their morning devotions. Kanto sketched off alone by himself while she and Mirrei did their lessons with Shep as their pacesetter.

"What did you and Kanto quarrel about now?" Mirrei asked. "His mood changed suddenly. He's been rather sulky, not his usual upbeat self."

"No crosstalk," Jhee replied.

"My time. My topics."

"We've only spoken or even seen each other today in passing."

"In passing, today. Not so last night."

"Nothing is happening with us."

Mirrei raised an eyebrow. "The root problem. Make something happen. Put aside your reservations. Teach him casting."

"I'm hardly a proper teacher."

"It hasn't stopped you with me."

"Men, men are different. Besides, I can hardly do so here, can I?"

"Sounds like excuses."

"I'll talk to him later, though, if it will ease your bothered mind."

Mirrei tapped the tip of Jhee's nose. "It would. That is all I ask. We shall speak no more of the menfolk for the remainder of our appointment."

"Clear and center your mind," Jhee said.

Jhee and Mirrei shook out their arms. Jhee instructed Mirrei how to plant her feet wide and drop her weight in to ensure she could not be uprooted while cyphering. Using his old battle drum and heavy striker, Shep beat it to set the tempo. They practiced grounding themselves for several minutes.

"Focus on directing your weight down through your anchoring gears."

When she instructed Mirrei in the cyphering forms, the forces trembled and echoed. Some residual effect from the tremors on the subtle energies. If the healing powers of this place weren't pure fancy, what impact might it have on the prime forces one drew on while cyphering? Was there more method than mania to the restrictions?

Flowers and Maker geld decorated the rubble in a section of the court-yard with no effigies. Was this where they found the Prospective crushed by falling debris? No trace of high velocity spatter. Jhee shielded her eyes as she scanned up the length of the spires. They cast long shadows. Brilliant, emerald and ruby coral clashed with those ghastly statues. Her mind began to work out the angles and trajectories required for anything which fell from a tower to land here or in the water.

Next she knew, she had her conch out. Mirrei and Shep cleared their throats. Jhee tucked it back in her robes.

Mirrei hugged Jhee's arm. "Someone died here."

"You'd be hard-pressed to find a patch of ground on or over which someone hasn't died," Shep replied.

"At some point," Kanto said, "but not weeks ago. No wonder the residents whisper about hauntings."

Jhee narrowed her eyes at the courtyard's far wall. Had she merely imagined what she saw at the courtyard shrine?

"Spirits and echoes of the past abound here," the prioress said.

The prioress approached Jhee.

"The abbess instructed me to give you a tour of the abbey," the prioress said. "She said you spoke about it after the feast."

"That we did."

The tour began at the gardens near their courtyard. They found Sister Serra overlooking a sparse contingent of Prospectives tending an herb garden.

"Justicar, what a lovely surprise. I was just about to make my rounds of the orchards and vineyards. Would you like me to explain to you our operations?"

"Please, denbe, can we?" Mirrei asked.

As much as Jhee would have liked to, she thought about how it might affect Mirrei to take a long journey in this damp. She wished she had had the presence of mind to see the litter prepared for their excursion. "Perhaps later."

Mirrei pouted.

Sister Serra took notice of her reaction. "A tour of the agri-pods then?"

Mirrei glimmered her eyes at Jhee. Jhee smiled. "Lead the way," Jhee said.

"One thing first." Sister Serra pulled out a magnifier and examined a vine bearing shriveled grapes.

"What are you looking for?" Mirrei asked.

"Noble rot."

Shep whispered to Mirrei, who asked, "For a new wine?"

Serra raised her head from the bunch. "Might as well put this mold and mildew to productive use. You know about viticulture?"

"Not as much I'd like. Why a new wine rather than increase production of Tranquility Gold?"

"The soil tutelaries responsible for the unique flavor of Tranquility Gold only inhabit the slopes. Not only is that area hard to work, but it's also at capacity. We can add the sweeter wines, which can only be made from grapes afflicted by a certain fungus, to our list of offerings."

Sister Serra winked. Jhee moved forward. Shep laid a hand on her wrist.

"Very sensible. I'm most interested in your sustainability and vertical farming."

"Blight destroyed part of our crops last year. Some affected fields became rice paddies. If we can increase the yields on the pods, we can protect them from the extreme weather."

Jhee stopped at a trellis of beige, wrinkled melons interlaced amongst spindly, vivid sea-green vines. The lattice occupied a sunny corner of the garden, not far from an apple tree and work shed. Underneath the tree, a stone memorial bench had been erected.

"Ha, lace root melons," Kanto exclaimed. He slipped between Jhee and Shep.

"This was one of Saheli's favorite spots."

"Secluded," Jhee said.

"She used to counsel many Prospectives here in private."

"Not entirely in private," the prioress said.

"Private enough. I didn't mean it like that."

"I'm sure you didn't."

"It saddened me to hear of Saheli's passing," Jhee said.

Their tour group rode a hand-operated lift up the agri-pod tower.

Sister Serra pointed across the way. "I saw her up there that day. She hailed me in the pods as normal. Then like that, she passed to the Makers."

The prioress scoffed. Jhee faked astonishment. "Is that where…?"

"A storm blew in after Saheli made the climb. We checked on her and found her passed out with the tower door open. Nectar drink and sticky paw prints everywhere. Drenched cat tore up the herb garden while we helped Saheli. It was good about keeping the crab-rats out but ate almost anything."

After Serra showed them about the agri-pods, they returned to the herb garden.

"What's up next on the agenda, Justicar?" Serra asked.

"The archives."

"Lethys's luck to you with that. Careful Justicar, you committed the most grievous of sins. You failed to condemn me one too many times. You'll be lucky if she lets you anywhere near the reliquary now."

~

The Middle Spire

The prioress brought their group to the archival wing. While there, Jhee decided to improve her map. A structure this old and storied was bound to have many hidden architectural features. She had best get started learning them now. She might be able to find the building plans, island survey maps, and tide charts somewhere in their records. By the time their company reached the archives, Jhee had to keep her hands tucked in her robes to keep them still.

The archivist popped her head out from behind an enormous book stand when Jhee and her entourage entered the library. The archivist's desk guarded the staircase to what appeared the only entrance to the library and reliquary proper. Anyone who wanted entry had to go through her.

She sniffed. "You."

"Sister Elkanah," Jhee said.

"What do you want?"

The prioress answered, "The abbess asked that I give the Justicar and her family a tour of the abbey."

"I, also, thought perhaps you might show us around your magnificent archive," Jhee said.

Sister Elkanah sniffed again. She directed a most scathing glare at the two men in Jhee's entourage. It wilted in comparison to the one she reserved for Jhee.

"We're quite busy."

Jhee glanced around at the mostly empty library. A few Professed and the odd Prospective occupied the rows of desks which at one point might have housed hundreds. Many tables bore scratches and peeling surfaces. One section, though, boasted new, gleaming counters with good indirect lighting.

The archivist tucked the book she had been reading under her arm. As they passed by the head desk, a knot formed in Jhee's stomach when she saw the archivist had several copies of Jhee's fictionalized account of her travels with Jeja of Marpele, "Dispatches from Arrow Point," arrayed on it.

"I take it you had time to review my requests again."

"I have. I had some concerns." The archivist stopped at the threshold of the archives and faced Jhee, the book she carried now fully visible. The faded cover of her grandmamere's screed on marriage, politics, and race confronted her. Jhee's stomach dropped through the floor. She almost smelled her hopes of extended time in the archives going up in smoke. "Quite controversial notions to be exposed to so young. A concern I had when I initially viewed your proposals."

"You looked into my family history."

"I was made aware of it and yours." The archivist held her chin up high. "Seeing firsthand, you do not hold to your family's controversial views on marriage, at least, has assuaged them. Nothing leaves the archives."

"May anyone who takes holy orders access the archives?"

"Yes."

Jhee continued when Sister Elkanah didn't elaborate. "I couldn't help but notice your carrels and duplicators. You do transcription and manuscript copying. I wondered if I might copy some of Thaedra's works. I understand you have some of the original founding texts, as well as one of the earliest reproductions of Thaedra's cyphering manuals and schematics. I heard of its famed translucent pages which glimmer in the light."

"Exposure to light and the elements can be extremely damaging to the text. Access to it is even more restricted. Duplication is on a case by case basis. While we have duplicators and conch image capture stations, not everything can be exposed to such direct lighting."

"Understandable. I might be honored to even see it from a distance."

"It's best not to be too enamored of the trappings of earthly wonders. The true wonders are the miracles of the Makers. Thaedra's schematics, while impressive, are the work of mere mortals. I debate they should even be housed with our most sacred of relics."

"You hold, then there is no divine inspiration to her discovery."

"We must concern ourselves more with following the path, which leads to reconciliation with the Makers. They are mostly secular works and, as such, must be put in proper context with respect to the teachings of the Makers. No males allowed in the arcane archives whatsoever or near our most sacred relics."

"Not even to provide more hands for transcription and preservation."

"The rough handling of their coarse, ungainly hands is as liable to pulverize as preserve our sacred relics. Women's slender, more graceful fingers are perfect for capturing the nuances of scripture and formulae and the fine art of restoration. No, the most sacred books and relics are reserved for the eyes of women alone. Particularly given the vast array of arcane knowledge they contain."

Jhee tucked her hands in her robes. This place and their backward rules. Kanto tugged on Jhee's sleeve and shook his head.

"My family and I considered an outing to explore the grounds and island a bit. Would it be possible to view any survey maps of the area? Or travelogues and traveler's accounts?"

"This isn't some holiday resort and the library some brochure center."

Sister Elkanah was pricklier than a pufferfish. Jhee usually had wheedled her way to the off-line catalogs by now. It didn't help the woman pierced her pressure points.

"What of the works of previous abbesses? I saw an example of Saheli's artwork outside the vizier's chambers. I heard some of her artworks along with her final sermon are housed here in the archives."

Kanto nodded at Jhee.

"I'm afraid males are not permitted to enter this part of the sanctum. Your husbands are welcome to wait here for us. We can circle back and pick them up later."

Kanto stepped up, "Denbe, denme and I need to choose outfits for tea with the vizier."

"The vizier?"

"Oh yes, Sister Elkanah," Kanto said. "My esteemed wife took tea with her last night. She invited us to dine with her tonight."

"Well, if the vizier, will allow you around her antiques, she must be reasonably confident you won't damage them."

"Nice to see the archives suffered minimal damage in the quake. Were you there during Saheli's final sermon?"

"All the most prestigious residents were."

Sister Elkanah drummed her fingers against the cover of grandmamere's book.

"Forgive my overstepping at the feast, Sister Elkanah. Sometimes my passion for Mechanism gets the better of me. What I really might like to read are histories about the island and the Mist Abbess."

"You'd do better to read the Cyclogenesis Sermons."

A recommendation tantamount to calling Jhee impious. She counted to three before she spoke again. "Who's your preferred sage? Kaerderon's my personal favorite. Perhaps you'd guide me to where they're kept."

"I don't have time for you now."

"It's important work you do here. Preserving all this history." Jhee moved to some structure prints and arcane manuals on a carrel stand. "Are these old, renovation plans for the abbey? This must be the original designs of the Coral Cloister. And this, the vertical farming tower. Does this describe the preservation process?"

Sister Elkanah slammed the screed on a desk. "I thought you were taking a tour. Then be about your business and leave me to mine."

Access to the archives had been within Jhee's grasp. She cast a forlorn glance at them and the archivist as the three left. Was Sister Elkanah's extreme reaction to the topic of the Mist Abbess more sinister than pious?

~

The Twin Spires

Every time Jhee wanted to inquire more into the details of the deaths, she remembered she had Mirrei with her.

"Are there lifts in the spires?"

"Stairs," replied the prioress.

Mirrei's labored breathing filled the corridor.

"Star Mirror," Jhee said, using Mirrei's outside name, "would you like me to have someone escort you back to the room so you can prepare?"

Mirrei curtsied. "If my denbe thinks that's best."

"I do."

Mirrei took her leave.

"I'll show you where Saheli died."

Jhee's conscience tugged at her start with the Prospectives' deaths. She considered exploring the isle and the place where the Prospective had drowned, but she should stay within the grounds so she would not be late for tea. "Would you show me to the Beach Tower?"

"Saheli collapsed in the Bridge Tower."

"I'm aware."

The prioress brought her to the Beach axis of the abbey, where they climbed the long, spiral stairway to the top. She unlocked a door, which led to a rotunda. Archways had been carved out and fitted with ornate railings to prevent mishaps.

"Is this door locked at all times?" The door did not show signs of forced entry. It had a flimsy lock that would not have taken much effort to prize it open.

"Usually, but it would not take much to open. We find many Prospectives and Professed come up here to think and reflect. Much like the *other* spire, which was one of Saheli's favorite places to seek solitude and contemplation."

Thick layers of pollen covered everything. Most of the footprints weren't recent, with Jhee's and the prioress's the only new ones. Jhee trailed her finger through the pitted, green dust covering the railing. That spoke of several cycles of rain and drying since anyone had wiped it. She tried to conceive a logical explanation. "You did not think it unusual for the Prospective to have come up here alone?"

"Alone, yes. If I may be candid, some come up here for much more unseemly pursuits, which is why we had to start locking it. The abbess and I possess the only keys and sign it out as needed to those who petition for its use."

Jhee dusted off her hands. The pollen had begun to bring tears to her eyes. "Are we so sure he was alone?"

"I keep the bed check. All the other Prospectives and Professed were accounted for."

"What of the senior clergy?"

"What exactly are you implying, Justicar?"

"I'm trying to learn the positions of bodies in the system." Jhee thought of what she had seen at the shrine. "All Prospectives are accounted for now?"

The prioress sucked her teeth. "Yes. And none are missing limbs, either."

"Mind if I have a moment alone to explore the spire a bit?"

The prioress gave a curt bow before stepping out. This spire afforded a fantastic view of the glory and majesty of the sea, the only power greater than oneself. Isles dotted the landscape off until forever: The Blessed Isles. She savored the salt on her lips. The view used to be all crystal blue waves and white sandy beaches at this time of day. She imagined how calm and meditative this place would be in clear weather.

The Blessed Isles. How many of those isles would remain once this was done? Lost to wind and erosion from the drenched shield. She remembered how far out you could see from the top rooms of her mountain home. No, she thought. They needed the shield to protect them from invaders who would violate their water boundaries and terrorize their lands. The barbarian threat was real. Yet, should they fight their own brother and sister races? Is that really part of the First Maker's Design? The shield was best for them and us. It removed the temptation to war.

Jhee pulled out her conch to note her findings. No signal and still almost full. She peered at the hillside underneath the spire. Around the edge of the bluff, she thought she could see flickering lights. The sea wisps?

She joined the prioress on the stairs. "Show me the Bridge Tower, please."

The prioress brought her to the other high spire. So many stairs. The space atop its height resembled the other except well kept. Archways had likewise been carved and fitted with railings. All except one which led to a little overhanging platform. The wind howled and rain pattered against the roof before accumulating to drip down onto the floor.

A view, as breathtaking as, the climb greeted Jhee. Jhee rested against the low rail. One overlooked nearly the whole isle from here. This spire's twin and the taller Storm Light Spire partially blocked the view. No doubt from the storm light deck little escaped notice. Mighty sea. High bluffs. Wetlands.

The Far Reaches, her household's home district or *nome*, existed near the recently constructed perpetual Storm Shield. It was remote even by the Outer Reaches' standards, quite literally the far end of the Reaches. It came as a shock to no one that the first phase of the Storm Shield project would run through their waters.

The billowing mass of the storm shield dominated the horizon. Lightning flashes from within brightened its ever-present glow. She squinted against an occasional glint from the solar array field when lightning escaped the bounds of the shield. Beautiful, vibrancy hid underneath new and near-constant fog and mellowing gray. The bright, cheery isle now plagued by storm and rain. Even when not storming, claustrophobic cloud cover persisted. How much more spectacular the view must have been before the shield? At the right time of day, in better weather, the light would be perfect for painting and photography. "Saheli made this climb, how often?"

"Every day, including the day of her transfiguration."

"She must have been most fit." Jhee pointed at scorched roofing tiles. "Is this where she ascended?"

"No, sometimes the reflections from a misaligned solar array get too hot."

Jhee held tight to the rough, coral arch as she inched out onto the over-hang. She found paint splotches and some scratches from Saheli's easel and tripod. A little lean—more than Jhee found comfortable—gave a good over-view of the domed hothouses. She gave a sigh once safely back on the landing.

"Fit and fearless." Further in the distance, away from the town proper, ramshackle huts and cook fires dotted the landscape. "Those are the refugee camps?"

The prioress's perpetual frown deepened. "The loss of landmass and rapid erosion near the storm zone has driven many closer and closer to high ground such as Torilsisle."

"The same happened on my home isle." Jhee remembered the prioress's comments about supplicants. "Many seek to take holy orders?"

"Saheli encouraged it. Pyrmo has been more restrictive. Males in particular."

"Strange so many young men taking vows."

"Those refugees left their homes for better lives. As a larger isle, Torilsisle has game enough and land for crops and flower beds. It is in no danger of being lost to the sea, which is why it sees so many on their way to elsewhere. The capital will not be able to accommodate them all. With proper education and training, some may find work on the shield or in mining. Some have made the calculation; it might be better to stay at places such as this."

"I've seen some of the places in the Far Reaches. The abbey is indeed an improvement from what many might normally expect."

The prioress expression and tone softened. "More than that, Justicar, as laypeople or charity cases, what we provided them was much more limited. Many joined the abbey to have full bellies. The abbey makes use of who it can. The refugees are cheap labor for fishing and farming. As Prospectives, they get an education, better quality food and accommodation, and to serve the Makers as they will."

"In that light, it does make much more sense." Jhee noted this on her conch. She returned to the platform and held her conch aloft. "High spires. High bluffs. So many dangerous heights on this isle."

"It protects our privacy and allows us forewarning should trouble come our way. With enough of us being veterans, I suspect any coming to do us harm as in the raiding days would no longer find us such easy prey."

"I suspect not. How long have you been prior?"

"I was raised to the priory upon Pyrmo's appointment as abbess. She held the position before me."

"Was it you who found Saheli collapsed?"

"Sister Serra. I arrived soon after. The horticulturist claims she came to return her cat. I insisted we take Saheli to the infirmary. Both claimed it unnecessary. Perhaps if I had been more insistent."

Jhee noted that too. Another failed transfer notice greeted her.

The prioress scowled. "Am I boring you?"

"I'm listening. I thought maybe I could get a signal out. Any updates on the antenna?"

"It's been too overcast. For a strong signal, try the solar array fields or storm light tower."

"Would you show me to where Saheli transcended?"

The prioress's stern expression returned. "This way."

The Coral Cloister Lesson Hall presented such an unremarkable back-drop to such a remarkable event. Clean-boards for instruction faced worn benches and chairs. Jhee considered how one might get from here to the courtyards or the abbess's chamber.

"What time of day was it when she transcended?"

"Afternoon."

"Any idea why Saheli collapsed?"

"Heatstroke? Dehydration? The double sunlight can become intense on clear days."

"Forward-thinking to have fruit beer on hand. Saheli must have gotten so engrossed in her work she forgot to drink some. What do you think about these rumors of the Mist Abbess?"

The prioress's face lost expression. "The abbey's history has not always been a peaceful one. When the barbarians sacked it, they slaughtered lesser spouses and children who had hidden here for safety. Prior to that, it was controlled by the Middle Pillarists during the atrocities. In those days, it was called Swordbridge. The Drakist Adepts renamed it along with what we now call the Beach Tower."

"Adepts? Yet, you eschew arcana."

"Our abbey was originally founded by ex-soldiers who had turned to the ways of spiritual reflection. Yet the space remembers. They say the barrier between the first realms of the dead and last realms of the living is thin here."

Jhee started calculating angles of reflections. "First Maker's Folly, is that the time? I'm afraid I must interrupt the tour. Would we be able to see the storm light tower tomorrow?"

"A second day away from my duties is unacceptable."

"Thank you for your assistance. I shall let the First Makers' Design guide my steps then."

8

FAMILY TEATIME

~

Make for Make

"You're late," Kanto said. "And you look a fright."

"I know, I know."

The small washbasin on a nearby table showed he had anticipated tardiness. Kanto spared her a frown but did not pause the painstaking process of lacquering Mirrei's nails. His had been freshly touched up and colored to complement his turquoise outfit. She cleaned herself while the rest of her cohort dressed in silence. Every now and then Kanto set the lacquer bottle down with a punctuated thud.

Kanto approached to brush her hair. Her headache had returned. When she began favoring the bridge of her nose, Mirrei appeared from nowhere again with the poultice.

After eying the poultice briefly, Kanto checked the time and sighed.

"You wore one the last time you saw her. We'll pretend it's your look." He found a scarf to match the robes he had chosen for her. "Early is on time and on time is late. I swear if we insult the vizier..."

Despite Kanto's fears, they arrived fashionably early. However, Mirrei alone spoke to her during the trip. Kanto was giving her the felled fish routine while Shep was Shep. He detested visits such as this. Both had brought an item to showcase their talents: Kanto his lute and Shep his kalacha war club, a further reason for him to be ill at ease.

Lady Bathsheba welcomed them with the more formal bows rather than forearm clasps.

73

"Your prompt response to my invitation was an unexpected delight. The watermarks, so elegant: Star Mirror, Bright Harmony, Dawn Wolf. Outside naming. Such formality. You are, indeed, a quaint cohort. I took the liberty of having a meal prepared."

"All honors to you, Lady Bathsheba, and I took the liberty of providing entertainment."

Make for Make. The tea table had been extended to make room for five. Opposite the table, a little performance chair had been set out. Kanto and Shep displayed the lute and kalacha on it for later. Lady Bathsheba gave Jhee and her senior spouse pride of place to either side with her juniors seated farthest away. Kanto offered to pour the tea. After tea and pleasantries, her spouses set up to perform.

Mirrei performed a Stations-of-the-Moons cypher. Jhee mouthed along as Mirrei performed each station flawlessly as they had practiced so many times. When she found herself miming along as well, she stilled herself. While the cypher was overly elaborate for what it did, it demonstrated many of the fundamental skills and techniques of the craft. At the close, the vase emitted a shower of shimmering cherry blossoms instead of the usual sparkles. Translucent blossom illusions evaporated as they landed upon the rug. The Stations-of-the-Moons was one of the required entrance cyphers for the magic program at the academy. A wide grin overtook Jhee. She, Lady Bathsheba, and Shep clapped in appreciation. Jhee perhaps with too much animation. She calmed herself when she saw Shep snicker. Kanto hovered about the edges, appearing whenever their teacups emptied.

Shep came to her aid with a distraction. "I must compliment the vizier on your collection of relics. Is that Hymn to Toril scrollwork on those aprons?"

"Indeed, it is. You have a discerning eye."

Next, Shep took center stage to perform a battle stomp. Kanto had retired to the wings to sketch and prepare for his performance. Shep looked to Jhee before he began. She gave a slight smile and nod of encouragement. He performed one of the stomps their old unit did for inspections or when dignitaries came to visit.

"Your performance of Stations-of-the-Moon was simply masterful, my dear."

"The vizier is most kind. It's thanks in no small part to denbe's excellent tutelage." Mirrei gave Jhee demure eye twinkles then a wink. Perhaps the young woman laid it on a bit thick.

Lady Bathsheba unfurled the finger maze on the table. "Justicar, I hope you don't mind me bringing out the finger maze you admired so much on your last visit. You and Star Mirror might be interested in trying it together."

Jhee and Mirrei finger cast through the levels of the finger maze. Lady Bathsheba watched with a visage of barely contained excitement. "She hopes to teach my fellow junior spouse as well. Denye's as likely to flourish under her direction as I am."

Lady Bathsheba regarded them with a bemused expression. "Nonsense. The subtleties, the nuance, the grace required of cyphering is too taxing for the male character. Common elemental grunt work is the only training suitable for men. Could you imagine if men were as proficient with fire as women? They'd fireball everything in sight."

"Yet, some men are proficient with fire and have yet to burn the place down."

"I owe that to most of the empire being on water."

With the question thoroughly answered as to whether Mirrei and Lady Bathsheba would get on, Jhee changed the subject. "How long have you resided here, Lady Bathsheba?"

"Longer than I want to admit. I retired from court after the death of my third husband. What a talented cohort you have. You have your males well-trained and well-appointed. A state I had not expected given our previous meeting. The traditional figure of your anchor spouse shows the markers of virility and fitness. I never quite went in for silver fangs myself. He does, however, make me see the appeal. Shame about his eye, though. Was it a consequence of his military service?"

"The vizier is quite astute."

"His tattoos and the recognition of the scrollwork. I've been around quite a few veterans."

Kanto began a performance of Freedom Flight, a challenging piece meant to impress.

"Your Kanto, on the other hand."

They lapsed into appreciative silence while he played. Kanto finished with a flourish. Lady Bathsheba clapped thunderously.

"Thank you, my dear. Your playing…. There are no words. Handsome, talented, and a connoisseur of tea. Such talent and good breeding. Rare jewels found in such a remote district. You will fit right in at court."

"Thank you. Such high praise. The vizier is most kind," Kanto said. He and Shep bowed then returned to the table.

"Come. Sit beside me." Lady Bathsheba and Kanto turned Jhee's way. She inclined her head. "Where did you learn to play so brilliantly?"

"Tutors. Though I am largely self-taught. Our corner of the district is so far off the main lanes. Not too many tutors were willing to make the journey. Certainly, none as brilliant or prestigious as you, my lady. My family could spare the expense. I was an exception. My dames were always great matrons of the arts. I was talking to my honored wife about improving the state of education in our district, particularly regarding art and music."

"Talented and civic-minded. This one is such a flatterer. Makes me feel almost like a young woman again. Justicar, I might have to borrow him from you." Lady Bathsheba drank from her teacup and nodded approvingly. "A perfect pour, precisely spiced. Hard to do with this blend."

"Thank you, Vizier. Black forest tea has such a dominant flavor; it must be delicately treated, so it does not overpower."

"My goodness, I just noticed the lovely foil work on your nails. I'm amazed it didn't get damaged in your playing."

"The trick is to apply another layer of lacquer once it has properly set up."

The two laughed and got on famously. Whenever the Lady so much as held out her cup, Kanto rushed to refill it. Shep from his newly demoted position gave Jhee another smirk. Perhaps Jhee had been too fast to rule out a match between Kanto and the vizier. Yet, she imagined the conversation with Lady Kaydence. Trapped at the isolated abbey with these sexist women was surely not what his grandmamere had in mind. The abbey was a woefully inappropriate place for him. This place is too small for her husband. She was too small for her husband. And if she were to be so selfish, the match held little socio-political advantage for her.

Jhee occupied herself during Lady Bathsheba's distraction with a closer look at the room details. The martial theme to the decor had not been what she expected from a music tutor. A jostle caused the finger maze to slip. She caught the finger maze and placed it with some architectural plans for an archive expansion on a nearby table. The speckled texture of a ritual collar gave her pause.

"Such sumptuous robes, this time, Justicar. Was it something I said?"

"No, Lady Bathsheba," Jhee said, then finished in her head, *it wasn't one snobbish thing you said it was everything.* She returned her attention to her companions. She hid her mouth with her cup so Lady Bathsheba would not see her frown. The Lady Bathshebas of the world did not worry about having much younger husbands. They viewed husbands as pets. There would be more women like this in the capital. Not the ideal situation she wished for Kanto. In the end, it would be his choice.

One insurmountable concern outweighed the others for Jhee. Someone here may have killed Saheli and the young men. Even if the deaths weren't murders, the clergy had little love for anyone save themselves.

"In my indelicate way, I thought I was doing you a favor. My warnings about court were not hyperbole. I also sought to test you. Conscientious officials are not always the norm. Are you also, a veteran?"

"Intelligence pool."

"Wealthy enough for your family to position you away from real danger." Jhee sipped some more tea. "Please, don't take that wrong. As an official, a vizier, I had a way out of combat. Like yourself. Someone as fearless and civic-minded as yourself, I might have thought you'd get a commission to the navy."

"I prefer solid ground."

Lady Bathsheba studied Jhee for a moment. "I continue to scandalize you. A privilege of getting older is no longer concerning yourself with trivia, niceties, or conventions. Those are young woman's cares and concern of court. I live a more rustic life here."

~

A Gracious Host

Their assembly ate a most excellent meal of crispy pork, braised rice and onions, yams, kale and fennel salad, and a marvelous poached tuna, accompanied by a humble decanter of Tranquility Bridge's Light. As expected, Mirrei favored generous helpings of salad and heavily salted pork in avoidance of the starch and other animal proteins.

"Pascoe standards. No land meat. Did I get it correct?"

Jhee dabbed her mouth with a napkin. "You did, my lady."

Lady Bathsheba addressed Mirrei, "Your wife mentioned you are into dietetics. Are you whose palate we are accommodating?"

"I'm afraid I can't take all the credit, Vizier."

"Was everything to your satisfaction, gentlemen?"

"The crispy pork was cooked to perfection," Kanto said.

Shep nodded enthusiastically. "It helps when you start with such prime cuts."

"It seems the privation which hit the rest of the isles has yet to do so here," Mirrei said. Jhee winced. Kanto pinched Mirrei just under the table. She twitched. "Everything was wonderful, Vizier."

"Yet, you did not touch most of the dishes."

"I'm watching my saline levels."

"Fresh Lung?"

"A mild case."

"Your Star Mirror is a true daughter of the sea, Justicar. Did you try the draught I suggested? I hear it works wonders on Fresh Lung as well."

"Not yet, my lady."

Lady Bathsheba twisted her napkin. "Make sure you do so soon."

"Have you spoken to the archivist yet?"

"It might take some more time. Elkanah has proved obstinate. You must have really barnacled her keel."

"Thank you, Lady Bathsheba, for hosting us," Mirrei said. "Might I ask from what home isle do you hail?"

"I am from Wilobeia."

"Of course! home isle of this magnificent tea. And if I remember my biology and geography correctly: Cheiropthys, the batfish or batwing maye, and Maate-Kheru Wilobeian, violet harvest nut, one of various plants called seed of enlightenment. Isn't everything on Wilobeia poisonous? My biology tutor joked it was like everything on the isle was trying to kill everything else."

"A studious one. I see why you and your denbe are so well-suited. How are your cyphering studies? Are you familiar with the basics of gyration?"

Mirrei grinned. "Complete with veiled hoods and protective circles for the menfolk. Talk about your ancient knowledge."

Jhee swallowed her bite of yam and wiped her mouth. "It's the tradition. I'd do you a disservice if I didn't instruct you in the proper forms and etiquette. Though, I try to adhere to more modern Mechanist methods."

"Ancients sometimes have knowledge we don't. We weren't here first. There are beings older than us. Forces beyond our comprehension. Not just in this abbey, but in the cosmos; beings older than when we emerged and slapped the title of Maker on everything. Remember it wasn't us who aligned the worlds and the moons."

"You speak of the First Ones, the Prototypes. A closer stream of distant knowledge intrigues me more. I heard a strange term, Mist Abbess. Does that mean anything to you?"

"A mythical figure who once ruled the island. I hear tale of a resurgence in her blood cult. They seek to revive the practices of the old days and bring back the sacrifices and orgies. There are tales of strange figures walking the halls at all hours of day or night. Perhaps these are the ghosts that you claimed to have seen. Nothing supernatural. Simply all too mortal beings bent on resurrecting their heretical deities. Rumors abound of strange lights and figures seen about the abbey and on the island. Hints of cultish, pagan rites being performed in the now."

"Surely you do not believe in the Last Hunt, Lady Bathsheba?"

"I believe they believe it. Which is more than enough."

"For someone who doesn't believe, this appears to unsettle you."

"I don't know about the deacons' malign forces or restless spirits, but I do know something's amiss here with respect to casting. You've been practicing here. Have you noticed the difference to the prime forces?"

"My cyphering did feel off."

"The abbey's restrictions on arcana have deep roots."

"How so?"

"The coral edifice showcases examples of the earliest preserving arcana used to speed the mineralization process and fetter the dead. The reliquary, much like shrines, serves to accumulate ancestral power. This abbey is a giant spirit battery, Justicar. Perhaps the lights seen on the marsh was just illicit revelers and pranksters. Or perhaps it's from some far deeper and darker powers from which this isle draws its healing energy. The ichor of a power which sleeps beneath the isle."

Jhee took the initiative to lighten the mood and steer the conversation toward less existential topics.

"Husbands, if you would delight us again with your skills."

"It is my honor, denbe," Kanto said. "Any particular piece?"

"Do you perchance know The Strawberry Letters?" Lady Bathsheba asked.

Kanto tuned his lute. Shep took up a position beside the chair.

"Would you happen to have any maps of the island?" Jhee asked.

"I have. Over here."

"I'd be delighted to see them, Lady Bathsheba."

Lady Bathsheba walked Jhee to a corner of her chambers. She opened a giant sharkskin bound atlas and leafed through it. "Do you still have the map I gave you? I have a few landmarks you might find interesting."

"Indeed."

"Here, have a close look at this one." Jhee leaned toward the bound volume. The vizier marked the map with several court symbols. At Jhee's puzzled look, the lady whispered, "We're not alone. I suspect I'm being watched. I've heard odd sounds while supposedly alone. You must forgive my behavior in our previous meeting, Justicar. I didn't know who might be listening or if you could be trusted. I thought it better for eavesdroppers to think us at odds."

"The lady is most wise," Jhee said. She glanced around now, suddenly paranoid rather than annoyed. At Jhee's nod, Shep whispered in Kanto's ear then performed a simpler, but louder battle stomp as accompaniment.

"The atmosphere here changed once Saheli was appointed. We had all expected it to be Pyrmo. I don't think the high clergy accepted the Chief Abbess chose an outsider. Beyond fell rumors of orgies and malign forces, the name you mentioned, the Mist Abbess, resurfaced shortly thereafter."

Jhee pursed her lips.

"I discovered these poking around the archives after we last met."

Jhee looked closely and found a proposal and blueprints for commercializing the orchards and vineyards, submitted by Sister Serra.

"Who else knows about these?"

"If I found these in the archives, it would be the easiest task in the world for Elkanah to as well." Lady Bathsheba quickly rolled up the map and snatched up the glow orb. "No. I've said too much."

Jhee gently touched her arm. "No. Please, continue."

"There's a possibility I hesitate to entertain. I'm not so sure my accident was an accident."

"Forgive my impertinence, Lady Bathsheba, but I must ask. Where were you during the other deaths?"

"Of course. I would expect no less. I was here in my chambers."

Jhee frowned and said, "All three?"

"Not a very good alibi. I know. Wait, when Prospective Leigh drowned, I had jammed a toe and was being treated at the infirmary. The physician or her assistant should be able to verify I stayed there until morning."

"I will check this out and get back to you."

"Please, do. The sooner you rule me out, the sooner you can focus on who might have committed these horrible crimes."

Mirrei's eyelids fluttered. She slumped in her chair. Jhee immediately rushed over. "Are you unwell?"

"Just somewhat achy and light-headed. I must have eaten something that didn't agree with me."

"Perhaps we should retire for the evening?"

"Will you be able to manage by yourselves, or should we seek out assistance?" Lady Bathsheba asked.

"I can make it," Mirrei said. "No need to fuss."

Before they left, Lady Bathsheba pressed several signets into her hand.

"Justicar, you might need these, if you're serious about education. For as long as you are here, feel free to visit and talk as you desire. I enjoy the reminders you give me of court. Such a joy to have those closer to my station to converse with and possibly a kindred spirit. Now, you must go quickly and return to your husbands and wife. Hug them and cherish them for dark days may be upon us again."

9

———

THE CLERGY

~

The Infirmary

As their cohort journeyed back to their room, Jhee kept a slow pace. Kanto and Mirrei had their arms linked with hers. Shep lagged. Jhee mused on the details of the case in between checking on Mirrei. Kanto was all grins and had a bounce to his step.

"No need to keep such a slow pace for me," Mirrei said. "I'm feeling better already."

"No rush after such an exquisite meal," Jhee said.

"Too exquisite."

Kanto eyed Mirrei. "A shame we had to cut the evening short."

"I, for one, had had enough. Not the least because of all those ghastly relics and artwork on the walls."

"Reminders of a more savage time," Shep said.

"Now you sound like the lady," Jhee said.

"I have a small confession to make, denbe," Mirrei said. "I thought you could use a reason to leave."

"I knew it," Kanto said. "You little liar."

"It wasn't quite a lie. Her outdated views and elitism had begun to make me ill. You wouldn't believe the things she said while you and Shep performed. I wasn't sure if I could stomach another moment of flattering her."

"Clever girl. I had grown rather tired with the evening myself."

Mirrei feigned shock. "No? Your eyes kept going that shade they do before you lose your temper."

Kanto snuggled closer to Jhee who patted his hand. "Lady Bathsheba thoroughly and entirely creeped me out with all her talk of ghosts and evil forces at the end though," he said.

Mirrei coughed. Jhee squeezed her arm in response. "She creeped me out with all her leering."

"Perhaps it was best we left before you descended into a self-righteous lecture, denye. I think we made a good impression anyway. Signet codes of introduction."

"Thanks to you, husband," Jhee said. A blush pinked his eyes. They exchanged smiles before he faced away. Jhee quickened their pace.

At the room, Jhee plopped in the chair. She fingered the access writ Lady Bathsheba had slipped in with the list of education contacts. If indeed Lady Bathsheba aimed to come off as a sexist snob and give the impression they were at odds, she had more than succeeded. She regretted her earlier ungracious thoughts which had accused Lady Bathsheba of snobbery. Reconsidering the meeting, Jhee may have taken the lady's words and actions the wrong way due to her beleaguered state of mind.

"You're the one looking wave-worn, now, denbe."

"I've been climbing stairs and visiting musty and moldy spires all day. While you may not have a headache, I do."

"I'd refresh your poultice, but our herbal stores are low."

Jhee changed from her robes into simple evening attire yet left the wrap in place as the poultice did help. She ran a thumb over the textured access writ. "Give me a list. I've meant to visit the infirmary, anyway. I'll see if they have some remedy for my sinuses as well."

In the hall, Jhee hesitated. She weighed the writ in her hand against Mirrei's list. Lady Bathsheba had drawn her attention to the storehouse at least twice. She consulted the map. The storehouse and the infirmary were on different axes of the abbey. One Prospective had died of sickness. They must have been tended by the abbey physician. The infirmary may also be where Saheli got her meditation aids. Jhee headed there.

A young, male Prospective sat the reception desk drawing anatomical drawings or nudes. No one else occupied the infirmary. He scrambled to his feet, shoved the parchments aside, and bowed, a protocol neither Jhee's office nor social status required. Nudes, then. She caught the whiff of robust, woodsy cologne. "Justicar, what ever is the matter? You've not taken ill, have you?"

"Not as such. I've been in and out of dreadful weather. Along the way, I developed a terrible headache. I also hoped to procure medicinal supplies. Is the physician in?"

The young man's eyes flared wide. "You actually want to see the physician? Perhaps, the Justicar, would rather see if it goes away on its own?"

"I'd like to see the physician this instant. Will that be a problem?"

"No. Not at all."

"What do you do here?"

He glanced at the pile where his parchments nestled. "I'm the infirmarian. I see to the non-medical needs of those confined to the infirmary."

A crash sounded from behind the physician's door then something thudded to the ground. The Prospective knocked. The door flew open. He jumped back as a short, graying woman barely taller than a shark dog stumbled out. "How many times have I told you not to move my equipment? And what's all this whispering out here? You best not have your friends here shirking their duties."

The infirmarian glanced at Jhee.

"Oh, a patient." The physician spat in her hands and slicked back her hair. She straightened out her robes before rushing to greet Jhee. A wave of the most horrendous body odor came with her. Jhee preempted her forearm clasp by initiating a bowed greeting. "He's as lazy as the refugees. I'm not like these other Sisters. I expect my assistants to work. These young men coming through today are nothing like they were in my day. You must be the famous Justicar? I'm Sister Zalver."

"I'd hardly say famous," Jhee said.

"Only to those such as myself, I suppose. I subscribe to the judicial law wire, followed the write-ups you did for Jeja of Marpele in Frontiers in Arcane Forensics, and read every 'Dispatches from Arrow Point' story twice. I absolutely loved your ingenuity in The Twelve Murders in The Manor. What brings you to seek my humble assistance?"

"That wasn't—. Never mind." What was she going to say? *That wasn't me; it was my literary counterpart.* Her fictional account had supplanted the truth in the popular imagination. Much as Jeja had wanted it to. "I wanted to pick up some supplies and perhaps get something for a headache."

"Come have a seat here." Sister Zalver urged her to an exam table. Jhee sighed with relief when the woman put on gloves before timing her pulse. She had Jhee's eyes forced open before she knew it. "Eye color bright and shiny. Good. Here, drink this draught."

"What is it?"

"Tranquility Gold mixed with ippi extract. Opens the blood vessels, gets the circulation going. Do be warned. It does have a purgative effect."

Indeed, ippi extract did. Drunken vomiting while light-headed was one way to alleviate a sinus headache, but not how Jhee wanted to conclude this evening. Sister Zalver was either a squib or charlatan. Jhee checked for the neutralizer inside her sleeve in case the physician poisoned her accidentally.

Jhee faced away to avoid her fetid breath and spit out the draught. "I don't recall seeing you at the feast."

"Slept through it. I've dealt with enough real barbarity to not want to watch fools play at it. No time for that nonsense."

"Since I've arrived, I've heard too many disturbing tales of the abbey's history. From massacres to the Mist Abbess. Have you heard of her?"

"More nonsense."

"I also thought I might ask you about the Prospective who died."

"Which one? Ha." She slapped Jhee hard on the back.

"Prospective Yaou. The one you treated."

"Oh, yes. He volunteered here from time to time. Sister Elkanah brought him in unconscious."

"Was his illness sudden?"

"Sudden upon learning the magnitude of his work. The number of men who come in here and then make miraculous recoveries. They fake illnesses to bypass their studies and chores. Well, I set them straight. Some even left the abbey never to come back."

"Yet this one died."

"True. Sad case. The young man's weak character and fragile nature caused him to nearly wither away."

"Do you know from what?"

"No doubt some mystery ailment brought by the refugees. Saheli allowed too many to take holy orders. I've treated quite a few. Mostly for mild cases of Fresh Lung. Though I did see a rise in the cases of coruscate syndrome and sprained middle toes. A simple draught of one of my Tranquility Gold remedies and they're fine to go about their duties."

"Coruscate syndrome? That's quite rare, isn't it?"

"Which is why I questioned if they were sick at all. Squalid camps are a spawning bed for disease and sedition, though. Yaou's case was different. I suspected Fresh Lung at first. Very similar to chronic wasting sickness."

Chronic wasting sickness the favorite diagnosis of many family physicians in the Far Reaches. Often it meant they had no idea why someone was deathly ill. In more extreme cases, it said they were too lazy to find out or paid not to disclose the true one.

"He was a refugee?"

"One of the good ones. Hard-working. Conscientious. Not like a lot of these other lazy Prospectives, I could name who seek accolades without putting in the work." The physician raised her voice at the last. "Sister Serra, the vizier, even the prioress, and Sister Elkanah consulted, yet still couldn't diagnose him. Rather than admit the work too stressful and his constitution too frail, he worked himself to death. Most tragic. Gave up the will to live poor thing. But that is the nature of the male disposition."

"You said you treated Saheli. What can you tell me of her health?"

"Healthy as a sea ox. I was monitoring her for acid reflux and a mild case of Brine Lung, which I treated with barley and morning seed."

Brine Lung was the complement to Fresh Lung, which afflicts those from inland or higher elevations when they move to the Outer Reaches.

"As for supplies, nothing doing. Our stores are low too. Someone's been stealing them." The doctor pitched her voice at the infirmarian. Zalver leaned forward. Face and breath mere inches from Jhee's nose. Jhee's eyes watered, and she held her breath. "Can't be too careful. Spies. Everywhere."

The infirmarian peered around the corner his face full of empathy and concern. Zalver wandered away. Jhee hied to the waiting room. The infirmarian inched a cologne bottle and manta silk handkerchief he had taken from a drawer towards her.

"I'm sorry, Justicar. I tried to warn you." The infirmarian lowered his voice. "Most know to seek others if really sick. For supplies, it's best to ask Sister Serra."

"Serra?" Zalver yelled and trundled into the room. "Speaking of lazy. That dirty, smelly hedie. All she does is tempt and indulge. You watch that one. Medicine isn't the only thing she grows in that hothouse of hers."

"Did I hear my name?" Sister Serra strode in with one arm balancing a cask on her shoulder while wheeling another after her. "Which is it today? Am I stealing your drugs or growing my own?"

"Both. A bit late for a delivery."

"I wanted to get an early start on tomorrow. I thought you'd appreciate an early resupply."

"That I would." Sister Zalver licked her lips and rubbed her hands over the spirits the horticulturist had delivered. She grunted. Zalver wheeled out the casks. "These feel light. Stealing this like you've been stealing my medicines, you drugged-out hedie."

"Clam up, old woman. No one's been stealing your drugs." Sister Serra turned to Jhee. "My deliveries are less frequent. Our cash crops haven't been the only things to suffer from the weather. We also keep the heavy pharmaceuticals under lock and key."

"I've got my eye on you," Zalver shouted.

"Well, remove it. I'm leaving, you old goat." Sister Serra lowered her voice, "Come to the pods later. I'll give you some real medicine."

"Bye, Sister Zalver," Sister Serra yelled on her way out.

Jhee turned toward a cordoned off infirmary section. "What's this area over here?"

Zalver guffawed. "At the moment, quarantine. It's where Prospective Yaou stayed while ill."

"Usually, a quiet room for patients," the infirmarian said. "Or where staff nap when we're busy."

"If the doctor would allow me?" Jhee asked.

The physician tossed Jhee a fresh pair of medical gloves and an infection mask. "Do be careful, Justicar. We don't know what he died of."

"I will."

"Did he leave any belongings?"

"His effects are over there. They were meant to go to the mortician," the infirmarian said.

"Should be the incinerator," Zalver yelled. "I meant to take them myself. I intend to fumigate everything when I get the time, but it's been so busy here."

Jhee contemplated the abandoned infirmary again.

"I've already disinfected it. Several times over," the infirmarian said.

"Like I'd trust you to do a job like that right."

Once Zalver wandered off again muttering, Jhee searched the sickroom's plain bed and chest. The same rough, simple sheets as the other Prospectives. Jhee flung open the wardrobe against the far wall. The interior held a few day robes. Their hangers scraped along the clothing rod as Jhee browsed through them. Plain, but fashionable. Not the sort of clothing clergy or laity would wear. "When was the last time someone stayed in this room?"

"Just before your arrival."

Jhee pitched her voice low. "Passing strange Prospectives chose to put themselves under the physician's care when they knew to go elsewhere if truly ill."

"Not everyone stayed away. Abbess Saheli for one. Vizier Bathsheba stayed here after her accident. Sister Elkanah often complained of cuts and rashes from dealing with the archives."

"Naturally, she wouldn't seek out Sister Serra."

"Her injuries reminded me more of those the gardeners get."

"Oh? The Prospective she brought in, what was his condition like?"

"I'm no doctor."

"You tended him nonetheless."

"He didn't seem sick. At least, not until the end. I think he may have been hiding."

"From who?" The infirmarian kept his eyes to the floor. Jhee approached him. "If you know something, you should tell me."

"On several of Sister Elkanah's visits, I found her in here. The last time was just after he died."

"Who does the bed checks? You or the doctor?"

"Sister Zalver, but she logs it. If you could not tell, she prefers I not perform certain duties. I checked the logs, though, none of our patients went missing."

"According to Sister Zalver. And her questionable faculties. Thank you." Jhee raised her voice, "Sister Zalver, I'll take these off your hands."

"Please, do."

～

The Morgue

Outside the infirmary, Jhee quickly went through the box. Nothing except a basic Prospective's robe and shift. Cologne emanated from the box and its contents. The infirmarian must have doused everything in the infirmary with it. When she shook out the clothes to check for hidden pockets, a peculiar woven bracelet with a thin coin-shaped charm clattered to the ground. She did not recognize the decoration on its faces. The likeness of some Lesser Island Maker or ancestor, no doubt, perhaps even Maker geld.

"Has that half-blind goat got you running her errands?"

Jhee vaguely remembered the mortician as one of the clerics who had danced and sang at the feast. "I volunteered. I was there seeking relief already."

"Brave woman. Worst smelling living person I've ever met. I asked for his personal effects days ago. Put them over there with the others."

"Zalver wanted to burn them. She thought they might be infectious. Did you perform autopsies on the bodies?"

"Pursuant to the Justicar's new directives. The prioress and I did. One showed the markers of being crushed by rubble. Prospective Yaou asphyxiated. Evidence of cyanosis. No fluid in the lungs."

"Abbess Saheli?"

"As best I could. Her remains were quickly interred in the crypts given the miraculous nature of her death, and the necessity to embalm before the crypts became inaccessible."

"Anything unusual about the body? Any signs of violence?"

"Nothing not in keeping with the spirited nature of her last sermon. She looked quite peaceful. Not like the poor Prospective who drowned, though. Crabs had got at the body. Hard to tell if he died of something else. I could send you the autopsy images."

"Dear Makers, no. I mean my conch is almost full, and I can't signal out to ether out my data. I'd like my senior spouse to review them, however. I'll give you a routing code for his device."

"If ya like."

Jhee noted the dates on the boxes. "Are these the effects from the others who died?"

"Ayup."

"May I?"

"If ya like."

Jhee recoiled from the mildewed smell of Leigh, the drowned Prospective's belongings. Her headache worsened. "The prospective who drowned. Where was his body found?"

"Out past the breakers on the far side of the isle."

Drowning. Breakers. Jhee cringed. Perhaps she would investigate into that locale later. "Ever heard of the person called the Mist Abbess?"

The mortician chuckled. "Zalver can't help yammering about conspiracies and secret cabals, can she? A tale to frighten misbehaving novices. Obey the rules or the Mist Abbess will get you."

Jhee closed the box. "Is this all their effects?"

"The abbey sells or salvages what we can. I do keep a log." The mortician brought Jhee her records. "Yes. Yes. I remember this. The one who drowned was found with a sizable quantity of minted shell on his person. As well as an antique chest containing more in his trunk. It's not unusual for refugees to have hard currency. It's traditional to donate it to the abbey, though, upon taking orders. Such a large amount of it though. I informed the prioress, and we logged it into the treasury. I believe I still have the chest as I was waiting for the rest of his effects. It seemed valuable like a family heirloom of some sort. I kept it in case we located his family."

She had seen stamped shells, the former hard currency, more and more. With the shield wreaking havoc on inter-isle communication, centralized banking and currency transfer had become less reliable. Shell promissory notes and markers had regained popularity.

The mortician led Jhee to a locker and pulled out a black lacquer chest of exquisite make. While she did not have Kanto's eye for finery, she admired the angular, scrollwork and craftsmanship.

What would a novitiate be doing with this? A holdover from the days prior to starting down the cleric's path? A prospective monk should have either left such items with family or given them to the abbey to do good works. She delved further into the man's belongings where she found a wrapped bundle of delicate and expensive silk containing another of those coin bracelets tied to a single shell of currency looped through with leather cord. She sniffed the cloth, a trace of musky perfume or cologne. Why would a novitiate have such an item? What manner of unnatural acts went on at this retreat?

Jhee held up the two bracelets side by side. "What do you make of these?"

"What have you got there?"

"I found them among the other Prospectives' effects."

"Maker or craft geld of some sort? I haven't quite seen this one before."

"Me neither. Mind if I hold on to these?"

"If ya like. Could they be from the reliquary or archives?"

"How would they gain access?"

The mortician chewed on her finger quill. "This is a peculiar structure honeycombed with nooks. During renovations, we often find old caches of weapons and food, sometimes valuables. The earthquake also uncovered a few more of its secrets."

"The minting marks are too recent."

The mortician chewed her quill more.

"What is it?" Jhee asked.

"I'm sure it's nothing."

"If you've thought of something, please."

"I didn't actually see the prioress log the money into the treasury."

"Why should that cause you concern?"

"I'm loathed to relay gossip, mind."

Why should anyone stop now? Jhee bit her tongue even though she wanted the mortician to be out with it already. "No, please, do."

"I heard Saheli caught her stealing."

Jhee pressed against her nose in hopes from some relief from the pressure. "You've been more than helpful."

"Sinuses?"

"I got a powerful whiff of the mildew."

"Go see Sister Serra. She grows the medicinal herbs for the infirmary, and I dare say she'd be better at fixing what ails you than Zalver."

"I'll take your advice. Soon. The prospective who they found crushed. What can you tell me about his death?"

"Buried by falling debris in the courtyard when the tremor hit. Suffocated, poor thing. Interesting if you think about it all three lost their breath."

Jhee went to note her findings and noticed her low battery. "Mind if I induct for a bit."

"If ya like."

Jhee input her notes manually. Dictation required power and space her conch lacked. And she still couldn't transmit.

"You'll not get nothing down here. Best try the storm light spire."

A long, arduous trek to the top of another spiral tower ranked low on the list of actions she wanted to perform. The prioress did mention the solar arrays.

Jhee charged her conch a few more minutes before heading for the nearest wing to the solar array. She stared at the door hearing the rain and crying winds outside. The Storm Child's rage had quieted some since she arrived. It was still guaranteed to be wet and miserable out, though. She clutched her robes about her and sighed before she stepped into the elements.

On a storm-rent night, the panels were a nightmare of reflections and shadows. The eyesight played tricks. Difficult to tell if someone stood amongst them. With an overactive imagination, perfect fodder for more eerie sightings. Jhee sheltered by the arrays for some protection from the wind and rain.

Creatures dashed this way and rustled that way through the weeds amongst the solar panel bases. Jhee hoped. The moisture beaded off them or ran to the ground in rivulets to puddle underneath them. She held her conch aloft. At first, she saw nothing then a single pip faded in. It acted a guttering candle flame in the wind. She exclaimed with excitement.

"What was that?" a snatch of words on the wind said.

A disjointed reply came chopped and sliced by the wind. "Nothing... crab-rats."

One of the eponymous crab-rats scurried by Jhee. She pressed her mouth closed to stifle a yelp. Who would come out here now aside from her? Those who wanted privacy and nothing but the winds and willows to keep their secrets.

Jhee doused her conch within her robes and dimmed her eye color. It took a moment for her eyesight to adjust. A little way off she saw the prioress talking to Raigen. Jhee murmured a concealment cypher. Before she completed her eavesdropping formulation, the pair separated.

The abbey door clanked open. Raigen went inside while the prioress remained a glow orb in one hand and a large bundle in the other. Jhee huddled closer to the solar array. The prioress went to the far edge of the array before giving a sharp whistle which cut through the storm noise. Another figure came from the mists, and she handed the bundle off. The prioress stopped before the door to the abbey and gave another quick look around. She peered in Jhee's direction for a long time then turned and went inside.

Jhee used the delay to examine the Bridge Tower from this vantage. A discolored patch corresponded to the scorched section seen on her visit. After some quick and dirty triangulation, she traced the faulty section of the array. Several had bent struts smudged with soot, a short-circuit perhaps. She captured an image with her conch. Saheli may have collapsed from sunstroke. Had Saheli's transcendence taken place in the tower, this may have accounted for the brilliant flash of light.

Jhee waited a little longer before she headed for the warmth and dryness of the abbey. Her measly long-range signal pip had gone almost immediately once she was inside. She contacted Bax and set him about the task of trailing Raigen.

Jhee yawned. Anything else she might do must wait until tomorrow, though. She returned to her spouses, soaking wet.

"Were the supplies underwater?" Shep asked.

"Don't even get me started. The physician tried to give me an emetic."

"Vomiting? For a headache?" Mirrei asked.

"Tomorrow, I'll inquire about topping up our stores with the Mistress of Horticulture."

10

THE ISLE

~

The Shed

Early in the morning, Jhee sought out the horticulturist. A few Prospectives who had been standing around talking hurried back to work. Jhee paused to have a gander at Saheli's favorite spot. Her mixed company on the initial tour meant she had not been able to investigate it as thoroughly as she wanted. Jhee rested on the bench and cast about her. White flickering from the ajar shed door drew her attention. She moved closer.

Sister Serra slapped Jhee on the back. She gasped hard to get her wind back. "None the worse for wear for your visit to Sister Souse, I see?"

Jhee felt a sharp pinch on her wrist. She found a bog gnat making a meal of her. She flicked its squished remains away. "Indeed. Your arrival was quite timely."

"I have standing orders with her assistants to call me if they're concerned. Try this. It's a mild analgesic."

The horticulturist handed Jhee a tube of spike leaf ointment.

"Zalver mentioned something about missing drugs."

"Not missing. Rationed. Besides Sister Souse isn't licensed to prescribe. Even if she were, we have doubts about how many of the pharmaceuticals would reach the patients. The prime suspect in the matter was the good doctor herself. She may have been a good doctor once until her senses started to go, and the self-medication. We cut back her supplies after a few mishaps."

"She's still allowed to practice. Why?"

"Same reason she got assigned: nepotism. We've been waiting for a replacement almost two long-years. Many doctors are moving inland. The Soothbringers have been offering free healing lessons. Penance they say. They charge no fees to learn or for their services. Though, the healing does involve the new science. We are an order who eschews arcana. Most healers have incorporated at least some of their techniques into their work. It's getting harder to find doctors who don't in some way."

"To hear her tell it, she still does a brisk trade."

"Sister Zalver's favored remedies use spirits of the alcoholic kind. In particular, she views our select blend as a cure-all. I suspect it's the only reason anyone still seeks her out for 'treatment.' Most learned to come to me or the prioress. Now, I have an extensive selection of mood-adjusters, medicines, and herbal remedies. Fill me in on the nature of the complaint, and I can narrow it down for you. For nightmares and trouble sleeping, I suggest tharos root, though it does vex the ability to cypher. For shakes and tremors, lilac acid tincture. Night flower for mania and midnight bloom for melancholy."

While her herbalism and pharmacology were a little oxidized, Jhee found no quibble with any of those suggestions; unlike what the physician had recommended. Jhee might consult an expert, Mirrei, or bring her along on a return visit.

"Something scholarly, perhaps. A study aid. I have several preparations good for memory and focus. Others which make one more receptive to learning, and creative and imaginative thinking."

"I think perhaps I should just stick to the items on my list."

"Your choice. If I may?" Jhee handed Sister Serra her list, who touched her chin and bobbed her head in approval. "Lashotic remedies. Solid choices. Portable and easy to store. You'll want them pre-dried and ready for transport. We'll have to go into the apothecary stores."

"If it's not breaking any confidences, mind if I ask what you prescribed to Saheli?"

"I'm no doctor. Simply a gifted amateur. Verdale, where I'm from, was teeming in plant life. A lot of it useful. A lot of it hostile. Mistake brightshade for blightshade, you'd regret it."

The bog gnats continued to buzz around Jhee. She swatted them away. "Am I clear on understanding that Saheli partook of brightshade?"

"Just so. It's one of those study aids I mentioned. It does have hallucinogenic properties though and is best not taken alone. Saheli took two seeds twice a week under my supervision for meditation purposes. We sometimes sought the four conjunctions together which lie deep in barbarian lands. All save one have fallen into their hands. The only way to visit them is via the use of ecstatics to open the mind and commune with the Makers through visions. Though, she had begun to develop a tolerance to it."

"Is that why you went up the spire to check on her and didn't want her to go to the infirmary?"

Sister Serra took up a glass pipe and packed the dried leaves into it. She rubbed her fingers together, which produced just enough flame to heat it. She took a deep drag and held it before releasing a voluminous cloud of smoke. "No one in their true mind wants to go to our infirmary. Saheli humored Zalver to make her feel useful. However, she also knew her, the prioress, and Elkanah to be tiresomely orthodox and inflexible. When I glanced over and found her gone, a closer look revealed her on the floor. You are right I did rush to the tower to search for any trace of seed of enlightenment, so they wouldn't know. Meanwhile, the cat licked everything in sight, including her spilled drink. It escaped when I opened the door."

Serra offered the pipe to Jhee. Jhee refused. The horticulturist's pungent scent and smell of smudging stick made more sense now. "I didn't realize Drakists were allowed to partake."

"They're not. I'm Pluralist. One of the few left here. The remnants of my order merged with the Drakists when our monastery was overrun. I hope I didn't overstep offering you the wine."

"Not as such."

"Demand has spiked, but I'm eager for more independent research on its healing properties. I admire anyone who would take a pleasure cruise on these waters." Sister Serra leaned over and whispered to Jhee. "Must make for passionate times with the adrenaline and fear. Your full marriage cohort indicates you to be a woman of appetite. One spouse no doubt deft and experienced; two whom you can groom and teach. Always mind the quiet ones."

Jhee waved away more gnats. Sister Serra looked unperturbed.

"I saw you grow lace root melons. May I make an addition to the list?"

"Feel free. Unlike my colleague, who is stingy with the fruits of her labor, I prefer to be generous. I consider mine a gift to all those who would ask."

"Would you have any of the taffies?"

"Another of our most profitable exports. I can't get enough of them myself. Here you are. Added to your requisition writ. If you'd like some now, I'll give you some of mine."

Jhee slapped her arm as another bog fly got her. Sister Serra produced a candy dish from under the workbench, and they each had one. "You were right about Sister Elkanah."

"She didn't let you anywhere near her precious relics. Once that humorless shrew makes up her mind, that's it. You're better off. Archives, relics are about death. My domain is alive."

"I came across something interesting, though. Plans to turn this into a health resort or commercialize the vineyards and orchards."

Sister Serra coughed. The pipe slipped from her hands. She reached out but nearly dropped the pipe again. She bounced it a few times before she found a cool place to hold it. Serra placed it on the workbench then blew on her hands. "Unmake me! Justicar, if you would be so kind as to pass back that spike leaf ointment."

Jhee handed Sister Serra the tube. The ointment's scent was sharp and bitter. Pyrmo's burn cream had a similar smell. "On second thought, I may take some brightshade."

"Like I said. A woman of appetite. I'll give you some from my own private stock. I appreciate your challenging of Elkanah's perspective. Smaller tin next to the taffies there."

Sister Serra indicated the tin under the workbench. While Jhee set about locating the tin, she examined container labels. No marked pesticides or substances which might be used to poison someone. "I also learned something of the Mist Abbess."

By the time Jhee rose, Sister Serra had brought out a wave skimmer. "I have to get going. The Wave Witch's up and the weather's decent enough. We should go skimming sometime. I know all the best spots."

"Wave skimming? That would be a hard pass."

"Suit yourself."

The horticulturist hurried off with her skimmer. Jhee muttered an oath at the closed and locked shed.

～

On a Mission

Jhee sought Pyrmo out next. "Blessed are the First Makers, Abbess."

"How goes your investigation, Justicar? You visited quite a number of our facilities."

"I wanted to get a proper sense of the abbey's arrangement. To grasp the design, you must first understand the system. The prioress was most helpful. A shame her duties prevent her from helping me today."

"Duties? The prioress asked for the day off today. I assumed to assist you."

"Perhaps I misunderstood."

"Par for the course nowadays. Unfortunately, she has become increasingly erratic. Pity. When she served under me while I held the position, she was quite reliable. I think she was more affected by Saheli's death than she cares to admit."

"Oh? Were they close?"

"Hard to say really. Saheli was a very hands-on abbess. She frequently counseled young men personally. She was very friendly, but not without secrets."

"Like most. Would it be possible for me to look at the treasury logs or perhaps the inventories and manifests?"

"Why look at those?"

"Simply being thorough. A routine question came up, and I want to verify it."

"Those records are confidential. I might be able to answer any general questions."

"The mortician said you sell off anything valuable the clergy possess when they die."

"Generally, yes. The Professed bequeath their belongings to the abbey. The situation is more complicated for the Prospectives. We generally give the family an opportunity to claim them. Although, with the large number of refugees fleeing most have no family to contact. Often their only belongings are sentimental."

"Anything that's not gets logged into the treasury, yes?"

"Yes."

"You said Saheli's belongings were interred with her or donated to the archives. What about the Prospectives who died? Were their valuables logged into the treasury?"

"The Prospectives? Valuables? Most are fisherfolk or shepherds. They had nothing more than a few trinkets. While every bit does help, their possessions were meager."

"No large amounts of currency?"

"Currency? No. Why would Prospectives have that here?"

"Why, indeed? Another curiosity came up during my investigation. I heard a strange term, the Mist Abbess. Docs that name mean anything to you?"

"A story to frighten young novices. There's a possibility I hesitate to entertain. The rumors of the Mist Abbess's return didn't happen until Saheli's appointment."

"Thank you, Abbess. With your permission, I'd like to continue my investigations."

"Of course."

The prioress had lied to Jhee about her activities. She never logged the large sum of cash the mortician found into the treasury. She also kept the tallies from bed check. The prioress's talk of ghosts could have been meant to scare Jhee away. Could she and Raigen have conspired in sending Jhee on a wisp chase? Perhaps Jhee would delve deeper into the prioress's activities.

~

Ask the Servants

"Ask the servants did you say, Bax? Lead the way," Jhee declared once she located her invaluable helper and family friend. Bax made as excellent a Justicar's assistant as he once made a criminal.

"They won't talk to you like that," Bax said.

With Kanto's help, Jhee had found her more unadorned day robes. She weighed the ability of her official robes' authority and dignity to loosen tongues against blending in. For now, she removed the sashes and any insignia of rank. She left her head wrap in place.

"It'll do."

After a few discrete inquiries, Jhee located the prioress by the storehouse. The prioress visited various provisioners and clothiers at the abbey and eventually the docks.

"I miss good old, grain bread. More and more it's that rice powder nonsense," said one fishmonger.

"Tried sopping up stew with it? Falls apart. Turns the whole bowl into mushy garbage," said another.

"Don't let it sit too long or dry out. It gets sticky. Like cement. Took two days to clean the bowl my youngest hid cause she didn't want to eat it."

"The trick is not to substitute direct," Jhee said. "Rice flour needs more yeast and starch. Coconut flour is very absorbent. Use less or put in more liquid." The fisherfolk glanced at her dubiously. "The First Mister likes to cook."

They nodded sagely. That rightly made more sense to them than a Justicar who might know how to cook.

"Bax, show me where the leaf mongers partake if you would." Bax led her through the hallways down to the cooking chambers to a rear enclosure sheltered from the elements. "I'm going to investigate the prioress. You keep following Raigen."

An overhang ensured privacy from the clergy's prying eyes. It also made an excellent vantage from which to mind the receiving area and await her quarry. A muddy well-worn path led the way with an occasional stubbed out butt. A few lay brothers and sisters toked on smoke root. When she entered, the nearest one dropped his and tried to stamp it out.

Jhee held up a placating hand. "I wondered if you might have an extra."

The staff paused dumbfounded. Then one stepped forward and handed Jhee an unlit, freshly trimmed root.

"Thank you." Jhee put the root between her teeth and used the young man's striker to light it. She dragged deep and tried not to cough. "My cohort doesn't like me to partake, especially on the yacht."

"One of the co-fathers was a stickler," another staff member said. "Drove our mother and the other father to toke in secret. When they had to get rid of theirs quickly, left a lot of half-smoked ones for me to clean up. Which I did."

The woman took a deep draw and raised her eyebrows.

Jhee nodded. "My grandmamere used to say smoke root kept evil spirits at bay."

"If only. It was spirits what got those boys. Maybe even the abbess," the second staffer said.

"Just the other day we had two Prospectives lured to their deaths," a third staffer said. "One got lured into the locked spire where he fell to his death. The door had been locked for some time, and there was still thick dust upon the ground. Now, how could that have happened save ghosts what led him there I tell you?"

"It weren't ghosts. It were the sea wisps. They led those poor men to their deaths. These young men about have them in a sore frenzy I bet you. They will take them under the sea to be their sea kings and spawn the next first fathers I tell you. Sea wisps beckon us back to the sea where we belong," the first staffer said.

"You don't really believe we were descended from mayes do you?"

"I believe what grandbabere and grandmamere told me. She said we were born in the sea and it ain't natural for us to be upon the land. That's what wrong with the barbarians. They don't spend enough time in the waves, and it has caused them to become uncivilized, especially the sky singers."

"The sky singers. You don't believe those old legends, do you?" the second staffer asked.

"I know we have the sky singers, the ground pounders, and them mixed fire children barbarians. That's what all I know."

"While I was out on the bluffs, I saw a pterosaur-like creature. One of the Unmaker's minions. I swear," yet another staffer said.

"No, it had to be Cheiropthys or the Wave Witch. Only she had the power to summon winged creatures."

The first staffer leaned in. "They say the blood cults are back and it's the Mist Abbess what leads them."

"Feh," the second staffer said, "best not to tarry with the Unknown Maker or worse the Unmakers."

"Sea wisps lured that boy to his death," said the first staffer.

"No," the second staffer said, "it was ghosts. They must have chased him up to the tower. How else could he have gotten in?"

"And caved in the cellar on that other one," agreed the third staffer.

"Did you hear one wasted away of fright?"

Jhee took a drag from her smoke root. "Ghosts. I think I may have seen some myself when I first arrived here. In the Zodiac Courtyard."

The second staffer nodded sagely. "Their favorite spot. They say that's where the Mist Abbess liked to perform her blasphemous rituals. That's where one Prospective died. Ill omen. It's the curse."

"The curse?" Jhee asked.

"The curse of the Unfettered Dead. I swear I can hear them whispering through the walls," the second staffer said. "Ghosts of those who died here don't like all these new, crude men."

"Reminds them of what they once were before they were cut down by the barbarians. Makers make the shield," said the third staffer.

"Makers make the shield," Jhee and the others repeated.

Had she seen an echo of some long-ago blood cult dismemberment ritual? The system remembers, and those who tinkered with the forbidden were most apt to leave traces not easily forgotten.

"This place sounds more frightening every day," Jhee said. "The abbess's death. These three unfortunates. You said sea wisps misled the one who drowned?"

The first staffer replied, "Wisp lights on the heath and the bluffs. Wisp lights have been seen for quite some time here. Boats used to be driven to their ruin on the breakers." Jhee closed her eyes tightly and shivered. "They say it was the ghosts of those massacred here in the past."

"The wisp lights led many a poor body to their death here. The young spouses and children who never got a chance to grow and play, now grow and play with the living to their detriment," said the last staffer.

"I've seen their lights out on the fields and bluffs myself. Especially the wood," the first staffer said.

The second staffer glanced back at the abbey. "The storm light's meant to drown out the false light of the dead."

The third staffer stamped out a root. "Best to ask the bilge workers near the harbor entrance. They found his body caught in some lobster traps."

The lights Jhee had seen from the first spire came to mind. "Did you know anything about him? Was he particularly careless?"

"Not more than most young men. He liked the bluffs though. He volunteered for any errands that took him out there."

Another staffer grinned. "Was it the errand location or the errand dispatcher?"

Jhee cocked an eyebrow. "You suspected him of an affair with the staff?"

The first staffer shrugged and gave a little glance up to the main abbey.

"Fraternization?" Jhee asked.

"Far be it from me to speak ill of the clergy, Justicar. But the horticulturist sure did need a lot of things from the seaport."

"Both deacons did," said the third staffer.

"More like the one wanted to know what the other was about. The Prospect who got sick worked at the archives off and on. Sometimes the agripods, too."

All staffers murmured agreement.

"What about the one crushed?" Jhee asked.

"He bounced around here and there. Restless sort. Not sure if this life was a good fit for him. But who am I to question the Makers' plan?"

At last, the prioress appeared. Jhee snuffed out her half-finished root. "I have to get back before I'm missed. Thank you, ladies and gentlemen."

The second staffer waved a smudging stick over her. "It'll cover the smell, Justicar. To protect you from the wrath of witches, wisps, and disapproving spouses."

Jhee gave a polite bow.

~

Blight and Bilge

The simmering sensation behind Jhee's eyes grew to boiling as she shadowed the prioress the rest of the day. The prioress paid the merchants and fishmongers with shell currency, no doubt the money stolen from the unfortunate, wretched Prospective's corpse. She did her best not to let outrage overtake her and confront the woman.

Finally, the prioress returned to the abbey. Enough time remained before dinner to undertake a visit to the bilges. The weather lightened to trickles, and the clergy went out to the fields to harvest what they could. Jhee conducted a personal walking tour of the island. Trailing the prioress had not presented the opportunity to appreciate its features. She strolled through the fields of grain. In the images she had seen, they were two or three times this height. For every cleric working, she saw one or two refugees. Some clergy even milled about and watched as the refugees worked.

She passed by the threshing shed and granary. What should have been floor to ceiling stacks of drying straw were barely half that. Refugees and clergy shoveled green, blighted plants into an incinerator. She picked up one of the stalks, some of them contained purple club-shaped growths: blightseed.

Some folk fished, lobster trapped, and hauled in the kreel nets. Others worked on a new drainage system for the bog trying to reclaim wetlands for expansion and to host more people.

The First Makers' Design guided Jhee's path to the bilges. The horrid, sweetly rank scent made the air a miasma. She covered her face, so she did not gag. She wished she had brought a smudging stick with her. She found the bilge workers on a break. She offered one her half-used root. She leaned forward and sniffed it deeply but waved it away. "No sparks or open flames while down here, Justicar."

"Of course. Later then?"

"Much appreciated, ma'am, but the smell gets in everything after long. What brings you down here, Justicar?"

Jhee put away the root as smoothly as she offered it. "Ghost stories. You know about the Prospective who drowned?"

"The morning crew found 'em. Glad it weren't mine. At least they found all of 'em. Sometimes you only find part. Finger. Toe. Dentures. You see a lot when you muck out the storm drains and inspect bilges."

"The staff thinks ghosts or sea wisps drove the young man off the bluffs or made him jump from the tower."

"Not sure how much ghosts had to do with it. Begging the Justicar's pardon. They found him beyond the breakers caught in some lobster traps wedged between rocks. He couldn't get that far out from even the storm light tower."

Jhee cringed, rocks, breakers. "The current, perhaps?"

"It's counter current. Only a few places he could have fallen to catch the right waters. The sloped vineyard, the bridge access way, or the lee of the isle. Most those is jagged rocks. Nothing can walk there but sheep and the surest of goats. He would of have to have been a ghost or wisp himself to survive walking about there."

"He didn't survive, did he?"

"No, ma'am, suppose not. Blessed be the Makers." The bilge worker locked her hands together.

Jhee did likewise. "Blessed be the First Makers."

11

GHOSTS

~

The Beach

Jhee awoke crammed between Kanto and Mirrei with the latter's arm flung over her face. She extricated herself as peaceably as she could. Her day robes and traveling robes had gone missing. She dug through the luggage around the room for anything resembling a simple wrap. The only other clothes of hers she turned up were the formal ones. She checked the dryness on her evening robes which hung near the fire. They were still wet. Beside them, the robes Kanto made had been cleaned and were dry as dust.

She found a fresh poultice waiting neatly on the table beside a full, clear, Adept teapot. She smiled and drew the teapot to heat the water. Shep joined her. As they drank the tea and perused the autopsy images, they sat hand in hand. He occasionally stroked her knuckles with his thumb. One Prospective had a peculiar tattoo on his wrist. Each had the more traditional jubilee tattoos which indicated the celestial phases and alignments of their birthday. Evidence of a brand which resembled those of the Medical Protectorate caused her and Shep to tense. It wasn't one, thank the Makers. Jhee brushed her fingers lightly over the failsafe sigil implanted in her arm. They touched escae before she left.

Planting herself outside the prioress's cell, bore Jhee the fruit she hoped. The prioress wandered to a side door in the Shrine Courtyard. One not on Jhee's map. No wonder she had tried to warn Jhee away from the place. It led to a little-used delivery canal under the abbey for cargo and fresh-caught sea meat. The channel must, also, serve as escape route or means to come and go from the abbey unseen. A scruffy old man awaited on a skiff piled with boxes and crates. The prioress boarded, and they pushed away from the landing.

Jhee examined the canal area. Not another vessel nearby. The spit of landing ended at the canal entrance. From there, her options were wade or swim. In either case, she could not keep up with them.

"Psst!" A sound came from the shadows deeper in the abbey's bowels. The drip and splash of a pole in water preceded a skiff piloted by Bax and Raigen gliding up to the landing. Jhee surmised Shep had Bax keeping an eye on her regardless of whatever other tasks she set him. However, why despite her charge did Bax and Raigen occupy this craft together? She had no time to ponder it now. She boarded, and they pushed off before the illumination from the skiff's lantern left sight.

The haggard man looked over his shoulder often. By the First Makers' whim, a light mist rolled in. She drew it to conceal their pursuit. The fog had the power of the great storm in it, she realized after she had extended herself to it. It tugged and fought and tried to wrench itself from her grasp.

With a last effort, Jhee prevailed. She sat back and rested. Bax and Raigen proved adept at navigating the shallows and masking their passage through the water. Her concealment was by no means perfect. They would be seen if anyone looked hard enough. Or if the mist wights inhaled. Had she also wrestled the last breaths of the dead as Reach lore would have it?

Their journey came to an end when the skiff ahead came to a stop on an isle no more than a sandbar. Gruff folk met it. Bax and Raigen broke off pursuit and put in at a nearby inlet out of sight.

"Get out here. We'll stow the skiff and meet up with you," Raigen said.

Jhee hopped out, flipped her robes inside out, and removed her insignia of rank. She remained overdressed anyway as she tried to blend with the crowd gathered to meet the skiff. These haggard folk were refugees. Burly refugees in clothes slightly less bedraggled than the rest helped the prioress unload the boat onto nearby sleds. Excited murmurs grew as refugees crowded the landing area. To Jhee's astonishment, a suspicious handful of aid workers drew the sleds away from shore. They came to a stop at a nearby supply depot. The prioress clapped, and the refugees queued up. A table had been set up where workers already started a sorting line. The prioress opened crates and boxes to reveal food and clothing. She distributed them to the line of refugees. Every now and then she pulled out a toy and presented it to a child.

A sizable crowd remained once the prioress's provisions came to an end. She shook her head and rested her head in her hands. After a body-shaking sigh, the prioress went amongst the crowd distributing the only goods she had in infinite supply, prayers and blessings. Even without supplies, a crowd pressed in on the woman, and Jhee lost track of her.

The refugees had noticed the fineness of Jhee's robes even inside out.

Their lean, starved faces pleaded with her. Jhee gave what she had on her person Maker geld, medicines, her medicinal inhaler. She even parted with as much of her clothing as was decent including Kanto's beautiful robe. She lost her poultice too. The crowd parted enough for Jhee to glimpse the prioress again.

In the confusion, the prioress disappeared once more. Jhee broke free of the crowd. She scanned the pathways through the tents and ramshackle huts. Most barely kept out the rain. Without her robes, she blended in better. She walked a few of the pathways between the tents. The sand was muddy and discolored. The air stank of urine and feces. A few aid workers distributed tarpaulins and beeswax to seal the plain cloth tents.

A gap opened between one set of tents and another. She spotted the prioress surrounded by a group of young men and women. They went to a flat bit of shore tamped down by many feet. Another crowd already awaited. The prioress clapped, and they formed ranks. Men, women, and children proceeded to do mediations in motion. The meditations Jhee did to clear and center herself for cyphering. The prioress made no effort to separate the men or boys.

The participants performed larger, more exaggerated gestures at full extension like the articles suggested. However, a beach full of people was much, much larger than the recommended five to six-person class size. Despite the admonition against cyphering and murky laws, the prioress proceeded to teach any and all cyphering, even men.

The sequences and cyphers were a hodge-podge at best. A pastiche cobbled together from many journals and articles about male cyphering. Jhee had planned on using many of the same moves in the system she considered for Kanto.

This close, there was no mistaking the aid workers' Pillarist garb; another reason why the prioress would not want her activities known. The aid workers were Soothbringers at least. The Doombringers had all but been eradicated. The Soothbringers had folded themselves into various other orders such as the Drakists and Beacons of Lost Sparks. Who else would be most equipped to teach cyphering indiscriminately?

The Middle Pillarists, more specifically the Doombringer heretics, were the reason for the cyphering laws in the first place. Technically, the rules against male education had been lessened and, in some cases, abolished. Poor men did not cypher and barely drew the elements. Much of the local populace still held to the traditions or distrusted male artificers. They looked askance at anyone teaching men such even though it was something the rich had done with their sons for quite some time now.

Gears ground and hitched in the environment. The unbalanced prime forces set Jhee's teeth on edge. Too many artificers in such a concentrated space. She hastened to test the air quality. The too sudden movement drew the prioress's attention.

The prioress gasped upon recognizing Jhee. She attempted to hide her motions.

"Justicar, please, I can explain," the prioress stammered.

"Later." Jhee queried the divine mechanism. Her mentor, Vizier Jeja, had been an arcane outreach counselor paid by the Central Authority to demonstrate the safety and benefits of cyphering. She had learned the signs when the environment spoiled, the symptoms of cyphering sickness. She had thought the program at the time had been meant to enrich the lives of the people. What it really was about was the Empire needed more artificers and adepts to work on the shield.

A man dropped to the ground and clutched his head. He convulsed. Jhee examined the man and cleaned the froth from his mouth. The air had the same wrongness, and depleted quality Jeja had taught her to look out for. They tended the man until he ceased his shaking and screams. Incidents like this only increased the stigma with regards to male cyphering.

"He should be fine. Cyphering is done for the day."

The prioress bowed profusely. "Justicar, if I may ask a favor. "

"You may ask."

"The clinic. Afterward, we can speak in private, and I will answer your questions as honestly as I can."

～

Mist Blind

The prioress escorted Jhee to a makeshift field hospital. For those taken by diseases, such as Fresh Lung, Jhee could do nothing. She healed apparent surface infections first. Then Jhee mended cuts and scrapes, a few broken bones and more apparent wounds. What truly ailed them she could not fix.

A group of grateful leaders met her and the prioress outside. They brought them to their meeting tent and fed them a thin groutfish stew and a hard, crumbly chunk of bread from their meager stores. It tasted the greatest of feasts to Jhee. She washed it down with a swig of the refugee's strong homemade liquor, squelch. It burned all the way down. She gasped and pounded her chest until the inebriation settled over her.

Jhee remembered the tattoo she had seen in Leigh's autopsy images. She noted similar ones on several of the people she treated. The thought of the autopsy images made her appetite flee. Another swig of squelch helped that, too.

Jhee listened politely and respectfully while her hosts talked.

"Our livelihood is dying. That drenched Shield. It scares the fish. We can also no longer go out as far for whale and other sea meat. Only the big ships with passes from the Imperial Authority. Makers make the Shield, anyway. Let's see if those stipple bastards can get around that."

"The whale and manta are being driven inland where they strand, or the ranchers get them. We could find more out further to sea, but we are humble fisherfolk who can't afford the license fees to venture beyond like the big ships can."

"Not unless we go in on the fishing combines."

"The rep from the fishing combine was here again."

"I'll be unmade before I let some inland bureaucrats tell me what to do on my own ship. No, ma'am. Begging your pardon, Justicar."

"I used to think they were a joke. I had my own ship. Why would I want to give that up to have someone else tell me how to run it?"

"Or worse, work someone else's so they can get rich while you break your back."

"I don't know anymore. The Imperial Authority doesn't seem to care about the little fish anymore. Only the whales."

Another elder drunkenly interrupted, "Arcana. Feh. I know how they built the shield. They used necromancy and deep magic to rouse the shell drake what lies at the bottom of the sea. It now circles about the isles churning the waters into this Maker-forlorn storm. That's what caused them quakes."

"They awoke the Storm Child in hir fury. We had two tremors and wyrm waves."

"The Wave Witch and Wind Witch have quarrel again."

"No, the Storm Child rides the shell drake."

After the second or third time losing the thread of the conversation, Jhee knew she needed to leave before she passed out there on the beach. She swayed as she rose and made her farewells.

The elder shoved a small carved piece of driftwood in her hands. "Be safe. That place is full of restless spirits."

Jhee reached into her devotion pouch for a tiny shell she had carved with Maker runes and cyphering primitives. She touched it to her esca then handed it to the elder in trade. The elder acknowledged the exchange with a nod. Make for Make.

As if Jhee were not already tired enough, she still had the prioress to deal with. A hollow stare was all it took to get her speaking.

"Allow me to explain."

"The mortician said Saheli caught you stealing."

"For this."

"You also took the cash from the dead Prospective's body."

"To buy more provisions. He was a refugee too once. When I revealed to Saheli why I stole, she understood. Saheli and I both thought the laws governing the teaching and education of men backward and archaic. Even when it came to cyphering. We resolved to teach any who would be willing to learn, and so we did."

"But your order eschews cyphering."

"We were encouraged by our success with the mundane educational program. This is our pilot program. With a fixed, controlled group, we hoped to better understand the dangers and the risks. Our first obligation and duty are to our community and the welfare of all the Makers' children. The knowledge could be used to better the lives of themselves and others, which is our foremost obligation. As clergy locked behind our walls, we sometimes become blind to the suffering of the people around us. These refugees reminded both Saheli and me of that. She even sometimes visited the camp herself. I do what I can here, but it's still not enough. Not only were we going to teach, but we were also going to lessen the tithe as a show of goodwill."

"I can only imagine how well that would go over."

"Which is why Saheli wanted it kept quiet until she was officially ready to announce it. Perhaps we could shame the other orders into helping. Once the decree went public, there was virtually no way to take it back."

"Save for the appointment of a new abbess."

Such a move narrowed down the suspect pool to any overly proud and comfortable cleric at the abbey. Jhee stroked her nose which the working conditions had shifted toward a muzzle. Rapid minor adaptations were a consequence of the shifting weather conditions this close to the Shield. Before the Storm Shield, it used to be subtler and more gradual unless you were adept at skin slipping.

"I kept track of every shell I took; all sales and philanthropy. And so did Saheli once she knew. We drew the money from a combination of slush funds, petty cash, and her revenues as abbess. We started tracking after we took over the books from Pyrmo. We almost had to. They had not been kept properly in years, perhaps decades. Inventory and audit were next on the agenda. Thanks to the current insinuations, all Saheli's reforms are now under evaluation. Some, if not many, are bound to be discarded. Pyrmo has already cut back on our charitable giving to the poor, and she never would approve of cyphering lessons."

"Or working with Soothbringers."

"These people are desperate. The traditional orders are failing them. Nearby cities consider them a nuisance. As do most of my fellow clergy. The other monasteries have largely ignored their and our pleas for aid. Only the Soothbringers have done anything for them. As a result, more and more follow them. Can you blame them, Justicar? Saheli and I tried to get them to join the Drakists instead. We could be doing more. Refugee housing programs. Or have the Professed and Prospectives help them build homes. Instead, we're hiding behind the walls of the abbey."

"I am not unsympathetic. The restrictions regarding this sort of thing have become more social than legal after the reforms of the Rescission Councils. Much as you informed me regarding your vows, this is a matter between your conscience and the First Makers. If you are going to continue the cyphering lessons in whatever capacity, you should consult with someone who has actual experience instructing others to cypher."

"Proper teachers cost money. Look around, Justicar. They can't do lengthy apprenticeships or hire enough teachers for the recommended student ratio."

The education report and the signets of introductions Lady Bathsheba had provided her sprang to mind. "A few isles have pooled their resources for cyphering instructors. I, also, have the personal contact information for Imperial Education Secretaries. A similar arrangement might be set up throughout the camps. In the interim, I offer my counsel. I'll instruct you in a few more healing cyphers and the warning signs for cyphering sickness and pollution. We can discuss a curriculum and a funding stream for both their supplies and education."

The prioress gave more profuse bows. She extended her hands to Jhee. They clasped forearms and touched foreheads. Jhee did not mind such a familiar gesture in such a circumstance. She felt the situation more than warranted it. The prioress hovered her palm over Jhee's esca. "The Makers' blessing to you and yours. We may not have always agreed, but I respected Saheli. She genuinely cared about the poor and not lining her own pockets or puffing herself up. Do you really think she was murdered?"

"All I learn makes it more and more likely."

On the beach, a leader, much younger than the others and who had spent most of the conversation silent, stopped Jhee.

"I have not heard anything from my brother. A man came to the camps. He claimed he could get him good work in the city as a cook or servant."

"I'll see what I can do."

Jhee watched the refugees with fatigue. Their blank, worn faces continued as an endless sea. She imagined this must be what the inhabitants of Antasia who tried to hold back the sea on their own or the lone elemental practitioners who tried themselves against the storms felt like. Would it ever be enough? Could she ever do enough? Her stomach felt knotted, and she wanted nothing more than to sit down and close her eyes to everything.

"Justicar, we should go," Bax said.

"Yes." Jhee turned for a last look over the camp. She faced the dim glow of the storm shield. The barbarians awaited on the other side. She must remember that. "Raigen?"

Jhee had meant to ask where the woman was, but that's all she managed.

"Later, Justicar. Later."

The Ghost Stories

Jhee slipped back to her room. Once again, Kanto remained awake, but this time with an audience. By the fire, her three spouses gathered with bowls of pork and rice. Shep perched on the edge of his seat. Mirrei clutched a pillow tight.

"What of the wicked monk who had mocked the Makers and aided the raiders?" Mirrei said.

"And the greedy priest?" Shep asked.

Kanto set down his bowl and leaned forward. Mirrei and Shep did too. "A cave-in had blocked one exit. The servants they mistreated sealed the other after them. They say they lost their way in the crypt depths amongst the very honored dead they betrayed. On many days, if you listen closely, you can still hear them searching, searching for the way out."

The three fell silent as if to listen.

"Let me out," Jhee whispered.

Her spouses jumped. Jhee gave a weary smile as she stepped into the room. Mirrei groaned and tossed her pillow at Jhee.

"Not. Funny," Shep said. "Did you two plan this?"

Jhee chuckled. Kanto gave a hearty laugh until he noticed her appearance. "My word, denbe, what happened? Your robes? The poultice? Were you robbed?"

"That pork and rice looks delicious," Jhee said.

"Sit here. Let me get you some," Kanto said. He sniffed her several times. "Is that liquor? Are you drunk?"

"Long story. Thank you."

Shep set down a washbasin and a cleaning cloth. "You're not hurt, are you?"

"No." When Kanto returned with a bowl of food, she devoured it. The water in the basin was too cold. She gazed at the fire yet did not have the strength to redirect it. She'd be surprised if she could even get a spark from an Adept stone.

"Look at me," Mirrei said. Her usually light and demure tone had gone replaced by one which Jhee could only describe as motherly and stern. She held up a finger and moved it in front of Jhee's eyes. After one or two passes, Jhee had to stop. "Jumpy tracking. Pale. Low body temp. Shallow breathing. Cyphering fatigue."

Kanto hovered and frowned, followed by dragging Shep aside for an animated conversation outside her hearing. Jhee picked up an uneaten roll.

"Wait," Shep said. Jhee bit into it and practically chipped a tooth. She tapped the roll against the table. It sounded fit for an Earth Adept's use. "Not everyone has adjusted their recipes properly for non-wheat flours yet."

She sighed. "Do we have any broth or soup?"

She put the roll into the soup and consumed it piece by piece as it softened.

"Kanto, not now," Shep said.

"If not, now, when? Before or after she slips away again without a word? Only to turn up like this? Or should we wait until she turns up dead?"

"Fine, we'll change the schedule. Here. How's this? The past couple of days will be my days or off days, and Jhee has my full permission to spend them how she wishes. Mirrei's days will be next since it's been a while for her and Jhee."

"For Makers' sake, Kanto, if it's that important, take my day," Mirrei said.

"All right Kanto then Mirrei. Agreed?"

"Agreed."

"Jhee?"

"Yes. Yes."

"There. Now everyone's happy or equally miserable. Take your pick."

"Shep, Mirrei, I ask a moment of denbe prerogative?" They had taken enough of the ire meant for her. They went to bed, leaving her and Kanto. "I'm sorry I left without a word."

"The timing on your return couldn't have been better, though," he said.

She quirked her mouth. "Where'd you learn that story?"

"From the Prospectives. You didn't expect us to stay shut inside the room all day while you run around. Don't worry, I had a clerical escort. I didn't realize how many of them came from isles like ours."

"Is that your way of saying you want to become a Professed?"

"And scandalize these poor, sheltered women?" Kanto made a grand sweep of his hand over himself. "They couldn't handle this. This is also not to be hidden away under ill-fitting cowls and cassocks."

Jhee rolled her eyes. "Spheres forfend you smile at one. She may faint."

"Wouldn't be the first." They laughed. "Denbe, I don't want to fight or nag."

"No, I have to do better by you." Jhee touched her chin then patted his hand. "Learn anything else interesting on your outing?"

"Here listen to this."

Kanto played recordings from his conch. Notes from a lute quavered and echoed in a way she never quite heard before. It sounded as if wind chimes accompanied them. Jhee squeezed her eyes shut. Men chanted. The sonorous tones caused her to think about a home by the sea, about footsteps that echoed in the too empty house. Jhee pressed her hands together in front of her trembling lips. Once she regained emotional equilibrium, she opened her eyes.

Kanto quickly glanced away. "The first is me in the Worship Hall. Eerie? The acoustical properties of the abbey are extraordinary. Our practice court-yard has a whisper wall where you can stand in one corner and whisper yet be heard by a person at the opposite corner. There is a certain step where you can clap and get an infinite echo. The weird shape of the building plays all sorts of auditory tricks. The wind blowing through an odd window or cracks might very well sound like moaning or scratching at the walls."

Jhee listened as further into the recording, the chants became sea songs and shanties. The refugees and the Prospectives were men like Kanto. The parallels between the missing young men and the deaths of the Prospectives weighed on her as much as her family duties. Refugees had gone missing, and no one noticed. Men died, and their Justicar had not noticed. Kanto had long felt neglected, and she had not noticed either.

Jhee folded her hands and faced away from Kanto. "Between Mirrei's health problems and Shep's episodes, you were the one I never had to worry about. I sometimes forget that you require my attention too, and for that, I am truly sorry. I never had to worry about you, and I took it for granted that I never would. Forgive me. We have not had a day together in a while. I intend to correct that. When your day comes, it will be your day and yours alone. We'll do whatever you want."

"Promise?"

"Promise."

Jhee had worked this all wrong. Despite the vizier's rebuke, she had still focused on the wrong death. She had avoided it, but she needed to plunge down into the drowned Prospective's death. She had set it aside long enough.

12

WISPS LIGHTS

~

A Goat Path

Jhee shielded her eyes to gauge the position of the dual suns. She might have time to check out the lee of the isle. She found the aforementioned goats and let them lead the way. The terrain became rockier and more treacherous as she approached. She turned to glance back at the abbey. Its shadows loomed large, yet not enough to reach this far. Even the storm light spire.

The small herd of goats wandered by her further out than she dared. They stopped and chewed on the hard scrub grass right on the verge of the cliff. One disappeared over the edge. The screech of child cut through the night.

Jhee whipped around to determine the source. The screech came again. It had come from the edge where the goat had fallen. She hastened over, summoned her courage, and peered over the edge.

The goat stared up at her from a series of steps carved into the cliffside. It gave another disturbing bleat as it descended further. She slumped her posture. The other goats trotted by her oblivious.

These steps may have been where Prospective Leigh fell. What was at the bottom? Jhee gathered her wits and courage to take the first step down. She thought to take the wet steps backward so she could look up instead of down. Or better still, eyes closed. Her Maker Within told her what a horrible idea that would be. Instead, she hugged the cliff and prayed the goat did not change its mind about its direction.

A fell, rain-soaked wind kicked up. Jhee accidentally glanced out over the

III

steps to the breakers. She flattened back against the wall. "Not today, Storm Child. Not today."

She brought her focus back to the stairs. She murmured the phrase her grandmamere had taught her for when the seas got too rough over and over as she descended. The peculiar way the waves broke seemed wrong to her. The closer she descended to the shoreline, the better visible a subtle glow from a nearby inlet became. A yellowish glowlight bobbed in the water atop a small buoy tethered in place.

At the bottom of the steps, there was no mistaking the opening in the rocks to a smugglers cove. A sea vessel, not imposing enough to be a pirate ship and devoid of ship-to-ship weaponry, moored at a makeshift dock. A few glow orbs lit it from inside. She crept along the cliff base towards the lights. She caught a strain or two of shanties. A group of smugglers loaded the ships hold with crates and several of the metal-bound casks with the Tranquility Gold, double-Drake brand burned into the oak along with some bearing the black label and orange brands. No sign any were armed.

Jhee crept closer. A gull bird nesting in the side of the cliff flew from its hiding place. The smuggler nearest her position gave the alarm. One grabbed a cargo hook.

She drew in her breath and took hold of the nearby winds. A gust sent them flying into the water. She felt the pullback as one or more tried too. A three-way struggle ensued between them and the storm. They were practiced, probably from wielding it to speed their passage. However, she gained her experience in battle. She allowed the storm to do much of the work, only insinuating herself when it turned the winds in her favor. Anyone who had not fled was now in the water.

With a lull in the winds, she had nothing to work with. The smugglers, instead of seizing the advantage, fished each other out. One, though, had fallen farther away than the others. The one she knocked in the water first had drifted away from the dock and headed for the breakers. She struggled and gulped.

Jhee froze. A young, teen's image begging for her help replaced the smuggler. Jhee was a pre-jubilant again, clinging desperately to a rock while the waves buffeted her. She began to shake.

Not today.

Jhee tore free from her memory-induced paralysis and thrust her will into the water. Against the arcane infused waters, the best she managed was to prevent them from drifting farther out. The other smugglers threw a line to the one struggling in the bay. Jhee collapsed to her knees. With their compatriot rescued, they turned her way again. She offered no resistance. She merely focused on the sea and the breakers. One of the smugglers raised a hand to strike her.

~

The Cove

"No," the smuggler who had nearly drowned yelled. She coughed and sputtered. "She saved me."

"Saved you? Captain, t'were her what put you in the sea, first," another smuggler said.

"Ain't Makerly to kill a magistrate. We're not murderers."

"What you propose we do with her?"

"Are you all right?" Jhee asked.

The captain nodded. She gained her feet and shook the water off her body hair. "Thank you, Magistrate."

Both smugglers had sea dog accents and pale body hair. Their eyes were a lighter more amber shade than those from around here. Jhee indulged her curiosity. "You are from the Gray Dale, captain …?"

"Yaren. Aye, that I am. Pardon, the reception, mum. You surprised us is all. What might a magistrate be doing about the beach in this weather?"

"I might ask the same of you fine folk."

She tugged on her ear. "We got slips. All forms and whatnot proper-like if you want to see them."

"Please."

The smugglers released Jhee. She dusted herself off as Captain Yaren led her to an alcove with a driftwood box. She opened it and pulled out a tiny, credential chip and a conch. At the bottom of the box, was some hard, shell currency. When she attached them, a manifest appeared. "There you are, Magistrate. As ye see, all taxes and duties, paid rightly."

Jhee gave the manifest a once over. The header was crooked. It had Penstock Freight's name, the shipping company it purported to come from, misspelled. The signature belonged to a notoriously corrupt dock master who had died two years previous. "What I see is a mediocre forgery."

Captain Yaren's eyes went wide, and she played with her ear. "Me crew have nothing to do with it. They loaded what were by their reckon a proper manifest."

"I'll take that into consideration should your help with another matter yield dividends."

"Aye, ask, and it be my humble honor to comply."

"Are you aware of the young man they found on the rocks?"

"We ain't had nothing to do with the death of that poor boy. We're Makerly devouts, we are."

"He had to have gone in the water around here. Any idea why he might be out this way?"

The captain tugged hard on her ear. "Admiring the view."

Jhee shoved her hand in her robes. "You try my patience, Captain. Your crewman's inner wrist bears a tattoo though he tried to remove it like the one on the Prospective's body. Likely a gang marker."

The captain's eyes flared. "Gangs?"

"That currency at the bottom of your chest matches the minting shape and denomination of currency also traced to the Prospective. Did you and your crew find him wandering out there and seek to rob him? He struggled, and you flung him to his death."

"Bite your tongue. None who be here is thief or robber of men. We're decent Maker folk. You ask the abbess. It were she what gave us the wine."

"Pyrmo?"

"Saheli. We're Makerly devouts, Magistrate. The tax on the wine were better spent on good works. We shared our custom and plied our trade to the benefit of Tranquility Bridge as much as our own. The abbess reckon it no crime we kept ourselves and our families fed. She saw we said prayers, made our offerings, and did our penance and devotions regular."

"Regular? How often?"

"Once or twice a long-tide until recently. Now it's that sour-faced woman what comes. Or we meet her by the solar arrays."

"The prioress."

"Aye, that be her. We sought to aid that boy's troubled soul. He paid us fair sum to take passage on our next lay out. Our lay out come, he never showed. We sailed ahead of a nasty squall. Not till our return did we learn his fate."

"Because of your operation here, you chose not to share your arrangement with the young man with the authorities."

"Beg pardon, Magistrate. Weren't our business. We told Saheli, and that were the last we heard of it. No other authority know enough to speak to us. We won't do it for them."

"Do you know why the young man wanted to leave?"

"Nay. He did seem sore troubled, though. We did our humble part to be fishers of our fellow folk as the abbess taught us."

"And for a nice fee."

"We do have families, mum."

Jhee imagined Saheli sitting up in her spire engaged in her works, seeing the strange lights as Jhee had. If she also had full access to the archives, she would learn the isles many secrets and inlets. An operation such as this would not escape so an involved an abbess as her. If Saheli not only benefited but supplied the smugglers, she had no incentive to turn them in except in the direst circumstance. And they had no motive to do her in as long as their arrangement held. It made it hard to believe they would kill Prospective Leigh for catching them. Why not merely tell the abbess and have her deal with it?

"How did he even know you were here?"

"A good question, mum."

The crewman Jhee singled out for their tattoo tried to hide behind another. "You there. Would you happen to know how he knew?"

"The abbess did not always come herself for the items she needed. She sent him down to procure them in her place."

"What items?"

"Fancy, expensive items. Sometimes… intimate items."

"I'll hear no false talk against the abbess," the Captain said.

"It's true, captain. The boy came here regular with a list and payment to get personal goods on behalf of his abbess. His words. I never brought it up with her myself due to the intimate nature of some of the items."

"He booked passage for himself and no other?" Jhee asked.

"Aye, mum."

"Thank you."

Jhee stroked her chin. The captain cleared her throat. "Magistrate, what might ye be doing about me crew and my humble person?"

"For the moment, nothing. Remain here should I have need of you again. If you flee, do know I have what I need to track you down."

Jhee touched their sailing vessel and performed the full hand cypher for a temporary illumination. The smugglers gasped. None of them seem to know the difference.

"Aye, Magistrate. Best hurry, mum. Begging your pardon, you ought not be out on the heath after dark. If not for sheer treacherousness of the footing, but what with the spirits and wisp lights about like what lured that poor, troubled boy to his doom. Best take a light and this sage."

Jhee tried to wrap her head around what she had learned. The Prospective wanted to leave the isle. Where had he acquired the currency to book passage and still have such a significant sum left over? Pilfering was not out of the question. He had a pipeline right here. His tattoo showed he had some form of gang affiliation. Could he have been profiteering off the refugees? Did they have those sums of money?

The missing men from the camps. Might Prospective Leigh have something to do with it? Trafficking? The same brand of robbery she accused the smugglers of.

～

The Wood

Armed with a glow orb and sage, Jhee made her way back up the stairs. She kept her gaze focused up and away from the breakers. It was almost last-sun or second sunset when she reached the top. Alone on the bluff, the goats have gone on along their way, she felt like relighting the sage. It had gone out during the climb though it continued to smoke. With the smugglers, prioress, and formerly Saheli running around here at night, she saw now why everyone thought the place infested with sea wisps. She gazed up at the moons in the sky. Full bright, when the largest shined its fullest. Sister

Serra's talk about astrological alignments and unleashed evil forces came back to her.

The dim-day—time between sunsets—had turned grayer. Jhee held her orb aloft to fight the gloom and made her way back towards the abbey. She thought of the sightings of spectral lights out here. Likely only the glow orbs of all the travelers between the abbey and the smugglers cove no doubt. Combine orb lights with a few mist reflections, and you had a recipe for sea wisps. Not to mention any gases which leeched from the wetlands or from underground mineral deposits.

In addition to the light and sage, the captain had explained to her the quick way to the side door by the solar arrays. The shortcut offered a different approach to the horticulturist's shed. Sister Serra was quick to illuminate the failings of others. What might she have to hide out there? Jhee examined the shed by the herb garden and the door that led to the solar arrays. She couldn't help but notice twice Sister Serra had prevented her from seeing inside. Serra was also rather cagey about her whereabouts.

Jhee glanced out into the gloom and thought she saw a light. She stared back at the warmth and safety of the abbey. Dare she? She did not believe in ghosts and spirits wandering about the grounds. If anything, her locating the smugglers, had made the notion less plausible. Regardless, she felt better with the sage in her pocket. She set off.

Clouds rolled in obscuring the moons. Light rainfall began. Despite the downfall, the vineyard remained clear of fog and mist. The light was definitely on the move. She maintained a constant distance. A concealment charm would not work in such an open setting. The night made a music all its own full of cheeps and chirps. Outside the range of her orb, splashes paralleled her. A frog loudly croaked its annoyance she had disturbed it. It hopped off to join its fellows in their night songs.

Jhee glanced frequently back at the abbey. She pretended she had not spent the day investigating the misfortunes of someone who may have stumbled or been pushed to their death. Possibly after being led astray by mysterious lights in the dark.

She swept the light frequently between the ground and the way further forward. She consulted her conch to gauge how far she might be from the edge of the bluffs.

The light ahead stopped. Jhee hid her orb in her sleeve and shaded her eyes. Whether what she followed was some moor phantasm or a more mundane entity, she preferred not to announce her location so clearly. Jhee held still. After a moment, the light began moving again. Jhee now proceeded with her orb partially hidden. If she stumbled and broke a bone out here, her cohort would never let her hear the end of it.

Amber-lit trees appeared in the distance, the orchard. The light continued toward it. As they approached, brighter lights flickered amongst the trunks. Murmurs and chants carried on the wind. Backlit by the counter light, Jhee's guide light became not a spirit or wisp, but a robed silhouette. Anger for even entertaining the notion fueled her pace. This accursed abbey and this drenched isle with its superstitious residents had her so wound up.

Jhee hid her orb able to navigate by the light from a bonfire amongst the trees. Rather than follow directly behind the figure, she followed at an angle until they reached a clearing. She flattened herself against a tree just beyond the ring of light. Robed figures circled the clearing, hands linked. Beside the bonfire, crossed beams bore a man strapped to them. A central figure in an elaborate headdress waited beside it. The headdress bore white on black markings with the cephalic lobes of the giant maye. The rear sported a whip-like, spineless tail. Jhee could not be sure, but she thought it was a representation of the Maye Queen.

The figure Jhee had followed presented the Maye Queen with a chalice and dagger. The Maye Queen held them up for all to see. Another figure poured burgundy liquid into the goblet. The Maye Queen went to the man on the cross beams. She cut the air in front of him with the dagger then tipped the cup to his lips. He drank deeply, gaze fixated on the masked figure. Once he had swallowed his fill, he ran his tongue over his lips and waited with parted lips.

With a last brandishing of the dagger, the Maye Queen slashed his chest. The man cried out. Jhee dropped into her first stance but hesitated. The man's cry had more the sound of ecstasy than pain. He still stared at the Maye Queen without fear in an almost trance-like fixation. A trail of blood opened across his chest. He even bit his lip as she drew the dagger over his flesh two more times.

The Maye Queen held the chalice to the wounds. She sliced her hand and dripped her blood into the vessel, too. She drank and then handed it to the next figure. They drank then passed it on to the following who drank as well. The Maye Queen pressed the blade to his lips. After he licked the blood, he arched his back and moaned.

The robed figures passed the chalice and chanted. They intoned a sequence Jhee had never heard before. After the attendees drank, they swayed in time. The Maye Queen tilted her face to the man on the beams.

"Warrior of Pain come to us. Warrior of Pain come to us," the figures chanted.

Mist snaked from the man's mouth to the Maye Queen's like reversed inspiration. When the Maye Queen stepped away, the man sagged against his restraints. Was this the Mist Abbess of which so many had spoken?

The Maye Queen's assistant presented her with a bit of cloth. They sang healing sequences and dressed his wounds. The Maye Queen placed a similar headdress with a tail spine and black-on-white markings, the Maye King, on the man.

"The Warrior of Pain is with us," the man said.

"The Warrior of Pain is with us," the circle of figures repeated.

The Maye Queen and her assistant cut the man down. Several figures with long staves pounded the ground. The other figures cavorted around the fire. Lady Bathsheba spoke of blood orgies. The Baqairu Blood cult rituals had been infamous for extreme bloodletting and cannibalism.

The capering figures stripped off their robes. Raindrops hissed on the bonfire turning into a woodsmoke-scented mist. The participants of the ritual began kissing and fondling each other. Scandalized, Jhee backed away.

This was just a bunch of dabblers partying. These people did not seem to be interested in kidnapping and killing Prospectives and refugees. Certainly, not secretly poisoning the former abbess. One of their revels may have gotten out of hand. A Prospective who partook too much stumbled off and slipped to his death. The theory still left the problem of the abbess and other two Prospectives. She saw no one involved who was not a willing participant. This made it no matter for the law. Jhee turned around and went back quietly the way she had come.

THE TEMPTING GARDEN

~

The Garden

The next morning Jhee found Shep sitting in the gardens. She tensed and froze when a salamander hopped away as she neared, but Shep didn't startle. He only turned her way, beaming. Her sigil remained inert, so she sat the bench beside him.

"Morning, dear husband."

"Morning, dear wife."

"How is Mirrei doing?"

"She seems better. She and Kanto are off exploring the courtyard."

The rains had picked up again today. The skies strayed beyond a mild overcast, but nowhere the previous days' gales. The Shield had added an extra layer of unpredictability to the weather. The high artificers had yet to perfect the formula. Artificers were still required to keep it operating efficiently. Soon enough, they expected to complete the perpetual motion sequence to make it self-sustaining. The derivations would be reintegrated every now and then, but it would hold on its own without constant tending. Barbarian raids and the need for measures like the berserkers, siren modules, and the other Medical Protectorate experiments would be a concern of the past.

"How are you faring?" Jhee asked.

"Dari and I went out for a run earlier this morn."

"Good."

Jhee expelled a breath relieved Shep answered the question she had not asked. The cramped confines of the yacht may not have suited him, but he had not complained. The weather had not afforded Dari or Shep enough time and space to roam as they would and relieve some of the pressure. They had needed more time above deck.

"We all needed off that boat."

"Did we? Or was it another way of avoiding Kanto?"

"You seem to have more than made up for it."

"My conversations with him regarding you are not substantively different than my conversation with you regarding him. He's young, healthy, and wants to please you."

"He was a fitting choice as second."

"Kanto deserves a say."

"What of the conversations between you and Mirrei?"

The look he returned had a tinge of anger mixed with bewilderment. "There are no such talks between Mirrei and me. That I leave to you. As that arrangement was made without my input, your other plans for her should be too."

"We owed them."

"Did we?"

"I owe them."

"I re-submit my previous response with the pronouns changed. Mai made her own choices."

Mai: their nickname when they were young for Mirrei's mother.

"She and her family were finally out of our lives." Shep's arm tensed. "One of my sisters contacted me the other day."

Jhee chocked her teeth together then pressed her mouth into a flat line. He did not need to clarify which; the one who had sided with Mirrei's family against them. If he wanted to depth charge the conversation, he could choose no better topic. "The archives were extraordinary. I think I may have scuttled my opportunity to visit them again."

"Well, dear wife, it's lucky I proved more charming. While you ran about the isle, I viewed the autopsy images and secured permission to perform an autopsy."

"Good on you. Aren't you industrious?"

"Isn't that why you keep me around?"

"Oh, is that why?"

Shep reached out and tickled the small of her back. She slapped his hand away with a laugh.

"Don't think I'm not angry with you for telling him about that place on my back."

"I see myself in him. I took pity on him. He wants to please you. You should let him."

Jhee and Shep had spoken of finding a training husband. She had agreed reluctantly, but she had still not thought Shep serious until he returned with Kanto in tow. "He's so young. They both are."

"Those are good things. New energy to revitalize the household."

"It's not that I don't appreciate their refinement and vigor. My tastes have always leaned towards a more rugged handsomeness." Jhee winked at Shep. He smirked. "I'm late for my lessons with Mirrei. Would you fetch us some breakfast and some treats? How about the lace root melons we saw during our tour?"

"I'll see to it."

Jhee and Shep held hands before she left.

~

The Refectory Incident

"I wonder what's taking denme so long with breakfast?" Mirrei said after the lesson.

"Perhaps he got to talking with the clergy. Many are vets," Jhee said.

Kanto scoffed. "Denme? Talking?"

"Fine. Grunting in the affirmative," Mirrei said. They giggled.

"Be nice, you two," Jhee said.

"Yes, denbe."

Jhee wondered as to Shep's whereabouts herself. He went to fetch their breakfast some time ago. The sigil on her arm itched. She pulled out her conch. It had died at some point during the night. Kanto offered his.

Bax answered instead of Shep. "Justicar, Makers' thanks. The refectory, quickly."

Yells and roars let loose in the background. The conch screen's image devolved into streaks and blurs. Jhee rushed to the abbey entrance.

Mirrei and Kanto had gathered their things. "Wait for us."

"No. No." The sigil on her arm burned enough to cause pain now. Jhee dared not bring them into a dangerous situation blind. She glanced around the courtyard. Their room would be more defensible, but dare she send them back unguarded? "Stay here. Don't leave unless, Bax, Shep, or I come for you."

"If someone's hurt, I can help," Mirrei said.

"Do as I say! Stay here. Both of you. Watch for anything… strange."

Mirrei and Kanto clutched each other. Jhee strode from the courtyard.

"Demons!"

"The Unmaking!"

Clerics and laypeople ran by her and away from the din of fighting. Jhee skidded to a stop at the refectory entrance. Several tables had been upturned. More diners sheltered behind them.

Shep whirled on her, his eyes fiery orange, teeth elongated. His nostrils flared. Deep, rapid breaths expanded his chest. His muscles had thickened, and his bulk had increased. A bench scraped against the floor stones. Shep spun towards the sound. Several clerics hurried away. Others had taken defensive stances. Shep hunched. His fingernails formed now into deadly sharp claws.

"No one move," Jhee said. She slipped a hand inside her robes to the sigil. "Shep, look at me. Please."

He snapped his head back in her direction. The Professed rushed him. He flung two aside then roared. His skin had taken on the black and sleekness of the orcinus, the whale crusher. More Professed surrounded him. He grabbed the heavy wooden table and hurled it into their midst. They scattered.

A few older Professed grabbed mugs which they struck against the table while they grunted in time. Shep paused.

With shaky gestures, a Prospective prepared to draw fire.

"No," Jhee yelled. Shep put himself in between her and the threat. He drew back to strike. Dari bounded into the refectory and hurled herself into Shep. He crashed backward. Dari planted herself in front of him with a warning growl. A Professed warrior tackled the foolish Prospective to the ground. Others piled on Shep. Jhee dug her nails into the sigil to activate it.

A dog-like yelp came from Shep. He stiffened then fell to the ground. He rapidly returned to his normal state. Jhee rushed over and cradled his head. Dari whimpered as she curled up beside them.

Sister Serra and several Professed came over. She held her hand above Shep's head. Dari snapped at them. "May we?"

Jhee nodded and petted Dari's head. Sister Serra examined him while the others locked their hands and chanted. Shep's eyes opened. They helped him to his feet.

Sister Serra and the Professed escorted Shep to the side.

The abbess arrived. "What has happened here?"

"I beg your forgiveness, Abbess. My husband, Dawn Wolf, had a mental crisis."

"Crisis? He went feral. I've seen it before," Sister Elkanah said. "You have a duty to report this."

"He did not go feral." Jhee paused to mitigate her tone. "I will, of course, report this."

"Must you really?" Sister Serra asked. "Your own husband."

"Because he is my husband, it is more incumbent upon me to pursue this. I must render judgment under the law without fear or favor even to him. I'll recuse myself from the case and call in another Justicar to render judgment once communications return."

"What if he regresses again?" Sister Elkanah asked. "Justicar, is he not guilty of crimes under the law? This man endangered the life of a government official as well as senior members of the abbey. He should be confined, not coddled."

Sister Serra tsked. "What of compassion, mercy, second chances, forgiveness, Sister? Do these mean nothing to you? Do the ways of the faith mean so little to you? This is a place of refuge for those with pasts they would rather forget."

"It's prophesied. The signs of the Unmaking. Saheli one who died by divine fire, the one who died by water, the one died by wind, and the one who died by earth. The last martyr, the last prophet. I don't want anything to happen to the pious souls who reside here."

"Neither do I," Jhee said.

"As you love and worship the Makers, your duty under the law is clear. As well as to the pious souls who reside here. Can we be sure he won't harm them?"

"Abbess, a statement from you will mitigate Dawn Wolf's sentence. In the meantime, may I have your permission to have him brought to the gardens? It will ease his recovery."

"He belongs in the Corrections Hall," Sister Elkanah said. "It was designed for situations such as this."

Jhee felt defeated.

"Justicar, if I may." To Jhee's surprise, Lady Bathsheba stepped from the shadows. "The abbey is located in a relief zone which places it under the Sanctuary statutes, am I correct?"

"Yes." Jhee's shoulders felt lighter. She repeated stronger, "Yes. Pursuant to the Fair-Weather Statutes, this is one of the few instances in which the Imperium does not maintain total sovereignty. The communications blackout or state of emergency means jurisdiction over certain acts reverts to local authority. Since I did not draw my weapons and no weapons were drawn by others. With no one killed or seriously injured, this is an ecclesiastic matter. This puts the crime in the sole jurisdiction of the abbey, more specifically the abbess."

They turned to Pyrmo. She squared her shoulders. "Then, I declare an apology and our forgiveness, constitute sufficient punishment."

"I must protest, Pyrmo. Are you to be as lax as Saheli? Shirking off serious infractions. No wonder why nether forces have taken anchor."

"Enough! I've made my decision," Pyrmo said. Lady Bathsheba and Sister Serra nodded approval. Sister Elkanah glared. "However, after some time to collect himself via reflection and communion with the Makers, he is confined to quarters for the rest of his stay. Except for an hour a day, in which he may visit the Maker's Shrine in the gardens."

Sister Elkanah gave a grudging nod. Jhee turned to thank Lady Bathsheba only to see her slipping from the refectory. She checked her pockets and found a message. The abbess collected Sister Serra, and they spoke to Shep at length. Tears formed in his eyes. The Professed Shep had injured joined those around him. Her view of him was now blocked. Jhee stepped forward.

"Here, Justicar, drink this," Bax said. He handed her a cup. She recognized the peachy smell of Tranquility Gold. She took a drink. Even watered down, the wine still tasted delicious.

Prospectives and staff had already started cleaning the mess. A growing pool of red liquid with bits of land meat on the ground caught her attention. The spilled contents of Shep's porridge bowl mingled with it. Blood. Shep had eaten blood porridge.

A cheer went up through the hall. Jhee whirled on her heel. The Professed and Shep took turns, consoling each other. He smiled and wiped his eyes. He headed her way.

"One moment," he said. He squeezed Jhee's hands before continuing passed her.

The abbess led him to the front of the hall where she announced, "Our guest has something to say."

"I would like to apologize to everyone for my disturbance, and I humbly ask your forgiveness in the Makers' names."

"I accept. Blessed be the Makers," Pyrmo said. She clasped forearms with him and winced.

Another Professed, one he had attacked, followed suit. "Blessed be the Makers."

After those he had injured had embraced him, a slow clap began. The clergy took up the applause. Jhee approached Shep, the abbess, and the horticulturist.

"Thank you for your understanding, Abbess."

"Understanding? Yes. I'd hate to have your explorations about the abbey hindered by a divided focus."

Jhee searched for Shep again. The horticulturist stopped her before she left.

"I have those supplies you wanted," Sister Serra said. "Stop by the agri-pods. I may be able to provide additional help."

"Thank you, Sister Serra."

~

The Temptation

After Jhee and Bax collected Mirrei and Kanto, they found Shep in the garden once again.

"So, what is my fate, Justicar?" Shep asked then tugged on his forearm hairs.

"This matter fell under the abbess's jurisdiction. She won't pursue any additional punishment. They explained the terms?"

"They'll give me until the rest of the day out here to reflect, but they have asked I remain in our room until we leave." Shep stared out into the distance. "A fair ask."

Jhee sat the bench beside Shep. She stroked his face. He kissed her palm and traced his eye scar with her thumb. He froze when he saw the discolored sigil on her arm.

"How bad?"

"Level two."

He stifled a sob. "I'm sorry. You and the others might want to secure separate rooms for yourselves as a precaution."

"No, dear one, no. The dish you grabbed was blood porridge."

"Makers." Shep tugged the hairs of his arm. "I like it here. It's very peaceful. A great many veterans reside here. It's good to be around others who know what it's like."

"Indeed," Jhee said. He took her hand and gently squeezed it. Despite what happened, she liked seeing how easy and untroubled he was. Her caretaker. Everyone's caretaker. She only wished she looked after him as well as he did the rest of them.

Jhee took a stand and dusted herself off.

Shep did too. "Let's go for a walk."

They walked through the courtyard and gardens. Shep's hands clasped behind his back and hers dignified and tucked into the sleeves of her robes. The minutes' respite, the privacy, the open space, and the beautiful surroundings emboldened her. She slipped a hand over and looped it through his arm. She kept public displays of affection to a proper minimum nowadays. She never wanted to make Kanto and Mirrei feel uncomfortable or left out, so she tried to maintain a certain equanimity to how she behaved towards them. Yet, her urge to be fair sometimes short-changed Shep. With the junior spouses elsewhere and the location so secluded, she indulged herself. Droplets of moisture glistened in his blue-gray body hair. Mindful of prying eyes, she reached over and stroked his forearm.

Shep pulled her into one of the alcoves. Jhee taken aback gave a quick glance around. They ensured no one watched before he slipped an arm around her waist. She and Shep nuzzled their noses together gently, before succumbing to a kiss. Jhee squeezed his upper arms for encouragement.

"I miss being alone with you," she whispered.

"Me too."

"One room. We'd have to be quiet."

"As I recall, I'm not the one who had trouble keeping quiet."

They shared another deeper kiss. Then stood for a moment with their escae together.

"Sometimes I can't breathe for wanting you."

They could find a discrete place now if they wished to find a few moments pleasure with each other. Behavior as fair to no one as it was improper. She had to conduct herself with the honor and decorum required of her office. She had to respect the abbey's rules. He deserved more than a few stolen moments.

"It's so tranquil here," he said.

"Perhaps we should forget the capital and simply take up on one of the nearby isles."

Shep smiled. "Yes, and we could work the seas and dive like we did as children. We'd fish and build a good home just the four of us with none of the pressures or intrigues of court."

"I don't know. For myself, I think I'd set up a cyphering school or a more permanent judicial arrangement helping refugees secure aid along with work credentials. Perhaps a tailor's shop or music school for Kanto. For Mirrei, a lab. No, a community center or garden where she could sell embroideries, do light healing work. It would be just lovely, don't you think?"

"Yes. Yes, it would."

Jhee and Shep stared at each other. Neither seemed convinced. She saw his scars, and he saw hers. As quickly as they had abandoned decorum, they regained it and want back to their proper distant postures. Nothing but a respectable married couple. The look on their faces returned to somber as the dream of a simpler life flew from their minds.

"Could you imagine Kanto here? Stuck on another rural isle too small for him or his vision?"

"No. No, I can't. He'd be bored beyond belief within a long-month."

"Less."

"He deserves a say."

It still felt surreal to be the head of household. Jhee's inheritance a fluke, the result of various coincidences and tragedies. She was not even supposed to be a justicar or magistrate. Her plan had long been to become a professor or fellow at some academy branch. Those were in the days of the Arcane Rehabilitation and Restoration Initiative. Before she enlisted in the military to follow Shep. She had been so young and naïve. True, the intelligence pool was usually a nepotist scheme to avoid heavy combat. It had been the best place for her considering. She took the work seriously, which did not go unnoticed. Her head for details landed her several, critical military intelligence assignments despite the cloud surrounding her. Perhaps even because of it. For information the Central Authority did not wish to entrust to conch, ether, or parchment, they used ciphers she designed and her encoding skills to hide their messages.

14

BROKEN PROMISES AND REMEDIES

~

The Fallout

Jhee stared at her conch, sitting alone on the charging station. Kanto and Mirrei had slipped out some time during the night. She paced and tapped her conch against her hand. Where were they likely to have gone?

Jhee yanked open the room door. They walked into view, giggling.

"Morning, denbe," Mirrei said. "We charged your conch for you."

Jhee turned the conch over and over in her hands. She still had not left the doorway. "Thank you."

The junior spouses' faces sobered as they brushed past.

"Mirrei agreed to take a look at our conchs."

"Where were you two? I thought I warned you not to go wandering about alone, especially you Kanto."

"Denye wasn't unaccompanied. He was with me. Kanto and I ate with the laypeople. Not everyone can be so lucky as us to eat from the high tables. What they have to eat was a water's worth less lavish than what we've eaten over the past few days."

Kanto wrinkled his nose and looked ill. Eating from the high table suited him fine. Therefore, it had to be Mirrei's half-drowned idea.

"Do your poverty tourism another time. I am well-appointed, and you are provided with the finest food, clothes, and medicine. And you always will be for as long as I can sustain it. You know how lucky you are. Can't you just enjoy it?"

"Pause, respite. Mirrei, could you give me a moment with our denbe?"

127

"Fine." Mirrei stomped into the next room.

"I suggested we give you and Shep some space," Kanto said.

"You should have informed me of your whereabouts regardless."

"Had you kept your promise, you'd know our whereabouts."

"My promise?"

"Whose day is it?"

The indignation which had stiffened Jhee's posture and made her so haughty drained away.

"You don't remember, do you? Today is Mirrei's day. Yesterday was mine. We moved around the days. Remember? Did it even cross your mind to ask me?"

"To spend the day with Shep? He was in crisis."

"About anything? You think me petty or insensitive. I am not without empathy. All you had to do was ask or inform me even. But I didn't even cross your mind. It was our day, and I got to spend it watching you sharing passionate embraces with another while plotting to send me away."

Jhee deflated even further. "The whispering wall."

"You're going to send Mirrei and me away once we reach the capital."

"It's more complicated than that. That was always the arrangement. In the capital, there will be those richer and more powerful than I. Or whose goals simply align better with yours. You want more than I can give you and you should have it. Politicking and power bring out the worst in me. My best life is a modest one. I'd still be a provincial official if I could. That would never suit you."

Kanto sighed and softened his tone, "How would you know? Did you ever ask, or did you just assume? I've committed to you and your household. A commitment I wish went both ways."

"Once we are somewhere with more options, I don't want you to feel obligated."

"Obligated? Neither Mirrei nor I want to be an obligation. What we want is your enthusiastic affection. What really happened to your belongings?"

"I gave them away."

"You what?"

"It had to be done. You wouldn't understand."

"What I don't understand is why you were wearing them in the first place. Those robes were not for running around in the dark or repairing ships. You even lost the poultice. Typical. It's not about the robes. It's not about days. It's about respect and consideration. You have no respect for the gifts we give you. You have no respect for us, or perhaps just me."

Kanto stopped. The truth of the thought fixed itself in his expression. Jhee realized too, seeing his reaction. He folded his hands into his robes and composed himself.

"I see," Kanto said.

"I've always been respectful to you."

He guffawed. "Proper, yes. Respectful, debatable. When we are together, you are always proper, a perfect gentlewoman. You were always perfectly proper. I could tolerate your reserve, your aloofness when I thought it simply your nature or a tactic. Some denbe do that, so none of their spouses know where they stand. In one glimpse, I saw otherwise. With him, you were vulnerable, open. I heard the desire in your voice. The way you spoke to Shep. The way you came alive in his arms for that one instant he kissed you. It's more than what I heard or saw. It's the affectionate and sometimes longing way you react to him. It's so effortless. He doesn't have to use tricks to stir passion in you. It's written in every way you touch each other. To sense the history there, to understand how he gets a part of you, I can never hope to...."

"Missing your day was unfair and inconsiderate. I remember we chose the day schedule because we thought it would be more equitable. Everyone received their own day instead of grouping it by activity. Fancy balls or political functions, which I hate and would have avoided, meant I might never spend time with you. I mishandled this. The respectful course would have been to ask to suspend the schedule during the investigation and not set up expectations for how much time I'd spend with you."

"Or as now, I'd be left the sole objector while Mirrei and Shep accepted it."

Jhee glanced at her personal effects where she kept the broken music box. It might make the perfect peace offering, but she judged the gesture too manipulative or worse, maudlin. Instead, she thrust a handkerchief at him. "What can you tell me about this?"

Kanto wiped his hand down his face then took the handkerchief with a sigh. "Nice scent, a Winter or Spring Forest fragrance, but the pattern's at least a decade out of fashion. Where did you get it?"

"I must have picked it up from somewhere. Is there anything I can do to make up for my oversight?"

"Is this where you attempt more matchmaking between the vizier and me? Or make another promise you break? Communicate with me honestly, so I don't have to assume or speculate and can serve your household properly. Unless... it's not about me, but you. You think I settled. You think this isn't where I want to be. It was. Until this moment. I'm not sure if I can do this."

"Will you be taking leave of us once we reach the capital?"

Kanto tucked his hands into his sleeves and stiffened his spine. "I haven't decided yet. If I may take my leave of you, denbe? Only to the next room."

"Of course."

"Thank you." Kanto stalked to the stool by the window and took up his sketchbook without further acknowledging her.

"Whelm!" Jhee said.

The Mineral Springs

Mirrei poked her head into the antechamber. Jhee remained in the antechamber where Kanto had left her, but she had settled into one of the tea nook chairs. He sketched furiously by the window.

Mirrei pulled up the other chair. "I trust you're in a better mood."

"Your trust would be misplaced."

"Let's relax with perhaps a soak in their open-air mineral springs."

"Open-air."

"It's not that bad out now. There's a nice mist to provide a little privacy. Hm? Hm?"

Mirrei leaned in and nuzzled Jhee's cheek.

"As you wish."

Eternal praises and the First Makers' blessings to the intrepid soul who had carved steps into some of the mineral springs. They made it so much easier on Jhee's knees and feet as she and Mirrei descended into the healing pools. After a few moments, her aching muscles relaxed. The young woman had been right, even with the drizzle and fog this had been worth the chance.

Jhee licked her lips. The minerals tasted sharp and salty, but sweeter than the salt taste of the sea air.

"Did you take your saline?"

"I must have forgotten in the excitement. Did you take your inhaler?"

"I must have forgotten in the excitement. Travel on the yacht had been so peaceful. To tell the truth, I had gotten rather used to not taking it."

The still, warm water had a particulate size too small to be detected by the unaided. Jhee murmured a basic cypher to enhance her sense of touch. Her skin tingled from the slight grittiness. Her imagination? The healing properties of the waters? She sighed. She might stay here forever.

Mirrei swam by her naked. On a sunny day, the waters may well have been crystal clear. Now, though, they had a grayish sheen which made them murky. Jhee barely made out the outline of her body. Wisps of steam rose from the pool's surface. Mixed with the fog, they caused a wavering haze which obscured the other springs. Jhee was glad Mirrei had the opportunity to take the waters with her. She only wished she could show her and Kanto the sights of the island. She felt terrible for them holed up in their room the entire time. And before that, cooped up on the yacht. It was bound to make them a little cabin cross. Here, she felt it a necessary precaution, though. She became all too aware of her bug bites again as the minerals irritated them.

Mirrei floated to Jhee's side. Her ears had perked up, and her pallor no longer quite looked so peaked. They shared a few kisses. "You're investigating a crime."

"A small matter."

"Murder."

"Nothing for you to worry about."

"Then why have you kept us locked away and under constant supervision while you run about the place tipsy turbulent?"

"I can't get anything past you, can I?"

"You don't have to hide it if you are."

"There seems to be something odd happening here. I'm just curious as to what. It will probably turn out to be routine. You know me. Looking for mysteries everywhere."

Mirrei tilted her head at Jhee. "You're a better liar than this."

"I found strange occurrences and incidents. Nothing I would stake my legal tabard and credentials on."

"Now, that was the truth." They left the springs and made their way to the nearby sauna. "Do you want another day off so you can work?"

Jhee grabbed a package of Tranquility Bridge's patented mineral salts. She poured the salts into the steamer and ladled water on to the warming stones. "That won't be necessary. The horticulturist offered me this. She called it 'seed of enlightenment,' a study aid."

Mirrei turned the plant over in her hands then took a good sniff. She wrinkled her nose. "Maate-Kheru Verdalia. Brightshade, sometimes called seed of enlightenment. A hallucinogen and natural insect repellent. Most plants of that Maker taxonomy are. Seems as though you should have taken some. You would have avoided your current discomfort. One of its derivatives also treats migraines."

Jhee put some spike leaf gel on her insect bites. "Explains why the insects swarmed me yet left her unmolested. Would you like to work the case with me?"

Mirrei swirled her hands throughout the steam. "I'm not sure what help I'd be. Another trip to the horticulturist is definitely in order. You look like you are in need of another poultice."

"I'm sorry I gave your previous one away."

"May I ask to whom?"

"Refugees. Their camps are on the beach on the far side of the fishing village. The conditions they live in... It'll break your heart."

"Then why should I mind if you gave it away? Seems they needed it more. Speaking of, don't forget to take your neutralizer and change out your spare."

Jhee had a quick puff while Mirrei popped a saline tablet. "Happy now?"

"Denbe, you told me the number one cause of death in our district was poison."

"Natural causes."

"You meant poison. Difficult to tell without autopsies."

"That it is. Good on you for catching that. Thank you for setting up that alert on my conch. For that and making me address them."

"If you are going to take the time to set them, you should not ignore them."

"I know. With the move and the travel, I had let them slide. Four people died in the few weeks before we arrived. According to the abbey's public records, the deadliest period since they had a boat capsize and a scaffolding collapse during renovations."

"Unusual enough for the search to catch."

Jhee smiled and nodded. Mirrei always the apt pupil. Jhee's quick praise of Mirrei made her pause.

"The poetess claims the deaths were murders."

"Do you believe her?"

"Unsure. What I do know about the poetess is she is an accomplished liar and Trouble Maker. I thought it best if I look into it."

"Flagging and addressing irregularities others missed or ignored is how you got your reputation."

Jhee sighed. "And our one-way trip to the capital."

"Who else can boast their wedding feast ended with half the guests arrested?"

Jhee shook the inhaler. It rattled lightly. "Don't remind me."

"Almost empty?"

"Ugh, greens houses again it is." Jhee dabbed gel on another bite. "Come with. You can pick up your supplies while I make inquiries and perhaps let me know what exactly she's growing in there."

"Thank you," Mirrei said.

"Thank me for what?"

"For losing that frown, that look. The piteous, worried expression everyone has around me."

"I'm sure they do not mean to offend."

"It's just tiresome. I do know what is going on with myself and my health."

"Do you feel I disrespect or am overly dismissive of you?"

"I know you can't abide foolishness. Foolish in your mind often equates to age."

Jhee took hold of Mirrei's dainty, slight hand and kissed it. It certainly felt a shade warmer and stronger than usual. "My apologies."

Mirrei tapped the tip of Jhee's nose. "Note, I only accept because I've seen improvement in your behavior. Towards me at least. Let's go."

～

The Greens Houses

The pair found Sister Serra waxing her wave skimming board and puffing on her glass pipe by the shed.

"Decided to take me up on my offer, eh? I could give you some seed of enlightenment for your man there. It works wonders for those afflicted with the war mind. Saheli found it most helpful."

"He wouldn't take it."

"Too proud, I suppose. Perhaps an elixir for yourselves then. I have many."

The Sister propped up the skimmer and offered them the pipe. Jhee waved away the smoke.

"Do you not partake at all or just when you are investigating? You think Saheli and those other Prospectives were murdered. You've been running about the isle asking questions."

"You are very well informed."

"I have my ways."

The wave skimmer propped up beside the work shed fell over. Mirrei held up her hands. "Sorry. Curious and clumsy."

"My wave skimmer. Do you skim?"

Mirrei sparkled her eyes and blushed. "Me? I could never."

"You should. Can't skim much since the weather turned bad. Although, knew some suicidal skimmers who would try. Makers bless them."

"I adore your extraction setup. Is this where you refine your guidance-seeking tinctures?"

Mirrei spoke softer as she moved down the work area away from the skimmer and shed. If Sister Serra wanted to hear, she had to follow.

"I've also been studying the mold and mildew affecting the crops."

"I remember. Noble rot. For your new wine, correct?"

"Among other things. I'm corresponding with pharmaceutical companies about the blight and major farming operations about hardier crop strains."

The lock on the shed hung unsecured. Jhee peeked. A black and white bundle behind a curtain caught Jhee's attention. Jhee moved aside a bit of cloth. She recognized the Maye Queen's headdress and robes. Mirrei pointed opposite Jhee's direction.

"Is this good for migraines? Denbe and I get the most terrible headaches."

"How do you normally treat them?"

"I make a sweet-smelling poultice. Lashotic."

"Of course."

"My, that's a nasty scrape on your hand. How'd you get it?"

"Hm, don't know. Running around in the vineyard somewhere."

Jhee returned holding the Maye Queen robe and headdress. "Or cavorting at a bonfire in the orchard?"

"Makers' whim," Sister Serra said. "It was a lark. We found some masks and did some rituals to the Warrior of Pain. No harm done."

"Sister Elkanah might disagree. These belong to the archives, correct? Along with your ritual implements: the ceremonial dagger and chalice."

"I planned to return them. Eventually. Because of who they're associated with, she didn't guard them closely as the others."

"How did you gain access without being seen?"

"This place is honeycombed with passages and exits. Escape routes put in after the massacres so that the residents could always have a way out."

"Did Saheli stumble upon one of your revels?"

"No."

"You involved Prospectives in your little revels?"

"Yes."

"Perhaps some of your participants changed their minds or had an attack of guilt. Were the dead Prospectives part of your little cabal?"

"No."

"They threatened to tell Saheli."

"No!"

"Maybe remorse so overcame them, they wanted to go to Saheli and confess their misconduct."

"Please, Justicar. You have it all wrong. Ask the mortician. We were both at the rite the evenings of the fall and the first tremor along with a dozen other village elders. Despite my boasts, I don't hand out medicine to or revel with just anyone. With Saheli, I finally felt like I had an ally. She was willing to honor other aspects of the Makers than the stern disapproving ones. I think she was one of the few who truly understood my path as ecstatic rather than ascetic. Saheli was open to the ecstatic path. What worth is it to kill my most powerful ally? I think Saheli made her wishes clear. She saw the pods and farming as the future of the abbey, not Elkanah's musty, old books and bones. The copy I got hold of must of been an old one. Saheli showed me her plan to enlarge the agriculture operations. A tasting room and shop to bring in more funds for the abbey."

"You ran to Sister Elkanah to gloat about it."

"No, but she found out somehow. Imagine how well she took it. I saw them arguing, and I caught her following the abbess. She's who you should be questioning. With Pyrmo in charge, Elkanah has exactly what she wants. A more conservative abbess with as much greed for relics as her. The sick Prospective was her creature. She used him to spy among other things. That is when she wasn't doing it herself. I wouldn't be surprised if she poisoned him. You won't tell Pyrmo or Sister Elkanah, will you? If the Justicar would see fit not to… should the Justicar be interested perhaps in attending herself I'm sure we could come to some reciprocal arrangement."

"Stop right there, before you sail into a bribery charge. I'll confirm your story first then decide how to proceed."

15

———

THE CHARMER

~

A Favor

Mirrei waited outside while Jhee got a quick confirmation of Sister Serra's whereabouts from the mortician. The woman perspired and stammered throughout but confirmed Serra's account of the revels in the orchard. She was full of profuse apologies for her behavior, regrets that Shep would not be able to autopsy the bodies, the state of the fields. Given enough time, she might have confessed to the assassination of Qamate. Perhaps indeed Serra and the mortician's frolics in the orchard had led to tales of the Mist Abbess resurfacing. With the two alibiing each other, there were two more suspects removed from her list. She might keep an eye on them all the same. There was still the matter of the contraband and wine smuggling.

"I hope that didn't upset you too much," Jhee said.

"You work is more exciting than I imagined. Who knew an abbey could be such a hotbed of intrigue and scandal? Fertility cults. Affairs. Rueful confessions."

Time to move on to Jhee's next likely suspect, the archivist. She had yet to speak to the woman since their first trip to the archives. Who would have thought she would have dreaded a visit a place full of so much history and knowledge? While she was there, she hoped to accomplish another task. Jhee needed a better map. This supposedly secure fortress of an abbey had more secret entrances and passages and back doors, so many no one could possibly know them all.

"I guess we better try to question the archivist now. I might prefer another stint with the bog gnats."

"You know it might calm the waters between you and Kanto if you ask him to help with the investigation like you did me?"

"I'm unsure. I tried to have him identify a clue, but just made muck of it."

"The last time we were at the archives, he buffered you and Sister Elkanah."

"Maybe you should ask him. I'm not sure if he's speaking to me right now."

"It will mean more coming from you."

Jhee and Mirrei returned to the room. Jhee sat beside Kanto. She cleared her throat and straightened her robes before proceeding, "Would you like to help me with my investigation?"

Kanto barely spared her a glance.

"I would like your help with my investigation. Please."

"To what end?"

"Sister Elkanah."

"Oh, so she is immune to your charms, then?"

"Please, be more reasonable than she is Kanto."

"I've been reasonable for months. Even after you married a new spouse before you'd even wiped our wedding contract ink from your fingertips. I've been reasonable when you flee my every attempt to woo you. Or meet it with panic or disinterest. I have tried base appeals to your lust. Flattery. I often wonder if you would have warmed to me if I held back or presented you more of a puzzle. You thought you had me solved the moment we met."

"People are dead, Kanto. I think we can agree that finding the killer is the priority."

"Well, I've been asking questions on my own, denbe, and you know what I found? Given her age and the other activities she got up to, it's no wonder Saheli died."

"Please, you mustn't go off investigating on your own. You have no authority to ask, and anything you find may be deemed unusable." Jhee added, "That goes for both of you."

"What do you want from me? I suppose you just want me to look pretty and act charming."

"No, I—"

"Do you remember our first tea? I dressed impeccably. For a change, I saw some glimmer of the attraction and fascination I was used to receiving. I was putting away the tea service after you left when I realized I had been sitting in front of grandmamere's antiquities collection.

"I'd hoped you'd be different than my mamere. House Kenyatta sires, denbe. Mamere was no exception. Officially, I have no baberes. Both sire and grandsire resided elsewhere upon the successful conclusion of their contracts. My dames had no use for them. Presumably, they settled down with those whom they loved and were loved by in return. My sire was particularly despised. He had produced female children for every dame except mamere. What she wanted was a daughter; a disappointment she never forgave my sire for or me. Being that I was not female, she had little time for me as well. Grandmamere, though, doted on me. She always kept a pouch of lace root melon taffies. Every time I told her something new and interesting about the people who visited us, I got one. I've always known what likely paths lay before me. From the moment, I understood what my chastity tattoo meant. I will not be treated as my sire was."

"My apologies. I have much to learn about having more than one spouse and many other matters. Please, help me with Sister Elkanah, and show me what you can do. That woman was insufferable."

Kanto chuckled. "Where would I have gotten in life if I didn't know how to flatter conceited old women? She's a territorial, rigid, self-important academic. It's no wonder you don't get along. On our way then. I'll help navigate these rocky waters. But you'll owe me."

"Owe you what?"

"I'll think of something."

Kanto's smile filled Jhee with the notion she'd made a Dismantler's Deal.

The Archives

The archivist popped her head out from behind the large book stand when Jhee, Kanto, and Mirrei entered the library. She sniffed. No one, least of all a Prospective, gained entry without her notice, yet somehow Sister Serra managed it when she stole the Maye headdresses and robes.

"You. Again," the huffy sister said.

"Sister Elkanah."

"What this time?"

"Might I have access to your archives?"

"Didn't your man just tear up the refectory?"

"Yes, but—"

"You must understand my first thought must be for the archives."

"That was an exceptional circumstance."

"I can't take that chance."

Jhee clenched her teeth then gave Kanto a pleading look.

"I understand your reluctance, Sister." Kanto cast his eyes down. "I assure you I have no interest in arcana or the like. My grandmere always said it was not gentlemanly to cypher. It's sage advice I've done my best to heed."

"Your grandmere sounds like a sensible woman, unlike some others. Come then."

"We weren't the most Makerly household, but we did have a collection of antiquities and relics for our Maker shrine as my denbe here can attest."

Jhee rushed to capitalize on the opening Kanto had provided. "I am given to understand you have a small library on local laws and ordinances."

The archivist snorted. "And you wish to view them?"

"I thought perhaps I could contribute: a small gift of my own writings on the subject and a few relics from my personal collection."

The archivist's eyes sparkled and widened. "What kind of relics?" she said with measured pauses between her words.

"Hand-carved, late century adjudication weight and scales set given as a gift to the third prefect."

"I am not interested in pagan idols. It would be inappropriate to have such things amongst our holy relics."

"These though are purported to have been blessed by Canon Oandzo."

"You have the provenance?"

"I have the signed note she sent along with the gift."

"I'd have to have it authenticated. Which texts were you interested in viewing?"

"A few manifests which may be vital to my work, some reference books, and perhaps Sister Niza's account of Saheli's death."

Sister Elkanah cut her a dubious look. "Make a new, formal request, and I'll consult the abbess and the vizier on it."

"Time is a factor."

Jhee fished the access writ the vizier had slipped her from her sleeve and placed it on the book stand in front of the archivist. Once the archivist verified the card, she snorted at Jhee again. "Hopefully, this one is better trained. The same rules as last time. Nothing leaves the archives. Duplication is on a case by case basis. We have a station for conch image capture. However, not all items can be exposed to such direct lighting. No males allowed in the arcane archives whatsoever or near the bones of our honored dead."

Glass doors which led to the staircase hissed open. Jhee and entourage crossed the threshold and traversed the steps to the library spire. Two paths flanked by tall stacks of shelves floor to ceiling diverged from the entryway behind the archivist. Jhee touched her palms together at angles for the First Makers' clasp. She brought her crossed hands to her esca before proceeding.

To Jhee's right, shelves bore every manner of chest and box. Stone, wood, polymer, colored glass. Some plain, some gilded and gleaming with jewels behind glass walls. Coffin-like chests. Funerary jars for the remains of the honored dead.

The right wing bore books in an endless array. Short, tall, fat, thin. Loosely bound sheaves of parchments. Document boxes. Aging conchs. Carved stones and shells whose weight and rough texture she already imagined in her hands. Or the slight scratching of parchment paper between her fingers. The joy Jhee experienced in the mineral springs did not compare to what she felt now. In this archive, she might genuinely remain forever. Hour upon hours spent with tactile, visceral representations of history held in her hands. Such fragile treasures like the heart of a lover.

Jhee inhaled deep the air's slight fishy tang. No doubt from the seaweed paper. A hint of decay and must from the flesh and blood and bones of canons and paragons reportedly housed here floated to her. Maybe the trace of an alchemist furnace or reagent created the sub-scents. One report she read of the archives said it housed the bones of a celestial.

As much as Jhee wanted to grab the nearest book or treasure and study it, she limited herself to the abbey's records and histories. She, Kanto, and Mirrei began to pore over books.

"Pirates and raiders destroyed or overran many other area monasteries," Kanto said. "Tranquility Bridge survived due to its unique location and large number of fighters. The Abbey of the Broken Sword was originally founded by ex-soldiers who had turned to the ways of religious reflection. They changed the Pillarist name Swordbridge to Broken Sword."

"And from that to Tranquility Bridge," Mirrei said.

Jhee turned a page of the text she read, records of building supply purchases. Curiously she could not find the architectural drawings she saw her first visit. "The Abbey of the Broken Sword at Tranquility Bridge. Technically, Tranquility Bridge is the name of the bridge, not the abbey."

"It says here that an untold number of spouses and children took their lives rather than be taken by the barbarians," Kanto said.

"That's the romantic interpretation, anyway. I doubt the children committed suicide. Which alone means whatever the prevailing narrative, the truth is there were a lot more murders than there were suicides. I suspect reluctant adults were helped along too."

"So, a massacre either way."

Jhee could not cast aside the notion she had been toyed with, led around. She had run around the isle chasing down every half-poached, fish-brained rumor when she should have been thinking smaller, simpler. Her curiosity had her chasing phantoms and tales. She must return to first principles.

One moment, it seemed as though the key to this case was Saheli's death. The next, one of the Prospectives. Somehow, she had gotten off course. Was she too focused on heresies, scandals, and grand conspiracies? Back to basics as her mentor Jeja Marpele would say when Jhee went too far chasing wisps down sea wormholes. First principles: most murders were simple. Committed by simple people for simple reasons. What came after was complicated. What was the simple truth here? Were these murders? She had yet to make that determination. She had lots of oddities and unanswered questions, but no definitive evidence. Nevertheless, her Maker Within whispered to her something didn't add up.

"I'm still not sure what we're dealing with," Jhee said. "One could have been an accident. One may have committed suicide. One may have been killed by an incompetent physician."

"And the abbess?" Mirrei asked.

"Possibly a heart attack or maybe she did ascend to the Maker Sphere in glorious light. Everyone loved Saheli. Loved her so much they can't help but make insinuations and cast aspersions."

"Well, denbe," Kanto said, "what I heard from the Prospectives is that the men who died were friends. What if Saheli killed them to hide she was having an affair with one of them? It proved too much for her fragile health, or maybe she committed suicide."

"A good theory I entertained, but one or more died after Saheli," Jhee said.

"Faked her death?"

"Reasonable premise. How?"

Mirrei jumped in, "Phosphorous or another volatile chemical. She may have had help. To refine brightshade into liquid form requires one of its derivatives. The horticulturist would have some if she cooks it herself."

"Volatile chemicals could cause too much heat and be too dangerous. Performers do use smokes and powders to make themselves disappear." Jhee tapped the side of her nose. "If perhaps she had a secret way to and from her chambers through which she sneaked the young men in, she could also slip away with no one the wiser."

Kanto said, "Pyrmo could have been in on it or knew about it. Staging it is how she burnt her hands. Now, that the abbess's chambers are hers, she would know of any such back exits. She and Saheli could have finished off the others."

"What if Saheli did not fake her death? What's the motive then?"

"Retaliation for the others? The drowned Prospective killed the others then Saheli or some combination thereof then committed suicide by flinging himself from the tower or falling off the bluffs while trying to make his escape."

"Also, another theory I entertained until I learned of his plans to run away. I, also, considered accidental overdose, due to Sister Serra's mention of her resistance but dismissed that too after more thought."

"Why?"

Mirrei answered without looking up, "Because it's next to impossible to overdose on that class of drug."

Kanto furrowed his brow, then propped his head up on the desk. "You make this look so easy."

Jhee set aside her book. "Likewise, your flair for style and diplomacy."

Jhee and Kanto locked gazes then hands. They shared a tentative smile.

"Aw!" Mirrei said.

Jhee cleared her throat and went back to her research on plant toxins. Brightshade which she knew the horticulturist grew. Or the blightseeds from the ruined crops. The archivist had access to the very text she read. Jhee eyed various places from which one may listen to anything they said.

"Makers' Mark, denbe, listen to this," Mirrei said. "'The big and sweeping movements are in keeping with the simplistic grandiosity of the male character. The subtlety and refinement of finger cypher are not suited for their clumsy, intemperate nature.' Now, I know where the vizier gets her backward ideas."

How many times had Jhee read some similar sentiment yet glossed over it? Now, confronted with an abbey full of women like this and the real-world effects, she had to grapple with how her silence aided the damage those attitudes caused.

"Are you aware Saheli was one of the leading signatories to the Nahele edict asserting there was no doctrinal or scriptural basis for the exclusion of men from cyphering?" Mirrei asked. "The abbey's practice of no cyphering began in their cloister school, was enacted to ensure a gender-neutral curriculum rather than directly challenge the inherent inequality of the ban. If they had included the practice of cypher in their studies, they would have been forced to exclude males from entry like the Tihalmec Imperial Academy. They maintained low-cost, high-quality education because they did not have to maintain the facilities for or hire experts in magical instruction."

"Seems she also sat on the Rescission Councils that overturned the bans. I may have even seen her there," Jhee said.

"You attended the Rescission Councils, denbe?" Kanto asked.

"As a member of Jeja's legal envoy. The law they passed to enact the ban had serious flaws which made their legitimacy shaky. This is the woman everyone is trying to convince me was a sex fiend of the highest order, who hated relics, was anti-education, and wasted the abbey's money. Either on the impoverished or expensive items for herself?"

"The aspects are not mutually exclusive. It could be how she expected them to show gratitude."

"True. She could have felt owed for her magnanimity. She would not be the first. If Saheli were this fiend as I've been led to believe, how could she have ascended in light to the Maker Sphere?"

"If you're interested in the arcane, denye," Mirrei said, peruse this."

"Mirrei, don't," Jhee began.

The door to the reading room burst open. Jhee tucked a ledger under her arm and jumped to her feet.

"Out," Sister Elkanah said.

COLLECTIONS

~

An Unfortunate Relic

"What? Why?" Mirrei asked.

"I'll have no fraternizing, inappropriate contact in my archives or ill talk of the abbey's esteemed leaders. Most of all no showing of new science texts to men. I warned you."

"How would you know if we were fraternizing or what we were discussing?" Mirrei glanced around. "Because you were watching."

"What of it? I told you my first concern was the proper reverence of the manuscripts and relics. I thought it prudent given the feral behavior your other husband displayed."

"Dawn Wolf did not go feral. Bright Harmony, Star Mirror, gather your belongings. We're leaving."

"No, you stay," Kanto said. "I'll leave if it will alleviate the Sister's concerns."

"And you with all your tempter's talk of not being interested in artifice."

"Get this through your narrow-minded head," Mirrei said. "You better get used to the notion of men cyphering, as the time's coming when as many men as women know how. And there won't be a single thing you can do about it."

"What a vile, disrespectful creature you are. You have no idea the disaster you court."

"Star Mirror, please," Jhee said. "We're leaving."

"Your spouses need discipline. I see where they get it from. If you weren't such a weak denbe, you would keep them in line. A few swats of the scourge or board might teach them some manners."

Jhee took a measured breath and initiated the tricky procedure to focus her siren module's calming abilities on herself, without making herself too docile. She suppressed the urge to use it on the archivist and be done with her once and for all. Any evidence gained through non-consensual use of the module gave instant grounds to appeal her ruling.

"That's enough, Sister Elkanah. Mind how you talk to my spouses and to me. I am still an Official of the Court."

"And nobility," Mirrei said. She folded her arms and raised her eyebrows. "Shame on you for turning away or trying to have imprisoned those like the refugees or our denme who need your help."

Sister Elkanah snapped her mouth shut. So much for trying to charm and back current information from her.

"Sister Elkanah, can you account for your whereabouts during the deaths of the Prospectives Leigh, Yaou, and Imsu?"

"Prospective Imsu died during the first quake at which time I and several others were trying to secure the items in the archives. Prospective Yaou's happened under Zalver's care, and she assured me it was some natural disease."

"I understood she treated you for scratches and skin irritation."

"Serra sometimes thinks it's funny to put itchweed on my finger quills."

"Did she do so while Prospective Yaou was there?"

"Yes."

"So, that means you would have had an opportunity to check in on him while he was there?"

"But I didn't."

"Wasn't he your assistant? I was under the impression he volunteered at the archives?"

"What of it?"

"You didn't want to inquire about the health of someone who helped you maintain the archive?"

"What if his ailment was contagious? An infection or mold might have detrimental effects on the collections. I didn't want to risk it."

"Then why were you repeatedly seen in the quiet room with him."

"Who told you that?"

"What of Prospective Leigh?"

"I'm not sure. I think I was performing devotions."

"In your room?"

"Yes."

"Alone."

"Yes!" Sister Elkanah snatched the ledger Jhee had slipped under her arm and jabbed her finger at the door.

Jhee stormed out of the archives. She would not be lectured about marriage by celibates. She could think of few practices which dishonored the Makers more.

"A celibate presumes to tell me how to treat my spouses. Kanto, you can have all the adept and cyphering lessons you want and more. I owe you that and another apology. I'm surprised anyone had bothered to report these young men's deaths at all. As they viewed them as too stupid or useless to be of concern."

How could she have contemplated for even a moment leaving Kanto here at the mercy of these fishwives? Mirrei suppressed a smirk.

"This isn't funny."

"No, it isn't." Mirrei continued to smirk. "Such a collection of bigoted women."

"These were my peers. Would I have even noticed a few years ago?"

Kanto snickered. As he continued, Mirrei and Jhee gave him dumbfounded looks. "I had matters well in hand with the archivist until you and Mirrei got up in your ether with her. Is this what it takes for you to respect my intelligence? Other women belittling it. The pattern emerges. You have no desire for pleasure or procreation with me, yet you feel free to hypocritically lecture the clerics on the celibate lifestyle. I'm leaving. Not that you'll have further need of me."

Kanto tromped off down the corridor.

At last, Jhee's anger flowed away. "It's getting late. That's enough excitement for today. Allow me to escort you back to the room."

"Where our adventure ends for the day?"

"I have a few more lines of inquiry to follow. It would put my mind at ease to know you are somewhere safe."

"Implying you will be somewhere not safe."

"I'm amazed at how quickly you've come to know me."

"Do remember I was a guest at your house for some time before our betrothal."

"How could I forget?"

Jhee and Mirrei returned to the room arm in arm.

"Kanto hasn't returned? He left ahead of us."

"Bax has eyes on him. He's talking to the Prospectives," Shep said.

***

The Storehouse

Jhee examined the procurement writ. She supposed now was as good a time as any to check out the apothecary. She hoped whatever Lady Bathsheba had tried to draw her attention to was still there.

A bored Professed unlocked the stores. "We're on the honor system for most supplies. Come up front when you're done and close the door after yourself. If any provisions you want are locked up, scan them, and I'll get them for you before you leave. Then I'll scan and close out your writ for you."

While nowhere near as magnificent as the archives, the shelves which lined either side of the storehouse boasted as much abundance. Jhee captured an image of the storehouse map posted by the door then set off down the aisles. Storage units brimmed with boxes of herbal and floral extracts. Dried leaves hung from hooks or vine ropes on every vertical. She used the illumination and magnification function on her conch to read tags and box labels. A thick layer of dust showed some had not been touched in ages. She had to dig through a few shelves to find the supplies on her list.

First things first: her promised casks of that most delicious Tranquility Gold. Mostly for her and Shep. A wine which surely should have met with even Shep's high standards. Though, she was disappointed he had not enjoyed it as much as she did. To be honest, the second taste she had the morning of the incident had been underwhelming. She located a cask, tapped the writ against it, then pressed a tag on it. She also wanted some of the must and unfermented nectar to study. She pinched the bridge of her nose. She gathered more raw ingredients for Mirrei's poultice.

Lady Bathsheba's draught recipe came to mind. She already had the nectar. What else did she need? Jhee snapped her fingers. Orange cider and black orchid tea.

Why had the Lady intimated she visit the storehouse? Why call her attention to the tea so ostentatiously? Was it meant to be a clue as to the doings of this murderer who stalked the abbey? Jhee would get to the bottom of it. If only because of professional curiosity alone. It was also her duty.

If only adhering to Jhee's familial duties came as easily to her as duty to empire and profession. How much misery would she have avoided if she had married a Crag Hall sibling as her family asked, not gone to war, or followed Shep? Uncharacteristic rebellion. She had thought to get a rise from them. She had always done as they wanted until she could not take it anymore. She had once sought to escape her rural district for life at court. A favor here; some discretion there. Which is how she acquired ministry connections at the capital. Then Central Authority had recalled the officials from the border districts as the Shield went up. All officials had to report to the court as soon as they could. And she did. She did as she was told. When Miramar learned of her assignment, she asked Jhee to take her daughter with her.

"You owe me, Jhee."

Their home island had half sunk into the sea by then. Jhee's home, which was on higher ground remained, but the displaced and homeless had grown. Miramar's house had sunk, and out of friendship and kindness and duty and loyalty, Jhee had taken Miramar and her daughter into her home. She gave them food and shelter. Jhee supposed it was why Miramar thought it was only natural to propose the match she did. Jhee out of friendship, also, chose to ask no giving or receiving of boons. Mirrei had much of her mother's looks. A fact which made the decision much easier on Jhee. She had been wary of taking a female consort at least before she had settled into her new assignment.

Jhee initially held the traditional, last position in her household for a more political arrangement at court similar to the one she had with Kanto's family. However, Kanto's social savvy and discontent with a modest life indicated he was already halfway to shore. She did not expect him to stay with her long once they reached the capital. She just hoped he would help her arrange his new situation. That way, she could reap a political benefit. She would probably do something similar with Mirrei. She would find them both spouses more suitable to their age and ambitions.

The orange cider Jhee spotted in a neater, more frequently used part of the storage room then scanned it and put a non-procurement tag on it. The black orchid tea she found by the lace root melon taffies in a locked, glass-front cabinet.

Jhee was in the middle of the pecking order and was not as overly ambitious as some. When opportunities presented themselves, she took them. She did not force them or jostle for position as others did. She rather liked her job as magistrate. She traveled from place to place on isles too small for much in the way of permanent structures. Especially with the Great Barrier Storm, those islands had become increasingly isolated, especially given the storm's effect on communication equipment. A measure designed to confound the barbarians' navigation systems. From time to time, shipwrecked barbarians washed up. They were also her duty to hand them over to the body catchers for transportation to the capital. She wondered what they did with them. Perhaps they would use them for the Medical Protectorate experiments instead of noble warriors like Shep.

Jhee contemplated the taffies, or if she truly wanted them. Did she really hope to buy Kanto's forgiveness with candy? It was the gesture she thought. A symbol to show she listened and was not wholly uninterested in him as a person. She tagged the sweets.

A door opened. Jhee assumed the storekeeper had come to check on her. Cool, outdoors wind moistened her face. Jhee stopped on the verge of calling out to the new arrival. The breeze, heavy with the scent of the smudging stick, whispered down the aisle. Shuffling footfalls, their gait halting, approached. The horticulturist? The poetess? Jhee doused her conch and ducked down an aisle.

~

The Complaints

A figure garbed in clerical vestments dragged a hefty, black keg over to the case. Still oblivious to Jhee's presence, the person stumbled to one of the giant barrels of beer and poured a tankard from the tasting spigot which she chugged in one go. She removed the stopper and used a sampling pipette to fill a flask she produced from inside her robes. She took a quick swig before screwing on the cap. Jhee followed the figure to the locked cases where she produced keys and unlocked them.

Behind the tea, rested more giant black kegs. The figure thumped a few before one had a hollower, heavier sound than the others. She paused and touched the scan tag Jhee had left. She spun around.

"Looking for me?" Jhee emerged from the aisle.

The figure lowered her hood. Pyrmo glanced at the flask she held then shoved it into her sleeve. She sighed, shook her head, and took it back out. "Alas, you've discovered my dirty little secret."

"May I ask what that actually is?"

Pyrmo's attention went to the black keg. "Tranquility Black. Moonshine. My own private stash. I am ashamed to have you see me like this."

"Let only those whose feet have never been wet lecture someone else on how to keep theirs dry. I'm afraid I will have to ask you a few questions regarding the death of Saheli and the Prospectives."

"Ask. Whatever answers I have, I will give."

"I've heard your account of when Saheli died. I'll need your accounting of the times leading up to the deaths of the Prospectives."

"My accounting? It's hard to say. I was well into my cups then. The night of the storm where the Prospective fell, I had been drinking particularly heavily. Likewise, the first tremor. As embarrassed as I am to say, I made quite the spectacle of myself. Far more than ever, the poetess did."

Jhee laid a finger aside her nose and tapped in thought. Pyrmo's contempt for the poetess then lay more in the distaste of seeing one's own flaws reflected back at you. "Can anyone confirm this?"

"Confirm? I would think half the abbey could. To the specific, though, the prioress was called to put me to bed like a child. Not my noblest moment, Justicar."

"I will confirm this with her."

"Of course."

"Did you have occasion to visit Prospective Yaou?"

"I did."

"May I inquire what you spoke about?"

"I am afraid, on that, I must be oblique. As the communication happened under the veil of counsel."

"He confided in you something for which he wanted absolution or advice."

"Why does it feel as if I am being interrogated?"

"Four people have died here in the past few months. To faithfully execute the task you set me, requires my due diligence."

"Your thoroughness is appreciated. Though had Saheli's miraculous death not had such a thorough accounting by so many witnesses, I might not have thought her long for this world. She was on the aged side. As for those poor, young boys, life is always short and harsh for those such as them."

"Still, I want you and the residents of this abbey to know you are not forgotten. To do less, would be a disservice to you and my duty under the law."

"I see. You shame me once again with your insight, Justicar. My personal failings have led to my not being as concerned with the affairs of those beneath me here at the abbey. I think we should both strive to do better by those under our care."

"I am glad you would agree."

The abbess unscrewed the flask's cap and proceeded to the nearest drain. After she dumped out the contents, Jhee nodded. Pyrmo grabbed the black orchid tea. "I will require this to sober up. I'd also appreciate your discretion."

"Once I have satisfied certain curiosities, we shall speak no more of this."

The abbess set aside the tea to clasp forearms and touch foreheads. The overly familiar gesture between them more warranted this time. Though the reek of smudge thick on Pyrmo—which now made more sense—worsened Jhee's headache. Despite that, the smell of burn cream and licorice overpowered it.

Jhee twiddled the letters on her conch to log the abbess's statement longhand, glad to have enriched someone's life. Given her domestic blunders of late, she luxuriated in a rare feeling of competence.

Although, if Pyrmo's alibi checked out, she might have been on the verge of eliminating her major suspects. What was it Raigen said Saheli suspected in her letter? Another authority undermining her. If anything Sister Serra said could be believed, Pyrmo made a prime candidate for this Mist Abbess character. If she and Sister Elkanah disapproved so strongly of Saheli's methods, Jhee could see them staging a coup. Though, would they have gone as far as murder?

Back at the room, Mirrei prepared Jhee another poultice. "Try not to give this one away."

Kanto returned to their chambers. "Mirrei, may we have the room?"

"Sure," Mirrei said. "Keep it civil, you two."

"Shall we try this again?" Kanto took the other chair in the nook. "I feel like you think I'm some kind of fool. I don't like you looking at me that way."

"From what I can tell, you are quite intelligent in your own way."

"My own way? What way is that?"

"Emotional. Cultural—"

"You made some impressive strategic moves in the positioning of your house like coming to the aid of House Foster in exchange for half their holdings. Underwhelming ones too such as not crushing House Diamante when you had the chance. How many times have they encroached on both your sea lanes and spawning beds since? You were an academic, though. Women like grandmamere would eat you alive. I would be the secret ingredient."

Jhee viewed him anew. What could she say? She had never discussed household strategy with him, yet he knew about some of her more oblique maneuvers.

"Nothing to say to that. Of course not."

Kanto rose.

"The choice to marry you was mine. Though, if grandmamere disapproved, she would have found a way to talk me out of it and likely make me think it was my idea. She is well versed in the art of letting other people have her way. Grandmamere still got the better of you in our marriage negotiations. Yet, she was impressed with how hard a bargain you commanded."

Kanto glided from the nook as Jhee continued to sit mute.

17

THE GUEST WING

~

The Performers

According to Sister Niza's account of Saheli's death, all senior clergy were present and in full sight of the others. While it's possible they were all part of some conspiracy, Jhee doubted it. With so many factions, the likelihood they conspired to protect the guilty party was nil. If either the archivist or the horticulturist had an advantage over the other, they would use it.

First, Jhee must confirm or deny the abbess's alibi before she entertained other theories. She tracked the prioress down in her cell.

"I caught Pyrmo sneaking liquor. She claims to have been drunk the night Prospective Leigh drowned and that you put her to bed."

"I did. It explained much. She was prioress before me. Saheli's indulgences extended to more than the deacons. She took the hands-on approach as abbess. No disrespect intended to Saheli or Pyrmo, but the abbey's finances were a mess and Pyrmo a disaster as prioress which makes more sense considering her problem. I may not have always agreed with Saheli's choices, but I trusted her judgment. Still, Saheli should have found a less challenging position for Pyrmo."

With each of Jhee's prime suspects providing alibis for different murders, perhaps there was some elaborate scheme by which they all did it. A cabal that conspired to keep the truth of Saheli's death private? While dramatic, with these players unlikely. A bit of the "Dispatches from Arrow Point"-era Jhee's mindset had sneaked out. She had proceeded with the hypothesis that if Saheli were indeed murdered the perpetrator had to be a clergy member.

Strangers such as the performers or refugees could not get close enough. Though, having learned of Saheli's personal approach to running the abbey invalidated that premise. Which raised another possibility: what if the principal victims were the Prospectives?

The suspect pool opened much wider. She may have been too quick to narrow her focus to the high table. A mistake she would now correct.

Performers do use smokes and powders to make themselves disappear.

She thought of Shep, Mirrei, and Kanto's admonishments. Had she been too quick to dismiss the Prospectives and the refugees based on age or gender? Or even the performers? She had been ready to condemn Lady Bathsheba for snobbery, but what of her own. She knew how easy it was to lay blame for everything at the threshold of margin dwellers. Maybe she was making the same mistakes with the perpetrator as she had with the victims. If not for suspecting them first, but for perhaps dismissing them as not smart enough. Members of the camps. Smugglers. Performers. She had cast aside her doubts on them for dubious reasons.

"What do you know about the performers?" Jhee asked the prioress.

"Not much. Some of them were refugees, and they sometimes did free shows there. They usually stuck to the port towns."

Jhee remembered the tattoos on the members of the camp, the smuggler, and yes, of course, one of the performers. This abbey had secret ways in and out aplenty. There existed smugglers and contraband. All that was required was someone on the inside. What better way to smuggle contraband or people to and from the abbey than via the performance troupe?

The prioress kissed her Drakist effigy. "The things they're saying about Saheli aren't true. She was good folk. Yes, she had her own ways of doing things, and even I didn't always approve. While her emphasis was on good works and labor, she valued knowledge too but understood formal education wasn't for everyone."

"'To every part, its place in the Design.' Thank you for your candor."

Jhee found the rather storm-tossed appearing Pyrmo in the Worship Hall praying. The black orchid tea rested beside her on the bench. She placed a gentle hand on the abbess's shoulder. Pyrmo started and gazed about her wildly.

"Justicar, why are you here?"

"Sorry to disturb you, Abbess. I had a quick question about the performance troupe."

"The performance troupe?"

"Did they perform here frequently?"

"Not at all. I believe this was their first time although the abbey is on their route. Though it was not my idea."

"Why the change?"

"The troupe leader's request. I thought with the special occasion, why not?"

Jhee tapped the side of her nose. "Thank you."

On Jhee's way to see the performers, she visited Lady Bathsheba to thank her for access to the archives and for her help in the aftermath of Shep's incident. She also might glean more information about the initial state of the system.

"You would have thought of it yourself eventually. You were under enormous pressure at that moment."

"Thank you then for hastening my recollection of the law. One more thing, whose idea was it to have the performance troupe play the feast?"

"Saheli and I entertained the idea. We knew they came through the area often. Pyrmo made it happen, though."

Jhee contacted Bax. "Have you found out anything new?"

"More gossip mostly. I've tried sending you field reports, but they've bounced."

This storm-blasted communication blackout had struck again. Laughter and clinking glasses carried through the connection. Were Jhee a less charitable sort, she would have suspected him of having been drinking it up this whole time. "Could you arrange for me to meet with the troupe leaders?"

"Of course. They were just here."

"What's your location?"

"We're in the hostelry near the guest annex. I can meet you and provide introductions."

"Splendid." Jhee whipped out the trusty, invaluable map and set off.

Scrapes and the odd rattle shadowed Jhee, as she met Bax in the guest wing. The troupe leaders were a married couple, the announcer and the assistant who held the fire blanket during Mr. Zane's performance. They greeted her with hearty smiles and wide arms. A distinct change from the other receptions she had received these past few days.

"Welcome, Justicar. Welcome." The announcer kicked out a seat and had already poured her a cup of whatever they had already been drinking by the time Jhee sat. "No empty cups at my table. One. Two. Three."

The announcer, her husband, and Bax knocked theirs back then slammed their cups down on the table. Jhee took a deep drink. She ascribed no other distinct taste to the alcohol other than burn. She squeezed her eyes shut to stop them from watering. The liquor paled in comparison to the refujuice she drank the day previous. She covered her cup when the announcer went to refill it. The obligations of politeness had been met.

"To what do we owe such a distinguished visit by such an important person as yourself?"

"I'm in need of some quick answers if you don't mind."

"Of course, not. We'd be happy to. Ask. Ask."

"How was it you came to perform for the feast?"

"I'd think many of the troupes which passed by this place had wanted to.

We'd often bypassed it ourselves. We might've done so again if two of our number hadn't mentioned their anniversary celebration."

"Two?"

"Yes, both Hethyr and Anshu mentioned the feast. They'd been after us to visit for some time. Although we'd make a few shell at the nearby town, it hadn't made sense until now. Holy places can be some of the cheapest patrons. There's something about celebrations which can prize open even the tightest clams."

Jhee nodded and took another polite drink from her cup. The announcer bobbed her head with satisfaction. Jhee's shoulders loosened as she settled more into her seat. Either the alcohol or the announcer's warm, melodic voice had wrapped a sense of welcome around her. "Do your performers give lessons or work by private arrangement?"

The announcer raised an eyebrow. "Some have been known to. Mr. Zane, for instance. Mostly, by prior arrangement."

"No chance of calling upon them, now."

"They may make an exception for an official visitor. The hall across the annex. Men on the left and women on the right. Ms. Hethyr and Mr. Zane are at the far end."

Jhee wrenched herself free of the camaraderie and rose to leave. Bax stood too with a slight sway. "Hold, my lady. Mr. Shep would have my hide if I let you go alone."

Bax, who had gone bright red and sweaty from the effect of drink, would be of no use to her in this condition. "In your current state, Bax, what help do you think you would be? No, Bax. Stay and partake with your friends. I only have a few simple inquiries. I don't intend to be long."

The performers' quarters were located across the annex from the owners. At least she did not have to ascend or descend steps. She held her glow orb aloft as she crossed the cloister, a long walkway of alcoves and columns, many filled with grotesque statues. She paused to examine one. They were eerily life-like with a similar finish to that of the abbey. She shivered.

The patter of footsteps came to a stop an instant after hers then went quiet. A drip of water rang oddly warped by the annex's weird acoustics. Had Bax chosen to follow her anyway? If he had, why would he not announce his presence?

Jhee tucked the glow orb in her sleeve and ducked behind a column. Once her eyes adjusted, she noticed a shadowy shape stealing down the annex. She waited for the figure to pass then doubled back along her route a few columns. She peered out again.

The whiff of something akin to sickly-sweet fennel came to her nose. A sharp strike to her head caused a flash in her vision. Her head struck the column. She swayed and slumped to the ground.

～

The Actor

Jhee awoke in a strange room. A young man, in a dressing robe, filed his nail claws at the desk beside the bed. He set aside the file to daub himself with cologne. "Oh, good, you have awakened."

She glanced around the room. One corner held hoops and poles wrapped in wick or topped with glow orbs. "Mr. Zane? How did I get here?"

"I heard a thud outside my door. I opened it, and there you were. I initially thought you had passed out drunk."

He addressed her with a tone, while demur, deferential, also conveyed no hurry or concern for having found a strange woman at his door. Jhee's head had the dull throb of a headache which had been her constant companion since her arrival. A hazy recollection of being struck returned. "Let me smell your cologne," she ordered.

"A fair thank you for someone who may have saved your life."

The room had the sooty smell of accelerant and old fire. It made her nauseated. Jhee clenched her mouth shut. Her head exploded in pain. She probed the tender spots on her head. "Do it this instant, young man."

Mr. Zane gave a crisp snap of his sleeve and held over with the small, cologne bottle. He removed the cologne's stopper and wafted the scent towards Jhee. Then he leaned in to let her catch his scent. Both scents bore cucumber undertones. Not a match for what she smelled before she had been struck. "I've known men who've received expensive jewels in return for less."

"Thank you. Forgive my rudeness. You should not have been the recipient of my ire. This stay has been bothersome in the extreme through no fault of yours."

She lurched to her feet. The room shifted as her perceptions righted themselves. The tenderness at both the front and back of her head stopped at the edge of her head wrap. The poultice must have cushioned the blows she took. It may well have saved her life.

"You should be compensating me for all the liberties you're taking, Justicar. What has you creeping about so late?"

"I was hoping to speak to Mr. Anshu or Ms. Hethyr. If you could point me towards Ms. Hethyr."

"Hetty." Mr. Zane rolled his eyes and adjusted his robes. "A subject of little interest to me anymore. She's a crude, stupid, ungrateful, clumsy beast."

"Yet, you did keep company?"

"When it pleased me. Which it no longer does." Mr. Zane moved aside the collar of his robe to reveal old burns where someone attempted to leave a drawer's mark or cypher's sigil. "She was abusive and consorted with criminals."

"She sought to bind you?"

"Don't all artificers."

"Only the weak ones."

"Fortunately for me, she has her sights on another."

"Mr. Anshu."

"He recently joined the troupe. Right before our arrival here."

"Is he any more receptive to this attention than you?"

Mr. Zane slipped one of the arm hoops from the corner over his forearm. He moved his arm in a circle until the hoop spun. "You would have to ask him."

The spinning hoops made Jhee dizzy. She stilled them by reaching out, then flopped back down on the bed. "I have asked you."

Mr. Zane sat beside her feet. "Justicar, may I talk candidly to you?"

"By the Makers, it's time more did."

"I imagine your position has you hear a great many shocking things?"

"On occasion."

"I couldn't help but notice your household arrangement. Mr. Anshu has drawn more attention than Hethyr's. I have found that I am fond of him as well, a fondness I believe he returns. An awkward situation has developed between Hethyr, Anshu, and myself. The fondness between Anshu and me has drawn Hethyr's notice to the detriment of her behavior."

"Oh." Jhee rubbed her hands against her thighs to give herself a moment to think about this new dimension.

"Hethyr is not the first of my admirers. They all, however, have been women. This affection for Anshu has upended me. I suppose for branch Drakists who'll take no mortal lovers of a different gender, there is no scandal. Although for the celibates here who take no mortal companionship at all, both paths make a widow of the life mate the Path Maker intended for me. I had never supposed a situation like this would arise outside of a household."

Jhee cleared her throat. Of all those to consult in affairs of the heart, Mr. Zane had chosen the poorest of experts. She should have excused herself and made an instant bid to leave. Yet, he had sought her counsel, and she owed him some answer. "Give it some time, and perhaps the feelings will pass. A string of admirers suggests dissatisfaction with each. Mr. Anshu presents an element of mystery and the unknown."

"You suggest perhaps my affection stems from routine and a desire for something new." Mr. Zane placed a hand on Jhee's forearm. He glanced down as he brushed her robes then up again at her. "Perhaps the attentions of a more established, smarter woman might snap me out of it."

And wealthier. Jhee had no doubt which trait of hers interested him most. "Even if the affection lingers, you must find your own path."

"You wouldn't find it a hindrance to my obtaining a proper place in a household. Say, yours, for instance."

Jhee removed Mr. Zane's hand from her robes and placed it demurely with his other. "I have no doubt of your resourcefulness to find a situation befitting whatever path your preferences dictate. My advice, being something of a traditionalist, would be wholly traditional and not as befitting the free-spirited nature to which you are accustomed. These cannot be matched to the mutual bonds within a household which are born of deep affection and a commitment to child-rearing. However, the law has minimal judgment to render on the mutual affections of informed adults. Now if I may, might you point me in the direction of Mr. Anshu."

Jhee hoped she had made seeking a placement with her sound suitably dull and proper.

Mr. Zane smirked and squared his shoulders at Jhee's uncomfortable reaction. "I thank you for your most learned counsel. Second door down. I would prefer it he not know what I confided."

"You can count on my discretion, young sir."

Jhee removed her head wrap and tucked it under her arm. She owed her continued health this evening to the young and love-struck. They had proved her the foolish one many times for discounting them. She had a duty to her constituency. One she had neglected too long. This made her all too cognizant of the trade-offs Mirrei and Kanto made to join such a household as hers.

Jhee had to do better by all those who depended on her, from the forgotten young men to the members of her household. She would uncover whatever unscrupulous behavior was going on at this abbey. She would deliver Mirrei and Kanto to the capital where they can reach their full potential and spread their wings and fly. Then she and Shep would return to licking their wounds together.

She made haste to the hall where she enacted a mild healing on her head injuries.

~

The Animal Handler

Jhee scanned her surroundings and kept constant watch about her as she went to Mr. Anshu's room. Due to the abbey's odd acoustics, every drip and scrape echoed and magnified, assaulting her hearing from every angle. She kept her hand on the knife up her sleeve. Some fiend had caught her unawares once. There would not be a second time.

No light came from Mr. Anshu's door. She knocked anyway. Her patience was thin, and she meant to have answers from someone, anyone tonight. "Mr. Anshu, this is the Justicar. I wish to speak with you."

Shuffling came from within followed by an unintelligible moan or grunt. Jhee took that as leave to enter. The room smelled of animal musk. The bed lay empty and undisturbed.

A shadow rose beside her. She turned, glow orb and knife at the ready.

Pale eyes peered out from a dark corner. Too pale to be folk. Itzil, the imposing bull hound from the feast performance, crept forward with a low growl. The buckles on her harness clanked on every motion.

Jhee reached for the door. Itzil raised up on her haunches and loomed over her. Its bulk filled the entire space between Jhee and the door. Itzil growled in warning. A rudimentary attempt to soothsay it with Earth also elicited a warning bark. Jhee closed her eyes and focused on projecting a calm voice.

"Easy, Itzil. Easy." Her voice came out calm and disappointingly normal, without a trace of reverberation. She tried again. Pain shot down her spine. She saw stars. The blow she took must have activated the anti-tampering protocols on her siren module.

Jhee hazarded a glance behind her. A driftwood wardrobe stood open. Discretion being the better part of valor, she ducked inside. Through the sword-shaped openings carved in the doors, she watched Itzil, who returned to all fours. Itzil curled up in front of the wardrobe doors and blocked Jhee in.

Any movement Jhee made, the bull hound barked or snarled. The moment Jhee squatted down, Itzil became quiescent.

Jhee must have drifted off to sleep because she awoke to the sound of jingling bells. She peered through the wardrobe openings.

Mr. Anshu entered the room. He jingled the bells at Itzil who sat up and panted. "Good girl."

Mr. Anshu took a seat at the dressing table and turned on the lamp. He took up the nearby towel and wiped down his face and muzzle. He removed his hairpiece and placed it on a wig stand. He unbuckled the straps on his armor to remove his cuirass and pauldrons. He scratched his scalp then dug at his golden, sparkling esca. Part of it came off in his fingers. Jhee fought back the bile rising in her throat.

Itzil growled at her movement. Mr. Anshu grabbed a knife and faced the wardrobe. No blood or fluids dripped from the esca. It was intact. Except now it showed its actual shape, the divoted star of a woman. Mr. Anshu appeared not to be a mister.

"Pardon me… ma'am."

"Who's that?"

"The justicar. I'd appreciate it if you called off your companion."

"Itzil, go."

The bull hound bounded to its bedding in the far corner. The animal handler opened the wardrobe. Jhee let out her breath. "Makers' blessings upon you, madam. Or should I still address you as sir?"

"The clothes are the lie, not my body. Please, explain your presence in my wardrobe."

"It was the safest place I fear from your companion's wrath. I barely made it with my life."

"If Itzil meant you true harm, I assure you would not have. She must have liked your smell or was otherwise feeling playful."

"That was playful?"

"You are still intact, aren't you?" The animal handler leaned in and sniffed. "Minty. A raw undertone. Do you own pets?"

"A shark dog."

"Shark dog musk. That must be it. Itzil is very docile with respect to other hounds, especially sharks and—" The animal handler's eyes brightened. "The man at breakfast. Your husband?"

Jhee nodded then sought to change the subject, "Perhaps I would have done well to bring some shark nip with me."

"Be lucky you didn't. Itzil detests shark nip. You still have not explained why you're here."

Jhee pointed at the knife the animal handler still held. "If you would. I have a few questions I wish to ask."

The animal handler lowered the knife but did not put it away. This close and without all her gear on Jhee again noted the similarity of hair color and ear shape to her glimpse of Mr. Akesheem. "You are some relation to Mr. Pol and his son?"

"I'd pity anyone with that bottom feeder as a father. I am Djet Anshula from Ebbingsisle. Aki is my brother, Djet Akesheem. Mr. Pol is no one's father least of all ours. Astute guess."

"The calibrations or alignments are the key. Alignments: You carry yourselves similar. Coloring. Ear shape. The unique shade of your eyes. Calibration: At the performance, also, Akesheem expressed no distress over Itzil's appearance. Yet, terror at every brush of Ms. Hethyr's flames."

Ms. Anshula fondled Itzil's chin and scratched her chin while she secured her harness to the wall. "My brother's met Itzil before. You had other questions?"

"First, how did your brother come to be here without you and in the care of one you describe as a bottom feeder?"

"Akesheem, in despair over a matter of the heart, left home. He struck up a friendship with Mr. Pol, who agreed to transport him to the capital and get him proper work papers without our parents' permission. If not work, then he would find him a wife or other accommodation. I understand his impulse. Our family is poor. Both our leaving provides relief to our family. More for our siblings' dowry. We could not afford dowries for them to marry."

"Dowry? Rather than boon exchange?"

"Things are becoming hard in the Outer Reaches."

Boon exchange was more common among those not well off. Despair over a matter of the heart. Jhee understood that kind of despair all too well, though.

Jhee rubbed her muzzle. Her thoughts went to Kanto and Mirrei. "This disguise?"

"Recruiters came to our isle offering work grants. The work grant was only for men who could already artifice. My parents could only afford teaching for me. My primaries are Earth and Water. A helpful recruiter suggested I disguise myself to participate in the free work exchanges where I could get advanced training with drawing to work on the wall. She got another recruitment bounty. While I assumed one of my other brothers' identities to support myself during my search."

"Earth and Water. Hence your rapport with Itzil."

"That and some early volunteer work with veterans. Itzil and I traveled, moving from work camp to work camp. I hired myself out as a drawer until I joined the troupe. There Itzil could be part of my act. I soon learned my brother had resolved to take vows."

"You asked the troupe owners to visit because you are of a mind to talk him out of it."

"If I can. To look after him, if I cannot. There is also the matter of a recruitment fee Mr. Pol paid my family. My parents wanted to make sure they would not have to give back the money if Aki took vows."

"So many amateur investigators running about, I feel I am redundant. Two by chance. One here for her mother. One here for her brother."

Ms. Anshula smiled. "The poetess. My brother's reaction to her has bolstered my hope of dissuading him from celibacy. A fact I just discussed with her."

"Feh. Celibacy. Does no actual meditation and contemplation take place at this abbey? What of Ms. Hethyr?"

Ms. Anshula snorted. "Hethyr? That brute. You won't find her here. I have seen Mr. Zane's 'love bites.' It requires much restraint on my part when I am in her presence. Just as well she has kept her distance from me."

Jhee tucked her hands in her sleeves. Then Ms. Hethyr had an independent desire to visit the abbey.

A knock came at the door. Raigen burst in trailed by Mr. Zane and Bax before Ms. Anshula responded. Itzil perked up.

"Itzil, down."

Raigen spoke, "Forgive my rudeness. We are looking for the justicar."

Mr. Zane stopped short at Ms. Anshula's appearance.

"It appears your dilemma has answered itself, Mr. Zane. So much for your attempts to scandalize me."

"Pity. I had begun to warm to the idea of something different."

"Off with you and your pretense of decadence and sophistication. It grows tiresome. Now, what has happened to put you in such a state?"

"Sister Elkanah has accused Sister Serra of heresy and wants to call the Invocation. The whole abbey is in an uproar. She has cited you as a witness."

"Me? Forge my patience in flames. This woman."

18

THE ACCUSATION

~

The Unmaker's Work

When Jhee entered the main hall, the abbess registered a mix of shock and relief at her arrival. Jhee took a position off to the side.

Sister Elkanah held the floor. "Serra is from Verdale where they still practice the blasphemous worship of those such as the Maye King and Maye Queen or their so-called Deep Makers. Here are some of her indecent effigies."

"*Toki* dolls. You plant them in the field for a good harvest," Sister Serra said.

"Profaneness and heathenism."

"It's no secret the Maker selection and exclusion process was largely political. I didn't know what else to do. I went with what I knew. The fertility rituals of my childhood isle. Maker geld and effigies and buried toki shell figures. Yes, I borrowed a few of Sister Elkanah's texts and researched a few more rituals. I figured what could it hurt. Ceremonies and sacrifices to honor the Maye King and Queen and the Warrior of Pain."

"Virgin sacrifices?"

"Yes."

"You see Abbess and Justicar? She admits participation in vile blood rites."

Sister Serra cleared her throat. "Not that kind of sacrifice."

The physician suppressed a chuckle.

"Oh," Jhee said.

161

"It is the Unmaker's work," Sister Elkanah said. "You shall not profane this holy place with such infernal practices. No wonder the abbey has been plagued by death and demonic forces. I call upon the Invocation of Xendatia to cleanse this holy place."

Everyone gasped. Professed and Prospective alike whispered amongst themselves, even the remaining senior clergy. The physician began to rock back and forth in her chair, shaking her head. Jhee had an accountability chain: audits, review boards, Chief Justicar councils. The Invokers did not. They worked by patronage. Once invited in, the Invokers would not stop.

Pyrmo stood. "Silence. I'm sure, Sister Elkanah, you did not mean that."

"This is not a laughing matter or a matter for play. You do not invoke the Unraveler on this sacred isle."

Pyrmo shook her head. "A member has called for the Invocation of Xendatia. I will retire to consider the matter."

"What is to consider? These fiends invoked the Unmaker on our isle. We must have a cleansing."

"You are not the abbess here, Elkanah."

"Perhaps I should be. I once thought your leadership would bring about a return to tradition and decency. Yet, the Unraveler's influence continues to rise. Perhaps I was wrong to support you."

"What of your sins, Sister Elkanah?" Jhee asked.

"My sins?" Sister Elkanah sputtered. "My-my sins are not at issue here."

"Unraveler? An interesting choice of appellation for the Unmaker. One I believe favored by the anarchist wing of the Pillarists. Whom I seem to remember you called the Doombearers instead of the more common term Doombringers."

The archivist's eyes went wide, turning a dark umber in the process. "How dare you?"

"How dare you, Elkanah?" Sister Serra said. "Everyone knows how jealously you guard the archives. Care to explain how I could have gained access to the archives under your watch?"

"Upon occasion, I had need to counsel one of my assistants. One evening after our conversation and prayers, I returned to find the archives had been breached."

"Conversation? Is that what you call it? In your chambers, no doubt," Sister Serra said.

"I am not on trial here."

"Perhaps you should be."

"I admit to one night having succumbed to the affections of one of these wicked, wicked men."

"Who?" Jhee asked.

"Prospective Yaou. I later realized someone had taken relics from the archives. My activities with the Doombringers were misguided. My sins, though, are not why we're here."

"All our sins are," Sister Serra spat. "The land suffers for our sins. The constant storms are drowning the fields, poisoning the crops and sea life. You'd know that if you poked your head out of the archives long enough to experience the world around you."

"I've experienced the ills of this world aplenty. This is about you and your shameful, wicked ways. If you had perhaps stayed on the true path instead of these false ones, the Makers would see fit to reward our isle with an abundance of something other than misery."

"Idolaters. You with your lust for relics and false piety. You've sown the soil with fallowness. The Makers want us to make, to produce. Yet you worship relics of the dead and practice celibacy. Then we threw up that blasted shield. And the land withered. Archives, relics, crypts, are about death. The fields, the orchards are life."

Pyrmo's hands shook, and her eyes smoldered almost orange. "Must I remind everyone final authority to start an invocation rests in my hands alone? I will give the Justicar some time to find out more before we have the whole isle crawling with Invokers and go staking people out to be godsparked. Most of us have seen enough death. Before we invite more, we must see what else there may be behind these deaths. The Justicar assures me there is no evidence of Unmakers and that what has happened was solely a mundane matter. Now, if you will excuse me."

Pyrmo left via the clerical door and jerked her head for Jhee to follow. Once inside the abbess's office, Jhee closed the door firmly behind them. Pyrmo collapsed in her chair. "I need a drink."

Jhee stepped forward.

Pyrmo tucked her shaking hands into her sleeves. "That's far enough. I've been true to my word and haven't touched any since you caught me. Please, if there is anything you can do to avoid our having to call the Invokers or the exorcists. I will not have them running through here, causing hysteria amongst the clergy. Have you made any progress?"

Jhee hesitated to voice her current inquiries into the performers. With the archivist on a tear, it would be too easy for them to become the shark's bait. If one did murder, only that one should pay. "Some, Abbess."

"Could Sister Elkanah be right about Sister Serra? At least for the murders."

"Possibly. For me to pronounce sentence yet or even make an accusation now, is premature."

Pyrmo brought her hands to her esca and murmured a prayer. "In exchange for the understanding and discretion you have shown me and my problem, I'll allow you more time to complete your inquiries and hold off on charging Sister Serra or calling in the Invokers. But please, I urge you to hurry, before this mess boils over. Sisters Serra and Elkanah publicly confessed to serious breaches of the abbey rules. At the very least, I'll order them confined to quarters where they can't antagonize each other. However, if anything else untoward happens, I'll be forced to Invoke the Xendatia Cleansing."

Jhee and Pyrmo returned to the main hall. The abbess announced she would not invoke a cleansing until Jhee concluded her investigation.

~

The Penitents

Sister Serra was taken away to be put under guard. She stopped Jhee as she passed. "Watch Elkanah. You surprised me in the pods when you said you found expansion plans for the archives. After Saheli died, I switched out the compromise plans for mine."

A tapestry at the far end of the auditorium rustled. Jhee crept toward it. The decoration flung aside, and the vizier beckoned her.

"Lady Bathsheba? What are you doing here?"

"I didn't hear back from you regarding my message. I wanted to speak to you about something I found. It's a matter of some urgency, but not out here in the open. My quarters. Meet me as soon as you conclude your business here."

Message? In all the commotion, Jhee had forgotten about the note the lady slipped her. Lady Bathsheba hurried off.

Sister Elkanah tried to slink away in the interim. The prioress met her at the entrance. "I suspect the Justicar has some questions for you."

"Thank you, prioress, I do. You uncovered hothouse expansion plans."

"Yes."

"You killed Saheli because you thought she was going to gut the archives and expand the fields and orchards."

"No. At first, that's what I thought. After I had confessed my transgressions to Saheli. She showed me the full expansion plan, including those for archives. True, I felt her too lax, but the dead cannot be improved only remade. A lesson I punish myself for not learning sooner.

"I understood the hard position she was in. It could not have been easy taking me in and keeping my secret. Was Saheli too lenient with the clergy and novices? Yes, but that was her way. Those writings, that heretical trash, could ruin her reputation. I should know. As a Doombringer, I thought I was on the side of the Makers, but now I see I was doing the Unmakers' work. I didn't want Saheli to go down that path. The Makers gave men and women roles and arts, and it was a mistake to force a misguided notion of arcane equanimity on them. One they were not ready for."

"Those writings? The missing sermon and Sister Niza's missing account?"

"What do you mean missing?"

Jhee held up the empty folder. "Quit your games and stalling. Show me that sermon and Scholar Niza's account, now."

"No," Sister Elkanah said. "No. It must be here."

"Check for yourself, if you don't believe me."

"That's not right. The boards, the papers on her desk were full of cyphers."

"Sister Elkanah, you've gone through quite an effort to conceal her final Sermon. Perhaps to cover up your part in her death."

"No, but I feared the roots of Unmaking taking hold. I won't deny being glad Saheli can't cut archival spending or sell my collections, only to see the monies diverted to the hothouses and fields."

The prioress clasped Elkanah's hands. "And outreach. Saheli wasn't anti-knowledge. Indeed, she had taken great pains to enhance our learning facilities. Overhauling our fee structure. Reducing both the tithe and the tuition. She wanted to make it more affordable and accept more male students. Maintaining the archives was expensive. By enhancing our crop production and selling off some of the relics and books, she could subsidize the classes. Pay more attention to the living than the dead and relics of the past. Divest some rare books in favor of textbooks. She planned to use the sale of rare books and relics to finance the purchase of textbooks and modern equipment. Workshops, labs, vocational facilities, adepts, and cyphering teachers."

Sister Elkanah snatched her hands away. "She wanted to dedicate more and more resources to refugees and teaching men arcana. I won't stand for it! It is because of my past I know the dangers and wickedness unleashed by teaching men artifice. She could not see what a dangerous path that was. I thought as she did once, except I was trying to doom the worlds. Then the first alignment came, then the second, and then nothing. The third and fourth Doombringer rebellions had accounted to little more than mobs and riots. Though still deadly."

"Now, Sister Elkanah, tell me about this stolen antiquity."

"I realize now I was being lured away from the archive. A few items were stolen: an early uncensored copy of the Grand Design; a gilded metal and hardwood strongbox with some personal papers and family tree; inscribed ivories; some drawing puzzles; and parts of a Pillarist, arcane polyptych. When I caught Yaou with a triptych—a piece of the polyptych—and the strongbox, he threatened to reveal our indiscretion unless I taught him how to decode and perform the cyphers therein. Saheli came upon us soon after and confiscated both. I couldn't very well tell her how he obtained them. Saheli already knew about my past with the Doombringers. She said this abbey was a place for second chances and atonement.

"Later, I confessed my transgressions and urged her to burn the triptych. An act I found myself unable to do. She could not either, I suppose. To destroy a relic, even a blasphemous one, was anathema to us both."

"And her missing sermon?"

"Being both familiar with male cyphering and having read the triptych myself, I recognized the source of her inspiration. She had taken the theorems and built on them. All believed she had transcended to the Spheres, while I knew the Makers struck her down for her apostasy. I returned later to destroy it and retrieve the strongbox. I found the triptych and strongbox missing. That profane relic. We should have destroyed it. It's dangerous. Anathema."

The sister's body language showed no indications of lying. "I'll discuss what to do with you with the abbess later. In the meantime, perhaps you should retire to your cell until then."

"You have no authority—"

The prioress touched Sister Elkanah's elbow. "Please, do as she suggests and don't force the matter."

Sister Elkanah stiffened her posture and strode from the auditorium.

Jhee pinched the bridge of her nose. "Still no closer to finding that storm drenched sermon."

The prioress contemplated the floor, then mumbled, "I know where it is. Or I did. I saw Sister Elkanah take the sermon. I used my master keys to take it from her cell, where I also found the account. To protect Saheli's reputation. I'm sorry, Justicar. I knew she'd destroy it. Maybe I should have let her. They'll use it to ruin Saheli's reputation."

Jhee huffed. "Where are they now?"

"I put them in the crypts for safekeeping."

19

THE EYE

~

Shapes in Fog

Jhee met Lady Bathsheba at the hermitage near the springs.

"Did you come alone?" Lady Bathsheba asked.

She peered out into night behind Jhee. Jhee did likewise. "As far as I know."

Lady Bathsheba pulled Jhee inside. She brandished an amulet. "If you be a spirit or demon, this talisman of the Wave Witch compels you to answer me now in the affirmative."

Jhee fixed the woman with an exasperated look. She brandished the amulet at Jhee again. "No. I am not a spirit or demon."

Lady Bathsheba visibly relaxed.

Jhee and Lady Bathsheba sat at the tea table assessing the merits of the tasty cod the monks caught today. The delicate, moist flesh practically melted in the mouth. It was so incredibly juicy. Jhee quite thoroughly enjoyed it. "Shep is a great diver. He has never caught something as succulent as this. But close, very close."

"Fresh-caught. I bypass the kitchens and pantries and acquire my food straight from the docks and market. More so recently. As a precaution."

The land meat, rotisserie goat, smelled like roast perfection. It's scarce she had any; even then seldom so rare. She had loved it as a child. The dietary minefield she had to navigate with her household made it simpler not to have any. Jhee closed her eyes and savored the delicious taste. If only it were rarer. She had it so infrequently, even more cooked than she liked, it was divine. "Divine."

"Glad you enjoy it."

They partook of some white abalone. Jhee politely held her wine cup. Between whatever she had drank with the performers and her blow to the head, she needed to keep her head clear. "I wanted to thank you so much for your help, Vizier. Especially with Shep's troubles. You mentioned a matter you wanted to bring to my attention."

Lady Bathsheba coughed. "You are welcome. It's been good to get out again. I swear I feel years younger. It's a good thing I'm not. I might well give you a run for your money with Bright Harmony or even Dawn Wolf a run for you. Were that I were a few years younger and not a hermit here, I would certainly have to steal him. My reclusive lifestyle is not a good fit for such a bright treasure such as him."

Jhee thought back to Miramar, Mirrei's mother and once her closest friend, standing alone on the docks the last time she saw her. That is who Lady Bathsheba reminded her of. The defiant Miramar. So many regrets. Nothing to be done about it now except move forward and try to do better. Jhee wiped her muzzle with the napkin.

Lady Bathsheba coughed again. She covered her mouth with a fist. "Pardon me. Something must have gone down the wrong pipe."

She took another drink from her wine cup. A coughing fit overtook her. Her pallor changed. Beads of sweat broke out on her forehead. Lady Bathsheba stared at Jhee with panic then gaped at their wine cups. She dropped hers and knocked Jhee's from her hand before falling into Jhee's arms. Her skin had turned a purplish color. She clawed at the collar around her throat.

Jhee produced her inhaler from her robes and gave the Lady two puffs. Lady Bathsheba calmed down. Her breath came in a steady though wheezy tempo. It took a few minutes before her color turned back to a color resembling normal. The lady reached out a shaky hand to the emergency call button.

Jhee brought out her conch as she went to the call button. She pressed the button several times. Nothing happened. Jhee swore. She got no response from Bax or Shep. She slipped Lady Bathsheba's arm around her shoulder. "You need help."

"Where?"

"The agri-pods. We need kinberry to counteract the effects of the poison."

Lady Bathsheba struggled against her. "Not Sister Serra. Take me to the infirmary."

"The infirmary then. I'll have someone meet us there with a counter-agent."

Jhee flung open the Lady's door. A figure in a bat-faced Cheiropthys mask stood there. The garish tongue hung out underneath a crest of extravagant plumage. There came a whir followed by a hiss. White smoke billowed from the mouth. Jhee coughed and waved her hand in front of her face. Warmth crept through her head. Her vision skewed. Jhee sank to her knees. The figure brushed past her. She reached feebly at a hem. It shook off her limp hand. Jhee captured an image with her conch before falling against the wall.

Consciousness came and went. Jhee felt like she was being dragged and sometimes carried. Drizzling rain driven by a chill wind passed over her skin. A cry went out. She found herself dumped on the wet, muddy ground. The air held the slight scent of sulfur and effervescence.

Raised voices argued. Then a loud splash. More cries.

Jhee stumbled to her feet. She could not tell if the fog came from her mental state or the weather. She staggered among pools of water. A satin bubble, brightly-colored, caught her eye in the nearby spring: Lady Bathsheba's robe.

The strands of the elements slipped through Jhee's mental grasp. She gathered enough to bring Lady Bathsheba within arm's reach. With a great heave, she pulled her from the water. Jhee collapsed backward, unable to do much else.

Weird phantasmal shapes in the fog swam before her in the mist. The image of that fiend, Hethyr, approached her out of the fog. Fiend. Abuser of men. Sister Elkanah burst from the fog. Jhee's eyes became too heavy to remain open.

Jhee sank under the ocean again, drowning. She couldn't touch bottom. The waves battered her about. Every now and then they slammed her against hard, sharp rocks. The impacts forced the breath from her lungs. Her limbs were so heavy. She could not fight anymore. Mouth clamped shut, lungs burning, she contemplated the briny depths below. As she decided to let go, an enormous, brilliant, scaly eye opened, bathing her in light. She opened her mouth to scream. Ocean poured in. A hand grabbed her collar.

⌣

Shadowed

"Justicar. Justicar. Wake up. Wake up."

A hand tapped Jhee's face repeatedly, but gently. She groaned and opened her eyes. The infirmarian's face hovered over her. She uprighted herself.

Lady Bathsheba lay on the bed in the quiet room. On the exam table beside Jhee, resided the prioress.

"Are they?" Jhee croaked.

"They're alive. Barely. Praise be the Makers."

"Blessed are the First Makers. What happened to the prioress?"

169

"No one's sure. She came to the infirmary shortly before you did complaining of shortness of breath."

"Similar symptoms to Prospective Yaou?"

"Maybe."

"Justicar?" Lady Bathsheba called out in a meek voice. She held out a hand to Jhee who took hold of it. "Thank you."

"Please, don't try to speak. I never thanked you for intervening on my husband's behalf. Thank you."

Jhee sat vigil by the Lady's bedside pondering the questions. This abbey, this place of rest and quiet contemplation hid so many secrets. If this was the prelude to the capital, the lessons learned here, she would not soon forget.

The door to the infirmary banged open. Sister Elkanah strode in triumphant with the remaining senior clergy. "Good. You're awake. This time I have proof Sister Serra is the fiend," she proclaimed.

She thrust a bit of torn silk at Jhee. "What is this?"

"I tore this off your *masked* attacker when I saved your lives. You should count yourself lucky Zalver and I had decided to shadow you to ensure you remained on a righteous path."

Jhee's face burned. "Is that so? What if I hadn't?"

"Then it would simply be more evidence for the Invokers of the Unmaker's work."

"I see."

"I'll summon the abbess and have her put Sister Serra in the Corrections Hall at once."

"On what proof?"

"I gave you the proof."

"You know this is Sister Serra's how?"

"I don't—. The mask."

"I assumed you inventoried your masks."

"Yes."

"How many were missing?"

"Three."

"You retrieved how many from the horticulturist?"

"Three. Which I put in the custody of the prioress."

Jhee displayed the images she had captured on her conch to Sister Elkanah. "Was this one?"

"No. But you saw—?"

"I saw a masked figure and at some later point you."

"Me? I rescued you. Why are you questioning me?"

"What proof do I have you weren't the one who attacked us?"

Sister Elkanah regarded the rest of her mob with a pleading expression. "Serra had the masks."

"Thanks to your accusation Sister Serra was under guard, which meant she could not have attacked us."

"An accomplice. One of her fellow debauchees. Several masks were missing."

"Which don't resemble the one in these images taken during the assault. May I further submit ghosts and demons don't have separable garments?"

Sister Elkanah tried one last feeble excuse, "But she stole my relics and violated the sanctity of the archives."

"A courtesy you no doubt repaid when you and your minions trashed her hothouse. Or do you claim to have neatly turned it upside down searching for your flimsy evidence? Her mischief and yours are matters for the abbess, not me."

Jhee marched to the dejected archivist. Her nostrils flared. She took a good whiff.

"What are you—?"

Cold and musty like her relics. It was not her. "Thank you for my rescue. Now, go before I change my mind. Be lucky I am more considered in judgment than you. I'm going to ask the abbess to confine both you and the horticulturist to quarters until I resolve this matter. Try my patience, and I'll have you confined to the Corrections Hall you clamor so much about with only a copy of the Cyclogenesis sermons."

"You can't do that."

"Try me."

Jhee ruled Sister Elkanah out as the person who bashed her on the head and nothing more. The scent of the attacker was so familiar. Yet, so far, she had not matched it to a culprit.

20
____

THE UNEXPECTED GUESTS

~

The Actress

Now that Jhee had dealt with both the archivist and the horticulturist, she needed to collect her thoughts and resume her investigation. Before all this nonsense began, she had been investigating the performers. Jhee replayed her misadventures in the fog. She had seen various figures: Sister Elkanah. Ms. Hethyr. With her compromised mental state, she was not sure which were real or imaginary. What she did know is, she had no good intelligence on Ms. Hethyr's whereabouts since the storeroom after the fire show and her heated exchange with Ms. Anshula.

Bax met her inside of the infirmary, grim and stone-cold sober. "I failed you, my lady. You'll go nowhere without me anymore."

"Ms. Hethyr's room. We'll get the prioress's keys to gain us entry if need be."

"At once, Justicar."

Jhee stalked over to the prioress. "Now, as for you. Niza's account mentioned calculations and a board full of equations. Yet, the images I acquired from Sister Elkanah show clean boards."

"The servants say the words faded away with her transcendence, leaving us with only the accounts of those present as to what was said," Bax offered.

Jhee fixed her gaze on the prioress who turned away.

"I wiped the boards and hid the images and calculations in the crypts. I knew what it was, but it was so brilliant I didn't want Saheli's last great contribution to the world destroyed. But if anyone else found it, it would jeopardize her legacy and consideration as a Canon."

"I'll need your master keys for the hostelry. Is every scrap with the sermon?"

The prioress placed them in Jhee's hand with a sigh. "Yes, I planned to move everything once the weather got better."

"Saheli wasn't talking about the pillars of society, she was talking about the pillars of arcana as envisioned by the Middle Pillarists."

"Now, you see why I hid it. Given Elkanah's past, likely she knew it for what it was, too. Who knew what she might do with them?"

They left the prioress and made their way to the performers' quarters. They knocked. Jhee double-checked for wild beasts before using the prioress's key to unlock the door. The room was sparse with very little personal in it. It had the same air of old smoke and oils as Mr. Zane's room. It contained a much more extensive collection of burn tools than his. Jhee sniffed among the few toiletries she found. Nothing matching what she smelled before her blow to the head.

"You should see this, Justicar," Bax said. She abandoned her search to kneel beside Bax and the open footlocker. She gave him a questioning glance. "It was open."

She hoped the footlocker contained nothing of actual probative value or else she might have to exclude it from her deliberations. "What did you find?"

Bax held up a simple woven shift like the ones worn by the Prospectives. "It is as you suspected, Justicar. Hethyr must be disguising herself as clergy."

Jhee laid the shift down and scrutinized it. It smelled of cologne. She found a name written on the inside of the collar. "There's a name written here."

"Prospectives are responsible for the washing of their own garments and vestments. They wouldn't want to get them mixed up."

"Leigh."

"The drowned boy."

Jhee dug around the chest to see if she might find one of those bracelets. Nothing. She paused to think. She pulled out her map. "Follow me."

"Where to, Justicar?" Bax asked.

"To the only places in this warren I haven't traversed back and forth a dozen times over now."

Outside Ms. Hethyr's room, they bumped into the trio of Raigen, Mr. Zane, and Ms. Anshula.

"I went to confront Mr. Pol and reclaim my brother," Ms. Anshula began.

"Mr. Pol and Akesheem are missing from their rooms," the poetess said. "It is as I feared, Akesheem shall be the next mysterious death."

"If he has harmed my brother," Ms. Anshula said.

Jhee held up a hand. "Do not finish that phrase."

Jhee attempted to reach her cohort via conch. The signal pip came and went. Ms. Anshula gathered a few weapons from her room. Jhee eyed her.

"A precaution," she said.

"To my room."

"What?"

Ms. Anshula's eyes widened. Jhee held up her hand. "First and foremost, we ensure the safety of those whose location we know. Come with me. I must check on my cohort. Then we formulate a plan."

Jhee took off, expecting them to follow.

A Game Interrupted

"Will denbe be here soon?" Mirrei asked.

"Soon. Never you mind. She has a great many duties to attend to, but she always returns safe and sound." Shep placed his next tile down. "Try that, Sprite."

"An amateurish mistake, Pup." Mirrei smiled and made her play. She knighted a single capture tile next to his stronghold tile. "Breach."

Mirrei turned over Shep's stronghold tile so, the bright side faced up. With that, she had him. He scratched his head and hunched his shoulders. He had missed her stealthy positioning of the capture tile. "Well, would you look at that? You have much improved since we've first played."

"Why do you think I never play her anymore?" Kanto said. He punctuated the statement with a few notes on the lute.

Shep smiled at his two junior spouses. He tried not to let on how worried he was for Jhee. He had not heard from her or Bax in quite a while. Usually, he'd be out there with her. He needed to be here though to protect them. She'd had multiple attempts on her life, yet insisted they were the ones in the greatest danger.

The conchs sat on a table near the one charging station. Not only was the amount of power the station put out barely a trickle it had to be split between three and four devices when Kanto did not monopolize it. He should check for a message from Jhee, but they had a strict no-devices rule during tiles.

Kanto and Mirrei cast frequent, furtive glances at each other throughout the evening. They reminded Shep of him and his sister with how they could bicker one moment then be back to school fish the next. He had not entirely worked out what mischief they had gotten up to. All he knew was they left early with Bax and returned late without him smelling strongly of drink. In the meantime, he had not been able to contact anyone to learn what was happening.

Mirrei laughed which soon degenerated into a coughing fit. Kanto gave her his usual sidelong glance. The coughing fit lasted a few moments longer and sounded wetter than usual. Shep reached out and felt her forehead. If he weren't so familiar with her condition, he might have attributed her turn for the worse to a hangover. Kanto ceased playing.

"We shouldn't have gone out today," Kanto said. His face concerned and perhaps guilty from having doubted her.

"You were right. I am the one confined here, not you."

While Shep did not say it, he second-guessed letting them leave the room. He should have stood firm against their pressure. Jhee had been worried enough by what was happening at the abbey to insist they always had an escort. With her and Bax indisposed and him obligated to stay in the room, he felt guilty that they had to stay by his side. They were back safe. He supposed that was all that mattered. He had needed the time to himself, too, to ensure if he was in the right frame of mind to protect them.

Rapid footfalls approached. Shep caught a muddle of unfamiliar scents. His tattoo tingled. His ears flattened against head.

"Both of you get to the far side of the bed away from the door." He motioned for Kanto and Mirrei to place the bed between them and the door. He rushed to his war chest. His war club lay on top since tea with the vizier.

The doorknob rattled and slowly turned.

~

The Dropped War Club

Jhee and company burst into her rooms. No one sat by the fireplace. A game of tiles remained unfinished on the tables. An unmoving shape lay on the bed. The sigil on her arm ached. Her heart dropped. She rushed forward. A grunt behind her caused her to turn. Raigen lay on the ground, disarmed. Shep stood behind the door, poised to strike again. His hands shook. His chest heaved. Sweat beaded on his face while his breath came in snort-like bursts. A dull red-gold fury glowed in his eyes.

"Shep, they're with me." Ms. Anshula inched back, palms wide and empty. She formed the first gesture of an Earth drawing. Jhee stroked the sigil on her arm gently. As she sang a few notes of Shep's favorite song, his eyes returned to their standard golden color. The war club dropped from his hands. They embraced each other. "It's all right. I should not have made you worry."

Jhee pulled against Shep's embrace. He held tight. Kanto and Mirrei poked their heads out from behind the bed. The tension drained from Jhee.

Hacking came from Mirrei who tried to suppress it. Jhee rubbed Shep's ears. He indicated his calmness with a curt nod then dropped to his knees. His hands raised in supplication.

Raigen got up, brushed herself off, and shook the remaining vapors from her head. "Justicar," Raigen said, "please. Time may be running out."

"A moment please." Jhee ushered Mirrei to the bed where she removed the pillows they had used as decoys.

Raigen held out her flask. "Try this."

"Why?" Shep intercepted the flask and had a tentative sniff. He and Jhee had more experience than they cared to admit with mystery flask games. His expression softened. After a taste, his face lit up. "Whoa, that's delicious. What is that?"

"Tranquility Gold."

Shep cocked his head back. "I had Tranquility Gold. That wasn't it."

"This is the Tranquility Gold served at the head table. Try this. This is probably what you had. And this, this is the Tranquility Gold being sold to merchants."

Shep tasted the second. He gagged and nearly spit the second out. "Oh, that is disgusting. Bleh. Those aren't the same. The second's watered-down garbage."

"What they sell to the general public is even worse."

Shep eyed the third cup before taking a sip. He spit it out immediately, wiped his tongue with a napkin, then washed it down with a drink of water. "That was like vinegar. That can't be from degradation of the harvest due to weather. Those were more what I expected from the first flask. It's been blended with low-grade wines."

"We can only hope. The squelchers on my isle used to get very creative."

Shep waved for Raigen to give him the first flask. He sipped the contents until his grimace went away. "Now, I understand the fuss."

Watered-down wines. Jhee cast her mind back to the storehouse and her discovery of Pyrmo there. "Could it be for themselves?"

"At the scale I uncovered, it would be a drinker on the order of Lethys and the Rum Toad," Raigen said.

Jhee guffawed. She supposed Pyrmo or Sister Zalver might have drunk a river of alcohol over the course of years. "Then the culprit must be pocketing the proceeds. Or putting them to other use."

"Perhaps I should not have sought Mr. Akesheem's help. It may be what caused those fiends to turn on him."

"Doesn't this give Sister Serra motive to kill Prospective Leigh?" Shep asked. "Tampering with the wine jeopardizes its imperial certification as a noble blend."

"Either he found out and was going to expose her," Jhee speculated and nodded.

"Or she learned he sullied the brand which she takes so much pride in."

Jhee integrated this new component of the machine. Pyrmo as prioress for years had been an excellent position to run such a scheme. Yet, as Jhee had learned, she must not be too quick to eliminate the others. The horticulturist was exceedingly proud of the abbey's wine. Would she dilute the reputation of the brand? The archivist might, both to embarrass Sister Serra and put the monies into the archives. The prioress and Saheli might have done the same. Hadn't the smugglers confirmed as much?

"Ms. Anshula, you and Mr. Zane stay here. Raigen, Bax, and I will continue the search for your brother and Mr. Pol."

"I'm coming with you," Ms. Anshula said. "Your male possesses a kalacha and the full gift of skin slipping. He can protect your cohort on his own."

Shep had returned to supplicating kneeling.

"He was a war chaplain and needs to recenter. I'll say no more of it. Please, I'm entrusting you with the protection of those who mean most to me."

Jhee took in all the faces in the room, especially the young ones. Her spouses who bore the hopes of their families. The dutiful daughter looking out for her family. The would-be lovers. These people had put themselves in her care. She did not intend to lose a single one. She strode into the hallway. Bax and Raigen fell in behind her.

21

—————

SECRETS OF THE DEPTHS

~

The Halls of the Tortured and the Drenched

"Another elementalist might have been helpful," Raigen said.

Their selected party, Jhee, Raigen, and Bax, headed for the central hall. Jhee compared her map to the one she had copied while in the archives. "With as wound up as everyone is, I fear what may happen if the wrong pairs of people interact. Where we find Mr. Pol, we may encounter Ms. Hethyr."

"Ms. Hethyr?"

"Merely a hypothesis. I suspect perhaps some alliance between Ms. Hethyr and Mr. Pol." Jhee traced a finger along a faint corridor not shown on Lady Bathsheba's map. "Now, follow me."

The archivist had been right about one detail. There had to be an accomplice. Her current surmise led her to believe more than one person perpetrated these crimes. Whatever scheme had befallen Saheli and these young men involved multiple people.

"Justicar, where are we going?" Bax asked.

"The crypts."

They journeyed back to the Prayer Hall back through the central hall. Jhee flipped through the master keys. None of them seemed to match the locks on either barred door. She returned to the first barred exit from the banquet hall.

"This way leads to the Corrections Hall," Raigen said.

"According to my examination of these maps," Jhee began, "there is an entrance to the crypts at the other end of the hall."

They stood before the massive door to the Corrections Hall. Jhee jangled the rusted lock which secured the chain wrapped around the handles in place.

"It's been locked and closed for years," Raigen said.

"Will that be a problem, Bax?"

"No, my lady." Bax knelt in front of the lock. Jhee moved the glowtorch closer so he could see better. Bax reached into his waist pouch and pulled out a fastened kit. He rubbed his chin, then produced a pipette and vial from the wallet. A thin trail of smoke rose from the lock as he piped a few drops of liquid into its keyhole. Jhee's eyes watered. Her pores burned. She covered her nose and mouth as the foul odor reached her. Bax placed an awl in the lock's keyhole. A solid hammer blow shattered the whole lock. The chains slid to the ground.

Raigen gave Jhee a confused look.

"Bax came before the judgment block as a thief," Jhee said.

"To spare me a more traditional punishment"—Bax held up his hands and showed them off front and back—"the Justicar paid my fines and took me into her service."

"Seems as though I'm not the only one who wants to keep their body parts intact," Raigen said.

Jhee pushed open the doors to the Corrections Hall. The miasma of dust and decay greeted them. An eerie silence hung about the place. They crept forward as anything else seemed disrespectful. An automated light guttered to life then returned to power conservation mode. She swept her glowtorch over the exhibits. They pushed forward.

"I was born to murder the world," a recorded voice blared from a loudspeaker.

Jhee yelped but had a cypher at the ready. The three faced outward in combat stances. Ominous, red light flared in the nearest exhibit. The shadowed forms shuddered and moved. It took a moment to realize the display was automated.

Horrible, garish creatures glowered at them from frescoed reliefs. Carved hands clawed from pits in the ground as if beseeching the passerby for deliverance.

Figures painted like barbarians, their faces formed into the most horrid expressions, wielded wicked-looking weapons as they disemboweled or decapitated warriors who tried to fight them. Their tongues lolled, and malachite eyes looked lustily at captured spouses and children.

They formed up their ranks as they continued. "You said you suspected an alliance between Ms. Hethyr and Mr. Pol," Raigen said.

"The performers' route provides a perfect trafficking route, and her tattoos tie her to local gangs. Mr. Pol has access to a steady stream of young men via the camps and the abbey. Ms. Hethyr might even be the Mist Abbess. Also, who's to say the Mist Abbess must be a woman? Anshula proved with some basic make-up and the right demeanor, people saw what they wanted to see."

Further along, the next exhibit gave the dangers of the Baqairu blood cults who, led by the Mist Abbess, had resolved to end the Flower Wars and bring back the days of the hunt and battle through sacrifice. The priest figures in their headdresses and masks cut and ripped hearts from bare chests and sucked the marrow from their victims' bones. Priestesses sucked the faces off victims and stole their breath or used fire and godspark to cleanse their bodies. The scene she had stumbled on in the wood had made a hedonistic mock of it.

Another voice-over kicked in when they reached the next exhibit. "The Final Sword. Even beyond the Baqairu death cultists, were the doomsday cultists. They wanted to end all existence, and their instruments of destruction were artificers. All who practiced magic in numbers saw how the lands and the areas around them suffered from excess cyphering. The Middle Pillarists known as Doombringers, based on the forbidden sequences from Thaedra's portfolio, innovated particularly devastating sequences that when used by male artificers left miles of destruction in their wake. They made no effort to preserve the environment. They encouraged male and female artificers alike to burst cypher. A process which often killed them and anyone in the area immediately around them. The area remained deadly for years afterward. Not a plant would grow, not a creature could flourish. To even move through the area, one could not survive. The land itself was hungry and drank the very life from any living thing unlucky enough to enter it."

A reverse spirit battery of sorts.

"My lady, what do you make of this?" Bax asked. He held his glowtorch over a giant, rectangular void in the dust in front of the Middle Pillarist exhibit. Jhee peered closer. The pattern in the dust came from something woven. Nearby a discarded Middle Pillarist prayer cloth and glow orb stands had been kicked aside. Brown droplets flecked the ground, ripped bits of fabric and scourge thorns scattered among them. The minute scratches on Sister Elkanah's arms and shoulders flashed in her mind.

"Sister Elkanah. She appears to have a different idea of how she should atone than her former associates."

The exhibit beyond this one came almost as a pleasant relief, depending on one's feelings about flying rodents. Cheiropthys the bat-faced Lesser Maker, his symbol, the sky fox, a gigantic, bloodsucking bat which dwarfed many hounds. The sky fox hailed from one of the aboriginal isles. A more tropical equivalent of Verdale with its host of deadly plants.

Next, came scenes of the counter inquisition's torturers. Then the Medical Protectorate doctors whose experiments and excesses had created unfortunate programs like the berserkers. Jhee turned away. Bax's torch swept over a scene of a physician dismembering a young man. He stifled a sob and covered his mouth in horror. She placed a tender hand on his forearm.

"You know the other name they had for the Corrections Hall," Raigen said. "The Halls of Torture and the Drenched. A holdover from another time when we focused on the fear of the Makers rather than the love of them. The custom was to lock young Prospectives in here to contemplate their sins."

Even as a learned woman, if locked in here long enough, Jhee would certainly rethink her life. This hall must have its own emergency power source. First Makers forfend these exhibits not work when you wanted to frighten prisoners or young Prospectives. Another pit of grasping hands bookended the displays. "Pleasant. Come, let's leave this foul place as quick as possible."

"Agreed, Justicar."

~

The Crypts

They found an archway at the far end with a pressure sealed gate. As Bax worked, vermin most likely crab-rats skittered in the darkness behind them. The wind outside had picked up. Loose tiles in the heights of the ceiling rattled. The blowing wind sometimes sounded like a whistle. Other times it affected the moans of the drenched.

The pressure seal disengaged with a hiss. They entered an airlock on the other side without a moment's hesitation.

"Reseal it. Pyrmo said the salt air could contaminate the crypts."

What Jhee really wanted to do was seal herself off from the images in the hall.

The airlock's dim, low-level lighting made a bright white contrast to the blood reds and fiery umbers of the Corrections Hall. Sea and storm air made a welcome change from the mustiness. A series of wind shafts and fans whined and groaned with every spin as they labored to keep a steady flow of air. The door out of the airlock showed more recent and frequent use likely for maintenance.

Steps beyond the door led down into the depths of the abbey. Jhee took the vanguard with her glowtorch outstretched. A fog, the folkloric last breaths of the dead, covered the lowest steps.

Warm, misty air tickled her cheeks. The back and forth seawater flow and air pressure gave the impression of the cave itself breathing. Jhee found focusing on the walls hard. The stony surface wavered as illumination sparkled through moisture droplets. Faint, cyan light emanated from the rocky strata comprising the vaults. She clutched her robes and recited statutes to her Maker within.

"Mr. Akesheem. Mr. Pol," Jhee called.

Frogs and water drips gave the only replies. They continued calling out for the missing men as they pressed forward. Dank air brought the swift return of Jhee's headache. Their footsteps sloshed through the water. Something brushed her legs. She did not even want to think about what sorts of unseen creatures swam at their feet. They turned a corner.

A sharp pain knifed through her esca and the back of her neck. What was it about this isle that made her head pound so? She squeezed her eyes shut.

Open your eyes and look, her Maker within said. When Jhee opened her eyes again, she was enveloped in mist. She must have gotten turned around in the fog.

"Bax, Raigen," Jhee called.

The breathing of the cave had grown louder. Caves, mineral springs, earth gases, bizarre construction. All manner of causes to trick the senses. Add in being primed to see oddities by all the rumors. No wonder rumors of the abbey's haunted nature persisted.

Emissary.

The mist grew deeper. Jhee forged ahead. She reminded herself of the weirdness experienced at the mineral springs. The sigil on her arm throbbed. Jhee thought it was because of Shep for a moment. Shep made it itch or burn. This sensation was different.

The bridge or the sword. Until all are one.

Jhee's ears rang. Her head pounded. It felt as if the world itself quaked.

A frog leaped off a most hideous green statue like those in the cloister and on the edifice. Jhee started.

Bax and Raigen called her name.

"Here," Jhee answered.

"We got separated in this labyrinth," Raigen said, as they joined her.

Bax clutched his thieves' tools. "Blessed Makers, places such as this are favored by bogglies and swamp goblins."

"It's just a statue. The hall we just went through should provide proof enough there are things far scarier than bogglies or swamp goblins."

Peculiar statues in shades from white-green jade to brightest emerald lined the passage. Unlike those on the edifice and in the cloister, these appeared more malformed or half-formed and melted. They moved further along. Raigen, who now led the way, gulped.

"Maker's Mark, that's disgusting." Raigen glanced around the passage her color turning ashen then covered her mouth as if choking back vomit.

"What is it now?" Jhee snapped.

"These aren't statues."

Jhee stepped in front of her. A placard which read "Saheli" hung above an alcove. The former abbess's body sat propped up on a pedestal, her mouth a rictus. Bits of skull poked through the face. Glittering, green coral and barnacles had grown over parts of her. In places, patchy fur and pale brown skin shown where the creatures had yet to take hold. Within a few more months or years, her mortal remains would be grown over as solid as the other residents.

"The 'honored dead,'" Jhee whispered.

Bile rose in Jhee's throat. She recited more statutes to remain composed in front of the Raigen and Bax. She set her jaw and cleared her throat. A chest Jhee presumed contained Saheli's belongings rested at the foot of the corpse. A mix of live and dead barnacles covered it. "Bax, open this if you would."

Bax gave her a wide-eyed stare but broke open the chest anyway. He scampered away. Jhee pulled out Saheli's scrolls, paintings, and crafts, one of which appeared a companion piece to the work outside Lady Bathsheba's chamber. Something nagged at her about the pieces, yet she could not quite place it. Opened eyes.

"Look at this etching. Do the cat's pupils strike you as particularly large?" Jhee asked.

For the pupils to be that large, the etching had to have been painted somewhere dark, somewhere unlike atop a sunlit spire in the afternoon—unless something else caused them to dilate. She gave a last look at Saheli's semi-encrusted corpse. The process appeared patchy and uneven as if a morbid piece of rock candy. By reflex, her hand went to her bruised head. Sights, smells, and sounds associated with her attack flooded back to her.

"You were right, Raigen. Saheli was murdered. We've had our audience with the mother who bears the secret of the depths. Now we need one with the mother who bears the secrets of the spires. We'll leave by the main entrance and drop off these troublesome items."

"My poem? You insisted we come here. Now we're leaving? What about Mr. Akesheem and Mr. Pol?"

Jhee rolled up the scroll with the sermon and Scholar Niza's account of Saheli's transcendence and replaced them in the small chest. She shook out a handkerchief. Jhee averted her face as she collected a handful of the dead barnacles. She grabbed her glowtorch as she hurriedly led them out the main entrance to the crypts. "There is nothing more we can learn here. I had thought Ms. Hethyr would have brought them here or the Corrections Hall as they are the only places forbidden to all. I assure you we will find them."

Bax and Raigen stared at her oddly.

"Your esca?" Bax said.

"What do you mean?"

"It's silver," Raigen said.

"What? I don't know. I must have been exposed to something in the crypts."

"Ours are fine."

Jhee took a moment to examine her sigil. Its color had changed too, having become silver and iridescent. She quickly covered it back up. "Problem for another time."

Her mind contemplated the geometric nature of the abbey again. This crystallizing embalming process sought to use the spirits of the dead to protect the abbey. The crystal coral may have explained why it felt so odd to cypher here. Were they atop some giant spirit battery? If so, what did it feed or power? Was this abomination Doombringer or Baqairu witchery?

They headed back to the room. Jhee dropped off Saheli's chest while ignoring the reactions to her esca.

Mirrei forced a smile. The one Jhee returned was equally forced. She had thought time off the yacht would do Mirrei good. Instead, Mirrei appeared to have gotten worse. Had this been Jhee's doing? Was the trip to the climate-controlled archives or exposing her to substances in the agri-pods too much for her delicate constitution?

Kanto double-glanced at Jhee but gave his seat to her without question. She picked up Mirrei's practically untouched kale and fennel salad. "You really must eat something," Jhee said.

Mirrei averted her head from the forkful of salad Jhee held out. Even Jhee blenched at the sickly-sweet licorice scent of the fennel. Mirrei managed a few sips from the cup of wine Shep handed over. A quick aroma of peach identified it as Tranquility Gold.

Mirrei licked her lips. "I input that I was sick out into the system, and the Makers implemented my design. I'll be fine. I feel stronger already."

Jhee patted the young woman's arm. She caught the smell of the fennel again. Jhee's hand went to her bruised head.

"Foolish. Foolish. Foolish," Jhee said. She hurried from the room. Bax and Raigen caught up to her. She swept across the hall and through the north courtyard. "I've had too many voices in my ear since I arrived."

"What?" Raigen asked. "Justicar, please."

"I allowed myself to be pulled into the deacons' drama and missed the obvious. I predicated my investigation on a false assumption. Namely, whoever killed the Prospectives killed Saheli, and whoever killed Saheli must have killed the Prospectives. Ms. Hethyr and Mr. Pol might have free access to the Prospectives, but even an abbess as open and friendly as Saheli would be cautious of them. Only someone Saheli trusted, with access to her food, and who knew her habit of communing with spirits in the spire could have killed her. It had to be a member of the senior clergy. Many of whom I mistakenly eliminated based on alibis for the Prospectives' deaths."

"Saheli died in front of many witnesses."

"Poison knows no hour." Jhee paused at the top of the Prime spire to catch her breath from the anger-fueled pace she had set to reach here. Once she had composed herself, she banged on Pyrmo's door.

22

SECRETS OF THE SPIRES

~

The High Chamber

Pyrmo opened the servant's door with a look of astonishment. "Ah, Justicar? Raigen? Why have you arrived via this entrance?"

"We've been to the crypts where we've searched Saheli's burial items and seen her corpse. I'm here to inform you of my current progress in the investigation and make an accusation."

"I suppose you better come in. I was deciding if I should have some tea." Pyrmo wandered away from the open door to make herself comfortable in her chair. A tea service and the box of black orchid tea sat on the lacquer table beside the chair. After she waved away some steam, Pyrmo sniffed it deeply. "Almost perfect. Now, what are you going on about?"

Jhee set her conch to record at the most space-conserving setting possible and handed it to Bax. "We've come to make you answer for your crimes. These two shall act as witnesses."

"Witnesses? Crimes? You'll have to elaborate."

"I have concluded my investigation into the death of Saheli. I'm here to hear your defense against the charge you murdered your predecessor, Saheli. Do you deny it?"

The trial in extremis was a few of the responsibilities of rural magistrates such as herself who needed to travel the Outer Reaches. She did have to record and send her records back to the capital for the legal archives.

"Who accuses me of such?'

"I do. Do you deny the charge?"

187

Pyrmo winced as she picked up her cup and spoon. "It's best if I drink this before it gets cold. I'll have to make sure to drink every drop, so I don't leave a mess."

"You also stand guilty of the crime of assault against an imperial official. It was you that struck me the blow to my head."

"Blow to your head? Where are my manners?" Pyrmo offered Jhee some tea.

Jhee refused. "Do you deny these charges? Do you deny you are the Mist Abbess?"

Pyrmo took a sip of her tea. "I assume you have proof. Or is it your habit to go about spewing slanderous claims?"

"The matter of the Prospectives remains an open question. I shall lay out my case if you wish. My primary concern is the location of Mr. Akesheem, who has gone missing along with your confederate, Mr. Pol. I shall show leniency provided we find him quickly and unharmed. You and Mr. Pol conspired to traffic folk and illicit goods, namely skimming and counterfeiting Drakist wines."

Pyrmo pushed her tea aside. She took out a flask and had a long drink. "Mr. Pol is a procurer. He lures innocent young people to the city with the promise of work. Then he sells them to any willing to pay. Artificers. Wealthy patrons. Middle Pillarists…. Medical Protectorate."

"For you as well?"

"Those were wicked boys who engaged in the most sinful of acts on this sacred isle," Pyrmo yelled.

Flecks of spittle flew from her mouth. She wiped it away with a sleeve.

"With this Mist Abbess or a senior member of the clergy."

"Malign practices and the lustful abound. It is their fault for having succumbed to the material temptations of the world, it was their duty to resist. If they had not indulged in such wickedness, they would still be alive."

"What of yourself and your love of drink and relics? It was your duty, your responsibility to care for them. The protection of all under this roof is your responsibility."

The abbess returned to drinking her moonshine with more speed and vehemence. "Celibacy and chastity keep the essence pure. I see no use to waste it on relations with the wicked. I may have failed much and not been as devout in my adherence to all the Drakist tenets, but I hold our vow of chastity most sacred. It is the fount from which the others derive. I heard some of the acts these boys were alleged to have engaged in. I assure you I would never sully myself in such a way. We even had to lock the towers to prevent their misbehavior. Disgusting. Wickedness, though, reaped its own harvest."

"Where are Misters Akesheem and Pol?"

"I'm afraid I have no answers to give on that subject. So comfortable."

Pyrmo nestled into her chair and drank her flask slower. "I'm still waiting to hear why you believe it is I who has knowledge of these transgressions."

"Once I realized you were the one who tried to kill me, the rest fell into place. I was confused by the smell you see. The odor of the smudging stick and spike leaf ointment dogged me since the night of the feast even though I did not realize it. A similar odor I smelled once more when I was struck. Both you and Sister Serra reek of them. In my various interviews with you, I kept noticing it. However, because Sister Serra and the previous Abbess were both in the habit of taking 'seed of enlightenment,' it made their scent sharper and more pungent and them like giant pest repellents. You, on the other hand, with your licorice moonshine and mints to cover the scent of your drinking, had a sickly-sweet smell. Much beloved by the insects. When you called me into the office post-trial, it was the only time I have smelled you in isolation without my poultice. The poultice I used for my headache masked the scent most of the time. The same dressing saved my life from your murderous strike."

Pyrmo's flask cap clinked against the flask body as she continued to drink. "I fail to see how that connects me to the murder of Saheli. My, that tea seems more appealing all the time. Perhaps it is a good idea to finish that instead. How could I have killed Saheli in front of the senior clergy without a hint of violence?"

"Here is where you were most clever. Saheli was not some frail, old woman with one foot in the grave as you tried to get me to believe. She daily climbed to the top of the Bridge Tower to paint and meditate. Having done it myself, I know the climb is indeed arduous. Anyone who spent much time up there, especially in warm weather might like to have a pitcher of refreshments with them. You also knew of her habit of taking brightshade. You knew she would bring something to quench her thirst while she did her crafts and surveyed the isle. You spiked her fruit beer with the similar, yet deadly ordeal oil or nightmare blight extracted from the infected crops. Among its effects is dehydration. To be sure she was quite thirsty, you also adjusted one of the solar panels to point at the tower. The warmer it got, the more she drank. The more she drank, the thirstier she got. Unfortunately for you, a sudden storm blew in. The horticulturist and prioress checked on her and found her alive with her cat lapping at her spilled fruit beer. She passed out but survived due to a combination of her good health and being on conflicting courses of treatment from the physician and the horticulturist. One treatment caused her to retain water, and the other acted as an antidote. I imagined you must have been shocked when Saheli came down from the spire and summoned the senior clergy into a meeting. You must have thought she was on to you, so you set about covering your tracks. You returned the volatile chemicals you used to concoct your deadly brew in the storehouse then ran out to the solar array to return the errant panel to its original position."

Pyrmo grunted. "You may indeed have me stuck at that. These are good supposes but supposes, nonetheless. I suppose you could autopsy her, but I suppose the encrustation process might make that quite difficult."

"Your cleverness failed with the quick embalming. You hoped it would hide the evidence of your crimes. Instead, the preservation revealed it." Jhee set the handkerchief with barnacles on the table beside Pyrmo. "Remember, how I noted the tendency of pests to be repelled by those who partook of brightshade. As you said, the barnacles and coral involved in the preservation process only thrive in a certain environment. Saheli's tissues proved to be too hostile for them to take hold. Even proved toxic to some."

The abbess slurped at her flask. A few rivulets slid down her chin. As she drew her sleeve across her mouth, her hand trembled. She held up her hands out, palms up. "You can't prove anything with a bunch of dead sea critters."

"Ordeal oil has similar effects to seed of enlightenment. If anyone did a toxicology, they might dismiss it for the more benign brightshade. The excited utterances Saheli made before her death. The talking to herself. Your ten-page commentary was nothing but the dying utterances of a madwoman high on a mix of hallucinogens. Your miraculous burns came not from the glorious light of transcendence, but Saheli's literal fiery speech igniting the chemicals you spilled in your haste."

Pyrmo had broken out into a sweat and looked distressed. Proof positive of her guilt. "You are that confident of what poison was used."

"You know what I did not find in the crypts with Saheli? The remains of her cat. It is a small matter to find where it's buried. Under her favorite tree, was it? Another effect of ordeal oil is dilated pupils. An etching I did find caused me to realize her cat may have ingested whatever Saheli had. I may not be able to autopsy the former abbess because of the preservation process, but I can necropsy her cat. Pyrmo you are confined to quarters for the attempted murder of an Imperial Official and the death of Abbess Saheli."

Pyrmo grimaced.

Jhee stroked her muzzle and conferred with Raigen quietly. "She made no mention of Ms. Hethyr. Help me search this room. There must be a clue here somewhere."

～

A Glamor

When Bax, Jhee, and Raigen's search turned up nothing of note, they left the abbess's chamber via the main door.

"What now, Justicar?" Raigen said.

"Mr. Pol. Bax, take her master keys. Secure this and the servant's door, so she doesn't leave until we return."

They searched Mr. Pol's room. They still turned up nothing.

"I must think. This all began when I saw the figure with a mask struggling with a naked, one-armed man. It did not match any of the ones we recovered from the horticulturist. It did not match the one in the image of my attacker."

One of them did, however, match the Medical Protectorate masks from the Halls of Torture and Drenching. Like that one-armed body on the table in the hall.

Jhee thought about the hall and the moaning of the wind and further to her encounter in the crypts with the breath of the isle. She shuddered. When had she decided to name what she encountered? A name tamed it, made it more tangible. Tangibility might also give it more power. The moaning winds became a more pleasant thought in contrast. The moans of the wind? The moans of the trenched. "What a fool I've been! We need to go back to the Corrections' Hall."

Jhee brought up the rear as they rushed back to the Corrections' Hall. Strapped to the table in the dismemberment scene which had so horrified them earlier they barely glanced, they found Mr. Akesheem.

Raigen gasped. "That fiend Ms. Hethyr has chopped off his arm and foot."

"Get him down quickly." The stumps appeared clean, with no outward sign of infection. Jhee geared up for a formulation which blended cyphering and fire drawing. "I can cauterize the wounds to forestall infection or sepsis. We're unlikely to find anyone capable of limb regeneration this far from the capital."

Jhee laid her hands upon the arm stump. Where she expected empty air, she contacted solid, soft flesh. She probed further until she felt the full outline of Mr. Akesheem's arm. She checked the space where his foot would be.

"How bad are his wounds?"

"His limbs are there. It's a glamor."

"Praise the Makers."

"Praise, indeed. Let's get him down." Jhee tried her conch. Low on power and barely any signal. "I'm unable to contact the Central Authority. With the abbess relieved of duty, who assumes control over the abbey?"

"I'm unsure. I'd suppose one of the senior clerics."

"Who are all under confinement. Save the physician."

"We have to take Akesheem to the infirmary anyway."

"She's as likely to kill him as cure him. Take him to my rooms. With Sister Serra unavailable, Shep and Mirrei might be the best healers at our disposal. I'll go seek Lady Bathsheba and the physician at the infirmary. One of them is liable to know how to bring up the antenna. We must inform the local peacekeeping authorities and the Chief Abbess at once."

The Uncomfortable Room

Ms. Anshula's head tracked Mr. Zane as he wandered to the fireplace where Kanto's robes hung. Mr. Zane raised the hem of one and let it fall. He addressed Kanto, "Beautiful work. Yours?"

Shep compared the performer to his co-spouse. Handsome. Sleek, athletic builds. Pampered and flawlessly groomed. Traits they shared with Akesheem from what he remembered.

Kanto looked up from his sketch pad. "The design and construction are mine. The embroidery. Star Mirror did that."

"The cuffs are perfectly shaped. I've tried starch and interfacing. What's your secret?"

"Wire."

"Wire? Yes, obvious and ingenious. The Justicar's feast robes caught the eye. Your work too?" Kanto nodded. "Bold designs for a bold denbe. Doesn't it worry you what she gets up to out there at night? It would worry me."

"Denbe can take care of herself. What do you know of what she gets up to at night?"

"Nothing except your wife found herself in my room so many times, I may ask to be put on the marriage charter."

"When was this?"

"Yesterday. She didn't tell you?" Kanto glared at Mr. Zane then at a handkerchief on the bedside table. "She was the perfect gentlewoman and took no liberties. Neither did I. The blow to the head she took that landed her in my room could have killed her."

The two men sized each other up. Eye contact passed between Ms. Anshula and Mirrei showing they shared the same opinion on the posturing.

"I could not abide a woman who kept my beauty hidden away for her eyes alone or would not let me use my own name around strangers."

"So, you claim Mr. Zane is your birth name?"

"Such nice clothes. And your denme here doesn't look like he has missed too many meals. You don't get a husky figure like his eating kelp and plankton. It requires lots of calories and protein. Your whole household seems well provided for."

Shep tucked a little coverlet over Mirrei who had retired to the bed with Kanto beside her on a stool. She looked paler than before but made no complaint.

"Sprite, I thought I asked you to keep Tunes here out of trouble."

Kanto grabbed Shep's forearm and held his gaze. Shep patted the younger man's hand for comfort, before returning to their guests who occupied the salon chair together. Shep went to the table and reset the tile board.

"May I interest either of you in a game of tiles?" Shep asked.

Mr. Zane rose. The animal handler, Ms. Anshula, held his arm. He sat back down. "Mr. Zane, perhaps you'd be more comfortable on the chair with me."

"Madam Anshula?"

"We're fine as we are."

Shep sighed. He prepared a cold compress and took it over to Kanto and Mirrei. As Kanto arranged it on her fevered brow, she assured them she was comfortable. The animal handler took a keen interest in Shep's every move. He approached her. She tensed and formed a rudimentary base for a cypher.

"You don't have to worry. I am a danger to no one here."

Ms. Anshula's expression remained hard.

"If it concerns you so much, play tiles with me. I find it calming and meditative."

Shep returned to the tea table. He placed his first tile then gestured at the empty seat opposite him. Ms. Anshula joined him. Mr. Zane stretched out on the salon chair with great ceremony. Kanto spared a last glance at Mr. Zane before jamming his conch's earpiece in his ear and snapping open his sketchbook.

Ms. Anshula cast a speculative eye at Shep and matched his opener.

"I know what you are: an augmented, skin-slipper. I worked with some on our home isle." Ms. Anshula jerked her chin at Dari. "Therapeutic companion?"

"You could say so. Is that how you came into possession of your rapport with Itzil?"

"My village had veterans, even those who went through the process you did. They made frequent use of my skills to reintegrate. Their hands did not shake like yours. I heard about breakfast."

"Their eyes likely have not seen what mine have seen. The trigger is unfamiliar blood. Strange environment. I know your scents now. You are also a command female...and an animal handler. If something were to happen, my instinct would be to obey rather than attack you."

Ms. Anshula played as terse and reluctant as she spoke. "All the same. The Justicar did not want to leave you alone with them."

"You're so sure it's me which worried her? Should you encounter Ms. Hethyr or the one who took your brother what would be your response?"

"No less than they deserved."

Yet, Shep was the one confined to quarters. "Consumed. That's the match."

"What?"

Ms. Anshula grimaced at the board. All her tiles had been captured or turned.

"No, that's not right," Kanto said.

Shep thought he meant how he had beat Ms. Anshula. When he faced Kanto, though, the younger man had his head buried in his sketchbook and an earpiece in his ear, brow furrowed. A slow smile appeared on his face. He nodded more and more then snapped his fingers. "Denbe's going to love this."

At last, Kanto pulled out his earpiece. He met Shep's gaze with a smug smile. Shep turned back to the tile board where Ms. Anshula still puzzled over her loss. Mr. Zane draped on her arm, stroking her hair.

"Denme, double-check this for me. So, I know I'm not imagining it before I show denbe."

Kanto thrust his sketchbook at him. Shep reached out. He did not know what meaningful input he could provide on a new clothing design or musical composition, but if it kept the peace, he was all for it.

A knock came at the door. Shep inhaled deeply. No alarming scents. He stood, but Ms. Anshula motioned for quiet. She positioned herself behind the door. He wanted to tell her there was no need. Yet, the doings at this abbey of late justified her caution. One might not be able to tell friend from foe.

Shep opened the door. Raigen and Bax bustled in with an unconscious Akesheem.

"Please, he's not well," Raigen said.

Shep checked the hallway. No sign of Jhee. A mere glance and Bax scampered out before Shep closed the door. He'd have his words with Jhee and Bax later. He directed them to the salon chair. "Here."

Mr. Zane vacated the spot as they laid Akesheem down gently. His sister gasped. "His limbs."

Shep's attention went to the young man's missing arm. Shep's hand twitched.

"A glamor," Raigen said. She poked the area. Her finger indented in the air.

Shep said a chant and marshaled himself to stillness. Had Mirrei not been in such a severe way, this glamor would have been of great interest to her. A quick examination showed the signs of dehydration, but no other illness or injury. Those glamored limbs though needed dealing with. "Raigen, have you any skill in elements or cyphering?"

"Some."

"I'm not sure if this is cyphering or a drawing trick with air. Work with Ms. Anshula to figure out how to undo it. I want to make sure he has no hidden wounds. The limb being invisible will make it difficult to decypher the sequences used to create such an illusion."

Shep provided the young man with a little reheated broth.

"Here give him some." Raigen handed Shep the flask. "You might want more yourself."

The wonderful peach bouquet met with his approval. He took a sip and found himself doubly stunned again. He administered some to Akesheem and more to Mirrei for good measure. They both quieted.

23

UNBROKEN CHAIN

~

Succession

Lady Bathsheba welcomed Jhee to the infirmary quiet room. Jhee's mind reeled from all the death and revelations. She only hoped her desk position at the capital entailed less such frightful chores.

"You look as if you should be the one abed, Justicar. Would you care for some kolal? It'll calm your nerves."

"No, thank you, Lady Bathsheba. I must inform you I've confined Pyrmo to quarters. It seems as though she murdered Saheli. I'm still unsure of her connection to the dead Prospectives, though."

Lady Bathsheba shook her head. "My word, that is dreadful. Truly. We were shocked when the Chief Abbess named Saheli, an outsider. However, it seems as though she was most wise. She might have known about Pyrmo's problem, or the firestorm if she had appointed either deacon. How may I be of help?"

"We need to raise the antenna, so we can inform the authorities. I'm also unsure of the abbey's succession hierarchy. I will likely need you to take charge of the abbey until a replacement can be dispatched or I sort out culpability amongst the senior clergy."

"Of course, I will do what I must. This is terrible business, really. I left court to be rid of such concerns, but duty is duty. How could these scandalous happenings have occurred right under my very nose? Had I paid more attention.... Instead, I chose to absent myself from the day to day affairs of the abbey. I believe some part of me suspected which is why I pressed you so on those three men's deaths."

"Please, Lady Bathsheba, there will be a time for blame, but it is not now."

"Yes. Yes. The matter of the missing young man."

"Missing? No, we found him. It will mean much if a former vizier, such as yourself, is there while Mr. Akesheem gives his recorded testimony. You may well have questions for him yourself."

"Indeed, I might. I have no doubt you will do a more than adequate job. However, I must see to the unexpected duties which have fallen upon my shoulders. Firstly, a headcount to ensure no others are missing."

"My thoughts precisely," Jhee said.

"With most of the senior clergy confined, I must wear many tabards from here out. So much to be done. So much to be done."

"It may seem a trifle, Lady Bathsheba, but the map you gave me proved most helpful."

"Sometimes it is the trifles which mean the most."

"Words to contemplate indeed. May I have your permission to grab some provisions from the infirmary's stores?"

"Yes. Yes. Of course. Whatever you need." Lady Bathsheba produced a set of keys from her robes and unlocked the cabinets for Jhee.

"Thank you."

"Now, you rest here and finish your kolal."

"I must return to my room."

"Stay here for a few minutes and catch your breath. You've had a hectic and punishing few days. Give your head time to clear before you return to your cohort. They'll need you at your strongest."

Jhee thought of Shep's disapproval, Mirrei's quiet admonishment, and one of Kanto's disdainful huffs awaiting her. "I suppose you're right."

After a few minutes of rest, Jhee rose. The prioress beckoned for Jhee to join her in the hallway. "I had another idea of how you can get a message out."

"Excellent. How?"

The prioress pointed to a view-screen half-hidden by an ornate drapery. "The old theological address system."

"Is that a viewer? Where is it getting its signal?"

"The short-range, inter-isle communication network. A holdover from the Imperial literacy campaign. It uses a series of relays. Easily accessible in remote regions. We use it as a theological address system, now. I understand you believe us to be technology resisters, but we have it for the occasions when the Chief Abbess makes a convocation or edict meant to be implemented at once across the various cloisters and monasteries or for group prayer. There are a few circumstances where we need one. They're only tuned to one channel: the private frequency of the Drakist Hierarch."

"You work on that while we see Mr. Akesheem to wellness."

~

The Testimony

Jhee returned to her room. "Lady Bathsheba has assumed control of the abbey for now."

With all these people in it, it rather resembled the docks upon arrival of the noonday ferry. Mr. Akesheem laid fitfully on the salon chair. Meanwhile, Mirrei rested equally as fitful on the bed. Jhee considered them and where her higher duty lay. Shep and Kanto tended both.

"Welcome back, Justicar," Raigen said.

"Did you decypher the glamor on Mr. Akesheem's limbs?"

"The invisibility made it nearly impossible to back form; your man Dawn Wolf was most helpful. He's also awake, now."

"Is Mr. Akesheem able to give testimony?"

Raigen and Ms. Anshula were aghast. "He's in no condition."

"An account of his ordeal, as horrible as it was, and while it's still fresh in his thoughts, is paramount." Jhee turned to Shep, who stood beside the man ministering to him as he did to everyone. He frowned then nodded. "Ms. Anshula, as his dame in absentia, may I have your permission to inspire him?"

"Inspiration? What is that?"

"An interrogation method. It is a little invasive, but it won't harm him. You may observe if you wish."

Ms. Anshula wrung her hands. "I'm trusting you, Justicar. I'll call stop at the slightest sign of pain or discomfort from him."

"A fair ask." Jhee hit record on her conch. It refused with a space too low prompt. Then the low power indicator. She dug a thumb into her arm to suppress the swear which almost passed her lips. She swept over to Mirrei's bedside where she deposited the conch on the charging station. Her skin prickled from all the eyes on her.

"Here, take my conch," Kanto said. "It has the archives on it."

"Thank you."

Music played from the conch. It sounded familiar. Now, she remembered. The refugee camps. "Is this music from the refugee camps?"

"Yes."

"When did you record this?"

"During the heresy trial. Mirrei and I, we sneaked out."

Jhee bustled him out to the corridor. "You what? By yourselves?"

"Afraid some dastard might brain us over the head?"

"I should have told you about that. I didn't want you to worry."

"Shouldn't I be worried? It seems you should be the one kept in this room."

"Was this your way of getting back at me?"

His eyes took on the glaze of hurt. "Did I need to?"

"If you are upset with me, there's no need to take it out on poor Mirrei."

He turned away from her and whispered, "Oh yes, poor sweet, innocent Mirrei? Who we've been looking after while you traipse about strange men's rooms, picking up their favors."

"What are you talking about?"

"This." Kanto faced her, eyes brightened by red. He waved a handkerchief at her. "This isn't mine or denme's. The second you've acquired that I know of. Why not accuse me of making Shep feral too?"

"Did you? Sabotaging my night with him worked to your advantage. Why not go farther?"

The look of hurt appeared again. "Perhaps my intent with tea was to have more time with you in a setting which showcased my talents. My intention, though, was not to usurp Shep's time. Why not ask him if he did it to himself to ruin our day together? That worked to his advantage. It was my day, remember? Of course, you don't. Or else you might not have spent it sharing passion with another while plotting to give me away like a gift you don't want. To be clear, denbe, I am a gift. It's to your detriment you don't see that I could be your secret weapon. Just like you didn't bother to ask me to give up my day and look after Mirrei so you can tend to Shep. Just like you didn't bother to ask me if I want to be remarried. That's your default operating mode. But that's a discussion for another time."

"Indeed, it is. Now, if you'll excuse me."

Kanto smoothed his robes and softened his tone, "Please, denbe, wait. I think you should hear this. It's important."

"I'm sure you think it's important, but others need my attention right now. Least of all your denye because of your irresponsible behavior."

He narrowed his eyes. "My behavior? If you're not being attacked, you seem to be wandering about a number of strange bedchambers at night. Despite what you think, I'd never transfer my anger at you to Mirrei or Shep, least of all endanger them. Never." Kanto paused and took a deep breath. "I'm not trying to fight with you. I think I can help."

"Help? You can help me by keeping yourself occupied while I get the young man's testimony."

Tale of The Low Chamber

Back at Mr. Akesheem's side, Jhee noted those present and had Ms. Anshula reaffirm her consent to the inspiration procedure. Jhee took a deep breath and made herself as relaxed as possible before she began. She opened his mouth slightly and exhaled deeply. A shimmer of air passed from her mouth to his.

"Brave, Akesheem," she said in a mild and comforting tone. She heard the reverberation as expected and felt no discomfort of her own. She stroked his head and ears. "Hear my words, Akesheem, you are safe and in the company of those who care for you."

Tension drained from Mr. Akesheem. His restlessness quieted. When his eyes opened, they shone a color more silver than gold. Like hers. At least, in his case, it was explainable.

"What are you doing to him?" Raigen demanded.

"Quiet," Shep whispered. He gestured for them to be serene. "If he is to be calmed, we must remain calm."

"Brave, Akesheem, please, give as full an account as you can of how you came to be in the Corrections Hall."

"Having recognized my sister, Ani, I resolved to have it out with her. After her performance, I slipped away from Mr. Pol to speak with her. My initial intent was to send her away. Then I heard Raigen's poem. Between my sister's counsel and Raigen's words to me throughout my stay, I was no longer as sure of my decision to take vows. I found Mr. Pol and confessed to him my doubts and my desire to possibly return home. He grew furious. He yelled at me and called me ungrateful.

"'We'll see what the abbess has to say about this. A great number of preparations had been made to much trouble and great expense. I've already received payment for you and spent it besides.' He also explained if I backed out now, my family would be forced to repay the sums he had given them."

Mr. Akesheem's coherence impressed Jhee. Shep and Mirrei working together to treat him must have been the cause.

The sordid tale continued, "He pulled my hair then dragged me to his room where he locked me in. Some time later, he returned. I thought we were going to see Abbess Pyrmo. He pulled me through the Prayer Hall and through a courtyard then pushed me through a door. We emerged into a dressing room with a curtained bed. I had never seen such a luxuriously appointed room. A voice which echoed from everywhere called to me. It said I should join her as her groom as the Father Maker joins the Mother Maker. How could I properly decide if I would know no wife other than the Mother Maker unless I knew what it was I gave up?

"I refused. Mr. Pol grabbed a cane from the wall and then a branding iron from the fire. 'He is willful. I know how to ensure obedience.'

"'His skin is far too pretty and unblemished considering where he comes from. Unmarked, he may be of more use to us later. Put him to sleep where he can reconsider his options: my company or the brand.' A figure wearing a Cheiropthys mask stepped forward. Smoke emanated from its mouth. I fainted."

"At first, he had called the voice the abbess. I thought they sought to make me take vows against my will. Later, while I was stripped naked in that room, Mr. Pol called her the Mist Abbess. It was then I knew they had something far more diabolical planned. I despaired of my very soul.

"I awoke later only to see you and Raigen pass me by in the Halls of the Tortured and the Drenched. I thought all was lost. I too felt like I had been tortured and drenched. Then by the Makers' grace, you returned."

"You are very brave, Akesheem. No one has the right to enforce such indignities upon you. Now, this is very important, did you smell anything when you were in the room? Smudge? Licorice? Accelerants?"

"No—Wait. The lovely aroma of flowers and woody cologne. The beautiful fragrance mocked the misery the room must have seen."

"What about Hethyr? Did you see her or hear her name mentioned?"

Mr. Akesheem shook his head. Jhee furrowed her brow. She closed her eyes and drew a deep breath. The inspiration left him. "Very good, Akesheem. You did very well. Rest now."

Mr. Akesheem drifted off to sleep. Ms. Anshula looked away with moist eyes. Mr. Zane held her to him. Itzil roared in the distance. The sound broke the tension. "Itzil hasn't been out in a while. I need to exercise her. She likes the Zodiac Courtyard. That's where I'll be if you need me."

"I'll come with," Mr. Zane said.

They exited the room with haste.

"One of the many hazards of keeping a bull hound in your room," Jhee said. "Bright Harmony, you may have your conch back now."

When no response came, she faced those watching. Kanto wasn't present. He must have gone with them. She sighed. Shep placed a hand on her elbow.

"Mirrei has gotten worse," he whispered. "She is ill with fever."

"I checked on her. She is young and resilient. She assured me she is fine. I have no doubt you can and will tend to her."

"I *demand* of you little, but on this, as denme, I insist. Talk to her more. It may do her good."

Jhee inclined her head. She pulled up a stool beside Mirrei and adjusted her compress. "What's all this fuss? Think of the shame if we arrive at the capital and the first action we have to do is petition the Soothbringers for their cures. If you wanted my attention, you just needed to say so."

Mirrei smiled. Jhee returned the gesture. "So."

Jhee noted Mirrei's embroidery hoop lying beside her sickbed abandoned. Her smile faded. "This embroidery looks to be your finest to date. The poultice I chided you for proved pivotal in my investigation. It may have even saved my life. Between the journey and the single room, our time together has been lacking and for that, I apologize."

"No need."

"You have your denyes worried to waves over you. You were supposed to be resting, and they were supposed to be taking care of you."

"Please, don't baby me. Remember what I said about your ageism."

"How am I supposed to react when you both behave like disobedient adolescents? What else did you expect? Running around in the cold and damp?"

"No credible source says being out in the rain affects your likelihood of catching a cold."

"Exhaustion does. Besides, you don't have a cold. You have Fresh Lung Syndrome. This water is much too riverine for you to traipse about."

"Hence, why I wanted to see the Soothbringer healers in action."

Jhee pulled a faded, wrinkled parchment from her breast pocket. She placed the letter in Mirrei's chilly, dainty hands. "This is the letter your mother sent along with you before her passing."

Mirrei grimaced.

"She made me promise when she gave me your hand in marriage, I would see you safe and given a better life in the capital. Which is precisely what I intend to do. Will you make a liar of me and shame us both in her eyes?"

Mirrei shook her head 'No.'

"Good."

Jhee gained her feet. Mirrei grasped her hand.

"It's not his fault. I begged him to come with. He didn't even know where the camps were. I knew because you mentioned it then I consulted an atlas while we were in the archives."

"Nevertheless, he should have known better. You're in no condition to go traipsing around the island. Your delicate constitution is not suited for such misadventures. How could he have been so irresponsible to risk your health like that?"

"Makers, you didn't say that to him, did you?"

"Not in so many words. I know about his history with his mother."

Mirrei sunk further into the bedding in relief. "Good."

Jhee patted her hand. "Before you two came along, Shep and I were quite lax in our devotions. I shall go to the shrine and pray to Pascoe and Lashae for you. I shall input that you are well into the system, and I dare the Makers not to implement my design. You must heed me and your mamere's spirit and get better this instant."

Mirrei nodded. "Make time for him. You've made time for everyone else. Now, do so for him."

"Rest. We'll discuss it when I get back."

Bax reported back the results of the headcount. All were accounted for except the criminals, Ms. Hethyr and Mr. Pol. And now her husband.

"Where do you think Mr. Kanto went?" Bax asked.

"Likely sulking. Who knows? Maybe he went to Lady Bathsheba looking to trade up."

"That boy idolizes you, Justicar."

"I'm sorry. That was uncalled for. I'm not in the right waters for one of his moods now."

"Drench it, Jhee!" Shep said. "Are you this blind? What better way for you to think him capable and clever than to help your case and uncover the murderer himself?"

"He wouldn't be that reckless, would he?" Shep gave her a hard glare. A young man trying to impress would be precisely that reckless. She and Shep went to Kanto's seat by the charging station. "His sketchbook isn't here."

"He had been working in it while listening to his conch. Trench, he mentioned something he wanted me to look over before he presented it to you. I forgot in all the commotion."

"Maybe there's a clue on his conch."

Jhee tried to listen, but the room held too many distractions. "I must excuse myself, so I can think about how we are to proceed. Bax, with me. The rest of you stay here."

"Yes, Justicar."

Jhee and Bax headed out.

Mirrei took hold of her hand. "Go after him. Apologize. Pray for me together."

Mirrei closed her eyes. Jhee placed the embroidery hood and box on a stool for when she awoke. She used her sleeve to hide wiping away tears. She paused an extra moment to compose herself. Everyone in this room looked to her to maintain the systems. She must not fail them.

24

THE CLOISTER

~

The Coral Cloister

Kanto paced out the length of the Coral Cloister. He had left in such haste, he had brought no instrument to test his theory with save his voice. Not only that, he left his conch behind as well. He swallowed hard. He opened his mouth then clamped it shut again. Instead, he clapped. He took note of the sound of the echo and sustain. He proceeded a few paces. Then clapped again. He repeated the routine about half the perimeter of the Coral Cloister. Each spot sounded the same so far. He pulled out his sketchbook.

Tap. Tap. Kanto's knuckles rapped against an annex wall. He knew he was being a bit of a brat. But after weeks cooped up on that boat to see how denbe favored Mirrei. If only she knew.

With Mirrei's arrival, Kanto's calculations changed. He was no longer as sure of what his role was to be in their family as he once was. Perhaps he shouldn't fight denbe's plans to remarry him. But drench it, that was his decision, and she had not even bothered to ask him if that's what he wanted. His grandmere for all her cunning had at least respected him that much.

"She'll hate this," Shep had said. *"She'll hate that I'm here. But she needs a more suitable companion for the state dinner."*

The arrangement with Shep had been standard. Kanto was to escort denbe to public functions and be the elegant, refined showpiece of her house in situations where appearances and tact mattered. Shep had no desire or inclination to do it himself. Having, also, heard about the refectory, if only secondhand, denbe could not risk such an incident at court.

Initially, it had been unclear if Shep intended romantic duties as well. Kanto suspected that had been an up-swell from grandmamere. He touched his side where the specialized, seahorse tattoo covered the nearly invisible scar from the "gentleman's" surgery he had as a child.

Grandmere must have up-swelled them as she had him. In the provinces, you sold excess. In the capital, they bought. "*No, he would not just be your companion for events or social secretary,*" she must have told them. "*Make him your husband. He would be your stream to riches. Claim his dowry and then remarry him for even more at the capital.*"

Tap. Tap. The columns sounded fine. Kanto walked the Coral Cloister again as he checked his notes.

How easy Kanto had thought it would be to win promotion to first husband. It took mere moments in the company of the vain, preening Mr. Zane to realize that's what denbe thought he was. A clownfish paddling for a wave to the capital. He understood now he needed to impress her. If he helped her crack the case, it might crack the ice between them.

Why did Kanto fight her so hard on remarrying him? He would find a rich woman, who kept him finely attired and supplied with taffies and cakes. Until he grew aged and fat and she threw him aside for another younger and more fit. He did not think denbe so shallow. One had to cast their gaze no further than her current first husband.

Denbe thought him shallow. She thought it was about the material trifles. It was about respect. She was no longer going to be a field judge. She would have to sit on the bench and render judgment. If she showed up to a court function in ripped, dirty robes and disheveled hair, who there would respect her? If she had to attend higher-ranking officials, would they submit to the judgment of someone who presented to them as beneath them? No. When she got to court, he wanted them to see what he had seen their first meeting, the small, unassuming woman who nevertheless owned the room. The one who made Shep's eyes brighten and sit up straighter when he talked about her and being her husband.

Kanto huffed and grimaced at the grim statues. Scarred, graying like Shep. If grandmamere's information was correct, not spending nearly enough time in the marriage bed.

Grandmamere had known the ways to hook Kanto. She filled his head with tales of a loveless marriage, a marriage of convenience, how he could give her love and care, and most importantly, heirs. What he knew was denbe and denme were not on the same wavelength about everything. Kanto's introduction didn't seem a matter of sexual satisfaction, and Shep had spoken of children and family. Yet, those seemed the farthest notion from what denbe wanted.

"What had happened to saddle such a smart, passionate woman with such an unsatisfactory partner as Shep. If my inquiries are correct, he's barely able to perform his husbandly duties. I fail to see what use Shep provides her that mere hired

brutes could not, yet she lavishes attention on him. She needs your political savvy. Younger, more handsome, more virile. It should be an easy task for you to become first. It should be child's play for you to supplant him."

Spousal promotion might have been an easy task if Kanto spent enough time alone with denbe. No sooner had they consummated, however, then Mirrei and Miramar arrived. He had made some measure of progress. He gained Shep's confidence enough to learn denbe's exciters and dislikes. He caught her eye more and more.

"Don't be another crisis she has to manage. I am the denme. If there is a problem, come to me first. I'll do my best to resolve it without troubling her."

What if the problem was the distance between Kanto and his denbe? Shep's attempt to be a well-meaning intermediary only heightened the problem. Could he even assure himself Shep meant well, though?

"Flatter her. Don't be a burden."

Shep's help always hung in the space between sabotage and self-destruction. Kanto and denbe needed to find their own accommodation. How to assert himself and his needs, though, without adding to her burdens?

Kanto wiped his forehead with a handkerchief only to realize it was the one denbe had 'picked up somewhere.' He shoved it back into his robes.

"Bright Harmony, what are you doing?" the vizier asked.

Kanto started. "Coming to see you," he quipped to cover his embarrassment and gave her a charming smile.

She tilted her head. "Is that so?"

He sighed. "There was something I wanted to investigate."

"Taking after your denbe, I see. I was on my way to speak to her. You shouldn't be about unaccompanied. Don't you know there is a killer about with a murderous desire for young men?"

Suddenly, Kanto felt childish and even worse foolish. What was he doing out here? *Well, denme, she'll hate that I'm here, too.*

"What was that?" The vizier clasped the codex and amulet closer to her body. She tensed upon scrutiny of every shadow as if expecting an Unmaker to leap from every single one. "Come, let us return you to her care forthwith."

She offered him her arm. He paused to consider if he should take it. The vizier was still a handsome woman. One, who were he still entertaining suit, he would not have accounted a hardship to be paired with. Yet he knew authoritatives like the vizier from years having to prepare and serve tea for grandmamere's visitors. To them with their cups held out, he was invisible except when they leered. He minded being invisible little. The better to serve his information gathering.

With denbe, Kanto minded being invisible much. He wanted denbe to see him and his worth. He had not accomplished what he set out to do. If he returned with nothing to show for his efforts, he confirmed his wife's opinion of him as shallow and frivolous. Maybe she was right. Maybe he was out of his depths. He was no investigator.

"I don't know about this, Bright Harmony. I think we should go. Now. As soon as possible."

Lady Bathsheba swiveled her head this way and that at the slightest noise. Kanto rapped one of the statues in an alcove. Tap. Tunk. A flatter thump than the others greeted him.

"In a moment, Lady Bathsheba. I want to try this one, last..." Kanto pushed. The statue rotated inward unexpectedly. He tumbled through the opening.

~

The Cellar

"I don't like this, Bax."

"Me neither, Justicar."

"Drench, foolish man. There's still a killer on the prowl."

With a taste for young men. Jhee and Bax made their way down to the central hall. She did not anticipate having to tell the vizier her husband had run off. Which outcome horrified her more? Him wandering around the abbey a step ahead of murderers? Or as she had wondered all along his interest in her had revolved around money and ambition? What if she did find him seeking the vizier's attention? She would simply have to manage.

Outside the annex, Cheiropthys emerged. From the Cheiropthys mask to the clothes, all remained as she recalled from when the character had taunted her and assaulted her amongst the mineral springs. However, he held Kanto's sketchbook. She gasped.

"Stop there!"

Cheiropthys dropped the sketchbook then turned and ran. Bax gave chase. Jhee paused to scoop up Kanto's possession. Their pursuit took them through the kitchens and across the courtyard. They ran the length of the outer perimeter. This time Jhee determined not to stop until she had unmasked that foul man.

She had to think this through and analyze the best course. With the abbey's layout, if they continued pursuit haphazardly, the figure could easily keep a step ahead of them. The same if she gathered others for a systematic search floor-by-floor.

In the cellar, they turned up the crab-rat they sought. Jhee charged. Cheiropthys fled. The fiend's shoes skidded on the rocks. She drew a burst of air. In the time it took her to stop and draw, Cheiropthys turned a corner out of her sight. The puff of air only blew around the dust where he had been.

She ran again. The glow orb lit tunnels meant she had no source of fire to use. His foot disappeared around a corner further down the hallway. They emerged into the cloister again, having traveled in a loop.

Columns and macabre sculptures surrounded the cloister. She stopped to draw. Cheiropthys dashed between the columns. The blast of air passed by him again. She ran to his former location. He crawled through a small archway in the wall. She squeezed through hot on his trail.

The archway led to food stores. Cheiropthys grabbed a rack of rice and pulled it down after him. Jhee scrabbled over it. Cheiropthys pulled more shelves of food down. Next, a rack of dishes. A few wooden bowls and utensils flew at her propelled by elemental force. She defended herself with a combination of covering her head and wind bursts. By the time she looked up, he had taken off again. Pots clattered to her left.

Cheiropthys made a whip-like motion. Pebbles pelted her. Many tiny without and much force behind them. She plowed through as another shield meant less speed. A small whir came from the mask. Jhee was ready this time. She spun aside and had a counter ready. She used an air gust to blow it back in his face. The masked figure leaped back. Only a thin, sputtering wisp of smoke came from the mask this time unlike the voluminous amounts previous.

Her attacker ripped off the mask to reveal an obsequious face with goatee. Mr. Pol doubled over coughing. He spared a frustrated glare at the mask before he hurled it at her. She ducked. He dashed down the hallway.

Jhee pursued again. His gender treachery and vile assaults upon innocent young men would not go unanswered. She would find Kanto even if she had to tear the whole abbey apart with her bare claws. Had Kanto's kidnapping been belated vengeance for spoiling their plans? Or as Jhee hesitated to entertain, a prize in and of himself. His refinement, his breeding, his gentle nature. To be despoiled by some cougar like the one behind the curtained bed. She had not appreciated him. She shuddered to think to what indignities the more aggressive deviants of the capital might put her poor Kanto through. Mr. Pol and whatever dark-hearted and cruel enterprise he served ended tonight.

At last, she corned Mr. Pol in the storeroom where the performers kept their costumes.

"You will answer for your crimes," she said. "Tell me my husband's location, and I shall be merciful and speak on your behalf in front of the Central Justicars."

Jhee gestured for Bax to circle around.

"Unfortunately, Justicar, I will not be going anywhere with you. There are far worse fates than imperial justice. You don't know the forces the one whom I serve can bring to bear. Look at what the Mist Abbess did to those who defied her. The previous abbess tried to oppose her only to be struck down, too. The Mist Abbess took us into the depths of the abbey and used her magical powers to influence our minds and see what she wanted us to see. She even roused the Storm Drake twice causing the earth to tremble and the waves to rise. I doubt I'd survive long enough to make it to trial. Forgive me if I pass on your generous offer."

Had Jhee seen such a creature herself, heard its snoring, felt its breath? What had she seen glimmering and shining on the walls of the crypts? Toril's resting place? The slumbering place of one of the lesser drakes? Some lesser kin to the Storm Drakes? If the greater drakes existed, it stood to reason the lesser drakes did too, perhaps slumbering beneath the isles. Alive or preserved as the honored dead were?

And once the fancy took her mind, she could not loosen it. Her vision sped down through the rocks of isle's foundation to some vast cavern to where Toril and his drake slumbered until the time of the great Unmaking.

"Please, I beg of you, tell me where my husband is."

Mr. Pol did not reply. More pebbles flew at her. His elemental skills were weak and overused. The bowls were probably the most damage he could muster. She might wrest control of the stones from him. A gesture not worth the effort compared to her air shields which he proved weak against.

Jhee, also, had a more mundane alternative. She reached into her sleeve for the handle of her knife. He proved to have no skill with air. If he wasted his focus on pebbles, he could not deflect her blade.

"You have nowhere to go, Mr. Pol. Please, surrender this instant."

He must be hiding in the niche. Jhee crept down the last few feet of the storeroom. She pulled out her knife. "Please, Mr. Pol, no games. All I want is my husband's safe return."

With a cry, she rolled across the opening of the nook; the empty nook. The yell died on her lips. Mr. Pol had gone.

She and Bax stared at each other. He could not have slipped past both.

"Perhaps he was taken by the ghosts."

"For the last time, Bax. There are no such things as ghosts."

"With all the strange doings around here and then, Mr. Pol disappears into thin air."

"I'll not leave Kanto in the hands of ghosts or whatever else arcane or mundane which haunts this place. Now help me search."

They tore the nook apart. Baskets and masks lay strewn everywhere by the end. Yet, not a single clue of where Mr. Pol had gone.

25

THE MIST PARTS

~

The Curtained Bed

Kanto favored his head which rested scant inches from open space. He scrambled toward the wall of the narrow landing. The Makers' grace alone prevented him from overshooting the landing to the steps or central shaft. He hastened to his feet and hugged the wall. What murderous architect designed such a stairwell?

He heard muffled voices the other side of the wall. He pushed on it. "Lady Bathsheba?"

Mumbled, distorted vocalizations answered him. He pushed on the wall again. He felt no other mechanism to open it. He turned his attention to the stairwell. The sensible course would have been to wait for Lady Bathsheba to figure out how to open the secret passage. Assuming she had even seen what happened to him. Or for denbe to find him. Dare he wait? This is what he had come to the Prayer Hall to discover in the first place, wasn't it? To investigate the discrepancy in the Prayer Hall's acoustics on his own and present his findings to denbe in a manner she would accept.

Kanto had lost his glow orb in the fall. After a moment, his eyes adjusted, and his esca provided a modicum of illumination. The gloppy contents of the broken polyglass sphere trailed down the stairs. A faint, warm glow emanated from below. He placed a hand firmly against the wall to his left and wriggled and shuffled forward. The coral rock walls scraped against his fingertips. He took the extra moment to test each step before he put his weight down. As he proceeded further down the stairwell, he regretted learning then retelling the ghost story of the lost cleric trapped in the walls. He started at the slightest noise. He repeated to himself the nature of the acoustics of the abbey. They magnified and distorted every drip or crab-rat shuffle into the roar of waves or footsteps of giants. Acoustic trickery. That's all it was.

Only crab-rats. Those were scary enough on their own. Kanto continued to feel his way towards the light. At last, he came to a wooden door. He pushed it open to reveal a curtained bed. A cozy fire burned nearby. Golden, glow orbs rather than the more traditional and stark blue were inset in sconces on the wall a giant, single glow orb in the ceiling. He expected a room like this to be cold and damp even with the fire. However, the Prospectives had told him in certain old parts of the abbey, the hot springs ran around or even through the walls.

Deep, high thread silken tapestries in green and golds hung from the rods near the ceiling. Furnishings made from hardwoods adorned the room, luxurious though dated. A cloying fragrance permeated the room combined with the smell of a mild, spring forest cologne, an expensive cologne with an airy woodsy scent only available via special order. Whenever Kanto smelled it as a child, he associated it with inland and the capital. A bouquet of sea roses graced the center of a black lacquer table.

The door creaked. Kanto whirled and ran. It shut and locked as he reached it. He tried the handle. It did not move.

The coral walls matched the color and orientation of the Prayer Hall above. A sideboard contained a staggering arrangement of food delicacies. Beside the bed, a clear decanter of Tranquility Red, the abbey's less well-known brandy, had been opened and allowed to breathe. A pre-packed glass pipe nestled next to an ash dish containing rare, aged smoke root shaved and rerolled into a tight tube. A silver tray bore Black Sea maye roe, white abalone, and algae toast points. The wall had made the passage to the Black Sea all but unnavigable spiking the price and dropping the availability of any products from the mayes of that region. Kanto's stomach growled. He scooped up some the roe with a toast wedge.

The table runner, with its dated scrollwork, caught his attention. He reached into his robe for the handkerchief. The pattern on it matched the runner. He sniffed the scarf. Woodsy notes. The curtained bed. Flowers. Mr. Akesheem's kidnapping account. The lair of the Mist Abbess.

"Please, indulge yourself."

The voice echoed from all corners of the room at once. Eerie screeches and deep rumbles accompanied by weird echoes. Acoustic tricks, Kanto reminded himself, due to the shape of the room and the Prayer Hall. Like the whisper wall. All the speaker had to do was stand in the right place.

"Where are you? Show yourself."

"In due time."

"Please, I wish to return to my family."

"Not quite yet. Soon I promise. Do not trouble yourself. For now, truly, indulge yourself."

The overhead orb faded out. The secondary spheres remained the only source of light along with a few companions on the table. He waited for a while. He took up one of the lamps from the table and went to the door.

Kanto examined the lock. A basic mechanical lock, easy enough to foil even if he did not have Bax's skill for it. He required something long and thin to work the tumblers. Mirrei had struck a deal with Bax. She formulated and supplied him with his lock-picking aides, and he taught them how to use them, including the mundane ones. The lessons their little secret because denbe would have been scandalized. Mirrei claimed you never knew when it might be useful. He, on the other hand, had done it to alleviate the monotony. Otherwise, he might have been driven mad with boredom while denbe tried to solve the world's mysteries. Mirrei turned out to be the one in the right.

Kanto scoured the room for something thin to fit into the opening and strong enough to manipulate the mechanics. He paused to consider how denbe might approach the search. He felt along crevices and walls and bedposts. He had much to learn from denbe. As he had from the hours he spent listening at his grand dame's feet. He sought to find interest in the subjects she found interest in. He sought to delight her with his stylish and bright clothes and his music playing. Some lessons went over his head. Many did not.

On the headboard, Kanto found a slightly raised lip. He worked at it a bit with a nail to reveal a small compartment. A thin bound notebook lay atop a sheaf of parchments. He leafed through them. Names, dates, a few symbols. The symbols must have acted as a shorthand for what they had done that his captor could use against them. He had found someone's favor lists, a potent leverage tool to share with denbe once he escaped. He tucked them away in his hidden, breast pockets. A tight fit as he had not made his as capacious as Jhee's.

Despite Kanto's ordeal, his robes while dirtied and muddied retained the impeccable shape to the sleeves had worked so hard to perfect. Wire. He picked at the stitching until he created an opening large enough to worry out the wire. He separated and twisted the wire into a shape suitable to serve his purposes.

Denbe's house needed him as well. She may have been an academic and not a politician, but it was a deficit he could help her correct if she allowed. On some sphere, she knew or else she'd never have agreed to the match.

As Kanto worked the lock, he glimpsed a brand beside the fireplace. He pushed away Akesheem's account. He shoved away the knowledge of the three dead Prospectives. A beauty such as himself did not come along often and would have been most valuable. The delicacies, along with his capture, proved the villain who held him, had some taste at least. He hated to think he would spend his last few hours with someone with bad taste. Simply unconscionable. He leaned into the lock picking. His pick bent.

Kanto swore. He calmed himself. He was Kanto, only son of House Kenyatta, son of Kaisonia, grandson of Lady Kaydence, and he would not die in some sleazy, underground boudoir decorated with dated, mismatched furnishings. His wife, the brilliant, powerful Justicar Jhee, would find him and make those who did this pay. She likely already searched for him. He refashioned the pick and tried again.

The proper clicks went off in the right sequence. The door swung open.

Kanto made a satisfied sound and stepped outside. A figure in a mask of the bat-faced Cheiropthys blocked his path. The figure chanted and gestured, a drawing. A small rock flew from the ground. He enacted a quick air burst. The drawing produced only an impotent puff which barely perturbed the rock.

The rock struck Kanto on the head. Kanto covered his esca. The figure closed the distance. A white plume of smoke emanated from the mask's mouth. The smoke hit Kanto directly in the face. He coughed. He felt light-headed.

"The playboy?"

"The favorite husband or the wife would have been better. Too late now. We'll make do."

The images and bright colors of the coral spun about Kanto. A moment later, he had a vague awareness of the hard-coral ground rushing to meet his face.

~

The Last of the Elixir

"Mr. Pol is still out there. And Ms. Hethyr. What if they have procured Kanto? He stormed off because we had cross words."

"It's not your fault, Justicar."

"Nevertheless, it is still my problem. Kanto tried to inform me about an issue important to him, Bax. I dismissed him. I should have listened. I should have made time. Come. We must hurry."

"Don't be worried, Justicar. Mr. Kanto probably just went to the springs or to visit with the refugees."

"My hope is you're right."

"Should we go back to the Corrections Hall?"

"No, Mr. Pol is unlikely to return there so soon. Not since we are likely to be watching it. Pyrmo. She may have answers."

When they entered Pyrmo's room, the former abbess was still slumped in her chair sleeping restlessly.

Jhee stalked over. When she touched Pyrmo's shoulder to wake her, she noticed Pyrmo's yellowish pallor. Her skin was cold and clammy. She shook and coughed.

"What did you take?" Jhee fumbled in her sleeves for her elixir. She had used it all on Lady Bathsheba. "Bax, hand me the spare elixir."

Pyrmo collapsed against Jhee. Jhee flipped Pyrmo onto her back. Bax handed her the elixir vial, and she tipped it to Pyrmo's lips. "Please, Bright Harmony and Mr. Pol."

Pyrmo coughed the elixir back out. "This life is just mist."

The abbess frothed at the mouth, shuddered, then stopped moving.

"No!" Jhee hunched over Pyrmo's lifeless body. "She was our last link."

Bax brushed her shoulder in reassurance. A flask weighted down a note on the lacquer side table: "Best not to leave a mess. You are shrewder and more resourceful than we gave you credit for."

Jhee examined the flask. It wasn't the one Pyrmo drank from earlier or in the storehouse. "This is a different flask. She was murdered."

She found the servant's door unlocked.

"I locked it I swear, Justicar."

Jhee believed him. They made a quick search of the crypts. Its mists now made her uneasy. A ringing, a quiver of eagerness filled it now.

Their urgency brought them to the mineral springs. Jhee's heart skipped a beat. She carefully examined each. Thankfully, she found them empty with no trace of Kanto. She breathed a sigh of relief. Now, they still had to hurry.

"Where else, Justicar?"

"Where indeed? This wind-blasted abbey has so many twists and turns and nooks to it. Let's limit his means off this rock then."

After Jhee and Bax alerted the licit boat captains, they rushed to the smugglers' notch. The captain and her crew worked the deck as if in preparation to leave. Upon sight of Jhee, the captain worried her ear. "Magistrate, we were just securing our ship."

"No lies right now, captain. You're clearly taking a lay out while the weather is passable. My husband is missing. Has he or anyone else approached you to book passage? You have seen no one unusual while you prepared?"

"Nay."

"May I have leave to examine your holds?"

"Now, wait one moment, magistrate. I reckon we've been more than accommodating—."

"As have I. No other authority has come to trouble you. If it were my intention, to change that I would have. I assure you my concern is larger than poaching or smuggling." Jhee and Bax did a quick search. They even ferreted out a few false panels and holds, much to the captain's chagrin. No trace of Jhee's husband. "Is the wine the only cargo you smuggle?"

"Nay. We do a little fishing what to feed ourselves and our kin with. Well, and the items what you already knows about."

Jhee cornered the gang-affiliated crewman she identified her last visit. "What manner of fineries did you procure?"

"All sorts. Caviar. Roe. Abalone. Forest Cologne. Sur Dale root and leaf. Jassar silks."

"Silks?"

"Aye, mum."

"Was it always Prospectives who came to procure the items?"

"No, mum. I weren't always required to bring goods in. Times they needed me to send items out. Them times it were either a man or a lady what gave them to me."

"Would you recognize either if you saw them again?"

"Aye, mum."

Jhee fished out Kanto's sketchbook. She leafed through the sketches.

"There, that be the man."

The crewman had stopped on the picture of Mr. Pol. Jhee continued to go through the images. "Her. She wore a cloak what kept her face hidden, but I recognize this symbol."

Rage threatened to consume Jhee. She resorted to counting and statute recitation to calm herself. Under the circumstances, she could not risk misusing her siren module on herself. "Captain, please, might you delay your departure in the chance I have need of you."

"Mum, we tarry for days at your say so while our family like t'starve and we sore miss 'em."

"I know, I know. Please, a little longer."

"An hour or two maybe, but after that, we will leave."

"If it comes to that, ensure none but your crew are on board."

"Ye have my word on it."

As Jhee left, the captain seized the crew member by the scruff and clout them on the ears.

~

Echoes at the Courtyard Shrine

Every distorted noise in the distance became the most horrid cries. What was happening to Jhee's rejected husband? What were those fiend folk doing to Kanto? Gentle souls like him and Mirrei would be mistreated by this world. The Makers put those like Jhee here to protect and keep them. She had failed. In her obsession with puzzles and the law, she had sore neglected both. Now

Kanto had met an unknown fate because she could not spare him a few moments attention. She did not want him to die in fear and hurt thinking they had not cared. That he would not be missed. Shep's mental health and Mirrei's physical health had deteriorated. Kanto felt abandoned and unappreciated.

Jhee conjured an idealized image of Miramar, Mirrei's mother and her childhood friend, in mind. From that image her recollection went on to the complicated relationship between Jhee, Shep, and her. Then settled once more on the image of Miramar standing defiant against the waves. Miramar had wished to sleep under the waves which held her loved ones and families' remains. The same waves which had claimed their home atoll soon after.

Jhee erred. It had been her responsibility to see her cohort safely to the capital as she had promised Kanto's grandmamere and sworn in remembrance of Mirrei's mamere. She had pledged to Kanto's grand dame and Mirrei's dame they would have the best she had to offer. She had meant monetarily. Yet, that turned out to be a pauper's meal which had done nothing to nourish their essences.

In her search, Jhee found herself at the courtyard shrine. She knelt and removed her headwear. She clasped her wrists. "First and Greatest Makers, I beg of you, please, let me find Kanto safe and unharmed. If you do, I promise to honor him and cherish him as I do Shep. I promise to respect his wishes and not take him for granted."

Jhee breathed in the breath of the salt and sea. She got the sense of being watched. The Forebears. *Those in the waves and those in the sky gaze favorably upon us in the liminal realm until the time of our Remaking come.*

Of her spouses, Jhee understood Kanto the least. She and Shep were content to sit and enjoy each other's company. She didn't feel this pressure to do "something." She and Mirrei could talk books or arcana. She and Kanto fought or walked on new crab shells around each other.

What did Kanto get from their relationship other than the obvious? Jhee did not know what he saw when he looked at her. There was the core mechanism of it. Shep saw her with an old lover's gaze, one born of youthful affection and years of bonding. Mirrei saw her with gratefulness or as a successful older woman to emulate.

What did Kanto see when he looked at her? This woman he had been sold to. Sure, she and his grand dame had dressed it up in pretty words and a contract, with other particulars of the arrangement worked out by Shep, Kanto, and Kanto's grand dame. But it involved an exchange of value for him, though not monetary. She had bought Kanto. And she planned to sell him again once they reached the capital. Older women passed men and women as young and cultivated as him around like fine art.

Kanto's disappearance was the same as it was with those missing young men.

We were so concerned with the death of the more prestigious individual, the fate and absence of the less prestigious nearly went unremarked and unnoticed. Another overlooked, passed over for more intriguing and immediate concerns. If some calamity befalls Kanto, I will never forgive myself.

"He hears things. He's very observant. Jhee, he's smarter than you give him credit for," Shep had said once.

What did Kanto see or hear that sent him rushing out into the night? Jhee brought out Kanto's sketchbook and conch. She cursed herself. She had predicated her search on Kanto's foolhardiness. What she should have done was trusted his talents, namely his ear and his eye. To combat the sense of impropriety she felt viewing his drawings, she skipped past any which appeared to have been drawn before their arrival. She came upon a sketch of the household in the courtyard. The illustration depicted her with the flowing hair of waves and seaweed common to the Lady of the Isles imagery from back home. He had drawn himself in lightly as a cupbearer with Mirrei and Shep as her standard-bearers. Roughed in around them were the wall with the abbey's sigil and the arches, pillars, and pedestals bearing several Makers' marks and offerings.

Jhee blessed him for his practicality and cleverness when she found a document entitled "Time Codes." Inside Kanto had recorded names and times codes for audio snips he had found interesting. The last two notes read "Whisper Wall" and "Dead Zone."

She listened to a few recordings of the Prospectives telling the stories of how they had arrived at the abbey. They relayed tales of tiny, overloaded crafts capsizing; the sounds of the screams and then the eerie silence; the image of hands scrabbling for any piece of flotsam only to disappear under the waves to never resurface. Jhee's chest only allowed shallow breaths. She imagined a calm shore to block out the images. She skipped ahead to the sea songs and shanties of the refugees at the camps. Waves and winds crashed in the background. She scrolled back to the Prospectives telling their stories. More waves and wind performed as undertones to their accounts.

She rewound again. The Prospectives stories had been captured inside the abbey either in the central hall or Prayer Hall as they undertook their duties. Where was the sound of waves and wind coming from?

Jhee stared at his sketch of the courtyard. Then she looked at the direction where she had seen the strange occurrence. The wall with the abbey's sigil. The bridge and the sword. So much had happened since she had arrived, she almost forgot about the mysterious sight she had seen her first night here. She examined Kanto's sketch again. In his drawing, the bridge and the sword were joined upright with the sword pierced through the bridge. The same as they were on the entrance gates. The mark she saw now, and on the first night, the sword and the bridge were separated. The bridge was oriented up and down and the sword horizontal. The crenelations atop the wall were offset from each other with one double row then a single. The drawing showed only two rows. It could have been a fanciful interpretation like his sketch of their family. Yet, he had been painstakingly accurate and literal about every other architectural feature he had drawn since he got here.

Lost Prospectives and whispers and music from within the walls. Walls more than two meters thick. Why build internal walls that thick? Jhee consulted her map.

Jhee approached the sigil. It was not single emblem hung or carved on the wall as she had assumed, but two pieces. She placed a hand on the bridge and the sword then rotated it.

"I have become something of a hermit."

"Sister Serra, the vizier, even the prioress, and Sister Elkanah consulted."

As Jhee turned, the sword and bridge rejoined. The wall reconfigured amidst a grinding of stone and dust. She rotated the emblem the opposite way. The masonry flowed aside to reveal a secret passageway. A slight breeze hit her face. From a few steps back, the wall appeared seamless except for the crenelations.

"I've barely left my chambers."

"The vizier and I consulted."

Jhee took up her map and a glowtorch. She passed through the opening.

When Jhee pocketed the conchs, her hand brushed the handkerchief containing barnacles. *"The second you've acquired..."* She compared it to Elkanah's ripped garment scrap. Similar, but not exact. She had gotten this one from Leigh's belongings. Where had the second come from? The infirmary.

The trick Kanto and Mirrei pulled with the pillows. *"...none of our patients went missing." According to Sister Zalver. And her questionable faculties.* How closely had she checked?

The opening led to a narrow corridor which ran alongside the principal axes. Jhee made her way along the passageway. Different colors and textures of stone composed the opposite sides of the passage. One side also displayed signs of weathering. The passage must have been added later. Every few minutes, she heard the sound of metal striking stone. As she got closer, the noises were preceded by a moist thud. Whack-shink-whack. Thud. Whack-shink-whack.

The passageway opened onto a hexagonal room. Just inside the entrance, a mechanized puppet missing an arm and foot lay propped against the wall. Meanwhile, the noises continued ahead. A figure in a mask stood before a coral altar. Her arm raised to reveal a bloody cleaver which she brought down on a slab of meat on the platform.

The masked figure doused the altar with rancid fluid from a black keg. She snatched up a cattle prod. Then with one swift motion set the table alight with godspark. Blue-green flames leaped into the sky. She removed her fanged, re-breather mask and apron which she threw onto the pyre. She spread her arms wide. The flames grew higher. She gestured in an upsweep. The fire consumed everything on the table and then vanished.

Jhee moved up behind her. Munching and squishing noises began.

"Nice trick. Since I doubt you discovered the secret of true making, I assume that leads to a waste chute. Am I in the presence of the Wave Witch, or should I say the Mist Abbess?" Jhee held her glow orb higher. "Or shall I call you vizier?"

26

THE LOW CHAMBER

~

The Low Spire

Lady Bathsheba turned to Jhee. She smiled at Jhee with a blood-stained mouth, a half-chewed heart in her hands.

"I have a flair for the dramatic. I do hope you were impressed." She gulped down the last of the heart. "Now, his spirit will serve me in the realms to come. Lady Bathsheba will be fine. I must congratulate you on finding my little hobby chamber. A gallery of horrors of some sort. I arrogated it for more pleasurable pursuits."

"I'm not so sure if the men you abducted thought so."

"Seduced. I'd never take you for such a prude, Justicar. You'd be surprised how agreeable they found my company."

"You or the gifts you showered them with?"

"Spoken with the contempt of finery and riches only capable by one who has never been without them. Rather than as achievements, comforts, you view my enticements as bribes. They're luxuries these men never hope to possess on their own; a glimpse of a life which under normal circumstances would never be theirs. Fine wines and delicacies. Delights they would have never tasted on their backwater, provincial isles. They were then more pliable and predisposed to the sorts of women they would meet in the larger towns. Once having learned some grace or refinement, they would be better able to make their way in the cities. It's a buyer's market out there. Oh, to be there myself. It is very similar to the learning husband situation most were already accustomed to. It's obvious you had similar plans for Bright

219

Harmony. Was what I did so much different from you? Was it also not how you married him in the first place? I gave these boys opportunities they would not have otherwise had. I was really doing them a service as well as my clients in the city."

"Spoken with the arrogance and self-delusion of every predator I've ever dealt with."

"Please, Jhee, I'm quite a cut above those provincial villains in your stories. Basic competence, let alone, dare I say it, genius, is a trait sorely lacking nowadays. Like Thaedra with her salon of great thinkers and talented students. The best and the brightest who drove each other to innovate and experiment. You yourself can attest to the insights we are still gleaning from their body of works. To be sure Thaedra was no Canon. I feel a kinship with her. You think Thaedra, surrounded by such young and vigorous company, did not succumb at least once or twice. I'm apt to think her salon was as much a dating pool as a place of study."

Lady Bathsheba bent by the puppet and deposited the recovered piece of the triptych or polyptych into a gilded metal and hardwood strongbox. The lady grinned and wiped her mouth with a silken, amethyst sash. A dark chunk fell from the altar with a wet smack: a partially charred hand. Jhee's heart dropped to the great depths.

"You fiend." Jhee drew the elements and slammed Lady Bathsheba against the wall with a burst of air.

Lady Bathsheba laughed and picked herself up off the floor. "You really must calm yourself."

The First Makers only knew what Jhee might have done if the altar were still ablaze. "Vizier Bathsheba of Toho and Wilobeia, by the power invested in me by the dual sovereigns of the Six Isles, I—"

"Please, Justicar, let's return to my chamber for some kolal before you finish your accusation."

Lady Bathsheba hitched up her skirts and walked past Jhee. Jhee opened her mouth to protest.

"I assure you it will be a career-ending phrase for you, not me. Shall we return to my chamber? I need to refresh myself."

Jhee stared at the smoking, blood-stained altar. She had promised his grand dame. His well-being had been her responsibility.

"They say this place was built by an evil necromancer, a rival of Thaedra. I fell in love with the acoustics the moment I arrived. One of the few compelling traits this backwater boasts. Aside from the ghastly statues. Most remarkable. In the Corrections Hall, you must have seen some of the more salacious, sordid episodes in this place's history. I'd say my activities barely rate in comparison.

"Now that you have explored more of the abbey, you simply must tell me what you think? I would love to compare notes. I'm still impressed. I only discovered it myself recently. I thought you were clever. The moment I saw your pretense of sophistication, I said to myself that is one clever girl. I was assured of it once I met your lovely cohort."

"The embracing couple," Jhee mumbled.

"Your cloister ghosts. Yes. Via my blunder then. Your sudden arrival prompted me to clean up after myself. I had been using the puppet as a decoy to fool the bed check and give the impression certain places were haunted. Then Pyrmo informed me they hadn't let your vessel sink as I suggested. I improvised as best I could, but not enough."

"All the talk of malign forces was you giving a good show. The Mist Abbess rumors didn't start with Saheli's arrival. They began with yours some long-months before. With the crop blight and weird chemicals, ghost hysteria hit Torilsisle, and you were all too happy to capitalize on it."

"Quite the contrary. I caused it. You said it felt strange to cypher here. The tremors resulted from my attempts to perform the incomplete rites. I knew I had missed some nuance. I had thought to search the archives again while everyone was preoccupied with the banquet. It took some time to locate the missing start sequence. Thank you for oh so helpfully pointed out part of the instructions were missing."

~

The Unraveling Tale I

Stunned, numb, Jhee allowed the vizier to guide her back to the hermitage. She once again found herself laid bare and belittled at Lady Bathsheba's table surrounded by her terrifyingly beautiful things. The vizier cleaned up as the kolal heated.

Jhee had failed. Her responsibility had been to see her cohort safely to the capital as she had promised Kanto's grandmamere and sworn in remembrance of Mirrei's mamere. She could not pry her attention away from the purplish, blood-smeared, and dirtied sash. Her tabard of office weighed on her like an anchor.

"I meant to have tea ready, but you arrived earlier than I expected. Why so taciturn? I'd imagined you full of questions and more talkative than this. This is the part in your stories I always loved, where Jeja would sit down with the villain and allow them to tell the story of why they did it."

Lady Bathsheba noticed Jhee's gaze on the sash. She snatched it up.

"Ah, amethyst. Bright Harmony's preferred accent color. No. No. No. My word, you didn't think? Justicar, what good would that have done me? He is far more valuable alive. More so than the panicky Mr. Pol. Men like him can be replaced as can men like the Prospectives. Unlike the irreplaceable treasure you don't make proper use of. Your disinterest shall we say in his obvious charms impressed itself even on me. With the care and work he puts into his appearance, it's positively criminal for you to neglect his efforts."

"It was Mr. Pol?" Jhee mulled over the thought. The finger claws on the hand had been dirty and ragged, which could have happened while trapped. However, they lacked nail lacquer and foil work traces. The clothing and the thickened body hair color had not matched her husband's. "It was Mr. Pol," Jhee asserted.

"Hopefully, now you are in a better frame of mind to listen to what I must say. Please, if you have any questions for me, now is the time to ask."

"Kanto, where is he?"

"We'll get to that." Lady Bathsheba poured kolal into both their cups. Jhee did not touch hers. "I am not petty or vindictive. What do you take me for?"

"A perverter and killer of men."

"You have me there. You would already be dead if that were my wish. We need to come to an arrangement. I am being courteous to you because you have been a worthy opponent. You should not refuse my hospitality."

"With all the poisonings around here, you shouldn't be insulted by reasonable precautions on my part."

Lady Bathsheba picked up her cup and drank. She grimaced at her cup. "A little bitter. Forgive the bad pour. Nowhere near the skill of your husband's. My palate's been off since my little dip."

"You mean the night you poisoned us."

"A bit of theater. Nothing more. Nothing we ate or drank was poisoned. Harming myself once was enough. A little fireroot on the fingernail, dab some in your eye or another mucous membrane. Sweats, complexion change, palpitations set in. Very dramatic. I do need to thank you for my daring rescue. The intent was to disappear with you as witness, not drown."

"Staged. Just like your accident before my arrival."

"Not entirely. I didn't realize the archivist was stalking you. I fell into the springs by accident when she attacked Mr. Pol. That ninny was so determined to catch the Trouble Maker she ran after him and left us to die. I'd say that's enough time for me to be showing signs of anything you suspect I might have added to the tea. Now, please, have some. It's so nice to have a proper tea."

Jhee made a show of picking up hers and bringing it to her lips. She was, however, not foolish enough to drink.

"There. Civility. While it is a bit of a relief to have everything out in the open, I'm curious as to how you figured it out. Was it only seeing me with the puppet?"

"'Sometimes it is the trifles which mean the most.' It's rarely anything obvious. Anyone can reckon the obvious. It's the details, the minutiae. Small misalignments are the elements most people miss. Tiny parts of the mechanism out of place create a need in me to figure out where they fit. I sometimes lose sight of the larger device."

"Won't you at least give me one hint?"

"Despite your efforts to convince me you were a reclusive hermit, a paranoid shut-in in fear for her life, it never quite felt right. Everywhere, everyone from physician to abbess greeted me with accounts of your active hand and participation in abbey affairs. Almost as if you ran it instead of the assigned abbess, a Mist Abbess, in effect. I suppose you could have done it via messages. Much like you did with your acolytes. Your appearance at the refectory after Shep's episode rang most falsely. No one seemed shocked by your presence. As if they were used to it. Why did you have keys to the infirmary stores? Also, I never mentioned Mr. Akesheem was missing."

"Oh, so thorough. I like it."

"After Mr. Akesheem's testimony, the brand which I had initially taken as some form of gang marker, turned out to be the marker of a different illicit affiliation. That and the visage on the wergeld bracelets I did not recognize."

"Not only tokens of my affection and nefarious power, but trackers. The 'Talisman of the Wave Witch.' I had convinced them it would protect them from the nether forces of the abbey and the marshes. Proof of membership in my salon."

"Along with expensive silks and cologne. I must have picked some up from your other acolytes. The infirmarian for one."

"If memory serves me correctly, artifice marks were considered the preferred way to put arcane enhancements on males in days past. In order for Dawn Wolf to so much as think of cyphering or be released from berserker service, what manner of implants and trackers might he have on him? Bright Harmony likely has a paternity stamp somewhere. Others put their mark on their property, I put my mark on mine."

"Just how many others are 'yours'? You seem to have hands in every spire."

"My acolytes strategically placed throughout the abbey helped me obtain people, the odd relic or two, the occasional drug from the infirmary or agri-pods."

"Did we miss anyone in your salon?"

"With Mr. Pol meeting with the wind and waves, all dead. I find keeping secrets easier the fewer who know. Pyrmo's suicide and Akesheem's rescue sent him into a bit of a panic. Men can be so emotional, don't you think? It always falls to us women to do the most vital work."

Jhee scoffed. "Suicide?"

"Pyrmo and I discussed her options in the past and agreed it was best. I anticipated she might lose her nerve, so I did it for her. A much more painful end than Saheli's, which could have been avoided if she had done it herself."

"The black orchid tea. So, you meant to kill me too?"

"If you drank the tea by itself, you would have been fine."

"Until you chose to administer the chaser."

"If. Merely a precaution."

"Her moonshine, the tea; a two-part reaction of creeper toad venom and toadstools."

Lady Bathsheba clapped and beamed with delight. "That's exactly what I used. Well done."

Jhee studied her cup, doubly glad she hadn't drunk any. "Why kill the Prospectives? It seems you had found an equilibrium. What changed?"

"Lot Number Fifty-one or the request for it. Mr. Pol procured folk. I procured other items. Rare books and artifacts. Exotic medicines. One of our regular clients asked us to procure a collection not a person: The Eclipse Chest, or effects and paperwork collection Lot Number Fifty-one. Lot Number Fifty-one was a strongbox containing various papers, relics, and a dodecaptych, twelve-part arcane manual, gifted to the abbey and thought lost. It turns out the reason no one could find it was the lot had been broken into pieces first then archived."

"The stolen items from the archives."

"Then Yaou found that drenched triptych in the strongbox. An early arcane manual of some sort. I'm not sure of who the author was. Certainly, not Thaedra. Maybe her sorcerous rival. Almost certainly, someone of the Pillarist persuasion. Keep in mind this structure's history. I was curious."

"With the sudden interest, you wanted to peek and see if you could gain some advantage."

"It was an unusual request, after all. This particular client had always asked for people. What would they want with a musty old relic? In fact, I had two competing requests come in for it. I concluded it must have some sort of significance and that it could be worth far more than I was being offered. I was curious as to what the object was and investigated further. Imagine my surprise when it turns out that I may found the legendary Altar-piece of the Creed or at least an early reproduction.

"I managed to learn one or two techniques such as that glamor before Yaou absconded with it. Along with a ritual, which I enacted. I awoke some-thing. I attempted the ritual again with similar results. It's then I realized the ritual was incomplete."

"Part of the instructions were encoded in the finger maze."

"Exactly. Now, you're playing your part. This is where you ask me why I invited your household to tea."

Jhee rolled her eyes. She knew why. "Why risk it?"

"I had read your requests. I needed our first tea to assess you. Were you a drunkard, a relic lover, lustful? I originally meant to scare you off until I real-ized you knew how to unlock the finger maze. The second tea for you to demonstrate how it worked.

"You are not mistaken in that most of my powers were trickery. While nowhere near as accomplished at the arcane as you, I do have some training. Mostly the parlor trick variety like your Star Mirror. I want to thank the two of you for showing me how to work the manual."

"I can't believe Abbess Pyrmo was a party to this."

"Don't be too hard on her. She was a thief and a smuggler from long back who was no good at covering up her affairs. She and Zalver had been pilfering from the abbey for years. Ever since she was passed up for promotion to abbess. Once she needed my help, I had her. It was a simple matter to compel her to kill Saheli once she had became suspicious. Then a recommendation to the Chief Abbess."

"You were able to assure the appointment of an abbess more accepting of your habits. The only snag was Sister Elkanah who continually wanted to confine everyone to the Corrections Hall."

"Then that Xendatia business. No one wanted Invokers running around. They only make a mess. She's been almost as much of a problem as Saheli. Every time I thought the matter sunk, another piece of flotsam surfaced to cause trouble. So many meddlers between her and your whole household."

"Dawn Wolf had secured permission to autopsy the Prospectives. You slipped him raw, land meat to stop it."

"Technically, the mortician did. Though she didn't know what would happen. The incident also split your focus, bought time, and gave me a way to ingratiate myself to you by helping."

"Not many know what he is, let alone how to involuntarily trigger a slip."

"It's not hard to deduce if you know what to look for. His tattoos. His military service. Knowledge of Toril. An aversion to land meat. Not many know about the last. I don't imagine many berserkers are eager to tell given the results. I've had occasion to deal with the Medical Protectorate. In fact, it's dealing with them that instigated this whole disaster."

"What about kidnapping my husband?"

"The plan was to catch one of your other spouses, the ones of which you're most fond. On my way to finalize the details with my accomplice, who should leap into the net, instead? My personal favorite among them. A sure sign from the Makers."

~

The Unraveling Tale II

The lady was a good storyteller. Now Jhee understood how easy it would be for the sheltered and lost to fall under her sway.

"You pitted Saheli and her former prioress against each other. Just like you tried to pit her against the smugglers. There is where your plan fell apart. The abbess befriended the smugglers because, for all her flaws, she cared about people. She remembered the first duty of the abbey as a beacon. You then used that to frame the poor abbess and taint her legacy, using her sympathy and mentoring of young men to paint her as a maneater. Saheli befriended most of those you sent against her."

"All it takes is one. Such as one drunk bitter, she had been passed up for an appointment."

"And you as the caring and sympathetic vizier suggested what remedy the poor put upon pious clergy should use against the heretical, radical abbess. You made the ordeal oil. Pyrmo wasn't in the storehouse covering her tracks. She was covering yours."

"They didn't need all that much convincing. Despite being a thief, smuggler, and drunk, Pyrmo still felt she should have been named abbess. Between you and me, I think she was more than happy to be rid of the excess males. It almost became a race to see who did Saheli in first. Elkanah, the reformed Pillarist, wanted heretics. Zalver wanted a villain, and I gave her one. Zalver self-medicated because she was once a Counter-Inquisitor with the Invocation. Did you know that? I suspect part of her misses it. She much like you was oh so eager to see Trenchmasons everywhere. Conspiracies always made for so much more juicy narratives than the mundane truth."

"Once Saheli confided her expansion plans to you, you had Prospective Yaou steal a copy. You showed the deacons only the parts of the plans guaranteed to infuriate them. When she announced her new reforms, Pyrmo's lucrative sideline would be threatened as would yours."

"It was bad enough to be exiled here, but to no longer be allowed to live in the manner to which I was accustomed. Her foolishness had spread to even my salon, some were even contemplating taking these silly arcana classes of hers."

"You were everyone's friend and confidante, whispering in their every ear. Including mine."

"The traditionalist and the fanatic in their pride and arrogance over their priceless relics and treasures. Poor, good-hearted reformist trying to save the world. The hedonistic Serra always craving new sensations and experiences. Last, the stressed-out magistrate who wanted nothing more than a shoulder to lean on and a brief escape from responsibility."

"Raigen's recitation about three broken vows: abstinence, humility, and hospitality."

"I specialize in matriarchal issues, Justicar. Those starved for powerful, maternal approval like Kanto or those drowned in maternal affection like Mirrei. You and Kanto have more in common than you think. Empty, distant households where you always had to be the adult. Imperial spouses confined as they were to the Imperial isles have similar weaknesses. Sheltered. Often overlooked and underappreciated. Allowed few if any visitors."

"Except for tutors."

"Except tutors. Sister Serra was an amateur at a game I perfected there."

"Lure them in with drugs and liquor."

"I've been cooking up mood-adjusters since before you were weaned."

"Young, unsophisticated men whose minds were altered by your concoctions would be impressed and have no idea your magical powers were no more than tricks. Then what happened? The novelty wore off, and your hold on them began to slip? You read the triptych and thought here was your chance to impress them and regain your power over them. It worked too well. They became terror-stricken and ran over half the isle yelling about demons. You had to silence them or risk what you had been up to coming to light."

"It's my fault for encouraging them. I indulged them, gave them the finest of everything. A few I even allowed access to the restricted archives. I allowed them the run of the abbey, looked the other way as they practiced minor arcana. You did well not to do so with your husbands. The Sages were right. Nothing but disaster comes of it. Look no further than that abomination they've constructed out there."

"Much better to initiate your own abomination here, by practicing arcana you don't understand. You provoked the drake. Using the triptych like a toy killed Prospective Imsu."

"We were in the Low Spire altar room. I began the ritual, and a tremor hit. Part of the ceiling collapsed on Imsu."

"To cover up his death, you brought him to the courtyard and pushed some rubble on him."

"Matters deteriorated from there. Leigh panicked. I scared him, poor thing, and he wanted to leave the salon. Meanwhile, Yaou stole part of the triptych."

"He wasn't frightened?"

"Quite the contrary. Yaou had gotten a taste for the nether arts. I got the idea to poison him after the second novitiate's death. I used an aerosol poison. I was feeling a bit clever, and it made a bit of poetic sense. One novitiate died crushed by stones. The other by water."

"Saheli met quite the fiery end."

"Happy coincidence."

"Still, murder seems extreme if not wasteful."

"The client is a piece of work. Someone you don't want to mist off. It's why I took such extreme measures to get the pieces back. Yaou's curiosity did him in and Saheli as well. I had the foresight to booby trap the triptych when I saw his too keen interest in it. I turned out to be right. After he stole the book, he tried to get Elkanah to show him how to use it by blackmailing her over their indiscretion. She turned out to be smart enough not to handle it. I was sure the archivist had it until Saheli, and now the prioress turned up sick. That idiot Pyrmo botched Saheli's murder, and she returned before I retrieved the triptych. Somewhere in the ensuing chaos over the abbess's death, the triptych got lost. Thanks to your deft skewering, Elkanah bared her soul in the infirmary where I could hear."

"Here I thought you considered yourself the only competent person on this island."

"I am surrounded by incompetent crabs who consistently seek to pull one back into the pot with them. I would think the abbess's death would be something of a cautionary tale for you, Jhee. No one likes a reformer. If I may give you some advice, stay out of depths you're not suited for. Stick to the rivers and the lakes you're used to. Don't be a waterfall chaser or wave maker."

The lady didn't need to tell Jhee that. Her whole dashed tenure as Justicar had been an object lesson. By the time of her reassignment, she had almost welcomed leaving for the capital.

"Many powerful interests are often invested in the way circumstances are. Tangle with it at your peril. I hope this teaches you a valuable lesson. The next woman may not choose to give him back. Considering your obsession with policies or the law and minutiae, you might have been better suited for a position as a librarian or scribe. My advice to you, given your lack of ambition and cunning, is to keep your head down and enjoy the life of a bureaucrat once you reach the capital. Perhaps find a wealthier benefactor or matron to protect you or else they'll eat you alive. Also, learn who counts and who doesn't. A lesson I forgot once and wound up here. And not a lesson I wanted to learn again. If some people counted and some didn't, do you think I would have gone unnoticed for so long?"

The lady frowned and held up her hand. "Enough. Tomorrow, would you be my guest for a game of three stack or tiles? I'd be interested in matching wits with you on a smaller scale."

27

GATEKEEPERS

~

The Courtyard of the Zodiac

The hen chimes rang from the spires to mark the morning hours.

"Shall we get some breakfast, Jhee? It is so nice to have someone to talk to."

"I intend to see you brought before a tribunal for murder, rape, and abduction."

"My accomplices are all dead. The boys in my salon were more than willing. As for the others... The boys never saw me until I wanted them to, and by then they were under my total sway. What proof remains points to poor Pyrmo and Saheli. Your words against mine, sage and former imperial vizier. In a capital case with such flimsy evidence, I rather suspect the worst they can do to me is force me to retire to some remote monastery for quiet reflection. Wait, they already did that. Perhaps they'll move me to somewhere better than this. In that case, it will be worth it. Though, I will miss the unique construction."

"It won't just be my word."

"Because you're 'secretly' recording our conversation? It would have disappointed me if you had not. I counted on it. Have you forgotten the communications array is down? Your recordings will not be transmitted until it is in operation again. Assuming some unfortunate sabotage does not befall it. It will though be harder to explain your genetic matter on Pyrmo's flask, the black orchid tea, and the poisonous toadstools she ingested. The same tea and toadstools on your writ and for good measure your prints on the case in the storehouse. You must have thought her greeting of you overly familiar. Although, she thought I meant to extort or frame you for someone's else's murder."

Jhee remembered the esca touch. They entered the courtyard by now bathed in the new, bright light of day. The rains had stopped finally. It seemed a mockery after the dark and horrible events of the evening.

"What a pleasant day. I just feel like singing. Which brings us to the matter of Bright Harmony's return. Bright Harmony. Outside naming. A tool of economic control. Your spouses given no opportunity to grow their own names and thus their independence from you. Yet you would lecture me on the proper treatment of young men."

Jhee and Lady Bathsheba ventured further into the Courtyard of the Zodiac. "Enough. How do I secure Bright Harmony's return?"

"Oh, fine. You will find that most evidence points to the unfortunate Pyrmo. The only solid proof you have of my involvement is my confession. The antenna doesn't come up until I say so. In the meantime, one of my admirers implants a simple worm, and the data is erased. As for the copy on your conch, you're going to remove that and destroy any auto-copies. In exchange, I'll tell you Bright Harmony's location."

Tampering with Jhee's evidence register. The vizier couldn't have hit Jhee harder if she had punched her. She needed to catch her breath.

"That's it. That's the look I want. Let's finish up, shall we, so we don't waste this marvelous day. This interference has cost me greatly. It will be some time before I can rebuild my salon. I am nothing if not patient. Slowly bit by bit, I will rebuild. If as stated you consider the deaths wasteful, I can assure you they 're not. I will be much more selective, and I promise to more closely monitor my excesses and those of my salon members. I can assure you nothing else like that will happen again. Thanks to our postmortem tea, I now know how the mistakes I made helped you catch me. I can assure you I will take many more precautions next time. Fate is a cruel mistress, destiny's a bitch, and coincidence is monster. Waves always break at the worst possible point with the wrong amount of force and at the worst time. Such are the vagaries of the sea and the Wave Witch. Now, if you would sign me into your case files."

Jhee held up the conch. Her stomach felt cold and sour.

"Must I remind you I hold your husband's fate is in my hands. You've already had a taste of what it felt like to lose him. Would you like it to be permanent?"

With her heart heavy, Jhee entered her code.

Lady Bathsheba took the conch from Jhee's hand. "Goodness, Justicar, do you ever delete anything from this? No wonder I couldn't transfer my map with the malicious implant. I had to settle for a short-range tracker on the portable. I didn't always know your whereabouts but knew your position well enough to arrange several strategic run-ins. First, the recording of my confession."

She made the delete gesture. Jhee winced.

"That's pretty drenching. That's must go. Oh, yes, that too."

A rapid series of deletes followed. Jhee's head swam. She closed her eyes only to see the image of the blood-stained, charred altar where Mr. Pol met his end.

The lady frowned and then looked angry. "Now, that's just speculation and unkind as well. Gone."

Another delete.

"That can stay. It points to Pyrmo so no problem there. Now, this. Definitely can't leave this one either."

Another deletion gesture. Each one felt a tear at the fabric of Jhee's very being. Preserve life first. Let Kanto escape this unharmed. Let it not be in vain.

"Gone. Gone. Gone. Like words in the waves and kisses on the wind. You are quite the little detective, Justicar. If I had not had so many fail-safes and contingencies, you would have had me dead to rights on a couple things. This has been an amusing couple of days. The most fun I've had in years because of you. No one else could have done it.

"I do hope you won't judge me too harshly. One must keep oneself amused somehow. It gets so terribly lonely out here with nothing but the near tee-totaling monks and nuns. I just needed something to ease the boredom only a fraction. I thought I had it with the salon. Then with the forbidden arcana. None of it did anything. Finally, when the deaths started happening, I had not felt that alive in so long. You kept me on my toes, and for that, I thank you. Plus, the lovely diversion. It was the most beautiful thing ever.

"It can get so boring here. My amusement with these eager young boys makes it tolerable. Valueless males foolishly committed to celibacy. A natural crime, as you said. I share your contempt for the practice. Don't you have any hobbies or bad habits, Justicar?"

"Your dislike of this lifestyle makes me think your retirement here was not entirely voluntary."

"I once taught music and etiquette to the future emperors and empresses. Until I chose the wrong participants for one of my special engagements; someone's favorite son or husband. On occasion, I craved the extra bit of challenge and danger from seducing men of higher prominence. Now I reside on a rock with rabble and caught between two nitwits quarreling over whether rocks or weeds hold the true path to enlightenment. All because a few noble priaps didn't know their limits. A circumstance unlikely to occur here with so many young men coming through here. So wide-eyed and desperate. There are always more Pols and Akesheems."

Jhee scratched her nose. She had begun to shake. "They are all disposable and interchangeable to you, aren't they?"

"They are nowadays. I simply put out my net into the waters, and they all practically jumped into it. They would not have made it at the capital. None of you belong there. But what else are they going to do with you after destroying your homes? You should not blame me, but the foolish feckless officials who put up the wall."

"I have seen war if the Shield prevents it so be it."

"At what cost? A gimmicky boondoggle of a public works folly they claim will protect us yet has done nothing but hurt our own people. It has destroyed so many homes. The smaller isles subsumed under wind and waves among them yours. From the birth defects and pod strandings to the Fresh Lung Sickness, suffered by your very own Mirrei. All so those cowards could gut our military and cede the better part of our world to the barbarian hordes."

"They built the Shield for our protection."

"They built it for theirs. To hide behind like the clergy. To prevent the reunification. To prevent the resurrection of the lost god. The sword and the bridge. Two halves coming together."

Jhee twitched from her own helplessness. Itzil's roar reverberated from the pen where Ms. Anshula must have left her. The Storm Shield. The trenched Shield. As always, it came back to the trenched Storm Shield. "I'd build the drenched shield myself if it prevents more atrocities like the berserkers."

"I met one of the last surviving doctors of Medical Protectorate involved in that. Now, she was scary. I like your wit and your fire, Jhee. Despite your crudeness, in my marrying days, I could have molded you into a fine second. If you are going to survive at court, you'll need to learn who matters and who doesn't."

Lady Bathsheba handed Jhee back her conch. "He's at the bottom of the Storm Light Tower. Have your representative meet mine at the tower steps so he can be safely escorted back into your care. Try not to lose him again."

Jhee contacted Bax and Shep and gave them the location.

"Such a lovely day, I recommend the maye eggs and lamprey, one of the few flesh dishes available here."

Lady Bathsheba gestured towards the gardens. Jhee obeyed. The vizier's overconfidence was earned. Jhee had only hearsay left.

"Lady Bathsheba!"

~

The Gate

"Lady Bathsheba! We are here to make you answer for your crimes."

Ms. Hethyr appeared with several villagers and refugees. Each armed with clubs and farming implements. Ms. Hethyr, however, carried two swords with a series of holes along the blades, wind swords. They threw the beaten smuggler and the infirmarian on the ground in between their mob and the two officials. If they were here, where was her husband?

"Tell the Justicar what you told us," Ms. Hethyr said.

"Leigh came to the infirmary complaining of coruscate syndrome, the code for proper identification and transit papers to the capital. He offered me the remaining proceeds from his medicinal sideline and gave me a silk handkerchief and expensive cologne as down payment. He didn't have to tell me where he got the items from. I knew. The same figure had presented me similar gifts when I first arrived. I was so young and naïve. Seems like a lifetime ago."

"Who was the figure?"

"We called her the Witch because of the mask she wore. She also had another name, though, The Mist Abbess. She instructed us in the finer things in life. How to speak. How to dress. Few of us who graduated her course remained at the abbey. It was too small after having seen what the world had to offer for those of us who had never seen such things. I didn't learn her true identity until she showed up in the infirmary."

The crowd advanced.

"Ms. Hethyr, wait!"

"Step aside, Justicar. Our quarrel is with the so-called Mist Abbess. I knew if I followed you, you would lead me to my brother's murderer."

"The garment. Leigh."

"Yes."

The vizier prepped a cypher. Nothing happened. "Protect me, Justicar. I lied about your husband's location. If they get to me, he remains lost, too."

Jhee maneuvered Lady Bathsheba behind her. Ms. Hethyr leaped forward. Jhee grabbed a tall torch stand and blocked Ms. Hethyr's strikes. The clash of torch stand against sword produced a clank and the wind swords distinctive whistle. Jhee pivoted, keeping herself between Ms. Hethyr and Lady Bathsheba.

"Stop this!"

Lady Bathsheba fled. The crowd hesitated.

"What are you waiting for? Go after her. Don't harm the justicar."

Jhee took a deep breath and projected her voice toward the crowd. "Halt!"

The mob paused. They murmured and looked at each other in confusion. Ms. Hethyr narrowed her eyes at Jhee.

"Ms. Hethyr, I can't let you do this."

Ms. Hethyr flinched and shook her head. "You can. I saved you twice.

Once when I brought you to Mr. Zane's door and second when Cheiropthys and the Wave Witch attempted to carry you off."

"You have my thanks and that of my whole house. Still, I cannot allow you to kill her. She has my husband captive."

"He is already lost as were our family members. Now let us do what needs be done."

Jhee leaned into the voice module. "Return to your elders. She belongs to the law."

The mob began to break up and wander off. Ms. Hethyr covered her ears and glared at Jhee. "Sorcery!"

Lady Bathsheba fled through the arch to the Zodiac Courtyard. "This way, Justicar."

"No, Vizier, wait!"

Jhee had no choice but to follow. One of Ms. Hethyr's blades whistled by Jhee's ear. She spun around with the candlestick and brought it up in time to block the second blade. She gripped the candlestick tighter or else she might go for her sleeve knives. Preserve life first.

Ms. Hethyr swung her wind swords. Jhee edged back from her to keep beyond the reach of her blades. The piercing sound of the whistle increased the faster Ms. Hethyr swung her swords. Her movements generated winds along with the high-pitched whistle. Jhee cleared her mind to grasp them.

One block and defensive counter after another, she met Ms. Hethyr's blades and attempts to blast her with winds. She edged herself and Lady Bathsheba back through a covered walkway.

"Remarkable," Ms. Hethyr said. "You are a demon and worthy adversary. But all this for her."

"She belongs to the law. It and only it will see her punished."

"I overheard you. She deleted all your evidence. She will never see justice, and neither will my brother or our families. Never."

They reached a closed metal gate, the only way out of the area they occupied.

"Nowhere left to go," Ms. Hethyr said.

Lady Bathsheba tried to cypher a few more times.

"Tharos root. Didn't you think your tea tasted a bit odd? I took a page out of your book, Mist Abbess."

Jhee seized control of the winds. She blasted Ms. Hethyr back.

Lady Bathsheba opened the grate to the side yard and slipped through. Jhee caught up to her just in time for the lady to barricade the gate. She shook the grate. "Listen to me, Vizier. Open this gate now."

Lady Bathsheba tossed a geld coin at her. "Thank you, Jhee. I will not forget this. If you survive Hethyr and the mob, put me on your favor list."

The crowd of angry relatives found them again, dragging the infirmarian with them. Jhee rushed through them to shield him. She grabbed him by the lapels. "Did she tell the truth? Is my husband at the bottom of the Storm Light Tower?"

The infirmarian started to cry. Useless. Jhee fought her way back to the gate. She rattled it again. "Vizier, get out of there!"

Ms. Hethyr groaned and advanced on them again. "I will avenge my brother. Even if I have to cut through you to do it."

Jhee dropped the torch stand. She took a deep breath and grasped her sleeve knives. For Kanto and her promise. Jhee's conch rang with Bax's tone. Then the sigil on her arm pulsed out a message.

Jhee dropped her hands to her sides. "No need. Put up your swords."

Ms. Hethyr stared at her, confused. "Pick up your weapon. I'll not slay you unarmed. In liking of your skill, you will not meet the Makers empty-handed."

"No. Put up your swords," Jhee commanded, changing the target of her inspiration to Ms. Hethyr.

Ms. Hethyr dropped her swords. The vizier grabbed the torch stand. She jammed the gate with it.

"Thank you," Lady Bathsheba said.

"Don't thank me. You are about to know what it is to be at the whims of animal appetites other than your own."

An ominous growl came from behind Lady Bathsheba. The smug expression froze on the vizier's face. Jhee withdrew her inspiration from Ms. Hethyr.

"Perhaps you can drug Itzil before she decides she doesn't like your stench any more than the rest of us."

"Shark nip? No, wait, she hates shark nip. You can't do this."

"You have a better chance than any of your victims."

Jhee folded her hands into the sleeve of her robes. She strode by a dumbfounded Ms. Hethyr. Lady Bathsheba's screams and the bull hound's roars echoed throughout the courtyard. Jhee winced at each one. The mob parted as she approached. They let her pass unmolested. Once out of their sight, she doubled over and emptied the contents of her stomach upon the ground.

Jhee read the message on her conch from Bax again. -We have him.

It did not note if they had found him alive or dead. She ran to the bottom of the Storm Light Tower. A group of Prospectives and Professed had gathered. She pushed through the crowd. The inner ring of the crowd consisted of those she had left in the safety of her room. They huddled around Kanto's blanket-wrapped figure. His skin looked deathly pale.

Her heart skipped a beat. Jhee dropped down beside him. "Kanto?"

For a horrible moment, nothing happened then his eyes fluttered open. His gaze focused on Jhee's face. He rubbed his wrists where he bore bruises from restraints. "I've found something new about an official we visited with. I'm going to want some melon taffies after this for sure. Melon taffies and little cakes."

Jhee laughed. She dug about in her sleeves and found a lone parchment wrapped melon candy. She placed it in his hand.

"And little cakes."

Jhee and Shep helped Kanto to his feet. They supported Kanto as they headed back to the abbey.

Ms. Hethyr and the mob had joined the throng of onlookers. Jhee paused.

"Now, you, Ms. Hethyr, have your own crimes to answer for. Not the least of which is your disgraceful treatment of Mr. Zane. At the very least you owe him an apology."

"I had been drinking, having just found out about my brother's death."

"That is no excuse. I'll withhold charging you pending Mr. Zane's input. I suggest you throw yourself on his mercy."

"I cannot face him."

"Try, and I may see fit to see my way to excuse your assault upon a member of the court."

Ms. Hethyr nodded.

Jhee and Shep returned Kanto to their room.

28

THE FIRST SPIRE

~

The First Spire

After Jhee had every healer on the grounds and even a Soothbringer examine Kanto, she remained by his side while he convalesced. Once he had a good meal, she brought him lace root melon taffies along with his little cherry, citrus cakes as promised. He also requested reading materials, namely later copies of "Dispatches from Arrow Point." Jhee, at last, had free access to the archives. She scoured their histories for any accounts that might shed light on what occurred in the crypts. Her search came up empty. Kanto ate his treats happily while he read, and they chatted.

"Definite improvement from your first ones." He set them aside. "I knew you'd come for me. I just had to have faith and hold out. Akesheem and I were lucky. We had people who cared enough to come looking. I think about others. The lost and forgotten. Victims of other Lady Bathshebas and Mr. Pols."

"One of the biggest tragedies about all this is that no one really cared about these men. No one took them seriously. They were dismissed, condescended to, and disbelieved. Had someone shown the slightest bit of concern, their tragedies might have been prevented."

"Isn't that what happened in the end, Jhee? Those who were concerned spoke up for them."

"Lady Bathsheba was right. It was my job to speak for these boys. A duty I plan to take much more seriously from now on. I'll count it amongst one of the many lessons she and you taught me."

237

Kanto snorted. He placed a hand on Jhee's arm. "This past day was nice."

"But?"

"It'll make it worse when you go back to barely tolerating or avoiding me. The only time I despaired was when I overheard my kidnappers' debate. They were disappointed they caught me and not Shep or Mirrei. Even strangers noticed how much more regard you had for them than me. Your history with Shep. The history between Mirrei's family and yours. I'm the only outsider here. You obviously mean Mirrei to inherit and Shep runs your household. Where does that leave me?"

"I hadn't considered that. My long view never accounted for you remaining once we reached the capital."

"These brutes bought and sold men. How did grandmamere frame selling me to you?"

"The Lady Kaydence had multiple tacks. A rescue."

"Grandmamere couldn't wait to get rid of me like you."

"Not that way."

"When you had no use for my savvy or physical charms, I thought perhaps what you needed was someone light and fun. Then you brought home Mirrei and proceeded to pass me over in household and political matters. I kept thinking it's me. I'm your equal, Jhee. I've read the accounts of your cases with Vizier Jeja. You know the power of expression and story to affect people. What is music and fashion if not another means of expression, of storytelling? I am a remora as attached to fashion and politics as you are to arcana and the law. I'm not some poor frail thing like Mirrei nor am I a sturdy pair of arms like Shep. What's more, you respect their interests more than you respect mine. Shep's interest in food and fauna or Mirrei's interest in medicine and flora won't be of any more inherent value than mine in music and fashion at court. The minutiae I value may be the only tool to help you survive there."

"This is precisely why I tried not to become overly reliant on your charms. I didn't want to build false expectations."

"Yours or mine? Consummation, instrumentation, and sensitization decrease your incentive to remarry me. At least, be honest about the true cause of your reluctance. You've always been of a mind for remarriage when it comes to Mirrei and me. Every night spent in your arms secured my place further in your household and hindered annulment, which makes remarriage for gain harder."

"You never answered if you wanted to take your leave once we reached the capital."

Kanto swept over to the hearth and gazed into the fire. "It's so easy for you to forswear our marriage. You're not invested. You never let yourself be. That stings most of all."

Jhee moved to stand behind him. She wanted to reach out, but it would just be too little too late. Maybe if she told him he was right. That seemed inadequate, as well. She balled up her hands and remained paralyzed by insecurity.

"'Don't be another problem she has to fix.' I've tried to play along with this idea you have of me as some empty-headed libertine. Perhaps I shouldn't have. It only seems to make things worse. You know you never had that way of undressing me with your eyes the way most of those who visited the grand dame did. I liked that about you. You literally liked your little obscure facts and figures, and it didn't matter what I looked like. I'm not sure if I'd ever experienced that before. When you visited our house to meet, I thought, me, you made a straight shark-line for our private antiquities collection. You were so adorable and awkward. Here you were, an accomplished official who had spent time at the capital, and you were so out of your depth but down to earth. Your head so full of facts and figures so full of the minutiae. That's how I first knew and saw the person who Shep described to grandmamere. I must admit to having been smitten. I decided then and there on the spot, I would marry you. Even if grandmamere decided against it. Do you know while she did want me to have a love match, she hedged her bets? She let it be known your house and mine might be coming to an arrangement."

"Plenty of takers I have no doubt."

"Plenty, too many to count. It was a bit of a frenzy for a while."

"No doubt, you could have done better than me."

"There you would be wrong; I could *never* have done better than you, because you were *my* choice from the very beginning, from the moment I saw you. Not grandmamere's, not Shep's. *My* choice. I know grandmamere, though. If she disapproved, she'd have found a way to convince me otherwise and make me believe it was my idea." Kanto hugged himself. "Jhee, where was this flattery months ago when it might have made a difference?"

"I don't know. I was just blind to your strengths, I suppose."

"I think it's more you don't reckon what I excel at as strengths."

"You know me so much better than I know you."

"Most assuredly from your lack of trying. Here, Jhee." Kanto produced a slim, leather notebook from an inner pocked and gave it to Jhee. "This is how the vizier kept herself protected. I planned to use these as part of my independence kit. Without me, you're liable to require them more than I."

"Favor lists?"

"Lady Bathsheba's. I've done my best to decipher them. I found them in that awful room she held me in along with her boudoir journal, where she rated the various merits of the men she 'seduced.' The possibility remains they are decoys or fakes so exercise caution if you choose to use them. Consider them a parting gift from me."

"I cannot even begin to account for all the ways I've wronged you as your denbe."

"You did the best you could."

"Thank you. May I give you a parting gift as well? Gift for Gift rather than Make for Make."

"As you like. Any gifts given I intend to keep, including clothes and other finery. The only matter I'll account you stingy is in your affections. Your other attentions were quite lavish."

"I thought you would want this. I should have given it to you long before this."

Jhee pulled out the cloth-wrapped bundle she had debated giving him so many times. The moment had never seemed right. Now, she no longer feared the gift might give the wrong impression. Since signs pointed to this being her last opportunity, now made as an appropriate a moment as any. She unwrapped the unadorned, freshly repaired music box and presented it to him.

Kanto's eyes went brilliant gold, bathing his face in a warm light. "Mamere's music box. It was smashed. Irreparable."

"With an isle full of Earth Adepts and enough motivation, even the most broken items may be fixed."

Jhee gingerly passed the music box to Kanto. He opened it and wound the tiny key. Bright, tinkly notes of an old melody filled the alcove. He choked back a sob.

Tears brimmed in his eyes. "Before she grew bitter and sick, I would curl up in her lap, and nestle my head under her chin. She would pick up the music box and turn the crank. The bright tinkly melody would float out. Thank you."

"Would you like to take the waters or a walk in the orchards? You and me. No one else. Right now."

"Include the Storm Light Tower, and I'll consider it."

Stairs and heights overlooking breakers. Jhee noted his folded arms. "Agreed."

~

The Dismantler's Deal

Jhee and Kanto walked through the Annex. Jhee's hands remained tucked into the sleeves of her robes while Kanto clasped his behind his back. "The building's structure, no doubt created with the tenets of sacred geometry in mind, played several visual and auditory tricks on the unsuspecting visitor," Jhee said.

"The Lady Bathsheba, armed with her theoretical music knowledge, was uniquely equipped to recognize and take advantage of it."

Jhee untucked her hands to initiate contact, then tucked them away again. "You were uniquely able to as well."

They concluded their walk on the storm light's observation deck and paused to watch the dual suns set. Jhee held back from the edge. Kanto offered her his hand. Gently, he eased her closer to the rail. Jhee gasped at the sight of the suns dipping below the horizon. They tightened their clasped hands.

"I asked one boon of Shep before he presented me to you. Non-negotiable. Tell me everything you love about her. I merely wished for you to view me with an inkling of the desire you have for him or even the way you do books in the library. I had hoped to substitute desire for respect. I am highly concerned with art and aesthetics. Pursuits you consider frivolous. I do understand weighty topics. Do you know the price my grand dame negotiated with Shep?"

It had not been money or wealth. Shep had the run of those. They had not decreased with Kanto's arrival. "Nothing monetary. He is a good diver."

"A bunch of sea meat is what you think you're worth?" Kanto sighed and shook his head. "You."

Jhee's mouth opened in shock. "Me?"

"He told her stories about you. She listened to the affection in his words. Her house is waning. Grandmere could have leveraged me. She had opportunities to make arrangements with wealthier, more prestigious houses. Such arrangements are fickle and subject to whim. I am young and beautiful. Now. What happens to me, once they are bored or someone more youthful or attractive catches their eye? My only hope was to have given them favored daughters. My grand dame may have been tough as fellstones, but she loved me. Rather than barter me like a commodity to save her house, she arranged marriage to someone kind and fair. Someone who might come to love me. Someone who would be as committed to me as I would be to her."

"I did not know."

"You thought all I cared about was the trinkets and baubles. My mother had no female heirs. My idiot cousins have already blown through their inheritances and are waiting for grandmamere to die. I wanted to help you build your house. I've done my level best to meet you where you are. Shep does not play the game as well as I do. He does realize what you do not. It must be played regardless. You need someone better at it than you two. From the questions he asked, I inferred my purpose. When you took in Mirrei, it strengthened my resolve to nurture this house. You demonstrated both your pragmatism and your generous spirit. Giving the daughter of your childhood friend a better life. Giving yourself a female heir for your holdings should you have no daughters."

"You never wanted to be married to a provincial official."

"Stop assuming you know my mind. Ask. What effort have you taken to get to know me? No, you assumed based on appearance. You did it to me, and those at court are going to do it to you."

"'Drown him in jewels and finery. Don't let him sit alone in a big empty house by the bedside of another dying woman.'"

"Grandmamere had just started using the chair before Shep's visit. She had a health scare."

"She said she fell on her way to religious devotions."

"She tried to feed me that hook too. She fell while visiting her lover."

"I suspect she'll outlive us all." Jhee ran her hands over the favor lists. "How would you do it?"

"Do what?"

"Test to see if the favor lists are fake."

"Call in a random marker. Nothing too big to guard against the list being authentic. Our dear departed vizier must have been embroiled in a massive scandal. These contain some powerful individuals. Court officials. Imperials."

"Either what she did was to someone of such stature, no one in that list could save her. Or of such a heinous nature, exile was her best outcome."

"Precisely. There's hope for you yet."

"We could exchange political lessons for arcana lessons."

"Do you not want to teach cyphering lessons, or do you not want to teach me? You haven't hesitated to teach strangers."

"Do you really want them? Or is it just a way to flatter me?"

"I've wondered what it would be like to learn. It is prudent to have options."

"I thought of something else we could do with these and her journals. Would we be able to track down where she sent the men she trafficked? Kanto, I don't know if there will ever be love between us. I will promise to no longer keep you at arm's length. I further promise to work harder to demonstrate the value and respect I have for you as a person. I'll first start with saying, 'Thank you.' Your skill and eye for details helped me dismantle the Mist Abbess's whole scheme."

"I suppose that's a start."

Kanto extended both hands toward Jhee's face. She stepped forward, and they briefly touched escae.

~

The Ferry

Jhee pushed open the doors leading to the docks. Sunlight and sea spray caressed her face. She breathed deep of the beautiful tang of the sea air. For the first time since their arrival, her sinuses were clear and her headache a memory. Eternal silence and the First Makers' curses to whoever designed this abbey. She swore by everything Made she might godspark the next person who so much as uttered stairs.

The foghorn for the ferry sounded. Between the weather and the uproar, the repairs to their travel yacht were still underway. However, if they delayed any longer, they would be late for festival season. The prioress followed her towards the dock.

"Thank you, Justicar, for all you have done on behalf of the abbey. I shall take over the running of the abbey until a new abbess is appointed."

"Think nothing of it. I shall tell the Chief Abbess she could do a lot worse than to perhaps appoint you."

"All honors to you, Justicar. You are most kind and gracious."

"I merely did my duty as an official of the court. Perhaps even my duty under the First Makers."

The prioress signaled a nearby Prospective to bring over the Eclipse Chest. "Here, Justicar, take this with you."

"Perhaps much grief and suffering would have been prevented if it were destroyed."

"Saheli wouldn't have wanted knowledge and history destroyed any more than you, especially on her account. However, it doesn't belong here. The temptation is too great. Raigen was right to mock us. Our order had three sacred tenets, vows to which we were to cling before all others: humility, chastity, and charity. We flouted them all with glee. We have already proved ourselves unworthy to safeguard them. You may be able to find them a better home in the capital."

"I'll consider the chest and its contents on indefinite loan."

Other lay folk loaded a supply of Tranquility Gold wine along with samples of the wild yeast cultures.

"Don't worry. Here's the bill. After all, that was the offer you made at the feast correct?"

Jhee steeled herself. She had seen the market prices for their increasingly rare noble blend. They might need to cart her to the infirmary once she saw this invoice. They should name it after her for the amount she was going to have to shell out. Jhee opened the receipt. A huge smile spread across her face.

The prioress grinned for the first time Jhee had ever seen. "I calculated the market rate for the wines and fees versus the industry standard for the services you rendered us."

Lay people loaded their belongings onto the ferry. Jhee tucked the small chest containing the relics, sermon, and triptych under her arm. The litter arrived bearing Jhee's younger spouses accompanied by Shep who had chosen to walk. Mirrei's fever had broken sometime during the night. The abbey's select blend had indeed worked wonders. And Jhee now had a container of both that and their traditional nectar to study or sample as needs be. The two couples, Mr. Zane and Ms. Anshula, Raigen and Mr. Akesheem, came down the stairs behind them to see Jhee and her entourage off. Ms. Anshula clasped forearms with Shep. She passed a vial to him which he pocketed.

"Are you sure we can't see you to the capital or perhaps another isle?" Jhee asked.

"No," Mr. Akesheem said. "I left home to find my way, and I have. Raigen has promised we shall build a new home and new birthline together."

"I have made similar promises to Mr. Zane. We shall go forth as a group of bright and brave companions to make our fortunes in the world. We will honor our parents and see their sacrifices earn dividends through our prosperity."

Jhee smiled. "I've often wondered at the romantic ideals of the young. You have restored my hope that indeed, romance has not died even in these changing times. I wish you all the luck and blessings the First Makers will see fit to have me give you."

Bax arrived.

"Is it done?" Jhee asked.

"Yes. The solar arrays have been recharged, and the communications array restored. You may transmit soon."

"Alas, what remains of my report to Central Authority isn't enough for Lady Bathsheba's full crimes to be known."

"Do you anticipate trouble?"

"Perhaps. Which is why I sent a copy of my report of the fate of a certain vizier to Jeja and asked for advice. She has agreed to act as my advocate should anyone become too curious about it. I also learned that she wasn't the only one to shed shark's tears at the news. She said, 'You should have spoken to me first, Jhee. I could have told you Bathsheba was a well-known predator.' Which leaves the matter of you."

"Me?" Bax stepped back and asked, "What?"

Jhee folded her arms and grinned. "I thought I set you to follow Raigen, not work with her."

"She... caught me." Jhee heard the hitch of wounded pride. Indeed, catching the infamous Shadowcat during his crime spree had required some cleverness on her part.

Dari barked. Itzil emitted a chastened yelp. Her harness clanked as Dari herded her away from the ferry and the gathered people. Despite Lady Bathsheba's fate, the much larger bull hound remained a comical sight being harried by a dog a fraction of its size. Jhee read through her report again.

"Lady Bathsheba met with an unfortunate accident while wandering around the cloister. She ventured out too soon having thought the storm ended and took a wrong turn into the courtyard where Itzil was housed. The frightened creature on edge because of the weather mauled her to death. Ms. Anshula, I will, of course, have to fine you for improper housing of and failure to secure Itzil, a dangerous animal, properly. If the family and friends of Lady Bathsheba wish for further redress, they can take up the matter with the courts. She likely had to renounce any outside family to retire here, and with the Sanctuary statutes in effect standing will be difficult to establish. A solid case can be made that only the Drakist Order and the abbess has standing to do so."

With Jhee's conch charged and no longer low on space, she transferred over Mr. Akesheem's testimony. The two critical pieces of evidence she had, namely Pyrmo's confession and his witness account had no explicit mention of the vizier. She had to classify Leigh's death under accident and negligence. A tricky descent, at night, in a hurry, weak frame of mind, during a storm. Yet, he would not have been out on such a miserable night if the vizier were not after him.

The litter was brought aboard the ferry. Jhee waited on the dock until all her retinue had boarded.

Jhee turned to Shep. "What did Ms. Anshula give you?"

"Some of Itzil's bioplasm."

She glanced down at her conch and all the messages that had flooded in once she had proper access to off-isle communication. Among them, the confirmation of their reservation at the resort run by an old schoolmate of hers. "Are you sure you don't want to come with us?"

"I want to stay here a little longer and get my head right. I'm not fit company for festivals, right now. I'll go on ahead to the capital and get the house set up while you and the denyes bond."

Jhee paused. People surrounded them, least of all the younger spouses. Her hands itched to pull Shep close. A gesture utterly inappropriate in such a public venue. She knew Kanto, in particular, to be sensitive how much affection she showed Shep.

When Jhee turned back to the ferry, Mirrei and Kanto watched her with eager expressions. They both nodded. Propriety be drenched, Jhee and Shep indulged in a public display of affection by touching escae. Mirrei and Kanto grinned.

"You are wind and waves, my lady of the Isles," Shep said.

"Beloved cohort are we ready to cast off?"

"Your timetable is our timetable," Kanto said.

"As you lead, we follow," Mirrei said.

Jhee smiled. She stood near the prow of the yacht as they pushed off. She took a last look at the abbey with its many spires and congruous frogman's antenna. The hothouse and the fields of sun panels. She stared at the statues adorning the edifice of the abbey. This was one way to prevent them from becoming mist wights, wisps, or part of the region's fog. She shuddered. After her experience in the crypts, she could not help it. She studied one after another to see if she could pick out which of the gruesome figures were honored or fettered dead or mere imaginative fancies. She waved at the couples until they had passed from sight. She smiled. All in a day's work.

Kanto and Mirrei held her arms. Jhee would not break her promise to Miramar nor Kanto's grand dame. *I will fulfill the promise I made to their dames to see them safely to the capital where they can decide for themselves what it is they want.*

"Kanto, you mentioned not liking our robes. Would you be opposed to designing us new ones?"

"I would love nothing more. I've been waiting for you to ask."

Vast waters of enormous change lay ahead. Who knew where they might land? What Jhee knew is her household must stay vigilant in the trying times to come at court. They set sail for the trials and intrigues of the capital.

The End: Book 1

Please, consider leaving an honest review on the bookseller's website, Goodreads, or BookBub so others can discover Justicar Jhee—and tell all your friends to download a copy as well.

ACKNOWLEDGMENTS

Adam C., Anne K., Molly K., Val A.

Justicar Jhee
and the
Hole in the World

-The Justicar Jhee Mysteries Book 2-

by Trevol Swift

To my mother and sisters for all those books they left laying around the house.

1
————

THE WELCOME

~

The Maid of the Mists

Jhee pointed the viewer at the stately villa where they would holiday for the next long-tides as artisans finished the last bit of construction on their new home on the capital island. She brought the viewer down so Shep, her senior husband, could see her face. "Our ferry arrived without incident, and we are safely at the resort. I wish you were here with us," she said.

Shep frowned. "Non-stop social engagements? I'll pass. You're in Kanto's world now. Allow him to show you around. This will give you more time with him in his element. It'll do you and him good to spend more time together especially in an environment that showcases his talents."

"It won't stop me from missing you anyway."

"Ether crest life never suited me, but it's cut to fit for Kanto. You three need time together without me. Besides, someone needs to oversee the final work on our new home, so it's ready for your arrival. You'll be so busy with balls and parties you won't even notice."

"Don't remind me."

"Jhee, it'll be fine. Between them, I'm confident they'll see you don't make a fool of yourself."

Jhee spun to capture the rest of the private island off the cape's view of Straya, the largest island in the Blessed Isles, even larger than the capital isle. A few buildings from Galleon City towered in the distance. She ended on the magnificence of the ocean and the harbor, a combination of both Makers' and mortal achievements.

Kanto and Mirrei approached. "Is that our absent, boring, old *denme* who'd rather babysit a house than ride the high crests with us?"

"Correction: who'd rather babysit a house than babysit you."

Kanto made the childish gesture of pressing his nose. "Fine. Then every stick of furniture must be precisely where I specified and every possession as I outlined or else I'll blame you."

"A fair turn," Shep said.

This was the first time Jhee recalled Shep not being there to act as a buffer or point of friction.

Kanto had spent days laboring and poring over manuals and catalogs and images of furniture. He would see their new home brightly and gaily and fabulously and opulently appointed.

Jhee had the utmost confidence in his design skills. He would know what every stick of furniture and window treatment would convey about their situation. They had spent their night together going over it extensively. He quizzed her on what impression she wanted their home to communicate to visitors. Jhee did not much care herself, but it made him happy. She wanted him to feel fulfilled and tasks like this delighted him. He vowed to make their new home convey the tone and image she wanted while also remaining stylish and opulent as befitted her rank.

"I've seen images of places like this. In my grandmere's day, this was all the rave. A stay at a posh resort, then you motor up to the capital and stay at your own place or rent a townhouse during festival season."

Jhee tried not to think too hard about what that said about her taste or her age.

Lady Delphine, their host, awaited them atop the sandstone and seashell steps to the entryway. Jhee held out her hands. "Oh, Lady Delphine, thank you again for hosting me and my cohort."

Delphine clasped her forearms, then pressed each temple against Jhee's. "Oh, you old fool. Come here. Come here. Shame on you for thinking to slip through our waters without a visit. So good to see you. It's the least I can do for the help you gave me when we were in the academy together. I couldn't believe it when you told me you had expanded your household. When do I get to meet the rest of your welcome entourage?"

"Momentarily. Shep sends his regards. He's overseeing the final transport of our belongings from the barges to our new home."

"How regretful. He will join us later, I hope."

"He'll do his best. Shep isn't much for the festival scene."

"Ah. I won't press." Lady Delphine linked her arm with Jhee's. "About those other matters we discussed, have you mulled them over?"

"While the situation has been a little hectic, I gave your proposal some thought. Let's see how the stay goes before making any final decisions."

Lady Delphine cleared her throat and glanced from side to side. "And the last matter? The death of the mining supervisor?"

"I had no immediate conclusions to draw from what you told me. I might have a better idea once I've examined the work sites."

"You will be discrete?"

"As much as I can be."

Liveried barbarian porters bustled by them and picked up their trunks and suitcases. Mirrei held Kanto's arm as they ascended the broad stairs of the front of the island resort. Mirrei had a figure slenderer and daintier than her mother at that age. Her gossamer champagne traveling robe hid her delicate steps. She appeared to glide up to meet them. The pale complexion to her fuzzy skin along with her light gown gave her ascent an ethereal quality. It reminded Jhee of the stories of the Maid of the Mists. Right near the top, Mirrei's steps faltered. She coughed and turned red. Kanto held her steady.

Jhee offered her arm and helped Mirrei up the mansion's broad steps. "You should have let me secure a mobility chair or litter for you."

"Nonsense, *denbe*," Kanto said. "Poor Mirrei didn't want all that fuss."

Mirrei cut Kanto a brief look. "My fellow spouse is right, denbe. What would your friend think of me if I can't manage the simple task of walking up the stairs?"

And any situation Jhee might later wish for them. "As you wish, my... dear," Jhee said, trying a less formal term.

Both Kanto and Mirrei pulled a face. Mirrei smiled wanly and gave a slight shake of her head. Jhee agreed. Too much. Jhee had only said it to please. Her affection for her had not become even that deep yet. It was an insult to Mirrei to pretend otherwise. She rushed to amend herself. "As you wish, my wife."

"Thank you, denbe."

"Yes, thank you, denbe," Kanto repeated. He smirked. Those two and their teasing.

"Will I have to separate you two?"

"No," Mirrei said.

The three of them finished their graceful ascent to the landing. Misty rain had replaced the torrential downpour which plagued most of their journey. The island resort rested far enough away from the storm curtain to experience lessened effects from its significant weather disturbances. Once the storm curtain stabilized, even the drizzle might stop.

Hopefully, the drier weather would ease some symptoms from Mirrei's Fresh Lung Sickness. The less saline waters of the inner islands did not agree with many. Mirrei, like Kanto and Jhee, was used to the saltier waters of the Far Reaches. Though, their Fresh Lung Sickness had come and gone rapidly. The damp also did not help. Much like the storms, hopefully, the younger woman's condition would stabilize.

Jhee checked her pockets to see if she had any saline tablets on her. Even if they did not have to manage her saline levels and ensure her diet heavy in rock salt, Mirrei never had the hardiest constitution to begin with, according to her mother.

Miramar, Mirrei's mother, had had a difficult pregnancy. Mirrei had been Miramar's only child. A miracle child, much like Kanto. That may have been why the two spouses had bonded so quickly. Still, it was one more child than she and Shep had managed. Perhaps that would change. Or perhaps that was indicative of what difficulties Jhee might have if their plans for Kanto proceeded.

"Lady Delphine, may I present you Bright Harmony, my second husband."

"A pleasure, Lady Delphine," Kanto said. He gave the most formal of bows before planting a kiss on the back of Lady Delphine's hand.

"Likewise, Bright Harmony," said the Lady Delphine.

"This is Star Mirror, my youngest spouse," Jhee said. Jhee used their outside name because neither had been formally introduced to the Lady Delphine. Once they had stayed under her roof, they would be less formal.

Mirrei curtsied. "Lady Delphine."

"Delighted, Star Mirror."

"Are we the only guests?" Mirrei asked.

"I dare say we have quite the full house. There's a rather crude business-man, a travel writer, an organizer for fishing combines, a free-spirited advo-cate, and a mining director. We're also hosting an ambassador to the barbarian lands. He is also a man of waves."

"More clergy. My, we'll have to be on our best behavior."

"I don't know about all that now. He seemed a perfectly reasonable sort. Some others though are quite the characters."

"Speaking of waves and devotion," Jhee said. "I'd like to pay my respects to your Makers' Shrine."

"I'll have you brought to it once I've shown you to your rooms and given you a chance to refresh yourselves."

"Much appreciated." Jhee lowered her voice, "A mining director? I see, now, why you wanted my assistance."

"I'd like to put the issue to rest before Styrling sends any more help," Lady Delphine whispered.

Lady Delphine wrapped her arm in Jhee's and bundled them up the stairs to the solar where drinks with ice melon balls in them awaited them. Warm sunny drinks for these overcast times, but Lady Delphine loved them so even when they were first-years together. Lady Delphine had also been assigned to the intelligence pool just as Jhee had. The compulsory military service every citizen had to undergo had better positions than others. The intelligence pool is where the wealthier could get themselves or their offspring stationed and kept off the front lines. Not so much for Jhee and Shep, though. The Path Maker had had different plans.

Jhee shuddered and tried to shake off thoughts of her and Shep's military service.

"We have much to catch up on," Lady Delphine said. "I've put you up in the Observatory suite: one master bedroom with adjoining suites. If that doesn't suit, we can rearrange. I'll have the last bed put away until you need it."

At their rooms, Jhee turned to Kanto and nosed him on his cheek. Kanto pressed his *esca*, the star-shaped Makers' mark that adorned Water Folk's forehead, against hers. "See, here in time for festival season. Just as I promised," Jhee said.

"I had no doubt you would see your promise fulfilled. If anyone could, it would be you, dear wife."

"Thank you for your vote of confidence. You'll be happy to know, Mirrei, besides following Pascoe food protocols, they operate as Blue Waters certified for environmental protection and sustainability."

"Excellent." Mirrei plopped down on the master bed. "Our own beds, again."

The yacht and the detour to the Tranquility Bridge Abbey had them sleeping double and sometimes triple. As denbe, the anchor spouse, Jhee was the only one who ever had the luxury of a bedroom to herself at any point since they left their home in the Far Isles. Though, if propriety would have permitted it, she would have allowed Shep to share it on her nights to herself.

Jhee looked over the invoice from their abbey stay. Now she understood more and more why so many rural Justicars were corrupt. The sum had almost matched the cost of booking the resort stay, due in no small part to purchasing Tranquility Gold at market price.

"Now if you'll excuse me," Kanto said, "I need to ready our outfits. I claim this space right over here for a sewing area and to do design sketches. From now on, it's off-limits to anyone but me."

"Far be it from us to interrupt the Maker at Making."

"Laugh all you wish, but I intend for us to make a splash and be the envy of even the most fashionable houses."

"Live your Make, *denye*, always."

Kanto and Mirrei waggled fingers at each other. "Pure truth."

Kanto pulled out various robes and laid them on the bed. He touched his chin as he pored over them, ever the fashion-conscious one. Jhee had better uses for her mind share. Let him and Mirrei tend to such matters, likely why the Makers had put them in her path.

Jhee cleaned herself up and went looking for the Makers' shrine to perform her devotions and thank the Makers for their safe arrival, as was her duty as the head of household. The shrine occupied a shell grotto off the central atrium. She gave of the elements of air, earth, fire, and water to the First Makers; the sweat of her brow to the water feature; incense shavings for the ever-burning candle; breath and warmth for the plants; a respectful touch of her esca to the ground for the Unknown Maker, so that one would not turn her way. Next, she paid devotion to the Lesser Makers. For Kanto, she jangled Maker geld coins and bounced a few off Futou's drum-like belly. She burned a scented prayer letter and gave an extra measure of laughter to Pascoe and Lashae for Mirrei.

Though now that Kanto had mentioned the subject, the suite provided them much more room than the yacht. Since they had space, setting up a workshop for her and Mirrei while they were here did not sound like such a bad idea. Although constructing a chemistry lab in your hotel room was a far cry from designating a makeshift sewing room. Jhee would have to ask Delphine if she had an area where they could practice.

With a few moments of quiet to contemplate, Jhee thought through the scant details Delphine had given her about the mining supervisor's death and minor acts of vandalism, theft, and a poisoning incident. Most disturbing was the mining supervisor's death. Her fall down the mineshaft had been called an accident, but with all the other happenings Lady Delphine suspected otherwise. She wanted to get ahead of the matter before Styrling Mining stepped in and made matters worse.

~

Hake Hill

Jhee leaned against the balcony railing to catch a bit of spray and morning suns before Kanto arrived for their walk. Gentle rain patter and crashing surf eased the tension in her shoulders. Two figures yelling and gesturing at each other caught her notice. The strong winds and surf cut off most of their conversation. She had been refining her eavesdropping cypher. A small wind drawing might produce more than a clipped word. She synced herself to the winds. Such a strong presence of the winds here was hard to control. While this might make excellent practice, it made for poor ethics. Jhee allowed the winds to slip through her mental grasp. Unaided, Jhee still caught a word or two.

"You need to leave."

"Why you?"

"I have no answers. Just leave."

One turned to leave. The other grabbed his arm. The first man pushed the second to the ground. "Nowhere near us again."

The first man ran full on down the beach. The second got to his knees. He punched at the ground then clasped his hands into the traditional angle of the Makers where he meditated for some moments. He must have been Delphine's aforementioned ambassador and man of the coif. Jhee stepped back inside. She heard the door of the residence open and slam.

The encounter on the beach stayed with Jhee as she and her spouses went on an excursion. Jhee hung back while Kanto and Mirrei rushed along the Avenue from store to store. She was content to let them have their fun though she wished Shep were here to help her keep herself occupied.

Kanto came to a stop in front of a luxury clothier. "Oh! Let's go in this one."

They dashed inside and wandered the aisles handling bolts and realms of vibrant, high-end cloth.

"Denye, look at this fabric. Have you ever seen anything like it?"

"No, it's got an excellent hand, practically slips through my fingers." Kanto threw the fabric about Mirrei. "It drapes wonderfully."

"This pattern reminds me of our house watermark."

Kanto and Mirrei emerged from the shop sometime later with several bolts of expensive fabric. They walked further along the Avenue. Kanto came to a dead stop. "You want to be bad?"

"Let's be bad," Mirrei said.

"Iced fruit and cream. Let's get iced fruit and cream."

"Yes!"

Kanto and Mirrei ran inside giggling. Jhee smiled and trailed after them. The three of them found a lovely little table overlooking the deep blue water. Jhee kept her gaze focused beyond the immediate drop and further out to the crafts in the water. The two younger spouses gabbed about the latest doings and goings-on at the capital.

"The famous Hake Hill row. I've always dreamed of being able to shop here," Kanto said. "You'll love the capital city with all the finest foods, fashions, and entertainment."

"No, she'll be too busy with courses. The capital boasts some of the finest schools and academies in the inhabited worlds."

Mirrei raised an eyebrow, then shook her head and smiled. "Who needs to plan the rest of their life when I have you to do it for me?"

"My lady Justicar," a voice called. "Look, sibs, aren't those our guests?"

Jhee turned at the greeting. Two young women and a young man, all quite fetching, approached them with a few shopping bags in their hands. The young woman in the lead waved her arm then hurried to greet them.

"What a pleasant surprise. I'm Erma. This is Semele and Vash. We're Lady Delphine's children. How wonderful to meet you."

"Ah," Jhee said. She clasped forearms with each of them. "A pleasure to put faces to the names."

"For us, as well," the young man, Vash, said. Vash was one of those she saw arguing from her window. She now wished she had used that eavesdropping charm. He ended his forearm clasp with a rather forward extra squeeze before his attention immediately turned to Jhee's spouses.

"Allow me to introduce my consorts, Bright Harmony and Star Mirror."

"Pleasure to meet you," Kanto said

Vash's greeting lasted that extra fraction with them too, so she assumed him to be too affectionate. "Such evocative outside name choices."

"We picked them ourselves," said Mirrei. Her gaze lingered on the young man's.

"We didn't give you our outside names. You must think us terribly improper. It's just mumsy told us so much about you. We felt as if we already knew you. Given how close you and mumsy used to be, we didn't feel the need to stand on ceremony."

"Now, correct me if I'm wrong. You were mumsy's society fellow in the Academy days?" Semele asked.

"That is indeed correct."

"Come with us and let us give you the grand tour of the city."

Jhee checked for her junior spouses' reactions. Both bore eager expressions. "Very well then."

The Delphines escorted them to the heart of the city after they finished their treats. Jhee and her spouses stopped dead in their tracks near the monumental Cetus Fountains in the square. A group of Doombringers preached openly and proudly about the Unmaking, and no one, including their escorts, broke their stride. Young Folk protesting drowned out their proselytizing.

"Philosophy Making in the public square, a proud inland tradition," Semele said.

Each fountain hosted a different preacher.

Dusty folk in work aprons fought to out-yell the Doombringers, "The Empire thought nothing of them when it built the wall and submerged their isles. If the Empire didn't want to house or do right by them, it should have thought of that before it destroyed their homes."

"Yeah, put them to work in the mines," yelled someone from the crowd.

"Them and the barbarians," chimed in someone from another.

A group of young folk with crimson and ocher scarves countered, "Where they can get not one lung disease but two? We don't need another drain on Imperial resources. We need to improve the working conditions in the mines."

"A drain on the empire's resources? The empire's the one who destroyed our homes, our livelihood."

A group with a banner depicting the ocean with a giant numeral one on it spoke up next, "But that's the game, isn't it? Keep refugees and the Fire Folk at each other, so the Empire can do as it wills."

"The only true unity is that of the Final Sword and the glorious forces of remaking," the Doombringers said.

"Blast this trenched drizzle," Erma said. "At least it's better than storms. When those rolled through regularly, it was a treat. However, everything is still moist and sodden. It's sinking into the food and draining the flavor. Meals need seasoning with twice as many sea peppers as before."

"I wonder what they are eating at the capital," Semele asked.

"I doubt the capital has all this rain," Jhee answered. She continued to marvel at the manic street preaching. "They are too far from the storm zone."

"Too true."

"What about you, gentlefolk?" Erma asked. "Looks like we had the same idea. I figure as part of your stay here we should get you started on joining the social scene at the capital as soon as possible. That way, you can learn who the players are."

Semele clasped her hands. "If you have time, stop by the street fair this weekend. It involves lots of local businesses. Mumsy, along with Styrling Mining, is one of the co-sponsors. It's to help raise awareness of Miners' Lung Disease."

"That and Fresh Lung Syndrome are causes of mine," Vash said. "I'm a fellow of the Breath of the Deep, a foundation close to my heart."

"Nice to know," Mirrei said. She fluttered her eye color. Vash grinned.

"If you're heading back, we'd be glad to accompany you," Vash said.

Mirrei glanced back at Jhee and Kanto. "No, we still have errands. Hope to see you at the villa later."

"I look forward to it."

2

———

THE RESORT

~

Weirs

The next morning, the weather turned bright. Jhee sipped her honey and herb tea. Mirrei and Lady Delphine's daughters played in the surf by the small seaside lawn to Lady Delphine's country estate. Vash joined the frolic. They, too, had welcomed relief from the rain. Jhee and Delphine reclined on the east lawn watching the tide roll out. The four waded into the waves ankle-deep crabbing and picking up other exciting finds from the beach with a beachcombing rake.

"Your Mirrei looks so much livelier since she got here. I see a definite improvement in the color of her cheeks since she has arrived."

"She might have acclimated to the climate further inland."

Jhee glanced out at Mirrei basking and frolicking among the waves. The image of Miramar on the shores of their home, which must surely have sunk beneath the waves rolled in then out of her thoughts.

"She might at that."

"It may also be as much to do with the company as the final arrival and subsequent stability of dry land after such a long water voyage."

"Indeed."

Mirrei, Erma, Semele, and Vash returned with a bucket full of crabs. Mirrei had hitched up her skirts, which held more sea crabs. They rushed towards the white table and chairs they had set up on the private beach. Mirrei dumped her catch into a nearby bucket. She leaned over and pecked Jhee on the cheek. Jhee brushed sand from Mirrei's face.

"I see we will probably have sea crabs for lunch," Jhee said.

"We used to roast crabs on skewers when I was growing up," Mirrei said. "I haven't roasted crabs since I left home."

"I'll have the staff set up a bonfire," Lady Delphine said. "We may have enough here to put on the dinner menu tonight."

"And don't forget the skewers," Vash said.

Mirrei smiled and then looked away sheepishly. "Should we invite Kanto, denbe?"

"Whatever you wish."

"We can play weirs while we wait," Erma said.

"That would be lovely," said Semele. "Mirrei, care to come with?"

"Come on. It will be marvelous," Vash said. "You can be on my team. This way, they can't gang up on me."

Mirrei hesitated and glanced at Jhee. Jhee tucked her hands in her robes. "We should continue your lessons."

"Oh, so soon."

"Yes, we only have so much daylight left. The currents will be too weak at night. At least for our current lessons."

"If you insist, denbe."

Mirrei fluttered the tint of her eyes at Jhee. Not fair. Jhee drooped her shoulders then nodded.

Mirrei and Lady Delphine's offspring took off down the beach again, leaving their haul of crabs snapping and crawling in the nearby bucket. Jhee smiled. Yes, this environment seemed to agree with her. It was good for her and Kanto to have friends their own age.

"I must thank you for the use of your boathouse as a workspace."

"No need. No need. To discuss our proposal. Are we still in agreement?"

"Such as it was. She seems to be happy and thriving here. But we shall see. I'll force her into no arrangement she does not want."

"Understood. Understood. I, for one, was never one to give any member of my family such autonomy. But that is part of what makes you such a better woman than I, Jhee."

Jhee tensed under the unearned praise. Better woman. Jhee tried not to scoff. Many on her home islands might have a word or two to say on the subject. Most of all, Miramar had she still inhabited this sphere with them.

Miramar had held her home together against all mundane assaults only to see it done in by the stroke of a finger quill. Not from a natural disaster, but because of some official who did not even know or care her family existed. Bureaucracy, the force of nature no one could stand against.

Yells of alarm carried from the weir court. Jhee and Delphine barely had a moment to look at each before they ran for the courts. Vash cradled a collapsed Mirrei in his arms. They quickly brought her to a lawn chair.

"What happened?"

"We were having a spirited match of weirs. She started coughing, then collapsed," Vash began.

Semele shaded Mirrei from the sun while Vash touched Mirrei's face and neck. "She's clammy and cool to the touch. I've sent for my bag."

They brought Mirrei to a lawn chair. An anxious Kanto arrived on the heels of the servant with the bag. He must have been watching them this whole time.

Vash, the house physician apparently, placed his stethoscope against Mirrei's chest and held her wrists and hands. Kanto hovered while stroking his lacquered nails. Jhee remained poised. Yet, inside her sleeves, where she had hidden her hands, she pressed her palms tight together.

After a few moments, Vash put away the stethoscope, patted Mirrei's leg, and smiled at her.

"So?" Kanto asked.

"Our Mirrei here will be fine."

"What sort of aftercare does she need?"

"She needs some rest."

Vash patted her leg again. Jhee noted the signs of discoloration on his fingers and the wear patterns on his bag. She knew he had attended the medical program at the Imperial Academy and had good marks. What she sought now was additional signifiers of technique and expertise.

Jhee tapped her nose. "You're the house physician. Clinically trained at Tihalmec Imperial Academy. At the capital or Galleon City?"

"TAGC. Galleon City."

"Whole health?"

"Epidemiology."

Kanto ceased fidgeting to position himself beside Jhee. Mirrei appeared mortified.

"You also volunteer at a free clinic."

"You're quite astute. I provide services two long-tides a moon. Mumsy says it's important to give back."

Mirrei's eyes lit up. She seized control of the conversation. "Admirable. I'm considering joining the Imperial Academy of Medicine."

Jhee nodded, satisfied for now.

"You are such a lucky young lady to have such a caring household to look after you."

"She is," Kanto replied. "Denbe, denme, and I see she gets plenty of rest and eats right. We look after her."

"I can tell. Your household gives our Mirrei such excellent care. If I say so myself."

"All this fuss," Mirrei said.

"If you wanted to show mercy to my sisters and give them the match, you could have just resigned."

"Resigned," Erma said. "Tosh. We were winning."

"Hardly. Mirrei here is a fierce weirs player."

"A stinger if ever I saw one," Semele said.

Mirrei blushed.

"You gave us quite the fright," Kanto said. He moved in between Vash and Mirrei. "You should not have exerted yourself so."

"I was just having so much fun."

"I'm afraid it's my fault," Vash said. "If I had known about her condition, I would not have been so active. I would have kept a better eye on her."

"I know. Which is precisely why I didn't tell you."

Mirrei smiled.

Jhee took hold of her hand and kissed it. "You must not frighten us again like that."

"I know. Simply little too much excitement. Please, oh please, don't let this ruin the crab roast. I was so looking forward to it."

"If you insist. You are sure you wish to do this?"

"Yes. Please, a clam bake would be a marvelous way to end this day."

"Only for you."

The Delphines and Jhee's cohort spent the day's remainder roasting crabs by the beach.

~

Moonlight Reflections

During the crab roast, Jhee slipped away and began to set up their boathouse workshop. It might make a pleasant surprise for Mirrei where she could work on healing sequences in peace.

"I'd wondered where you'd gotten to," Mirrei said.

"I was hoping to have it set up before you noticed."

"Care for a walk along the beach?"

Jhee hesitated. Mirrei twinkled her eyes and pouted. Again, not fair. "How can I deny you, dende?"

As the narrow strip of beach tapered near a quiet little grotto, Jhee reached out and held Mirrei's hand on impulse. They smiled at each other. Mirrei leaned in. Jhee turned away and walked on. Mirrei stopped her, then leaned in for a kiss again. Jhee allowed herself to savor the moment. Then like the roar and sound of the surf, the moment evaporated to be replaced by another.

"I couldn't think of a better end to the day," Mirrei said.

"Seconded."

Though Jhee believed Mirrei the most likely of the two younger spouses to stay, she had kept Mirrei at a respectable remove because of more than allowing her some independence. She was not sure if what she felt for the young woman was only some residual of her feelings for Miramar. If so, it was not fair to encourage an attachment based on false pretenses, not when they were about to settle some place where there were better opportunities for her with those richer or those who would love her for who she was.

Would this ever not be awkward? Would Jhee always be reminded of Miramar and her betrayal of her? Jhee had loved her mother so much. So much she wondered if she could ever separate the two entirely in her mind and soul—which is why she always felt so guilty whenever she and Mirrei were romantic. Were her feelings for Mirrei or the residual of what she felt for Miramar? Perhaps she would never know.

Back in the suite, Jhee raised her head from her notes when Mirrei emerged from the dressing room in her nightgown.

"Will our home in the city have access to the beach?"

"No, but there is one nearby."

Mirrei's shoulders sagged.

"Once we're situated and I'm surer of my position, I might look into acquiring a beachfront vacation estate. And Lady Delphine says we have a standing invite to visit her whenever we wish."

"All right, then I shall speak no more of it."

"It was so good to see you laugh and play today."

"It was great fun. Sorry to have worried you."

"Now, now, go straight to bed. We'll skip the lessons tonight."

Mirrei hopped into bed and pulled aside the covers waiting for Jhee to join her.

"You should rest. I have more ledgers to look over."

Mirrei cocked her head at Jhee. "I won't break. My day. I say what goes on my day."

Consummation had been Mirrei's idea. Jhee understood the nuances involved and that their marriage was primarily one of convenience. It could have been chaste. Jhee had only delicately inquired into whether their match was Mirrei's preference. She supposed her keen interest in Vash had answered her question, another reason Jhee believed their match would not last long. Mirrei might be better off with another situation. She entertained getting another marriage for Mirrei. If their pairing was not Mirrei's prefer- ence, she knew they would have to arrange another marriage for her, one she would find more satisfying and passionate. She owed the young woman at least that much. She wanted her junior spouses to be happy. While she was not always the most conscientious denbe, she did not want to be entirely unconcerned with their happiness.

Mirrei attributed Jhee's hesitation to a belief the young woman too frail. Her reluctance had a more bittersweet cause. Too often, when she looked at Mirrei, all she could see was the junior's mother.

Jhee beckoned Mirrei toward her, "You may not be strong enough for Drawing, but I have a lesson to offer you tonight. These right here are the listings of our seabeds and shipping lanes and the deeds to some smaller atolls we owned. We still own them. It's just they are now storm-wracked or many feet underwater."

"I remember."

Mirrei touched the picture of one atoll: Talas island.

"Yes," Jhee said and turned away. Talas island where Mirrei's family home used to be and Jhee's.

"I remember when mamere and I came to stay with you. You two fought like seals and whales."

"Much like when we were young."

Jhee thought about the day when Miramar barged into their highland house with Mirrei in tow. She strode right past the staff and dropped her day bag in the middle of Jhee's entryway. She dared Jhee to kick her out. Jhee hadn't.

"I want to be open about the household finances with you. This may be your job one day. I spend a lot of money on Kanto."

"I understand. He's high maintenance."

"Your expenditures dropped off rapidly after you first got here. I initially thought I'd have two high-spending spouses to account for. Though, I don't mind. I am prepared to spend as much money on your interests and hobbies. I'd up your allowance, but you and Shep barely spend any of it already. And ask for even less little else besides. I initially gave you all the same allowance. Perhaps you can help me come up with a more equitable balance."

"Switch over to gifting and shopping trips. Those are fun, and to be fair, he spends as much of his allowance on us as himself."

"Case made. You have such a quick, detail-oriented mind. Should you change your path, I'd be more than happy to help you get your legal tabard. I still harbor hopes of a joint legal venture."

They walked through her investments. Jhee explained how she tended towards the more practical and old-fashioned. She liked to keep her investments in tangibles like food and shelter and sometimes safety: commodities people always needed. She saw too many prominent families ruined by speculative investments in next-wave, dodgy technologies. While it had paid off spectacularly for some like the Zeloachs, more often it led to ruin.

Mirrei was attentive, but soon, Jhee heard a light snore. Mirrei had fallen asleep on a stack of shipping reports. Jhee slipped them from under her head and coaxed her to bed where Jhee joined her.

~

Beach Lesson

Kanto accompanied Jhee and Mirrei down to the beach where she had decided that the ocean grotto would be an excellent locale for another lesson in drawing.

"We are sure your element is wind, yes?"

"Yes, teacher," Mirrei said jokingly.

"So, this would be a good place to practice, especially if we want you to expand into other elements for drawing. This is a liminal space where wind and sea meet."

"You sure it's proper I'm here," Kanto said.

"Yes. We will obey the traditional forms, but I will not dignify this no-male-arcana nonsense any longer. You will see what you will see."

"As you wish, denbe."

"Now shall we begin?" Jhee asked.

"Yes, teacher."

Jhee and Mirrei took a stance. They moved and flowed their arms with the wind and the waves. Kanto studiously kept his gaze averted. Jhee's clock wound back to other shores years ago: Miramar and Jhee at their morning practices while Shep watched in an utter flouting of convention. The similarity dashed her concentration. She overextended her reach but caught herself before she lost balance.

Mirrei paused but said nothing. Kanto glanced her way.

"Kanto, why don't you join us?" Jhee motioned for him to take a stance. She reset and dropped back into a neutral position. "Don't think I won't be as hard on you as I am on Mirrei because you haven't been practicing as long as she has. This space has other limnalities: the sand, the soil, the rocks from the grotto. Good for a male to sense. Clear and center your mind. Focus your weight down like an anchor stabilizing your position in the Mechanism."

They moved their arms back and forth.

"This is the place for big movements. Finger arcana is not strong enough to manipulate this amount and strength of winds. No mortal menfolk can draw the seas. No mortal womenfolk can draw the winds. Move the air around some, but you must understand your limitations. That is the lesson. Meet the vast glory that is the sea and the winds and realize your place under heaven, under the Mechanism, under the Makers. Here is a place to truly learn the Makers' magnificence. It is meant to be humbling."

Jhee placed her hands onto Kanto's arms to correct his form. He tensed. He still seemed uncomfortable with arcana. Traditional women who instilled in him the idea of male artificers as evil had raised him. Drawing probably seemed so as well. Though they had loosened the restrictions on male drawing, the cyphering laws were in flux. Cyphering and derivations for men were still in a legal gray area, one where she did not want to lead her spouses astray. As an officer of the court, she had to uphold the law even if she thought it was wrong. Perhaps she should still exclude Kanto from watching the cyphering lessons even if she only intended to teach him to draw until the laws settled.

For their lesson proper, Jhee started with synchronating the area. It would give them a baseline to work from and gauge if they had to fight any other artificers' influence. She applied the prime forces within to the gears of the Divine Mechanism. Another external factor beyond the Shield countered her. She pinpointed a source that emanated from the direction of the grotto. Odd. Perhaps she would check it out later.

While they gave their lesson, they had drawn the attention of the children who greeted the ferries on their arrival, offering to carry bags for coins and treats. Many had swarmed their cohort the day they arrived on the docks. They watched in wide-eyed fascination as the lesson continued. Jhee moved the lesson in full view of the children. She slowed to give the children a chance to follow their movements. She pitched her voice loud as she explained the actions to Mirrei and Kanto.

"Now. Feel the rhythms of the waves and the winds. Feel them moving through you. Feel the sand and the earth. Experience their weight holding you down. Grounding you to the land. These are our lands and our waters. We are the Water Folk. The other barbarian races may have taken over the rest of the world, but these lands and these waters more than any others are ours."

Wind drawing was Jhee's primary ascendant though she had gained secondary dominance in fire drawing because of her service. She commanded the elements which research increasingly tied to the women of their people. Researchers found mastery of elements such as water and earth to be most dominant in men. Hence, why men had become increasingly vital to the Shield project and a dilemma since male arcanists had been banned for almost four generations. In theory, the ban did not prohibit them from learning elementalism. In practice, most dampened that training for men too.

"Water and earth for you, the male. Fire and wind for you, the female. All elements working in concert. That is how achievements like the Shield are Made. Its completion represents the ultimate devotional act."

The Shield, though, needed ever more water and earth drawers. With the focus on training practitioners to build the Shield, fire drawing had fallen back in importance. Since it was also a product of the winds, it needed wind and fire drawers specialized in lightning. Given the papers Jhee had written on the subject, the Shield commission had asked her to consult on the Shield project. Which she would have happily done if not for her duties to the law and the courts.

Again, Jhee's mind went back to the abbey. She regretted that she could not find a less violent way out of that. She prided herself on solving problems with intellect. If she someone called upon her to judge herself, what would have been her finding?

After a while, they had a whole group of children doing their best to follow along or at the very least, mimic their movements.

Jhee made minor corrections to Mirrei's forms, as well. She and Mirrei harmonized and synchronized with the winds and the warm sun above them. They dug their feet into the ground and felt the sand squish between their toes. Water gulls screeched and wheeled around the skies above them. Crack-crack went the shells of the clams on the rocks lining the shore as the gulls dropped them to get to the treasure inside.

The visit with the Delphines had the underlying end to feel out what Mirrei wanted. Kanto had made himself plain frequently that whatever his affectations, Jhee was his choice. Lady Delphine had both eligible daughters and a son; an ideal situation in which Mirrei could find herself and express her needs. It did not have to be either-or. But she needed to give Mirrei an opportunity for another arrangement that better suited her nature. Jhee then could make arrangements everyone found acceptable.

Jhee thought about the situation she sought for Mirrei and Kanto. He had put a full stop on it, and she had finally listened. Mirrei had still voiced little opinion on the matter. Mirrei was young, and she deserved a better situation than to be saddled with two broken and aging anchors such as Jhee and Shep. Jhee figured, though, this was the least she could do. She had made a promise to Miramar, Mirrei's mother, that she would see the young woman to the capital and installed in whatever situation she wished. She owed them and their family that much.

Once the lesson ended, Jhee sent her spouses back to the villa and approached their audience. Some ran away. The rest swarmed her again vying for some change or candy. She pulled out a lace root melon candy and a low denomination shell. "All right, these go to the person who can tell me anything about the mischief happening over at the worksite."

Jhee had an immediate taker. A precocious little girl with a mix of barbarian and Water Folk features, elongated, droplet-shaped esca but golden eyes and pure-toned body hair, grabbed the candy and the money. The barbarians, also known as the Fire Folk, oddly enough had an esca shaped like a droplet, while the Water Folk bore ones shaped like a star. Perhaps there was some irony to that. The next difference was usually to be found in eye color.

"It's nature wisps," the tiny girl said. "I've seen them sometimes. Hovering over the equipment at night."

Jhee produced another bit of candy and money. "Now, these go to the person who can tell me anything about the supervisor that died."

At this, most of the children fled. The little precocious girl stood her ground. She grabbed the candy and money again. "Come with me."

The little girl led Jhee in the direction the Prime Forces had pulled her earlier. Just as during the lesson, Jhee felt a distinct energy shift in the forces within around this location. The Prime Forces were aquiver here. Jhee outpaced the girl as Jhee tracked them to a source, a crude shrine.

Votive offerings had been left for the Mischief Makers and other Lesser Makers by the work crews or locals. Small traces of incense and peppermint lingered. Inscribed shells and remnants of candle wax surrounded a nearby sheltered hollow. The high tide crashed against the rocks behind her. Jhee was mindful to not dwell on her proximity to sea and waves. A litany of cyphers and statutes distracted her from speculation about the dangers the watery vastness held.

In front of depictions of the Singers of the Sea family: the Witch Sisters, the Storm Child and hir pet shell drake, the Lady of the Isles, the Maid of the Mists, Grandmother, Whale Rider, Pearl Diver, Star Stealer, and the Moon-wave Runners, had been placed fruit geld. The hair and gown of wispy clouds and rain common to the Maid of the Mists imagery stood out from the other members of her family. A protective hex mark encircled her. The locals must genuinely believe this to be the work of glitch or mist mites. Most modern communities put up a shrine to Maker Supreme when they're being terrorized by criminals.

The girl placed one of her candies on the shrine. "You can feel them can't you? The nature wisps."

"Nature wisps?" Jhee repeated.

"Everybody knows about nature wisps. They also like to hang about the Shield poles. All that mining, it made them restless. That's why they been messing with the site. Company's been digging too deep. They might go down and hit the mother or the root."

"Mother? Root?"

"You really don't know nothing."

"I suppose I don't."

"The mother or the root. All the miners know. That person died messing around the without the wisps' blessing. They offended the Singers of the Sea. That's what got them killed. They didn't do their devotions proper. Not like me. My 'mere showed me how. She was mine folk. Made her sick. She died. Since then, that's why I help people—to get extra money. You need a guide? Me and a few others we can show you around."

"Perhaps later."

"Suit yourself. If you change your mind, just come back to the docks and ask for the Latchers."

"The Latchers? That's what you're called?"

"Yep. You just let me know if you need anything. Me and the others we know where everything is, where all the stuff goes. We can help you out with whatever you need."

"I will at that."

The girl smiled, bobbed her head, and ran off. There were so many orphans. Were there always this many, or was that just the result of the displacement caused by the Shield? Netherwise, Jhee marveled at the resourcefulness of children. While tracing the flow of energy around here produced a resonance within the system, Jhee was not sure what to make of the girl's stories. She doubted haunted mines were the problem. Jhee suspected she had just been scammed out of candy and coin.

3

BAD COMPANY

~

Worksite Woes

Jhee met Mirrei at breakfast. "It's your day. What do you want to do? They have a lot of lovely museums and libraries. One local gallery even has a copy of Oandzo's original Grand Design, one of ten in existence. As well as the Orgonne treatises and the Chronicles and The Principles of The Blue Light. And a copy of Selisse's interim bible."

"Oh, I promised the Delphines I'd play weirs with them today. Sorry. I forgot."

"Apology accepted. You've been playing an awful lot of weirs. I would have never figured you to have taken to a sport so well."

"Neither did I. Rain slip?"

"Of course. Of course. It's good to see you out and about with people your own age."

"Glad you understand."

While Mirrei and the younger Delphines played weirs, Jhee used the opportunity to tackle the ongoing trouble at the mines Lady Delphine asked Jhee to investigate. Jhee had Lady Delphine walk her down to the site.

"The mining supervisor's accident was an exception. Mostly, it's been just mischief," Delphine said, "but I'm afraid someone else might get hurt if the equipment breaks at the wrong time. Not to mention the poisoning, lost nearly a dozen miners for a week."

Jhee returned to the beach. The drawing sensation she felt had piqued her curiosity, especially with the work site around the bend from the site of their

273

arcana lessons. Near the grotto's entrance was the mine site. The Delphines' family business used to be mining before outfits like Styrling bought most out. Many families needed to change how they defined themselves nowadays.

The assignment to the capital came at just the right time. Kanto and Mirrei had shown signs of discontentment and boredom in their simple home on the heights. Kanto had redecorated continually, citing how dreary the place was. Yet, every attempt fell short of the idea he had in his mind, and he started over. Sometimes Mirrei helped. She preferred to explore the house finding new nooks to read and the caches of Jhee's books. On her good days, she even walked the grounds. Eventually, Kanto had decorated anew rooms he had finished and Mirrei reread the same books.

Jhee evaluated the damage to the heavy equipment. The electronic control panel on the heavy equipment had been fried. This had to come from a massive electrical overload as if lightning had struck the equipment. The ground and the vegetation showed no fulgurites or evidence of scorching. Whatever phenomenon occurred here had been confined to the equipment. No wonder everyone suspected glitch mites or nature wisps.

A glint on the ground under the generator caught her eye. She found a foil candy wrapper among the dirt. Jhee picked it up. It smelled heavily of cloves. A strong flavor like that had to be an acquired taste. Jhee suspected the only glitch mites afoot to be the little sea urchins who hustled her out of candy and coin. Poisoning, though—even more than the supervisor's fall—hinted at something larger or more sinister.

A loud break whistle pierced the air. Jhee offered a few devotions to the Singers of the Sea, topping off her prayers with a small offering to the Grandmother.

"Oi! Fancy Lady at our shrine." Jhee lifted her head to see an older pale skinned miner emerge from behind a support pillar. "Few folks the likes of you know how to show proper respect for Grandmother Whale Crusher."

"I'm from the Far Isles, the Reaches. You always wanted Grandmother Orcinus's blessing before you headed out into unknown waters. Who might you be?"

The old timer nodded. "Nix. Pod leader."

"So, you're like the Grandmother of the miners?"

"Yes, ma'am. Not sure as I deserve the title at the moment. You some high-crested investigator the lady brought in or are you mine company folk?"

"Lady Delphine's an old friend. She's worried about what's been happening around here lately. Might you part the waters about the subject for me?"

"It ain't us, if that's what you mean," the miner snapped. She eyed Jhee again then hastily bowed and snatched her soft cap off her head. "Begging your pardon m'lady."

"No offense taken. Why don't you just tell me what's been going on?"

Nix spoke with a rapid patter it took Jhee a moment to get. "My family's worked these mines for the Delphines for generations. Ain't seen nothing like it. At least, not since the stories grandmere told of the mining war days. Malfunctioning equipment. Foul tastes and beer that sours overnight. Missing tools. Sure signs we are beglitched. Like our gear and our site have drawn the notice of the Unknown Maker."

"Beer? You drink beer on site?"

"It's hot, thirsty work, m'ladies." The old timer bowed her head to Lady Delphine who waited at a respectable distance while Jhee worked. Delphine, sensing she might still have a chilling effect on the investigation, slipped away.

"So, you have a little something to quench your throats."

"Yes, but not in the mines. I sees it's only after we finish for the day if I can, ma'am. Danger. Dehydration. You got to stay crisp down there. Not just your life, but that of your fellows depends on it."

"Likewise for the mining supervisor?"

Nix squeezed her hat. "Company folk. They take care of their own. We take care of ours."

Miners lined up to drink from various coolers. "I'm keeping you from your break."

"Not at all, m'lady. I like to wait."

The initial rush at the shared coolers subsided. Jhee joined those gathered around one then waited until Nix drank before doing so herself. Some miners seated themselves on the non-working equipment pretending not to notice them conversing, while others were blatant. A few presented geld and libation at the shrine.

Jhee and Nix walked a few feet over with their cups. "What about folks getting sick?" Jhee asked.

Nix shrugged. Another glance at the shared coolers brought back Nix's comment about the soured beverages. Jhee downed the cup of brown liquid lest she contemplate too long about what it might be. The pleasant tang of chilled kolal leaf tea greeted her palate.

A group of miners congregated around a cooler at a remove from the others. The group remained small. If any excess wandered over, they were turned away with a furtive glance or two in Jhee's direction. The two miners staffing the cooler were studious about avoiding eye contact with her.

"Would you it bother you if I mixed a bit?" Jhee asked.

"No, m'lady. You need anything, come direct to me."

"Thank you. I will." Jhee drifted over to the out-of-place cooler and held out her cup. "May I?"

The eyes of one of those manning the cooler went bright umber and wide, making a severe contrast to their grimy, rose dust-streaked face.

The other answered, "You wouldn't like it, m'lady. Weak tea. Us is the only few what could stand it."

"As you wish. Did the mining supervisor like it?"

"Um, yes ma'am."

A few more discreet questions away from Nix confirmed Jhee's suspicions. The mining supervisor and the ill had drank from the same cooler, one known to be spiked with squelch, homemade liquor.

The break whistle sounded again and Jhee found Nix again. "Thank you, Grandmother."

Nix gave a gap-toothed smile as she donned her soft cap again. "Ma'am, about the mining supervisor."

"Any idea why she fell?"

"No, ma'am I just question the timing; off hours."

"Do company folk often go into the mines off shift?"

"Their business ain't none of mine unless it affects the pods. They give us a thorough going over of when we go in the mines and what we take out. Not so, Styrling folks."

"The mining supervisor may have been stealing templarite?"

"Someone had been going in the mine off hours. I just know it won't us. You don't take from the mines without proper devotions to appease the glitch mites and mine sprites. It may be her carelessness what drew Old Unknowable's notice."

Jhee found Delphine on the ridge above just out of sight.

"Anything?" Delphine asked.

"The mining supervisor liked to drink and was prone to visiting the mine after hours. As for your other troubles, there's some indication the mining supervisor may have also been stealing. All the accidents and the sabotage may have been a cover for her activities."

"Employee theft. So, it could have just been an accident? Styrling might accept that. What of the poisoning?"

"I may not have the full solution to your glitch mite problem, but I believe I know what made many ill: spoiled, alcoholic tea coolers."

Tension drained from Lady Delphine's posture. "Styrling suspected a work slowdown. That made them more anxious than the supervisor's death."

"Because they viewed it as a prelude to greater organizing action. I'll keep my eye out for any other answers."

"Homemade liquor." Delphine smirked. "Remember that one time we punched up the punch at that Academy reception?"

Jhee chuckled. "Don't remind me. I was sick for two whole days."

"Me too."

～

On the Town

Jhee stepped out into the hallway. Vash stormed by her. Then turned. "I'm sorry. Good morning, Justicar."

She noted he held a slip of bio-film in his hands. He twisted it and twisted it.

"I had a weirs date with Mirrei. Please, give her my regards and my apologies."

"I will. Is everything all right?"

"No, Justicar. No, they are not. Pardon my abruptness. If you will excuse me, I'm not fit company at the moment. I need to speak with Mumsy."

Erma walked by brandishing her weirs racket. She registered mild concern as Vash stormed by her. "I wonder what that was about."

"It would seem he cannot make your weirs date."

"Well, we will somehow persevere without him. How are you this morning, Justicar?"

"Fine. I was contemplating taking a constitutional."

"Perhaps you would like to join us for weirs. I can only assume Mirrei gets her extraordinary talent at it from your instruction."

"Alas, no such luck. I am quite the horrible player."

"Oh well, suit yourself. We'll go threesies."

Kanto entered the corridor from the adjoining suite.

"Kanto, we're going to play weirs," Erma said. "Would you and Mirrei care to play doubles?"

"No, thank you, I have other matters to attend to," Kanto said.

Jhee leaned over and said, "You should. It will be fun, and it will be good for you to spend more time with those closest to your own age."

"No. Thank you. Besides, if I didn't know any better, I might think you were still trying to get rid of me."

"Of course not. I made you a promise. I would never do such an action or even entertain that idea again."

Once Jhee dressed quickly and plainly, she headed down to breakfast. The ambassador browsed the buffet table while appearing decidedly dour. After she assessed the buffet and picked a few fruits for herself, she also sampled the buffet's new herbal orange tea. She had developed a taste for the beverage. A splash of Tranquility Bridge's nectar would go along with it nicely. She would make a cup for her and Mirrei. Jhee's sinuses had swollen. Not quite in headache territory, but she did not want to let it sneak up on her. The open sea had not agreed with her.

As Jhee went about gathering breakfast, the ambassador approached and spoke before she could politely affect an escape. "Justicar, allow me to introduce myself formally. Ambassador Naiman."

"Ambassador Naiman, how are you this morning?"

"Contemplative." He continued to pick at the buffet listlessly. The cast of the Ambassador's teal colored eyes softened. Teal eyes, but a star-shaped Makers' mark. Either he had spent extensive time in the Scorched lands or…. Faint rosettes dotted his body hair.

"You, Ambassador? Are you a barbarian?"

"Yes. Though, I find that term to be a bit of a misnomer, don't you? Have you visited the other continents?"

Jhee throat went dry. She swallowed.

"Only briefly," Jhee said and left the "during the war" part of the statement unspoken. The Makers' mark along with eye color was one of the more prominent means to distinguish between the various Folk. Water Folk had golden eyes while the barbarians had teal or greenish eyes. Both eyes gave off a slight bit of illumination. That was one of the creepiest things from her service. When you went into a night raid or on one of her missions, all you saw in the darkness was those greenish eyes staring back at you. Was that experience as unnerving for the barbarian soldiers as well? To see a slew of golden eyes in the blackness coming at them. Perhaps the barbarians did not fear Water Folk as much as the Water Folk feared the barbarians. The barbarians and the Other Folk who lived off world had resoundingly thrashed the Water Folk.

"I see. You're from the outer islands? Visit any interesting places on your journey here?"

"We recently spent time at the famous Abbey of Tranquility Bridge."

"With their famous blessed wines and healing waters?"

"The same. I understand you to be a man of the waves, too, Ambassador."

"I trained as a vicar and chaplain before being appointed an ambassador. Though, unlike the monastics, my Path Maker emphasized working with the community at large. Because I drove a water junk during my conscription, I got a water taxi license. I used to help the elderly run errands and transport them to doctors' appointments."

"Ah, the Formalist tenets of outreach and service. You come from a ministry which practices being amongst the populace, unlike Drakists."

"No offense to the seclusionists, but what good does faith do you and your community alone on an island? Faith needs to be put under pressure and challenge, but only enough to temper it. Now, though, how much is too much? How much temptation goes too far? At what point does seeking to test faith weaken it and have the opposite effect of what you were going for?"

"All interesting questions."

Vash entered the dining hall. The two men caught each other's gaze. Vash glared then left.

The ambassador frowned. "Begging the fine lady's pardon, I have other less spiritual matters to contend with."

Mirrei came down the stairs happily chatting with Erma and Semele. She rushed over and slipped her arm into Jhee's.

"For me?" Mirrei purred.

"I have some nectar stashed in our room if you want it."

"Thank you. I've just become a fiend for these orange tea and nectar healing draughts. I think I owe them my improvements these past long-tides."

"My hope is you're right. It is one reason I put aground there. It might have been one of the few things to make what we went through there worth it."

"Also, you and Kanto getting along better, too."

"Yes that too. What are your plans for today? I spoke with Vash, and he told me he had to cancel."

"I know. It's a shame. Semele, Erma, and I will persevere without him. We're going to head into town and perhaps catch some shows."

"Would you do me a favor?"

"Anything."

"Invite Kanto. I've tried to encourage him to do activities on his own, but he doesn't listen to me."

"He doesn't listen to me either. I'll see what he can do, but likely all he will do is sulk, anyway. He's been such a wipeout lately."

Later, Jhee went to the villa pool to find Kanto swimming, Mirrei and the Delphines having long since left. He emerged from the pool lean, sleek, and glistening in the suns. It reminded her of being a quarter jubilant and watching along with Mai, their nickname for Mirrei's mother, as Shep approached them the first time fresh from diving. He dumped a bucket of fresh-caught sea meat before them. Fearless Mai had leaped to her feet first and offered him a towel.

Jhee stood and offered Kanto a robe. He slipped into it, pulled her gently against him, and muzzed her cheek.

"Thanks," he said, in a low voice. He arrayed himself on the beach chair beside hers with a confident smile. By the secluded poolside, she allowed her gaze to linger in a brazen manner she would have been too embarrassed, too scandalized to do only weeks before.

"Didn't you want to go into town with Mirrei and the Delphines? I thought they invited you."

"No, I figured I'd find my own amusement today."

"I have some meet-and-greets to do around town. Would you like to come with?"

"Isn't this your off day?"

"Yes, but since you didn't go into town with them, I thought I'd offer you another outing. Unless you want to lounge around by the pool alone."

"Not at all. While this is your day, I'd very much like to spend it with you if you'll let me. Your day, your say. I'd be delighted so long as you don't consider this me impinging on your personal time."

"Consider this business, not personal. I'm going to chat with the local dignitaries. I need my secret weapon with me."

Kanto grinned. "In that case, I'd be delighted. Let me go get changed. Come with. If you know who'll be meeting ahead of time, I can brief you."

They walked arm and arm back to the observatory suite.

After they returned, Jhee showered. She emerged to find Kanto organizing her papers and ledgers.

"I hope you don't mind. Perhaps we should go over your holdings again. I'm concerned about the water rights dispute you have with those spiteful Brackfins, and now it seems the Foresters are making a claim too."

"Surely you must want to do something other than pore over these musty old ledgers. Mirrei and the younger Delphines will be doing more crabbing and weirs later. You can always join them."

"I much prefer to spend time with you if I may."

"As you wish."

"Please, denbe, I want to understand our holdings. I don't want you to give me anything which will hurt you to give."

"If you insist, my dear husband."

Jhee patted Kanto's hand affectionately. He covered it with his other and stared at her long and intently.

"It is not my day," he said. "Perhaps we could get a bit of an early start to it, anyway."

"Tell me about the new furnishings you got for our new home."

"Well, as it turns out, I got an excellent deal on most of the driftwood pieces. The old master recently died, and his son took over. He is still under apprenticeship, but his work is every bit as good as his father's. So, it's undervalued. However, he wants to get his name out and established and gave us a deal on some sets so he can have his work on display in the capital. I think it will suit your aesthetic very well. We should not just imitate the fashions of the capital but seek to bring aspects of our home districts into the forefront and make a fusion of the various styles. A mind burrower to keep the Far Reaches and outlying islands in their thoughts whenever they see us or our home. A way of showing the capital what the future could be and perhaps how much of a forward thinker you can be."

"That sounds wonderful. I often forget the little nuances, and you never fail to remind me."

"And I always will, my denbe."

$$4$$

DIVERGENT STREAMS

~

Street Fair

"Denbe, can we attend the street fair, instead? Please, please, oh please."

"It's your day. I suppose I can indulge you. The museums waited this long. I suppose they can wait longer."

"Thank you." Mirrei gave Jhee a tremendous kiss. Jhee upturned the corners of her mouth to cover her disappointment. The girl had been cooped up so long at home and during their journey. Jhee could let her live some. The capital had bigger, better galleries. Mirrei grabbed Jhee's hand and pulled her to a table selling turquoise and sandstone jewelry. Despite herself, Jhee enjoyed it. The blending of cultures and great food and music. Mirrei danced while Jhee stood on the sideline. Every so often, Mirrei sought to entice Jhee to join in by flashing the golden light of her eyes. Jhee continually declined.

"Yoo-hoo, my lady Justicar," came Erma's voice. She waved excitedly to Jhee from further up the lane. "Kanto, look who we found."

As she continued to wave, Erma and her sister cut through the crowd along with their reluctant companion Kanto.

"Glad you could make it. Having fun, I hope?"

"Oceans of it," Mirrei said.

The three chuckled and clasped hands.

"You have got to see this sand painter," Semele said.

She and Erma grabbed Mirrei and dragged her back through the crowd, leaving Jhee and Kanto to studiously avoid interacting. The travel writer had hir conch aimed at what Jhee believed to be another guest from the villa. The man, who operated a table at the fair, grew wide-eyed with Jhee's approach and cracked a huge smile.

"My lady Justicar, you can't imagine what a great pleasure it is to meet you. I'm Lake, the fishing combine rep." The fishing combine representative grabbed for Jhee's hand. Kanto intercepted the gesture with his own outstretched hand. He pumped Kanto's hand vigorously. "Such an honor. Would you like to sign our petition? I'm here trying to recruit people for the fishing combine—a small group of fisherfolk who decide on fishing rules and pool resources for beyond the Shield fishing licenses. The fees are prohibitively expensive for the individual fisherfolk. Together we can accomplish what none of us can alone. The power of the school of fish protects the individual fish contained within. Let me get you some literature."

The travel writer held hir conch closer. "This will make great local color for my piece."

"When will it be published?" Lake asked. "We can really use the exposure."

"Still at it I see, Lake." A jovial woman stuffed the remains of her apple fritter in her mouth and wiped her hands before offering one to Jhee. She sidestepped Kanto's attempt to intercept her. "Sianna, director of company relations for Styrling Mining and Staffing, and this is my associate Inksy. And you are the indefatigable Justicar from the Sixteenth District."

Jhee took Sianna's hand. Inksy hung back and said nothing. "Allow me to introduce—"

"Bright Harmony. My pleasure." The woman clasped her hands behind her back and rocked on her feet. At Jhee's confused look, she said, "I'm staying at the resort with you."

"That's odd. I don't recall—"

"I keep odd hours. Toodles and enjoy the fair."

The pair walked away. Inksy gave a brief look back at them and popped a mint.

"How rude," Kanto said. "I have to catch up to my hosts. Maybe we'll all supper together later."

Jhee encountered other guests at the gaming tables though they had not been introduced. One woman had a large supply of winnings in front of her. She wore a headscarf with an end that dangled down her left side and over her shoulder. This guest at the villa had made no secret of her comings and goings, unlike Sianna and her companion. A heat shimmer around her made it hard for Jhee to focus on her. She picked up the dicing cup and shook it near her ear. "Six, did you say? No, sixteen? You sure?"

"Dumb, rotten luck. That's all it is," grumbled a rough and burly man at the end of the table. She recognized him as another guest, a businessman of some sort. He stroked at his bushy mustaches. "One more throw."

"Perhaps you should be giving more offerings to Lethys and her luck wisps." The woman put down her money and the next person rolled. Sure enough, sixteen came up. Jhee approached. "Hello-o, fellow guest. Advocate Farkhande. I just adore street fairs, don't you?"

"I haven't attended many," Jhee answered.

"What a shame indeed. Just as well you're attending this one then. You are missing quite an experience of culture and atmosphere. It's good to remember ways different from yours exists. The gossip wisps sure are abuzz today. They are having the time of their lives. Keep an eye out for those Mischief Makers. If you see one, make sure you show them proper respect and give them an offering. You'll thank me later and save yourself a lot of trouble in the meantime."

"To the trench with those dice." The mustachioed man tore his promissory stubs into tiny bits and scattered them to the winds. Jhee watched awhile longer. His luck did not change. He pressed his hands together at angles then took a drink and poured one into another glass for the Unknown Makers. "Who are you again?" he asked Jhee.

"One of your fellow guests at the villa, Mister…?"

"Eldjin. Ah, yes. The Justicar. How fitting cause it's a crime how fast my fortunes turned."

"Your name. I feel I've heard it beyond the villa."

Lady Delphine approached the gaming tables in the company of an athletic, younger woman wearing a sporty sailing ensemble.

"Well, if it isn't my favorite guests all in one place," Lady Delphine said. "Allow me to introduce the heritage committee liaison, Oriel. She helped organize all this and convinced me to sign on as a sponsor."

"Not single-handedly," Ms. Oriel said. Her voice was throaty and soothing. "All I did was help an already finely tuned endeavor run smoother."

At some point, the travel writer had wandered over. Advocate Farkhande offered xe the dicing cup. "Care to try your luck?"

"No, I already know it's bad," xe said.

"Justicar, what about you?" Jhee also passed. "Well, I'm going to go spread the love. Hope to see everyone at the fundraiser."

"Will we see you gentle folk there?" Ms. Oriel asked.

Jhee shook her head confused. "What fundraiser?"

Ms. Oriel gave the formal touch of her heart to both Jhee and household to convey she did not know how familiar of a greeting to provide her with. The woman was familiar with court etiquette and from the middle ranks. Jhee inclined her head to show basic familiarity was sufficient.

"You haven't heard about the fundraiser? Well, Justicar, allow me to tell you all about it. On behalf of the Breath of the Deep, I've organized a charity event at the local observatory. The proceeds go towards the local free clinics as well as fighting and researching Fresh Lung Syndrome. We'll also be auctioning a few Mechanist artifacts."

Jhee clasped her hands, and her ears perked up. "Mechanist artifacts?"

"Yes. I'll send you invites and put your names on the list."

"Truly, I am in your debt."

"My pleasure, my lady Justicar." Ms. Oriel gave a quick touch of heart. "Now, I must be going. Waves to damp. Preparations to finish."

Farkhande went to Lake's table and picked up his sign-up board. After she applied her signet with much ceremony and vigor, she flipped the tail of her headscarf over her shoulder.

This confirmed it, Jhee thought. All the other guests were a bunch of weirdos and cranks, not at all the guests Delphine's family hosted in their heyday. Was it due to changing times or changing family fortunes? Another consequence of the vandalism, harassment, and sabotage happening at the resort?

Not long after Lady Delphine left, invites arrived via ether.

"Stall the wall! Stop the squall!"

Out of nowhere a stream of protesters, swept through the fair. If Jhee had eyes on her spouses, she lost them here.

$\sim$

Protests

"Stop the wall! All Folx unite!"

After she got cut off from the Delphines, Mirrei wandered the stalls and small tucked away shops of the Furnace District at the edge of the fair. The colors and scents of the Fire Folk fare bore earthier notes than Water Folk food and dress. Both though had a love of spice.

Mirrei stopped at a food cart temporarily turned into a stall which emanated the most wonderful, mouth-watering scent of bay and cape root. "Sea meat stew and a lamb and crab skewer, please."

The woman and man team working the cart served orders fast and furious; the man performing entertaining flourishes with the ladles, spatulas, and spices, while the women displayed various tricks cutting and seasoning the meats. The dishes had Mirrei sweating and wiping her brow. She contemplated not finishing them, but she had no means to save them for later. The marvelous pepper taste and guilt over wasting the fine meal made her persevere. Afterwards, her head and sinuses felt fit to explode as if she had sneezed dozens of times in succession.

A mix of Folk at a sidewalk café nearby cheered. A skinny-framed man with very short, light brown hair and modest clothes watched from the door. He gave a slow clap. "For a moment there, we didn't think you were going to make it."

A protester tried to shove a flier in Mirrei's hand. The cart vendors shooed them away with their utensils. "Trouble Maker! Trouble Makers!"

Xe melted back into the flow of people. Another wave of protesters swept by. A fight broke out.

"Quick, in here." Semele beckoned to Mirrei from the doorway the man had occupied. They watched the fray from the safety of the club.

More chants floated in from outside. "Stop the wall! All Folx unite!"

"What are they protesting?" Mirrei asked.

A woman with messy, reddish hair and a cut over her eye answered, "The wall isn't safe. The effects on the ecosystem and as well as the islands deliberately sunk, the displaced wildlife, and the destruction of coral reefs pose a health hazard. The winds and rains it generates could create a self-sustaining vortex which will be subject to thermal runaway, resulting in a cascade effect that will suck in and destroy all the Blessed Isles."

"My word," Mirrei said.

Erma treated the first woman's cut. "Must you always be so alarmist? Some are protesting for better working conditions in the mines. There's been a spike in Miners' Lung Disease since the last big orders came in."

"Why're you explaining anything to this guppy, Wynne?" the man who had laughed at her earlier asked from a stool at the bar. He knocked back a shot. He swept his gaze over Mirrei. "Hey, guppy. Let me guess. You're here to soak up the exotic, barbarian culture."

"Guppy?" Mirrei asked.

"This is Star," Semele began.

"Star. Just Star," Mirrei interrupted. She did not want him knowing even her veiled name.

The man smirked. "Name's Chappy. I own this and another establishment. Can I get you ladies a drink?"

"No. We should probably be heading back."

"Suit yourself."

~

"Stop the wall! The wall is death!"

The stream of protesters cut Kanto off from his hosts. He spun around. He had no way of returning to where he last saw Jhee or Mirrei. A man had taken up a position on the rim of one grand, marble Cetus fountain in the plaza.

The man pointed into the crowd. "What of you, brother? You look well kept. What's your name?"

Kanto looked around. He noticed all eyes had focused on him. "Bright Harmony."

"Veiled names. What era are you from? Is that name your family's choice, your anchor's, or yours?"

He had always imagined himself the center of attention, just not like this. "All."

"Well, aren't you a fine pet?"

Kanto wrinkled his nose. He should have known. "Feh, CARPs. I enjoy being taken care of, and I like nice things. My path isn't yours."

Core Andro Rights Proponents wouldn't be happy unless he came home stinking of the sea every day. Indeed, the plights of men who were not in such a favored circumstance as his motivated him. Men who had been forced to flee and wound up as refugees or Prospectives at Tranquility Bridge's abbey. If they were fortunate. Others wound up worked to death or as bed slaves. He'd rather his silks and colognes, instead of cassocks and the burnt flesh scent of a brand.

~

"The wall is death! All Folx unite!"

Jhee worked her way through the protesters to an eye of calm at a nearby shrine. This disruption felt like the first time in forever she had a moment alone. The journey via yacht from their former home to the capital had been long with several interesting stops along the way. While she had her own stateroom on the ship and her master bedroom at the villa, Mirrei and Kanto were still a constant presence.

Ambassador Naiman's path had converged with the miners, and they had fallen into a civil conference. They were a mix of Fire and Water Folk, though identifiers other than their eye colors and Maker's Mark had been obscured by the dust of their trade. With their reddish shade, glowing eyes, and esca, they conjured images of Trench bound wisps.

The shrine Jhee occupied only contained altars for the First Makers. She placed a cypher inscribed shell on the shrine's Unknown Maker space and offered common devotions to the First Makers for Kanto and Mirrei before trying to reach them via conch.

How did Jhee proceed with the dendes' marriage arrangements? Kanto had elicited a promise from her she would not try to marry him off. Would he still be so eager to stay once they reached the capital proper? There he would be surrounded by an excess of well-appointed lords and ladies.

The idea bothered Jhee a little. A fact which surprised her. She had done her best to maintain a distance between them for just such a possibility. The business at the abbey taught her to value him and in a smaller way Mirrei as well.

Advocate Farkhande stood at the center of another group, listening intently to their concerns; more common laborers and farmers from their aprons and overalls. While Jhee hung back, Jhee listened in to their griev-ances. Had Jhee been called to adjudicate she likely would have found in their favor. In the Far Reaches, most everyone made their living directly from the sea. Open field farming was practically unheard of. What farming there was, took place at sea or on terraces like those surrounding their former home. Shep's family had been quite renowned for their dive farm.

For so long, it had been only Jhee and Shep. Then almost overnight it was the four of them. The dendes' energy and fresh outlook had become a welcome addition. New blood may have been just the component their household needed. It would be disappointing to see them go. She and Shep, while still short of three jubilees, had lived a fair bit. They were set in their ways and had a routine that worked for them. Kanto and Mirrei were younger and had much to anticipate in their lives. It felt like holding them back to obligate them to stay.

The travel writer had climbed an awning to capture images. Lake, at last, found a receptive audience for his combine amongst the protesters. The fisherfolk had locked arms to form a protective wall around his table as he preached about the benefits. Jhee understood the fisherfolk's lot the best. But by the time the Shield had come, her family with their dubious history and relatively new noble status had already diversified from fishing.

The Shield had changed much in the Reaches and Jhee was one of few who had a legitimate means out. Jhee knew full well the reasoning behind the commitments her new spouses and their families had made. Still, arranged marriages; she detested the practice. However, her attempt to flout it had caused so much misery and strife. Their families had reached arrangements, and for all the best reasons: giving the two a better life. At what cost, though? Jhee had been clear and upfront; they were under no obligation to stay. Should they wish to break their marriage contracts early, all they had to do was come to her. She would not pursue legal action against them or their families to force the return of dowries. She asked them at least to let her negotiate their new marriage contracts so she might benefit from their remarriage.

Jhee got a message through to her spouses. On the other side of the protests, they rendezvoused and sought transportation back to the villa.

"Stop the wall! All Folx unite!"

"Stall the wall! Stop the squall!"

Kanto plopped back into the ferry's cushions. "Let's never do that again. I had a run in with a core rights proponent, CARP, on the way here. They don't respect me any more than the ones they claim to be rescuing me from. What's so enviable about being some diving boy who showers off sea brine every day?"

"Like Shep," Mirrei said.

"I didn't mean it that way."

"People are desperate and worried. Who knows? With the way the wall has spiked food prices, being a diver could make one's fortune, and it's probably a lot safer than the mines."

"My biggest worry about the Shield is that it won't work," Kanto said. "They say the barbarians have already found a way through: cheap sailing vessels without any modern navigation equipment to be fooled by the Shield's defenses."

"Wouldn't they be dashed on the rocks?" Mirrei asked.

Jhee tensed. "Not if their ship were the right size and made of metal which they have in abundance unlike us."

Kanto frowned. "All that money and resources for a defense system that can be defeated by technology older than the Prototypes."

"On a lighter note," Jhee said, "we've been invited to a high society fundraiser. The proceeds go toward the local clinics and the Breath of the Deep Society. I'd say that splits the difference between both of your concerns."

Mirrei sighed.

"Next Startide," Kanto said as he went over the fundraiser invite. "Less than a week, way too little time for me to finish outfits for us myself. I'll compose our response at once, then work out particulars. I saw a few boutiques along the lane. I'll make inquiries with them. If this is the major event it's supposed to be, they may be swamped too."

~

The Boutique

The transport bearing Jhee, Kanto, and Mirrei came to a stop in front of a boutique on Hake Hill in Galleon City. The boutique boasted a much more modest and rustic storefront than its modern peers along the row.

"I don't see why we need to purchase new outfits for the fundraiser," Jhee said. "I much prefer your designs in both look and comfort."

Jhee also considered the expense involved.

"As much as I would like to have constructed our outfits for this event," Kanto said. "There simply is not enough time for me to design and make outfits for each of us. There was barely enough time for me to locate a boutique up to my standards who can guarantee completion in time. This should be just a quick fitting, and then we shall proceed to other activities."

"They could have at least traveled to the villa."

"No, they couldn't. This saves time."

The chauffeur helped them out of the transport. A shopper from the boutique approached them, lighted umbrella at the ready, and escorted them inside.

"Denbe," Mirrei said, "you of all of us shouldn't balk at spending more time in the city. What was the most time you've spent in a city?"

"I spent some time in a city at various intervals, such as during my final confirmation to the justiciary."

"What about when you were in the academy or during your service?"

"The Academy was outside of town. I boarded there and went home when I could much like Lady Delphine. On one of my assignments during the war, I did have to live in a small apartment. I did my best not to leave."

"You never visited the city for fun?"

"We went out on the odd night in my academy days. The Academy had an extensive library."

Kanto returned from speaking with the boutique owner bearing sea-green robes with gold and blue embroidery. Assistants brought out daises.

"Up." Kanto pointed Mirrei at the dais. She hopped to. "Of course, our denbe would prefer to spend her time with a conch to her face."

Quick as a flash, Kanto draped her in the robes and then Jhee. The owner brought over her tailoring kit and started to pin and fit their robes. Somehow Kanto now had hold of a tailoring kit and was pinning his own robes on a dais of his own.

"Once we are done here, what should we head next?" Jhee asked.

"You tell us, denbe," Mirrei said, "you're the one chatting up all the guests and street guides."

"I'm sure I don't know what you mean."

"You've been in detective mode since we got here."

"I have not."

Both Kanto and Mirrei frowned at her.

"Fine," Jhee said. "Maybe a little. Delphine's been having problems at the mines. Equipment going missing. That sort of thing. Minor problems."

"So minor she put you on the case?"

"I provided a satisfactory answer."

"But?"

"It has too many dangling threads."

"Dangling threads the scourge of both your work and mine," the boutique owner said.

Kanto chuckled. "That's our denbe: always working; always a puzzle to solve. Woe betide anyone who tries to keep her from it."

Jhee forced the conversation back on track lest the oddities at the mine take over all of her mind share. "I suggest we visit some museums. Galleon City is a city teeming in history and a blend of unique cultures."

"We only made it through half the famous Hake Hills shops our last trip, Mirrei. Care to shop the other half?"

Mirrei folded her hands. "I had another idea in mind. The clinic Vash volunteers at isn't hard to reach from here."

"Ouch!" Kanto set down a pin and tenderly poked his side. "Tailor's maxim."

"You move, you bleed," the boutique owner said. She walked over and did a quick re-pin on Kanto. He nodded approval. She whipped the robe off and then returned to Jhee and Mirrei. "Please check that the pockets are where you like them."

The pockets were precisely where Jhee liked them. "I believe we can do that. I'm very interested in seeing what sort of facilities they have. It'll give me a better idea of what sort of donation to give."

"You mean it?" Mirrei said.

"We'll see."

They finished their fitting.

"I'm going to look for some odds and todds pieces for our house. Meet you for the ride back?" Kanto pecked Jhee on the cheek. He and Mirrei gave their characteristic finger waggle goodbye.

"Hey let me go!" a child yelled.

The shopper had the Latcher girl from the beach by her collar. "Pardons my lady, this little crab-rat was trying to harass you."

"Was not. I have something important to tell the lady. She knows me. We've done devotions together. We're like this."

The Latcher girl entwined her fingers.

Jhee held up a hand. "You may let her go. I know her."

The shopper released the girl who smoothed her ragged gown. The shopper returned to holding the umbrella with a disdainful look.

"What do you have for me?"

The girl stared fish-mouthed at Mirrei for a moment. "Wave Wanderer ships have been spotted out to sea. Near the mines."

"Wave Wanderers? You mean Water Nomads?"

"So you do know some stuff after all. What's more they've been coming ashore."

Jhee paused. Water Nomads live nearly their entire lives on ships. "Any idea where or why?"

The Latcher girl cleared her throat and cupped her hands. Jhee fished out a melon candy and some shell.

"Something to do with the observatory opening. The mines have been going crazy. The crystals have been singing. It has to be their water songs."

"There's only been the one death at the site?"

"I suppose. At least not that's not normal. The mines is rough. It kills up and grinds up a lot of folk. Like my 'mere and my 'bere."

"I'm sorry to hear that. Who takes care of you now?"

"I do."

"May I ask you to keep the information flowing?"

"Sure, as long as you got the money and candy. It ain't just for me, see. It's for the other kids. They helped me get the information. They should get some reward, too."

"Would you tell me if the Water Nomads leave?"

"Sure." The girl held out her hand for another candy. Jhee gave her another one. Jhee had created a worse melon candy fiend than Kanto. "Thank you kindly, ma'am. The Maid of the Mists guide your steps."

"Why the Maid of the Mists?" Jhee asked. The usual saying was to have the Makers' Design guide one's steps.

The Latcher girl looked over Mirrei again. "Full Makers don't come near us folk. All we got is the Singers of the Sea. The Maid of the Mists keeps her eye on the nature wisps. They're her companions. You keep going in the mines, best get her on your side. If you want them to go away, it's best to ask her. You need anything else lady?"

"That will be all for now. Thank you very much for your help."

"You sure talk funny."

The little girl pressed her nose at the shopper before running away. Jhee had the transport take them to the docks where Vash's clinic was.

"What an adorable little operator," Mirrei said.

~

The Clinic

The clinic's large cubic structure rose out of the water like some square behemoth. Engineers built the clinic on flotation moorings, which could raise and lower with sea levels. On the seaward side were moorings where junks and more modest river transports sailed up to deliver patients or fisherfolk stopped in for quick visits.

"Here you go." Vash handed a little girl a candied plum stick. He turned to the girl's father. "Have you been giving her the antibiotics like I prescribed?"

The man bobbed his head. "Dey. Dey. The medicine though it's not working."

"I'll write you another prescription."

"Dey. Dey. Thank you again, doctor."

"Ah Justicar, Mirrei, what an unexpected surprise," Vash said.

"I hope you don't mind," Mirrei said.

"Not at all. Quite the bit of excitement at the street fair."

"Indeed. You look a little busy. Injuries from the protests or the Miner's Lung Disease swell?"

Jhee was taken aback then remembered between Mirrei's interest in healing and being an apt pupil she would notice the signs of disease in others.

Vash nodded. "Those and a Fresh Lung Syndrome outbreak. Though there is some debate whether it's an outbreak or the result of an increase in the number of salt-to-fresh displaced persons."

"Fair assessment. Fair assessment," Mirrei said.

"Speaking of which, how is yours doing?"

"Oh, much better."

"Please allow me to show you around. We have a fully committed practitioner of the Pillarist healing who volunteers twice a long-tide as well as me and several other Academy doctors. We lost a doctor last week and had to scale back our hours from a full day cycle to dawning, day, and setting."

Jhee positioned Mirrei in between her and Vash and kept half a step or so forward.

"How many surgical facilities do you have?" Jhee asked.

"Three currently."

"I noticed the modular construction," Mirrei said. "It lets you add more as the need arises?"

"Just so. Or subtract them. We're retrofitting some moorings to full mobility. Once that's complete, we will be able to sail at least a part of the clinic down the waterways to reach more folk, perhaps even the Wave Wanderers. The clinic design is based on Water Nomad structures."

"Tell me more about the clinic's operations."

"It's quite dull. really. Not the sort of pursuit to interest a jet-streaming heiress such as yourself. I, for one, would not hesitate to leave it behind if the right situation presented itself or should my future wife insist. I should think a proper wife would insist I devote myself to her needs and those of our family."

"What happens to the clinic then? Or your patients?"

"Who's to say? It's likely to close. Since I would no longer work there, mumsy is likely to withdraw her support. Unless perhaps I could convince my denbe to help. Some sweet, compassionate woman who truly wants to help people. Either way, it would hardly be my responsibility anymore. Let Oriel see to that. It's her job after all."

Jhee rounded the corner and saw a young man having a heated discussion with a weaselly woman in expensive but tacky clothing. She noted how the woman held her arm favoring her side, not as if with an injury but as if with a weapon.

"No more excuses. My patience is wearing thin," the weaselly woman said.

They went silent when they saw Jhee. The woman gave the man a smile, patted her flank, and then dashed off. Vash and Mirrei caught up to Jhee.

"Is there a problem here, sir?" Jhee asked. She walked forward to where the woman had been. Rust-colored powdery flakes covered the floor. A disposable napkin bearing a stylized letter Cee lay among them. The logo matched the local business who had provided linens and music equipment for the fair. Jhee picked up the napkin. Writing scrawled on the back read: Pool. Underground lake. This blight of a city consumed in a pillar of light. Mineral sands. Starry eyes.

"No, my lady. No problem at all."

"Bastian, this is the Justicar and Star Mirror. They are friends of my mother who are staying with us for a few weeks. I was just giving them a quick overview of the facilities."

"Pleased to make your acquaintance."

"Bastian here is a volunteer who donates his time to the clinic just as I do. He also volunteers technical work for the Breath of the Deep Society."

Mr. Bastian bowed slightly. "I do what I can. Excuse me miss, my lady, I couldn't help but overhear. You have FLS?"

"Why yes I do."

'Might I ask you a few questions?"

"Um sure."

"Where are you from?"

"Talasisle."

Mr. Bastian leaned in. "Lived there your whole life?"

"Just about."

"How long ago did you start showing symptoms?"

Mirrei backed a step away. "I've shown some my whole life, but much like everyone else it got worse as we journeyed inland. Here, though, it only troubles me a little."

Mr. Bastian had closed the distance again.

"Vash," Mirrei cooed then sidled over to his side, "can we finish the tour?"

Upon closer inspection, Jhee located a struck-out artifice mark, on Mr. Bastian's wrist. Was that the bloodsucker tattoo of a paid remora? "Yes, I'm sure Mr. Bastian has duties we're keeping him from."

"There are still some preparations I have to make for our upcoming joint gala."

"No worries, chum," Vash said. "Be about it."

Before Mr. Bastian responded, Ms. Oriel arrived. "Ah, my lady Justicar, lovely to see you again. I was just getting more testimonials filmed and picking up the commemorative crystals for the fundraiser. The area children made them as 'thank you' gifts to our donors. What brings you here?"

Jhee poked her chin toward where Mr. Bastian and Mirrei waited. "My dende wanted to tour the facilities."

Ms. Oriel frowned for an instant then returned to a cheery expression. "Hm, well, we shouldn't waste anymore of my lady Justicar's time. Bastian, could you bring these boxes to the vehicle, please?"

After Mr. Bastian left, Vash looked apologetic. "Our volunteers can be a bit passionate."

"I hope you like what you see here, my Lady Justicar, and we can look forward to some plump, juicy bids on our items."

With a formal touch of the heart, Ms. Oriel departed. After the tour, Jhee and Mirrei fought their way through another wave of protests to their transport where Kanto awaited them.

"Stall the Wall! Stop the Squall!"

"Fishers' rights! All Folx unite!"

A crowd of protesters blocked the road on their way back to the villa.

"My apologies, my Lady," the transport driver said. "These protests have been going on for several long-tides. It'll take me a few minutes to find a different route."

"See, I knew we should have taken the water taxi," Mirrei said.

Kanto wiggled his shoulders and adjusted in his seat. "Well, we wouldn't have missed the last ferry if someone hadn't detoured to visit a clinic."

Jhee stared out the windows at the faces as they passed by. Angry, twisted expressions met her gaze. Didn't they understand? We needed this shield. It was the only means to stop the coming war with the barbarians.

5
____

THE MIXER I

~

The Ride There

Contorted yelling faces again greeted the transport Jhee and Mirrei caught to the gala. Jhee stroked her chin in contemplation while they hurled slogans at them.

"Complicit! Oligarchs! The wall is death! One Folk! All Folk! Free the waves! Free the winds! Free the rains!"

"You live in your glass houses, but the wall is a lie. It's not meant to keep them out, but us in. Resist and wake up. We must stop the wall at all costs. Wake up guppies. Join the revolution. The time is now."

"How rude. They're protesting a charity event. We're trying to help," a fellow transport rider said, a low-ranking vizier judging by his badge and creme sash.

"Absolutely," a woman passenger chimed in. "There's a right way and a wrong way to protest."

A slim, brown-haired man, who wore clothes befitting the middle ranks, contrasted with the motley protesters that surrounded the gate. He barely batted an eye at the disruption but fixed Mirrei and Jhee with a long, direct stare as their water taxi passed the guard tower.

"If it weren't disruptive, it wouldn't rightly be a protest, would it?" Jhee asked.

Advocate Farkhande flipped the ends of her scarf over her shoulder. "That's always been my take on it."

Mirrei leaned back against the seat. "They want better lives. Like the refugees."

Jhee patted her hand. "Conditions will get better, once the Shield stabilizes."

"Didn't you tell me, denbe, 'Justice procrastinated is justice abdicated?'"

Jhee nodded.

Advocate Farkhande nodded too. "And patience can sometimes be deadly. More deadly than anything."

"Lobster drivel," the vizier said.

"What they were saying," Mirrei said. "'The wall is death.' What do you suppose they meant?"

"Hard to say, really," Jhee answered. "Many believe we shouldn't close ourselves off from the barbarian lands. It will lead to stagnation of the bloodlines, inbreeding. The inbreeding we had always been careful to avoid. The tampering with the weather. There's also the massive amount of male elementalists involved. The arcana. Many still don't know enough to know elementalism and cyphering are not the same."

"I'm not sure I do either. With the Shield up, the Other Folk may never get to go back and see their families again. They'll be stranded inside the Shield with us."

"In a way, that's how it's always been. It's the compact we made with the Other Folk: what washes up on our shores is ours. Even them."

"That's sad. It hardly seems right."

"They have to try hard to reach the empire. It doesn't just happen. The rules are clear: any who are not Water Folk who lay eyes on the Blessed Isles may not leave."

"Why?"

"I," Jhee started. "I don't know."

Mirrei's eyes flashed at the admission. She and Kanto always looked to Jhee for the answers. A better denbe might have had a more reassuring response to give her. It stunned Jhee too to realize she had always taken it as a given Imperial isle trespassers may not leave. Of all the assumptions for her not to question, why that one?

"Tell the truth, now, Justicar," Advocate Farkhande said, "because the previous policy was worse."

Jhee lapsed into silence as she had too often when it came to the treatment of the barbarians.

~

Fundraiser Arrival

Jhee and Mirrei disembarked from their water taxi. They had taken earlier transportation to the Observatory fundraiser with Lady Delphine's entourage not far behind. Yet, somehow, their large, ungainly retinue overtook them. The Delphines and Kanto had already queued up at the Foundation Members' entrance. The usher examined Jhee and Mirrei's invites and directed them to a longer queue separate from them while Advocate Farkhande and their other transport passengers joined the shorter line. Kanto furrowed his brow at them and raised his hands askance. Jhee shrugged.

Their queue barely moved. The security guards kept their heads down and focused on the invites while others thoroughly searched everyone who reached them. Jhee glanced over to the queue with the Delphines and Kanto. It had moved significantly faster. The guards were affable and mostly waved everyone through with the most cursory of searches. Kanto spared another concerned look before the guard swept his group inside where the porter announced their entrance.

"The pre-approved line," Mirrei said. She palmed her esca.

Was Jhee supposed to submit their credentials ahead of time? She smiled apologetically at Mirrei who returned her smile and took Jhee's arm so they might walk into the event together. "I think I may have erred."

"I'm sorry. The fault was mine," Mirrei said as if she had read Jhee's thoughts. "I should have sent ahead to pre-approve our credentials. Kanto explained it to me. Even reminded me twice. This will simply not do. This is one of my duties for our night and I washed out."

Jhee patted Mirrei's hand. In that, they were alike. She forgot about such details, too. "Don't fret over it. If you weren't here, I still would have forgotten it entirely and been waiting in this line anyway."

"Hence," Mirrei said, affecting a haughty accent, "why it is one of my duties and my responsibilities to see that an official such as yourself isn't seen in a queue like this. Not the most auspicious start to our introduction to courtly society and the social scene. Won't do at all and the shame is mine."

Jhee smirked. She would trust her younger spouses' judgment in this. Etiquette such as this had been part of their training. It certainly had been for Kanto, yet another reason they agreed to take him on as a husband. At least, that was one of Shep's motives. She could merely guess at the rest. They had found his role in their household, and she would honor him and let him do it. Plain and simple. Now, on the other hand, she had Mirrei.

Mirrei. The stickier issue. Jhee had returned with the young woman suddenly as Shep had unexpectedly shown up with Kanto in tow. Though, not at the same time, as Jhee had resolved to have only one additional marriage. She had already taken Kanto on months prior, but she simply could not refuse Miramar's request.

"Have you been enjoying our stay?" Jhee asked.

"It's going well. Lady Delphine and her family are very kind and generous. Her daughters are a hoot. Vash is caring and such a gentleman."

"Excellent. I'm glad to see you getting along. There is a chance her daughters will join the Military Academy."

"And me too unless I want to be conscripted?"

"Not necessarily. The shield has the conscription rules in flux. You and Kanto, being married, may no longer be under its strictures. With tightened requirements for recruitment, they no longer need to go as wide with their requests for service and fewer of us need to figure out how to serve or game the system to get them and theirs out of it."

"Leaving the poor most at risk still. I suppose my Fresh Lung Syndrome likely would have kept me out anyway."

"They find ways for those who wish to serve, to serve, even if they have a disqualifying condition."

The event organizer, Ms. Oriel, appeared at the doorway. She spoke to the guard who pointed at Jhee's queue. The woman hurried over her face a mask of distress. She unhooked the sealskin rope and walked Jhee and Mirrei over to the other entrance right past the rest of the line. "Apologies for the miscommunication, my Lady Justicar."

The barbarian porter announced Jhee's formal title in a booming, clear voice. "… Justicar of the Far Reaches, Talasisle, and sixteenth district and her escort, Star Mirror of Saphiria and Talasisle, beloved third and promised liege."

Beloved? Jhee winced. That had not been the impression she meant to give at all. The official designation should have been Bonded. Now, everyone would be under the misconception that they could not engage Mirrei directly. Jhee would have to field inquiries and act as her social secretary unless she wanted the woman to spend the whole event unapproachable.

Jhee did not even know what she was doing or what role she had intended the young woman to fill. She had not thought it through far enough. She only knew she had a debt and obligation to meet. A debt she could never repay. Mistakes she could never atone or make up for. This was barely even a down payment.

"No frowns," Mirrei said.

Jhee grunted as Lady Delphine's daughters sprinted by her, followed shortly by Vash. Kanto remained behind with Lady Delphine. He flashed his most winsome grin and gestured to the door with his wine glass. The younger Delphines and Mirrei chatted and giggled as excited and thick as coral in a cluster. A word drifted to her about the protests, the Shield, the refugees. She cast about her for someone else to converse with. She knew no one else here, save Lady Delphine. As long as Kanto accompanied her alone, Jhee had to maintain her distance according to household protocol.

Erma linked arms with Mirrei. "Our brother mentioned you have Fresh Lung Sickness. I can't imagine all this rain helps."

"It's all right," Mirrei replied. "I simply need to manage my salinity levels."

Semele quirked an eyebrow at them. "You even sound like Vash."

Jhee afforded herself of the exhibits. On display were some of the older telescopes once housed in the observatory's three domes and images of the former lead astronomers and their families. She tried not to get too far ahead and herd their assemblage along as she took in the exhibits.

The observatory itself was an architectural marvel with its multiple levels some of which were recessed into the hillside on which it sat. In the middle, a grand staircase that fluted outward in a pearlescent curve almost like the entire round hallway had been made of glowing mother of pearl inlay. Electrified glow orbs with bioluminescent light brighter than the basic honey and clam liquid variety led the way. A grand, crystal chandelier dominated the refinished dome above the great room. Depictions of the phases of the moons, the other inhabited worlds' transits across the sky, and other astronomical phenomena had been painted on the dome's surface.

The porters and attendants all wore matching fur and gilded gem uniforms. Many of them were barbarians. Occasionally the more high-ranking ones were traditional Water Folk who wore similar uniforms but just a little bit more ornate and with more insignia. They all bore the same logo and name: Inkerton Event Solutions. They provided the staff and catering for many high society events and always with barbarians dressed smartly in elegant, urbane attire. It was weird she had not really noticed that before. She also noted many of the service staff to be smaller and possibly shabbier Water Folk. Mostly male. Again, more people coming from the provinces to the capital for work. Her mind went back to Tranquility Bridge Abbey and to Mr. Pol, the widower, and the smuggling and trafficking of people and the refugees.

Kanto stepped away from Lady Delphine. As soon as she saw the opening, Jhee approached her. "Save me," she said.

Delphine laughed. "Were we ever that young?"

"Never."

The gang of four walked from exhibit to exhibit whispering and laughing. Mirrei behaved so alive and engaged. She would make a good heir for her fortunes. Jhee decided to scale back on their lessons at least while they were here. Kanto slipped back into the group once they had merged.

They heard more than one attendee remark sentiments such as, "Are those images of men cyphering? Scandalous."

"Think of the children," Erma said while smirking.

Mirrei and Semele giggled.

"It wasn't such a laughing matter not long ago," Delphine said.

A timeline wall showcased artifacts relating to arcana or the science of the Shield. Images and implements of early arcana tables, including recently dusted off illustrations related to pre-ban male artificers. A case featured a few yellowed gyration veils and sun-faded mats with protective circles, both implements meant to shield the men from harm. Several images showed rows of men practicing cyphers in formation.

"Arcana still isn't well understood," Jhee said. Jhee walked them through the timeline. "Pillarists had everyone convinced male artificers were going to break the world. The ensuing panic saw many men who practiced jailed or worse. The elimination of male practitioners shifted the arcane window and arcana in general might have died out."

One wing lead to a rotunda with an inertial pendulum and another housed an aquarium. The younger folk had lapsed into more subdued conversation by the time they had visited every great room exhibit and wing —except for one wing which remained unopened. The plaque read: The History of Galleon City.

"It's good to have this reminder of how fortunate we are and how grateful we should be," Mirrei said.

Semele took her hand and Erma's. "And how far we can go in our persecution of others."

"Don't think we just reserved our prejudices for the Other Folk," Kanto said.

"Hardly," Delphine said. "Your denbe and I were mid-toned. We would have barely passed the parchment test."

"Parchment test?" Vash asked.

Lady Delphine looked embarrassed. "A remnant of another time."

Jhee took a drink. "Rumors were you only gained access to certain social circles if you were dark enough. The débutantes took a piece of parchment paper and held it beside your face. If your complexion was lighter than the parchment, they did not let you join."

Vash blanched, and Lady Delphine rubbed his back. "Water Folk really did that to each other?" he asked.

"I saw no actual evidence of it being practiced, but the most elite were all darker toned."

Lady Delphine raised a glass. "Enough of that, this is also a celebration. As the Mechanists say: to being remade magnificent."

~

Brief Interlude

"Ah Lady Delphine, thank you so much for coming," Ms. Oriel, the event organizer, said. She graciously clasped forearms with Lady Delphine. "Erma. Semele. Vash. Great to see you."

"Oriel, this is our guest Bright Harmony. You remember the Justicar and this is her consort, Star Mirror."

"Pleasure to meet you, Ms. Oriel," Mirrei said.

A young man of similar age and dress to the event organizer came over,

Mr. Bastian, the volunteer from the clinic. "My Ladies, allow me to introduce my fiancé, Bastian."

"Ladies," he said with a slight bow.

Kanto gave him the once over, gaze lingering on the wrist tattoo, and made an unusually territorial bow.

"We've met," Jhee said. "At the clinic."

"Ah, yes. Not the ideal way I wanted to make your acquaintance, my lady. I realize now how my questions must have sounded." Mr. Bastian slipped his arm into the event organizer's. He coughed. When the coughing did not stop, he covered his mouth with a handkerchief. "Excuse me, ladies."

Ms. Oriel followed him through a nearby archway. She returned a short time later.

"Pardon my sudden departure. Fresh Lung Syndrome. It was his plight which first moved me to get involved with this cause. You might say he is the reason we are all here tonight."

"Oriel, may I impose upon you to give my old friend the Justicar and her wife a private tour and allow her to see the telescope? She is a practicing artificer and big matron of heritage Mechanics."

The event organizer's eyes, and smile grew brighter upon mention of Jhee's matronage. "I'd be delighted."

The musicians started up, and the dancing began. Mirrei sipped from her fluted champagne glass while Jhee tapped her foot along and bobbed her head. Mirrei plucked another glass from the tray of a passing server. Something about the man had caught Mirrei's attention. Jhee couldn't help but notice, too. She had a more immediate concern. Jhee downed her glass of champagne in a single, long shot. She glanced at the dance floor and swallowed the lump in her throat. She held out her arms to Mirrei. "May I?" Jhee asked.

"I'd be delighted, denbe."

Mirrei stepped into Jhee's arms. Jhee swept her around the dance floor. Jhee tried not to move her lips as she counted steps. "I haven't danced so much until recently."

"You're doing great," Mirrei said.

"Even in my academy days, I didn't dance this much. Even though they had a ball almost every long-tide. Unless you're too much like me, you will love it."

Mirrei's smile was half-hearted. "I suppose. I might prefer the company of a good book while in a comfy chair."

"That's my girl. That was my preferred way to spend the evening. Tihalmec Academy's library is extensive with complete access to the ether collections housed at the other branches. Their physical volumes are available via loan unless you want something from their rare volume collection. I made more than a few trips to the other branches for just that reason."

"I can completely see you poring over volumes in your free time. You must have been over the Spheres."

"I was."

"May I?" Vash asked.

Jhee waited for Mirrei's reaction to the offer. Mirrei eagerly tapped Jhee's waist beneath the concealment of Jhee's sleeves. Jhee stepped aside and allowed Vash to take her place. Mirrei winked before Jhee went to find a place off the dance floor to stand. Ambassador Naiman and one passenger from her transport, the vizier, examined an exhibit dedicated to barbarian workers. Eldjin, the mustachioed villa guest, trailed after them doing the most obvious job of listening in she had ever seen.

Advocate Farkhande swept through dancing by herself or possibly with the wisps. The same shimmering haze Jhee noted before. Jhee's esca tingled and she felt light-headed. She decided she needed some air. A breather was not to be had. Instead, the mayor cornered her and went on at length about how Jhee should set a story in Galleon City. Eventually, Jhee excused herself.

Jhee came across the ambassador who appeared to be doing his dawned best to ignore his companion, the vizier from the transport. The expression on Ambassador Naiman's face was part beleaguered, part disgust. Eldjin appeared to have abandoned their conversation to socialize with other officials.

"What do sand slakers know about great architecture?" the vizier scoffed.

The ambassador gripped his tumbler tightly. "This may surprise you, Vizier, but the Fire Folk are civilized. We have cities with buildings, modern conveniences, and everything."

"Yes, I've heard about your building dedication ceremonies. I hear barbarians celebrate the start of work on a new building by killing and burying some unbedded fellow under the foundation."

"Alas, I think the Vizier is mistaken. That practice was only done on the spring festivals by followers of the Maye King over a hundred years ago."

Jhee interjected, "Around the same time, the Water Folk did as well. I also believe Water Folk from the Qibarei isles had similar practices. And I believe it was the The Djararo of the Far/Middle Isles, Water Folk, who were known for sacrificing people to volcanoes."

The vizier shrugged. "I suppose it's all the same in those backwater isles. With all that interbreeding."

"If I remember correctly, in the past this area had a tradition of when a powerful chieftess died, they buried her husbands alive with her."

The vizier shook his head and walked away.

"I like how he slipped in that nice two-tap with the last insult."

"I must commend you, Ambassador, not just on your patience, but on the remarkable accomplishment of keeping your hems clean."

"Oh?" The ambassador glanced down. "Yes."

"The main walkway near the transports has turned into a virtual lake. I'm

not used to maneuvering in these longer robes yet. I suppose in your homeland the problem would be sand."

"This is my homeland."

"When you said you were a barbarian and with you being an ambassador, I—" Jhee gulped. "My apologies. I should know better."

"Fire Folk on my father's side. My mother, whom I never knew, appears
to have been Water Folk."

"Imagine the scandal."

"What could she have been thinking?"

"You never know. She could have been in love. You know how these
matters can be. A lonely isolated woman and someone offers her the gift of
friendship and something more."

"That's what I've always hoped. I'd like to think there was some affection
in my conception and not violence or coercion."

"Here's hoping you are right. I thank you for humoring a bigot, and I
don't mean the vizier."

After the ambassador left, Kanto drifted over to Jhee with a drink. He
faced away from her as he spoke.

"How are we making our way home then? Do you wish for me to ride
back with you or them?"

"We shall see."

Mirrei ran over to Jhee and took her arm. "Thank you, denbe. That was
such fun."

"You dance divinely."

"Vash is an expert partner." Mirrei nodded at Kanto. "Not perhaps as
great as you, denye. Oh, Kanto, we are having the most marvelous time.
Why did you leave?"

"I had responsibilities to attend to. I saw our denbe left to her own
devices on a night when she is not supposed to be."

Mirrei dropped her gaze for a moment showing she had taken Kanto's
gentle rebuke. She went back to beaming happiness once again. "Denbe,
would it be all right if I made the return trip with the Delphines? There is
something I wanted to discuss with them."

"Star Mirror." Kanto tightened his mouth then gave a weary sigh while
mumbling something about completely inappropriate.

"*Bright Harmony*, it's not your night," Mirrei said.

Kanto looked away sheepishly. Mirrei returned her attention to Jhee. Her
expression showed such excitement and expectation. Jhee sighed. "As it
pleases you, dende."

"Oh, thank you so much. Denye, would you do me the favor of accompa-
nying her back to the villa in my stead?"

Kanto bowed. "As it pleases, my denye."

Mirrei kissed Jhee's cheek then Kanto's and ran off to rejoin the
Delphines.

The weaselly woman from the clinic strode into the fundraiser. She raised a glass at several folk, among them the unpleasant vizier from the transport ride. The vizier began to continually adjust his sash of rank. Jhee later observed the weaselly woman and vizier in conversation. Eldjin upon seeing them made himself scarce. Jhee thought perhaps she had uncovered a loan shark or gangster. The woman's presence at the clinic made so much more sense now.

6

THE MIXER II

~

Indisposed

Jhee did her best to pay attention as Kanto introduced her to another dignitary or minor official. This one the minor lord of that region. This one in charge of draining rights for the city. And this one handles building permits. While this one was the fourth cousin once removed from the emperor or empress and fiftieth in line for appointment to the Imperial Palace, yet farther outside the succession pool than Jhee. Her eyes glazed over and wanted to roll back in her head. She made small talk where she could. Often in situations such as this, his prompting proved invaluable. He, however, kept a close watch on Mirrei and the Delphines. A feat Jhee had done her level best not to do. He had failed. Eventually, they were alone. Kanto sipped his drink and stared daggers as Mirrei slipped her arm in Vash's and smiled and laughed with the Delphines.

The musicians finally began to tune up. *Thank the Makers.*

Kanto smiled and patted her hand. "You did well. You didn't look too terribly bored."

"I'm sorry. I didn't mean to be rude."

"Denbe, I say this with all due humility, most of these guests rank beneath you—to a remarkable degree. They may peer down at you because you are from the Far Reaches, but put plainly, your status is higher than theirs. You should assert it more. Some of them really weren't worth your time, and for some, it may be too soon for them to know where they stand with you."

305

The band went into a rendition of the Dawning of the Night music and stanzas of Canon Chaisen. Jhee started tapping her feet.

"Shall we?"

Jhee nodded. "We shall."

Kanto spun her about the dance floor. Dancing was one of the many skills required of a consort such as him. His dancing was almost as good and practiced as his lute playing. Jhee was awkward. When she missed the step, he did a slight flourish which covered the gaffe. When she hesitated unable or unsure how to move, gentle guiding pressure on her back made it clear how and when to move. She only wished she made him look as good.

Jhee sneaked a few glances over at Mirrei. She danced with several individuals. Eventually, Vash swept her into his arms. He swirled and twirled her about the dance floor as expertly and deftly as Kanto swept her. Not a missed step. They seemed in perfect harmony. Jhee smiled. She had to keep herself focused on her current companion.

Kanto's embrace had tensed. Every so often he winced.

"What is it?" she asked.

"The musician's instruments. They 're out of tune or something is wrong with the musical equipment. Every few bars, the stringed instruments hit a false note with too much feedback and resonance. All this moisture might affect the acoustical properties. I hope my lutes won't be affected."

"You have such a practiced and attuned ear. Leave it to you to notice a detail like that."

"My musical ear is a skill I pride myself on."

"As well you should."

"I must excuse myself. There is only so much of this I can take. I only hope my lutes won't be affected."

"Would you like me to come with?"

"No, I'm going take a moment to refresh myself. You stay here and try not to be too bored without me."

"I make no promises."

Kanto scampered off. It might be a good time to refresh herself as well. Jhee found the facilities marked Neutral. Jhee used the screened stall, and as she washed her hands, Mirrei emerged from another one. She rinsed her hands and began to fix her make-up.

Mirrei had ceded her night to Kanto likely intending to have it to herself without Jhee hovering. Jhee contemplated saying something. It would not technically be a breach of etiquette as Kanto had excused himself and she would only spend a moment with Mirrei.

"So, you are enjoying your evening?"

"Yes. No need to worry about me. I saw both you and Kanto nearly straining your necks to watch me. Please, enjoy your evening together."

"How are you feeling?"

"Very well. No need to worry. I'll inform you if something changes."

"Be sure you do. A valid emergency is a perfectly valid excuse to violate the rules. Or a genuine change of circumstance."

"I know. See you later."

Mirrei finished up the last touches on her make-up. She swept out of the facilities. Jhee finished up the last bits of her toilet and then left too. When she emerged, Kanto was there to take her arm. "Have your poor sensitive ears been revived, dear husband?"

"Much better. I will find some way to ignore it. Once you hear it, though it is hard to unhear."

"I am that way about cases sometimes."

"Believe me, I know. I love the way your mind works. I like the way you watch and take everything in. So, did your talk with Mirrei reassure you?"

Jhee raised an eyebrow.

"I saw her come out."

Jhee nodded. "Just so. Forgive me. Please, don't feel pushed aside. I did not mean to violate your time."

"Not at all. I would have spoken to her myself too if she had let me."

"Shall we return to the great room?"

"Let's."

Jhee and Kanto danced and danced. She even pushed Mirrei out of her head for a few minutes.

"She abandoned you on your night together," Kanto said. "It's the height of rudeness. Why aren't you more upset at this?"

"Kanto, please. Allow her to enjoy herself."

"Well, aren't you going to put a stop to it? Not only is it indiscreet, but they also nearly killed her inside of a long-tide."

"Kanto, don't you feel you are being at least a bit dramatic? Perhaps we should return to the manse. We've hobnobbed enough for one evening. We should have some time alone. I thought a night out such as this would be enjoyable for you. And her. I see now it was a mistake. Our announcement. You told them to use the term beloved."

"I thought it was appropriate."

"Won't you please allow her to enjoy herself? I wanted her free to explore her options without having everyone she speaks to filtered by me." Jhee sighed and sought to redirect Kanto's focus. "This is our night now. Amuse me with the latest fashion or gossip. Who are the two most prominent officials you know who are rumored to have affairs right now?"

"Explore her options?" Kanto repeated. "I see. Our stay is multifold. I should have understood sooner. No wonder you've been encouraging us to accompany them places without you. Should the Mistress of the House herself, her daughters, or an Aunt come to call while we are here, inform them I cannot make their acquaintance. I am indisposed. I've taken ill."

Kanto set his drink down on the bar. He walked out of the front doors, and Jhee followed sparing a last glance at Mirrei and the Delphines.

"Wait, were you going? We haven't had the private tour yet."

"Bright Harmony's taken ill. Something didn't agree with him. Please have a transport brought around."

"As you wish, my Lady Justicar."

The sounds of protest carried from further down the drive. Jhee had not wanted to brave those crowds again so soon. Kanto stayed by Jhee's side in sullen silence. She wracked her brain for a way to get Kanto to change his mind. If he gave the Delphines a chance, he might grow to like them as Mirrei had.

The valet approached them. "Your pardon, my Lady Justicar. We are experiencing transport delays because of the protests. It may be another twenty minutes to half an hour before we can have any of the private shuttles brought up."

"What of a water taxi?"

"I'll call one."

"Call one? There's one parked right there." Jhee pointed to the water taxi idling nearby with its lights off. She started down the lane to the seaside pick-up. "Come along, Bright Harmony."

"Let's just wait for a transport. In the meantime, we can return to the opening."

"Weren't you the one eager to leave?"

"Not if it means traveling in some creepy, trench cab. Besides, I'm not inclined to wasting the pretty or brave the protesters again so soon. They've been known to throw gross substances on the finely dressed people. Also, I've reconsidered leaving Mirrei alone in the company of those Delphines."

The valet squinted down the lane. "I don't recognize their service mark, and they appear to be off duty. If my lady would allow me to check it out first?"

The valet overtook them. Once he had gotten halfway, the water taxi's lights came on, and it sped away.

"How rude," Kanto said. "I did not want to ride in some scummy taxi anyway. I can already imagine it. The second we got inside the doors would lock and speed us through the Hole in the World to the Unmaker's discard pile or the Trench itself."

"Such a vivid picture you paint."

"I try. You win, denbe. Back inside to the horrible music and company we go."

The Viewing

"You've returned," Ms. Oriel, the event organizer, said. "I'm glad you've changed your mind. We're just about to start a private tour for the Breath of the Deep Society donors."

"We're not members."

"Yet. I think we can make an exception. Don't tell anyone. Keep it between us, though."

Jhee smirked. The woman was persuasive, she could tell you that. The Delphines opted out. Ms. Oriel led them along to where a group of the fabulously rich gathered at the base of one of the astronomy towers. A woman in a rumpled, ill-fitting gown shuffled from foot to foot. She greeted Ms. Oriel's arrival with a look of sheer terror.

"Hello everyone. Yes. Yes. Gather round. I see you have already met Levinia. For those of you who might not already know, she is the Observatory's lead astronomer. She led the charge on all our restoration work here at the Observatory. Without her bringing me in, I suspect our beloved observatory would still linger in a state of disrepair."

A smattering of applause came from the crowd.

Ms. Oriel's conch went off. She tried to ignore it. She pulled it out to silence it, then changed her mind. "I'm sorry, I have to take this. Levinia, I turn the tour over to you."

Ms. Levinia's eyes went wide. She turned and began up the stairs. As she rattled off dry statistics about the observatory, Jhee stared up at the dizzying height of the dome. Why did it always have to be stairs? "Above you, gentlefolk, hangs the historic Planetarium Chandelier, lovingly restored to near original condition. After a cleaning, it went missing. It was thought to be lost until maintenance crews found it stashed in an observatory storage unit."

At last, they emerged from the stairwell to the telescope dome. The lead astronomer's eyes had taken on a bright sheen as she went into detail on the telescope's lens size and viewing capabilities. Jhee rested against the inner viewing chamber. She was careful not to lean against the dome which could move at any time. What she wanted now more than anything was a chair. A close second, an opportunity to look through the drenched telescope already.

"All the telescopic domes were refitted with composite materials after their metals were stripped for the space effort. With the increased light pollution of the city and the Storm Shield, the telescopes will now be used for terrestrial photography. I'm sure you are all now more than eager to take a look."

Jhee straightened in anticipation. Kanto had spent most of the time hiding chuckles. She was almost as glad his mood improved as she was for a chance to look through the telescope. She waited for all the other tour participants to go first. Finally, her turn at the viewfinder came. She squeezed one eye shut.

The rocky craters of the fourth moon came into startling view. She took in a breath and flailed for Kanto to look. She smiled when he gasped at the sight. He took hold of her hand and squeezed gently. Kanto turned back to her, eyes bright and full of wonder. He went back to the telescope again, his breathing now almost as labored as hers was from their climb.

As the tour continued, he stood closer than he had at the start. His other hand covered the one she rested on his arm.

Ms. Levinia gave a planetarium presentation and a brief description of the celestial finds that had been made by the observatory's previous astronomers.

Ms. Oriel clapped. "Rest assured. These are still astronomical telescopes. So, no spying on the neighbors even if they are pointed landward. We can, however, see the Styr Mine or the royal game preserve."

Jhee had not noticed her return.

"The Styr Mine," Ms. Levinia said, "the Hole in the World. The civilized world's largest source of templarite, the Empire's indispensable mineral, used in everything from your conch to the Shield."

"Our best view though," Ms. Oriel said, "doesn't require the telescope and can be seen with the unaided eye. If you'll please follow me, gentlefolk."

Their tour guides led them to the roof terrace of the observatory. Two majestic clear pillars rose out of the ground a few miles away. Within each, whirled two waterspouts. Now and then a peal of thunder and flash of lightning would strike them. The waterspouts spun and twirled but did not move far from their centralized location. The bottoms where they touched the waters wandered some but not far. In between them sat the relay station so small and unassuming nestled between the two towering giants of water and electricity. This was truly a technical marvel. Further beyond them, she could just make out the shadow of the Great Tether to Heaven.

"Behold, the Double Tines, the heart of the defense grid, better known as the Storm Shield. This vantage affords the best view of them in the whole region, perhaps even on the entire continent. Each tower is named after one of the legendary double drakes thought to encircle the isles."

After a few minutes to marvel and sip champagne, Ms. Oriel started taking them back down the stair.

"Oriel, about those Breath of the Deep visitors' logs," Ms. Levinia began.

Mr. Oriel checked her timepiece. "Not now, don't you see we have an important guest? Would you mind showing the Justicar the Mechanist pieces while I finish up the tour? Please."

Before Ms. Levinia could argue, Ms. Oriel took off.

"Come with me, please," Ms. Levinia said.

Ms. Levinia led Jhee and Kanto to a climate-controlled vault. In the viewing room, she carefully arrayed a series of Wondrous Age-era astrological tools.

Jhee clasped her hands then touched them to her esca. "The First Devotions. Each piece supposedly designed and hand-crafted to exacting specifications by Parul, one of the earliest devisers of the Mechanist movement."

"They're on loan from the Imperial Collection. Would you like to examine them?"

Jhee's breath caught. "Yes, please."

To see an early set of Mechanist devotional tools up close, would be worth the donation the event organizer would likely solicit at the end of the tour. Kanto accompanied her to the viewing room where they were instructed in the handling procedures. She would have thought he'd find this incredibly boring. He somehow cut a dashing figure even in a smock and Thindril gloves.

"They must be at least a thousand years old," Jhee said. "A minuscule amount in geological time, a considerable amount of time even with our current lifespans. They use indirect methods to date them rather than risk damaging their integrity via chemical analysis. Be as gentle as you would with me while handling them."

Kanto grinned. Technicians brought in a portfolio, one of five copies of the original specifications. Jhee held her breath, clasped her hands then touched them to her esca again, as they set it in front of her. The portfolio displayed on a thin bio-film screen which had thousands of hairline cracks from age and a few creases. It ran on solar power, its cells probably depleted and at the end of even their most optimistic lifespan.

"Please, examine it closer," the astronomer said. She handed Jhee a magnifier.

Jhee waved Kanto over. "It's on a dedicated reader for confidentiality. Those creases date to its creation. They say one of Parul's first assistants made them. Stands to reason, to them confidential or not it was simply another tool. It was bound to get damaged as they ran their experiments."

They held the magnifier together, and Jhee thumbed through the portfolio gently. The screen barely produced enough light for viewing it by. She pointed out the infamous Bebhinn transposition error which was only caught after several years of it already being part of the curricula and how it was a miracle the Imperial Academy had not been blasted to the moons by then. Kanto's eyes shone with eagerness.

"So much history," he said. "No, stories. So many stories. You teach me so much, denbe. Subjects I would have never been interested in on my own."

"You do that for me."

Jhee and Kanto browsed through the portfolio more. Ms. Oriel entered. "I hate to pry you away, but I have to be there for the chandelier dedication."

"Yes. Yes. Of course," Jhee said and sighed wistfully.

7
____

THE MIXER III

~

The Mechanist

Jhee and Kanto emerged from the viewing room having divested themselves of gloves and smocks.

"I brought you in to get us funding, not to go into business for yourself. I intended this to be a community event for the underprivileged, not another private matronage affair," Ms. Levinia began.

Ms. Oriel silenced her. "I trust you enjoyed your private viewing, my lady Justicar?"

"Very much so," Jhee replied.

"Lady Delphine mentioned you were a matron of the arts."

"Yes. Indeed."

"Using templarite from the local mines, the Imperial History Museum was one of the first to restore a portfolio to operation on its own original power source. Our work with the telescopes and chandelier restoration pioneered technologies that allowed us to assist."

Ms. Levinia blushed. "I can't take all the credit. Bastian assisted me. He's insightful on technical matters. If the Justicar will excuse me."

The lead astronomer hurried off, leaving only Ms. Oriel to answer Jhee's questions.

"Templarite. I imagine it was quite expensive."

"Well, Justicar...."

"If I wanted to start an organization like the Fresh Lung Society, how would you recommend I go about it?"

Jhee nodded along as Ms. Oriel laid out the process in sensible and direct terms until Kanto began to fidget.

Quick as lightning, Jhee produced a code chip from her sleeve. "Here's a routing code for my charitable trust's business office. Provide them verification access for the financials of both the observatory and the clinic. Once they sign off, I'll authorize a donation."

"Right away, Justicar. And thank you. Very generous of you."

"Not at all. Consider it an audition. If I like what I see, perhaps we can work on other ventures together. What I was most interested in, Ms. Oriel, was starting a charity to help the refugees. I also wanted to investigate schools and funding streams for teaching the men cyphering."

"Cyphering. Forward-thinking. We can help the men learn other modern trades, too."

"The Shield will need people to maintain it, and well, I can't think of a more future-forward skill for the men to learn than cyphering or drawing."

"We are of similar minds."

Ms. Oriel and Jhee discussed the matter a little more before the other woman took her leave.

"That was brilliant," Kanto whispered and nuzzled her ear. "I'm almost done documenting my recordings from the abbey. Do you think a heritage foundation might like it if I donate some to their collection? Remember how I wanted to work with educational institutions? This event has given me several ideas on how to get involved in charitable causes of my own. I think I might work with organizations designed to help refugees. The serving staff seem happy. Are they the lucky ones? How many might otherwise wind up in pleasure houses?"

Jhee released a breath she had not realized she been holding. She smiled approvingly at Kanto. "That sounds like a wonderful pursuit."

"One moment, I left my conch."

While Jhee waited for Kanto to return, Jhee paused on the mezzanine landing to admire the historic chandelier. Ms. Oriel and Mr. Bastian enjoyed cocktails at a nearby table further along the mezzanine railing. Ms. Oriel pulled out a jewelry box and presented it to him.

"Thank you. It's beautiful. She's right, you know? This is exactly the opposite of the event we wanted."

"It's events like this one that fund those."

The organizer's conch chimed, and she answered it. Her posture tensed. She gestured with more and more emphasis until at last, she shoved the conch in a concealed pocket. By the time she finished the conversation, Bastian had donned the plain but elegant lapel pin topped with an oversized crystal.

Ms. Oriel began to unclasp the pin. "You know what? We should probably put it in the security vault for now."

"Oh, I wanted to wear it the rest of the evening, you could show us both off."

Ms. Oriel leaned forward and lowered her voice, "I know what you've been up to and who with."

Before Jhee could move closer for a better listen, Kanto reemerged and hurried Jhee down to the main event.

"Step lively, Jhee. That's the vizier of building permits, the land development consortium head, and that's the vizier of mineral rights. Oh, and the mayor. You should definitely talk to them. They can help you in your dispute with the Brackfins. I'm sure if you put in a word or two, they might find in your favor."

"I've already had the displeasure of meeting the building permits vizier this evening."

"How bad?" Jhee pursed her lips. "We'll approach the consortium head then."

"You know so much about the household affairs."

"Yes, ever since you and I reached an accommodation, it's been easier. No more gleaning snippets from your paperwork or secondhand tidbits from Shep. I did my best to hide my intelligence from you."

"You didn't need to. You know I love intellectual stimulation as much as any other stimulation you might provide."

Jhee raised an eyebrow.

"I know that now. But I grew up being told that women would not want me to be smart. It was in my best interest to be a reflection or mirror of my spouses, see to their needs, and not be too intimidating."

Jhee found Mirrei once more in the crowd. "Well, no more. Remind me to have you sit in when next I discuss household practicals."

Kanto dipped his head. "As it pleases, denbe."

Jhee caught the weaselly woman from the clinic stalking at the top of the stairs to the mezzanine. "Enough stalling. You better come through or else."

"Bright Harmony, wait here a moment."

"What? Denbe, where are you going?"

The woman paused upon sight of Jhee. Her eyes widened, and she scuttled away. Jhee chanced upon Bastian on the lanai contemplating a glass of scotch on the rocks.

"About what you saw at the clinic," Mr. Bastian began.

"A clinic in an impoverished area. An attempted shakedown by a criminal element?"

"Precisely so, my lady. We try to keep them at bay as best we can."

"Not anymore I suppose."

"Hence, our drive to move the clinic."

"Say no more, Mr. Bastian. Relief may be on the next tide."

"If you say so, my lady. Do you believe in divine retribution?"

"I believe mortal retribution hits us faster."

"You're a Mechanist, Justicar," Mr. Bastian said.

"Yes, and an artificer."

"You know what is to be tasked with the conception and design of a devotional creation. Maybe you've even experienced the wondrous elation and closeness to the Makers which comes from a well-designed piece or simple yet elegant equation."

"Yes."

"What do you do when that feeling betrays you? When what you've wrought turns on you? When your beautiful equations go to pot, and they leave you with nothing but wreckage?"

"My mentor used to say, you can't always account for every eventuality. If you try, you could drive yourself to madness."

"What if a gunner had not misread a radar signature and led to a ship of pilgrims being blown out of the sky? What if the Bebhinn transposition error hadn't been corrected before the worst happened? Don't forget the Althan Astrolabe which had a tiny flaw. It was off by a mere two degrees, and it caused the Migdal disaster. Or the Trishanku serum contamination incident caused when technicians did not destroy one unsterilized batch? How do you think the architects of those disasters felt?"

"I am fortunate to have never faced a situation like that."

"Not even your mentor's final 'Dispatches from Arrow Point' case." Jhee's mouth twitched. "Don't you worry that with all your judgments you might have made a mistake? That you might have destroyed someone's life?"

"I can't let that stop me. If I'm too afraid to do my duty and render judgment, I'm no good to anyone. Least of those I might help. I must do my best to help those I can, to render a good judgment with the best available information and without caprice. I can only pray that if I am wrong, the First Makers see fit to make my mistakes known before too much damage is done."

"And if they're not?"

"I must do what I can to make amends."

"Would that were always the case. Some wounds are not so easily mended, my Lady. Please, enjoy the rest of the fundraiser."

Mr. Bastian headed inside. He remained on the mezzanine admiring the chandelier as Jhee returned downstairs.

"My lady Justicar, good to see you again," the mayor said. "Enjoying the fundraiser?"

"A lot more than the fair, so far," Jhee said.

"Oh yes, those nasty protests and strikes."

"It's only natural for folk to want to strive for better positioning in the Prime Maker's showcase."

Advocate Farkhande said, "We do not understand what sort of effects all this arcana can have on those who performed the work and on those who live near the constructions. What manner of artifice is it? The most sacred and reserved kind. With all these men cyphering."

"The loosening of restrictions on cyphering came because of the Storm Shield. I see it as a good thing. They needed the males' skills, and so it led to their liberation from useless traditions."

"At what cost?" the Ambassador said. "They may have released the men from their restrictions, but for the wrong reasons. This may be a problem, and they are as likely to put them back for the wrong reasons."

"Wise words," Advocate Farkhande said.

"Wise words to consider indeed, Ambassador." Jhee placed a finger on her esca.

"That's all I can ask."

"There are other rumors I heard from the nature wisps. There are those concerned about health effects. A massive working of this kind with all the various cyphering, drawings, weftings involved. And let alone one which affects the weather. Some say we are reaching too far. It's hubris. We are violating the Makers' realm, and they will punish us for it."

Jhee's vision refused to focus on the advocate. "It is also the First Makers' design that we create and innovate."

"My, what an interesting, auspicious gathering," Sianna said. She and her silent companion deposited half-drunk glasses of champagne and some shiny, pocket trash on a champagne server's tray and joined their conclave. "What sort of nasty rumors are you going on about, Advocate?"

"Nothing to concern you, director," the ambassador said.

"Everything to do with the mines concerns me and Inksy. Isn't that right?"

"Heh." Inksy's breath held a strong odor of cloves. She grabbed another glass of champagne. She downed it without bothering to remove the strong-flavored clove candy she sucked on. Jhee could only imagine how revolting such a combination tasted.

Sianna faced Jhee. "I thought it was a core Mechanist principle that society work like a finely tuned machine with everyone in their place, and any part that violates that was an anathema?"

"Were you eavesdropping on my conversation?" Jhee asked.

"No, of course not. But I couldn't help but overhear."

"There's room for both. The Grand Design is nothing if not expansive."

Advocate Farkhande turned toward the ambassador, "So, on another topic, I heard they hospitalized another half dozen in accidents down at the mines."

"Yes, quite terrible, really. I'll likely be representing the Fire Folk in arbitration against the mining company. Conditions in the mine have deteriorated with the increase in production and have become more dangerous than ever."

"It's a pity their labor contract prevents them from suing."

Sianna grabbed another glass of champagne and Inksy. "I get it. We'll go somewhere more welcoming."

~

Dye Hard

A murmuring arose from the attendees.

Jhee and the private tour attendees ran to the side of the terrace. From their vantage, they saw the outline of a figure scaling the side of the observatory dome. The climber noticed the scrutiny and gave the onlookers a cheeky wave. On the ground, security had gathered. Jhee looked at Kanto.

"What is she doing?" Mirrei asked.

"Whelm and waves," Erma said. She and Mirrei gaped at each other. Erma's color had drained. "She's crazy."

"Hold my robes," Jhee said.

"You're insane," Kanto said. "You can't honestly be thinking of going out there."

Jhee inspected the side of the building. She plotted her hand holds and foot holds. All around the Observatory she saw solid ground. No sheer drops to the ocean. She closed her eyes and steadied her nerves. If Jhee swung her leg over the railing, she might climb the face of the building towards the vandal. She respected the Makers of Heights; she did not fear them.

Jhee glanced back at Kanto's terrified expression. Instead of going over the side, the observatory offices had some nice, sensible windows from which to converse with the activist. "Hail friend."

A fresh, friendly face with golden eyes and watermark peered up at her from beneath ginger, shaggy hair tight in a bun. She had a fading cut on her forehead. "Hello, my lady."

"What do you think you're doing?"

"I thought it might be a nice night for a climb and to display this banner. It won't take a moment. You should probably wait inside. I wouldn't want you to get hurt."

The wind caused Jhee to yell to be heard. "You have no equipment."

"Neither do you."

"None needed where I stand. Care to join me?"

"Do mind, my lady. This is rather distracting. I need to focus on the climb."

"Perhaps you would let me throw you a rope?"

"Nay. I just need to concentrate."

Jhee went over the response time in her head. The security forces on the ground had moved an airbag into place underneath the activist. Not enough and too many things could go wrong with the placement. She had to hope they saw Jhee and figured out how to get to the office.

The activist continued to climb. Jhee went to the stairs and found the next flight up. As she passed by the mezzanine landing, it was now empty. She poked her head out another window.

"You sure I can't offer you some assistance?"

"My lady is too kind. I'll be right down in a jiffy. One way or another."

"That's what I'm afraid of."

The activist chuckled. A sudden gust of wind caught the banner and threatened to take flight with her. The activist flattened herself against the building murmuring and pressing her fingers into it. The building was stonework. She must have been an earth elementalist.

Jhee breathed deep to engage the Divine Mechanism and link her prime forces within to the breeze. The winds died down. She guided the winds to push the activist towards the building, a feat made difficult by the height. The wind vortices around tall buildings could be mercurial creatures. Their sudden appearance had surprised more than one wind elementalist.

"Handy trick," the activist said.

"Same." Jhee pointed her chin at the activist's climbing skills. "I'm a certified wind guider."

"I can't say as you can do lots of fancy wind motions climbing the side of a building."

"Perhaps you could come inside, and we could discuss elementalism techniques."

"No thanks. Maybe once I'm done here. My lady must be aware she is splitting my focus which will make it hard for me to deal with events should another gale like that occur."

"Many pardons." Jhee ducked back inside. By now the security team had entered the building. She heard their pounding footsteps on the stairs. She met them on the landing. "Follow me."

Jhee led them up to the roof access door where she and her tour had so recently used. They burst onto the roof deck. The activist clipped a carabiner to the side of a banner. She unfurled the banner and leaped off the side of the building.

The 'Free the Fire Folk' banner caught the winds, and she floated down from the spire beyond the observatory hill to some lower depth Jhee could not see and out of sight. By now, Erma, Kanto and Mirrei had reached the roof deck.

"Denbe, are you okay?"

"Yes," Jhee reassured them.

Erma ran to the edge. Mirrei joined her and leaned over. Too far over for Jhee's taste. "Was that not the coolest thing ever?" Mirrei said.

"Yes, that was not the coolest thing ever. Hopefully, the authorities will find her safe on the ground and not dashed upon the rocks."

Erma's ashen face showed she, at least, agreed with Jhee. She fled the roof deck.

Kanto gaped and gave Jhee back her robes. "Denbe, you might have climbed out there with her if we weren't here."

The realization she would have hit Jhee then. She shut her eyes. Dashed upon the rocks. She paused and took several breaths. When she opened them again, her younger spouses stared at her with concern. She straightened her posture and tucked her hands in her robes. She endeavored to project strength and self-assuredness. They visibly relaxed.

"Now shall we return to the festivities?"

"I can't possibly think of a thing they could do that might best that."

"Me neither," Kanto agreed.

Jhee had been about to say how the last thing she wanted was for them to try. A scream cut her off.

"Whelm and waves. What now?"

Jhee paused at the stairs contemplating yet another trip up and down them. She soldiered on. After a brief pause, she hurried down them as best as the unusual length robes would allow her. How much air could the robes catch? If she leaped over the railing, could she parachute down to the ground floor as the activist had? She would rather not find out and so confined herself to descending the stairs the healthy way.

Chants arose from the stairwell. "Stop the wall. The wall is death. Stop the wall. The wall means death. The wall means death."

"Don't they know this is not the time? This is a charity event," Kanto said.

Jhee shrugged. "I understand their frustration. Justice procrastinated is justice abdicated. 'Patience can sometimes be deadly. More deadly than anything.'"

As Jhee and her cohort emerged into the great room, the chants and commotion died down. Ocher and crimson dye clouds, colors of the protests, glimmered in the air. The sheer terror Kanto displayed at the prospect of them staining his robes eclipsed the one he displayed moments before. He stopped them from going any farther.

Eerie stillness and silence reigned. Protesters had filled the reception area. Activists swathed in the orange tabards had stormed the observatory opening with packets of colored dust. More carried banners, the same thin man who had eyed Mirrei and Jhee by the observatory gates among them. Spills of dye littered the floor. Someone coughed. Attendees batted at their clothes. They left glittering dye halos. Everyone else had frozen in place.

Few people's attention was on the activists or the be-glittered dignitaries. Jhee stepped forward. She followed their gaze upward.

Mr. Bastian's body hung from the ornate, crystal chandelier beneath the great room's skylight. A long, thin crystal shard protruded from his chest. Officials and security guards alike stood about covered in pigment, making no effort to do anything about it.

One of the chandelier's moon crystals crashed to the ground. Everyone leaped back. Some shielded their eyes from the shards. A barbarian sprang into action before Jhee and with a simple gesture redirected the shards safely.

Jhee returned her focus upward to discern anything else. The light fixture lazily twisted this way then that. Blood from Mr. Bastian's wound dripped down into the mess of dye and crystal in a spiral.

One tremulous drop at a time the blood dropped and congealed into the crystal dust. A steady drip continued with an ominous Tick-Tock, death's metronome. Glints and reflections sparkled through the skylight down on the body as if haloing Bastian in light like a divine celestial being. He had become celestial artwork with a morbid beauty to it. Now he was one with the First Makers. Perhaps he had even earned his place in the Prime Maker's showcase, part of the divine clockworks as he may have wanted.

The chandelier jerked then dropped a few feet. Another barbarian jumped to the fore. Their eyes had rolled into their heads and their hands held up straining to keep it from crashing down. Guests huddled together almost as afraid of the staff as the chandelier.

"Move back, everyone," Jhee said.

A barbarian server spoke, "My lady Justicar, we need to secure the chandelier."

"Come with me. No one disturb anything else, and security call the imperators. This may be a crime scene."

8

THE INVESTIGATOR

~

Detective Mode

Jhee hurried to the door porters. "Make sure no one leaves. Tell the valets. No transports brought around. Nothing. That is an official request."

Several barbarians followed Jhee to the landing where they stabilized the chandelier. Jhee examined Mr. Bastian's body in its resting place. A crystal lance pierced his body. A reddish-green powdered substance blanketed the floor in the lance's direction's likely trajectory. She pulled out her conch, careful not to disturb anything and took a visual record. One of the musician's instruments lay broken nearby.

Mr. Bastian had his whole life ahead of him. An occasion to look forward to with his impending marriage. A life full of possibility snuffed out so soon —too soon like the anonymous young ones out on the streets now dying unsung—such a waste, an utter tragic waste. Jhee clasped her palms together at angles for the First Makers' blessing and touched her hands to her esca before proceeding. May Mr. Bastian be remade magnificent. Jhee rejoined her dende on the ground floor.

"Disgraceful," Kanto said, having found three blue-gray exhibit blankets. He cloaked them with two. "Denbe, is he…?"

"Dead? Yes, it might be a murder. We are all witnesses or suspects."

He clutched his throat. "This evening is nothing if not exciting.

"I've noticed a trend. My nights with you often are."

"Flatter all you wish. I'm still terribly cross with you."

Jhee patted his hand and stroked along his ear ridge. He purred a little and snuggled against her.

"My night, my rules?"

"Always."

"Fine. My new rule for tonight is Mirrei rides home with us once we are free to leave."

Jhee stopped stroking his ear.

"Now come with me to see if she is all right."

"I will add a rule of my own then. Don't mention what you figured out to Mirrei. I don't want her to feel pressured. By either of us."

Kanto huffed. "Agreed."

Mirrei's eyes lit up when she saw them. She made a beeline for Kanto who mantled her with the remaining blanket. She pulled out her conch. "Did you take notes? I took notes. We should compare them."

And like that, Kanto's mood shifted. Kanto suppressed a giggle and they took each others' hands. "You know I don't take notes. That's more you and Jhee."

"No comparing of what you saw," Jhee said.

"Of course," Mirrei said. "I forgot. We want to capture our recollections but not compare them. We should keep our statements separate and not coordinate them, so the investigators can get as pristine a recollection of the facts as possible."

Jhee nodded. "We're potential witnesses. We have to avoid contaminating our statements."

"Our first time as witnesses," Mirrei said.

Kanto lowered his voice, "Or suspects."

"I know. Isn't it exciting?"

Jhee cleared her throat. She wanted to chide them about what a serious matter this was. Someone's death was not a cause for delight no matter who they were. She stopped short because she thought about Kanto's ordeal at the hand of the foul villain at Tranquility Bridge. He seemed none the worse for wear aside from occasional nightmares. If he could find it in him not to be reminded of his ordeal in a situation such as this, she did not want to make the connection for him. She had suspended the schedule to give him extra attention following his plight.

Jhee documented the blood pattern and inhaled, testing for unusual smells. If she had means to get an air sample, she might have been able to get Mirrei to do a chemical analysis once they returned to the villa.

"If only I had my field kit," Jhee murmured.

"Left side," Kanto said.

Jhee made a face at him.

"Check the left side of your robes." Jhee patted around and pulled out a small, whale skin case. "Mirrei, check your right side."

"A field assay kit?"

A tailor-made moment, as if the First Makers had designed it. Jhee felt a presence behind her. The mayor and several attendees craned to observe her working.

"What are you doing?" the mayor asked.

"I'm just noting the peculiarities that's all."

"Do you already have an idea about who might have done it?" one attendee asked.

Others nodded enthusiastically. "We want more than anything to know what you concluded."

It dawned on Jhee this was not her jurisdiction nor responsibility. She herded everyone including the dendes away from the evidence. "I'd rather not say. This is a matter for the local law enforcement. Perhaps later once I've spoken to the lead investigator who should be here any moment."

The mainly barbarian staff had thinned. Not good. Not with the tie between the weapon and the barbarians. Jhee approached the head porter, a Water Folk woman in a blue and beige, IES uniform.

"Excuse me."

"Why yes, ma'am. How may I help you?"

"Weren't there more staff here?"

"I'm sure the other staff are just in the kitchen, ma'am. If you need something, I might be able to get it for you."

"I asked no one to leave."

"No one told us, ma'am."

"I noticed not all your staff are barbarians."

"Yes, some are conscripts from the Outer Reaches."

"I see. With all the influx of people, good work is hard to find."

"I assure you, ma'am, this is good honest work."

"I did not mean to imply otherwise. You also employ barbarians."

"Has someone done something? Is their service not satisfactory?"

"Nothing of that sort."

The woman visibly relaxed. "We work within the guidelines of the Rabe documents, ma'am. Our staff are raised in the state-run schools for the betterment of their respective peoples, our tax and foundation dollars well-spent on those unfortunate enough to have laid eyes on the forbidden empire. If you're concerned about the drawing, don't worry, the ones who drew will be spoken to."

"I'd say they should be commended."

Another porter dressed similarly to the one Jhee spoke with approached them. The head porter held up a hand to cut her off.

"Any other questions, ma'am?"

"No. Just make sure no one else leaves."

"Of course, ma'am. Right away, ma'am."

By the time of the imperators' arrival, Jhee noted the sudden absence of most of the staffing service. Inksy approached a group of staff by the kitchens and whispered in one's ear. The stragglers set down their trays, and she walked them into the kitchens. Jhee hurried forward.

Sianna appeared in front of her. "A murder. How unexpected? Coconut cluster."

Sianna held out the confection to Jhee. Jhee waved it away and tried to sidestep her.

"I'm afraid we have a bit of situation here," Jhee said. "The facts of the crime had certain elements that may point to barbarian involvement."

"The coconut clusters really are amazing. I think it might be best if we separate out the staff. Until the imperators get here to maintain order. Shouldn't you let them handle it? Your family's waiting for you."

Jhee frowned and returned to her spouses.

Fire Folk. The barbarians. Called by some the bastard races. Their skin color differed from that of the Water Folk. Their skin lacked the bluish black hues of the Water Folk and instead tended towards tans and more temperate greens. Quite dull if you asked Jhee. Their eyes were also different. Rather than the divine pure and proper gold of the Water Folk, their eyes shone mundane blue-green, sometimes brilliantly so—a feature inherited from the exiles mixing of bloodlines.

At last, came their *escae*, the Fire Mark. Unlike the star-shaped mark of the Water Folk, theirs was pear-shaped. The teardrop shape bridged the difference between the round and marquise shape of the Air Folk and Land Folk exiles. The missing wedge on those such as the Air and barbarian males evoked a crescent shape. An incomplete shape unlike the more perfect full escae of women.

"What did you want with the staff?" asked the mayor. "Are they involved?"

The security guards dragged a protester limp and singing loudly towards her.

"We found this one hiding in the Galleon wing, Justicar."

"We did it for the cause, and we'd do it again."

"So, you confess?"

"One Folk! One Wave! One Force! One Rain! One People! For the cause," the suspect belted out.

"Your cause? Is that your excuse for murder? Enough foolishness from you. If you're so eager to confess, the imperators will be here shortly."

"Wait, murder? What do you mean?"

Jhee jammed her finger up at the chandelier.

"No. Wait. I had nothing to do with that."

"You can explain yourself to the magistrate."

"Lady, dear lady. I beg of you. No, I implore you to hear me out. I had nothing to do with this. I killed no one. We just painted a little sign on the galleon. That thing's offensive and should not be put on display. Free the Fire Folk! Solidarity now! One Wave! One Folk!"

Jhee caught movement from amongst the staff.

"I advise you to be silent. Last thing we need is another riot here."

"Please, put in a good word. Perhaps you know my mama or papa. They are good folk. It will just kill them to know I've been arrested."

"Then you should have thought of that before pulling a stunt like this or perhaps even murder. Explain yourself to the imperators or your advocate. I have no jurisdiction and can do nothing for you here. Now, do be silent."

"Best listen to the Justicar, my dear," Advocate Farkhande said.

"Yes, ma'am, if you say so, ma'am."

"And you, Justicar, mind you don't exceed your authority. By what right are you detaining everyone here?"

Jhee pursed her her lips, but she had the law on her side, "Extraordinary circumstances."

The advocate raised her eyebrows, and the corners of her mouth upturned. "I'll still be monitoring you."

～

The Inquester Arrives

A woman walked in wearing waist-length robes and a short, neat haircut. Jhee watched as she flashed her credentials to the Imperator on duty and spoke to security. Her eyes narrowed. She swept her gaze in a lengthy, slow assessment of the room and attendees. The woman paused in front of the wing entrance for the unopened Gray Galleon exhibit. She leaned in to read the plaque. Her posture stiffened. She turned sharp on her heel back to the crowd.

An Imperator and a security guard produced the suspect. "There's been a mistake," she said.

"I've been told you confessed," the woman replied.

"To the graffiti. Not to killing anybody. I'm a Makerly woman. I have no truck with body desecration or murder. We only want all Folk to be free and to see this obscenity is not displayed in our fair city. It was a lark, a bit of laugh."

"No one's laughing. Hold this one aside while I deal with the rest of the guests. And keep everyone away from this area until the criminal sciences unit gets here."

"Yes, ma'am. Very well, ma'am."

"You got to believe me. I had nothing to do with that," the activist said as she was dragged away.

"I'll try to get you a representative," Advocate Farkhande said. "Remember to say nothing else until they arrive."

"Advocate Farkhande, how unexpected to see you here," the credentialed woman said.

"Inquester Paij, I could say the same. I'm here on business. I had an injunction to deliver. If you ask me, that vessel should be melted down for slag."

The advocate gestured at the closed wing.

An imperator handed an evidence bag the other woman. "We found a discarded server's uniform in the galleon wing."

Jhee, confident she had identified the lead investigator, approached her.

The woman sent the Imperator away with a pat. "What can I do for you, Lady...?"

"Justicar of District Sixteen. Inquester, I wanted to inform you I secured the crime scene and made sure no one touched anything. Allow me to share with you what I've observed so far. I saw a powdery rose substance surrounding the body and on the mezzanine. I also saw a suspicious man at the gates, who I also think was dressed as a waiter—Inquester, shouldn't you be noting this down?"

"My Lady, I assure you your testimony statement is being duly recorded."

"Sensor suit technology?"

The inquester seemed taken aback. "You know about sensor suit technology?"

"Inquester, I am a Justicar."

"District Sixteen? 'Dispatches from Arrow Point.' I've read some of your tales. Aren't you a bit out of your jurisdiction?"

"I was attending the event as a guest. You understand I'm a trained observer, yes?"

"Ah yes. Of course. Forgive my rudeness, but it's a lot different when you are part of the story rather than a dispassionate observer."

"Your words are quite true. As I was saying. I separated the witnesses as best I could and ensured no one left."

"Thank you for your efforts, Justicar. Very conscientious of you. We will take it from here."

Jhee sighed. "Another observation. I observed a suspicious woman in rumpled robes coming down from the mezzanine after a tense exchange with Mr. Bastian. If you get a chance Inquester, I advise you to check out the victim's fiancé's clinic. I saw Mr. Bastian being shook down by this woman, a criminal element. She left behind a powdered rose substance similar to that near the victim's body."

"Thank you again. I assure you I will do that."

"Inquester, I don't have the feeling you are taking me seriously."

"I assure you, ma'am, I am. Justicar, forgive my rudeness, but you'll find we do things a bit differently on the main isles. We move slower and let the evidence dictate the course of the investigation. We try not to get ahead of it."

"I understand entirely. I underwent training beside the Imperators at the Emerald Isles Academy as you did."

Inquester Paij wrinkled her brow then held up her hand. "My class ring. How did you know who I studied with?"

"You also are practicing certain containment procedures, in particular methods favored by and taught only by the lead instructor at Emerald Isles Academy; idiosyncratic to the Sarlan's school. But yes, I take your point that amateurs should not go stumbling around. As mentioned, I'm a trained observer. I am offering you my services."

"Justicar, may I be candid?"

"This is you being oblique?"

"Please, Justicar, leave this to our division. Should my conclusions come under review, I don't have a fortune with which to pay the fines or the favors enough to squash them. I must rely on division resources which demand I follow proper procedures. I can't in good order afford to bring on a whirlpool investigator."

"In the interim, may I tell you what I observed?"

Jhee listed off some of the findings she noted. The Inquester smiled and nodded obligingly. Occasionally she rolled her eyes. She only humored Jhee.

"I realize this is awkward, Inquester. But I would ask that I be afforded at least professional courtesy."

The Inquester sighed. "Of course, ma'am. Take me through what you saw slowly."

"Before the presentation Ms. Oriel took me and my spouse on a tour of the museum. We were also allowed a private viewing of some of the rare exhibits. After, I observed Ms. Oriel and Mr. Bastian fighting and her giving him a bit of jewelry which I note is now missing. She also got a phone call on her conch that made her very upset. She excused herself, and we didn't see her again until shortly before the auction."

"What was the event organizer's demeanor?"

"She appeared upset, but not flustered. Her left sleeve was torn. It hadn't been when she left. She showed no markers of exertion. Not at all like someone who just murdered their fiancé."

"Yes, ma'am. Yet you understand, as do I, the overwhelmingly domestic nature of most killings."

"Indeed. Besides, I spoke to Mr. Bastian after that and he was very much alive. However, there are anomalies to this one that aren't factoring cleanly for me."

"I have a few questions for you, Justicar."

"Ask."

"Why exactly were you there?"

"Lady Delphine and I are friends, and she invited us as her guests. My dende and I had just attended a private artifact viewing when the nonsense started."

Inquester Paij adjusted her suit cuff. "Why would the event organizer take you, of all the dignitaries here, on a private tour and allow you to see rare artifacts?"

"I am something of a history buff and a Mechanist. I believe Ms. Oriel wanted to flatter me."

"For a donation."

"Precisely so."

The mayor beelined for them. Much like a bee sting, Jhee expected nothing pleasant coming next.

"Excellent! I see you are already hard at work on solving this horrible incident. I trust you, and the Justicar will bring it to a swift resolution. She did brief you?"

"If I may, madam, the Justicar and her family haven't been cleared."

"Piffle. You don't think one of the most prominent Justicars in a generation up and committed murder at a charity function in front of a bunch of witnesses."

"Witnesses of which, the Justicar and her family can be counted among. Should we go to trial, the testimony of a trained observer and expert as herself would be most invaluable."

"Almost as invaluable as an inspector's I would say, and they aren't prevented from testifying on cases they've worked. Two words, Paij: Gray Galleon."

The mayor left. The inquester pursed her lips at Jhee.

Jhee tucked her hands in her robes' sleeves. "I know you can't officially bring me on to the case until my family and I are cleared."

"Hang back. Say nothing."

～

Irreplaceable

Jhee and Inquester Paij went about collecting statements. Jhee did her best to be unobtrusive. While she observed the inquester at work, she kept her quiet.

Inquester Paij turned to her. "I trust everything met with your approval?"

"Inquester, you need no approval from me to do as you would."

"I know that look. But?"

"I noted that the porters' cuffs were dirty."

"Mm, I did too."

"Yet, you didn't ask about it?"

"No. Now, we just have a few more suspects to question."

"I, suggest we—you—speak with Ms. Oriel."

"As for speaking with the victim's fiancé, would you know where I could find her?"

"Now that you mention it, I haven't seen her since we discovered the body."

"Convenient that."

"Perhaps so."

They found the distraught Ms. Oriel being comforted by the lead astronomer in the latter's office.

"He was just fine a few minutes ago. We were making plans for our post-wedding retreat. He said he wanted to visit the new megaresort on isle three. Maybe even visit Tether Island. We discussed visiting the barbarian lands. I wanted to tour the Shield. The telescopes don't do it justice. I can't believe this happened."

"I know. Me too," Ms. Levinia said. "To say nothing of the damage to the Planetarium Chandelier, it's near priceless. Bastian's help had been invaluable on the chandelier restoration and telescope upgrades. That chandelier is irreplaceable."

"Bastian, too," the inquester began. "I understand this is a difficult time for you and will do my best to make this brief. Did the deceased have any enemies or anyone who might want to do him harm?"

Ms. Oriel rubbed her esca and shook her head. "No, everyone loved him, he was very unobtrusive and very quiet."

"Mind if I ask how you met?"

"He volunteered for the clinic. I was there capturing footage for Friends of the Observatory and the Breath of the Deep Society."

"Forgive me," Jhee said, "I thought you said you became involved with the Breath of the Deep Society because of Mr. Bastian."

"Oh no, well partially. I was already working on the Observatory restoration committee. They did a joint fundraiser with the Breath of the Deep Society. Many members are on both boards."

"Ah yes. Thank you."

"What about you, miss?" the inquester asked. "How did you meet the deceased?"

"Me. Oh, the same."

"Wait," Ms. Oriel said, "wasn't he your date at that investor cocktail party we held to kick off the restoration?"

"No, you must be mistaken. Oriel, will you be all right? I have to go inspect the telescopes for damage."

Ms. Oriel nodded.

"Don't go too far, miss," the inquester said. "I might have some additional questions for you."

Ms. Levinia bobbed her head before rushing off. Inquester Paij nodded at an Imperator who followed her.

"May I ask where you were during the incident?"

"I had to go to the vault for something. By the time I returned, all Trench had backed up. I couldn't find Bastian in the commotion. Then I saw his body."

"Thank you, very much," the inquester said and waved over a constable. "I may have more questions for you later. Meanwhile, this officer will take you to your office where you can rest."

Jhee waited until Ms. Oriel had gone. "I can confirm some of that."

Inquester Paij stroked her upper lip. "Bastian is a handsome and likable man much like your husband, Justicar. Did you also find him unobtrusive and quiet?"

"Inquester, what are you implying?"

"About your talk with the victim. Witnesses said they saw you and the victim on the terrace alone. Bastian was an event walker until he and the event organizer became engaged. Did you meet your husband under similar circumstances? Your husband has a similar background, I presume."

"You presume too much, Inquester."

"Simply, doing my job, my Lady."

"Mr. Bastian had a coughing fit. I was just inquiring how he was. Like my youngest consort, he suffers from Fresh Lung Syndrome."

"Which I would argue, precludes him from climbing up to the top of the rafters to vandalize the chandelier."

"Not without the aid of heavy mobility equipment such as the restoration crane."

"Restoration crane?"

"The mechanical crane the observatory has to do maintenance on the dome and clean the chandelier and skylight, and most importantly restoration on large artworks, such as the Great Galleon."

The inquester realized Jhee had taken control of the conversation and switched topics to regain it. "One of the other witnesses mentioned an incident at the clinic where Bastian seemed to show undue interest in your wife. I can't imagine the event organizer liked that too much or you."

How had she learned so much so fast? *Ah,* Jhee thought, *the sensor suit technology had real-time statement collation.*

9

———

THE MERGING STREAMS

~

The Eel

Inquester Paij pushed the arrested activist out of her office ahead of her. Advocate Farkhande and Ambassador Naiman followed.

"Advocate Farkhande, I really must object to your presence here," the Ambassador said.

"She's wanted here. Not you," the activist replied. "At least the advocate's fighting for the little *guls*. You rolled over like a logging dolphin. Convinced us to agree to live near a bunch of cancerous crystal pylons. Got yourself a nice ambassadorship out of it."

"You'll be notified of your judgment date. Stay nearby and keep out of trouble," the inquester said. Farkhande walked the activist out.

"If that will be all, I'll take my leave too," the Ambassador said.

"So, she didn't do it?" Jhee asked.

"Ah, Lady...?" Inquester Paij paused. Jhee stared at her. "You and your cohort have been cleared and are free to go."

"Oh. I'd been asked to remain."

"Well, not at my request."

The mayor and Advocate Farkhande strode into the squad room. "Ah, Inspector, it was at mine," the mayor said.

Farkhande hopped on a nearby desk and swung her feet.

"Madam Mayor," the inquester said.

"I've been told the Justicar is not a suspect."

"No, but—"

333

The mayor smiled. "Excellent! May I inquire what your interest in this matter is, Justicar?"

"None I suppose," Jhee answered. "This matter has interesting aspects. It might be good for research."

"The Justicar hinted to me at the event she is working on a new story. Since she is not a suspect, then there should be no problem allowing her full access to your investigation, Inspector."

Inquester Paij rocked back on her heels. "Ma'am?"

"This death has indications arcana was involved, yes? The Justicar is already familiar with the case and an expert in arcana. We need to pool resources into solving this horrible mess."

Jhee's eyes widened, and she gaped at the inquester. She exaggerated her genuine shock, hoping to show she in no way asked for this.

"Mayor, I really couldn't. I'm sure the inquester here will do a great job alone. My family and I are on vacation. My spouses would prefer we get back to enjoying our holiday. They simply would not have it."

"Nonsense. I want the best and the brightest on this at once. The more of you, the better. The last thing we need is a scandal riding the tails of this other unrest. Together you should come up with a solution faster than either of you alone. I hope for a speedy and satisfactory conclusion to this mess. I mean it inspector, see the Justicar gets full access to your investigation." The mayor faced Jhee. "Try to portray me competently when you write this up in one of your Dispatches. I'll want an early copy of the story when you release it. Autographed. Now if you'll excuse me."

Jhee stood there awkwardly with the inquester and the Advocate once the mayor left.

"I had no part in that," Jhee said.

"Looks like that eel bent back on you, didn't it."

"Indeed, it did."

Advocate Farkhande, listening nearby, coughed loudly for attention. "Have you seen the way they portray local law enforcement in those?"

"Believe me, I have."

The inquester's narrowed eyes directed at Jhee made her opinion clear. Advocate Farkhande swept aside her scarf's dangling end.

"Then stop acting the fool. You of all people could use some good publicity. Maybe bilging off a media personality isn't the best idea right now?"

Paij rolled her eyes Sphere-ward. Advocate Farkhande hopped off the desk and gave Jhee a once over. Jhee remained impassive.

"I understand, Justicar, that you are versed in the new science."

"I've studied and been a practitioner many years."

"One wonders why the 'new science' is not simply called 'science,'" the inquester said.

"I have read your papers on forensic arcana. Illuminating." Advocate Farkhande paused as if listening to something. "The wisps say I should keep my eye on you. They know why you are afraid every time you peer over the edge into the depths. Deep forces have turned their gaze towards you."

The advocate left. Jhee turned to the inquester. "Should I ask?"

"I never do. She's good folk. I think. You really writing a story?"

"No."

"Of course. I heard you already met Wynne. She's one leader of our merry bunch of Mischief Makers."

"The building climber."

"Yep. Let's go have a chat with her. They hang out at Chuc's."

Chuc's turned out to be an underground cavern converted into an establishment for dancing and playing billiards. Folk scattered or melted away as the inquester's transport came into view. The suspicious reception she and the inquester received spoke volumes about the patrons who frequented the establishment, at least, during the day.

The crowd left a clear path for Jhee and the inquester to enter. Inside, they found the protesters clustered around a table.

"Wynne?" Inquester Paij asked.

The protesters were studious about not reacting. Jhee picked out the building climber and made eye contact. She nodded at Jhee, "What can I do for you, officer, my lady?"

Jhee took the lead, "I'm glad to see you made it down safely."

Wynne shrugged.

"Could we ask you a few questions?"

Wynne shrugged again. "Might as well before you get less than polite about it."

"Might I ask how you got onto the grounds?"

"Talent."

"So, you just went over the wall? No one let you in?"

"Your words, not mine."

"Perhaps your little stunt was a distraction for the murderer," Inquester Paij said.

"Distraction? Yes. Murderer? No."

"For the dye gag and defacing the galleon," Jhee said.

Wynne shrugged again.

Inquester Paij sighed. "We're wasting our time here."

"Again, your words, not mine."

Jhee nodded. "Perhaps. Our friend here isn't planning on wandering far. Correct? We can return if we have additional questions."

The pair made their way outside. The inquester spoke, "That went about like I expected. Guess where we head next."

"To have words with the other side of the crowd that evening."

The Marina

Jhee and Inquester Paij's quest for interviews led to the marina where several more prestigious fundraiser attendees had gathered to watch the regatta.

"Detective, can't you see we are terribly distraught?" the first noble asked.

"Inquester. Yes, I do. But a person lost their life, and it's my job to get to the heart of it."

"Humph." Tall and thin with olive skin and mid-back length, lank, dark brown hair, the Lady had an angry feel about her. Her alert black-gold eyes barely registered the inquester's presence. She raised her binoculars. "Come on. Come on."

Jhee invaded her field of vision. "Please, my Lady. Inquester Paij simply wants to ensure our safety. The sooner we conclude our inquiries the sooner you can get back to watching the regatta."

The noble's narrowed eyes calculated her relative rank to Jhee and if she could dismiss her. "As you wish. Ask your questions."

Jhee made introductions then allowed the inquester to lead. The nobles became more responsive once they noticed Jhee's polite deferral to the inquester while Inquester Paij bristled less and became more assertive. Though, her posture remained tense, and she fussed with her sensor suit's cuff link.

They at last went to question the vizier with whom Jhee and the Ambassador had the contentious exchange. While the inquester asked her standard questions, Jhee observed his demeanor. His perfectly pressed, fabulous clothes were slightly too big. The discolored hem of the vizier's robe also caught her attention.

"Inquester, permit me to ask a question?"

The inquester's eye color fluttered through a spectrum of exasperated hues.

"Vizier, did you go to the mezzanine?"

"I was in the great room all night."

"My, vizier, looks like you picked up a nasty stain on your hem."

"Oh, for the love of the Makers."

"Allow me. Strange, I thought I saw you slip out." Jhee had porters a locate a member of the housekeeping staff to clean the stain. She palmed the handkerchief with a sample of the stain before housekeeping left. The vizier's conversations at the fundraiser had put his prejudices and biases on full display. In her experience with those like him, showing you were like-minded exposed weaknesses in them. "Can you believe Team Nordale didn't even qualify this year? I have to say these 'social experiment' crews will get you every time. What would those Folk from the Scorched Lands know about sailing, anyway?"

"Exactly. If you must know, official-to-official, I was meeting with my bookmaker. I lost big on the qualifiers for the regatta. We met at the side entrance in the Galleon wing. I must have picked it up there."

"Name, so we can confirm this," the inquester said.

"She goes by Queenie, but don't tell her I said anything."

So, Queenie was the name of the weaselly woman from the clinic. "You have my promise," Jhee said.

"Thank you."

The inquester turned to her after they moved on. "What was that about? I had just gotten used to your blessed silence."

Jhee and Inquester Paij took their leave. "The hem of his robe. It was stained the same as at the fundraiser."

The inquester's expression was abashed. "I hadn't noticed it until you pointed it out."

Once outside, Jhee produced the handkerchief bearing the stain sampled from the vizier's robe. Its gray-green residue matched the stains the porters bore back at the fundraiser. She handed it over to Inquester Paij. "Several of us had those stains at the fundraiser. I had attributed it to wading through the lawn to reach the transport area. There was ankle-deep water all over there with no way around. Why is it still discolored now?"

"He also could have taken a skiff."

"Just so. A skiff." Jhee placed her finger alongside her nose and thought a moment. "There was also a gray-green stain on his sleeve."

"That I noticed. The same color as the corrosion on the galleon. Coincidence?"

"I think not."

"Definitely worth a follow-up. I'll have this sample analyzed." Inquester Paij fidgeted for a moment. "Thank you, Justicar. You were actually very helpful."

"My pleasure, Inquester."

～

The Crane

While Jhee and her spouses were out shopping, she received a summons from the inquester asking to meet at the observatory. Before she went inside, she went to the side of the building the activist had climbed. The wall kept her holds. She had used drawing on a manufactured structure and overcome all the resistance that imbued in a material. Manufactured walls not only bore many imprints, they often involved multiple elements. Either Wynne was an epic elementalist, or she knew cyphering.

The creaking and sweeping sounds of the sea and the haunting echoes of the gulls and sea life outside followed Jhee into the great room. The restoration crane occupied the center, and someone had raised the chandelier. No one was around. Jhee looked around a little suspicious. She heard a squeal and a bit of creaking rope and metal.

"Inquester?"

"Up here."

Dust and debris drifted down from the ceiling. Jhee shook her head as grit landed in her eye. Exactly what she needed. As if her eyes were not already bothering her enough this trip, she would be flushing them out from now until the next feast day. While she enjoyed the city, the strain on her allergies she could do without.

Once Jhee's vision cleared again, the inquester waved from the power lift platform that Jhee mentioned the restorers and others used.

"This thing is great!"

The inquester operated a joystick, and the lift moved up and down. She let out a little laugh.

"Inquester," Jhee said in a no-nonsense tone.

"Oh? Sorry."

The inquester lowered the platform. She shrugged when Jhee folded her arms.

"You could have at least waited for me," Jhee said.

The inquester smiled, and they shared a chuckle. "Care to do the honors?"

Jhee took the controls from the inquester, and she had her own fun as she hoisted them back into the sky. Meanwhile, Mirrei and Kanto lounged by their lonesome, ignored on the ground with only their conchs for amusement.

Inquester Paij said, "I gave this lift and the area a quick overlook. Anyone could come in here and use this thing. Let alone someone who might have as much access as the event organizer. But that's not all I found. Have a gander."

Inquester Paij pointed out voids in the dust on the mezzanine catwalk which would only be visible with a Height Maker's view. Jhee strained over the railing for a better look.

"Careful now, Justicar," said the inquester.

A gasp from her young spouses brought Jhee back to her senses. Below her, Kanto and Mirrei had snapped out of their disinterest. Jhee planted her feet firmly on the platform. Instead, she pulled out her conch and brought up the zoom and magnification function. Footprints, eight inches, stride, shorter than two feet, possibly the event organizer's, but there was no way to be satisfied. Estimating body size and height from stride length and shoe size was an inexact science. But more importantly, the crystalline rose substance that Jhee had been finding everywhere covered the catwalk.

Another glimpse of Kanto and Mirrei's anxious faces told Jhee this would not work. Jhee lowered the platform long enough to release them from their obligation to stay and insist they finish shopping without her. She would contact them to meet for dinner and drinks later.

Jhee fished out her forensic kit. Inquester fished out hers. They had nearly the same kit.

Inquester Paij and Jhee's minds worked alike. A deduction the inquester may have made too had she not spent such effort resenting Jhee's presence. Jhee had spent hours yesterday on a project that might extract her and the inquester from the predicament the mayor put her in and ease the way between them. She had the proper credentials. They must protect the law and the case. A murderer would not go free because the judiciary viewed her presence as a violation of procedure. To preserve the integrity of the case and for her evidence to be admissible, she needed to be authorized to be at the crime scenes and use arcana.

"Inquester, I wanted to do this by the guides. I started a formal request to work this case with you through the Central Authority and assignments clerks."

"Here I was thinking my opinion didn't matter."

Jhee presented the inquester with her formal credentials via ether. "It not about your approval. My dedication is to the law. I don't want the case integrity compromised."

The inquester read through the signets on her conch. "Neither do I."

"I hope this goes some way towards putting us back on the right footing."

Inquester Paij accepted the credentials with a nod. "Want to help me lift the prints?"

"Yes!"

Jhee nodded excitedly. She and Paij busied themselves imaging the scene. Despite Jhee's insinuations otherwise, she was only familiar with Sensor Suits in theory. She had not seen one used in the field. They compared notes and went over the evidence practically giddy and laughing. It was so good to have this meaningful dialogue with someone on her same level.

Mirrei and Kanto resumed shopping. "Let's hit some places in the Furnace District," Mirrei said.

"Let's not."

"Aren't you curious about what sorts of fabric or design ideas you could pick up from the Fire Folk?"

Mirrei waited and watched him think it over. At last, he shook his head. "No, we shouldn't stray too far without denbe."

"Too far? It's just up the road. I'll go by myself then, if you're too scared."

Kanto sighed. "Stay out of trouble and meet me back at the square by first setting."

Mirrei kissed Kanto on the cheek. "You're the best denye ever."

"Just go and don't make me regret it."

Mirrei marveled at the dizzying height and closeness of the architecture.

She wondered if she could find that one food cart from the street fair again. Mirrei rewarded herself with a pat on the back and two skewers once she had. She skipped the stew.

Protesters still passed through the area around the carts but the tone was much more subdued. A group even occupied some tables at the sidewalk café, Che's, she had taken refuge in during the protests. One of them must have recognized her because they waved her over. She hesitated then approached.

"Was that your first action?" one asked.

Mirrei nodded.

"They're not usually that intense."

"I bet it was the Squids. They pay folk to agitate."

"Stick with us. We mostly sit- or lay-in."

"Your next time will be easier."

Next time, Mirrei thought. *Would there be a next time?* When she had tried to get involved at the abbey, she ended up bedridden. She was done being confined to a bed. She intended to spend her time having fun.

"No thanks," Mirrei said. She still had time to hit up a few smoke and candle shops she before getting back to the square.

～

Like Knows Like

The event organizer, Ms. Oriel, had been scarce since the murder. Grief-stricken, according to colleagues.

"This was the last thing the observatory needed. Oriel was supposed to help save it not drench it," Ms. Levinia said.

"When the Justicar left the viewing, she mentioned an argument between you and Oriel."

"It wasn't an argument."

"You mentioned something about her going into business for herself," Jhee said.

"I was just venting."

"What about Bastian?" Inquester Paij asked. "How well did you know him?"

"Not well," Ms. Levinia said.

"Really? Didn't you hire him to accompany you?"

"I'd hired Bastian as a remora, a paid companion and guard for social events. I'd had several confrontations with the protesters. He also turned out to be rather technically inclined. I assumed he worked as a remora to put himself through school. He assisted me with operating and maintaining the telescopes. He even helped troubleshoot the Planetarium Chandelier. The highlight of the event was supposed to be treating our guests to a presentation, not Oriel's auction. I originally meant the fundraiser to be a benefit for FLS/MLD sufferers. They would be the first to see the Planetarium Chandelier restored to working condition. At least, that's how Bastian and I originally planned it."

When Jhee and the inquester went to question Ms. Oriel at her apartment, they found no one there. Their next stop was the clinic.

"Have you seen Ms. Oriel recently?" Jhee asked Vash.

"Well no," Vash said. "Now that you mention it, I haven't seen her since that ghastly business at the fundraiser. Any progress on finding the killer?"

Inquester Paij continued the questioning. "Please, Sir Delphine, if you would just answer the questions and point us where she kept her things."

Vash led them to the employee locker rooms. "I'm still not sure what you are hoping to find."

"Do you have a key to this?"

"Yes."

"Open it, please."

Vash unlocked Ms. Oriel's locker. Inquester Paij recorded the original state of the locker before she poked and prodded about. She handed the camera off to Jhee as she removed the contents of the locker. At the bottom of the locker, the inquester found a pair of shoes coated in rose crystalline particles. She projected a virtual overlay of a ruler and the prints from the catwalk and compared them. "I'd say that looks the same."

Jhee noted the shoes of other sizes in the locker. She tugged at the inquester's sleeve. "Inquester."

"A misdirect. She wore oversized shoes to throw us off."

Jhee kept her counsel. That was a possibility. She had to admit she had nothing more to go on than her gut at this point. It still did not seem to add up. Why would she leave the shoes here where anyone could find them? She did not know Ms. Oriel, and the inquester's methods were sound. Everything by the guides. Nothing she would not be doing herself. Did she just not want Ms. Oriel to be guilty because she showed Jhee some priceless artifacts?

"Your reasoning is sound."

"So glad you approve. Sir Delphine, we will have to look at your records. Give us everything you got on the event organizer."

"Unfortunately, Inquester, our records are private and confidential. It will require an official writ of inquiry from the Imperial Circuit, not local. We are under the Empire's Health and Redevelopment Philanthropy division."

"As you wish."

"Perhaps, I might be of assistance. I know people on the Imperial Circuit, Inquester."

"Just what I hoped you would say. I intend to put all your fancy connections to work."

Inquester Paij and Jhee checked out Ms. Oriel's temporary office while

Jhee sent messages and contacted folk. Jhee disconnected from the last one. "We can have a writ, but it might take up to a long-tide."

"Wraith and wrath," the inquester said. "Beats never, I suppose."

Jhee noticed a glint from the waste bin beside the desk. Jhee bent over and examined it. It was another shiny wrapper like she found at Lady Delphine's work site. Was Ms. Oriel connected to the vandalism and sabotage?

"Inquester." Jhee pointed out the wrapper. "I found a similar one near some vandalized equipment at Lady Delphine's. Ms. Oriel could have let the protesters in. Perhaps she had a hand in the street fair protests, too since she also organized that event, too. Whether it was for the publicity or the ideology remains to be seen."

Jhee examined the Friends of the Observatory tour itineraries. These were well outside of observatory hours. She found Advocate Farkhande's name listed several times.

"I'm no expert, but these payments don't seem like a normal event organizer's fees. What do you make of this?"

The inquester handed Jhee an inscribed branch painted in bright blue and yellow. She recognized the markings as the Failed Prototypes' work. Jhee held a late-era prayer rod. "An artifact of the Failed Prototypes. You would be correct, Inquester. I think Ms. Oriel had been selling private tours and access to the restricted exhibits to wealthy patrons."

The inquester took the rod from Jhee. "New motive. Bastian caught the event organizer compromising the foundation."

"That is also a plausible explanation. As plausible as any we've had so far."

The inquester's eyes flashed. "What is your brilliant analysis since you keep throwing cold water on mine?"

"I don't have one yet. I'm still gathering data."

"The mayor did not seem to have a lot of patience with us gathering data. You are supposed to be speeding things up not slowing them down."

"That is not my intention, Inquester. I'm simply trying to be thorough and properly situate all bodies in the system. A person's life may depend on it."

"A person's life may depend on bringing this character in. She may well be out there stalking her next victim. We have a duty to protect the public first."

"I understand, Inquester."

"Are you sure you do? I didn't want you on this case to begin with."

"I understand that, too. Please, I am not deliberately trying to slow down your investigation. You should proceed however you feel you must."

The inquester rolled her eyes. "'Madam Mayor I've made an arrest in the case. Yes, Oriel, the event organizer.' 'Do you know how much good they have done for this community and how many feathers you will ruffle?

Justicar, do you agree with her assessment of who the killer is?' To which you would say?"

The inquester pointed the rod at Jhee. Jhee winced at her indelicate handling of the ancient artifact.

Jhee took it back from her carefully. "I take your meaning. This is your investigation, Inquester. I would not gainsay or undermine you in public."

"Only in private."

"Would you like the honest answer?"

"I would like the benefit of your skills. You have good instincts and eyes. If I didn't trust in those, I would have put this to bed already. Which is why your doubts are making me doubt. If you say we should keep looking and there is more to this, I can't help but agree. It seems a little pat to me too. I, though, have to go strictly by the book. We need a plausible reason for not running with this lead."

"You collected samples for arcane and forensic toxicology tests, correct? Well, the most accurate labs and the premiere company are on the far side of the island. They are in high demand. It could take long-tides for the results to return. In the meantime, we should continue to work the evidence we have."

"Ah, I take your point, Justicar. You have a surprisingly devious mind."

"Like knows like. You are not the only one who's used to dealing with recalcitrant or entitled nobles trying to steer an investigation."

"All right, let's go over the evidence again together and see what we missed. You're not the only one whose instincts are warning them away from a quick arrest."

"Thank you, Inquester."

"Your reasonableness is infuriating, you know that?"

Jhee smiled. She knew.

10

THE WATERING HOLE AND THE DIVE BAR

～

The Watering Hole

Jhee and the inquester met up with Kanto and Mirrei at Che's, a mid-scale club. She bought the first round.

"Open us a tab, if you would?" Jhee asked the barman. "Didn't I see you at the Observatory fundraiser?"

"No, my lady. Not my sort of affair. They don't let the likes of me in except through the servants' way. If you attended the street fair, you might have seen me there."

"Perhaps that's it."

"Begging your pardon, my lady. This doesn't seem like your sort of affair either. I try to run a top-notch place, but the more dignified types like yourself pass my place by."

Jhee examined the branded napkins in the napkin holder, he set out for their drinks. The stylized letter logo matched the one on the napkin with the note written on it from the clinic. Jhee indicated her companions. "Just soaking up the local flavor. Young spouses, you know how it is?"

The barman looked dubious but let the matter pass. Jhee returned with their drinks.

Kanto wrinkled his nose and used a handkerchief to clean off his glass. "This place is quaint."

"I don't know. I think it's charming," Mirrei said.

"To the shock of no one. We should leave before anyone important sees us here."

345

"Learn anything else after I left the observatory or did you just continue to amuse yourself with the crane?" Jhee asked.

Paij laughed. "It's okay; I get to have a little fun now and then."

The inquester had been right. It was fun.

"Bright Harmony, Star Mirror, would you be dears and grab the inquester and me more ales?"

"Of course, denbe."

The Inquester stared too long after them and wiped ale foam from her mouth. "I must say Justicar, after working with you, I never pegged you as the sort to have trophy consorts."

Jhee frowned. A bowl of shiny candies sat on the bar. They were luxury candies meant to lend the establishment a posh air. Jhee tried one and nearly coughed it back out. Black pepper clove was one of her least favorite tastes. It reminded her of the home remedies grandmamere swore by and always fed them the instant they got a sniffle. She discreetly spit the candy back into the wrapper and had a drink to wash away the taste.

"Sore subject, I see. This doesn't seem like your sort of place, Justicar. Why are we really here? At first, I thought it was to humor your spouses, but now I'm not sure."

"I'm following a hunch. Inquester, I beg your indulgence as I humor a notion."

"I can't bring hunches or notions to the station. Sorry, but it's looking like I will have to bring Oriel in. Unless you want to clue me in on what about this place piqued your interest?"

"I thought you said you did not want to get ahead of the evidence or be part of the story, Inquester."

"Why don't you let me be the judge of that?"

"Still seems like there's more we're missing. The calibrations on this are off. Why would Ms. Oriel go through all that bother? It doesn't make much sense."

"Unfortunately, it doesn't always have to."

"Then there's this." Jhee placed the clinic napkin on the bar and slid it toward the inquester. "I found it after I saw Mr. Bastian and Queenie, the weaselly woman, the first time."

"'Pool. Underground lake. This blight of a city consumed in a pillar of light. Mineral sands. Starry eyes.' What does this mean?"

"I don't know, but I'd like to find out."

Jhee's junior spouses returned bearing more drinks. The inquester pounded hers back then slammed the mug down on the counter. "Well, once more off to the streams. I'm off to track down the event organizer. Catch you at to the station, ya?"

"At some interval, Inquester."

"Bright Harmony. Star Mirror. See you again sometime. If you'll excuse me, I've got me a suspect to go capture."

Like that, Inquester Paij was gone. Jhee brooded and monitored the other patrons.

"If you wanted to go with her," Mirrei said, "you could have. We must schedule another play date for you."

"No, I'd rather spend this time with you."

"That would be so sweet if I believed you."

"What will it take to convince you?"

Despite Kanto's gripe, Jhee and Mirrei drifted around the bar a while longer. She took pity on Kanto and sent him back to the villa, though Jhee remained, and Mirrei kept her company. They drank and danced.

To their shock, the inquester returned as they were leaving. She looked keeled. She was alone. The inquester paced, as Jhee and Mirrei hailed a water taxi.

"Well, it looks as though no one can find the event organizer. I can't think of a clearer sign of guilt than that, can you?"

"Surely there must be some explanation for this, Inquester."

"And she can explain it to me when she's in custody. I'm putting out an alert for her. Presumed dangerous."

"Inquester, please."

"Justicar, she is a person of interest, but she could very well be a killer. I have to act in the best interest of safety. Please, if you'll excuse me. Also, if you see the event organizer, call me immediately. This is no time for any of your 'Dispatches from Arrow Point' heroics."

Jhee sighed. "I assure you, Inquester, I am a creature of comfort. I do not go in for heroics."

"Creature of comfort? A creature of comfort with quick throw sleeve knives. I peeked at your service record, Justicar. I mean the parts that weren't redacted. Now off you go."

The inquester shut the taxi door after Jhee, and it sped off. She thought about the evidence they had found. Was Ms. Oriel guilty? No. It just didn't seem to add up. Jhee was missing something. She just knew it. She couldn't figure out what, but she had a duty to the law and the order of the state, city, and the Empire. If she found Ms. Oriel, she would do her duty.

When the inquester questioned Ms. Oriel, she mentioned how she had gone to the vault. She had also mentioned something about putting Mr. Bastian's lapel pin there. The Observatory was likely to have several vaults. What had Ms. Levinia said about the Planetarium Chandelier? They had found it moldering in one of the observatory's storage units. It was worth a shot.

They arrived at the villa. Mirrei exited; Jhee didn't.

Mirrei took that as her cue. "Go," she said.

Jhee's first thought was to investigate her theory alone. Though, she hoped to find Ms. Oriel before the local constabulary. The fear of bloodshed after a high-spirited chase too often proved founded. It was no longer her and Shep anymore. Jhee had to cut back on the foolishness such as looking for a killer in the middle of the night in a dark and damp cave. She had also promised to respect the inquester's jurisdiction. She took out her conch. "Inquester, I think I might know where we can find the event organizer."

~

The Dive Bar

Mirrei stood on the veranda watching as Jhee's taxi sped off. She thought about what to do with the rest of the evening. If she returned to the suite, she had a plateful of Kanto's pouting or ignoring her to look forward to. After all his yammering on about enjoying himself in a major city, Galleon City did not agree with him. Perhaps nothing short of the capital would meet his standards.

The Delphine siblings stumbled onto the veranda dressed for a night out. They exchanged cheek kisses with Mirrei. Erma leaned against a porch column and sparked up a smoke root. Semele held out her hand. Erma passed the smoke pouch to her.

"You want to douse this place and go somewhere more exciting?" Semele said. She took hold of Mirrei's hand.

"Like where?" Mirrei asked.

Erma offered Mirrei the root. "There's an underground club in some closed mine tunnels."

Mirrei declined. "Sounds touristy."

Smoke root exacerbated her Fresh Lung Syndrome. Not to mention what frolicking in a mine might entail. The last thing she needed was to contract Miner's Lung on top of FLS. She probably should have gone inside by now.

Vash answered, "Not this place. What do you say?"

The sisters and Vash regarded her with expectant, pleading expressions.

"Please, please, please," Semele said. Her necklaces clacked and her skirts bounced as she did a little stompy dance. She even used Mirrei's own eye flutter trick against her.

Mirrei bit her lip. No wonder denbe always caved. "Let's go."

They arrived at the busy club swarming with folk from every walk of life, from jet-streamers to street urchins. They didn't have to wait in line and were escorted right inside to a booth in the upper area. The Delphines introduced Mirrei to their friends Deziree and Taral.

"There are a lot of Fire Folk here," Mirrei said. She tried not to act like a gape-mouthed grouper. Tunnels led this way and that presumably off deeper into the mines.

"Miners," Wynne replied. She stepped out from the crowd. "They make the best Earth movers. The Storm Shield needs its minerals. Contracts with the 'heritage' schools allow a loophole in the wage laws. Companies can pay them even less than skilled refugees. I remember you. Your wifey had my friends arrested."

"Hey, take a dive, Wynne," Chappy said. "Hope, she didn't bother you too much, miss... Star, right?"

Mirrei nestled into the semi-circular couch, so it was to be all flattery now that he knew she might be important.

~

A Watery Hole

Jhee and the inquester slogged through dankness and night to the vault entrance. The sounds of the surf crashed against the beach in a darkness still teeming with life. Birds called. Breezes whistled through rock openings. Sometimes she found the subtle ocean scents comforting. Not now, not with her drenchable eye allergies acting up. It was like they were burning out of her sockets. This was the last thing she needed. They found the vault locked up tight.

Jhee explained why she thought Ms. Oriel had come here. "She mentioned the water storage facility that they had for rare objects and decommissioned telescopes and how they reminded her of the secret little spot she had on the beach where she and Mr. Bastian would go. It made a great hiding spot. It's also where they kept some of their observatory's rarer finds, to prevent them from being damaged and/or stolen."

Her eyes watered something fierce almost blinding her. She rubbed at them which only made it worse. She shone her flashlight in the darkness and continued to slosh through the cave and wade through the ankle-deep water. To the Trench with these allergies, the ankle-deep water, and her long city robes. How could they stand these gowns? She thought about that one official's hemline and the cuffs on the porters and service staff at the grand auction.

"I don't know, Justicar. This seems like a long shot."

"Please bear with me, Inquester Paij."

Their journey led to an unused portion of the mine beyond the vault sections. Jhee swept her glowtorch around. She laid a finger aside her nose in concentration. Her burning eyes and her allergies proved too distracting.

"Hm, I thought she would be here."

"Wep, Justicar, we gave it a tilt. But now let's leave it to the professionals."

Jhee raised an eyebrow at the woman.

"Sorry. I know you are 'the professionals' too."

Jhee rotated for a moment casting about the space. She made a quizzical sound, pondering what had she missed. They turned and started to leave the cave.

Inquester Paij tripped and fell. "Unmake me!"

The inquester fished around the water for her conch. At last, she got a hold of it, and by chance, it flashed against the wall, and she saw a half-lit shape in a fissure.

"Inquester, wait! What's that?" Jhee showed her light over what she thought she saw. Ms. Oriel hung from the wall pinned to the rock wall, like an insect in a collection. Jhee gasped.

"Drench," the inquester swore.

~

The Tadpoles

"This definitely puts a new wrinkle in things. The event organizer was our best suspect for Bastian's murder," Inquester Paij said.

The two colleagues stood on the beach as the criminal sciences unit recovered Ms. Oriel's body.

Jhee tucked her hands away within her sleeves. "I suspected something was off. But I had hoped I was wrong. I would have preferred to be wrong given the loss of life. Now, I have to figure out what perturbed me about Ms. Oriel being a suspect."

"Well, what usually bothers you when you are looking for clues?"

"Mis-calibrations. Imbalances. Something missing or something that doesn't add up. Ms. Oriel was jealous, yes, but it seemed as if more was happening there, more than mere jealousy. After Mr. Bastian was dead why would she still chase after him or this other person?"

"Maybe we should search for the other woman or man? The event organizer kills Bastian out of jealousy, and the lover kills the event organizer for revenge."

"Plausible. But still the character of the murders. They were very impersonal. I think that's what's missing. They were dramatic, overly so, meant to send a message or to shock. Neither strikes me as a crime of passion. They had a very deliberate nature about them especially with the religious staging of the bodies."

"The wall activists. Not that poor sod we arrested. She was a patsy if ever I saw one."

"I agree with you on that one," Jhee said.

"So nice of you."

Inquester Paij shrugged. "There are all the other activists like Wynne. Where do we even begin? There are so many of them in the city. Also, the lot of them who stormed in here that night. Who's to say that one was the only one got somewhere they shouldn't have?"

"That is a suspicion of mine as well. The person who displayed these bodies wanted to make a statement. 'One waters.' Why would killing Ms. Oriel forward such an agenda?"

"Killed for what she knew? New idea. The event organizer was the original target. Bastian surprises the killer and gets done in. We go chasing off after Oriel. Once the heat is off, the killer goes after their original target, Oriel."

"That sounds plausible as well. All these theories sound plausible. We might want to start by eliminating the most implausible. Who would want to kill Ms. Oriel then?"

"Someone who did not look too kindly on her mishandling indigenous artifacts or fleecing them for these charities. How much background research do you do on the charities you donate to?"

"My charitable trust performs financial checks on the various organizations I support. I have no problem giving away my fortune; I just want it to go to helping people."

"Maybe that's it. Someone finds out what wave witchery the event organizer was up to. They don't take kindly to the misuse of funds. Especially, if they could not really afford them. You told me how persuasive she could be."

"Charm the skin off a sea otter."

"Maybe she was too charming. Someone came looking to get their donation back. Stumbles upon Bastian in the dark, perforates him only to find out it wasn't the event organizer."

"I like it, but it doesn't quite track either. Perhaps if we did a walkthrough of the crime on scene to see how plausible it is to mistake the two."

"Concrete. Actionable. Now, our streams are merging."

Jhee and the inquester returned to Ms. Oriel's apartment. The door was ajar. Through the narrow crack in the door, Jhee saw the apartment's turbulent state.

The inquester made a silencing motion and drew her sidearm. She motioned for Jhee to stay back while she crept into the apartment. She spoke into the cuff of her Sensor Suit. "This is Inquester Paij at forty-four Stack Street, apartment two-oh-one, requesting assistance."

Jhee readied her siren module to enhance a disarm command and prepped a cypher. She got three uses of the module at full-strength, full-compulsion with diminishing returns thereafter. The inquester swept and cleared the apartment. She holstered her weapon.

"All clear." She raised her cuff. "Request for assistance canceled. Send a dust-up team to my location."

The inquester noted the positioning of Jhee's hands.

"Cyphering's useful and all but I haven't seen an artificer who can stop a bullet."

"True enough, Inquester. But in anything short of such a situation, which is most, it does well in a pinch. I take it your suit has kinetic displacement shielding."

"The latest and the greatest. Wep, it looks like somebody got here before us. What do you suppose they were looking for?"

"I wish I knew, Inquester. I wish I knew."

The inquester started walking through the scene. "Well, whatever it is they didn't find it."

"Can we be so sure?"

"Nope, we can't."

The inquester picked at a vase on the shelf. Chillenster. Expensive. "Being a fund raiser pays better than I thought."

"Inquester, may I have your permission to synchronate the room?"

"Can you magically tell who did it?"

"Inquester, you've seen my methods. I would think by now I'd have earned a little less suction from you. I'm eliminating options. If arcana has something to do with this, I'll get impressions. Some may even be detailed enough to know a category of arcana to pursue, but not who performed it. I have some theories on if it will ever be possible. Arcana is a lot less arcane than most think. We are only beginning to scratch the surface."

"I think I'm going to wait until the arcane forensics unit shows up. Yes, Justicar, we have one, fledgling though it may be."

"What I want to do is not much unlike the criminal sciences unit. You don't like arcana do you, Inquester?"

"Not so much. What I don't like even more is having everything become a nail to its hammer. I prefer technology. Less destructive. It's much more egalitarian. But arcana's the wave of the future isn't it?"

"Both can be devastating. As for egalitarian, that's one condition I'm hoping the Shield will fix. I hope it will show the value of allowing males to cypher and draw."

"You are quite the optimist. The Shield has brought nothing but misery to the city. Crime, murder, riots, and protests. Nobles from the Imperial isles are sheltered from it."

"Inquester, I'm from the Far Reaches. My ancestral home, our lands, are sunk beneath the waves."

"Lands? Ancestral home? The tragedy."

"Does this mean no more consultations and beer?"

"Depends. Will it involve a visit to your noble estates?"

"Yes, but with your behavior, it's liable to be the one underwater. The Reaches are sheltered from nothing. Not storms. Not raiders or pirates."

Inquester Paij held wide her hands in a gesture of surrender. "I accept my rebuke as much deserved and fairly meted. Consider my sucker shots binned."

"Now watch me work and squish it."

"Yes, my Lady Justicar."

The fledgling arcane forensic team arrived, and it was indeed fledgling. It comprised a handful of anxious techs using store-bought, stock kits. A beleaguered expression appeared to be the only one they had. They tried to set up a synchronance perimeter only to have the other forensic techs and investigators disrespect its boundaries. Two techs struggled to keep their stanchions upright, a young man and woman who looked as though they had newly graduated the academy. She had case notes older than them.

Jhee lent her aid. "How many cases have you worked?"

"Dozens. Simulated."

"How many field cases?"

"Three including this one," the young man answered.

"Arcane forensics is a new specialty at the Emerald Isles," Jhee said.

"Our shift commander was among the first graduating classes. It's an honor to meet you, my Lady Justicar. I did a paper on the role of arcana and forensics in the 'Dispatches from Arrow Point.' I practically grew up on it."

Jhee could believe it. Men were excluded from the field until the laws changed. The tech must be younger than Dispatches.

In due time, Jhee and the flustered technicians obtained an arcane map of the apartment which they could use for reconstructions at the lab.

11

A CHANGE OF COLOR

~

A Fitting Demonstration

"Can't this wait, Kanto?"

"I refuse to show up to court for the height of the festival season with all of us still decked out in mismatched country robes. Now that we are on solid ground, I can do something about it."

Kanto sighed and checked his conch. Jhee set her teacup down. She contemplated speaking but picked up her cup again. She glanced at her conch then took another sip of tea.

Kanto pursed his lips, his golden eyes taking on a reddish hue.

"Perhaps we should proceed without her."

"She could have at least informed us she wouldn't be here."

Jhee's first instinct was to defend Mirrei and make more excuses—Mirrei's actions had disrespected Kanto enough already. That angered Jhee more than anything. She nodded. "I'll address it with her when next we speak. She should not be so inconsiderate."

Kanto studied her, and his expression softened. She had acknowledged his injury, not minimized it, and let him know what she would do to correct it.

"Denbe, I'm sorry to be so crisp on this," he said. "I'm losing track of the fittings she's flaked out on without so much as a word or by your leave. I put a lot of thought and effort into these ensembles. They tie together with a unified house theme while taking into account our individual styles. Do you know how hard that is to pull off?"

355

"Why don't you explain it to me?"

Kanto carried on for a while, and Jhee did her best to follow along. The color symbolism and the motifs made the most sense.

"This bores you."

"No, actually. Color symbolism and motifs come up often in textual analysis and in more elaborate illuminated works."

Kanto smiled. "Come on. Up you go. Tell me about the case. I know that look."

Jhee mounted the dais and Kanto draped her in fabric. "We found Ms. Oriel dead. She was our prime suspect."

"Um hm," Kanto said a series of pins held between his teeth.

"I was skeptical it was her and had just come around. Now we're back at square one and I don't know where to start."

"Why were you skeptical?" Kanto mumbled.

"Her means, motive, and opportunity were weak or nonexistent."

The door to the observatory suite burst open. Mirrei bustled in with her weirs gear. She wore her play jacket with the hood pulled up over her head. "Sorry. Sorry, kin. Lost the time."

Jhee let out her breath. "No harm done. Right, Kanto?"

Kanto showed his teeth, his mouth still full of pins. Mirrei grabbed Tranquility Bridge herbal tea and cookies from the table.

"I think you owe us an apology for keeping us waiting without notice."

Kanto nodded.

"Yes. Yes." Mirrei swallowed the cookies. She clasped her hands. "Honored denbe, dearest denye, my deepest apologies for my inconsiderate behavior."

"Now, how about a sincere apology?" Mirrei still had not taken off her jacket. Jhee noted the green smudge on the hood. "Mirrei, where have you been, really? And why won't you take off your jacket?"

The young woman's eyes went as wide as tea saucers. She hunched and slipped the hood back to reveal hair dyed deep rose and light sea-green. "I used my personal palette, so it wouldn't clash with our ensemble."

The pins spilled from Kanto's mouth. Jhee moved forward. A pin stuck her in the leg. She flinched.

"Tailor's… maxim," Kanto mumbled.

"The dye is temporary," Mirrei said. "It should wash out in a few days."

"The cut," Jhee began. She cast about for an affirmative statement. "The cut is flattering."

"I thought so too. The shorter length frames my face just so. Shorter cuts are all the wave inland. What do you think, Kanto?"

His mouth hung open. Even as Mirrei helped gather the pins, he gaped. Jhee imagined the lecture brewing in Kanto's head about the scandalous cut, *"Improper, it was just improper."* Jhee pleaded with him with her eyes not to make a scene.

"It's... nice," Kanto said after regaining his power of speech. "Now, get on the dais. I need to make some... adjustments to your robe."

Relief flowed through Jhee. She hung her unfinished robe on the nearby mannequin. For a moment, she considered having a custom fitting double commissioned once they arrived at the capital. Though, the thought of standing half-naked in front of strangers for that long made her uncomfortable.

Jhee squeezed Kanto's shoulders to thank him for being civil. "I'm going to turn in early. I have an appointment at the local imperator branch tomorrow. Mirrei, we'll discuss your apology later."

~

"ALL RIGHT. Here allow me to show you how to position your stanchions properly for maximum coverage," Jhee said. An ASU tech held out the stanchion. Jhee brought it to one corner of the ASU lab and directed other techs to do likewise. "We want to put them at the corners of the room and hopefully the winds will have been right. This should maximize the coverage. What we are after is the direction of effect and its target. Which would likely be inside the room and the perimeter, so if someone cyphered into this room, we'll catch it. It carries some risk that the artificer may have cyphered from the ceiling or through the floor but if there's an artificer who can levitate or dematerialize, we have much bigger problems."

That got a little chuckle from them.

The ASU's shift commander addressed the untrained onlookers who had begun to gathered, "Arcana leaves behind echoes much like how every material contact leaves a trace. Arcane forensics looks for signs of drawing and cyphering. Elemental drawing disturbs the natural flows of elements. So, you look for elementals out of 'alignment.' And more complex drawings involving cyphers leave 'Makers' marks' on the elements in the area."

Jhee joined the shift commander at the control panel. "We activate the grid to get a pre-cyphering reference level. You put in your credentials so you'll be in the exclusion list."

The arcane crime scene techs gave a backward glance. Jhee smiled, donned safety goggles, and nodded her approval. They tried with drawing to recreate patterns from the textbooks. "Arcana does not always require arcana or technology to detect. Direct observation is the first and simplest way to determine if arcana has been used."

Jhee demonstrated draws and cyphers and had them compare it to some non-arcane types of fire and water damage.

"Now, our first victim was hurled into the chandelier by a crystal projectile from the balcony, approximately here," the shift commander said. She went to the approximate location where Jhee had found the red dust trail the night of the fundraiser."

Jhee rolled up her sleeves and then clapped her hands together. She clapped them together again. She hummed and started thinking about the sound of the ocean. Think and be the wind and the air. Air and the wood specialty of Earth were common to concealment formulations. She hummed and focused her mind. She reached out to the high waters, the fluid prime forces that flowed beneath existence, the motions of the Divine Mechanism which connected all things. As she shifted through the arcane reconstruction for residues of arcana use, she found no sign anyone had been here to go over the scene and hide evidence. No one had used arcana in that apartment recently.

By the end of the synchronance, a small crowd had gathered to watch her work.

The inquester gave her a bit of mocking applause. "You had everyone spellbound. What were you saying about you not being a whirlpool investigator?"

"Not a whirlpool. I love to teach or lecture as the spouses might say."

The shift commander clasped Jhee's forearms. "Many thanks. I've tried for months to get the rest of the department to attend a primer."

A uniformed imperator rapped on the glass. The inquester spoke with them for a moment then returned looking dour.

"Inquester, a development with the case?"

"Your wife has been arrested for disturbing civic peace."

Jhee pinched the bridge of her nose. "Whelm and waves. Where?"

"Near the Styr Mine project. They arrested dozens. There was a clash between One Waters or Folx United kooks and the miners. I know the detention facility they'll have gone to and the bull who runs it."

$$\sim$$

The Jail

As the jailer on duty led them down to the confinement chambers, Jhee still pinched the bridge of her nose. Her naïve, sheltered Mirrei arrested. The jail's air tasted of body odor and bleach with a vomit chaser. The cold and the smell caused moisture to build in the corner of her eyes. By the time the jailer brought Jhee and the inquester to the end of the hallway of cells filled with protesters and activists and other sorts of criminals, Jhee wiped moisture away every few moments. Lest they think she was crying.

"Over here. I put them in their own cell as a professional courtesy," the jailer said.

They came to a cell where Mirrei and Semele sat alone. They stood as Jhee and the inquester accompanied by the jailer on duty came into view. She would not meet Jhee's eyes as the jailer unlocked the cell door.

"Star Mirror? Semele? What is the meaning of this?" Jhee asked.

"Justicar, it was all my idea," Semele said.

"Somehow, I doubt that. I've informed your mother. And she will deal with you later. Star Mirror can speak for herself," Jhee said.

"Can I?" Mirrei asked. Her face flashed with anger. Jhee braced. "We were at the protests because the wall is wrong."

"You're young. You don't understand."

"Don't I? What don't I understand? That we are destroying people's homes and burning out their children because we're so scared of the big bad 'barbarians' who are kicking our butts? Well, maybe our butts need to be kicked. We tried to conquer them and the other inhabited worlds. Then there was that galleon. Ghastly. They packed in there like cattle to be shipped to a hostile, strange environment rather than stay."

Jhee let Mirrei's words sink in. She had never heard the young woman talk so passionately about anything. How had she missed this? "I'm bailing you out. We'll discuss this further once we're at home."

"I'm staying right here."

"Surely you don't mean that, Star Mirror? This is no place for someone with your condition."

"I'm staying as long as everyone else is here."

Mirrei folded her arms over her chest and sat down defiantly. Jhee turned to the jailer on duty. "Forgive me for disrespecting your house," she said.

She formed her fingers and did a simple cypher. When she was done, there was a dent in one wall.

"There," Jhee said. She held out her wrists to the jailer on duty so she could be restrained.

The jailer's eyes turned molten gold. She fixed Jhee and the inquester with a death glare before sighing. The inquester mimed the gestures for wiping her hands and out to sea. "Under the statutes on the destruction of Imperial property, I am taking you into custody. It is your right to contact an advocate unless you waive your right to do so. Any word or deed from you from this point on will affect your defense at your judgment date until you assert either right. Do you understand?"

"Understood."

"All right, let's get you up to the front for processing."

After booking, the jailer deposited Jhee in the cell opposite Mirrei and Semele. "Behave."

Jhee rubbed at her stinging eyes once her hands were free again.

"When was the last time you took your allergy medication?"

"A few days ago. This isn't about me. When was the last time you took your saline?"

"I'd been feeling so good lately. It slipped my mind." Mirrei folded her arms. She glanced at the wall dent. "Why would you do that?"

"To end up precisely where I am now. They can't put me in jail for nothing. Requests for voluntary remand require several long-tides to approve.

Property damage and disruption are minor offenses which don't involve assault upon the good persons of this jail. The best I could come up with given the time-sensitive situation."

Semele laughed. "Your anchor is insane. I love it."

"Is she right, denbe? Are you insane?"

"Simply concerned. Also, this is important to you, and somehow, I missed it. Even once you changed your hair, I wasn't listening, but I'm listening now."

"I only watched the protests. I stopped to help the wounded after the fight broke out, then the Imps showed up. You were right at the abbey. Kanto and I were being misery tourists. I wanted to do something. There's so much I didn't know about, that I have never seen. All the suffering. I just wanted to do something. Other than throw a few shell at a charity. Kanto is a man of many waters: music, clothing, drawing. Shep makes food to die for and is good in a fight. You are this great, warrior detective. And what can I do? Swoon. I can't fight or take up arms, but I can do this."

Whirlpool investigator? Warrior detective? Why was everyone under the impression Jhee committed so much violence? Given her druthers, she would be the first to run from a fight. She spent most of her time diffusing fights and violence. Many conflated her mentor's background with her own, due in part to her writings. But even Jeja's exploits she had embellished to make the stories more exciting.

Jhee gave a bittersweet smile. "I remember those days. Star Mirror, I forget how sheltered you've been. How you want to have a mind and life of your own, while I keep trying to fit you into my mold. You are still discovering who you are and so am I. You want to know one thing you can do that we can't?"

Mirrei stared up at her with those young innocent amber eyes expectedly.

"Heal people."

Mirrei laughed a little. Sometime later the jailer on duty arrived and unlocked their cell doors.

"You three have been bailed out and are free to go." Mirrei started to protest. "Arrangements are being made for the other protesters as we speak. Now. Get. Out. Of. My. Jail!"

Kanto and Lady Delphine waited at exit processing. He sniffed. "By the names and countenances of all the Makers, what have you two done? Vandalism. Disturbing civic peace. I have half a mind to leave you both here overnight."

"Then you should leave because we are of a mind to stay here overnight."

"Nonsense. You are both coming home with me this instant. If either of you does anything to get yourselves arrested again before we leave, I shan't forgive either of you."

Jhee deferred to Mirrei. Mirrei swallowed. A jailer with a group of detainees crowded them out of exit processing. Behind them, more awaited. "We can go."

Jhee's conch shook.

-She likes port. It better be the best you can find. I'm partial to stouts.

Kanto held his peace until they reached their rooms in the villa. "Never pull anything like that again. Promise me."

"I promise," Mirrei said. She and Kanto pressed their escae together and embraced.

"Jhee?"

"Would you want me to lie?"

"What am I going to do with you?" He frowned. They touched escae then their lips. He sighed after the kiss ended. "I see now why Shep grayed so young."

Jhee's sheltered, fragile Mirrei. Mirrei had been more than that for a while now. If she had ever been. She always chafed when Jhee babied her; Jhee had just not seen it. She was too caught up in her own emotions.

Jhee glanced at Mirrei and could not help but be reminded of Miramar and the wages of their families' feud.

~

Talk and Collapse

Jhee went to Mirrei's room later that evening. "Mirrei, may we talk?"

"If you are here to read me, Kanto already did."

"No, not that. I want to talk about us and our family situation."

"Go ahead."

"Are you happy here?"

"I'm very grateful to you, denbe, for taking me and mum in and for making me part of your family."

"That's not what I asked. I asked are you happy?"

"I'm as happy as can be under the circumstances. One look around this city and its people, shows me how lucky I am to have found such a caring and generous denbe as you. Children and lesser spouses talk. Kanto and I lucked out with you. Both you and Shep are considerate and involved in our lives."

"You are still avoiding the question."

"I'm trying to be happy."

"You are young, Mirrei, and I am getting older. I would like to see you established with a good situation should the worst happen. Our agreement stands. If you want to be released from our marriage contract, I won't stand in your way."

"It's not that. I'm just not feeling fulfilled, I guess. Like how Kanto is with his charitable work."

"Why don't you do what Kanto is doing with the refugees and education? We'll meet with our charitable trust director and identify some charities and programs you can work with to help people."

"I don't throw myself into healing the way he does into fashion. It can't be my entire world. Not like fashion and parties are with him. You're hard to keep up with and approach sometimes. You're always so noble and do the right things. It's hard to relate."

Noble? Her? She had to look no further than the wreckage of three families to know the lie of that. "I'm as flawed as anyone. I want you to feel you can talk to me. What you see now isn't always who I was. It was a process, a journey. I have to remember you weren't there to see the falls and the stumbles. Perhaps we could go over options for your future. Maybe a stint at the Imperial Academy. Now that we are near the capital, you could enroll in the ether academy. I'll fund everything. That way you could become a doctor or anything."

"Anything?"

"Anything except arctic studies. You'd freeze your snout off. It's viewed as a punishment. Although at least one graduate in my class was genuinely excited to go. It's viewed as a bilge assignment. The program you put your children or spouse in if you want to get rid of them or have them out of sight, out of mind."

"Do you want me out of sight, out of mind or do you think I'm an embarrassment?"

"Absolutely not. I couldn't be prouder of you if you were my own blood or your accomplishments mine. It is a good thing you know your own mind. It will serve you well, especially if life turns out not to be exactly what you hoped. Besides, it would be hard to put you out of sight with that hair."

"You don't like it."

"It's an adjustment. Though, I meant what I said about the cut."

Mirrei chuckled then her expression sobered.

"This holiday has a familiar feel to it. Like my first stays at your home when we were 'courting.'"

"When did you figure out why I wanted you to get to know them?"

"The crab roast. You don't flirt with me, you flirt with the others. You flirt with the inquester. But not me."

"I'm not flirting."

"Engage in playful banter with underlying sexual tension. Now, who's avoiding the question?"

"I want you to know what options you might have."

"I'm aware. Thank you. I'm going to spend the rest of my night in my room. Meet you for family breakfast."

"It's a date."

Jhee left and gently closed the door after her.

Jhee picked up her conch. She composed an apology for the jailer along with a delivery of a case of Imperial Isles Signature port. She also sent a "thank you" message to the inquester. A cheeky message arrived from her financial manager shortly thereafter. She almost ignored it. Jhee pinched the bridge of her nose upon seeing the remits which had the manager in an uproar. Jhee's funds had bailed out the whole jail.

~

KANTO MET Jhee at her door the next morning and escorted her to the dining room to meet Mirrei for breakfast. Mirrei sat, her head propped up on her fist. She absently poked at her kreel and porridge with her spoon.

"Morning, wife," Jhee said and kissed her on the cheek. It felt a little warm. Kanto likewise gave her a quick muzz on the forehead.

"Morning, kin."

"You look tired, Mirrei. Did you not sleep well?"

"I spent most of the night thinking."

"You know what?" Kanto asked. "Let me go get you some orange tea. That should perk you right up."

"Thank you," Mirrei said as he ran off.

"Is this about the Shield?"

"I can't stop thinking about it. And how we need to do more."

Jhee took hold of her hand. It was a little warm too. "Are you sure you are all right? You don't look well. With all your running about did you take your saline dosage?"

"I don't recall. I'll go do it now. Then I think I'll retire to our rooms for a bit."

Mirrei stood and swayed. Jhee caught her before she completely collapsed. They took Mirrei back to her room and called Vash.

"It seems like just another Fresh Lung Sickness flare-up," Vash declared. "Get plenty of rest for the next few days and keep up with your saline regimen."

Jhee slipped her hands into her robes and paced. She continued even after Vash had left.

"You can say it," Mirrei said. "You were right. The jail was no place for someone in my condition."

"I can't see what would be gained by me scolding you. You are a grown woman."

"Nevertheless, you were right, and I was wrong."

Jhee sat down on the edge of the bed. "I don't care about that. I care about you. Mirrei, I want you to take care of yourself. You are blossoming and becoming so independent. Once you leave us behind, I don't want to worry about you."

"I would never do that."

"Never say never. I'll let you get some rest."

Jhee rose then noticed Mirrei's slippers. The bottoms were stained rose. The clothes she wore yesterday were also covered in rose dust and smelled of the smudging stick.

"Your clothes reek of the smudging stick. Have you been smoking?"

"I can't get anything passed you, can I?"

"Smoke root plus your extra exertion might explain your collapse."

"Not me, I swear. Erma and her friends do, though," Mirrei said then cocked her head. "You have that look."

"What's this stain on your shoes?"

"I don't know. I must have got it while we were running around somewhere?"

"Somewhere? Like where? It's important."

"I don't know. We covered a lot of ground during our march. Why? What is it?"

Jhee furrowed her brow. "It's nothing. Just rest."

Jhee excused herself. She called the inquester on her conch. "Hello, Inquester, do you have footage of the arrests from yesterday? I also need to know where they arrested Star Mirror and her friends."

12
———

THE DEEP DIVE

~

The Lament Cypher

Mr. Bastian's apartment was freakishly bare and neat except for a houseplant with brown leaves dying from neglect. It appeared he did not spend much time here. Movement drew Inquester Paij to the window. When she opened it, a domestic sea-lynx hopped inside.

The sea-lynx hissed and flared its head crest when the inquester reached for it. Jhee enabled the animal protocol on her siren module.

"Come here, little one," Jhee said spending one use to sooth the creature. The sea-lynx purred and Jhee stroked its crest. The animal protocol did not require filling out forms after using it. She found more of the rose crystalline powder. "What's this you are covered in?"

A key reading 'Sandoval' hung from its signet collar. Jhee and the inquester turned the apartment over from stem to stern. While they scoured the bedroom, the apartment door opened. Someone began rummaging around the apartment. The sea-lynx screeched. Jhee flicked on the light. The intruder froze, the hissing sea-lynx held at arm's length.

"It seems your luck still has not changed for the better, Mr. Eldjin," Jhee said.

"Justicar?"

"Unlike your bad run at gaming, this is an actual crime. Why are you burglarizing this apartment?"

"I wasn't burglarizing. I was investigating. Like you."

"Investigating what?"

365

Mr. Eldjin released the hissing ball of reptilian fury. It ran into the bedroom. "The competition. The bid which won the Shield contract was the lowest. Way lower than it feasibly could be. It means somewhere along the way someone had to cut corners. To a dangerous degree."

Jhee frowned at this less fanciful implication of the dangers of the Shield. "Ah, Eldjin-X, the losing contractor for the Shield. You would say that."

"You are right. But tell me this. Why has no one been allowed to see the contracts or the specs for the Shield? The labor receipts? I may have a harpoon to hurl, but it doesn't mean I'm wrong. The mortal toll; they have to be grinding up and burning out practitioners at an alarming rate. Also, what of the physical tolls. It has to be maintained around the clock until it can sustain itself. My bid was so high because I tried to do right by the workers and their families. My estimate included the costs of care, pensions, dependent care and survivors' benefits for spouses and family. There is no way the winning bid took that into account."

"So, you are doing this out of the goodness your heart?"

"Hardly. His design used synthetic crystals made from compressed dust."

"His design? Mr. Bastian's?"

"Vilmar. The winning contractor. Compressed dust is a fraction of the cost of whole crystals of those sizes, but the dust is toxic and leads to respiratory illness in miners. To get Blue Waters certification, his contract then needed to provide extra pension and medical benefits for the miners and their family. Someone waived the provision. I just want to find out who it was. Those provisions were part of the reqs for the contract. If their bid didn't include them, how did their bid get approval? Someone had to waive that requirement. I think the Delphines called in a favor and got Vilmar awarded the contract."

For years, Jhee had swam in a sea of conspiracies surrounding it. This felt different. Mr. Eldjin might have inside knowledge. Her frown deepened. Jhee thought about Mr. Bastian's remora mark. Was she wrong about what it represented? "And Mr. Bastian?"

"A technician with some company in charge of the project. He said he wanted to help me. He needed my credentials to the bid system. We were looking for the proof templarite mining was unsafe, and the government covered it up. He said he had research data. Oriel hid it. We just don't know where. My competitor must have silenced them both. Maybe even the mining supervisor, but I heard Lethys was more of a stranger at her gaming table than mine. What are you going to do?"

"I'll look into it."

"That it?"

"I'll look into it. That's a promise." Jhee yelled over her shoulder, "Inquester Paij, I trust you'll see to this matter."

"Yes, my lady. And you, Eldjin, you will go with me for detention. You were trespassing."

"Wait, you were there this whole time?"

Inquester Paij escorted Mr. Eldjin out. Jhee would have to investigate his accusation further. This did not bode well for Lady Delphine. Jhee wandered about the room. Lady Delphine had been on the council that decided the contracts. Other officials Kanto had introduced her to at the charity may have had a hand in the decision. Was there a connection there? In the bedroom, she came to a stop in front of a wall mural.

A depiction of the cataclysm that destroyed the Failed Prototypes' civilization, Findar-beneath-the-Waves, hung on one wall. It had sunk beneath the waves amidst a torrent of godspark and ash allegedly because of hubris. Her foot contacted a valise overflowing with paperwork. Jhee pulled the valise from under the edge of the bed. More paperwork trailed with it. She was still organizing it by the time Inquester Paij returned. "Over there."

Jhee pointed at a shoe box of medical bills she had placed near the lamp. "On top, you'll find a recent transcode message."

"'We regret to inform you your fourth stage aggressive Miners' Lung dementia has progressed to a terminal stage.'"

Jhee found receipts for wigs, many water taxi trips, and hair dye in the closet. What were you up to, Mr. Bastian?

"With his advanced Miners' Lung Syndrome, he couldn't be running around the exhibits. He would need to enlist someone else for that. The activists?"

"Could be Ms. Levinia."

Jhee pulled a disposable conch from the bottom of the valise. When she turned it on, a video played. It was motion-activated security film of Mr. Bastian talking to someone off-screen. "Careful with that. Look around us. One mistake in calibration and you could start a chain reaction that would set the whole thing off."

"Inquester, look at this footage. What do you see?" Jhee pointed to the standing lamp. "Look at the way the shadow falls, that's not right."

"That's not this apartment."

Jhee crawled over to the financial papers. She flipped through them on her hands and knees until she found a lease. She flicked it with her finger then shoved the lease at the inquester. "A-ha."

The inquester rocked back and forth on her heels. She took the paper with a hooded glance at Jhee. Jhee realized how she must appear knelt amidst a storm of papers framed by a painting of a world-ending squall. She rose, dusted herself off, and tucked her hands in her robe.

"It's not for this apartment or Ms. Oriel's."

"Sandoval's long-term vault storage."

It took two more uses of the siren module on the sea-lynx to tranquilize it enough to get the key off its collar. Each time the effect diminished. A fourth use might not work or do irreparable harm.

The key from the sea-lynx's collar unlocked a storage unit down on the mine docks. The vault workshop was not so modestly appointed as the apartment. Antiquities, knick-knacks, rare books had been pushed aside and piled in dusty heaps. Engineering books though had been arranged on the shelves with great care. An entire wall of the apartment was covered in bio-film filled with equations and schematics. Mr. Bastian must be more than a technician, an engineer perhaps. Whose lie was it? Mr. Eldjin's or Mr. Bastian's? Jhee filed the tidbit away for later. Over the top of the brain-storm wall were written the words, "This was to be my hymn to the Makers."

Articles and clippings about the Shield and the protests occupied one wall section. Another had geological surveys. While another displayed refraction indexes; half-lives: exposure rates. Each one had other words or phrases scrawled over them. "Not right." "It doesn't add up." "Complicit." "Liars."

"Who would want to kill a dying engineer?"

"He looked as though he did not have long for the world, anyway. You see, Justicar, everyone has something to hide."

"That goes without saying, Inquester."

Jhee and the inquester explored the squatter's workshop. The designs for devices, including one Mr. Bastian labeled a synchronator, screamed unhinged as if conjured and written straight from the depths of the Unmaker's Trench. Some were lightly penciled in, some traced over and over again. Frequency equations and more frequency equations accompanied numerous charts about body types, weights, and sizes. "Not right. Not right" was scrawled all over images. Mr. Bastian sought an answer only his disturbed mind could fathom.

This reminded her of one of her academy mates. Doli Monkfin had a breakdown third year. She had gotten into numerology arcana, and became obsessed with number patterns, formulas, and something called the Lament Cypher: a derivation so intricate and detailed that if you attempted to solve it, you went mad.

It appeared as though Mr. Bastian had found his own Lament Cypher. But what was it about?

Bits and bobs of tech sat on the workshop in various stages of construction along with signs of his Mechanist devotions. A hardware equation deriver which if properly designed and calibrated could do a thousand times more calculations than software worked continuously. There were frequency textbooks thrown about with treatises on toxins. A book on the bed, on the table, tons on the workshop's table beside stacks of periodicals. Passages had been marked ranging from catering, food prep, food-borne illnesses to home brewing and bottling.

The living area, though, contained little other than an unassuming chair, table, and cot. Everything there was basic and functional, reminiscent of a prison cell—a prison of his own mind and Make. The disordered signs of a disordered mind. Was Mr. Bastian always this obsessed or was it something that happened to him because of his advanced Miners' Lung condition?

Scale models of the Shield tines, pylons, and the relay station rested on one table. 'Free the Fire Folk' had been scrawled on the surfaces. Jhee touched it. Still wet. This must have been done recently. Mr. Bastian was a wall activist. Something or someone had accelerated his descent into madness. Had Mr. Bastian been planning to poison them all, or something else? It seems they had dodged a lance.

~

The Weirs Court

A knock at the suite door interrupted Kanto's sketching. He recognized Vash's knock pattern by now. His was better. He set aside his sketchbook and headed for the door. Mirrei hopped by him, still putting on her shoe while managing her weirs bag.

"Weirs. Must go. Bye."

"Weirs? In your condition?"

"What exactly is my condition, Kanto?"

"Didn't you just have a 'health scare'?"

Mirrei horn glared him. "Suck silt."

"Bottom feed, you little faker."

"Which you were fine with when it gave you an opportunity to spend more time with denbe because you thought you could use it to usurp Shep."

"You're not my denbe or denme."

"Well, you sure as water are trying to act like mine."

"Someone must."

"It doesn't have to be you, Kanto. You're allowed some irresponsibility. I'm going. You can come with if you're that concerned. You might even enjoy yourself."

"Fine. I will."

"Fine."

"Oh, so the weirs courts are underground now?" Kanto said after they stepped inside Chapman's Underground Club. This was leagues worse than that horrid little bar they met the inquester at.

After they entered the hangout, everyone cheered. "There's our hero of the day. Healer, our failed banner hanger, and bail provider."

Mirrei took the drink the man behind the bar offered and kissed him. "I can't take all the credit. My denye's the one who bailed everyone out."

Kanto grimaced.

"Fine, then, all hail...."

"Bright Harmony."

"Your wife doesn't even let you use your own name in public. Has she kept you bred or bled, so you never have time to pursue your own interests?"

Another drench CARP. "Denbe is very supportive. If she weren't, Star Mirror wouldn't be hanging out here, and you Trouble Makers would still be jailed."

"Star Mirror?" the man behind the bar asked. He chuckled. "Any denye of *Star Mirror* is welcome here, too."

Mirrei pinched Kanto's arm. He gave her an offended look. Why pinch him and not laughing boy? Two jet-stream setters with red-tinted eyes and a flask in hand abandoned their card game and wandered over to them.

"Oo, Star's brother-groom," the woman said. "I'm Deziree and this is Taral. We've heard nothing about you. Means we get to figure it all out ourselves."

The man who accompanied her wore a bespoke vest and a dapper waved coiffure. He gave Kanto a once over. "Exquisite fabric, golden thread, black pearls in the embroidery."

As the pair assessed him, they passed the flask back and forth.

Deziree nodded. "Tailored beautifully. Don't recognize the designer. Oo, but maybe that's the point. A trendsetter."

Kanto refused when they offered him the flask. "I only drink champagne."

They giggled and went back to their card playing.

"These are my friends. Don't embarrass me," Mirrei said. He gave her a sidelong glance. Embarrass her?

After taking a seat away from the bar, they treated Kanto to the uncomfortable sight of Mirrei snogging Semele and the barkeep, Chapman. Kanto continued to sit there; he played with his cuffs, unsure of what else to do. This far underground his conch did not work. He saw a bio-film periodical sitting on the bar. It took a few pages for him to realize its erotic nature.

"You look sad sitting over there all by your lonesome. Wouldn't you be more comfortable over here with us?" Taral asked.

"I'm fine where I am," Kanto said.

Erma patted the stool beside her. "Don't worry, sweetie. You're safe with me. Alas, so too with your lovely sister-wife. I say personal companions are much like driving transports: best when they confine themselves to a single lane."

"Don't you find that view limits your ability to find a situation outside your mother's household?"

"Plenty of such situations exist. Mumsy is quite aware of my interest in those with more mammaries than fewer."

Semele came over to the bar to grab a drink. "Mumsy's greater disappointment is their financial accounts don't have at least as many digits. Vash is the hope of our family in that regard."

"Her biggest disappointment is our association with those who protest her livelihood."

Deziree sat beside Kanto. She smiled then leaned in to kiss him.

"I'm married," he exclaimed, "and so is Star Mirror. Get your things. We're leaving."

Mirrei rolled her eyes. "You can leave if you wish. I'm enjoying myself for once."

Kanto walked towards the door but thought better of leaving Mirrei here with these reprobates. He stormed onto the balcony that overlooked the rest of the underground club. The club had not opened for the evening yet, but a few staffers were there to make last-minute preparations.

Vash joined him. "I'm sorry if what you saw in there made you uncomfortable."

"We should go. This is all very improper."

Vash moved closer to Kanto. "Winsome Bright Harmony, every aspect of your appearance designed to entice. Yet, in which direction? Do you seek to lure more to your house or to be lured away?"

Kanto attempted a coy remark, "As my anchor wishes, so shall it be."

"Tell me of them. Should you or Mirrei find a place here, they would seek to fill their household numbers?"

Vash laid his hand over Kanto's and leaned in. "Envision an alliance between us. A united front against any other suitors, perhaps, should it come to it, we might even force out an unwanted one."

An offer to usurp Shep and be co-anchors was sure to follow. How long before he would seek to be anchor himself? Or bring in another to force him out. Kanto considered the offer. How Jhee looked at Shep even now? Their relationship was better since the abbey, but nothing like the longing looks or easy touches she shared with Shep. How long, if ever, might it be before they shared that rapport? Sooner, if Shep were not there. Vash didn't want Jhee. He would be no threat.

Vash watched him with an open, expectant leer as if he knew the options Kanto weighed in his mind. Vash it seemed was more interested in a wifely benefactor rather than a wifely companion. The cold, mercenary nature of it rankled Kanto. He did not want to be a family with this man in any capacity. He did not want to expose Jhee to his fickleness or be a part of his treachery.

Kanto yanked his hand away and swept back into the main room. "Star Mirror, are you ready to go?"

What offended him more about Vash's behavior? The very act of it or its crude mockery of how Kanto often found himself obligated to behave.

Mirrei stomped over to Kanto. "Why are you being so impossible? I invited you along, so you could have some fun."

"Our definitions of fun differ."

"I thought being turned away from denbe's bed less often would make you less insufferable not more." Mirrei sighed and grabbed her coat. They hailed a water taxi outside. Kanto paced. "I thought you of all people would want to try new things."

"Not infidelity."

"I see, which is why you constantly try to nose in on days with denbe that aren't yours."

"What? I do not."

"I can't remember the last day she had with Shep or me where you weren't hovering trying to get her attention."

"As well I should, given how quickly you strayed."

"Run, tell denbe all about it then. It will provide you the perfect opportunity to spend more time with her. I realized how smitten you were with her despite your complaints. I thought with time I too would develop the same affection for her as you and Shep did."

"Revered Makers, look at your hair. It's like I don't even know you anymore."

Mirrei grabbed her bag from coat check, popped a clove candy, and waved a smudging stick over herself. "As if you ever knew me to begin with."

"You're shaming our denbe. We have an enviable situation with Jhee. Why are you trying to ruin it?"

"So, it's 'Jhee' now?"

"You could call her Jhee, too."

"It wouldn't feel right. I don't think we're there yet. Even you have to see what she's doing."

"Even me?"

"You know what I meant."

"Yes, I know precisely what you meant."

"I'm sorry."

"Jhee needs time. I don't think she really wants us to go. If she were serious about this, she'd hire a professional arranger."

"I don't want to sit around a mansion for the rest of my life embroidering. Being kept like two pond fish."

"Learning to sew was for me. I did it for the enjoyment, the craft, and the achievement; a matter of pride. While we weren't poor, it was the only way I might get to wear some of the latest fashions from inland. I like being the one taken care of for a change. I like that Jhee spoils us."

Mirrei scoffed. "Being told what to do. What to eat. How to dress."

"Not being the one who must decide what another eats, having to dress them."

"Being mothered all the time."

"Yes. Not having it always fall on you to take care of someone else. She's our denbe. We must respect her."

"I do. While I complain about denbe, she's always been kind and understanding. I just wish she wouldn't smother me so much."

"If she hovered half as much over me as she did over you, I'd be ecstatic."

Mirrei sighed and took Kanto's hand. "I told you about my mother. You know what she was like. In her way, denbe's just as bad."

"I don't like being left to my own devices so much. She's running around town with that investigator. You're off who knows where. I swear to the Makers I will put a tracker on you both if you don't check in more. I never thought I'd miss Shep's presence. Once, I thought it'd be great to be somewhere so lively. Now, I find it's the loneliest thing ever."

"Have you spoken to denbe about children?"

Kanto's hand went to his chastity tattoo. "The time never seems right. We're still getting to know each other. We're still getting used to the way everything changed since the abbey."

Mirrei degenerated into one of her signature coughing fits. At first, Kanto ignored her. He hesitated a moment. The deep gasping and wetness of phlegm which accompanied the coughing marked this one as authentic. He rushed over and put an arm around her. He was one of the few who could distinguish the two.

"You didn't fake your collapse, did you?"

"I'm fine."

"How long have you had this cough?"

"The protest action and the arrest proved more taxing than I expected. Don't tell her about any of this. Keep all this amongst us," Mirrei said. "Please."

Kanto grudgingly agreed.

13

A PRACTICED EYE

~

Ill Fitting

"The length of these robes. I'm not sure I like it. They feel too long," Jhee said.

"They wear their robes longer inland," Kanto replied. "Presumably, because it's drier."

"I don't imagine they do a lot of wading like back home."

"Yet, somehow you managed it. Also, please, don't give them away this time."

Jhee looked in the mirror at her gorgeous robes, and she looked at Mirrei's robe sitting on another chair unused.

"Don't worry," Jhee said, "she'll be here. I'll talk to her."

"Don't. Don't. Let her have her fun. You're right. I'm being selfish. She never got out much; she has a right to live it up a little. Like I always thought we would once we got to the city."

"I thought you wanted to attend the festivals and galas."

"I did. And I do. Just not alone. I wanted us to attend together as a family. Denbe, I know you were just flattering me at the observatory. I want to introduce you to new experiences, so you can appreciate them like I do. Think of our lessons, how you taught me about how to recognize the feel and movements of the different elements."

"Tell you what? Why don't I attend one of these with you?"

"Jhee, you'd hate it. It's gossip and schmoozing. You barely made it through the fundraiser."

375

"Maybe I'm not looking at it properly. I like to people watch and figure out the relationships between people. So, I'll go to people watch."

"Thank you, Jhee."

Kanto started pinning the robes. Jhee thought through the case out loud. "We've got one murdered fiancé. Possibly having an affair and who is caught or at least suspected by one dead event organizer. The inquester thinks it's possible it was a case of mistaken identity. The Gray Galleon project was very controversial, and there is also evidence Ms. Oriel was misusing Findari, the Failed Prototypes, antiquities. Maybe someone killed her and strung her up to find out which unauthorized people she let see them."

"It sounds plausible. Struck over the head in the dark. They have similar body types."

"That is my assessment as well. Make the pockets higher. Conchs are getting bigger and heavier. They pull down and hang too low."

"I'm proud of you, Jhee. Old you would have simply dealt with it. Also, we must fix it, so it doesn't distort the lines and designs of the robes. I can't have you looking like some marine rustic. I would never live down the shame. My denbe will be the most stylish well-appointed official at court, or else the Trench will have more residents. I'll put my mind to the length dilemma later. What is it you say Mr. Bastian did for a living?"

"An engineer. Though, more recently, he offered his services as an event walker until he met Ms. Oriel. He may have also found some work as a sire."

"Unsurprising."

"You knew."

"Suspected. Body language. His positioning regarding her. Always ready with an arm when she entered or exited a room."

"You positioned yourself similar to him. There's also your seahorse tattoo."

"If you want to know something, Jhee, ask."

"Would that be proper? Only if you wish to discuss it."

"Grandmamere always wanted me to have options. I had private instruction. It wouldn't do for me to be seen attending the training. I also needed to know who to look out for. Men who make the leap from remora to mister are not uncommon. I had my gentleman's surgery at a young age. Then I undertook limited engagements to have resources for my independence kit. I have friends there, which is how I found out about Shep's inquiries. He looked so out of his depth during his interviews. Being sired, I could already be counted upon to have an impeccable pedigree. To be honest, Grandmere or I could have told Shep anything, and he would have believed it. Mr. Bastian didn't show the markers of formal training. Strictly amateur."

"How do you know?"

"How do you know who trained an investigator? His lanced-out tattoo for one."

"The astronomer also called him a guard."

"Ah, that explains the shoes." Kanto sighed. "His footwear. A formally trained remora is an accessory counseled strongly on all aspects of appearance. His shoes were sensible and very worn. Unsuitable for a society event. An upper-class remora has no such considerations. If they have occasion to go anywhere which required shoes like that, an advance team has already cleared and made a proper place for them to walk. They may buy them or wear them to appear humble or relatable, but not enough to show signs of wear. Again, at least not without the deliberate efforts of servants."

"They have their servants make their clothes appear worn?"

"For 'authenticity' and 'character.' You can't merely look like some aristocrat who bought cheap or modest clothing to appear poor, you must look like you wear them."

"I'm glad I have you to explain these matters because that would never occur to me. Now tell me more about these pre-frayed shirts and garments."

"I preferred to do it myself. Collars with just the right amount of fraying. Creases in just the right place."

"Why does that not surprise me?"

"You were born to be a denbe, Jhee. You think you understand what it means being groomed as a dende because you pretend interest in our pastimes. It's obvious when a conversation or subject is of no interest to you. The trick of it, the art, is for your denbe to not know it. You must sell them on your interest. Any but the most self-absorbed denbes will suspect, but you must allow them enough doubt to assuage their guilt. True denbes are deferred to. They take a certain amount of agreement for granted."

"I'm sorry."

"No need to apologize. Our accommodation must go both ways. I accept it's your nature. It's who you are. Certain details will always be beneath your notice. This is because of Mirrei, isn't it? Despite our agreement, you still may want to get rid of me. Is that why you insist I hang out with those awful Delphines? Vash is the worst. He tried to kiss me."

Jhee flinched and got stuck again.

Kanto looked aghast. "I hadn't meant to blurt that out."

"My apologies. I didn't know."

"No reason you should. I suppose he could write it off as trying to get my approval. You do not understand half of the tricks denmes try when approving minor spouses."

"I don't suppose I do."

"Some can be quite bold. More than one grabbed my rear. They try to take other liberties, too. One husband thought his approval warranted dropping his robes right in the middle of grandmamere's receiving room."

Jhee thought about minor spouses and some of the behavior they got up to. She knew it was a common tactic of minor spouses to ingratiate themselves with spouses other than those they married to secure their position.

"What Mr. Bastian did had an honest integrity to it. On the other hand,

Vash, with his clean looks and good breeding, will leech off some prominent spouse until they tire of him. He's a chum."

"A chum?"

"They call everyone 'chum' or 'kin' and are drawn to status or riches like sharks. Isn't that what you thought of me, of us? What's worse, Mirrei's started acting like a chum too. Stop trying to sell us off."

"I'll quit pressuring you to mingle with them."

"So, you and the inquester are like whales in a pod?"

"Not quite. I empathize with her plight, being tugged in so many directions. She has a tough job, but she is a more than competent investigator."

"If you say so. Just so you know, I'll outfit her as expertly as I outfit you."

Jhee glanced down. Kanto raised an eyebrow.

A New Tack

The inquester and Jhee broke out the case files in the former's office. While they reviewed their findings, the inquester's conch clacked. She answered.

Inquester Paij put away her conch. "Nothing mysterious about this cause of death, Justicar. Good old-fashioned projectiles to the chest. Not mind bullets. Tangible objects fired from a traditional firearm."

"Interesting you say mind bullets. Some elementalists have been able to enhance the speed and accuracy of gunshots."

"Must you scuttle all my theories? Am I allowed no comforting certainties?"

"May I review the findings?"

"Knock yourself out, mayor's friend who must be allowed complete access to my files."

"You need to come up with new material."

"No can do. My humor is all middle- and low-class. Since we can't afford to keep buying new jokes, we reuse ours until they wear out."

"The rest of us suffer in the meantime."

"Speak for yourself, Justicar. I'm a laugh riot. Okay, what are we looking at here?"

"One possibly jealous event organizer and a fiancé possibly having an affair. We've got a bunch of Findari artifacts. And some choppy record keeping."

"Certainly adds up to motive. What about means? The last anyone saw of Oriel that night was shortly before she left you to go prepare for the auction. Enough time to sneak up to the mezzanine and confront Bastian. They struggle and argue. She stabs him."

"Then drags his body up to the chandelier with no one seeing her. Even with the crane that seems a hard ask."

"True." The inquester made a shooting gesture. "Blasts them over there with air drawing. No need for the crane. Oriel may have known how to cypher. Though, to hang them from the chandelier and make that tableau. How much arcane strength and hard work does that take?"

"A minor wind charm can give one strength enough to lift the body. A skilled drawer could even draw the body up there. Air makes it more likely to be a woman. Did the ASU find any evidence of cyphering or drawing?"

"Everywhere. The whole area tested positive for arcana."

"Yes, the restoration projects would lead to confusing positives. They would need earth drawers to maintain the integrity of the vessel and the chandelier crystals." Jhee touched her chin and mulled it over. "Maybe it was one massive blast that propelled them from the balcony to the chandelier. Not of air, but of earth. It would explain the crystal dust. They needed to form the lance out of something. The noise downstairs would cover any sound. An earth drawer that powerful lends itself to a male drawer. Arcana is distinguished by the sexes."

"But with men being forbidden from cyphering and drawing, it's my understanding that women also had to learn earth and water if only as their tertiaries."

"True. Water and earth are not my strongest elements, but I have some skill with them. I might conjure something up even with my limited skills."

"So far our suspects-other-than-Oriel list has been narrowed down to nearly anyone."

"We need to go back to first principles then: means, motive, opportunity. I might want to cross-check the personal records just to be sure. One matter is for certain though. If they used air, the killer is unlikely to be male. Even with the loosening restrictions on cyphering, the highest demand for male artificers is water and earth. There remain serious superstitions about men being taught to draw air or fire. Heavy restrictions remain on those. And some forms of cyphering are likewise off-limits."

"So, empty nets again. What other woman then would have a motive to kill Bastian?"

"Ms. Levinia. I'd know that longing look anywhere. Perhaps this other woman whoever she is?"

"You don't think she is the other woman?"

"Perhaps. The 'longing' aspect suggests something one-sided."

"Are we so sure it's a woman? All we know is Oriel suspected Bastian of being unfaithful. There's nothing that says who she suspected it was with."

"Inquester, remember when I told you, I saw a criminal element hanging around the clinic. Perhaps that is it. Mr. Bastian could have been killed as a warning to Vash and Ms. Oriel. She still did not get the message, and the criminal element kills her."

"I could see that."

"Did the forensic accounting come back on Ms. Oriel?"

"Yes. It seems the only things of the event organizer's that was not a complete mess was the charity finances. She was conscientious about that at least. The clinic on the other hand. That's a different story."

"May I see the records?"

"Please do."

"Here. What's this?" Jhee held up an out-of-place invoice for a medical supply distributer. "There was a suspicious character hanging around the clinic the day Mirrei and I went to visit. I overheard them arguing. They may have been shaking the clinic down for medicine or supplies."

"That tracks. What if Oriel began to refuse? First, they kill her fiancé then Oriel?"

Jhee put her hand over her mouth. "I had a more horrible thought. What if the lesson wasn't for Ms. Oriel? What if it was for Vash? I think we need to speak to him again."

"I'm thinking you are right."

The inquester keyed her conch. Jhee folded her hands inside her robes. She did not even know how she would explain this to Mirrei. She was so fond of Vash. Would Mirrei think the accusations malicious or made of jealousy? Would she believe Jhee is acting out like Kanto? She could not think about that right now. They had a suspect to question.

Jhee browsed through the case files a few more times trying to find out what it was she was missing. It all looked cut and dried. The evidence pointed to one suspect and then another. If Ms. Oriel had not turned up dead, she would have still been their prime suspect.

"Only one of the clinic trio is left to shine sunlight on the matter," the inquester said.

Jhee nodded. "Vash."

～

The Ink

After Vash and his advocate arrived, Inquester Paij escorted them to the interview suites.

Inquester Paij sat across from them and rested her elbows on the table. "You're comfortable, aren't you? You don't need a drink or anything?"

Jhee watched the interrogation from the other side of one-way glass. She did not want her presence to be a distraction. She wanted this to be legitimate and by the guides. An outburst from her would not be the act to scuttle the case. A keen advocate might even argue she unduly influenced Vash.

"Inquester, to what do I owe the pleasure?" Vash asked.

"Oriel has been murdered."

Vash played with his signet ring. "My word. How did it happen?"

"we found her pinned to a cavern wall near the templarite mines. The cause of death is still indeterminate."

"What can we do for you, investigator?" Vash's advocate asked.

"We just wanted to give your client a chance to mention something now which if he relies on it later might harm his defense."

"I don't know what you are talking about, Inquester," Vash said.

His advocate put a hand on his arm. "Inquester, precisely what are you hinting at?"

"It has come to our attention that certain unsavory types have been hanging around your clinic. I'm saying this is your client's opportunity to come clean about anything which may concern him about the goings-on there. Perhaps someone who comes around frequently making demands."

Vash leaned over and whispered in his advocate's ear.

The advocate turned to the inquester. "My client has something he needs to tell you."

"It was an inherited problem. Almost from the moment we opened the clinic, they started hanging around. Equipment started to go missing. We had several break-ins. It continued that way until someone showed up in person. She made it clear many of the problems were her doing. She could stop them in exchange for a favor or two now and then. Maybe some medication. Perhaps treat a few of her personnel. We agreed."

The inquester sat back in her chair. "Then what happened?"

"With all the influx of new patients and then our funding went south, we weren't getting as many resources as before, and we had to make them last more. She came back and said she could put us in contact with another supplier who could give us supplies for a discount. We had no other choice, don't you see? Then that's when we noticed why the drugs and supplies were so cheap. They watered them down. The supplier had cut the medications with something and was selling the excess to others, double billing for the same amount of supply. We wanted to stop. We begged to go back to our old supplier, but by then we were in too deep."

The advocate touched Vash's arm. "Inquester, my client is a victim in all this."

"Did Oriel know?" the inquester asked.

Vash nodded. "Though, it didn't sit right with her. Eventually, we stopped paying. She had even written up a new contract with our old supplier. Even though we weren't paying anymore, all the intimidation had stopped dead calm. I assumed she had made some other arrangements with them until… We hadn't made our order for weeks when 'our friend' showed up to ask why. She and Oriel had it out. She threatened Oriel."

"Why didn't you come forward before now?"

"When Bastian was killed, I didn't make the connection. Afterward, she paid us a visit at the clinic again. But now that you've found Oriel's body, I put it together. I waited because I'm afraid for myself and my family and my friends." Vash glanced at the one-way glass. "Justicar, are you back there? I just wanted to protect Star. She threatened our families."

Jhee folded her arms. She did not look forward to telling Mirrei about this, not one bit.

"We'll check your story out. You are free to go for now. Don't go far. We may have follow-up questions for you."

Vash hunched. "Where would I go? This is all I know."

He and his advocate stood and left. The inquester joined Jhee in the observation room.

"So, do you believe him?"

"It tracks with what I saw. One of his patients complained that their medicine was not working effectively."

Vash and his advocate stumbled back into the interrogation room. Sianna and Inksy close behind them.

"What is that?" the advocate asked.

Inksy answered. "An imperial writ which allows us to hold you as long as we want until the imperial guard comes to take you into custody."

Vash's advocate leaned back, "My client has been nothing but coopera-tive. This is outrageous—"

Sianna cut him off, "Then you won't mind taking the time to cooperate with us. You're dismissed, Inquester. And please clear the observation room on your way out."

"Well, we've done all the interrogations they will let us do today."

Jhee and the inquester headed to Paij's desk. "There's rude, and then there is those two."

"You've never been privy to the delight that is working with the Squids."

"Not since my days working as a Military Police Magistrate." Jhee thought for a moment. "Since Vash and the Inkertons are tied up for the time being, we could go check on Ms. Oriel's files at the clinic."

"You're such a bad influence on me."

"Like knows like."

~

The Makerly Steward

At the health clinic, Jhee and the inquester accessed the clinic's terminal via her sensor suit's link.

"I hope you meant what you said about the writ," Inquester Paij said.

"Why?"

"I copied the signet from the Ink's writ to gain records' access. Here, can you make sense of these?"

"Salinity tables. Wind dispersal patterns. Charts of the currents and waterways. Maps of the Fresh and Miners' Lung outbreaks."

"Makes sense, tracking the outbreak of a health crisis. Do you think they were looking for a patient zero?"

"It is a possibility."

"Let's have another gander at those lockers."

While they made another pass on Ms. Oriel's and Mr. Bastian's lockers, a steward grunted and pushed a squealing cart into the employee locker room.

"Oi, what you doing here?"

The inquester tapped her lapel insignia. "Galleon City Imperators. We're investigating—"

"All the dead folk. You won't find nothing there. That volunteer, at least, kept his things elsewhere. What you need to be investigating is who stole my uniform?"

"Someone stole your uniform?" Jhee asked.

"That's what I said, didn't I? At least, the other supplies that went missing made sense. Squishies could sell those."

"So, you had a lot of break-ins and thefts?"

"Not as much anymore. Shame about the passionfish though. They was a cute couple. Just when this ship had righted itself again."

"I heard they were a dedicated pair," the inquester said.

The steward shrugged. "Ain't Makerly to gossip, mind, and that volunteer and the money lady worked hard to keep this place going. But something odd about them."

"Odd, how?"

The steward motioned them closer. Jhee and the inquester leaned in.

The steward continued in hushed tones, "Times the man acted more the doctor than the doctors. Other times he acted more a squishy than the squishies, if you know what I mean. I also wondered if maybe he was the squishy behind the thefts, what with all the places I found him where he ought not be. But I ain't one to gossip."

Jhee nodded. "Of course."

"I caught him at the incinerators once, hiding stuff in the medical waste."

Jhee cast her eyes from side to side. "Do you know why?"

The steward smiled. "No, but I think I know where he kept his things. I told his fiancée, the money lady. I don't know if she claimed them or not."

"Would you show us?" the inquester asked.

The steward lead them to a locker hidden in the storage room. Jhee said, "Thank you. We'll let you get back to work."

"Let me know if you find my uniform in there."

Inquester Paij proved to be a deft hand at picking the mechanical lock. In the hidden locker, they found various reagents and cannisters of powders, including a cache of templarite dust. They also found a log with dates, patient names, with what looked like various templarite dilutions, and results. Among the entries, they discovered the mining supervisor.

They gathered the new evidence and went back to the inquester's office.

A cross-check of the patients' names with public records produced a disturbing result: most had died. The cause of death most frequently listed was Miners' Lung Disease. In addition, Mr. Bastian's results bore notations about mouth sensations and detectability. His secret workshop had contained treatises on toxins and catering. He had experimented with ways to hide the taste of templarite. A liquid solution with high alcohol content proved least noticeable.

"The bad squelch," Jhee said aloud.

"What's that?" the inquester asked.

"Have you had large incidents of food poisonings?"

"We've been having problems with a bad batch of squelch going around. We've had trouble tracking down the makers."

"I think I know why."

Jhee slid Mr. Bastian's notes toward the inquester who read over them quickly then captured them with her sleeve recorder.

"Why would Bastian or Oriel poison miners? To drum up business for the clinic?"

"To slow down work at the mines?"

"If they were in on the sabotage together, then they may have planned something for the event." Inquester Paij plopped the arrests records for that night on her desk. "That is until the merry dusters pulled their stunt."

"To the contrary," Jhee said, "it would have made them perfect pseudopods."

"Then why didn't they go through with it?"

"Maybe they argued, and Mr. Bastian wound up dead. The event organizer did not strike me as particularly tech-savvy. She might not have been able to pull it off without Mr. Bastian's expertise."

"Then she goes looking for someone to replace him and gets a bullet for her trouble."

~

Tailor's Maxim

Jhee dwelt on how narrowly her household avoided both Mr. Bastian's schemes. Then her thoughts flowed into what Kanto had said about the inquester during their last fitting. She laid a finger aside her nose. A pin stuck her in the side. She flinched.

"Tailor's maxim," Kanto said in a scolding tone.

"You know I have no designs on getting another spouse."

"What if Mirrei's stay with the Delphines goes as well as you hope? She will be happy. She will have found her bit of belonging. But what about you? I know you need a form of intellectual stimulation you won't get from Shep or me."

Jhee stilled Kanto's hands from his pinning. "No. I will just focus my attention the two of you if Mirrei leaves. I won't just run out and try to acquire another. That is not me."

"If it's so easy for you to get rid of her, would it be so easy for you to get rid of me?"

"You're not going anywhere unless you want to. I've said it before, I'll repeat it. I'll say it a thousand times until you believe me."

Jhee put a finger under Kanto's chin and raised his face. He pressed his muzzle against hers.

"Jhee," he said. "You and this family mean so much to me. I want nothing to happen to our family. You three are my world. You, Mirrei, and Shep are my household, and I want no others. She is irreplaceable as are you."

"I understand. You must leave off Mirrei and the Delphines. You must let her make her own decision on this, agreed?"

"All right, denbe."

Kanto and Jhee embraced, and he clung to her. "It means a lot you try. I don't know if I say that often enough."

"Will it always be enough?" Jhee asked.

"What do you mean?"

"Will it ever wear on you I must try or be forced? Will it bother you to have a spouse not as enamored of a pursuit as you are? Who can't find the same joy in an activity you do?"

"Does it bother you? Why are you asking this? Are you still wondering if I want to be elsewhere? If I did, I wouldn't choose the Delphines. You're better appointed than Lady Delphine. Your holdings are worth three times hers, and her family's influence has faded. There's little for you to gain via spousal price. I don't know why you considered the match in the first place."

"You truly were humoring me all those first moons."

Kanto winked. "You enjoyed teaching me, so I let you."

"Fine, Maker Foz, then you have to help me with ledgers."

Jhee hopped from the dais. She whipped off the fabric and handed it to Kanto. He should learn this. She needed to adjust to the idea Mirrei might not be there to help her with the accounts. She had always figured Kanto would be the first one to leave.

"Most expensive vacation ever. Look at this charge here. Thousands for bail. The whole jail, Kanto?"

"I wanted you freed. They were being obstinate. Apparently, you and Mirrei roiled their oceans. I'd call those her charges or yours."

"You made a good case. Settled." Jhee produced a list she had compiled of every judicial caseworker she knew. "However, you need to help me make calls to these folks. Ensuring most of those bailed out return for their judgment dates is our only means to recoup some of the expense."

After they called a quarter of the list, Jhee and Kanto returned to the accounts.

"Ms. Oriel wasted no time cashing my donations." Jhee grimaced. "Whelm and waves, these charges for spa treatments cost how much?"

Jhee examined the charges closer. These weren't household charges. The Fresh Lung Clinic's records had somehow gotten mixed in with hers. "If three thousand shell is what the clinic charges for services, they should never want for funds."

"May I see that, Jhee? Spa treatments are my area of expertise."

"I defer to the master."

Kanto chewed on his lip. "These charges make little sense. For instance, see here this charge for three thousand shell for a massage. An all-day session with Mr. Andre one of the best in the known worlds, booked moons in advance, referral only, costs fifteen hundred. And look how often these charges are. Anyone this high in the demand doesn't have time to meet with anyone except his regulars or most valued patrons this often."

"Maybe Vash is one of his most valued patrons because he's paying him three thousand shell."

"Fine. The price I mentioned is for a full day. Now look here at Vash's clinic appointment schedule. A spa visit and then he's seeing patients less than an hour afterward. Paying this amount for less than a full day is preposterous. He only uses it for a half-hour at most. What would be the point? Here, compare the charity, clinic, and the Delphines' finances."

Kanto confronted her with a conch displaying financial transactions.

"Kanto. How did you get access to these?"

"While I tidied up for our fitting, I noticed them amongst the documents you left about."

Jhee shook her head. She had to take better care with evidence now that it was no longer her and Shep.

"No. Please, hear me out. The additional clinic records, I asked your charitable trust director to request. The Delphines have some huge liabilities. There is no way they could have afforded such a huge donation. I went looking, and I found a series of suspicious donations to the charities account and mysterious deposits to Vash's clinic in matching amounts. Vash may be embezzling from the clinic. I thought Vash was just a cad. What if he's a killer?"

"Even should all this prove to be true, we may have compromised the means to prevent him from doing more harm. I can't go to Inquester Paij with this."

"Can't you handle this yourself?"

"This is not my jurisdiction."

"Can't you handle it some other way? Mirrei may be in danger. Why won't you protect her like you protected me?"

"I hope you are not implying what I think you are. Your disrespect for the law shows disrespect for me. And this obsession with undermining the Delphines shows a disrespect for Mirrei."

"Like the respect you had for the law at the abbey that nearly got me killed or the means with which you dealt with the culprit? Like the way you treat Mirrei as some wilting weed. If only you knew."

"Knew what?"

"Nothing, Jhee. Nothing. Handle it as you see fit. I pray Mirrei does not pay the price for your self-righteousness."

"Enough, Kanto. I think we need to draw tonight to a conclusion. You should return to your room."

"But—"

"Fine. Stay if you wish. I'm going for a walk, and I don't intend to return until you're asleep."

"Please, Jhee, just look."

Always a step back for every step forward with him. Jhee took the records from Kanto. She furrowed her brow. These were indeed worrying. Weird liabilities. Weird assets. Deposits. All highly confidential. If he had poked into Imperially protected records, though.... She backtracked the document custody chain to compile her account of the mishandled evidence. On closer examination, these weren't records she obtained working with Inquester Paij. Of course. Her requests for authorization before she donated. They did not need an Imperial Writ. Ms. Oriel had handed their records over.

Jhee hopped to her feet.

Kanto who had hovered over her shoulder jerked back in surprise. "Ow! What? I think I stabbed myself in my chastity mark with the pen. Not quite a Tailor's Maxim, but close enough."

"'You move. You bleed,'" Jhee repeated. "Not a bloodsucker. That's it, Kanto. That's it!"

Jhee reached for her conch.

"Jhee, where are you going?"

"I've got to go see an expert about a tattoo."

"You're getting another tattoo?"

She pressed her esca to Kanto's.

"What was that for?"

"Being you. Also, send my charitable trust director, no everyone at the trust, a nice gift. My financial adviser too."

14

STINGRAY

~

The Stingray

A place the size of Galleon City likely hosted a branch of the Manray Society gentlewoman's club with its attendant Whisper Room. Jhee met the inquester for brunch outside of one such place, the Stingray Club. The inquester fidgeted and looked uncomfortable. "Members only. They don't give my kind membership."

"You're my guest. Where I go, you can go."

Jhee and the inquester walked inside. The concierge greeted her with a smile. She turned a large bio-film ledger her way. "Sign in please."

"Thank you. I've brought a guest for brunch."

"Very well. Sign in, Miss. Would you like me to go over the Stingray Club rules?"

"Would you."

"All visitors are expected to adhere to the decorum standards as befits a gentlewoman. Male visitors and young children are only permitted during special events or through prior arrangement. Full conch use is only allowed in the dining hall. Only in quiet mode. Absolutely no imaging anywhere on the premises. Beyond the dining hall, device disablers are employed, and only basic communication services will be available. In the event of an emergency, additional services will be allowed, but only at the discretion of management."

They took a small table in the solar overlooking a small cove. Jhee was distracted and unable to eat her steak and sea quail eggs and whale milk with a light bit of watercress and cured maye sausage. The inquester, however, had a big healthy appetite.

The inquester gestured at Jhee's plate with her fork. "You going to eat that? Mind if I?"

"Go right ahead, Inquester."

"Thanks." The inquester speared the food from Jhee's plate. "A separate person has to have killed Oriel."

"What would be the motive?"

"Revenge for the Bastian killing. There're also all those barbarians around. One of them might have gotten it in their head to take revenge for the Gray Galleon."

"Fire Folk."

The inquester raised an eyebrow. "Yeah, Fire Folk. It's one thing to know such a practice existed in abstract. It's another to see it up close and personal like that."

"That sounds plausible."

"What's your theory?"

"I'm still trying to work that out. I think the same person killed both. We just have to figure out the hidden reason."

"Other than their being engaged. You are like a tyro, a newling. There always has to be a greater mystery than the obvious. Start simple. Go cautious."

"First principles my mentor used to say. I like for details to add up."

"A holdover from your arcane training no doubt. People and the real world are messy. Spells and potions aren't."

"Spoken like someone who has never dealt with many equations. Some simple cyphers made me long for third-year chemistry."

The inquester grimaced. "That bad?"

"Worse."

The inquester sopped up the last bit of egg yolk with a roll. "Grain bread. If I get to eat like this, you can have access to my case files anytime."

Jhee raised an eyebrow.

"Just a joke. You don't think much of me do you, Justicar?"

"I'm sorry if I gave you that impression."

The inquester waved off her response. "You are much more polite about it than most. You are one of those proper types who believes discourtesy is the greatest sin you can commit. Although you do and think many discourteous things. Fire Folk you call them now, but you think of them as barbarians. And you and me, we can pal around and go gull over investigation techniques, but at the end of the day you are grandly named, and I'm plainly named. Part of you believes in your inherent advantage to me or else you'd renounce your titles and land."

"I believe in the comfort and protection title and lands can provide."

"Fair enough. In a district where people live far away from each other, and there is not a lot of oversight, you can make logical leaps you can't back up. In a district like this where everyone's brushing fins and living gill to gill all the time, and I've got fifty bosses, simple and cautious is the best way to proceed. Everyone thinks they are my boss. Everyone second guesses my conclusions. I'm not empowered to render judgment as you are, and I have to walk many people through my evidence chain and my thought process."

"Every isle."

"Come again?"

"Are you familiar with the Fair-Weather statutes, Inquester?"

"Yeah, folk law."

"It's a fancy way of saying every isle has its own rules. Usually determined by its ruling family."

"You're not in the boonies anymore, Justicar, where you have sole authority. We have a centralized legal process here. I don't just have to convince myself. I have to bring my evidence to a tribunal and a bench of justices." Inquester Paij took a sip of kolal. "Under your tenure, I noticed an uptick in the number of bodies lost at sea in your home district, even before the wall."

"The corrupt are cunning. Poison was the preferred method of murder in the Far Reaches. With corrupt Justicars and personal security forces, they often labeled deaths without obvious signs of trauma or which took place in private spaces natural or accidental. A central authority with which to report deaths did not exist. Coroners, medical examiners, and appointed magistrars could often be convinced to look the other way. With help from the previous governess, I had implemented mandatory autopsies on all deaths."

"Unintended consequences."

"Just so. If those were the crimes I'd be forced to investigate, perhaps it's just as well they summoned me to serve at the capital. The Reach families need to get used to not being the final authority on everything. I need to get used to it, too. Even justicars will go away soon as law enforcement and arbitration are standardized under the Central Authority. I didn't mean to overstep. I'll do better."

Jhee looked around at those staffing the Stingray Club. They did not have the Inkerton Event Services logo, but that of another company Jhee knew was similar. She could not help but think of what had got them here. What indignities had they suffered to be allowed to interact with the rich? She bet it was sold as some manner of honor. Some staff were the sons or daughters of minor houses getting in a little extra work or networking in before they could get memberships themselves. If one could not be a member, the next best thing was to work here.

The inquester looked at Jhee and noted where her eyes went. "You are finally starting to get it. I think there is hope for you yet, Justicar. Perhaps I am being a little harsh. Therein lies the rub. Fire Folk. It doesn't quite roll off your tongue yet, does it? Many still call them Stipples or Dapples, not in polite company so much anymore. This is what I have to deal with. I have to deal with them as they are. Are they abused and exploited? Yes. But you also have to deal with what that does to them as a population. Bleakness, hopelessness. Many are trapped between two bad options: the police or the smugglers and gangs. Call them barbarians or call them Fire Folk but it won't change their lot in life. The only thing that can do that is action."

"Where do you stand on the Shield, Inquester?"

"I have no opinion on it really despite how it might seem. I understand the impetus for it entirely. But like so many things, it is a double-sworded fish. For every problem it seeks to stop, it creates another. One I have to address."

"Thank you for your candor."

"Thanks for introducing me to these sausages. Makers, I don't know what I did without them in my life. So, Justicar, what exactly are we doing here?"

"Waiting."

The inquester speared another sausage. She motioned at the waiter. "Orange juice. Thanks."

"Also, would you bring a selection of periodicals from the bear's den." Jhee picked more at her food. "Bastian's shoes. Kanto said his shoes did not match his professed occupation."

"That's an interesting theory."

"What if it's true?"

"We already know Bastian was leading some dual life. The question remains why?"

"Why indeed?"

The inquester's conch clacked. Other diners gave them dirty looks before she silenced it. "More results from the lab. It's confirmed, cause of death was slugs to the chest. You may find this interesting though. The slugs were magicked."

Jhee turned towards the inquester. "That is indeed interesting, Inquester. I'll want to examine them immediately if you'll permit it."

"Do I have much choice?"

"We all have choices."

"Ain't that the truth. However, they aren't always good ones, are they?"

"No, Inquester, I don't suppose they are."

"Might I ask you a question, Justicar?"

"Of course, Inquester."

"How did you become a Justicar?"

"The person who preceded me had to resign in disgrace. Oddly enough they meant my appointment to Justicar as a fluff assignment. It was meant to be relaxing to appease my family and berth me out of the way." And to keep her out of the trouble Jhee was liable to get in by coming to the Stingray.

Perhaps Paij's scenario where Ms. Oriel was the intended victim and Mr. Bastian's death mistaken identity bore reexamination. In which case, Jhee might do well to stop poking into his background. "Ms. Oriel and Bastian were of a similar height and build. A matched set we used to call them in my youth. Their offspring would be as well."

Inquester Paij shrugged. "Topic change accepted. Some like the same. Some like different."

"What about you, Inquester? Are you married?"

The inquester raised an eyebrow. "One mister, though he says I'm married to my job. I don't know how you manage it. I've had trouble enough maintaining one relationship over the years."

"It was just Shep and me for a long time. Now, we're just finding a way. They have reduced my duties. I will now be an official of the court at the capital. It will not require so much travel as my old duties did and I can dedicate more of my time to my household. Even now, a policing system like that here in the city will be rolled out in some fashion to all districts and regions. Especially given the amount of power a person in my position has the potential to wield. Which is part of what caught up my predecessor. He was like a textbook case of the numerous capricious and petty ways the holder of the office could wield their power. I expect the Justicar system to be abolished in not too many more years particularly with the population being concentrated more in large cities."

"I can see that. You said your family wanted to dry dock you?"

"There was a political matter that affected my ability to be assigned any rank in the capital. This was a compromise. Meant to place me somewhere, I would be mostly unobtrusive. My family needed something to do with me. I had some small skill with judging matters and getting to the truth of things. When I returned from the academy, I had done well in my civil service boards, and I had done my time in the service. I had developed something of a reputation though in my early years. I had a keen mind for sorting out the truth of disputes, except when it came to personal matters."

"Why does that not surprise me? So, you were observing and deciding things from when you were a wee little thing, huh?"

"Yes, indeed, Inquester. I wasn't supposed to inherit. I had several siblings older than I and more beloved. However, most of them were killed in warring and fighting. I was not smartest or bravest. I just paid more attention than most and made the logical connections others often had trouble making."

"Do you mind if we keep the questioning going?"

"For now."

"Is that how you learned arcana? Making the connections no one else would? You have such a traditional mind. It seems odd to me you would go for arcana."

"I learned most of my cyphering and drawing in the service."

"Oh, those classified missions I'm not allowed to read."

Jhee made her face impassive.

"Ah, gotcha. Did you learn as part of your normal service or as part of your super-secret spy training?"

Again, Jhee made no expression and did not change her body language.

"So intriguing. I almost learned. I mean I know a few crude cyphers. They require us to learn some things in the academy."

"I had learned some drawing and cyphering before my academy days. Most of it crude and of limited use, for farming and the like. One of the few reasons I have at least some expertise with water even if only as a tertiary focus."

"That seems par for the course. Myself, I'm fire. Such as it is. I can't do much more than snuff a candle flame."

"Sometimes that's all you need. A spark on a bit of kindling or under-brush and whoosh! Up everything goes."

"Like the city. You are correct, Justicar. I used to do parlor tricks with it, not much more. You got any more tips on how to use next to nonexistent drawing?"

"I'm full of them. A puff of air to clear something off or move something aside. Even as little as a breath. Then there is earth drawing. That one proves to be trickier. It is one of the more difficult of the elements to master. Any obstruction whatsoever can disrupt control. It also seems to be the most loca-tion dependent. Some people have trouble controlling soil from different regions. Sterile soil with few contaminants is the easiest to manipulate. Unlike fire and water though, carrying around a bucket of soil sticks out and draws attention to itself."

"I guess it's just as well the menfolk are best at it. With all the bulk of theirs to carry it with and crevices to hide dirt."

Jhee cracked a smile.

"Finally. I was beginning to worry, Justicar. I talk a good game, but I pride myself on my humor."

"In my later years, I've never been much of one for frivolities. I apologize. Your humor is quite amusing at times. It's just it might be much funnier if I weren't the brunt of it."

"Ah, okay, but you know I have to bust your pouch."

"Yes, as a test of what kind of person I am. Can I give as good as I get? Will I shrink away? Will I blow it out of proportion? I've often thought of doing a paper on hazing rituals."

"What a way to kill the mood."

Jhee laughed. "I got you."

The inquester wrinkled her snout. "That wasn't funny."

"Not even a little? Just a wee bit."

"Not funny."

"A scoche. An iota."

The inquester shook her head, but the corners of her mouth were upturned. "We're going have to go soon. Let's settle up and get back to the station."

Jhee stopped the inquester when she reached for her conch. "My treat, Inquester."

"I will be so spoiled once this is over. It's back to boiled squid and fruit chutney."

Jhee grimaced. "How ghastly."

The waiter returned with a selection of bio-film publications on a polished, silver tray. Jhee leafed through them until she saw one with a clipped corner. "This one. Thank you."

"Would the lady like to read it in the Whisper Room?"

"Yes. Thank you."

"Follow me if you would, ladies."

The waiter strode towards the far arch of the dining hall without regard to if they followed. Jhee left. The inquester downed the dregs of her juice and wolfed the last bit of sausage before she hurried after them. The waiter continued down a curved stair. Once the waiter reached an onyx black door, she paused for them to catch up. An attendant in white robes and black gloves stood as they approached. The waiter departed. Jhee and the inquester's conchs sounded to let them know they had lost signal. The attendant held out her hand for their conchs.

"Sustained silence is the rule of the Whisper Room," Jhee said.

Jhee set her conch to quiet and motioned for the inquester to do the same. She tucked the periodical under her arm. The attendant paused, looked her and the inquester over before she dropped her hand. She inclined her head and led them inside. She indicated two empty chairs by the fireplace.

A couch in the far corner was occupied and a settee by the window.

Jhee pretended to read the real estate brochure for a few moments before setting it down on the table beside her chair. A woman in a short robe and pants switched out the magazine for hers as she passed by without so much as a look. The inquester caught Jhee's gaze and leaned forward to ask if they should follow. Jhee lifted one finger from the armrest to indicate they needed to wait. She fanned through the pages of the replacement periodical. No inserts. The inquester gave her another glance.

The room attendant reappeared. Outside, Jhee saw movement from an alcove with a milky white glass door. Jhee made the slightest head motion towards the milky door. The attendant kept her focus elsewhere as Jhee and the inquester turned away from the stairs.

The woman in short robes sat on a bench toking on a cheap smoke root. "He's a ghost. Not surprising with all the people moving in from the Outreaches."

"Unofficially?" Jhee asked.

"He worked for MANTEL, all right, as a line engineer."

"Why would they wipe the records of a line engineer?"

The woman stubbed out her root in a caramel colored clay dish. "They wouldn't. I wanted to warn you in person, though. They pushed back. Your activities have not gone unnoticed. I'm bowing out. Good luck."

She left. Jhee walked to the dish and picked up the smoke root. She rolled it between her fingers. Too springy. Jhee tapped out a small rolled bit of bio-film. She slipped the roll in her pocket and lit up the root.

"MANTEL? Did she say MAN-flipping-TEL?"

"Keep your voice down. You've heard of them?"

"Of course I have, but not officially."

The inquester took the root from Jhee and puffed on it. They left out the smokers' entrance the opposite of the way the woman had gone. "My aunt used to talk about places like this. Tell me again you were some desk jockey in the war."

"Tell me more about your aunt."

"Story for another time."

"The same."

"The mister is going to kill me, for more reasons than one," the inquester said. She had one more delighted toke on the smoke root before her attention alighted on the pocket where Jhee had placed the roll. "Line engineer?"

Jhee stared at the Shield in the distance. If Mr. Bastian worked for MANTEL, the struck through sigil on his wrist was not a sucker or a spider as she originally thought. It must have been an octopus and that meant he had been part of the Octopus Inkworks research groups. "Lead engineer. I think there may be some catastrophic flaw with the Shield."

"Storm Child's rage," the inquester swore.

15

THE ACTIVIST

~

Mine Chase

Mirrei walked into the game room at Chuc's with Vash's arm loosely about her waist. Erma and Deziree sat at a table playing cards while Taral and Semele lazed about on a windowsill.

"I've brought your 'weirs' partner," Vash said.

Mirrei gave him a "thank you" muzz to the cheek.

"See you in a few hours. Try to stay out of trouble this time, chums."

As much as Mirrei liked his work at the clinic, Vash had quickly become a bore full of constant questions about denbe's holdings and homes. As soon as he found himself a proper wife, he intended to quit work at the clinic and devote himself full time to her. Talk of the clinic made him uncomfortable. Whenever she tried to talk about the clinic and the work he did for the community, he quickly changed the subject to her wealth or denbe's. He seemed particularly interested in denbe's.

How Vash spoke during Mirrei's first to the clinic proved most telling. Any interest Mirrei had in Vash soured the moment he sought to use the clinic as a bargaining stone in courtship and a sweetener to predispose her to his suit. *"I, for one, would not hesitate to leave it behind if the right situation presented itself or should my future wife insist.... Either way, it would hardly be my responsibility anymore. Let Oriel see to that. It's her job after all."*

"Did you hear about what happened?" Deziree said.

"What this time?" Mirrei asked.

"Another food riot down at the docks," Taral said.

"We need to plan another action," Semele said.

"We need to lie low. Mamere and babere threatened to enroll me in Arctic studies at the Imperial Academy," Deziree said.

"Mine threatened to put me out to sire," Taral said.

"So, we sit around on our anchors like a bunch of frightened brats, is that it?" Mirrei asked.

A sniff of disdain escaped Deziree. "We don't all have powerful and indulgent shell mommies like you do, Star."

Mirrei coughed. "She is not my mother and doesn't control me."

"I didn't mean anything by it, Star."

"I hear there's a sit-in at one of the wall's broadcast pylons," Semele said.

Taral nodded. "Yeah, we can go there."

Chappy picked up a glass and started polishing. "And do what?"

"I don't know. Amplify their voices."

Mirrei pursed her lips. Chappy smirked. "He's right. How about we do something else? We make a splash. We make a banner and hang it from the top of the substation?"

Chappy set down the glass and fixed her with an unwavering stare. "The last time someone did that your wifey got them arrested for murder."

"They were stupid. We'll be smart. Unless one of you is planning to murder someone, we should be fine. What do you propose?"

Chappy shrugged. "I'm just a lowly barman. You're the great activists."

After a few more minutes of debate and apathy, Mirrei took a water taxi to a substation protest check-in without them. It was just a game to them. They were dabblers who could walk away once the going got a little rough. But not her, she was truly committed. Next to the signage table, Mirrei found the first aid tent and volunteered to help. While she organized medical supplies, she watched signs parade by. "Stall the wall." "Death wall." "Tear down the wall." "Free the winds." "Freedom for the Fire Folk." "Solidarity now." "One waters."

Shortly after midday, the march leaders had them head out.

"Star!"

Erma, Semele, Deziree, and Taral waved at her, signs in hand. She smiled. They ran over and joined her.

"You were right. We need to do this."

"We're with you. All the way."

They marched from the park to the up-link substation's front gates. They added their voices to the crowd and did what they could. Mirrei had a coughing fit. She found a place off to the side where she used her saline monitor to check her salt levels. She took a couple saline lozenges.

"You don't look so good, Star."

"I'm fine. So, are we going to do this or what?"

They rejoined the protesters.

Mirrei looked out at the faces of the counter-protesters and curiosity seekers. So many folk just stood by watching. They could add their voices to hers. She still felt a little light-headed.

A member of the onlookers caught her attention. Why had her mind singled him out? His stance. Shep's primer on body language and violence. His posture was rigid and his face impassive. No hate. No curiosity. Unlike those around him. What else? Denbe's lectures on how to observe bubbled to the surface. His clothes were all wrong for the setting. Oversized and too warm for this weather. The rain had stopped. His arm was held oddly stiff at his side. What was that in his hand?

Mirrei dropped her sign. She ran forward. One constable stopped her.

"That's as far as you go, Miss."

"Imperator, please. Get everyone out of here."

"So, now you are concerned about protests?"

"No. That person." Mirrei scanned the crowd. She found the person again. She pointed at him. He noticed her and began to flee. "Stop him."

"He has as much right to be here as you. Unlike you, he's minding his own business."

"You don't understand. I think he's here to do violence."

"Sure. Sure. I recognize you. Didn't we arrest you and your friends last long-tide?"

"Yeah, then you should know who I am. My wife is a Justicar. She's friends with the mayor and Inquester Paij. She'll vouch for me, but please we detain that person."

"Fine, I will call her. To come down here and get you before you get your-self arrested again."

Shouting interrupted the imperator. A fight had broken out between a group of Water and Fire Folk in mining gear and another in makeshift armor with their faces covered by scarves. The imperators moved to separate the folks striking each other. Their interference became a conflagration amongst the original combatants, giving them a common target. And like a fire, the fighting spread.

A surge of protesters rushed the gate. Armored amateur militia tried to hold them back. The constable rushed to intervene. Mirrei dove through the crowd to find her friends.

"Hey, come back here."

The constable swore as they dodged a bottle. Mirrei located her compatri-ots. Via looks and gestures, they coordinated to pull the injured from the melee. Within minutes they had formed a small, sheltered area for the wounded.

She caught sight of the man from earlier taking advantage of the fracas to slip inside the substation. She took off after him.

"Star, where are you going?" Deziree yelled.

Mirrei slipped past the chaos into the substation, applying the secret lessons on shadowing from Bax. The man had reached the central power room. He laid out a parchment and attached a data shell to the console. He pressed buttons attempting some procedure on the controls. Mirrei spotted an alarm on the wall and hit it.

The would-be saboteur spotted her. He snatched the parchment and data shell then bolted. Quickly he ducked through a bank of power regulators, disappearing.

Mirrei squeezed through after him. She found herself in access tunnels. She listened then chased the suspect as he ran. Her head was positively swimming by now. The tunnels gave way to unfinished rock. She doubled over to catch her breath. Her breathing resonated throughout the cavern and filled her ears. So many crisscrossing catwalks. She held her breath while she listened closer. Only distortions from drips and the struggle outside reached her.

Each step became an agony. Each breath became a chore. Her extreme vulnerability and isolation hit her then. Old mine tracks led off into unlit, unused passages. The tunnel walls changed from the smoother walls of the heavily used tourist section to rougher hewn surfaces made with pickaxes. They were no longer in the substation, but a mine. How far down had she gone? If something happened to her, would anyone be able to find her, or would she just wind up another lost soul the likes of Kanto told stories about as cautionary tales?

Mirrei turned to leave. She spotted the suspect at the other end of the catwalk. He hid his face. Yet, Mirrei wanted a clear description for denbe. She struggled forward, and the figure backed away. She stumbled forward arm outstretched. If only she could just get a look. Spots swam before Mirrei's eyes.

Star, the name she used with the activists, echoed from shadows. Was she imagining them calling for her?

Mirrei blinked her eyes. One moment, she leaned against the shaft wall, hoping the light-headedness would pass. The next moment she had slid to the floor. A fuzzy blob loomed over her then ran off. Her wheezing filled the shaft. She could not get more than a sip of air at a time. She was still wheezing when rescuers found her. Her eyes fluttered closed.

~

The Hospitalization

"Justicar, it's Mirrei," Inquester Paij said.

Jhee rolled her eyes. "She got herself arrested again so soon?"

"Mirrei's been taken to the hospital. She and her 'weirs' club are in the hospital. There was some kind of incident at the substation. She and her friends were injured. We're still trying to figure out the details. They found them passed out in the back room at Chuc's; a known hangout for the more violent radicals."

The inquester's tone was somber her words carefully chosen.

"Thank you very much, Inquester," Jhee whispered.

"Justicar—"

Jhee disconnected. The conch slipped from her loose grasp. She sat down with a long exhale. She had to go see her. Jhee had disconnected from the inquester before she learned to which hospital they had taken Mirrei. What had the inquester said? They found them at the dive bar. That area was poor and underserved. Lifesavers would have taken them to the clinic if they were poorer. With their families means and influence, however, they would get private expedited transport to a top medical center. The nearest to that area was Makers' Care. Another center might better serve more specialized trauma. Jhee stilled her shaking hands. It would be Makers' Care; no other choice fit the givens.

Her conch sounded as if on cue. Sure enough, it was Makers' Care. The doctor she spoke to was very matter of fact that Mirrei's family should come at once. She called for a water taxi. She tucked her hands in her robes and went to Kanto's room to inform him what had happened. He smiled upon seeing her at first. His eyes narrowed, and he began to frown.

"Mirrei has been hospitalized." Kanto flinched. "A water taxi will be here soon. Come to think of it we should pack a day bag for her and us. Would you mind gathering anything of hers you think she might want or need?"

He studied her. His frown deepened. "Jhee, sit."

"I can't. I need to see to a few matters before we depart. Among them, inform Shep. He would want to know."

"No. Sit."

Jhee sat as he instructed. He touched his esca to hers. He gripped one of her hands tightly. "I'll contact Shep and pack us a day bag. You sit here until the water taxi comes."

Jhee closed her eyes and sighed. She felt almost as if in a dream while they rode to the hospital. She only felt awake again once the physician explained the extent of Mirrei's condition.

"This is probably one of the most aggressive cases of Fresh Lung Syndrome I've ever seen. You said someone examined her a few days ago?" Dr. Pike said.

Kanto gasped.

Jhee put an arm around him. "She had a fainting spell. The house physician at the villa, Vash, examined her and said it was nothing to worry about. That she had just overextended herself. We increased her saline regimen, monitored her, and everything seemed fine. I thought she was getting better. It was her first relapse in some time. The journey here she had been feeling poorly. However, once we arrived, she seemed to perk right up. Mirrei was getting her color back. She was very active in sports and humanitarian work. She really seemed to come alive here," Jhee's voice trailed off.

"Well, this condition has proved unpredictable. Not to mention the spontaneous occurrence in her friends. All from the main isles, you said?"

"Vash, Erma, and Semele are, yes. They're from right here on the cape. The others I don't know."

~

Mirrei's Confession

"I'd asked the First Makers for you not to get yourself arrested again," Jhee said. She took Mirrei's hand.

"What a way for them to implement your design."

"Precisely my thoughts. You keep reaping a harvest for seeds of misery you've never sown."

"By that, you mean the repercussions of your feud with mamere."

Mirrei lapsed into silence. Her mouth twitched as if wanting to say more. "What is it, Mirrei?" Jhee asked.

"As our house took on more and more water, she would see yours on the hill and talk about all the things your family had taken from ours. After they were kind enough to take you in. Every time our travels took us within sight of your home, she would point up at the house on the hill and say, 'There. There lives the fiend who ruined our lives.'

"When mamere and I stayed at your home the first time, I was trembling. Here we were at the spawning bed of the monster, the evil, Trench-hearted villains who had tried to destroy our family. I expected giants or creatures resembling leviathans from the deep. Horrible blood-stained fangs and claws. We announced ourselves. You opened the door yourself in a dressing gown and slippers with a shark-skinned volume tucked under your arm. You were soft-spoken. I almost mistook you for a servant. And I thought this, this is the woman who mamere cursed nightly so vehemently.

"My mother, nay the whole reaches, painted you as some fiendish cross between a seductress and an ogre who'd destroyed our family out of jealousy, and Shep as a disloyal lech. You were small. Almost pathetic. That's when the seed was sown that it was all small. And pathetic. This grudge which threatened to engulf both our families, our isles. I soon realized I wanted no part in perpetuating it."

Jhee supposed it was progress that everyone thought her a seductress now. Initially, no one but Miramar thought she seduced Shep. Perhaps Miramar had seen something between them that no one else had. It hurt that the first thought on everyone's mind was Shep had tricked her. Maybe he had.

Jhee reached into an inner pocket and extracted Miramar's somewhat rumpled letter. She read from it as she had so many times since Mirrei came to live with them. "... protect and honor my daughter," Jhee finished. She left off the last part as she usually did.

"You owe me, Jhee."

"Mamere's letter. You never read all of it aloud, especially the last part."

"Because when I share it with you, I want it to be about her love for you and not whatever transpired between us."

"'She owes us.' That's the way mamere always put it. What did you owe her?"

"The short version: I stole her fiancé and bankrupted, nay crushed, your family. I had to break my betrothal to do it, which gave your family an unlikely ally in the merchant kings and queens of Crag Hall."

"You, denbe? Hard to believe."

"Which part? That Shep might desire me more than your mother or my fortune is the result of others' misery?"

"I didn't mean it that way."

"Of course not."

"The problems in our home weren't about resources. Life at Crag Hall was never as full of privation as she made it out to be. They made a decent living as merchants. We just weren't rich like you. That's what bothered her the most, I think."

Jhee kept her own council. Almost every shred of her wealth was geld minted from the weakness of others. Even she had gotten her strikes in. The Mitsus and Crag Halls would never have been able to force Miramar and Mirrei from one home after the other without Jhee's machinations from long ago.

Mirrei took Jhee's hand. "Don't blame yourself. You've never struck me as vindictive. It seems petty, cruel, beneath you."

"It was. I can be both cowardly and cruel. You've just never seen that side of me. I was young and stupid. We all were."

"You've always been so gracious to me. I'm not sure if I deserve it."

Mirrei looked pained.

"Do you want me to fetch the doctor?" Jhee asked.

"I kissed Shep. When we first came to your house, I tried to seduce Shep. We weren't engaged yet. It was before I knew him, before I knew you."

"During my nights with Kanto, Shep took abrupt efforts not to share a bed with you alone. Which meant he had concerns, if not about his behavior, then yours. Even if he hadn't told me, I would have guessed on my own. And the fact you may have oversold how frail you were."

"You knew yet you said nothing. Why?"

"Not the whole time, but I caught on soon enough. Who am I to judge? Mai—Miramar, your mother could be intense. You wouldn't have been the first to embellish the truth for a little relief from her. Also, when you first became part of our household, you may have felt you needed to do it to get extra attention. An impulse I understand too well. Until you came along and stole my thunder, I was a world-class hypochondriac."

"Like knows like."

Jhee flashed back to young adulthood and her home and the silence, the disinterested parents who wanted nothing more than to lose themselves in memories. Was that what it was like growing up with a bitter, obsessed Miramar? How much of the hardship of her upbringing laid at Jhee's feet? "I can only imagine what it was like living with her like that for all those years."

"Please, denbe, tell me what happened between you."

"I was jealous of Mai. I always was. She was popular, and had a loving, if demanding, family."

"Don't. You don't have to play the villain to protect my mother's memory. I know who she was. You never badmouthed her. You've been very gracious. Mamere was jealous of the life you and Shep had together. The life she could have had with you, together. If she had stood up to her family."

"I wish my turn as the villain had only been play. Everyone had to pick a side and my family crushed anyone who chose wrong. Families who had been our friends for years. Families who had risked their lives in the search for my missing sisters. And families who had lost children just like my parents had. The worst part was, it was the most alive, the most united, I had seen my parents in years which is why I reveled in it too. So, if your mother hated us, hated me, she had good cause. For I am indeed the engineer of her misery and likely yours as well."

"If you hated each other so much, why did I also see you and she kiss that night?"

"Your mother and I were friends, more than. I was enamored of her and Shep or the idea of them. I wanted that for myself, and I took it. It was petty. It was vindictive. And we're all still paying the price for it. Well, she's dead now and no need to speak ill of her."

Mirrei winced. "Neither she nor I deserve your gracious words."

"Nonsense. You are probably the only true innocent in all this."

"That's the last thing I am. The obsession with the past went both ways. She said I reminded her of you. And you both tried to mold me into a shape not quite mine. You think you were the only one obsessed? You need to stop trying to make me into your very own little nerd. My mother already tried that, to turn me into a cutting of you so she could punish me in your place."

"Enough old pain for now, only some sweet dreams. Good night, Mirrei."

16

____

THE SQUELCH MAKER

~

The New Arrival

Jhee and Kanto continued to sit with Mirrei. Two days later, Jhee returned to Mirrei's room where Kanto lovingly brushed her hair as usual.

"You won't believe the latest gossip," he said to her. "The Damsels over on Isle Quiescence are in a feud with the Makos of Presque Isle. They had this long-standing marriage pact who knows how many years ago. But the youngest son you see decides he wants to be a whale rider to impress his fiancée. He had gotten it into his head or had heard her parents talking about how they no longer considered him a suitable match. Although I heard that she told him flat out she thought he was beneath her. Anyway, her family has a whale preserve. He and two friends get drunk and sneak into the whale pens with nets and riding hooks. I suppose they fancied themselves the remaking of Whale Rider. They climb into the water with the whales. The whales panic. One of them leaps up into the air, spins, and flops back down right on top of the son who had managed to rope and ride one of the other whales. He was severely crushed, and they injured both the whales. He has no breeding potential anymore. They are out two prize whales. Now the families are arguing back and forth over whose fault it was."

Jhee leaned against the door frame and smiled. Mirrei turned her head towards Jhee and gave a wan smile. She watched quietly as Kanto told her more stories. Every now and then Mirrei giggled a little, but a coughing fit shortly followed it. Jhee walked up behind Kanto. She put her hands on his shoulders and squeezed them gently. He touched her hand.

405

They took turns reading to her, Kanto from the gossip sheets and Jhee from the latest academic and forensic journals.

They heard footfalls at the door and turned. Shep stood there. He opened his arms, and Jhee ran to them. Kanto approached them quietly and respectfully. She composed herself and brushed away her tears.

Shep crouched beside Mirrei's bedside. "Hey, Sprite, how you doing?"

Mirrei's head turned towards his voice. "Been better," she mumbled through the haze of medication.

"You know there are better ways to get me to hurry back," Shep continued. "Wait to see the new house. You won't believe it. It should meet even Kanto's high standards."

"Is it our fault Mirrei and I are the only ones in this household with a decent sense of fashion and style?"

Shep shrugged. "Hey, Sprite, do you mind if I sit here with you for a while and give Tunes and Puzzler a rest?"

Mirrei moved her head the barest amount up and down. Shep gave them a single nod that said they could rest assured. He would be there. In the hallway, Jhee placed an arm around Kanto's shoulders as he shook and cried.

"It was that drench Vash! She was supposed to be with him. He said he would take care of her. Now, look at her. You just simply can't let her marry him. He'll kill her just like he did Ms. Oriel and Mr. Bastian. I went on one of those 'weirs' dates with them. It was nothing but debauchery. I told them I wanted no part of it. She, she made me promise not to tell you. Denbe, I'm sorry I didn't tell you. I'm sorry. I'm sorry."

Jhee rubbed Kanto's back. "This isn't your fault. You think I hadn't surmised they weren't playing weirs, anymore? Especially once she got herself arrested. You have nothing to be sorry for."

Shep approached them. "Go. Get some rest the both of you."

Jhee opened her mouth to speak.

"I demand it. It's my day today."

Jhee nodded. Shep procured them a transport, and they headed for the villa. The driver of the transport navigated past all the roadblocks and protests. Jhee's thoughts threatened to overwhelm her. She had to find stillness, so she could help her household.

"Driver, pull over please."

"My lady?"

"Pull over, please. Ground level."

"What's wrong?" Kanto asked.

The driver maneuvered to a pull off on the side of the transport lane.

"Nothing. I want to walk the rest of the way."

"What ever for?"

"Driver, bring him to the villa." Jhee smiled for Kanto's benefit. "Don't trouble yourself. I'll be there soon."

"If you insist."

Jhee squeezed his hand. She grabbed a lighted umbrella to protect herself from the light drizzle before hopping out. The transport merged back into the transport lane and sailed off. As she walked, Jhee gazed at the rich green trees lining the hills. Sometimes they gave way abruptly to a sharp drop. She cleared, centered, and directed her thought to the Wave Makers. The Wave Makers had claimed their due from her family and more. She took a step closer to the edge. For a few moments, she opened herself up and merely listened. The sounds of the sea called to her. Did she hear her siblings and her parents laughing in the surf? Jhee opened her eyes and returned to a safe distance from the waves.

Back at the villa, Jhee could not sleep. She crept to the boathouse Lady Delphine allowed them to use for a workshop. She pored over journals and sheets, then her healing derivations. Finally, everything she had learned about the curative properties of Tranquility Bridge's golden nectar. She had uncovered actual healing benefits to it, though she was no chemist or epidemiologist. That was more Mirrei's bailiwick.

Jhee hesitated in front of Mirrei's portion of the workshop they shared. If Jhee disturbed anything, Mirrei was likely to feel her privacy violated. Not much matched the feeling of returning to find one's belongings not where you left them.

If circumstances had kept going as they were, Jhee would be freed of worrying about Mirrei's space. That's what Jhee planned. Mirrei would be married to someone more suitable whose age and interests better complemented her own. She would lead or build a robust, thriving household that would one day return House Mitsu to its former glory.

None of that would happen if Jhee selfishly clung to the poor girl like a needy lover. She must let Mirrei thrive and flourish in whatever manner she saw fit. This was not her choice.

Along with casks of Tranquility Gold and samples of the wild yeast cultures, Mirrei's section contained glass jugs stoppered with corks. Tubes in the corks led to another lower set of jugs. Jhee took a whiff. She recognized that smell from the academy days. The only ailment that cured was boredom. She examined Mirrei's makeshift lab or should she call it a still.

Squelch. Mirrei's work? Jhee took a sip. She screwed up her face. If her eyes now resembled swirling fireworks after a swig, she would not have been surprised. Then the buzz arrived. Strong, but tasty. Better than anything Jhee and her classmates whipped up in her day. It tasted much like the refu-juice the refugees had served her on Torilsisle but went down much smoother. Was that where Mirrei got the idea? She had gotten sick like this after she and Kanto sneaked off to visit their camps near the Shield. Was it because of the squelch?

Jhee set the jug down. She would bring a sample to the hospital just in case. As Jhee gathered a sample, she found another foil wrapper in the trash.

Jhee did not want to go to bed, but was there anything more she could do tonight? Jhee just stopped at a loss for something else to do.

The idleness became too much. Jhee wrote a series of prayer letters then sought the shrine. She waved the letters through incense smoke to scent them before burning. She summoned happy memories of Mirrei and Mai so that she could complete proper tribute to Pascoe and Lashae.

For Mai, she thought of their swim team days. Miramar and Shep competed on the school team while Jhee managed.

For Mirrei, the times they spent in their home library. Jhee had taken an instant liking to the young woman. Cultured and well read. Simple clothing. After a few months of dealing with Kanto's pretensions and hectoring, it was nice to have someone around who had nothing to say about her clothes or hair or image. With whom she could discuss the classics and philosophy. Jhee gave the Makers her laughter and letters.

Chimes answered from somewhere in the distance. Jhee turned her attention to Futou, his effigy forever poised in the process of ecstatic drumbeating.

Kanto would be devastated if Mirrei left them. But Jhee could not let that sway her, she must do what was best for Mirrei.

Jhee was not oblivious to what was happening with him. The two had grown so close so fast. Jhee tossed geld and hummed until she could be alone with her thoughts no more.

Jhee had to learn more about the true Mirrei. She had an idea where to start. The wrapper in the trash: she had seen many in a dish at Che's.

~

The Dive Bar Revisited

Che's had been a dead end, but the same man owned both, a man named Chappy. Chappy, the man who had rescued Mirrei and her friends, hovered while Jhee poked about the dive club, the infamous game room at Chuc's. Cigarettes, joints, booze, and a snooker table occupied the space. Not all that different from Stingray Club with the same manner of doings as the older set it would appear. Their very own junior Stingray Club.

"I wanted to thank you for bringing Mirrei and her friends to safety."

"No need."

"They're lucky you were there. I figured you for one who stays behind the bar."

Chappy tucked his hands into his trouser pockets and kicked at the floor. "She was here right before it happened. Giving everyone what-for for turtle shelling. Don't worry, m'lady. She's feisty, a fighter. She'll come through just fine."

"The First Makers' Design be done. May I look around?"

"Uh, sure."

One part of the dive club stood on its own, a giant wall painted with slogans. "Miners Unite." "Free the Fire Folk. The Wall is Death." "Free the Waters." "One Waters. Fishers. Miners." Protest signs and that ridiculous banner they tried to hang over the plants lay crumpled. Were they insane? Why would they do such an act again so soon? She taught Mirrei better than that. Perhaps the repeat action was her lot's idea. Mirrei understood better how not to get caught or at least she should have. Repetition was a sure-fire way to get caught. Mirrei needed to vary her methods. That way no one got too used to one tactic and could counter it. One must do the unexpected. This would keep the imperators on their toes. Jhee smiled at the irony of her thinking about ways to teach Mirrei to flout the law. Ironic.

Jhee examined their materials and propaganda; hiding among them was a shiny wrapper for black pepper clove candy, but no dish of the candies themselves. Mirrei had hit it off with the Delphines as she hoped. They had practically accepted her into their family. Jhee wouldn't be surprised if, within a few years of marriage, Mirrei would run the entire household from offspring to dame. She might expect no less of a woman who learned from both her and Miramar. A woman. Jhee, at last, thought of Mirrei as a woman. Some part of her had always thought of her as a girl.—the girl she may have had with Miramar or the one they all might have had together. Jhee owed Miramar so much. This plan had worked out too well.

The apparatus in the corner caught Jhee's attention. The equipment much like what occupied the work shed she and Mirrei kept at the villa. Jhee realized she wasn't alone. Wynne, the activist who escaped at the observatory, sat at the bar. She looked like fifty knots of rough seas.

"Nice still. Star's?" Jhee asked.

"Only in the loosest sense. She has a secret ingredient. Everyone loves it. All efforts to reproduce it, not so much. Her squelch recipe pulled the Fire Folk and other miners in like the tide. It reminds them of what they drank back home. You're Star's denbe."

Wynne gave Jhee a slight chin jut of recognition and challenge. Her face was heavily bruised and bandages wrapped her head.

"I'm here to help Star and wanted to thank Chappy again. I understand he was the one who got Star and her friends to safety."

A flash of anger reddened Wynne's eyes followed by a wince of pain. "Chappy? It was Vash who saved them. Chappy was LAS. He only turned up after everything was over, apparently to take the credit."

Lost at sea. Chappy had lied. "You were present for the attack on the substation? Did you hear about what happened to her and her club friends?"

"I'm sorry to hear she's sick. She was good folk."

"Is. I don't suppose you want to help me save her?"

"Sure. Sure. What can I do?"

"Walk me through everything that happened at the substation protest."

"I saw her run off, but I was in the middle of a scrap with some scuttle miners Styrling hired to cross the labor lines. Some say she went into the substation. She'd passed out in the mine maybe trying to run away from the Imps and Squids. We found her before they did. Then the gas got deployed. They brought her and a bunch of other folk feeling fog-headed and woozy back to the med tent. I wound up at crit care on the crag getting patched back together after of bunch of scuttles with gas masks, who didn't look much like miners, jumped me. They found a group here passed out after they came here to regroup. We've been maced and gassed before. Some milk and a few hours and most folk are okay. Not this time. I'm not sure gas was the only thing they hit us with."

"They're escalating."

She clutched her side and grunted. "Well, we're not going to take it lying down, I guarantee you that."

To get a proper sense of the arrangement of all bodies in the system, Jhee needed to visit the substation.

At the substation, guards challenged Jhee. She flashed her credentials. They made her wait while they called it in but eventually allowed her on the premises. The fence which normally surrounded the substation had been knocked down in places.

Guards shadowed her as Jhee paced out the perimeter to get a sense of the size of the lot. She engaged the gears within and synchronated the area with an arcanum trace. The presence of the templarite dust and deposits caused a tricky-to-account-for reverberation. With the aid of onlookers, Jhee proceeded with due care and deliberation in a grid across the yard and noted the levels on her conch. This felt good. This was a finite, measurable action she could perform; a part of the Divine Mechanism she could know.

Emanations consistent with the Shield readings covered the middle of the space the protesters had occupied. That made sense given the proximity to the substation. Jhee studied the grid more. This level in the center was significantly higher than the residual in the rest of the area. The tract of land had been irradiated. The characteristics matched the trace radiation from the substation. She sought to discover the source. The faint trail did not lead toward the substation. As Jhee walked the affected area, the surface under Jhee's feet felt buckled. She bent and placed her hand against the shell concrete. Hardened, concentric ripples scarred the surface texture as if a pebble had been tossed into it only for the oscillations to freeze in place. The perimeter of the disturbance matched the concentration spikes. Their path dropped in from the sky.

First Makers, Styrling was escalating. The substation fell under the extreme trespass statutes. According to law, once the protesters had gained access to their property, they were within their rights to use enhanced force from gases to sonics, as long as it was "non-lethal." Had the crowd control measure Styrling used almost killed Mirrei?

Sianna and Inksy awaited Jhee at the villa. "Have a nice chat with Wynne and visit to the substation?"

On a mental boil because of the substation, Jhee's patience evaporated. She stomped over and spun Sianna's bar seat towards her. "Enough with the veiled barbs. Out with it."

Inksy stepped forward. Sianna waved her off and pushed several images toward Jhee.

"What are these?"

"Images of your wife in the company of a known Folx United radical."

Jhee recognized the person in the images as Wynne.

"Here she is entering the substation. I understand her prints were also found in the control room along with some sabotage tools."

Jhee pushed them back. "Fine. Threat made. I swear if Star Mirror dies because of whatever you deployed on the protesters, I'll dedicate myself to dismantling both your worlds. Your careers. Your reputations. Your well-being. Nothing of yours will remain safe from me. Just ask the Reaches. I'll save you the trouble of spying on me. I'm retiring for the evening. We've got an early day tomorrow."

17

QUESTIONS

~

Awakenings

When Jhee entered Mirrei's room, she found several orderlies trying to restrain her. "Mamere, mamere, is that you? Mamere, mamere, come back, please. I'm sorry. I'm sorry."

At last, Mirrei collapsed back on the bed. Jhee brushed damp hair away from her esca.

Mirrei swallowed. "Did you see her, denbe? Mamere was here. She was here."

Jhee pulled the parchment from her pocket and unfolded it. "You remember this don't you?"

Jhee began to read from Miramar's letter. Mirrei reached out and grasped Jhee's hand. "There's something else I need to confide…."

The feeble gesture caused Jhee to stifle a sob. There was almost no strength in the grip. "Whatever it is, can wait until you're better."

"If I'm going to die—"

"You're not going to die."

"If I'm going to die, I want to die as myself without so many lies between us. You'll never know how grateful I am to you or how much I don't deserve it. I lied, denbe, about my mother's last words. She didn't want you to take care of me or see me safely anywhere. I only said that to get you to take me in. With her not there, I couldn't remain at that house anymore even. I had nowhere else to go, and you had been so kind to me when we stayed with you. You were the last place she wanted me to go."

"The letter?"

"Fake."

Jhee crumpled the letter and chucked the letter over her shoulder. "Thank the First Makers."

Mirrei furrowed her brow then chuckled. A moment later, she winced in pain. "Don't make me laugh."

"My pardon."

"You're relieved?"

"I suspected it to be a last attempt by Mai to manipulate me from beneath the waves. I didn't want to sour your memories of her, though."

"No chance of that. I wanted to tell you every time you read from it to give me a pep talk. I thought you needed to believe it was real more than I did."

"Perhaps I did at first, the more I read it though, the more it felt wrong."

"I composed it based on old love letters she wrote."

"To Shep. That explains much. I wrote those. Your mother was accomplished at many things. Expressing herself through words was not one of them."

"The letters I found weren't to Shep. They were to you."

Jhee gaped in stunned silence.

"Her feelings towards you were a lot more complicated than you know."

"I'm beginning to see that."

Mirrei coughed. "Some part of me can't help but feel I deserve this. That it's punishment, divine justice, for exaggerating the extent of my illness all these years. I wasn't always sick as a child. I had a persistent state of mild, ill health which came and went. They fought often. I got sick once, and for once they stopped and were kind to each other. Mamere wasn't always the most engaged. When I got sick, she was so attentive. The talk of divorce stopped. Next I knew, I was sick a lot more. The magnitude of that sickness grew whenever divorce was mentioned. Not by my design mind you, but as I would learn later, my father's. Though, false doctor's visits became my father's and my own little secret. Once he passed, I found it to my advantage to keep the ruse going. I think she realized eventually and turned it to her advantage when dealing with her adversaries."

"So, and the fainting and ill health when you visited, were mere theatrics?"

"Mostly. Though, I found, when we stayed with you, a pall lifted. I genuinely felt lighter and more at ease. I blamed our home. At your house, I suspected what a toxic environment my home was. When the opportunity came to leave it, I ran."

A mausoleum out in the shoals was an apt way to describe what Jhee's home in the Far Reaches became. For Mirrei to see it as a refuge, buoyed Jhee's burdens. "After everything I've done to your family, I'm glad I enriched your life too."

A nurse came in and administered a sedative.

"No, babere, no more medicine, please," Mirrei murmured.

Jhee held the young woman's hand. Mirrei smiled and drifted to sleep. She remained asleep as the hours passed and they put her on a respirator. Jhee switched seats with Kanto and held up several bio-film periodicals. With the additional equipment, conch use was now restricted.

"Look what I brought. Frontiers in Forensics and Historian Daily. It's like you told me when we met, 'The least you can do is keep your mind sharp.' Not as exciting as Kanto's fashion books. A few pages of this and you'll hop right up out of that bed and flee screaming."

The inquester cleared her throat. Jhee let go of Mirrei's hand and set down the trade journal she had been reading to her.

"How is she?" the inquester asked.

"She is on an extreme replenishment course and requires a lot of rest. Her Maker within has been running on reserves for who knows how long."

"I'm sorry to hear that, and even sorrier to disturb you at a time like this."

"I need to do something tangible right now." Jhee paused at the echo of Mirrei's words from the jail cell. She shook her head. "What is it?"

"I was going to interview her friends. One of them woke up and is talking. I wanted to know if you wanted to come with."

The inquester stepped outside.

"One moment. Kanto."

"Jhee, no," Kanto said.

"It won't take long I swear."

"What if...? What if...? We might need you. I'd never forgive you if... You'd never forgive yourself."

"I must go. What if this provides the key to why she became so sick? I need to find out what happened to her. I need to see this through."

"Go. Shep and I will take care of our sister-wife while you go run off chasing villains."

Kanto broke away and returned to Mirrei's bedside.

Jhee stared at him for a moment, but he had already turned away. She took a shaky breath and joined Inquester Paij. The inquester handed her the case files.

"It seems one imperator had a run in with Mirrei at a rally right before she fell ill. She said she saw someone suspicious. Someone she thought would do violence. The imperators thought she was just causing more trouble. Then later on after the rally, the cleaning crews at the substation found this."

Inquester Paij handed Jhee a bricker, a programmable electromagnetic and incendiary mechanism. She used to plant similar units on comm towers in the war. This one was lighter and shaped more like a puck.

"A sabotage device. Do you think it belongs to the killer?""Possibly. Maybe he recognized Star Mirror and tried to finish her and her friends off.

They saw something they shouldn't have. Maybe they can identify the killer."

Jhee wiped at her eyes. She composed herself as best she could. This was indeed good news.

"I ran down the leads you told me about and looked into those items you found at their dive club. It turns out the stuff on their clothes is a match to the substance we found at both murders. It's templarite. The mineral used in the Shield. I have to tell you, Justicar, it doesn't look good for Mirrei and her friends. This evidence—it might be the motive. It might tie them to the murders."

"Mirrei is a hero. She may have saved many lives."

"Or...." the inquester trailed off. "Star Mirror trained in medicine and chemistry, didn't you say?"

"They were just making homemade squelch." The inquester made a face. "What is it?"

"The prevailing theory on what felled the protesters is a bad batch of squelch like at the mine."

"One: the mine poisoning happened before our arrival. Two: Mirrei—Star Mirror did not chase a punch bowl into the substation. She chased a person. Three: I've sampled her squelch, and I'm not ill."

"You admit though she has the skills and training."

"Where is this coming from Inquester? Don't answer. Allow me to guess, someone showed you images of her talking to Wynne."

The inquester rocked back on her heels. "You understand, Justicar, I have to examine every possibility no matter where it leads."

"My wife is not a murderer or mass poisoner, Inquester, and neither are those nitwits she fell in with. None of them except her has the imagination to stage the scenarios we've seen, and frankly she wouldn't be so stupid as to leave incriminating evidence lying around."

"Fair enough. One other is awake. Would you like to go interview them?"

Jhee squared her shoulders. The law. She had to respect the law. The law was finite. It was definite. It was fallible, but it was the duty of those like her and the inquester to help it obtain the divine state of perfection they knew it was capable of. Trust in the First Maker's Grand Design.

"Let's go."

~

Questioning

"My lady, how is Star doing?" Erma said.

"The truth is not good. She's slipped into a coma. Erma, Semele, I will need you to tell me the truth. What were you up to?"

"We weren't up to anything, we swear. We had all had a good think and reconsidered what we were about after getting arrested. Not Star, though, she was just as committed as ever. More so."

"That sounds like her. Stubborn like her mother."

"Yeah," Semele said, "rather than give up she doubled down. She shamed us into going to the next rally. We were there with her when she ran off. She was complaining of feeling light-headed. She said it was nothing, and she slipped off to adjust her saline drip. Next thing we know, she's running around saying people are in danger. We didn't know what she was about. When she was gone for too long, we went after. That's when we found her."

"Later after the action, we went back to our dive club. We had a few drinks and a smoke or two. But not Star, she only had a little now and then. We were feeling a little soggy and next thing we know, we wake up in the hospital."

Jhee thought about it. That sounds like her Mirrei. She was taking after Jhee. Maybe too much and it might have gotten her killed.

"Erma, Semele, this is very important—did you see or notice anything unusual once you got back to the hangout? Something that should be there that wasn't. Or something out of place."

"I don't know. Wait, the door. The door wasn't how we left it. I thought nothing of it at the time. The dive club is a public space, and we aren't the only ones who come through there. Most people know it's where we like to hang out. So, they don't mess with anything. We have had none of our things tampered with in a while."

"And where was Wynne?" the inquester asked.

Erma's eyes flashed red. "She was getting her head bashed in by Imps and Squids. They took her to Crag Critical Care. She can't afford a place like Makers' Care."

"Erma, you recognized her while she was climbing," Jhee said. "Your concern also seemed profound. You and Wynne?"

"The perfect choice for a rebellious daughter. It's been over-not-over for some time."

Inquester Paij fiddled with her sensor suit cuff. "Was it you who sneaked the Folx Uniters into the fundraiser?"

"It was me," Semele said.

"But I knew. They didn't inform us about the base jumping and defacing the galleon."

The inquester and Jhee left and went to the room across the hall. Deziree, another of the Dive Club miscreants, proved less helpful. She gave them nothing but Maker Foz worthy rejoinders and retorts. Jhee recited cyphers to restrain herself from activating her siren module and compelling the girl to tell them what they wanted to know.

Jhee yanked the pillow from under Deziree's head. "I have scant patience and time so I can't abide with your lies and disseminations. You will answer truthfully, or I'll have Dawn Wolf dissect you while you are still alive."

The inquester pulled Jhee into the hallway. "Justicar, I think you need a break. I invited you along as a courtesy, but I can only give you so much leeway."

"I'll pay the drench fine."

"Not on my case you won't. Take a walk. Now."

Jhee went outside for a constitutional around the hospital. With measured breaths, she focused her siren module's calming abilities on herself. As wound up as she was, accidentally making herself docile might have been an improvement. Those foolish children. What have they gotten themselves involved with? What had they gotten her naïve Mirrei involved with? Her naïve Mirrei? More like her drinking, smoking, homemade drug making, know several ways to sneak in and out of a building Mirrei. She must not do this. She must not infantilize Mirrei.

The rose substance. Mirrei's merry band of mischief Makers could easily alibi each other, and that was the problem. It was a hit to all their credibility. If means could be proved for one, it could be proved for all. Mirrei though had not left Jhee's sight for most of the evening, though. Or Kanto's. Even if she had, Mirrei would not have been a party to murder. But Jhee did not put it beyond her to cover for the others, though.

It was sloppy and most of all stupid—the last word she would apply to Mirrei.

Jhee found Inquester Paij with the last of Mirrei's club Taral. The inquester gave Jhee an inquiring once over. Jhee put her hands together to show she had composed herself.

"Star wasn't there. I mean we hadn't seen her for a while by the time they hit us with the wobble ray. When we found her later, we assumed she'd got hit with it, too."

"Assumed?" Jhee asked. "So, you didn't see her get bombarded?"

"No, ma'am."

"I've heard enough," Jhee said. "For now. I'm sure the inquester will have more question for you later."

~

Questions of a Queen

Jhee returned to Mirrei's room with a much calmer head. Shep kept watch over Kanto and Mirrei while they slept. Inquester Paij motioned to Jhee from outside the observation windows, and Jhee joined her in the corridor.

"We're tracking Bastian's conch. Someone turned it on."

"Great news, Inquester."

"We're about to close in on the location. Justicar, I could use your help."

"I'm sure you have it all taken care of and are more than capable of handling it yourself."

"I think I might require more unusual help."

"Ah, my cyphering expertise. I thought you disliked arcana."

"I dislike my team and me getting shot more."

"As you so eloquently stated before arcana can't stop bullets. Very well, inquester. Keep in mind though I'm not a gun on a stick. I'm not a super weapon, just another hand in a fight. My offensive powers are even more constrained by line of sight than my detecting powers."

"Fair enough. I'll get you some protective gear."

"That'll be peachy."

Shep regarded Jhee with a sigh. "A firefight. You are heading into a firefight now? Possibly gunplay. Now?"

"Please, Shep."

He spoke in almost a whisper, "I've lived through this before when we were in the service. Kanto hasn't. Mirrei hasn't. They need you. What happens if she wakes up? Is that the first thing I will tell her when she asks for you? 'She got her fool self shot trying to avenge you.'"

"I'll be behind the others. Watching their backs."

"You, bring up the rear? I'll believe it when I see it."

"Please, just keep them calm and watch over them while I do this."

Shep sighed and nodded. Jhee took a last look at Mirrei before she left. Kanto caught her gaze. He scowled and showed her his back.

Jhee needed to do this. In the end, she could count on the law. Always. Always. This was her calling.

The inquester led Jhee to the trace team's transport. The location of the signal had stopped.

"Any more movement?" Jhee asked.

The inquester nodded to the trace team member to let her know it was appropriate to answer.

"Not yet. It's been in the same spot for about an hour now."

"Okay. Everyone suit up and move out. We're going in. Whoever this is may be armed and dangerous. They have already killed two people that we know of."

Jhee put on a displacement vest. She drew a pure rune on it. For protection. No rune stopped a bullet though. Arcana was not a cure-all. She also drew some runes on her hands.

As they closed in on the conch location, they heard yelling and breached the door. Queenie, the weaselly woman from the clinic, was there shaking the depths out of Ms. Levinia. She let go of Ms. Levinia and held out wide her hands when she saw them.

Jhee checked Ms. Levinia. "Are you all right?"

Ms. Levinia rubbed her neck and nodded. Inquester Paij snapped the restraints on Queenie then warned her against self-incrimination. Despite that, Queenie proved cooperative. The savvy, career criminal wanted no part of high-profile capital murder charges.

The woman had a mid-sea accent so thick you could smear it on bread double. "The Queen had nothing to do with these nasty, nasty murders. She does not kill. Corpses can't pay. Accidents are another story. The Queen got an invitation to meet one of her clients there. He had a small personal loan payment to make. Several did in fact and so the Queen figured she would collect them all at once and make a delivery."

"Vash said you threatened his family and that the same thing that happened to Mr. Bastian and Ms. Oriel would happen to him."

"It was puffery. Once folk assumed the Queen was responsible, a lot of slow payers got quick. However, it came with other drawbacks."

"Did Mr. Bastian owe you money?"

"He owed the Queen something much more valuable. He offered, amongst other things, a device to bypass the Shield. And He also promised a weapon that would bloodlessly and instantly incapacitate someone."

"What did he want in return?"

"For us to stop leaning on his girlfriend and at first, just templarite dust, later several large flawless templarite crystals. Those caused the Queen approach other parties, who are displeased her side of the bargain has not been fulfilled. Their connection at the mines fell down a shaft. Your mining supervisor owed folks much less pleasant than the Queen. She hopes not to find herself at the bottom of the shaft with her."

"The aforementioned other drawbacks."

Queenie raised an eyebrow and gave a coy quirk of her mouth.

18

NOT TODAY

~

Interrogation and Workshop

"Vash, if you are in any way involved with what happened to Star Mirror, you need to tell me now."

"I swear to you, my lady, I had nothing to do with it. I went to Bastian and Oriel's apartments looking for something else."

"What?"

"Bastian had images of me and someone."

"A lover?"

Vash twisted his signet ring. "Yes."

Jhee narrowed her eyes. "Please, Vash, I have no time for games."

"The ambassador."

"Why would you go through all this nonsense for an image of you and the ambassador?"

"I won't say any more."

"Vash, Star Mirror's life is at stake because she fell in with you and your family. I thought you would protect her. I trusted you and thought she would be happy with you. Now I don't know what I was thinking. You need to tell me what you know so I can save her life."

"I'm sorry, Justicar. It's not my secret to tell. I just can't."

Jhee stood up in frustration. She stormed outside to the roof. She stood face to the sky, feeling the gentle mist on her face. Jhee recited statutes and cyphers. Vash's terseness was a blow. What could he possibly be hiding? It wasn't a lover. She knew that from his body language. But what? What could be or who's that important he would not tell her?

Bastian and Vash primarily knew each other through the former's volunteer work at the clinic. Did the secret pertain to the clinic? Other than Queenie's extortion, that is. Jhee examined the prospectuses and other promotional materials for the Friends of the Observatory and Breath of the Deep charities. The clinic is also how Bastian and Oriel met. Maybe Jhee could view the connection from this angle.

Vash featured prominently in the clinic's welcome footage. Toward the end, Vash and a handful of community leaders, including Ambassador Naiman, posed with individual children thanking prospective donors. Jhee found no trace of Bastian in any of the shots. The promo terminated with a wide group shot of VIPs and children. Ambassador Naiman and Vash framed opposite sides of the shot in a similar stance.

Even at opposite ends of the room, tension and avoidance radiated from the pair. Vash might have told part of the truth. Jhee had seen him and the ambassador arguing. They weren't lovers. The body language had been all wrong. They had also avoided each other since then.

Ambassador Naiman's awkward final waves to the camera matched. Jhee switched back and forth between Vash and the ambassador's 'thank you' segments. Now, she saw the resemblance, as if they were a set, but in different palettes.

Family. Vash was dedicated to his family. Jhee thought back to the altercation on the beach. The few words she caught. *"Why you?" "Stay away."*

Other aspects of Vash and the Ambassador Naiman's features tickled at Jhee's recollection. Then Jhee thought about what the ambassador had said about his heritage. Half barbarian. On his father's side. Jhee performed a quick calculation of the ambassador's age. Ambassador Naiman like Vash had to be born about the time Jhee and Delphine left the academy. A scholarship student who worked the grounds had Delphine's eye. She tried to hide it. Jhee knew about them, one of the few.

Jhee went back inside and daubed the moisture off her face. She confronted Vash. "He's your brother."

Vash looked aghast. "How did you? Yes, ma'am. Bastian, much like you, thought it was romantic."

"Because you had tried to kiss him much like you had Bright Harmony."

Vash twisted his signet ring more. "Yes, ma'am. It wasn't. The ambassador came to me and told me who he was and how he had been forced to get involved in the Shield negotiations because of our parents. He wanted to come clean. I tried everything to convince him not to."

Jhee loomed over him. "Vash, now no more lies."

"I wasn't only after the images. I'm not a credentialed doctor. Mumsy had always been reluctant to let me marry. The arrangements always fell through for one reason or another. When Naiman came to me and told me who my father was, I understood why she found fault with so many of the offers. It all made sense. I dropped out of the medical academy."

Vash pressed his hands flat on the table and Jhee seated herself.

"Bastian had obtained copies of my transcripts showing I hadn't completed all my coursework. I trashed the event organizer's apartment. I thought they might be there. Then I tried Bastian's apartment. They weren't there either. Then my sisters told me they had seen Bastian drifting around Chappy's Underground. I found a trail that led to his storage container. But the proof he claimed to have wasn't there. I found something else. He had all these weird designs and photos."

Jhee returned to Mirrei's workshop. She rubbed her eyes. It had been such a long day between Vash's betrayals and lies and her shattered vision. She had hoped to find Mirrei a place where she fit in and could be happy. Much like Kanto though, she knew it would not be with the Delphines. How far would she go? Once Mirrei recovered, Jhee would have to grapple with whether she would give her blessing if Mirrei wanted anything to do with these cads. Would she force the issue? She could sue Mirrei to remain married. Something she had promised not to do. She had promised to respect Mirrei's desires. And if she still desired to join the Delphines household? What would she do then?

If Mirrei recovered. Jhee sat down at Mirrei's work area. She looked over her set-up. Mirrei specialized in potions and healing draughts and chemical analysis. They had been putting her through the correspondence courses to get her chemistry degree and possibly a medical license. Jhee had the image of her helping her with cases. Once properly certified, Mirrei's findings could be used as testimony in court. As is, Mirrei's help was mostly unofficial.

From the looks of that dive club, Mirrei had other plans and found alternate uses for her skills.

Jhee held two such different visions of her relationship with Mirrei in her head. In one future, Mirrei and all of them were part of a crime-solving family who dedicated themselves to the law and justice, each with their own little niche. In the other, it was back to just her and Shep while Kanto and Mirrei were off somewhere else living their lives happy. Could she and Shep go back to how they were before those two came into their lives?

Mirrei's first love was medicine similar to how Jhee's was the law. Understandable given her condition and how much of her life she spent "sick" and cooped up with books and knowledge.

Jhee spied a little cask of Tranquility Gold. She drank a little to settle her nerves. The sip tickled all the proper keys. Smooth, fragrant, and peachy unlike whatever Mirrei had whipped up at the dive club.

After Jhee moved papers around Mirrei's desktop, she found notes and derivations Mirrei had worked on for Tranquility Bridge's nectar. Was Mirrei trying to replicate that as she had the refugee's squelch?

Jhee continued to sip her wine as she thumbed through Mirrei's research.

Thorough research it was. Mirrei had been documenting the properties of the nectar. The famed curative effects may have not been merely a placebo. The fermenting element gave you a mood boost. Meanwhile other factors increased immune response.

"Jhee?"

"Ah, Delphine, I believe I've solved your glitch mite problem."

"I'm sure it can wait. How is Mirrei?"

"In a coma. The haunted mines were nothing more than youngsters partying. Apparently, mines have become pop-up nightspots popular with the miners, activists, and the jet-stream set."

"Good to hear it's not Makers' feedback for my sins."

"It may yet be, but that's not for me to judge. You must have noticed the similarity between Vash and Naiman. Tell me about their father. Geology student who also worked the grounds?"

"Vulcanology and mining studies. Scholarship student. Even back then Vilmar thought big. He designed an early defense grid prototype based on pyroclastic clouds. Brilliant. Vash resembles him more than Naiman does, aside from the obvious."

"You kept the socially acceptable child and sent the other away."

"You're a fine one to judge me. I wasn't the only one in an illicit relationship. Which attracted you more? Your family's likely disapproval? Or stealing him away from Miramar?"

"It wasn't like that. Entirely. Do you know how much damage you caused by not keeping mum?"

"You caused. It was your lie and your broken promise."

"I had been waiting until the right waters."

"Tell yourself that if you must. I vowed never to regret my decision especially after witnessing what happened in the Far Reaches when you followed your heart."

Jhee pinched the bridge of her nose. If only that business had been as noble and romantic as it must have seemed from the outside. "It may not have happened in that manner if you hadn't breached the levee about my marriage to Shep."

"I hadn't meant to, for what it's worth."

No one else knew they had eloped. Only Delphine, her roommate, who was there when Shep showed up at academy to whisk her away. Was it a preemptive strike? Delphine had outed her and Shep before she could tell anyone about Delphine and the handyman. It all made so much sense now.

"You'd worried I caught on to you and Mr. Vilmar. You wanted to neutralize me and have me kicked out."

"I'm sorry. I hadn't realized that you had left the grounds as some grand elopement. The sweep team spotted me with Vilmar later, so we told them we were searching for you to divert suspicion. That night changed us, too. Your scandalous marriage put many ideas into Vilmar's head about our future. Mine, as well. They clashed. I guess I'm just not as strong as you. I couldn't put my family through that. First, I maintained Vash was sired. Then I arranged siring for Erma and Semele as well to maintain the pretense."

"Appears you looked forward to marrying into the Portshires as much as I did the Crag Halls."

"Less. He was a Portshire-Crag Hall."

"Endless talk of furniture supply chains instead of fabric."

"And wood importation. You must not forget the wood importation."

Jhee and Delphine laughed.

~

Researchers

Jhee awoke the next morning rubbing her aching neck. She had fallen asleep in the workshop. The scent of Kanto's favorite cologne rose from the blanket which had been thrown over her during the night. She gathered the research on Tranquility Bridge's nectar. She would consult with Mirrei's doctors about using the nectar as a treatment—as long as it did not hurt. Mirrei loved it so much. A little orange tea and nectar surely would not hurt her. Yes, she would ask the doctors if they could bring Mirrei her favorite tea.

First, though, Jhee made a stop at the main villa. She brandished Mirrei's notes in Vash's face as he ate his morning shrimp. "Did you help Mirrei with these?"

"My lady—"

"Did you help Mirrei with this research?"

"We made a sterilization series and tried it on some cultures at the clinic. The clinic isn't outfitted for research though. Is it appropriate for us to speak?"

"I'm a guest at your resort, and you're the in-house physician, or so we were all led to believe. How could you have missed it? How could you have missed the signs she was so ill? Fraud. Charlatan."

"I didn't miss it."

Jhee threw the research at Vash. She tucked her hands in her robes as she visualized cyphers and statutes. Vash gathered up the mess and set her down in the solar. "Forgive my outburst, Vash."

"I didn't miss it. There was nothing to miss. It also doesn't explain my sisters and the others. I dragged them out of there. I'm not a total incompetent as a doctor, my lady. Fresh Lung Syndrome is a catch-all term, a lazy diagnosis for a group of ailments being suffered by those coming from the Outer Reaches or a holdover from the deep ages of medicine when they had vague ailments for the gentry as well. Chronic wasting sickness. I was gathering the data. Fresh Lung Syndrome is just an immune response. Their immune systems were failing. The doctors were blinded by the fact the victims were poor and from places with atrocious health care. So, they would just write it off as Fresh Lung or exaggeration or depression because you know the poor are always sick."

"That's incredible. Why did no one tell us?"

"Snobbery. Incompetence. Even the rich doctors didn't know. To them, it might have resulted from bad food. They saw you were from the Outer Reaches and that was it. Problem solved: she had Fresh Lung Syndrome. I wanted to help people. I had come around. Often, I, too, misdiagnosed it. I also thought the outbreak came from so many migrants, but it made little sense. The variety of symptoms did. I thought it was just because of being over-diagnosed and as a catch-all. Then I noticed there seemed to be a pattern with the symptoms. All the various diseases being attributed to Fresh Lung could have one underlying cause. Immune system breakdown. Fresh Lung was not a disease itself but a state of compromised health. The patient got it and then could be fine unless an opportunistic infection came along. At which point, their body could not defend itself and thus all the different things called Fresh Lung."

"That's amazing. But then what do we do about it. That means the nectar could help. It's an immune booster. Vash, come with me. I want to take another look at the dive club."

"But?"

"Do you want to help Mirrei and your sisters or not?"

"Yes."

"Then behave like it. You've taken up enough time already. Now, come on, and no more of your foolishness. Fussing about after you has already cost me enough time away from my household."

Jhee and Vash headed to Chuc's place. Vash brought them in via the private entrance. Chappy hurried away from two passed out patrons at the bar.

"My lady, what time is it?" Chappy asked.

"Early. Late. Depending on your perspective," Jhee answered.

Jhee browsed the drugs and paraphernalia on the table. "Grab these items. We need to test each one. One of these might be it."

What else was Jhee missing? While they were at the dive club, she pulled out her conch. She played the footage she had taken at Mr. Bastian's. How had Mirrei gotten sick? She suspected the Inkerton's crowd suppression ray. But in case she was wrong, Jhee should test out other possibilities. All the talk of murder, suspects, and going on a wild wisp chase after Vash had consumed her.

As Jhee approached the sleeping pair near the still, Chappy hurried over and blocked her. "Now wait a moment, Justicar, you have no cause to take that without a writ. I'm not responsible for what my patrons—"

Vash held up a hand. "Public health matter. Anything we take will be confidential."

Jhee cleaned out a bottle and gathered a sample from the still. They brought their collected samples to the hospital.

"Doctor, are you familiar with Tranquility Gold nectar wine?" Jhee asked.

"Why yes."

"I was wondering if we could administer some to Mirrei."

"I don't think it's a good idea to be giving home remedies to someone in her state. Her system is so weak. Any shock might prove too much."

"The curative benefits may not be a fish wives' tale. There's been legitimate research into it. Mirrei's own experiments and studies by the Imperial Academy have proved its genuine health benefits. A pharmaceutical company had already been making overtures to the abbey's clerics. Here, examine the data."

Jhee shoved the bio-slips and bio-film papers into the doctor's arms. "I'll take a look. But Tranquility Bridge's nectar is rare and expensive."

"We have a supply. Mirrei uses it in her orange tea and home healing draughts."

"We'd need a more sterile form."

Jhee held up another bio-film. "I found this article on how to produce a sterile sample of fermented nectar. We also have wild yeast culture samples."

Dr. Pike cast a glance at Vash for rescue. He delivered a summary of his findings.

"Yes. Yes. I'll read through the data," the doctor said.

"Thank you, doctor. Thank you."

~

The Trap

Jhee and the inquester sat in the darkened transport waiting for their quarry to arrive.

"So, do you think this will work?"

"I have full confidence this will work. In the excitement, I nearly forgot about how I first got involved in this matter, the mining supervisors death, the sickened miners, and the glitch mites. The key to catching the murderer is to also catch the mine saboteur. The incidents are linked by a desire to disrupt mining and wall operations. I think they were going to try another dry run at the street fair, but the riots canceled that. Their next chance was at the fundraiser. They may have sought to try again at the substation. If the data shell figures into that at all, they'll come back for it."

They had laid a trap by feeding a story to their major suspects.

"The inquester and I attempted to catch the killer when they tried to sabotage the telescope controls yesterday. They got away. However, they left a data shell in the

console they used to hack into it. I have a sample of other incriminating code on another data shell from the substation. Once it arrives, I'll be able to compare the two and find out who amongst you was the last to use the satellite repositioning terminal to target the worksite with the EMP signal."

Jhee picked up her beef and goat cheese sandwich and took an enormous bite. She was eating so unhealthy without the others to scold her. Kanto would talk about if she gained weight it would ruin the lines of all his carefully made robes. Shep would say how she needed to slow down and pace herself and take the time to enjoy what she had already accomplished. What was the point of the comfortable life of mental exercise and fitness she put herself through if she would simply fail to do the work when it came to her body? Mirrei would weigh in on her choice of meat. Jhee had to let their opinions slide off her. She needed comfort food more than their approval now.

Around midnight, their waiting paid off. A slight, black-clad figure crept up to the observatory waving a conch light. An experienced burglar this wasn't. As the would-be burglar struggled loudly with the lock, Jhee and Inquester Paij opened the transport doors and crouched behind them. The inquester lined up her shot before she flipped on the transport headlights.

Ms. Levinia gasped when she saw them. "I can explain."

Inquester Paij closed the distance and subdued the woman with minimal fuss. "Spare us. I'm putting you under arrest for the murders of Oriel and Bastian."

"Wait, I had no reason to kill either of them."

"Why is that?" Ms. Levinia bit her lip. The inquester pushed her toward the transport. "Fine, say it to your advocate after a night of Imperial hospitality."

Ms. Levinia's eyes purpled with fear. "Ow, the restraints are too tight. Jail? I can't go to jail."

Jhee adjusted Ms. Levinia's restraints, so they were more comfortable. Jhee said in strategic sympathetic voice, "It's that or tell us everything this instant."

Ms. Levinia crouched toward Jhee. "Fine."

Inksy strode up with another meddlesome imperial writ held high. "We'll take it from here, locals."

Jhee snatched it and read it over. Everything seemed in order. Inquester Paij reluctantly released Ms. Levinia to the Squids' custody. More Inkertons rushed past them to secure the scene. She raised her face to the sky and contemplated the Grand Design and Divine Mechanism to calm her thoughts. They had been so close.

"Well, it was a game plan, Justicar. But if it's not Levinia, I don't think they're going to show now that storm Styrling's made landfall."

"Just give it a little more time, Inquester."

"Sorry. I'm calling it a night."

Jhee folded her hands inside her robes. What had she missed? She knew the murders and the worksite problems were connected. What had she overlooked?

"Unmake me," Jhee cursed. They walked out to the curb.

Perhaps she should head back to the hospital. Do as Kanto suggested: pray and spend what time remained with Mirrei while she could. Jhee opened her eyes when a nearby transport door slammed. She barely made out a figure cast in shadow by a water taxi's front lights paying from the curb. How fortuitous. The figure froze as she approached perhaps concerned Jhee meant harm. She squinted past the lights and held a hand to hail the taxi driver. A perturbation in the system struck Jhee, a misalignment she could not quite name.

Jhee walked toward the water taxi. A moment later, the gears of the Divine Mechanism aligned in her thoughts. Who would taxi here at this time of night? Jhee quickened her pace.

The figure at the taxicab fled. Drench. Jhee gave chase.

"Justicar!" the inquester yelled after her.

"It's them!"

Jhee continued without knowing if the inquester followed. The figure raced down the street towards the Stones footbridge. If they made it there, they could cut across to the plaza and get lost in the crowd.

The suspect sprinted up the iconic Fairgull Steps. Jhee cursed loudly. More stairs. Why did it always have to be stairs? This drench city. So busy was she lamenting the stairs, she did not realize the suspect had taken a different turn. Not towards the Stones and its bustling street and pub scene, but away from it and towards the bluffs.

They reached a chasm. The suspect leaped. Jhee went right up to the edge to gauge the distance. One look down made her head swim. The gap dropped to rocks and white surf. Jhee wheezed, grabbed her chest, and staggered back. Try as she might she could not force herself to approach the edge. In the distance, the object of her pursuit rapidly receded. She backed away and attempted to make the leap blind. She stopped short of the edge again.

Storm Child. Storm Child. Not today. Not today.

The inquester caught up to her. Jhee remained there trembling. Somewhere as if through distant fog and waves, she heard Paij's voice.

"I'll see if I can figure out what taxi company that was and question the driver."

Jhee raised her face to the sky again. *Storm Child. Storm Child. Not today.*

19
——————

THE RENT VEIL

~

More Questioning

Jhee sniffed and rubbed her eyes.

"Are you sure you are up to this?" the inquester asked.

"It's allergies. I'm sharp. I can do this."

"Maybe you should—"

"Inquester, I'm fine. Now, what are the facts? We have a disgraced engineer trying to redeem himself for his part in the Shield debacle. A contractor who knew something was amiss but couldn't prove it. A contractor who covered it up to hide his use of blackmail to get the contract. The ambassador with blackmail material of his own. Who had cause to kill both Ms. Oriel and Mr. Bastian? We have Mr. Bastian's as yet unidentified partner."

"Do you think Bastian knew what the partner had planned?"

"Perhaps. His obsession was such I'm not sure if he would have cared. We also have three key pieces of evidence. The proof of Vash meeting with the ambassador. The data Vash and Ms. Oriel were gathering which showed the locations of the Fresh Lung outbreaks and the connection to the substation. Mr. Bastian's filter design prototype and a map showing the substation locations."

It had become clear to Jhee there was some link between FLS and Miners' Lung. Mirrei had already hallucinated. Was a descent like Mr. Bastian's something Mirrei had to look forward to? Jhee had read all the literature she could. She trusted the arts of science, medicine, and arcana. Their confusion on the malady had her worried. She believed in that and the law to find

431

proper solutions to people's problems and as long as they trusted and worked the system properly. Their virtual ignorance on a topic which turned out to be so close to her and relevant to her interests had her shaken.

Inquester Paij rocked back in her chair. "I think it's about time we get some of these folks back in for follow-ups. We have enough to see if it might shake something loose."

Jhee wasted no time once the first callback, Chapman, arrived, "What about you, Chapman? I knew I'd seen you at the fundraiser. You helped cater the event, so you could easily grab a uniform and pick up a tray. No one would even look twice at you."

"You're right I was there. The activists had to get in somehow."

"As someone in food service, you'd know about food handling and food-borne illnesses."

"I make killer crab puffs, but not the way you're thinking. The instant I saw the body, I ditched my uniform and left. I knew the Imps and Squids would look to blame fighters for the cause."

"That leaves you plenty of time before that to kill Mr. Bastian."

"But I didn't. Ask the serving staff. Ask their handlers. They do regular headcounts and staff searches. During one, they looked closer at my identification. They held me aside so IES agents could question me. I slipped away while they were otherwise occupied by damage control."

After a few more questions, they sent Chapman off, but told him to stay close. The shift chiefs confirmed some of his story.

"The Styrling duo could corroborate or disprove the rest, but Lethys's luck getting them to come in for questioning," Jhee said.

Inquester Paij leaned back and smiled. "I don't know. Let me worry about that."

They spoke with Ambassador Naiman next.

"Ambassador, you had motive because Mr. Bastian had linked you to the improper contract to build the Shield."

"I could care less about the wall. Or the coward who claims to be my mother. Her and that family. My concern is the workers being exploited by both the state and companies such as Styrling Staffing. It's a travesty. Men like my father who are stripped away from their homes and forced to serve vain, careless women like Lady Delphine. Do you really believe that nonsense about the staff being prisoners who saw the forbidden isles? You know how hard this place is to reach from the other continents."

"It was plenty easy for the barbarians to get here when they wanted to raid and destroy."

"Do you buy that swarms of Fire Folk are braving the ocean just to come harass us? They are not coming to us. We are going to them. That is the truth of it. The inquester knows, don't you? The Galleon's a drenched tomb, a testament not of faith or resilience but hate like the wall."

Jhee rubbed her eyes. "Please, Ambassador, you must tell me what you know at once. My understanding and my patience are at an end. I'm about to get not so nice. I understand your grievance against Lady Delphine. Believe me, I do. But bribery, blackmail? Is that any way for a man of the waves to behave? You should set the example for others not flouting it."

"Like the example the noble Water Folk set."

Jhee tucked her hands in her sleeves. "It is within the Makers' Design for us to strive to improve ourselves and others or else be remade."

"In the Water Folk's image, via conquest. We are not an example. If anything, we proved their point. We cast out the Air Folk and Land Folk, for being too violent. Look at us, we are press-ganging their children into service. Are we any better? Look at 'disasters' like the Gray Galleon. Is that noble, and decent of us? Is that behavior worthy of the Makers' Criterions as we like to call ourselves?"

"Folk have a right to protect the sovereignty of their lands by any means necessary. We do it, the Fire Folk do it, even the Other folk."

Weariness then resolve played across Ambassador Naiman's features. "By any means necessary? Do you hear yourself? To what end? Total control over the Water Folk. It helps them control you not the Fire Folk. Don't be so naïve, Justicar."

A resolve of Jhee's own overtook her. "What do you want me to say, Ambassador? We're hypocritical bigots, me included? Fine, we are. What now?"

"That's always the question. I wish everyone would admit it as easily as you did."

"Then what? How do we move forward? Don't you think I wish I could take a pill or discover a cypher that would make all my conflicted feelings about Fire Folk go away or undo the horrible acts I countenanced as a Water Folk because of them. Tell me what to do, and I'll do it."

With the admission from Jhee, the ambassador's posture relaxed. "I wish I had the answers for you. I initially took up the wave coif searching for answers of my own."

Jhee re-centered with silent prayer and concealed finger-cyphering exercises. She had lost control of the conversation. In the process, she had created an opening with which she could draw more information from Ambassador Naiman.

"The off-world expeditions were misguided, wrong. But separating ourselves from the Other Folk via the Shield is different," Jhee said and pivoted to the immediate matter. "Time is scarce. I need to know why were you in the closed wing."

The ambassador acknowledged the impasse and accepted the topic shift with a calm response, "Because I was working with Advocate Farkhande to help the Fire Folk escape their contracts. They're made to sign onerous agreements tantamount to indenture. They charge them for food and lodging. And get them so far in debt they can never get out. Workers then often will send money to other relatives. I know because me and my father did every-thing we could to not wind up like that. Before I took the coif, I've worked as a cleaner, drove a taxi, and did cooking and maintenance. They will never see the end of service to Styrling. You should look over some of their contracts. It's a virtual prison sentence."

"I will, Ambassador. I will."

Jhee hung her head. She thought about the staff at the observatory fundraiser and the galleon. She suspected as much, and she had turned the other way. Jhee would do so no longer. "I still have to ask you for corrobora-tion of your whereabouts and who you were with."

"I was meeting with my folk smuggling contact. They may not back me up, given their line of work and their cultural traditions."

"You book them passage with Water Nomads."

Ambassador Naiman nodded.

Jhee took down the details. She and the inquester proceeded with their follow-up interviews. They were soon treated to another visit from Sianna and Inksy.

"Right on time," the inquester said. "I'd figure this would get their attention."

Jhee admired the inquester's ploy. If she had tried to call in Sianna and Inksy directly, they likely would have refused or stalled.

"Inksy and Sianna, you keep two floating to the top like dead fish. What were you doing at the mine site?"

"Same as you, investigating. Styrling Mining had leased it from Lady Delphine. But we've been plagued by accidents and equipment failures."

"The same for Ms. Oriel's offices at the clinic and the observatory?"

Sianna looked taken aback. "Styrling Mines is known for its great phil-anthropic contributions to many causes. As you can attest, she could charm the skin off a sea otter."

Jhee frowned, while Sianna looked smug.

~

A Sympathetic Ear

The Styrling pair substantiated Chapman's claim, which also explained their movements. They claimed not to have enough time to debunk his disguise but provided no other helpful details. The inquester motioned Jhee aside.

"I arranged for Levinia to be kept in temporary holding. I'll keep our friends here."

"While I go have a chat with her."

The inquester nodded and slipped Jhee an earpiece. After having let Ms. Levinia contemplate her accommodations for a few hours, she appeared on the verge of mania. Again, she huddled against Jhee for support.

"You said you had no reason to kill Ms. Oriel or Mr. Bastian. You need to tell us the full details of why you and Ms. Oriel were arguing."

"We resolved it."

"That's not what witnesses said. They said you and she parted loudly and angrily."

"Oriel caught up to me later, and she said I was right. The restoration project was mine. She had found an even grander use for her talents. She said she would credit me for the restoration as long as I kept quiet about her sideline."

"Then why were you skulking about?"

"Because I knew you'd find my fingerprints all over the chandelier winch and data shell with the backdoor program I implanted. I wanted to remove the traces of my break-in before anyone found out I did it."

"Why implant it at all?"

"To gather intel for the exposure piece. Bastian and I whipped up a means to spy on Oriel. Before Oriel and I had calmed our waters, I thought publicizing the Friends of the Observatory and the Breath of the Deep impropriety was my only means to finally get the recognition I deserved. The journalist had started to get impatient. Xe suspected I had perhaps oversold how big the scandal was and what I knew. Bastian used my credentials, and we installed a means to monitor the observatory's restricted feeds from a remote location."

"You wanted to embarrass or discredit her. Why not just kick her out?"

"The foundations most influential members viewed her like unto a Miracle Maker. She turned the benefit Bastian and I planned into a fundraiser associated with the Gray Galleon which drew the protesters and remade it into a spectacle. Oriel was taking credit for the restoration projects, selling exclusive access. I located the original chandelier in storage and spent years getting the funding together to restore it and the observatory. I worked and slaved over it. Oriel was just supposed to be the mistress of ceremonies. Instead, she swoops in at the last moment to take the accolades and line her pockets. I wanted to find some proof. I just wanted her to share credit like she promised she would. But I swear I didn't kill her or Bastian. I did go to her office to gather data. Then I heard them on the landing. They argued. It was about a woman I think then Oriel left. Before she did, she said something like 'I know what you've been up to and who with.' I thought she had learned about me and Bastian. When they left, I exited as fast as I could. Next I know, they find Bastian dead hanging from my life's work."

"I witnessed the exchange. There's no way you could have heard what they discussed."

Ms. Levinia hunched and gave a sheepish expression. "Arcane eavesdropping."

Jhee pursed her lips. "Do you have any corroboration of your whereabouts?"

"Afterward, I got drunk and went to record voice-overs for the observatory tours. I may have left an unflattering drawing on the board complaining about the restoration and recorded a few sarcastic messages. They may have a time stamp. I'd also started complaining to a journalist. Xe told me xe was a covert exposure journalist working on a shocking scandal. Xe's interviewed me several times about the observatory. I used to meet hir at a boathouse at the Delphines."

"Where is xe?"

"I don't know. After I spilled my guts in more ways than one, I woke up in the boathouse. I haven't seen hir since."

Jhee slipped back to the interrogations. She tapped her ear and nodded to confirm she recorded her exchange with Ms. Levinia. The inquester had moved on with questioning.

"I object to their presence here." Advocate Farkhande pointed at Sianna and Inksy. "I have a matter before the courts in which they are explicitly named. We wouldn't want this case or that tainted by impropriety or allegations of intimidation."

Sianna ran her tongue along the inside of her mouth. "Of course."

Sianna and Inksy bundled out.

"That includes watching from the side room or accessing the footage," the advocate called. "My team and I will be second-checking."

Jhee and the inquester did their best to appear disinterested.

Advocate Farkhande grinned at them. "Tell me you haven't always wanted to do that. You may proceed."

"Tell me, Advocate, how do you explain your name on these 'after hours' itineraries?" Jhee asked.

"I was there but only acting as an intermediary on behalf of those who wished to see the artifacts."

"Can you tell us who?" the inquester asked.

"Confidentiality oaths apply. Since you have the itineraries, I'm surprised you haven't deduced who on your own."

"Our records showed you called Oriel just before Bastian's murder."

"Making sure we were on the same sea about the Galleon Wing. Even for private viewings."

"And the green corrosion on your robe?" Jhee asked.

"I saw that detestable vizier sneak in the Galleon Wing. I thought perhaps Oriel had ignored our understanding. It turned out to be him and that quirky Queenie woman."

"Did you overhear their conversation?"

"Something about building permits."

"Are you sure?"

"How could I be wrong about something so banal when the wisps have so much more interesting things to say?" Advocate Farkhande paused as if listening. "The eye of the drake knows. The wisps have something they want you to see. All you have to do is open your eyes and look."

"Farkhande, enough with the wisps already," Paij said.

"Fine. Let us speak of more relevant details, perhaps of cures hiding in the wrong hands. Curing people who weren't sick is hardly profitable."

"No, it isn't. Curing sick people on the other hand."

Advocate Farkhande gave a bittersweet smile at Jhee's realization. "Now, the coverings are falling from your eyes, Justicar. When it's the wretched and destitute being hurt, no one cares as much. If it is as you say Justicar, how much would it have cost to implement the fix once they found out? How long did they know how to fix it? Someone had been too cheap or callous to implement the solution, while all those people were sick or dying."

Jhee finished for her, "On the other hand, make the right people ill, and they'll be clamoring for the cure."

"What if Styrling or MANTEL wanted to hoard the cure?"

The inquester scoffed. "It's the oldest conspiracy theory in the book that the powerful have the cure for a bunch of diseases and are just keeping it for themselves."

"Is it?" the advocate asked. "I can't tell you anymore. Either charge me or let me go."

"You can go, but—"

"Don't go far. Justicar, the wisps want you to keep going. Balance the scales. Close the circle."

The advocate left humming. The shimmer remained a moment after her. Jhee's esca and arm sigil tingled.

"Justicar, I don't know. Everyone's stories pass inspection," the inquester said, her voice breaking Jhee's fascination with whatever forces followed the advocate.

Jhee swore and touched her chin. Another dead end and she was nowhere near finding the murderer or helping Mirrei. What to do now? Where else did she turn? "Think. Think. Who else had reason to do so and why?"

"Perhaps you need to wind it back a bit."

"I'll wind it back once I've found the killer and Mirrei is cured." Jhee scowled at the inquester. The inquester's look of affront said it all. Jhee sighed. "I apologize, Inquester. This case has gotten too personal for me."

"Which is why I think you need to go back and see your family. Spend some time with them and get your head on straight."

"Yes. Yes," Jhee said. She rubbed at her burning, irritated eyes. First, she should go back to the villa and clean herself up and get some eye drops. It would not do for the others to see her in such a state. She had to project strength for them. They needed her. If she panicked, they would panic.

The Fallen Scales

"The eye of the drake knows. The wisps have something they want you to see. All you have to do is open your eyes and look.... Balance the scales. Close the circle."

Jhee went back to the villa and took a shower and put on a fresh change of clothes. She picked up a few things for Kanto and Shep as well. Advocate Farkhande's cryptic words nagged at her all the way back to the hospital.

Not quietly enough, Jhee stole into Mirrei's room. Shep awoke. His one good eye bright gold and the other much dimmer watched her in the dark. Kanto slept in a chair beside him. Jhee placed a finger to her lips. Shep went to her, and they embraced.

"Any change?" Jhee whispered.

Shep shook his head. Kanto's cherished, recently restored music box rested lightly in his lap. Jhee moved it to Mirrei's bedside table as a precaution. Kanto stirred. He gestured for her to wind it. She opened and cranked it back into working condition. The simple tinny song played in the darkened room, as the three of them watched eerily still Mirrei. The music box's melody drowned out the machines monitoring Mirrei's vital signs. Kanto took Jhee's hand and gave it a squeeze.

Jhee awoke to find Mirrei's doctor standing over her. With her head, she signaled Jhee should join her out in the hall. Vash stood by quietly.

The doctor cleared her throat. "Vash walked me through the clinic's research and what you showed me. Her immune system is compromised. You also said it involves another device."

"A standalone synchronator that doesn't need an artificer or stanchions."

"If we could get the device to examine it and figure out what frequency it's operating on, we might develop something that might help Mirrei without too much risk. Her research was thorough."

"I know. She was a conscientious and proper student. I expected nothing less from her work."

"Our experiments on cultures in the lab showed promise. However, when we administered the treatment to her. It barely made a difference. She responded well enough at first to the nectar treatment, but it's like her immune system is under assault and the nectar can't keep up. The most optimistic thing I could say about the nectar is that it doesn't hurt."

Back in the room, Kanto and Shep had awakened and pulled over the wheeled table with a turtle hidden-image puzzle over to Mirrei's bedside. Kanto also had the gossip sites open on his conch. "You see that? That's why siring should be done by contract. Official and legally binding. Good contracts make good sires. The norms and standards are you stay away unless contracted again, but you get the unscrupulous sire or dame who attempts to profit after they have rendered their services," Kanto finished.

The puzzle comprised a turtle painted on a tray and a colored see-through shell broken up into pieces. Jhee picked up a piece and searched for where it fit. As participants assembled the colored lens, the shell revealed a new image. She tried to wrap her head around what they had created. It wasn't until she rotated the puzzle did it make sense. She had been looking at it all wrong. Like everyone did with Mr. Bastian. Somehow, she was not seeing the whole image of the man.

Jhee located Vash in one lab desperately working on a cure. As a major donor to the hospital, Lady Delphine had him granted temporary privileges as a lab assistant. So long as he had the supervision of a credentialed doctor and did not treat or get directly involved with any patients' care, he could use their facilities.

"Any progress?"

Vash shook his head. "The poisoned squelch theory is consistent with our findings, though. We've been testing every sample we could get our hands on."

"What if we're looking at this all wrong?"

The doctor helping Vash chimed in, "How do you mean?"

"What if Mr. Bastian wanted redemption, not revenge? What if he wasn't trying to poison the miners? Maybe he wasn't trying to harm the mine personnel but help them by inoculating them against MLD."

"We've already concluded the squelch might have been him testing delivery methods," Vash said.

The doctor nodded. "Either their immune systems were too far gone. Or, if the solution meant to respond to the radiation with a counter wave. If the wave was out of phase, instead of making it better it made it worse."

"The other mystery though was why were all these people's immune systems compromised. There was no rhyme or reason. Oriel and I started tracking their connections and various contacts. We started tracking where everyone was from. Our data was on those data shells. A pattern started to emerge. Yes, it's true most Fresh Lung Sufferers came from the Outer Reaches. But not all of them came from regions with saltier water. We overlaid the map of the Fresh Lung outbreaks and the water salinity tables. They did not match up. When we reached a dead end on our own, Oriel threw herself into the fund raising. She wanted to surprise Bastian. Instead of a party, what if she got extra funding for cure research? Bastian had similar renderings at his place. Except he had a map of all the Shield substations and pylons. Those corresponded with the Fresh Lung outbreaks on a nearly one-to-one basis."

"The Shield—the wall is causing Fresh Lung Syndrome," Jhee said

"The Shield is compromising people's immune systems."

〜

The Rending of the Curtain

The Storm Shield, the wall, was the death wall its detractors had proclaimed.

Jhee needed to sit. The previous governess, an aggressive proponent and strong supporter of the Shield, spent a large amount of time touring and inspecting the facilities and construction sites. She had also died of FLS.

Jhee thought about Mirrei's family home. It had been right by the Shield. Jhee's family lived not only at higher elevations but more inland. The lavish homes on the beach her family had eschewed as the sea took its due. That was the key. Mirrei had grown up right next to the Shield. It also explained why she did seem to get better when she stayed at Jhee's house. She had also started getting better when they headed for the capital. She suspected Miramar had been doing something to the poor girl, or it was just pure happiness at being free.

Then Jhee had the yacht captain sail closer to the wall, and Mirrei took ill once again. Also, after Kanto and Mirrei had sneaked off to the refugee camps on Torilsisle.

Mirrei got better once again here in Galleon City about as far away from the wall as one could get. Except for the substation. The substation.

How close was too close to the substation? Only Mirrei was inside for any length of time. What had happened in the meantime to fell them all at once? The crowd dispersion device. There was still something Jhee was missing, some key to the puzzle.

Jhee concentrated on the recordings of Mr. Bastian's properties while dissecting aspects of their extended conversation at the fundraiser. He was the engineer who screwed up the Shield. He was obsessed with redeeming himself and waking people up. The synchronator would show them what the Shield did. No, not reveal what the Shield did. Mr. Bastian wanted redemption. Olipo, the name of a Lesser Maker recognized by Mechanism, was scrawled in block letters across one schematic. Olipo sometimes went by the title "The Tinkerer" or "Fixer." The Fix. A cure.

Surely curing people who weren't sick wouldn't do anything. No, it wouldn't. Curing sick people would. The synchronator. It could not just heal people but make them sick. The synchronator could have stopped the Fresh Lung Syndrome. Someone had been too cheap or careless to buy the fix, and all those people were sick or dying. She was weary of the fight with the Other Folk. If the authorities had only told them, Jhee might have gladly accepted the risks. Many of them were. Many of them would.

They could have protected themselves. Moved themselves away from the pylons and the barrier itself. Correction: those with enough means, like her, could have. For as many refugees as there were, how many had stayed behind? Because they would not or could not leave.

Jhee met with Mirrei's doctor and hid her hands in her robes as she spoke her speculation aloud. "Doctor, is it possible she is being bombarded with radiation?"

"Well, we shielded her from most forms of radiation and electromagnetics, and it helped. She responded very well to the isolated environment. However, we have yet to identify the specific frequencies doing the most damage. If this is indeed caused by the Shield or substation like you say it is, they are putting out powerful, broad-spectrum signals designed to penetrate through everything. Nothing we have here can counteract it for long without knowing specifically which frequencies to block."

"It's not enough to block the signal you need to send the counter wave."

Doctor Pike nodded. "You said you saw plans for a device? It would help if we had access to that device or the Shield technology itself. We may be able to synthesize something from the nectar and the device."

"The synchronator? That's what I dubbed it."

"We need to do tests. We can buy some time by leaving Mirrei in a medically induced coma. I don't want to try an unproven treatment on her without a minimum of testing. For that though, I will need the inducement device to test cures against."

"The Shield tech is classified, state secret."

"Without it, I don't think we can treat her. Keep in mind however, the hospital has legal obligations and cannot be found in possession of or use any restricted devices or any improperly acquired equipment."

Jhee folded her hands inside her robes. Mr. Bastian's Shield technology synchronator might fulfill those requirements. He had developed it on his own while volunteering at the clinic. "Don't worry, doctor. I will get you what you need. With Mr. Bastian's schematics, I can commission a new synchronator or build the drenched device myself if I must."

"We may not have that kind of time."

"Also, we run the risk he may have modified the designs in the meantime. We need the working prototype."

Jhee returned to find Ambassador Naiman saying devotions with Kanto and Shep. The ambassador excused himself. She cast her eyes to the floor. "I have to leave again. I'm on the trail of something that could help Mirrei."

"Jhee," Shep said. His pale, gold eye trained on her.

Kanto pursed his lips, tears streaming down his face.

Jhee rushed to head off their objections. "I know what you're going to say, 'What if it doesn't? What if you are wasting precious moments you could spend with her?' It's a possible treatment. It might cure her. I have to try."

Jhee turned to leave.

"Are we allowed no say before you leave?" Kanto asked. He cranked the music box. "Do you know how this got broken?"

Jhee held her tongue. He faced Mirrei and set it on the bedside stand.

"I used to play this for my mamere. One day she lashed out at me and struck it from my hands. She dashed it to smithereens. Every craftsman said it was irreparable. But you, Jhee, you fixed it. I don't care what it is, Jhee, or what you must do to get it. If there is a cure for Mirrei, find it."

"I will."

Kanto spoke without turning, "You won't come back without it?"

"No."

Shep put an arm about Kanto's shoulders. "Do what you must, Jhee. In the meantime, Kanto and I will address our pleas to other powers."

He and Shep knelt by Mirrei's bedside and raised their hands in supplication.

"I swear," Jhee said.

20

____

RACE FOR TIME

~

A New Search

Jhee pounded on the door at Lady Delphine's house. The servant answered.

"Justicar, how may I help you?"

"I need to speak to Vash. Is he here?"

"One moment, mum."

A groggy Vash descended the stairs, rubbing his eyes. "My lady, what's happened?"

"I need to access the clinic's patient records." As she spoke to Vash, she thumbed through the various crime scene images on her conch. Vash stared at her. "Examine the patient records from the clinic."

"Justicar, you know I can't. The medical ethics oaths I swore—"

"Apply to a valid doctor, not you. I don't need personal or specific infor-mation. I just need you to check your records. It's important. It might save Mirrei's life."

"As you said, I'm not a valid doctor. I've been suspended and no longer have access to the clinic's records."

"But you have personal records, don't you? Also, if I understand it correctly, you're suspended pending medical review and have limited access to aid in your defense."

Vash pulled out his conch. "The best I can do is check the records myself. But it will be the most basic information and no patient identifying information."

"That's fine. That should be all I need."

"What am I looking for?"

"Any case of Fresh Lung remission." Shock anchored Vash to the spot. "Now, please. Yav-yav."

Jhee took her time on each image. The suspicion she had seen the synchronator prototype when they searched Mr. Bastian's storage workshop had a hold to her. Sometimes the best way to hide something was in plain sight. Where might one hide a large data crystal? Among other crystals. The observatory's mineral rock collection or the chandelier, the mines.

Vash ran a few searches. "That's right. We had a few cases. Especially recently, we thought we had misdiagnosed them. I remember this one in particular."

Jhee tried to seize the conch. Vash pulled away. "Forgive me. Who was the volunteer who worked with them when they came in?"

"Allow me to check the shift logs." Vash did more searching and scrolling. "Bastian was on duty or had some contact with all of them. My lady, what's this about?"

"I think Mr. Bastian had discovered a way to treat or cure Fresh Lung Syndrome and he was using your clinic to test it out on patients."

"My word."

"If we could find the treatment he was using, we might use it to treat Mirrei."

While Vash continued his search, Jhee scoured her record of Mr. Bastian's experiment notes for hints about his treatment methods. He referred to the silver or sparkling eyes. It may have been a code in case his notes fell into the wrong hands. Was it mechanical or a substance? At last, she found references to a silver eye housing. She viewed the images of Mr. Bastian's apartment walls full of not only formulas, but schematics. If sabotage was not his goal, then what were the schematics? The treatment must be based around a device.

Jhee compared the footage of the apartment, the workshop. What was it? There was something here. She did not know for sure what she sought, an item out of place, a commonality between the two locations. An object missing which should be there would be the hardest to notice.

Because of Jhee's captures not being the highest quality, the process was slow going and headache-inducing. If Mr. Bastian had come up with apparatus to arrest the effects of the Shield, then what was he doing at the Observatory? What was he up to? Jhee pored over Mr. Bastian's obsessive scribblings. Now, she saw it; several references to some device called a synchronator. Jhee needed to examine the originals. She contacted the inquester. "The last time you and I checked the clinic records we'd been looking for deaths. Don't you see? We had it backwards. Do you still have the evidence we collected from the hidden storage unit in the evidence room?"

"Justicar, I hate to tell you this. Inkertons showed up with an Imperial writ."

Jhee felt punched. She hoped the inquester was not about to say what she thought she would say.

"They've confiscated Bastian's research equipment and his notes."

Jhee expelled a breath and collapsed down hard on the desk. Mirrei's cure. Their last, best hope for one.

Blessed be the First Makers. They who created the waters. Know the waters. Trust the waters.

~

The Race

Jhee recited several litanies to the First Makers and Lesser Makers. Then she switched to listing statues to calm her Maker within.

"Justicar? You still there?"

"A list," Jhee said. "They needed to have provided a detailed confiscation writ. Do you have it?"

"I can get it. Hold on. Transmitting."

As she read through the confiscation log, she paced. Nothing matched what she sought. The clicking her thought processes did to show a misalignment in the system began.

"Meet me at the warehouse."

The clicking continued as she and Paij met at the warehouse. "Something's not adding up and my Maker within is screaming at me. May I see an inventory of the workshop or do you have sensor suit footage I can view?"

"I can do both. I'll collate the lists. You review the footage." Paij operated her sleeve controls then pulled a microcrystal from her sensor suit collar and handed it to Jhee.

Jhee attached the microcrystal to her conch and they both delved into their assigned tasks.

"Got it," Paij said after a moment.

"I may have as well. Here. Look." Jhee squinted at the controls and scrubbed the scene backward. "What's that on the worktable?"

"Don't know. Nothing like that is on either list. Let me access that footage we found on the scene."

Jhee played the footage Bastian took alongside the footage of her and Paij collecting evidence.

"There. You see it?"

"Yep," the inquester said. "The lists of confiscated evidence don't match ours either."

"Someone else got there before Inkerton did."

"It must have been the killer."

"But why would the killer take all that stuff? It's of no use to them."

"No use if you want to make a profit, but what else could they use the data for?"

"Access to the substation. Our friends are chasing wisps into whirlpools."

The inquester rocked back on her heels. "Bastian found a way to transmit his fix and his cure to the Shield substations via an access terminal or pylon. But his discovery could just as easily transmit malicious code to all the substations and bring down the wall. I suspect Bastian had been duped by his accomplice."

"Ms. Oriel suspected Mr. Bastian of having an affair and followed him and found the storage locker."

"Or realized he had been using the clinic patients as test beds. Remember what Oriel said, 'I know what you've been up to and who with.' Either way, she located the storage locker. After Bastian's death, she puts two and two together with the map and shift logs and returns to the storage locker. She may have surprised the killer."

"They kill her and hear someone coming and have to get rid of the body quick. They leave the data behind to dispose of the body. Before they can come back, we've found it and sealed it off."

"Precisely. The killer though still has a mission to complete."

"Bring down the Shield."

"This may be their last chance before the security exploits are fixed."

"We find the killer. We find Mirrei's cure."

"Let's go. I'll drive," the inquester said.

Later at a lot overlooking the substation, Jhee regarded the impressive panorama with detachment. She attempted to marshal the Prime Forces within her while Paij had an animated conversation on her conch. Paij. When had Jhee began to regard the woman so informally?

The inquester slammed her conch down on the dashboard. "Inkerton Enforcement Services and their lawyers are stonewalling. They'll be no help."

"Did you tell them we suspect someone might try to sabotage the Shield?"

"I told them. They just don't care. They say they'll handle it."

"Of all the times to be playing politics! Don't they know people's lives are at stake?"

"Maybe you should sit this one out, Justicar. I can handle this. You go be with your family."

"I'm of more use here. I can't do anything for Mirrei in the hospital. But this, this might be her cure."

"If you say so."

"Where would they go?"

"Their real aim."

"The substation."

"I'm on it. I'll contact the courts for Imperial entrance orders."

"And I'll see what I can do as well, Inquester. I'll inquire if any of my judicial contacts will issue us one as well."

Jhee and Inquester grabbed their conchs. Jhee soon reached the end of her most likely prospects. Now, she had to use her favor lists if she wanted that order.

The inquester gripped her conch. Her clenched teeth spoke of her weighing if she should hurl it. "Looks like we must go rogue on this one. Inkerton Enforcement's lawyers filed an emergency injunction preventing us entry into the substation or within a hundred feet."

"I'll call in a few favors."

"Maybe we don't have to enter. Maybe we can do it from here."

"What do you mean, Inquester?"

"I mean we have you. You're an artificer. All the relay station is, is just that: a relay station. You say you can do magic detection or whatever. Can't you just whip up something like the ASU team has? We wouldn't even have to enter the substation. We set up a perimeter and triangulate."

"Not at this scale. That's not how arcana works...." Jhee took in the view before her again. They had a whole city full of stanchions in the form of the defense grid pylons. Jhee began going over possibilities. Could she combine a method like her eavesdropping formulation with a synchronance perimeter made from the pylons? "You might have the right of it. But I won't be able to pinpoint an exact location."

"We don't need one. We just need to get close enough and do it the mundane way. The imperators will set up a perimeter. Then we can trap this murderer."

~

The Gyro

"Inquester do you have a light flight vehicle, preferably a stealthy one?"

"I have something better. Come on."

Back at the evidence warehouse, Inquester Paij brought her to vehicle depot next door.

"You'll love this," the inquester said and slammed the button to open the hangar doors.

The doors revealed a small, three impeller, wind arcana gyrocopter.

"Blessed be the First Makers," Jhee said.

"We seized it in a raid," Inquester Paij said. "Can you make it work?"

"Can I ever." Jhee rushed over. As she ran her fingers over smooth, white composite material, she familiarized herself with its design, controls, and operations.

Despite its name, the gyro maneuvered as smooth as silk. Jhee barely had to spend any mind share fighting the internal stabilizers, unlike the models she had flown in the service. They approached the tines like the quiet before the storm. Thunder and lightning surrounded the clear waterspout towers. Between them, the deadly, relay station presented itself as so benign and innocuous. Once, Jhee had been so proud and amazed by the heart of the defense grid as a display of Water Folk cleverness and ingenuity. Now, what amazed her were the costs and the untold victims of their arrogance and hubris. Jhee turned away and thought of Mirrei and Shep. He was the real reason she had such high hopes for the Shield. Everything that had happened to him during his service to the empire. All to protect themselves from the Fire Folk. She had been so eager. She had hoped for something, anything to prevent that kind of carnage again. But was the wall so much better? Not that she could tell. Had they just traded one evil for another?

Jhee and the inquester touched down outside the injunction's radius at a good vantage point with which to cast their data net. If the killer so much as gave a cross look to the data stream, they would know. They had to bide their time and wait. Jhee thought about Mirrei lying there in that bed. What was she thinking? Was she dreaming? Jhee's scientific training said she wasn't. A coma was unconsciousness, a state where no conscious activity took place or activities such as dreams. Jhee did not like Mirrei just lying there surrounded by darkness in an abyss or nether realm from which there was no escape. She needed to get this cure. She wanted to see Mirrei laugh and embroider and do all the things a young woman her age should even if it was without her.

Jhee shook loose the morbid thoughts. There would be time enough for that later once Mirrei was back on her feet. She could already see her bright, smiling face. Beaming full of joy. That's the way she wanted to think of Mirrei. That's the way she wanted to think of Mai. Not as some cold bloated corpse beneath the sea.

"What happened back there at the Fairgull chasm?" Inquester Paij asked. "You let them get away."

"The redactions to my service record aren't what you think. My family had enough influence to have certain embarrassing aspects hidden. I was in the intelligence pool because they couldn't trust me on a ship. Vizier Jeja, on the other hand, was an even larger force of nature than I depicted. In 'Dispatches from Arrow Point,' portraying myself as on par with my mentor was wishful thinking on my part. Much of those stories were."

"Fish flakes," the inquester sad. "I told you I know what a place like your gentlewoman's club is. I also know they're not in the habit of welcoming military disgraces. Couldn't trust you on a ship, but your flying was calm pool. You don't want to tell me that's fine, but don't feed me a load of fish food."

"Nevertheless, I assure you, Inquester—"

Jhee's skin tingled then her makeshift detector pinged. Jhee straightened up. Something had disturbed the relay network. She engaged the gears of arcana within her. She became a conduit for the prime forces of the Divine Mechanism to work through her. Like the pieces of a magnificent clockwork, she traced a pathway through the system to achieve her goal.

The inquester set down her kolal. "That's it?"

"Someone's tampering with the tower security. It'll take me a few minutes to triangulate." Jhee would have preferred a full grid. But with the time and resources at her disposal, she had had to settle for a basic triangulation system which only allowed her to be so accurate regarding the location of the saboteur.

Jhee closed her eyes and stroked the waves of air and the waters coming at her. She circled to divine the direction where the signal was the strongest. She continued to spin around.

Jhee and the inspector hopped out of their aircraft. Jhee pointed her conch in the direction and watched the beeping on her screen. Someone was definitely trying to access the relay station's terminal. It might take a while if they were not skilled with programming. Mr. Bastian had done the programming and may not have been able to walk the accomplice entirely through the process of how to use and upload the code to the substation's systems. So, they would have extra time to track the person attempting to do the sabotage.

"Thank you for how understanding you've been, Inquester."

"Let only those whose feet have never been wet lecture someone else on how to keep theirs dry."

"Wet feet. Wet hem. Clean hems."

"We've assumed everyone has been getting the rose dust from somewhere they've been. What if it's from how they got there?"

"The water taxi."

The inquester palmed her esca. "Who else would have an excuse to know and meet with all the players."

"They could also have brought people like the ambassador to someplace dry."

"So, it has to be in a cab. What cab company?"

"Do we have Mr. Bastian's financial records still? Remember he had all those charges from the same water taxi service. Can we get an emergency order to look into the ambassador's finances?"

"I might. If you've got any favors left, I'd call them in too."

Jhee wracked her brain for details about the encounter at the observatory with the taxi and the killer. The odd water taxi at the fundraiser sprung to mind, followed by the taxi at the sight of their first trap again. The door. Its window had been open. The patron had been reaching inside for something from the front seat. Though the taxi had been lit and running, the driver's seat was empty.

Jhee went over the events at the fundraiser again. She did not want a repeat of the myopia at Tranquility Bridge which put her family in danger.

The murderer had already tried their sabotage at the observatory and the substation. Those places would have heightened security. Additionally, as she constructed her detector, she learned not every pylon had active access terminals. That left limited places for them to go for another attempt. What else was part of the defense grid and not on total lockdown?

They left their vantage to head in the direction the detector pointed. After a while the signal switched from one active pylon to the next. Then another. By the fourth, Jhee deduced where the path of pylons led. She gazed at the structures towering over the city and staring right at her.

The inquester traced her eyeline. "Oh, no. You know we can't go anywhere near—"

"You know this is our only chance. We have to get the killer before Styrling does."

They took an underground shortcut to head their quarry off.

All that remained now was to wait. Exhausted, Jhee found a darkened vantage near the bank of switches and dozed off. A rustling awoke her sometime later. A technician tried his access signet against the maintenance hatch.

Jhee hit the activator for the safety lockdown. The set of blast doors between the tines sealed shut as Jhee and the inquester sprung their trap. Jhee squinted into the dim light as recognition dawned—recognition, but not surprise. "You can do away with that ridiculous disguise. It's over."

21

THE RACE CONTINUED

~

Runway

Ambassador Naiman paused and removed his wig and cap. "How did you know?"

"Clean hems," Jhee said. "The skiff way was soaked because a mix-up triggered the lawn sprinklers. Everyone's hems got dirty."

"Except mine."

"You must have arrived via a different way. My mind also kept coming back to how did the killer know we were going back to the secret workshop to get there ahead of us and Inkerton."

The ambassador nodded and lowered the zipper on his coveralls. "Drench. I'm sorry."

"You were there to provide comfort to my family. Bright Harmony invited you."

"I did not mean to abuse my authority. I was there to help and comfort you and yours. After I had gone for kolal, and when I came back, I saw you consulting with Vash and a doctor. I'd also seen you and the investigator talking."

"So, you hid and listened in."

"Just so. How are you doing, Justicar?"

"To be honest, Ambassador, not well. It could have something to do with my spouse being about to die because of your foolishness."

"Sorry, I did not mean to expose her or any of them. Maybe Chappy. I've had to live my whole life with the activists thinking they are better than me, questioning my loyalty because I want our people to have a decent education and jobs."

"My wife is dying. Do you understand that? She's *dying,* and that device you stole might be the only option that can cure her. I don't intend to stand by and watch that happen without first going through you to prevent it."

The ambassador raised a conch and pressed an icon. The passageway doors opened. He dashed through then re-activated the blast door system. He progressed several airlocks ahead of Jhee and the inquester before they closed the bulkheads again. "I'm afraid I can't return it, Justicar. I'm trying to prevent a hundred, a thousand Star Mirrors. So, I must stop the wall. I must bring it down."

Inquester Paij placed the cuff of her Sensor Suit against the panel. "The override function will take time to counter. Keep him talking if you can."

Jhee moved next to the door. "I'm afraid I care about only one Star Mirror right now. I'm thin on patience and tolerance about now. The inquester here will arrest you. But first, I need you to turn over Mr. Bastian's prototype synchronator right now."

The bulkhead opened. Jhee drew air to burst herself through before the system locked them again. Likewise, the ambassador had advanced another chamber. The inquester gritted her teeth from a chamber behind Jhee before going to work with the Sensor Suit again.

"Please, Justicar, I'm appealing to your sense of All Folk solidarity. We need to stop this wall. You've seen the costs. If it's allowed to stabilize, there's no telling the amount of devastation it can wreak."

"It's wreaking plenty of havoc in its unfinished state. What of all those poor people near the relay station who are already suffering? The device you have can allow it to fix the victims. Many of whose lives you tried to improve in other ways."

The bulkhead opened again. Jhee narrowed the chamber gap between her and the ambassador, but Inquester Paij remained stuck another chamber farther behind.

"You sound like Bastian. He couldn't see the bigger picture just like you. It's not about fixing the wall. The wall can't be fixed. It has to be blown apart wind by wind and drop by drop. Didn't that galleon tell you it's folly for the Water Folk to recapture the past? The Other Folk are here to stay now. We should welcome them and make our peace with them."

"Some of us have tried and perhaps we will once they are ready and are civilized."

"Like my mother? I had to see her. I stayed under her roof. Watched her with her family. All without letting on who I was. You sound like her. She slummed it and slept with a barbarian, but she couldn't keep me. Not with eyes this color or the markings on my skin. Unlike Vash. The whirlpool of fate spun out a random biological collection of eyes and markings such that Vash is *Vash,* and I am *me.* It made it so some were born inland and others outland. I do this as much for the Water Folk as the Fire Folk. Look at the cost to the people, some of them from your own home district. We need to accept defeat and embrace the Other Folk. Do you see, Justicar? The wall is evil."

"Why would we want open transportation between the two realms? So more of the Other Folk can become stranded on our shores and be raised in the imperial run schools to be servants. Would you have more children like yourself stuck between two worlds? With parents unable to express their love for each other? I met your father. He was the caretaker's son. They stayed on the grounds. Your mother and he used to talk all the time. They were inseparable."

"So inseparable she turned him and me away."

"You don't know what it was like back then. She had to, but I'm sure she didn't want to. I'm sure she thought about you every day."

"Justicar, you are such a terrible liar. But I appreciate your attempts to make me feel better. Do you know how I found out who my mother was?"

"Please, tell me about it."

"He wanted the wall contract. He looked into who was in charge and who knew who. Well lo and behold it was his old sweetheart. In the end, I became a bargain stone to him. He used me to convince her to assign him the contact. Then he botches the project. It was typical of him. He made his fortune just by being good enough and cutting corners on the rest. All those people, poisoned. He should never have been awarded that contract. He might not have if not for my participation. It was then I realized how much like him I was.

"I had just concluded my part in the galleon deal. They got me to sign off on the retrieval by promising me money for a clinic and schools, but it all goes to a shell company. The various tribes are fighting over the money. They're excommunicating and disenfranchising those whom they disagreed with to get a bigger portion for themselves. It turned into a nightmare.

"I tried to make something good out of the wall, but it all turned to slush like everything the wall touches. It can't be fixed. It can't be redeemed. It just has to be torn apart. We can't make amends, Justicar. That's what I learned. We can't undo the bad we've done. All we can do is resolve to make the current life as best as possible now. If I can do my part in making that happen for others by destroying this wall, then that is what I must do. Tell Bright Harmony I'm sorry and to keep faith. You are not abandoned by the Makers. Tell Dawn Wolf there was nothing he could do about it either. And you, Justicar, I want you to forgive yourself. You were young and foolish. It was something small that spiraled out of control. It took all of you to make into the mess it became. You were nothing more than children, and the adults around you let you down. How were you to know they would not calm down and act no better than children themselves?"

"Ambassador, please, stay and let's talk about this."

"The dead cannot be improved only remade. The time for talking is done. Time for remaking has come. Once we put our plan in motion, I didn't want anyone to stop it."

"So, you killed the only person you knew could lift the lockout. What you didn't know was he was working off code Ms. Levinia designed."

"You're lying."

Inquester Paij opened the blast doors again.

Ambassador Naiman barreled down the passageway. He hit a button to re-trigger the lockdown sequence. Jhee sped through the closing doors. She was only one airlock chamber behind the ambassador now. She drew the winds to give her an air-propelled burst of speed. The ambassador made it to next chamber. Jhee barely slipped into the chamber behind Naiman. Inquester Paij was stuck another two chambers behind her.

"The wall went right through the Water Nomads' sacred waters. You needed to accelerate the timeline especially once Advocate Farkhande's injunction against the wall went down in defeat," Jhee said.

"We only got one tilt at this. We could have wasted it on the off chance it cured everyone. Or we could use it on the certainty it would stop the wall. Bastian, however, still thought the plan was to fix the wall and cure the sick. Bastian wanted to run more trials. He did not much like going down in history as the man who poisoned a generation. He viewed fixing the wall as his redemption. But you and I both know, Justicar, there are some actions you just can't repair."

Jhee activated her siren module. "I know that. I do. Please, Ambassador, I am begging you. For the life of Star Mirror, I'm begging you. Tell me where the prototype is."

The ambassador considered it.

An alarm warning about the pressure and air levels blared out of the address system. The swear she said at the top of her lungs had been just as drowned out as the ambassador's response. Jhee became short of breath as the ventilation system depressurized the compartment. The ambassador snapped out of her influence. That was one use down.

The doors opened. The ambassador bolted to the next chamber and re-started the lockdown. "Or you'll do what Justicar? You respect the law. Even if you don't always play by its rules. You will not harm me, a man of the coif. Not a devout woman like you. It's almost over now. You should go. There's nothing more you can do here."

"What about Ms. Oriel?"

"Oriel was what the mining company might deem an acceptable loss. She came back and found the secret workshop. She also accidentally caught footage of me meeting with Bastian and our underworld contact at the clinic."

"Ms. Oriel caught you and him together and assumed you were having an affair."

"At first. Oriel caught on and realized Bastian had found a cure. Ever the glory grabber until the end, she tried to extort me into licensing it and putting her name on it. In the beginning, she was an integral part of the plan. I introduced them, you know? I told him to get close to her like Levinia so we could get access to her credentials and use the clinic as a staging area. But I didn't realize Bastian would use it as a testing ground."

The inquester signaled Jhee. They were almost through the lockout. Just a few more minutes.

"What I don't know is was the mining supervisor you or Bastian?" Jhee asked.

"Bastian. According to him, that was an accident," Ambassador Naiman said.

"Her fondness for drinking on the job. If she caught him supplying the miners, or he caught her stealing sips, she'd want more."

"He didn't give me the details."

"Again more time pressure."

The ambassador held up his conch triumphantly.

"It doesn't have to end this way," Jhee yelled.

He pressed the send button. The conch he held emitted the no signal noise. The next door slid open. Ambassador Naiman slung himself to the companion tine's shaft, using a mix of air and earth drawing to outrun her. Jhee slipped into the chamber behind the ambassador. Jhee gaped as she caught her breath. Not only had he used interfering elements, but on manufactured metal. Jhee ran forward before it closed again. It slid closed again trapping the inquester only a room behind her. The inquester began working on the next override.

He pressed send again over and over. "What did you do?"

Jhee gathered her breath, "Take me to where you hid the prototype."

Ambassador Naiman winced and grimaced. He gazed at the tines. His body shaking.

"You think the miners will thank you for destroying their livelihood?"

"They'll be free of the mines and Styrling. If they won't thank me, maybe the communities devastated by the wall and the pylons might."

This was her last chance. Jhee increased the attenuation on the siren module. "You know their hearts better than I. Will they see it that way? Communities who view templarite deposits as blessings given them by the Makers as much as we in the Reaches view marine life."

The ambassador turned away from the tines and took a confused step toward her. Jhee held her breath. He shook his head and turned back toward the tine's base. She had used it too many times in succession on him. If she upped the attenuation to overcome his growing resistance, she risked turning him into a blathering idiot. She swore.

"Ambassador, why did you become a man of the coif?"

"To help people."

"Then be a helper and not the man who left my wife to die in a cavern or killed two people. Let your desire to help conquer your desire to punish Delphine and the system. What you are doing will hurt so many more people. You are not stopping anything. You stop this wall, and they will just build another. Meet me halfway. Work with me, and we will do our best to make a good world for the Water Folk and the Other Folk. We will build bridges instead of make swords."

Ambassador Naiman hurled the useless conch at the tine's base.

"I would love to believe you. I've taken that bait before, but not this time. The hole in the world isn't the mine, Justicar. The hole in the world isn't out there, it's within. Though we can build bridges, more often than not we make swords. I'm sorry, Justicar. Star Mirror seems like she cares about the plight of the Fire Folk. I may not have been able to plant the code via the substation, but I found an alternate way to still stop the wall and help the miners and those affected by the pylons. You are a clever and smart investigator, and if you took me in you could get me to talk and tell you where I hid the synchronator. Goodbye, Justicar."

Ambassador Naiman spread his feet and arms apart. Particles coalesced from the air and accumulated on his hands. He turned his hands as if winding a giant clock key. A burst cypher, a self-destructive arcane technique pioneered by Doombringers designed to inflict maximum damage to arcanists and environment alike.

Jhee dropped into stance for the counter. She exhaled strongly and turned her hands opposite his. His face strained. His body shook. More particles streamed out of the air. Jhee's legs wobbled. She drew upon the prime forces within to replenish what he took. Her body burned like she was being scoured with electrified acid.

A sniper round went through the ambassador's head. His body fell to the ground. Jhee collapsed to her knees.

~

Outside of Bounds

"No," Jhee said. "No. No. No."

The inquester overrode the last door and entered the column with Jhee and the ambassador's body.

"Justicar, are you okay?"

"Who? Why? He hadn't told me where the synchronator was."

"We'll figure it out, but for now, we better get out of here."

Jhee stared at the ambassador's body. They still had no idea where to find the synchronator, and time was running out for Mirrei. Jhee had to think. Where would the ambassador have hidden it? He hinted he had another endgame in mind. What was it he said? He found an alternative way.

"Wait. Wait." Jhee pondered then addressed to the inquester, "I don't quite think this is over. The ambassador, I think he may have discovered another way to destroy the defense grid."

"Makers, no."

"There has to be a clue where he's been and what he did with the prototype." She examined the soles of his shoes a combination of dirt and plant matter and more templarite dust. She began checking the ambassador's clothes and body.

As Jhee tried to order her thoughts about where the ambassador may have hidden the rest of the crystals and the synchronator, a loud bang sounded. Alarms went off. Armed Squid troopers wearing tact gear burst into the chamber.

Two Squids approached with a digital parchment held high. Jhee tensed in anticipation of the now familiar refrain. Forge her patience in flames, she practically knew their script by rote.

"Pursuant to this imperial order and the imperial seizure act, Inkerton Enforcement Services has been authorized on behalf of the empire to take over this matter. I'm afraid Justicar and Inquester we must ask you to leave," Sianna said.

"You can't. You don't understand," Jhee said. Jhee started to fight and protest. "We haven't found every device, and the ambassador may have been planning another attack."

"We'll take it from here. I assure you the matter will be thoroughly investigated, and any additional devices found in due time."

"In due time? My wife is dying now."

"Just be glad we're overlooking your violation of the injunction considering your assistance stopping the radical."

"This passage is one hundred-twenty feet away from the nearest substation."

"Justicar," the inquester said. "This looks official. Let's leave them to it. Come along, Justicar. I'll take you home to your villa."

The inquester grabbed Jhee and started to drag her out. Jhee began to protest. The inquester caught her eye and shook her head. The inquester brought Jhee out to the gyro. Jhee climbed in the seat morose and somber. The inquester slipped into the driver seat.

"Why didn't the conch work?" Jhee asked.

"I copied the Stingray Club's jamming signal."

They flew away from the perimeter via the gyro's backup motion drive and a stomach dropping series of hops. The inquester thankfully brought the gyro to the ground on a nearby outcropping. She pulled out a conch. The inquester extended a tray from the console and placed the conch on it. "I took this while they weren't looking. It's encrypted so we won't be able to look at the data, however. But we can get its unique signet without an imperial access order. The prototype isn't on him. So, where is it?"

"Good question. I must think. Where would he put it? How else could he destroy the grid? He was not the tech-savvy one. That was Mr. Bastian."

The inquester hrmled. "Okay. The ambassador didn't have much time to hide the synchronator since we stopped him at the observatory. He also needed to be at the hospital in order to not raise suspicions."

"Let's just hope he did a poor job of securing his conch."

Jhee took out her quick unlocker. The inquester waved it away and touched the sensor suit's cuff to the ambassador's conch. Jhee watched the lights and characters spin. And spin. Her heart began to sink. They would have to bring it to the techs to have them unlock it.

There had been more templarite on the ambassador's shoes. It couldn't have been from the workshop, because they had that place sewn up tight.

"Where are the source crystals for the pylons mined?" Jhee asked.

"I don't know. Maybe in the Rose Hills."

"Too far. Where did the templarite dust originate if not there? Everyone else with it on their shoes and clothing, got it from being in the water taxi."

"Or did they? They were also at the clinic and Chuc's. Could it be that simple?"

"Would the ambassador have gone back there with us crawling all over it?"

"We can go look."

"But if we're wrong, we've wasted more valuable time. I need to make a better educated guess." Jhee took a beat, so impatience would not in fact cost them more time. "You said we could get the unique signet? If the ambassador used the location services at all, we might track his movements. Conch only use a handful of methods for location tracking. We can figure out the conch's unique signet and the services he used. We track him via the infrastructure without having to crack the conch."

"The data the Imperium doesn't track and isn't supposed to keep a record of."

"Correction, Inquester, doesn't track or keep record of after a long-tide. We won't be able to know where the ambassador has been past a long-tide, but all we need is the last couple of days since he eluded us at the observatory."

"Precisely. Exactly. However, no doubt it'll involve violation of the privacy protocols and use of infrastructure controlled by the Imperium and by extension our Styrling prickle fish. If there are any favors you have left, call them in. Also, what about his room at the villa? There might be a clue there."

"Good thinking. Likely our friends already searched it, but they didn't know what they were looking for then."

"Show me the evidence manifest again." Jhee stared at the list again for the hundredth time: receipts, disposable conch, workshop footage. What did she expect to see now that she hadn't before? She remembered the disposable conch's footage of Bastian and presumably Ambassador Naiman speaking in his workshop.

"Careful with that. Look around us. One mistake in calibration and you could start a chain reaction that would set the whole thing off."

"The synchronator is like radiation shielding. It can still bring the Shield down. The ambassador wasn't the technical one, so it had to be a solution he figured out from a layman's knowledge. They made it from an unstable crystal. The substation needed to be run by the crystal. Without the crystal, the Shield would break down. A chain reaction. Destroy the crystal mines. The synchronator was a resonating device. It shielded. What happened if you overloaded it? It was still tuned to the same frequency as the Shield. The synchronator prototype could be reprogrammed to send out a feedback signal without much trouble. All you had to do was put it near the signal boost, and you could create a feedback loop.

"The hole in the world. The Styr Mine. I think that's where he planted the synchronator. He was going to stop the power sources. While without Mr. Bastian's access to the substation and code he can't shut down the Shield digitally, he can destroy its fuel source. With a chain reaction created by resonant vibrations from the synchronator, the templarite will start a cascade explosion."

"An explosion like that could take out half the drench isle, Water Folk and Fire Folk alike."

"It's even worse than that I'm afraid. That same mineral is used in many of our screens from conchs to viewers. The chain reaction could spread far beyond to the pylons and the tines."

"If the tines and the pylons keep the Storm Shield in place, what happens if something destroys them?"

"The storm gets to wander where it will. Years of captured storms suddenly freed. Utter devastation."

"Merciful Makers, was he insane?"

"Not insane. Bitter and desperate perhaps. It's even more imperative we find the synchronator now. Every moment that goes by means more than Mirrei having less and less chance of waking up. We can't wait for the formal investigation."

"The scene integrity."

"The ambassador is dead, and this may never go to trial. Preserve life first. Make the case second. The case always comes second to someone's life, Inquester. That's the way I was taught."

22

____

WAITING

~

Sterling Eyes

Jhee and Paij could not remain in the gyro on the outcropping overlooking the tines forever. Jhee contacted Shep via conch. "Shep, where are you now?"

"I'm back at the villa. Taking a rest. Kanto is at the hospital still with Mirrei."

"I need you to search the first floor harborside suite. It's Ambassador Naiman's."

"On it."

"Company may arrive soon."

"Understood." Shep's image shook and his quick footfalls carried through the conch's microphone. The image became blurry. The tune and hiss of a lock sounded before his face came back into view. "What am I looking for?"

Jhee pulled up Mr. Bastian's designs. "We are looking for any sign of where he's been over the past few days or any piece of technology that looks out of place or a rectangular enclosure thirty by fifteen centimeters on a side housing an eight-centimeter diameter crystal—."

"Small box, large crystal. Got it."

Shep began to scour the ambassador's room. Meanwhile, the inquester's console retrieved the conch's signet code. None of Jhee's judicial contacts answered her calls. Jhee considered who really owed her. Zeloach, whose son had been falsely convicted by the last District Sixteen magistrate, was not part of the judiciary. However, she would not need a writ.

461

"I may know of a tracking method that does not require an imperial order," Jhee said to the inquester.

The Imperium controlled the skies and the towers; they were much laxer about the sea and the ground. The Zeloach family had been tinkers who maintained the heavy machinery in the Outer Reaches. They had kept every-one's equipment, running from the farmer and fisherfolk to miners and ship-pers. It had afforded them service contracts with many houses. Still did. As times had changed, they had branched out into communication infrastructure. With the airways unsafe and most air travel grounded, they had the only means of running communication lines under the ground or along the sea floor.

Jhee contacted Zeloach, her contact with access to the imperial location grid, and she was all too eager to help. "Do you still have the waypoint grid system in case the broadcast power goes down?"

"Yes."

"Can you track a conch if I gave you its signet code?"

"I can, but our system is less accurate than the air track grid used above ground."

"What if I also had a time and location I know it was present?"

"That is a fur of a different stripe. With that info we can narrow down where it's been to within"—Zeloach paused, and the clack of keys came across the sound channel—"say ten to twenty meters at any point after."

"Accurate enough. Do it, please. Also, thank you."

"Don't consider this a favor sunk. I'll always be on your lists."

One of the first things Jhee had done when she took over the justicarship was review the old cases. It had not been her intention, but so many had come to her. If she thought the previous Justicar was corrupt, she did not know the half of it when she began looking into his so-called judgments. If he had not already bankrupted his house, what she uncovered would have done it. She had sometimes even paid for some appeals out of her own pocket for the more impoverished families. First Makers knew she needed the goodwill after how her family had behaved.

She had restored justice and order to District Sixteen and then came the Shield. Many of the families she had grew up with had moved their homes inland. Winter or seasonal homes closer to the capital had now being retro-fitted to become permanent residences. And as residences changed so did jobs and expertise. Lesser houses who once made their livings from spawning beds and kelp farms now had to adapt. Many had taken up posi-tions within the government infrastructure which had grown to accommo-date the centralization of power into large population centers.

"Jhee," came Shep's voice. "I haven't found a device like what you described. I did, however, find a lot of notes about mirrors, crystal stars and silver eyes and a list of suppliers."

Jhee went through her finger-cyphering exercises to calm her mind and steady her nerves. She tucked her hands into her robes to stop herself. Mirrei's plight had thrown her off.

"I think company's arrived, Jhee."

"All right, Shep, get out of there. Did you remember to cover your tracks?"

"I'll do my best."

Shep disconnected. Jhee needed to cease her reckless, unordered behavior and use the wits the Singers of the Seas had given her. Mirrei's life depended on it.

"I've got it, Justicar. The location data is coming in," the inquester said.

Jhee examined the incoming data. The ambassador had visited the templarite mines and a custom crystal, lens, and mirror supply company which was consistent with what Shep found. The ambassador had remained committed to the last to completing his mission: destroying the Shield. So, what would visiting those locations have to do with bringing it down? Power source. And where would he leave Mr. Bastian's shielding synchronator?

"That's it," Jhee exclaimed.

"Uh oh," the inquester said. "Shep isn't the only one with company."

The inquester pointed and engaged the gyro's motion drive. The Ink's troopers had spotted them. Some ran toward them. Others hopped into transports. The inquester sped off. "I guess they figured out I have the conch. Without you at the helm, we won't be able to outrun them in this contraption. The motion drive is no match for their pursuit cruisers."

"Don't outrun them. Hide. I know a place."

~

The Root

Jhee directed them to the Maid of the Mists grotto. The grotto provided just enough concealment to house their transportation. Jhee hopped out.

"All right, Inquester. This is where I leave you."

"I'll buy you what time I can. Where will you go? Wait! don't tell me. The less I know, the better. That way I can't tell them what I don't know."

"Thank you, Inquester."

The inquester tapped her temple and sped off. Shortly, Jhee heard the Galleon City Imperators' sirens and saw the weak, distant reflection of alternating emergency lights.

Jhee searched around in her robes for one of Kanto's infamous hidden pockets. She found one tucked under the armpit. This time with a bandanna and a bit of concealing make-up and facial hair in it. She slipped off her robes and flipped them inside out. He thought of everything. He must have taken the story of her disguising herself at the refugee camps to heart. Maybe he wasn't so bored by her work. She had never given him enough credit for his cleverness. Her mind popped back to the night of Mr. Bastian's murder and how she and her two younger spouses had worked as a well-crafted machine.

Jhee stared at the Inkerton Enforcement Services security sticker on the building with its unblinking eye atop a watchtower design. IES. Eyes.

"All you have to do is open your eyes and look."

What had Advocate Farkhande been trying to tell her?

Something about the clinic's financial records and Mr. Bastian's receipts nagged at her. His workshop was also close to here. The Sandoval Storage business address matched that of one of the shell and dummy companies Vash had used to hide his transactions with the clinic. She had seen it some-where else. The catering company who Ms. Oriel had used to pilfer her money from selling access also gave a similar address. The addresses were all postal rentals.

Jhee traced the physical location to a small ocean-side storefront near where they found Ms. Oriel's body and right next to where the observatory stored their decommissioned equipment.

The Delphines' old mining operations were right around the corner. Jhee took off for the worksite. She examined the underwater storage tanks and found nothing. What else was nearby?

The subsistence mines. The mines other than those leased by the Delphines to Styrling were exhausted. They did not produce commercial-grade crystals anymore. Individuals mined enough crystal dust to eke out a living with, if not the Delphines' blessing, then their forbearance.

A sound behind Jhee startled her. The Latcher girl stared at her.

"Quickest way to the main shafts?" Jhee asked.

"Transport bins." The girl brought her to a motorized vehicle attached to carts on a track. She pulled the pin to separate the mine carts. "You can tell me, you're a Singer of the Sea, right? The lady with you at the shop was the Maid of the Mists? Tell her I did my devotions proper."

Jhee sped to the mine entrance near Lady Delphine's. Amongst some miners having a drink, she found Wynne, who asked, "What are you doing here? And dressed like that?"

"I need your help. It's urgent. Ambassador Naiman implanted a device to blow up the mines. I need help to find it. Crystal stars. Does that jog any memories or have anything to do with the Shield or the One Waters move-ment, Folx United?"

The activist eyed Jhee.

"Please, my only concern now is saving lives. I have no time for anything else."

"Okay but only to help Star. We uncovered one of the smaller companies who helped build the wall. They were only a two-person den, with a small ocean-side storefront and a bunch of rental boxes. Not worth the time to protest. We needed to make a big splash and take our fight to the heart of the big corporations. Not harass little guls."

"Thank you, thank you so much." Small fries, little guys her behind. That company was a front, one of the various places nobles like Vash and the others laundered their money through.

"Everyone fan out."

"I need the device intact. Will that be a problem?"

"Trench yes, but we'll try, anyway. The last time a member of your household yelled about imminent danger they turned out to be right."

"You know these mines better than anybody. Where would he plant it for maximum destructive effect?"

"Deep underground. As deep as you can."

"Does it have anything to do with this?"

Jhee showed Wynne an image of the number and message on the back of the napkin from Che's. Pool. Underground lake. This blight of a city consumed in a pillar of light. Mineral sands. Starry eyes.

Wynne passed the image along. When it got to an old timer, the color drained from her face. "Merciful Makers, the mnemonic we use to locate the root crystal."

Wynne looked ill. At Jhee's desperate look, she explained further, "The entire city rests on crystal beds, the root or mother crystal. This must be its frequency signature."

Jhee's stomach sank to the depths. "Without support, reinforcement, the literal foundations of the city would be pulverized, turned to dust. Millions perhaps more would die. The land might be made uninhabitable in a way the Pillarist Doombringers could have only imagined."

"Yeah, well, welcome to Galleon City, a monument to short-sightedness, bad decisions, small-picture thinking, and heinous choices."

"A disaster that size with us trapped inside the storm wall could cripple the empire. It would be equivalent to a volcanic eruption. Monhar-before-the-light and Findar-beneath the-Waves all over again."

"Never thought he had it in him."

"You sound impressed, almost like you admire him."

"It's dedication I grant you, but not if it blows our people to the high heavens. Becoming a shared fine mist of cremains is not the sort of oneness I'm after."

"I need a direction toward the root of the crystal, can you guide me?"

Two older miners brought Jhee to a larger tunnel. They took a sitting position on either side of the tunnel. Placing their hands on the ground at their sides, they hummed. Their hum resonated in the ground at her feet.

"Follow the beat to the heart."

Jhee took off into the darkness following the pulsing beat.

Jhee dove through the mine tunnels. She blocked out the echoes of the beat coming from down the side tunnels and simply focused on the resonance at her feet.

As she got deeper, a beeping echoed from down the tunnel. That must have been it.

Jhee covered her ears as the ringing got louder. The synchronator must already be powering up.

She kept charging down. The narrow tunnels opened up into a large chamber. A massive crystal formation supported the chamber. At the top of the formation was a small machine wired in. That must be the synchronator. Luckily it wasn't a bomb, so it shouldn't be hard to shut—

The synchronator finished beeping and whirred to terrible life. A vibration began to echo throughout the chamber. Was Jhee too late? The crystal began to tremor and spark. Jhee reflexively covered herself to block the falling shards.

The tremors subsided. Had the synchronator failed? No, Jhee felt its external pressure. Its pulse was being canceled by another, the pulsing beat she followed here. She could only conclude it came from the miners. The miners were countering the vibration. They had given her a chance; she couldn't waste it.

She climbed up to the synchronator. The controls' intuitiveness matched what one expected of an engineer. She hoped she could get this device shut down before the Squids started pulling the miners away from their suppression.

She started fiddling with the controls. Sequences she had studied backwards and forwards from Mr. Bastian's sprang to mind. None of them worked.

Two sets of footsteps approached. Squids? The miners were still holding the synchronator back. Jhee began to rush through the shutdown. All the time preparing to defend herself. The air was thick with the crystal dust, heavy to draw. Gathering up enough to use was a laborious process.

Two miners entered the room. The two large Fire Folk wielded pickaxes. Whether they agreed with the ambassador or the Doombringers, Jhee must work faster. The pair began to clamber up the crystal root. Jhee unleashed an air burst to push them back. Charged with crystal, it came out much more violently than expected. The pair reeled back into the cavern tunnel.

The reprieve gave Jhee time to finish the shutdown sequence, but she still needed to disconnect the synchronator and escape. When the pair returned, she used the siren module and gave the command to "Flee!"

Feedback surged through her siren module. One turned and ran, but the other continued to climb. She swayed and scrabbled at the crystal.

Jhee arrested her fall but had slid within reach of the remaining miner. Jhee kicked down and got her in the face a few times before she caught Jhee's foot. The miner was much stronger than Jhee and held her grip. She swung her pickaxe at Jhee, who pushed herself back to avoid it.

Jhee struggled to gather another air burst. At this range, it might be enough. The miner pulled herself up to the top of the crystal and raised her pickaxe. Jhee seized upon the opening. She unleashed the small burst she gathered right at the miner's stomach. The miner fell backward off the crystal root, slamming into the ground below.

Jhee disconnected the synchronator. The synchronator comprised a fist-sized crystal housed in an electronic lattice much like an inverse of the bricker left at the substation. Her siren module still rang. The ringing brought her to her knees. A trickle of blood ran from her nose. *Close the circle. Fill the void. Until all are one.* She forced herself to her feet and fled past the writhing body of the fallen miner.

~

The Vigil

Jhee burst into the hospital emergency room. She roamed the hallways seeking Mirrei's doctor. The people regarded her with caution. The sight she must have made, wild-eyed and frantic.

"Doctor Pike?"

Mirrei's doctor came out and stared at her in bewilderment. Jhee's slovenly make-up used for disguise remained as did her wrong sided robes.

"Doctor Pike, I have it. I have the device which can treat Mirrei."

The doctor gave her the once over. Jhee took out the shielding synchronator and placed it in her hands. The doctor waved over an orderly. "What is it? How does it work?"

"It's a frequency jammer. You said you put Mirrei in an isolation chamber. This has the right frequency. It should stop the assault on her system." Jhee pulled out a data shell. "Here is the data. Someone used them to successfully treat the sufferers of Fresh Lung Syndrome and Miners' Lung Disease. Please, doctor, hurry."

"I'll get this to the lab."

The doctor took the data shell from Jhee.

Jhee entered the isolation ward. Kanto sat outside the polymer tent, a fashion book in his lap. He gently fiddled with a grooming kit. He rose when she entered. The beep of the meridian rate monitor was steady but slow. Jhee hugged him tight.

"Is it over?" he asked.

"Yes. It's over," she said. "I won't leave again."

Kanto hugged her tight then regarded her appearance. "You look a fright."

"I feel a fright. Any word from Shep?"

"He said he was on his way back from the villa. He said you were on the trail of something that might help her. Did you find it?"

Jhee put her arms around him. "I did."

"Will it work?"

"I hope to the Singers of the Sea it will."

Kanto cranked the music box. "I see you found the surprises I left for you in your robe."

"They were very helpful. Pivotal in fact. The disguise bought me the time I needed to find Mirrei's cure."

"You should go refresh yourself. I can't take care of you right now. I don't have the energy to fix you up too." He toyed with the brush from the grooming kit then stared away from her. "When mamere took ill, I cared for her every day. I bathed her, groomed her fur, and did her hair. She would have made quite the image on the social scene. She always took great pains with her appearance. I used to groom her after she had her stroke, sing, and play my lute for her. They won't let me groom Mirrei. When I play, I'm not sure she can hear it anymore."

Jhee had heard the story from Lady Kaydence, Kanto's grandmamere, when she gave her the music box. After his mother got sick, he would sit beside her bed, brushing her hair, reading to her. Just before he would take his leave for the night, he would play the music box for her. One night in her anger, she lashed out and knocked it from his hands shattering it to many pieces. He could not bring himself to throw them out. Instead he collected the pieces and kept them in an old box where Lady Kaydence found it.

"You were a good son." His hand tightened on the brush. Jhee covered it with hers. Kanto shook his head.

"Sit." Kanto offered her his seat. Once she made herself as comfortable as possible, he undid her hasty bun. He gently stroked the brush through her tangled hair. "You were right, Jhee. I had it backward. Vash wasn't embezzling money from the clinic for his independence kit. He was propping up the clinic with it. Someone else was draining the accounts. In my desperation, I wanted it to be him."

"I should have been more skeptical. Kanto, I owe you an apology on many things. I viewed you as the irresponsible one, the one who instigated the trouble you and Mirrei found yourselves in. Mirrei was the instigator. You went along to keep an eye on her."

"Sometimes. This mischief-making we did could be fun, and it was always interesting." He rested his chin on her head. She grasped the arms he slipped around her in a reverse hug. Shep arrived. They acknowledged Shep's arrival and continued to watch Mirrei's tent. Shep laid his hands on them to let them know he was there. "I love this family, Jhee and I love you and even dour Shep. Even if he doesn't quite know how to run a comb through his mane on the regular."

Jhee smiled weakly. "She will be fine."

"My denbe, the Mechanist who always wants to find a way to fix matters. Jhee, when you say it, I can almost believe you."

"You took good care of Mirrei in my absence. You've always taken the best care of her. Thank you. Now, allow me."

Jhee squeezed Kanto's arms again. She took hold of Mirrei's hand, so much slighter and the fur drier and much more brittle than she remembered.

The doctor returned shortly to transfer Mirrei to the isolation chamber. Jhee put an arm around Kanto. Shep stood behind them with a hand on each of their shoulders while the doctors began the treatment. She pecked Shep's hand and held Kanto tighter.

23

THE FIRST MAKERS' DESIGN BE DONE

~

A Slow Recovery

Mirrei was in and out of treatment for long-tides. She seemed to make a remarkable recovery. She was still not at peak efficiency. After a long-tide or two of treatments, she could visit the grounds. Jhee entered the sea garden courtyard. Mirrei and Shep sat at a table playing tiles and laughing while Kanto did sewing nearby. Mirrei perked up and smiled at her. A nice kettle of orange tea and Tranquility Bridge's nectar next to them. Jhee sat down and poured herself a cup. She studied it and contemplated all she had learned.

"Drink up," Mirrei said. "This stuff will give you life."

Jhee grinned. "Don't I know it. Well, aren't you looking quite the picture."

"I know. Isn't it wonderful?" Kanto said.

"I feel great. Better than I have in a long time. Kanto was just filling us in on the latest celebrity gossip."

"Was he now? So, who did what to whom?"

"Well, the third Earl of Ylush from the Summer Isles had her husband moved out of the whole household and took up with a fisherman. They were trying to foster children, and it turned out the husband had certain predilections. She claimed. She found out about it and filed for divorce to protect her children, she said. The scuttlebutt though is it was because he could not give her children and the offspring she fostered are in fact hers by said fisherman."

"My word, that sounds scandalous."

"I know, doesn't it?"

471

Mirrei slammed down the last tile. "I win, Pup."

"Well, I'll be," Shep said.

"I told you not to play her," Kanto said. "I tell you never to play her."

Mirrei grinned. "You and I both know he lets me win."

"I do nothing of the sort, Sprite. Those are one of the ironclad rules. That violates the rules of all sportsmanship. Good or bad, you do not throw tiles. Always play fair."

Mirrei quirked the side of her mouth.

"Honest. I never throw a game of tiles. It's a hard and fast rule."

"Denbe, join us for a game?" Mirrei asked.

Shep moved aside, and they mixed up the tiles again and made space for Jhee. Jhee and her household played tiles, and she explained what had happened.

"So, the murderer wasn't Vash?" Kanto asked.

Jhee played her tile. "It was the ambassador. Mr. Bastian was the engineer whose muck-up caused all this. He had made a mistake in calibrating the Shield to use synthetic instead of natural crystals. The crystal dust caused excess radiation leakage because of refraction. Not only was the radiation orders of magnitude stronger than predicted, the safety zone around the Shield was much greater. As a result, the wall radiation eroded the immune system. Mirrei had grew up too close to the wall because her mother refused to leave her home and move inland like most others. When she came to live with us, she began to get better. Mr. Bastian had found a cure for the Fresh Lung Syndrome and was experimenting on the patients at the clinic."

Kanto capped it. "Perhaps I should apologize. I was so convinced."

"You wanted it to be true. Vash was just an unwilling dupe. Mr. Bastian and the ambassador played him to get access to the clinic. Vash is not entirely off the hook. His medical credentials are incomplete. And there is the mess that is the clinic's finances. It may take long-tides or even moons to find out."

Mirrei's tile placement hemmed Jhee in again. "It's a shame. The clinic was helping people. With a few adjustments and a proper doctor, it could be a great help to people up and down the waterways."

"I know, but the scandal. I don't know how it will survive."

Kanto nodded. "I'm sorry, Mirrei."

"You should be. Not the least of which because I'm about to wipe the tiles with you." Mirrei tapped her tile against her chin. "The clinic's needed now more than ever. What happens to the patients in the meantime?"

Jhee placed a rescue tile to divert Mirrei from Kanto.

"Mistake," Shep taunted.

Jhee pursed her lips as she tried to think her way out of the trap the other three had laid for her. "Unfortunately, they will have to rely on public or faith hospitals."

"Who put up all sort of conditions on their care," Mirrei said.

Jhee at last broke her pieces free. "Unfortunately, unless they can find someone with credentials to take over. They will have to close the clinic. Vash will likely land on his feet for his work on the FLS cure."

Mirrei gave an extended sigh. "My cure."

"The cure worked."

"What if it hadn't? How do we know all the people Mr. Bastian tested it on are really okay? Or won't have unintended side effects? The later patients are fine. What of the early ones? Before he perfected it. Look what happened when he tried it on the miners. A cure tested on the disadvantaged without their consent just like the wall's effects. The contractor? Styrling Mining gets away with poisoning all those people?"

The headlines held misleading news of the sabotage plot. However, a blind item proclaimed how they had found a minor error with the wall, and they were retrofitting some of the pylons. Also, the minor flu outbreak among the miners had burned itself out.

"In a shocking turn, the recent terrorist attempt to sabotage the Storm Shield uncovered a potentially hazardous flaw. The authorities are taking steps to correct the flaw which may have caused potentially hundreds of people to get sick."

"In other news, the opening of the controversial Gray Galleon exhibit has been pushed back again because of a court injunction and continued protests..."

With resignation, Jhee nodded. "For the most part. The Imperial Courts will impose fines in lieu of confinement. It likely will include a trust to treat Fresh Lung sufferers and provisions for the pensions and death benefits they should have included as part of their original contract bid. However, having to pay after the fact still has netted them large savings as it will require some expertise to determine who is eligible. They might stall for some time, and many may die without them having to pay out a dime for their treatment. For what it's worth, thanks to the efforts of the activists and people like you who supported them, their gambit will cost them more than it saved."

Mirrei frowned. "If those such as ourselves hadn't gotten sick how long would it have taken before the problem was addressed? The shield company only needed to put a couple million shell worth of extra dampeners on the pylons, but they didn't. Then we get a disaster that makes Trishanku a pygmy sea drake beside the shell drake. Companies like Styrling take those chances with our tacit approval."

Silence reigned for a time as they played.

This time, Shep blocked Jhee's tile break out. Jhee squinted at him. He raised an eyebrow. "I'm just happy you're still here to beat me at tiles, Sprite."

"Breach, Pup," Mirrei said.

Jhee chortled.

"So very happy," Shep mumbled. He studied the board as if trying to puzzle out his defeat. "Someday, Sprite. Someday."

"What of the Planetarium Chandelier and the Gray Galleon?" Kanto asked.

Jhee folded her hands. "Well, it looks like the Imperial Historical society will take over the observatory and do a thorough accounting of the assets. They'll go over Ms. Oriel's finances with a fine-tooth comb to find out who paid her and for what."

Mirrei breached Kanto's tile stronghold. "Such a shame. It's the Findari's history. It belongs to them. How selfish of her not to respect their privacy."

"What will happen to the Mechanist Devotions?" Kanto said. Freed from his obligation to play by his sound defeat, he had taken out his sketchbook.

"The Imperial Historical society will see they're returned to the Imperial Collection. They will spend some time unwinding the finances of the charity. I had my accountant looking into it already when I was looking to donate."

"Overrun, denbe," Mirrei said and dispatched Jhee, as well.

~

Recriminations

Shep, Kanto, and Jhee read to Mirrei and kept her abreast of the latest goings-on. Mirrei rested her head on her hands as Kanto went over the latest gossip. She smiled and nodded. Jhee noticed though she no longer paid as rapt attention as she once did. Mirrei turned more and more inward.

The Delphines visited, Erma and Semele at first.

"It's nice to see you looking so well. You'll be back in the fight in no time."

"Or kicking our butts at weirs."

Mirrei giggled.

Lady Delphine spoke to Jhee off to the side, "I suppose I owe you a thank you. You got to the bottom of the harassment."

"I don't feel as if I did you a particular favor with that. Thank you for squashing any lingering issues and clearing the roadblocks with the prototype."

"I figured it was the least I could do for all your family suffered at the hands of mine. I'm sorry. All the grief he caused your family. The many people he harmed."

"Have they made arrangements for his body?"

"His father is handling all that. He refuses to give me any of the details which I suppose is only proper. If I cared while he was alive, I would have made the effort."

"I can't imagine what it was like or how hard it was to make such a decision."

"I wonder what might have happened had I chosen to raise him and defied my family. If I wouldn't have put him and his father out to begin with so many years ago. But after witnessing what happened in the Far Reaches...."

Jhee shrugged. "Some part of me still wonders if it was all worth it."

"I wouldn't trade my children for anything. I shouldn't have traded Naiman. But Vilmar knew the only way for them to stay was as servants or else risk having our secret exposed."

"It's best not to be too obsessed with past mistakes or it may consume you as it did Mr. Bastian and Naiman. Consider, for the damage he did, his efforts encouraged Mr. Bastian to find the cure. One which might never have been discovered without him."

"The error might never have been made without him. Vilmar's shoddy work caused this mess. A contract he would not have gotten if it weren't for me. He said I owed them."

Sentiments Miramar had expressed to Jhee often enough in person she had not questioned the faked letter. "The question though remains what are you going to do about it. Lady Delphine, you are smart and resilient. You will find a way out of it for you and your family."

"The same old Jhee. Always so affirming. Thank you for all your work."

"Flog yourself over if and maybe elsewhere. You'll find my sympathy strained to its limits. Thank us by using your remaining influence to save the clinic."

"Mumsy," Erma said, "what's this we hear about you and the Justicar being the sort who spent their time reading instead of attending the dances?"

Jhee and Delphine rejoined their charges. Delphine poured them the several glasses of melon drink. "Is that what she told you? Even though your denbe and I barely passed the parchment skin color test I told you about, they knew better than to invite two Trouble Makers like us. We spiked a punch bowl once. This one was quite the Trench Trawler. The way I remember it we didn't attend many of the dances because we were deep drunk in the graveyard from drinking bathtub squelch while reciting bad poetry."

Eventually, Vash showed up.

"You are looking well, Mirrei," he said.

"No thanks to you," Kanto retorted.

"I deserve that."

Kanto sniffed.

"May I have a word in private with Mirrei?"

Kanto opened his mouth, but Mirrei preempted him, "Whatever you have to say to me you can say in front of my household."

"First, Kanto, I wanted to apologize about my forward behavior. The revelation of my parentage knocked into me hard. All the lies, the betrayal. I simply wanted to see myself out of my mother's house and influence. I thought my mixed breeding might hamper my ability to find a situation elsewhere."

"So, you thought to 'ingratiate' yourself through junior spouses in order to join another family."

"Mirrei, Star, I just wanted to apologize to you for not being the man you thought I was."

"Would you give me more credit than that, please? I knew the man you were after our first walk with all your talk of finding a wife and abandoning the clinic. I needed someone to help me sneak away from denbe, and you served that purpose. Who you should apologize to are your patients and the community."

"I didn't think my lack of credentials should matter. It was only one or two courses. I was fully qualified. They were getting better care than they could have afforded otherwise. I thought what could it hurt?"

"It hurt. You hurt many people. Least of all me. I'll live, Vash. I'm rich, and I'll get the best care. What about your patients though? What are they going to do now? How can they ever trust anyone to help them again? Your foolishness and your stupidity nearly cost those people their lives. As if they don't have enough to deal with already. Did you even think about how this would affect them?"

"I know, Star. I know."

"Go, Vash. Don't come back here again. I don't want to see you anymore. Your sisters are welcome, but not you."

"Star."

Kanto rose and laid a hand on Vash's arm. "You heard her. She would like you to leave."

Vash turned on his way out. "It was selfish, I know. But I had to view lives like his up close. I had to know what my life may have been like if it had been me instead of him. I also thought I could help in the meantime."

Mirrei faced him. "Thank you for getting me and the others to safety. Thank you for your work on the cure, but I still need time."

Vash bowed and left.

Kanto reached out and touched Mirrei's hand. "You okay, Mirrei? I know that must have been hard for you."

"Spare the shark's tears, Kanto. You never liked him from the beginning."

Kanto recoiled then nodded. "Nevertheless, you did. The last outcome I want is to see you hurt."

Mirrei backed her mobility chair up and rolled out of the sea gardens leaving Kanto there to stare after her.

Jhee placed a hand on his shoulder. "She'll be fine. She'll come around. Mirrei needs some time."

"She's right. I should have been happy for her."

"You were right about him. Partially."

"That seems so unimportant now. I would be wrong if it meant she had one less moment of pain and distress over this."

Jhee pressed her esca to his. "This is what makes you such a good co-spouse."

The Sea Garden

In the mornings, Jhee had taken to doing her devotion in motion exercises in the hospital's sea gardens before visiting time. Occasionally, her husbands joined her. Though, she was alone when Inquester Paij arrived. They sat down for some morning tea.

"The mayor sent me to remind you she wants an autographed copy of your next 'Dispatches.' She also said make sure you portray her realistically and not as some clueless bureaucrat. To the mayor's point, have you considered writing up your more recent cases? How about 'Dispatches from Galleon City' where you'll follow the cases of a savvy, beautiful investigator?"

"You and she can't have it both ways."

The inquester chuckled. Jhee slid an engraved envelope across the table to Inquester Paij. "What's this?"

"A probationary club membership. You must wait a year and get another sponsor for full membership, but I'll know you'll manage it."

"What I would love is access to that quiet room. Does it come with that?"

"No, but I'm sure you'll manage that as well."

"Thank you. Though, 'Dispatches from Galleon City' has a nice ring to it."

"I have a suggestion, Inquester. Why don't you write up your own adventures?"

"I'm not a writer."

"Neither was I according to my critics. And from the feedback I get on those old stories, I never was or will be. One last matter, there's a group of children known as the Latchers who hang out by the arriving ferries. You'd be doing me a favor if you kept an eye on them. For a little candy and some change, they can be quite helpful."

Jhee and Paij had a pleasant tea where they spoke of everything except work. As their conversation wound down, Advocate Farkhande arrived.

"You shouldn't receive any flow back about the synchronator provided it's turned over once you're done with it. Ask your friend Lady Delphine to exert influence on your behalf if need be."

"There's much more beneath the surface with you, Advocate Farkhande."

"I'm just a well-meaning crank. Just like you're a harmless, bumbling, rural magistrate."

"On whose behalf were you acting as an intermediary with the observatory artifacts?"

"The only ones with a true right to see them. I have friends who enjoy the sea more than you."

Jhee held back a retort about that being a lower bar than Advocate

Farkhande might reckon. "Water nomads. If your head scarf were removed, what Makers' Mark would I find?"

"Not the one you're expecting, but good guess. And if I were to inquire about the scar on your neck or sigil on your arm?"

"Understood." Advocate Farkhande played with the ends of her scarf, but did not leave. "Was there something else?"

"I might need your intercession on another matter. The labor negotiations with Styrling have stalled. An arbitration is scheduled for later today to see if we can break the impasse."

"You wish me to use my influence with Lady Delphine on your behalf as well."

"Only if you feel comfortable doing so. Another quick, legal mind for support is appreciated."

"What if I side against you?"

Advocate Farkhande listened to the air. "The wisps say I can trust you."

Jhee scratched her esca which had itched. "The wisps, huh?"

Advocate Farkhande shrugged. The arbitration proceedings were already at full pressure when Jhee arrived. Nix and the mining pods were there along with Sianna, Inksy, Lady Delphine, and Folx United. The various sides yelled over each other. Delphine brightened at Jhee's presence and torpedoed towards her.

Wynne hobbled over on crutches. Her assistance in the mine had exacerbated her injuries. Jhee's expression changed to concerned. "This is just a scratch. I'll be back to jumping off buildings in no time. They're closing down the mine to cover up the incident."

Sianna and Inksy joined them. "Advocate Farkhande got her wish. The Styr Mine will be closed indefinitely."

"Are you two happy now?" Nix asked. "This is your doing Wynne. You and all your agitating, If your mother and father were here...."

"They'd be coughing their lungs out," Wynne finished.

Delphine clutched Jhee's arm. "The mining families that worked there and called our isle home for generations will be out of work. The mine closing is liable to hurt my family just as much. I can't survive just off the resort."

Sianna swept a hand at Wynne's side of the room. "All those mining families you claim to care about, out of work. Their communities gutted."

"We'll be alive and healthier," Wynne said.

Nix balled up her soft cap in her fist. "You think they'll see it that way. Your problem is you never think things through."

Sianna nodded along. "How do they work now? How do they feed themselves and their families?"

Jhee said, "Spare us your shark's tears for the miners routine. How long before you replaced them with strip mining and heavy equipment? You'd have done it already if you could. No one can stop the progress of the Divine

Mechanism no matter how much they try. It'll grind us all up eventually, you, me, the miners."

Wynne stomped her crutch on the ground. "You'd do better to bring the miners to the table than to spend so much energy on lies and intimidation aimed at holding back the tides of change."

Sianna narrowed her eyes. "I could say the same of you. Well, I'd say that just about concludes our business here. Thank you, Lady Delphine. Those melon drinks were quite refreshing."

24

STAR

~

The Shattered Image

Kanto held the door as Mirrei piloted her mobility chair into the villa. "Don't worry. I got this," he said.

Mirrei focused her gaze forward.

"Shep went back to oversee the last bits of getting our house ready. He's sure you will love it. The design already included assistance ramps and easy open doors to account for the mobility chair. So, even if you still require one by the time we leave, you should still be able to navigate around like an expert."

"That was very nice of him. But—"

"But what? I can't wait to see our new rooms. Aren't you excited to see yours?"

"Sure," Mirrei said.

Jhee brought Mirrei into the common room.

Mirrei lifted herself out of her mobility chair. Jhee and Kanto rushed to help her to the nearby chaise lounge. Kanto fluffed her pillow and made sure she was comfortable. He flitted around then said, "I'll return shortly."

Kanto went into the small kitchenette. Mirrei's gaze swept slowly over the suite, her expression neutral. Jhee's heart tightened. "On second thought, I'd like to spend some time on the patio."

"Of course," Jhee replied.

By the time Jhee had taken Mirrei out to the patio, Kanto returned with three glass dishes and the tiles set. "Look what I got? Iced fruit and cream. I

481

thought it might make a nice treat for when you got home. Don't you like it?"

"Yes, but."

"Don't worry. I cleared it with your doctors."

"Thank you."

Kanto scooped the dessert into their dishes. They ate their iced fruit in cream and played tiles with Mirrei immersed in an uncanny silence. Kanto continued to chat, but he would catch Jhee's eye with a concerned expression. However, whenever he spoke or faced Mirrei his face was always the image of cheerfulness. Mirrei's wasn't.

Mirrei tapped her utensil against the empty glass dish. She hummed a bit.

"It'll be about a long-tide before we head to our new home for good," Kanto said.

"That's nice."

"Mirrei, what is it?" Jhee asked.

"I don't." Mirrei placed her spoon down. "I won't be going with you."

Jhee took a deep breath. There it was.

"What do you mean you won't be going with us?" Kanto asked. "The doctors said you were fine to travel."

"I am fine to travel. That's not it. I—"

Mirrei looked at Jhee for support. Jhee just nodded her head.

"I won't be moving to the capital with you."

Kanto's smile froze in place. The corners of his muzzle twitched. "You're talking nonsense. Sleep on it. This is nonsense. You are talking crazy. A night's rest and you'll reconsider. You are still a little tired and unused to being out of the hospital."

"Kanto, listen to me."

"I am listening and what you're saying is preposterous."

"No, Kanto. I've thought about this for a while now. I don't want to move into the capital house. I just need some time to myself to think about what I want to do with my life."

"You can do that at the capital in our new home. Jhee, tell her."

"Kanto," Jhee said. "Don't."

"Tell her. Tell her to stop this foolishness, right now."

"Please, Kanto," Mirrei said, "this is already hard enough as it is."

"But why? I mean aren't you happy with us. I thought you were."

"I've been looking into the requirements for Imperial Academy of Medicine. They have a program, an internship."

Jhee caught her breath and tucked her hands inside her robes. This had been some time in coming, but still, she was not prepared for how much it affected her. Kanto stared at her. The plea for her to make it better, make it not true in his gaze. Jhee felt compelled to say something.

"We talked about you attending the Imperial Medical school in the past,"

Jhee said. "Our new home in the city is right by the Imperial Academy. There's a branch within easy travel. I mean you can go to the capital and enroll in the Imperial Academy. You can finish medical classes there and still come home to see us."

"I've been thinking about the clinic and all those people who will be without care. They fixed the mobility devices on the clinic. It can become a teaching hospital. They found another doctor to staff it. The new staff will take it up and down the waterways to treat the Fresh Lung sufferers who can't come to the city. They will bring the cure to them. I want to help them."

Kanto seized at the thread of hope. "You can help them in the capital."

"To what end? I've been cooped up and kept for so long. I was so scared of striking out on my own, but now I want to do something else. I want to see more of the world now that I'm cured."

"Don't worry. We can find another assistant willing to take it over. It doesn't have to be your responsibility."

"I want it to be my responsibility. The Imperial Academy has a study abroad program. The coursework I've already completed meets the requirements. I can take classes via conch like I've already been doing. We'll provide medical treatment, and while we do, I will pursue my medical credentials. My work on the clinic will count towards my residency requirements and practical experience credits. In the meantime, I'll be able to help people— help them in a way I never could before."

Jhee could not face Mirrei. She did not want her to think Jhee questioned her judgment. But she needed to at least try to preserve their family. "Are you sure this is what you want?"

"I don't want to be stuck at home again. Mamere kept me locked up in that dank, old house. I used to think, 'Of course, I'm sick cooped up in that house.' It was as if the sickness was in the walls. I wondered if it were cursed. I was glad when it started to sink, and we had to leave. I was so grateful to be gone from there. Once the gratitude wore off, I started to wonder is this all there is?

"I thought I could make this work, but I can't just move from her cage to yours. You can't imagine what a relief it is to know what was wrong with me has a name and more so could be cured. For the first time, I get to travel and see more of the world."

It dawned on Jhee she felt the same about her childhood home. For many years the richest and most prestigious families built their residences on the low-lying isles with plenty of beaches and shoreline; in a few places, even on Folk-built islands raised from the sea by mortal hands. That had been the Maker's Mark among the newly rich. Higher, rockier homes like her family's 'summer home' had been sniggered at and called ghastly, garish, gothic. Then came the Shield. In happier times before the feud, their family had acquired another home on one of those trendy mortal made isles. It was underwater now too. She now identified the emotion she felt the last time she had seen her family's waterlogged seaside manor: relief.

"Tell her she can't go, Jhee. Tell her." Kanto clenched the tile. He punctuated his words by jabbing it against the table as he continued. "Tell her, as her denbe, you order her to stay here with us."

Jhee faced Mirrei. Jaw clenched, eyes fiery orange and defiant, Mirrei dared her to do so; dared her to forbid Mirrei and to have Mirrei never forgive her thereby perpetuating the cycle. *"...she turned in time to see the towering wave bearing down on her. Defiantly, she faced it as it crashed upon our dock. That was the last I saw of her."*

The account of Miramar standing on the shore the raging ocean behind her savage winds whipping her hair about her had sold Jhee on the letter. It's how she wanted to imagine Miramar had died, defiant and as large as life to the end. Jhee had made a promise to her memory in the name of that image. Even if Mirrei had lied about that, Jhee owed Miramar, nonetheless. No. Jhee would not let her regrets rule her choices forever and continue to ruin Mirrei's life. The image of Miramar shattered in her mind to reveal only Mirrei before her. Jhee broke eye contact.

Mirrei nodded.

She piloted her mobility chair down the patio ramp to the garden. Kanto stared down the incline where she had left then turned to Jhee. His lower lip trembled. Kanto glared, hurled the tile down on the table, and stormed back into the suite.

~

The Sponge

"Would you mind another visitor?" Jhee asked after she poked her head into Mirrei's room at the villa.

"More geld for the Merry Maker," Mirrei said.

Jhee and Erma piloted Wynne into the suite. The building climber still bore bruises, cuts, and other lingering injuries from her beating at the substation. Jhee left them alone to talk. Soon after, Mirrei summoned her back.

"Come with us, denbe. We need you to help us conclude an investigation."

Not long after, Jhee and Mirrei entered the game room at Chappy's Underground Club. Mirrei had spent the whole ride on her conch, inviting all her activist contacts to meet her there. Quite a crowd had gathered to meet them. While Mirrei received warm greetings, Jhee's reception was much icier. A few fled. Most though fixed Jhee with horn glares or tried to crowd her. Jhee decided to just follow the young woman's lead. But despite the paperwork, Jhee readied to use her siren module just in case.

"Well, if it isn't the guppy and wife," Chappy said.

"Well, if it isn't the tattlefish," Mirrei responded.

"I presume you'll be swimming along upstream soon. Have you come to tell me the secret ingredient for your squelch? All my efforts have resulted in a brew affectionately likened to bilgewater."

"And let you continue to leech off the accomplishments of those better than you?" Mirrei addressed the miners and Weirs' Club. "Ask yourselves who knew where we would be that day? Who else knew the miners were meeting there that day? The Imps and Squids were waiting for us. Also, didn't it seem to you like we were targeted? Of all those who got arrested or got away, why us? They had opportunities to arrest others. They let them go to chase after us."

The Folx Uniter who had been suspected of murder at the fundraiser stood. "But the protest at the observatory fundraiser? He pretended to serve drinks to sneak us in."

"He convinced Semele to help. He was there dressed as a waiter not to help protesters but to meet with his handler, the mining rep. It was a trap to sell out the leaders. Whoever he let inside; he did to cover his exit."

"He rescued your group from the Squids," another remarked.

"Vash did that. It's what Chappy does best: misdirect."

"You're not going to believe this guppy, are you? She'll be here and gone with the tides. You know me. I'm part of this community. We're the ones who did the work, and no one is calling us heroes. How do we know it wasn't her?"

"On cue." Mirrei pitched her voice to the crowd again. "Did you see how deftly he did that? The substation protest wasn't the first time the Imps and Squids were a step ahead of you. Who was present every time your groups met? Who so generously offered his establishment for your use? He's a fake; a phony who filches others' accolades; a traitor to the cause."

"'The cause?' Are you the Justicar now? You're not unique. I've seen women like you before. Guppies like you are a pittance per school. You're a tourist who wants to be a great liberator; a faux activist. In a month, you'll be at the capital living the ether life having forgot all about the plight of the poor miners, the refugees, and the Fire Folk. Once you move on, the rest of the fish have to figure out have to survive your wake."

"He's right. I arrived yesterday and will be gone tomorrow. I can walk away anytime, but this is your lives. It's up to you what happens from here. I'll step back and follow your lead."

Click. Click. The gathering had gone silent. The activists parted. Erma assisted Wynne to the fore, her crutches clicking on the back room's floor. "Keep going, Star. You're doing fine. I saw you, Chappy, with the Styrling Mines duo, twice. Once, while I was sabotaging the loader. The second was at the substation protest action. I thought they didn't see me. Next thing I know, I'm getting jumped at our next action."

The crowd fell in behind Wynne. This merely confirmed what Jhee already suspected about the link between Chappy and Styrling. His establishments were the only ones that carried those clove candies. It also explained how he "slipped through their fingers" at the fundraiser.

Chappy hunched his shoulders. "The Ink's bounty was money too good to pass up. It beats shaking down small fish to have protests of their business stopped."

"Would you like to do the honors, dende?" Jhee asked.

Mirrei smiled. "With pleasure. Inquester, did you get all that?"

"Every word." Inquester Paij emerged from the crowd. "Chappy, you're under arrest."

"For what?"

"For extortion and squelching."

Lake, the fishing combine representative, and the travel writer burst into the club. "Imperators, arrest that man."

"He's already under arrest," Inquester Paij said. "Wynne, expect a visit from me later."

Wynne waved farewell with her crutch. "Looking forward to it, Inquester."

"Thank the Makers," Lake said.

"I can't believe we missed it," the travel writer said.

"You will still mention the fishing combines in your exposure piece, though?"

"Why did you want him arrested?" Jhee asked.

"Kidnapping and assault. The bar owner kept us locked up for days because we uncovered his involvement in misdeeds at the observatory. Levinia gave me the scoop, and we went on the quiet to ask around."

"Not quite quiet enough," Lake said.

"Wait, you were passed out at the bar when I dropped by a few days ago," Jhee said.

"Not passed out. Drugged," the travel writer said. "We must have gotten too close. This story will be just the break I need to stop writing travelogues and break into exposure journalism."

Lake took the travel writer's arm. "You said the combine's involvement in uncovering a scandal would get our work out there. You told me you already were an exposure journalist. That's the only reason I went with you."

The travel writer cleared hir throat, "I'm quite sure I didn't. I'm not responsible for what you inferred. Lake, didn't you have a proposal you wanted to bring to the Justicar and the miners?"

Lake screwed up his mouth then turned his attention toward Jhee.

"We heard about the mine closing. Well, one way you can save the mines… ask Lady Delphine to cancel her lease with Styrling and lease it to the miners instead. Make a mining combine like I'm trying to do with the fishers."

Erma shook her head, "Styrling would sue us both into oblivion. Wouldn't they?"

Jhee tapped a finger aside her nose. "Let me and Farkhande look at your lease agreement. I bet we can break it if they don't intend to mine. We can make a good case that they broke the lease by closing down the mine."

Miners clapped Lake on the shoulder. "Explain how these combine things work?"

Lake and the miners wandered off. The travel writer chased after them with hir recorder. Wynne chuckled.

Mirrei muzzed Jhee on the cheek. "You were right, denbe. That was fun."

Jhee offered her arm. "It's a classic and one of my favorite tricks. Wynne, that was brave of you. If you require help with any fines or fees related to your law-breaking, I'm sure Mirrei will step up. I'm sure her allowance can cover it."

Mirrei went wide-eyed.

"Don't bother," Wynne said. "I don't think anyone will press charges against me, and if they do, I got the fees covered."

At Mirrei's confused look, Jhee offered, "How do you think she's been getting access to the work site?"

Mirrei rolled her eyes. "Erma and Semele."

Wynne and Erma caught each other's gaze then looked away. "And you thought I was just using you for after hours access to the work sites?"

"Well, you were, weren't you?" Erma asked.

Wynne grinned, her eyes tinging pink.

$\sim$

Under Wraps

On the ride back to the villa, Mirrei was thoughtful. She gave Jhee a few hesitant glances before speaking.

"Denbe, you're very level and fair about things. Why do Fire Folk keel you off so much? Why are you so invested in the wall?"

"I fought the Fire Folk for many years, either in combat or stopping raiders, so did many in the Reaches. I've killed them. Befriended them." Jhee pulled back the sleeve of her robe to reveal several tattoos along with the command sigil on her arm. "It's hard to turn that off."

"We started it."

Jhee shoved her hands into her sleeves and pressed her palms together tightly. "Regardless of who started it, the situation is complicated. If it weren't for our navy and now the barrier, we'd be the ones serving them food and cleaning their houses. Maybe those of us left behind in their lands do just that. Maybe there, we wear the funny uniforms and are housed by the state. Or maybe they treat us with the compassion and dignity we can't quite manage for those left behind here. I'm not unsympathetic to their plight. They took their due. They hold the other continents. They carried off my family members. They took back their lands and then some. It is best for both our people to stay away from each other to the extent we can. We've earned our peace and I want no part of anything that disrupts that. I earned it with Shep's scars and mine and the lives of my sisters."

"I'm sorry."

"Don't be. Believe me, I also know the raiding went both ways, as did the trade. I don't know if they've stolen as many of our children as we did of theirs. It's different for the younger set I suppose. The wall's been up in some form most of your lives."

Mirrei bit her lip. "It's not just that. The distance, the respite from fighting has forced people to re-evaluate. So much about the past is coming to light and no longer sublimated. The Galleon City reconciliation project has all these records. Water Folk call ourselves the Makers' Criterions, but some of the things we did... Advocate Farkhande hinted that the previous policy regarding those Fire Folk who came here was worse. Was she was right?"

"They still call Other Folk who land or wash up on the shore driftwood. In gram-gram's day, there was a standing Imperial order to kill them on sight. And all Water Folk who traveled to their lands 'should henceforth consider themselves banished.' Those who sought return should likewise be killed."

Mirrei gasped.

"The policy had more lip service than enactment paid to it. Trade was the true concern of the policy, to limit the financial resources of rivals to the Dual Sovereign's rule."

"We were so cruel and then we were beaten."

"You wonder if maybe the Other Folk know something we don't. They're the winners. We're the losers. It's natural to want to emulate them."

Mirrei nodded.

"I never believed in the Pillarist Soothbringers' Ten Thousand Temples vision, a network of sacred spaces across the inhabited worlds dedicated to the Makers or the Seven Underwater Temples either. Enlisting is just what you did as your duty to the Empire and to show your pride at being Water Folk. Serving is also how you made a name for yourself. My family, especially had something to prove, not far removed as we were from gram-gram's piracy and gran's monogamist preaching. We had to wash the stink of disreputableness off our name."

Mirrei slipped over and hugged Jhee tightly.

Jhee ended the hug and patted her hand. "That's enough of that now. I just want the fighting to stop. And I don't know how we do that with both sides as bitter and dug in as they are. Maybe the Pillarists and their universal adoption of penance have the right of it. Neither side can make it right, but maybe we can make a new way. A new way to bring equilibrium to the system, if you are an example of our future."

Mirrei's eyes took on a shade between the pinking of embarrassment and brassiness of pride.

The transport pulled up to the villa. Inksy opened the door for them.

"We need to talk," Sianna said.

Mirrei paused and eyed the two mining company troubleshooters.

"It's all right," Jhee said. "Go inside. I'll be along shortly."

"Follow us."

"No, you follow me. We'll speak in the boathouse." In the boathouse, the pair looked around. "I assumed you've already searched here, and you have found no more data about the defense grid."

"We had to be thorough," Sianna said.

"I know. I saw your thoroughness all over the news and my shoes along with the ambassador's brains."

"We kept it quiet because of the panic. People wouldn't believe the problem was just some math error or shielding. Not to mention a male engineer made the 'error.' They would blame the use of male arcana. People's minds would go back to the Middle Pillarists. We couldn't take the chance of another Doombringer Uprising, once it got out that a male engineer no less, made the error."

Inksy crunched into her clove candy. "You stumbled onto something, Justicar, that few people are supposed to know about. The existence of MANTEL is a state secret, let alone any of the shareholders. As an officer of the court and a former intelligence officer, I can't impress upon you enough that it remain that way."

"I told you I can't stand the smell of those candies. Spit them out. Get rid of them," Sianna said.

Jhee waved them off. "May we skip the threats and flattery? How soon will 'the error' be repaired?"

"Almost immediately. You have our word. Eldjin-X just received a loan to buy out Vilmar's company. The Shield maintenance and any additional work will be done by Eldjin-X using a hybrid design."

"There is another matter we should discuss: how you weaponized Mr. Bastian's mistake. You deployed an experimental crowd control device on protesters, my wife amongst them; one based on the Shield's design flaw. It nearly killed her because she was already weakened by Shield exposure. It might risk the health of many Fresh Lung or Miners' Lung sufferers."

"Extreme measures on our part were justified. A mining supervisor was killed. We didn't know if it was miners or activists," Inksy said.

"The mining supervisor's death may have happened in multiple ways. Between her drinking, stealing, and gambling, she was on a self-destructive spiral. Bastian's notes had her listed as suffering from MLD, too."

Sianna interrupted Inksy's reply, "We can consider that 'experiment' a failure in exchange for your discretion."

Jhee had to accept it at that. She had pushed as much as she dared. Anything else she might do could cause a visit from the Abyssal Constabulary.

Before the pair left, Inksy pulled out a pocketful of wrappers and tossed them in the bin. A few of the foil wrappers escaped on the breeze. Jhee kept it to herself how the wrappers had marked places they had visited. She might need that advantage if the Path Maker crossed their streams again.

25

A NEW LETTER

~

The Cuttlefish

Mirrei was waiting for Jhee when she entered the suite. "So, how did it go?" she asked.

Jhee began changing into her night garments. "They're satisfied. I also got them to depth charge whatever they used on the crowd at the substation. For the moment."

Jhee flopped on the bed. "I think I'm going to clamshell up with a good book for the next day, then visit every gallery and museum I can before we leave."

It hit Jhee that the "we" no longer included Mirrei. Now she just felt awkward.

"I'm still getting used to it, too," Mirrei said.

"I take it you have no interest in visiting them with me before you leave."

"We can if you want."

"But, you really wouldn't enjoy it. Not like I would."

"But I would enjoy it, nonetheless. The same way I enjoy everything I share with a member of this household. Clothes and creative works to die for; soul nurturing food; arcane and legal brilliance; you even have a master thief. Everything this household does is excellent and comes from such a genuine place. All your caring does, every one of you. It didn't feel like an angle or that I was being wielded against another. I gave you each what you wanted. For you, a bookish companion and ingenue. I gave Kanto what he

491

wanted: a sister and model. Shep, I could never quite figure out if what he wanted was you or my mother."

"Bluer skies were never seen. Have I ever seen the real you?"

"More often than you might believe. That's how it works denbe, I find and amplify in myself the parts I think the person I'm with most wants to see. Do they want the party girl? The student? The sibling they never had? You were all so honest and genuine from the moment I first arrived. I began to feel sorry for taking advantage of you and intimidated. Then the fear and dread set in. Would you accept me if you knew? Ironic, as I didn't really know who I was myself. I had been playing a role for my whole life."

"That I understand too well."

Mirrei flopped on the bed beside Jhee.

Jhee propped herself up on her elbows. "Bookish companion? I guess your herbal knowledge didn't come about from texts and a keen interest in healing."

"Most of it. I read a lot as a child. There was scant else to do when they kept me trapped in that house or while waiting for my next doctor's visit. The rest, I had to pass the time somehow."

They shared a chuckle. Then a kiss, then a night in each other's arms.

THE DAY CAME for them to see Mirrei off and Kanto had still not come down. Shep glanced at his conch and then at Jhee. He had hurried back once they informed him about the course correction Mirrei extracted from the Path Maker.

"We'll give him a few more minutes," Mirrei said.

Shep pursed his lips. They waited a few more minutes. "I'll go see what's keeping him."

"No, I'll go," Jhee said.

Jhee and Mirrei found Kanto in his makeshift sewing room ironing fabric. "Mirrei has to leave, Kanto," Jhee said. "Don't you want to see her off?"

"No."

He drew his heated iron back and forth over the robes putting a crease in them so sharp you could cut steak with it. Mirrei entered the sewing room behind Jhee. She walked over and admired his work.

"I wanted to see you once more."

"If I had known it would be for a three-part look rather than four, I would have cut these differently and spent less time matching colors and prints."

"I see you've been working on a new set of robes."

"They were for you. The hems and sleeves required your detail work. I designed these pieces to complement your embroidery. Which much as I hate to admit, had just the right character to put them over the top."

"When I find somewhere new to settle, you can send them to me there."

Kanto stopped ironing. He picked up the robes. He looked her dead in the eyes and tore them. "These robes are for family. You're a stranger and thus entitled to none of the benefits of my work."

"Kanto, please."

"I had just gotten her to stop trying to send us away. Then you leave. I seem to be the only one trying to hold this family together. Am I the only one who likes the family we made?"

Mirrei stood defiant. "This isn't about you, Kanto. It's about me and what I need. I have to live my Make."

She grabbed his chin. "You and Jhee see me similarly: as a doll. For her, I'm delicate earthware, fragile, a legacy she has to protect. To you, I'm more of a mannequin for you to dress up as the sisters you never got to know. Is it too much to ask that you of all people be happy for me?"

Kanto picked up another robe and started ironing.

"I give up. What can I say, Kanto? I can't be your doll. I can't be the sister you never had. I can't be the friend denbe never reconciled with. I'm just me, the cuttlefish, the sponge."

Mirrei turned on her heel and left the sewing room. Kanto bent his head over the ironing board. A sob shook his body. Jhee walked over and lifted his face.

"I'll miss her too. We shouldn't keep her here if she doesn't want to stay."

He pulled away.

"We shouldn't make it easy either. She has to know you care. Fight for her. She's testing you to see if you'll fight for her and you're failing her."

"Mirrei is not you, Kanto. She's had a foot on land ever since the start. A fact I would have known before if I had listened to her. It'll be best for you to let her go with joy."

"I don't accept this. I won't. Is this about what's best for me, or your redemption?"

"Please, Kanto, you may only alienate her further. Read this, please. Mirrei wrote this while convalescing."

Jhee removed a letter from her inner gown pocket and rested it on the ironing board. A genuine letter written to replace the fake.

"'I'm a sponge. I'm a cuttlefish. Kanto wants a sister. I'm a sister. Shep wants a wounded creature to tend. I'm a sickling. You want a pupil. I'm a pupil. You two want a child. I am a child. My mother wanted revenge. I am revenge. I'm the healer. I'm the one down for the cause. I'm the pretentious heiress. I am the cuttlefish. I am the sponge. Forever changing myself to suit my surroundings. Soaking up everyone's expectations.'"

Kanto flattened it. After he gave it a once over, he returned to ironing. "Perhaps you should go as well and leave me to my work."

～

493

Strange Goodbyes

Jhee, Shep, and Mirrei transported her and a few belongings to the clinic. The rest of her belongings they packed for transport to their mansion in the city.

"Maybe you should donate them. I know many people who would love to have some Kanto originals."

"We'll hold on to your possessions just in case."

Shep hopped on board the clinic. He went over it from stem to stern. Its actual crew looked at him quizzically as he attempted to help them with the cast-off. Mirrei grinned.

"It'll do," Shep said. "I just wanted to make sure these dry landers knew what they were about. I also checked your quarters. I left you an emergency kit. And a waterproof instruction list from the Prepared Watchmen. It has some survival tips just in case you get caught or stuck somewhere. That way if something comes up, you'll have what you need to handle it."

"I also wrote some notes for cyphering exercises to keep your skills up," Jhee said and handed her two sheets of bio-film. "They should work in close quarters. You should practice for a minimum of half an hour a day. That should be enough to keep your skills up. The second sheet... A donation in your name to a refugee center, the Fresh Lung Research Foundation, and the Miners' Health Fund. I wasn't sure which was your favorite, so I donated to all three. I was going to buy a necklace or other trinket, but I figured you might enjoy this more instead."

"Thank you both for everything."

Mirrei hugged Shep. She stepped in front of Jhee and then pressed their escae together. "Goodbye, denbe."

"Goodbye, dende."

"I'll never forget what you've done for me."

"Don't make it sound so final. We're not divorced yet."

"If I need that to change, you'll be the first to know."

"Good. I intend to drive a hard bargain. And don't get complacent just because you are on a floating hospital. Monitor your salinity levels and keep up with your saline regimen. Who knows what the composition of the water will be like wherever you make port."

"Don't worry. I will."

Yelling came from behind them. Kanto stood at the edge of a pier. A water taxi sped off behind him. He waved, a box under his arm. With a disdainful look and wrinkled nose spared for the dock, he took a step forward. He took a deep breath, hitched up his robes then rushed down the crowded pier.

"Star. Star." Kanto stopped short in front of them. "Star. Star. I was afraid I missed you."

"You almost did."

Kanto gazed around the dock. "I guess you are serious about this, aren't you?"

"Very."

"If this is what you say will make you happy, I have to accept that. To be honest, I resented you a little when you first arrived. I had just married Jhee, and now she had another spouse who took away my time. I didn't want a denye at first. But then I got to know you. I never knew how much I wanted a denye until I had one."

"Like whales in a pod. Bonding over questionable mothers and a new wife uncertain of our new roles and our position in the household."

"I know. I was a clown fish. I'm sorry. You forgive me?"

"I don't know. What's in the box?"

"Star, you will love this."

"You don't have to call me Star. I think I'm done with that phase for now. Mirrei is fine."

"I didn't want you to leave without giving you this, Mirrei."

Kanto presented her with the box.

Mirrei opened it. It was the robe he had torn. He had patched it with more practical fabric.

"I turned it into something more suitable for your new role. It has detachable sleeves and a convertible hemline and extra pockets. Someone who doesn't know how to take care of her hems inspired it. All this fuss about clean hems, dirty hems. And vents under the arms for better airflow and temperature control. At least you can be the most well-dressed doctor or intern on this floating tub."

"Thank you."

"And you better call me, you hear? Every night. I intend to bend your ear every night. You may not live in the capital, but by the Lords of the Sea, you will hear every juicy bit of gossip I offer. And you dare not say a word about it."

Jhee laughed. Mirrei did too. Shep gave a curt nod which caused the two to break out into hysterics.

"I also wanted to let you know about a few charity events. They will provide supplemental funding for the clinic. You know what else, I've decided you are not the only one who can help people. Besides starting my charity for refugees and an activist bail fund. I will inquire into commissioning more of these tubs. That is if yours works out. So, you better make it work. Who knows how many other countless lives are depending on it?"

"No pressure."

"No pressure."

Kanto hugged her and whispered, "I'll miss you."

"I'll miss you too."

"Live your Make, dende."

"Always."

Mirrei gave a last look to Jhee as if waiting.

Shep gave Jhee a gentle shove. "Drenchit, Jhee if there is something you want to say. It's now or never. You might never get another chance."

Jhee tucked her hands in her robes at first. "What if I lied as well?"

"About?" Mirrei asked.

"Releasing you with joy."

"Tough."

"I don't know if I'm supposed to fight for you or let you go, but it matters to me you're leaving." Jhee hesitated then held out her arms. Mirrei fluttered her eye color through a spectrum of ambers. Jhee dropped her arms. "Not fair."

Mirrei touched her esca to Jhee's. "Jhee, your timing sucks. Maybe we'll discuss it when I get back."

Jhee smiled. "Maybe?"

"Maybe. That's all I can promise, for now, Jhee."

Jhee kissed Mirrei's slim hand. "Yes, my dear."

"That time I think you actually meant it."

The four embraced one last time.

Mirrei remained on the stern of the barge-like clinic. It lurched, and the crew with long poles pushed it away from the deck. The engines kicked in and began to froth the waters. The three waved at her from the pier. Even when she had left the stern, they waved and waved. She grinned and waved back at them. Mirrei oriented toward the horizon with a look of hopeful determination on her face.

The End: Book 2

Please, consider leaving an honest review on the bookseller's website, Goodreads,
or BookBub so others can discover Justicar Jhee—and tell all your friends to
download a copy as well.

ACKNOWLEDGMENTS

Adam C., Anne K., Elizabeth Frenette., Mark S., Val A.

Justicar Jhee
and the
House of Sorrows

-The Justicar Jhee Mysteries Book 3-

by Trevol Swift

To my secret weapon Adam.
To all my family's past and present service members. Thank you.

1

———

~

Living History

A seaweed-paper planner with several dates circled and a note reading "Pick one" awaited Jhee in her favorite chair. Jhee placed the planner on the end table and plopped into the cozy chair by the fireplace of their townhouse. The note had been written in Kanto's precise ornate hand. Both note and planner bore matching amethyst scalloped designs. The dates, Jhee presumed, were for counseling sessions. Kanto had been getting treatment for the lingering effects of his ordeal at the abbey. The process had prompted him to get on Shep and Jhee about their own neglected mental health and hygiene. Jhee admitted with a veteran's service center so nearby she had no excuse not to avail herself of her earned aid. But she had so much work to do between the academy, the law clinic, and consultant work.

Shep settled into the cushioned chair beside hers. He plopped a similar planner on the end table with hers.

"Where did he leave yours?" Jhee asked.

"On my exercise equipment. I have to give him points for persistence and knowing his targets."

"Could he be right? Perhaps we need to talk more about our experiences during the Flower Wars."

"Or how close we came to losing Mirrei."

"I'm not sure if I need the extra stress at the moment."

"Right or wrong, we agreed to be more open about our service, among other things."

Jhee rubbed the bridge of her nose. "I know. We should have just said 'no' if we didn't want to do it. Part of me wants to do it."

"And part of you wants to let the Trench swallow the anchors of the past."

"Yes."

Jhee and Shep brushed *escae*, the four-pointed, iridescent Makers' mark Water Folk bore in the center of their forehead. She briefly touched the scar that ran through Shep's right eye, which made it dimmer than the other. They nestled back into their chairs.

Between counseling and the reconciliation and living history projects, Jhee and Shep had over-committed on a topic they rarely spoke of in-depth: their service. Had keeping their experiences to themselves been proper or had doing so made it worse? Jhee extended her hand into the space between their chairs. Shep clasped it and stroked her knuckles with his thumb. Not long after, humming announced Kanto's return.

"*Denme*," Kanto said and squeezed Shep's shoulder. Then he planted a kiss on Jhee's lips. "*Denbe.* I see you both got my little reminders."

Kanto draped himself in his fireside seat opposite theirs. The embroidery on his amethyst and citrine robes echoed the decoration of the planner and note.

"Subtle," Shep said.

"Never," Kanto said. "So?"

"Give us a moment, we're still coming up with excuses to put it off."

Kanto grinned and shook his head, then hopped to his feet. "You two are incorrigible. Dearest wife, dearest brother-groom, when you come back from your night out, I expect the most amazing tale ever of why two are breaking your promise to me."

Shep grimaced. Jhee took a breath. Kanto knew how to hit them where it mattered. Shep and Jhee seized their respective calendars, circled their dates with finger quills Kanto provided, and handed them in to him.

Kanto peered at the calendars and nodded. "Excellent. Enjoy your evening out."

Once Kanto left, Shep and Jhee turned to each other.

"Drench, he's good," Shep said and raised an eyebrow.

They laughed.

For their night out, Jhee and Shep chose a gourmet restaurant a short transport ride away.

"Elaborate about what we ordered," Jhee said.

"Green beans almondine with a light caramelized butter glaze served alongside pan-seared whale-auroch with water chestnuts in oyster sauce with just a hint of truffle oil."

"Land meat? Are you sure about this?" Jhee asked.

"Trust me," Shep, her senior spouse, said. "The chef gives it a quick sear to seal in the flavor, then covers it just slightly with juices and simmers it in a covered pan."

The waiter arrived with their meals in short order. Shep took the eating utensils—knife and nail pike—sliced a piece of the red meat, and used his index finger to spear it with his nail pike. His teeth clinked on the pike as he slid the juicy morsel into his mouth. Jhee tensed and held her breath. As she watched for signs of an involuntary shift, her fingers hovered over the fail-safe sigil on her arm. It remained cold and inert.

Shep swallowed. "Delicious."

He sliced another piece, then held it out to her. As she took a bite, they held each other's gaze. The tender whale-auroch had just the right amount of sear and seasoning.

Jhee had not had meat this rare in so long. She had indulged when she could during her stay in Galleon City, but Mirrei's ethical concerns put the damper on any enjoyment from the experience. Jhee found it hard to savor the meat while her youngest spouse watched with mild distaste.

"The trick to the perfect plate is not dissimilar to the trick to a perfect pour." Shep shimmered his amber, glowing eyes at Jhee. "Then there is the pairing of a wine to complement a brilliant meal. They have a lovely tasting selection for each course. They also have an exclusive house red I wanted to sample."

After the meal and several glasses of excellent wine were consumed without incident, Jhee's worries had dissipated. Despite the location, she and Shep indulged in hand-holding and a few kisses. Mere months ago, as a field Justicar in a rural district, she would have been scandalized to publicly carry on in such a way. In the capital as an academic, though, no one batted an eye at her behavior.

A few doors down, they visited a family-run zoba tea place crammed next to a darkened shop offering tailoring and shoe repair. Their introduction to the tart and tangy beverage was easily one of their best discoveries since moving here to the capital. The capital rarely seemed to sleep. Even now, pedestrians and transports moved by them often. This activity and closeness was a contrast to the ocean expanses of their former home in the Far Reaches. Though, when a Storm Wall fueled gale hit the Reaches, it made even full-sun's bustle appear tame.

Jhee swirled the zoba berries at the bottom of her lidded, clear tea bottle. "How fortunate I am to be surrounded by such experts with respect to food and drink."

"Want to know another aspect of the perfect meal?"

She passed the bottle over to Shep, so he might have the last sip. "What?"

"The right companion." The smoldering tint to Shep's amber eyes suggested they should pay and make their way home. On the sidewalk, Shep swept Jhee into his arms and planted a kiss on her in full view of Makers and masses alike.

A man with a messenger bag and delivery logo on his jacket jostled them as he passed.

"Oi, sorry fel," the messenger said and patted Shep's robe a couple times.

As the man walked on, Shep immediately checked for his wallet, keys, and digital conch communicator. Jhee and Shep both recognized the old pickpocketing ploy. Shep removed his hand from his inner pocket and gazed at a glinting object in his palm. The command sigil on Jhee's arm switched from normal to burning hot.

Shep bounded after the messenger then grabbed him by the lapels and pinned him against the building, all with frightening speed. "What is this? Who sent you?"

"A *gul* just paid me to plant it on you as a gag."

"Who?"

"A gul. I don't know—an older lady with graying hair, maybe a little nervous."

"Shep, enough. Let him go."

Jhee got Shep to release the messenger. Shep held up his hands and backed away a few steps. While he paced like a caged animal, Jhee checked the messenger for injuries. The messenger had sustained some slight scratches and a bump on the head. Jhee apologized and also slipped the messenger a twenty-shell note.

The messenger rolled his head from side-to-side while rubbing his neck. He whispered to Jhee, "Your mister's got quite a temper there. Maybe he should see someone about that."

Shep fixed his good eye on the messenger to let him know Shep had heard that. The young man swallowed and scurried off. Jhee waited until the tempo of Shep's pacing slowed.

"Mind telling me what that was about?" Jhee asked.

Shep opened his palm to reveal a miniature representation of a kalacha war club, the preferred weapon of the berserker regiments. "Someone has a poor sense of humor."

"The berserker corps regiment pin. Who would send that to you?"

"I don't know." Shep's nostrils flared, and his eyes narrowed at something over Jhee's head, but he did not go on full alert. "Someone's there. The scent seems familiar."

Jhee turned. "Who's there? Show yourself."

～

The War Buddy

"Hey, *guls*, I see you got my message," a hesitant voice said. The figure of their old war buddy Ursula emerged from a shadowed doorway. She wore her hair in a slick ponytail. While her jacket was too baggy and loose-fitting, her other clothes appeared well-fitted, new, and clean, unlike the last time Jhee saw her some years ago. Overall, Ursula came across less frantic than their previous meeting. However, her gaze never settled in one place for long.

"Ursula!" Shep swept her up in a big hug and spun her around. "Urli-bird! You old sneak."

"Sorry if my message upset you."

"You could have delivered it yourself."

Ursula shrugged and kept her gaze on a constant move. "Too many people. I'm not doing good with crowds these days."

"Understood."

"You two, though, are looking good."

"It's all surface waves, we assure you," Jhee said. She and Ursula hugged. "How are you doing?"

"You know. Hanging in there."

"Come on. Let's all go for a walk. We can catch up."

"Sure."

They grabbed another round of zoba teas then went for a stroll through the park along the lakebed. Few people would be there this time of night. They reminisced. Several times Ursula paused as if she wanted to say more.

"I owe you, Urli," Shep said. "What's going on? Why did you have a regiment pin planted on me?"

"I had to see your reaction. It was stupid. I didn't mean to upset you."

"Forgiven. I can't count the number of times you saved my skin over the years."

"Or you mine," Ursula answered. "So much has happened since we last spoke. I wouldn't even know where to start."

"Whatever you need, ask," Shep said.

Shep handed Ursula back the regiment pin, but she refused it.

"Keep it as a reminder," Ursula said.

Shep glanced back at Jhee. He frowned. That sounded like "goodbye" to him as well.

Ursula stopped to give them a long once over. "I still can't get over how good, how together, you two look," she said.

"You know how it is," Jhee replied, "the cozy life of an academic and civil servant. What are you doing for work these days?"

"A little this. A little that. I'm in a similar line as you were, Sniffer, private inspector work, and the like."

"My field work isn't so far in the past. Is there anything else we can do for you? Do you need a place to stay?"

Ursula smiled. "No, I got that covered. That's just it. For the first time in a long time, I can see a way through. I'm here to check in on you two. Thanks for the offer, though."

Shep pulled up his collar. "We're good."

"I guess that means you found your way through, too. The last of the unit, except Cap. It's been so long since more than two of us have been in the same place together."

Their walking slowed. Jhee allowed them to get a half a step ahead. Jhee had been their unit's liaison and wasn't a berserker, a war-trained full skin slipper, like Shep, Ursula, and the others. She accounted it an honor they viewed her as part of their unit if only partially.

Ursula glanced around her. "I have to get going."

"Make for Make," Shep said, invoking the tradition of hospitality in exchange for the berserker pin. "Take our private c-cards. Contact us if you need anything. Please."

Jhee handed over a numbered credential card to Shep, which he put together with his and a hand-carved shark's tooth. He touched them to his *esca*, Makers' mark, before presenting them to Ursula.

Ursula took the pin back long enough to touch it to her esca then stuffed Shep's offering in her coat. She turned to Jhee and pulled an object from the devotional pouch at her waist, likely Maker geld. Jhee dug out a geld coin she had stamped with the gear emblem of Jhee's path, Mechanism, which she brought to her forehead. Perhaps the Prime Maker's design would guide Ursula to the other side of her difficulties unscathed.

After Jhee and Ursula exchanged coins, Ursula seized her in an embrace.

"The Makers have blessed you. Don't forget that." Ursula refused to release Jhee immediately. "You enjoy the rest of your evening," Ursula said.

At last, Ursula released her. Jhee examined the small, smooth object she had been given. It turned out to be a circular, hardwood disc carved with the batfish or maye. While Jhee did not remember which specific Makers Ursula honored, she knew it wasn't the Maye King or Queen. The maye, though, was Ursula's preferred berserker form.

"Urli?" Jhee began.

Ursula had already slipped away. Jhee and Shep tried to locate her but lost her tracks by the lake along with her scent.

At home, Jhee and Shep concluded the evening in her bedchamber. Before turning in, Shep went downstairs to grab them some iced sweetberries and cream. Jhee tidied up their discarded clothes along with others she had strewn about while getting ready for dinner. A shiny, jet black data shell clattered to the ground. It may have been one of hers or her students from the legal clinic. She threw it in her valise for later. Jhee took out Ursula's hardwood disc with the maye and wondered.

The Curious Academic

Days later, Jhee still puzzled over Ursula's visit and hardwood disc carved with the maye. The batfish or batwing maye was a sizable cartilaginous fish similar to a shark. Ursula used to leave this symbol to mark trails when scouting. Ursula had marked a trail for her, but to what? A few long-tides—weeks—passed, and Jhee all but forgot about it. She settled back into her regular routine of lecturing, advising the Academy's legal clinic, and giving arcane forensic seminars.

"We conclude from these records that the person was murdered," Jhee said. "Or more precisely, there is a high likelihood of their having been poisoned. And that concludes our virtual autopsy. Questions?"

Jhee signaled her teaching assistant to increase the lecture hall's lighting. Several hands in the arcane forensic seminar raised. Nevis, her colleague from the local Justicar's office who had been sent to evaluate the symposium, gave a grudging nod from the front row then scribbled on her evaluation sheet.

After the seminar, Jhee checked the time and gathered up her materials and slides. Plenty of time remained for her consult with the imperators and then refresh herself before tonight's evening out with Shep. In her haste, Jhee knocked over her valise and lecture materials. As she gathered up her fallen valise contents and slides, the jet black data shell she found the other day caught her eye. Following several failed attempts to decrypt it at home, Jhee thought to have someone at the office or clinic try. She stooped to pick it up. A floorboard creaked on the other side of the lecture bench.

Jhee grabbed the data shell and straightened up. A Water Folk individual standing by the lecture bench leaped back. She eyed Jhee and waited, hat clutched in her hands, looking sheepish. "Begging your pardon, Magistrate."

"Did you have questions about the seminar?" Jhee asked.

"Nay." Jhee gave the stranger a once over. Her clothes were threadbare. She continually twisted and worried the brim of the hat she held around in a circle. A sharp breath of the sea wafted from them. This was not a typical student or attendee. "This ain't about tome learning. You sees, a mutual friend gave me this card. She reckoned you might could help me."

The slight accent and pale body hair were peculiar to longshoremen and sailors from the Dales nicknamed sea dogs. The old sailor handed Jhee a credential card. After a quick inspection, Jhee realized the sequential number matched the one she had given Ursula.

"I have to head to my legal clinic. Walk with me." Jhee grabbed her valise, and she headed across the quad with the sailor. "What can I help you with?"

"I suspect this sea dog what I know be a med divisioner," she said using the sea dog dialect.

"I see," Jhee said cautiously. By "med divisioner," she meant a member of the Medical Protectorate. Between renewed interest in the Flower Wars and Medical Protectorate's recently uncovered unethical experiments, an obsession with war criminals had wormed its way into the popular consciousness. Folk had begun seeing them in every flower bed and suspecting every reclusive neighbor. "Have you brought your suspicions to the imperators?"

The sea dog handed her a copy of the complaint. "They laugh me off. I wants be sure before me goes back. I follow't along with your arcane detecting talks and be read your 'Dispatches from Arrow Point' adventures. Might I use some cypher or whatnot to prove me true?"

Jhee wrangled a few more details out of the sailor, but nothing that rose above the level of general war criminal hysteria. They arrived at the legal clinic where Jhee's grad students were sorting the files the Inquesters had brought with them. Consulting with Inquesters, the investigative ranks of law enforcement, comprised the other part of her new Justicar duties in the capital. At first sight of the Inquesters' insignia, her walking companion stopped short.

"Well, mum, many thanks for your time," the sea dog said and turned tail.

Had it been a generalized distrust of law enforcement officers that sent the sailor fleeing, or did she have more specific cause to avoid them? Hopefully, Jhee hadn't handled the card or incident report too much to get usable prints from them. Jhee tapped a finger aside her nose and proceeded to her consultation. A grad student handed her a stack of case files, and she went to work.

"There could be no denying it," Jhee said after examining a few reports. She peered through her magnifier at the images. Because of the lividity and bluish lip pallor shown in the images, Jhee suspected poison. Several victims' skin and body hair also bore pinkish blotches. This pattern seemed familiar. Jhee consulted the diagnostic tip sheet she had compiled over the years and compared it to the victims. Once she determined the cause of death to be poison, she had reached the end of her official mandate as consultant. All that remained was to turn her findings over to the local constabulary.

"Not all of these folk died of natural causes. You may be looking at a Maker of Death situation here. The calibrations and the alignments are key. Calibration: no common industrial link prior to their hospitalization. Alignment: all these victims show exposure to a rare pesticide present nowhere in their environment. This is a pattern I've seen before as a field Justicar in the Far Reaches."

"Folk can be so predictable. They always think they are so clever and have committed the perfect crime. They think they will be the ones to get away with it," the investigator said.

"Quite right," Jhee agreed. She tidied the bio-parchment printouts and handed the files back to the grateful investigators along with the clinic's and her grad students' findings.

"Thank you, Justicar. With your help, hopefully, we have enough to put this gutter guppy away," said the partner.

"My pleasure, Inquesters. Drop by anytime you need my help."

Later, Jhee might ask Shep what he thought. She had no doubt of her conclusion but missed talking through cases with him. Jhee pulled out her conch and recorded a summary of her notes. She double-checked her determination for good measure. Her notes concluded with the recommendation that a full murder inquiry be undertaken at once.

The Inquesters thanked her again before they left. Jhee basked in the sense of accomplishment.

Another conclusion expertly reached, but the job still felt half done. The urge to do more than make a determination had Jhee drumming her fingers on the case folder. She snatched up the folder again. Why give them the cause of death when Jhee could also give them the murderer? Jhee started running down the local suppliers of said pesticide. Only a few manufacturers produced it, but it had been prevalent amongst the older families. The pesticide mimicked the symptoms of a heart attack and was hard to detect. Until Jhee had helped discover additional markers that differentiated the pesticide-induced heart failure from a more typical one. With their favorite means to hide their crimes less effective, many in her home district switched to some form of direct violence. While the pesticide had a commercial use, it was an artifact being kept alive mostly via the Trench market by murderers. Had she single-handedly put a whole industry out of work? The Wolphin family from her home district might think so.

Unintended consequences. An interesting conundrum for another time. Jhee paused for humility's sake. This was not about her patting herself on the back; it was about getting justice for those who had no one to speak for them but her.

According to the wall-mounted clockworks, she had some time before she had to meet Shep for dinner. Jhee laid out the data shell, the card, and incident report. She plugged the data shell in and started another decryption protocol on it. While it worked, Jhee played with Ursula's disc.

Jhee continued to go through her files and review death records. A banded bruise on a body with the cause of death marked as accidental made her pause. Banded bruises like these often came from fingers. She projected the autopsy images and notes on the wall. She re-checked the cause of death and the findings on post-mortem lividity. With this heavy bruising and these injury patterns, how could someone have called this an accident? This person was badly beaten.

The coroner who called this an accident or natural causes had to be blind or corrupt. Some coroner late for a dinner or event took the word of a family member or authority figure. Jhee grabbed her conch to query the coroner.

She noted the time. A few minutes and she might be able to tell which one this particular coroner was, and then she could hurry to meet Shep with time to spare.

Jhee now took her time and carefully went over the autopsy findings. She pored through reports from the time the body was found until autopsy. As she did so, she recalled Jeja's lessons on first principles and smiled. *Don't assume. Let the evidence lead.*

Sometimes the mortuary staff mishandled bodies, and without due diligence, post-mortem damage could be confused for pre-mortem. The logs showed no discrepancy. No mentions of anyone dropping the body. No gaps in the timeline. If the marks didn't come from post-mortem mishandling, that made it more unlikely this man died from an accident.

Jhee brought up full-dimensional images of the victim's body. Blunt force trauma to the head, contusions: she examined each injury's characteristics. Other bones showed evidence of old breaks and fractures, not all of which had set properly. From the depressed knuckles and metacarpal fractures, she determined this man might have been a pugilist of some sort.

A check of the fighter's lists, public records, and footage proved him not an extremely good or popular one. From his record, a minor one. He had a few low-level bouts, which he had all lost. He acted as a meat bag for up-and-coming fighters and a sparring partner. No fortune and glory for this one, his story ended in some dirty alley, and the injustice of his death may have gone unnoticed without her due diligence.

Jhee dictated her findings. *Should she investigate this one herself?* She checked his records for family. None. The matter had kept this long, and no one was breaking down the door to solve it.

This was not Jhee's mandate, and she was not a field Justicar anymore, she told herself. Her duty was in the lecture hall or lab like she had always wanted or to consult as the Empire required. She had gone from the assistant of the intrepid Jeja of Marpele to a bureaucrat and academic. This had always been the Path Maker's plan: the original course for her life, a position in academia. She slipped off her fingernail ink reservoir and laid a finger along her muzzle. Jhee missed the old days when she solved the crimes and judged them by her lonesome, but her life had changed. She longed to see a whole case through and not just review others' findings. This had to suffice. She had a household, a family to consider. Though, she might ask Shep, with his greater anatomical knowledge, his opinion on the autopsy injuries.

Family. Shep. Jhee viewed the time with horror. Her conch chimed, and she answered.

"Jhee, where are you?" Shep asked.

"At the legal clinic. I lost the time."

"Get moving. They won't hold our reservation much longer."

She grabbed her valise and dashed out the door.

2

―――――――

～

The Caretakers

From the moment Jhee left her office, it was as if the Maker of swift travels conspired against her. Maintenance and construction delayed the routed transports. When she went on foot, she found herself caught up in the chanting crowds. Had she missed notice of a game, concert, rally, or other gathering happening at the university tonight?

A viewscreen Jhee glimpsed through a window displayed empire-wide protests over the latest revelations of the Medical Protectorate's atrocities. Morbid curiosity held her transfixed. The Medical Protectorate's Surgeon General had committed suicide after tests proved the grisly remains uncovered on Knifefish Island were related to the Haddondeep incident. Jhee closed her eyes. Deep inside a lock within released. A sense of ease and relief diffused through her. One architect of the Medical Protectorate's abuses, a caretaker of the House of Knives, was dead. Jhee walked the rest of the way in a daze.

When Jhee reached the grill, Shep frowned at her from the sidewalk. "They gave away our reservation."

"Dear one, I'm sorry."

"It took months to manage this. This is one of the best chefs in the Empire. During her soft launch." Shep sighed. "We might be able to get a table at the eatery up the street."

Jhee hung her head. "Wait, let me fix it."

"It's fine. Just forget about it."

Jhee wanted nothing more than to make this better. She strode into the restaurant, past the line of diners waiting for a table, and approached the grillery hostess.

"May I help you?" the hostess asked.

Jhee affected her most official attitude. "We had a reservation."

"Of course, you did."

"Justicar, party of two, reservation for last-sun."

The hostess glanced at the time. "It's first-moon."

Jhee pointedly displayed her family and academy signets. Then, as she rarely did for personal reasons, she removed her billfold and brandished her Imperial Justicar credentials. "I know. Isn't there something you can do?"

The hostess flashed her umber-hued eyes and continued to appear unimpressed. If it weren't for the paperwork it would entail, Jhee would have used her siren module to command the woman. Instead, she displayed an instant note for fifty shell.

After the hostess consulted her seating chart and reservation listing, she said, "We had a cancelation. I can get you a table for two in the back. That's the best I can do."

"Thank you."

Jhee motioned for Shep to join her. A waiter led them to a table near the kitchens. Shep frowned. They sat down to their meal. They browsed the menu together, and Jhee, as usual, took his suggestions.

Every time Shep attempted to explain some nuance of the meal, a member of the wait staff burst out from the swinging kitchen doors with a plate of steaming hot food. Shep's mouth turned down at the corners, and eventually, he dropped into a sullen silence.

Jhee wracked her brain for a conversation topic other than the *dendes*—her junior spouses Kanto and Mirrei—or work.

"I located a rare collection of items from an estate sale. I believe it possesses some personal effects from one of Thaedra's students. Apparently, she was quite the cryptologist. The collection may contain the rudiments of what later became the first set of cyphering windings and gyrations. It'd be interesting to see how it all took shape. Many have a conception of arcana having sprang fully formed from Thaedra's head. Instead, from what I've learned, it was a collaborative effort refined by her with the help of her students. It's like what I want to do with the clinic and my teaching. If I could have just a tiny fraction of the impact on my students as she had on hers…. I don't know. I'd consider it one of my life's greatest achievements."

"Waiter, salt," Shep said. Jhee swallowed her wine as the scandalized waiter hurried to comply. Drench. Adjusting the seasoning of another chef's food. Shep was more keeled than she thought. "Is that what you were doing instead of meeting me for dinner?"

"No. I got preoccupied by some unusual cases… The Architect of Sorrows committed suicide."

Shep tensed. "So I saw. I had trench all to do while you kept me waiting."

Shep sank into an even deeper silence than earlier. They passed the rest of their meal without speaking. She picked up her glass of wine. A waiter bumped their table, and she nearly dropped the glass.

"I know this wasn't quite the night out you had in mind."

"Jhee, I told you about this *months* in advance. You knew how important this was to me. The head chef did a live cook demonstration."

Shep pushed food around his plate with his nail pike. Jhee folded her napkin in her lap and gave him her full attention, so he knew he was being heard.

"I had everything planned. We had seats front row center to the grill. Right over there." Shep jerked his thumb at the centralized grill in the middle of the room, now long cold and practically empty. "I had wanted to see the chef create a meal for months. We would be in the center of it all." Shep sighed. "Never mind, it's fine. Let's just finish our meal."

Once they finished eating, Jhee paid, and they left without saying much more.

"I understand how disappointed in me you must be, Shep. I'm sorry."

"The tardiness and absences are worse than when you worked in the field."

Weariness laced through his words. Jhee had no idea what else to say. When she went to take Shep's arm, he barely noticed. This passivity disturbed her more than if he had been loud and belligerent.

"Shep, please, yell, scream, something, just don't withdraw."

"Hey, guls," Ursula's voice called. Ursula's sallow gaze regarded them from a face haggard and bruised, unlike when they saw her last. Stains and small tears marred her clothes, while the tie on her ponytail barely held. "Did you see the lead item on the news? One down, a dozen more to go."

"Would that the rest of them were all dealt with so easily," Shep said.

"Makers make it so."

The two spat.

"You're looking more... wave-worn since last we met," Jhee said.

"Well, you know how it is. I haven't been sleeping much lately. I wanted to thank you guls for your Makers' blessings. It helped more than you know."

"A sailor came to see me at my lab about some med divisioners. They said you sent them."

Ursula's face became even more gaunt, and her gaze darted about.

Shep frowned at Jhee. "Come, have a bite, and a good night's stay at our place. There's a veteran's service center right up the road."

"You know I hate those places."

"Can we get you a ride somewhere, maybe?"

"No, thanks. I'll be fine."

Ursula seized both in a hug. "Until we are all remade," she said, then scampered off.

Shep stared after her long after she left.

"What do you suppose that was about?" Jhee asked.

"Don't know. I won't be good company for the rest of the evening," he said. "I'll call for a transport to bring you home."

Shep went to the edge of the transport lane and took out his conch. She turned to him when the transport arrived. He assisted her into it then shut the door before she could argue. The transport sped her home.

The automatic lights turned on when Jhee stepped into their townhouse's sitting room. She found Kanto asleep in her chair.

"Mamere, mamere," Kanto murmured in his sleep.

Jhee laid her hand gently on his shoulder. Kanto started awake. "Why are you sleeping out here in the dark?"

"I must have fallen asleep after talking to grandmamere."

"And how is the Lady Kaydence?"

"Ornery as ever."

Kanto's shiny, golden eyes dulled as he drifted into reverie.

Jhee said, "You were having a nightmare about your mother? Today is the anniversary of her death."

A disappointed expression came over Kanto's face. "I was hoping Mirrei would call. She must have forgotten with her hectic path as an activist healer."

"She will. I'm sure she had a good reason." Normally, Jhee might have said she would talk to Mirrei about being more considerate and not defended her third spouse. But after the muck Jhee made of this evening, paying lip service to scolding Mirrei was a feat of hypocrisy even Jhee couldn't accomplish.

Kanto glanced at the clockworks and yawned. "Where's denme?"

"Trenched if I know," Jhee said. She took a breath to calm herself.

"But you went out tonight together?"

"He needed to blow off some steam."

"Because you let matters slip again."

"Not exactly. Partially. Yes. We'll talk more about it later."

Kanto rose and offered her his arm. "Perhaps, what we all need is a good tuck away?"

"Perhaps what you need is someone to talk to about your mamere? I'll have tea brought up."

~

Bars and Hammers

Should I track Ursula down? Shep thought. Despite what she said, Ursula may have needed a friend as much as he did right now. She had been a big help to him when he first arrived. It was she that had referred him to the exposure therapy group, which had broken him of his extreme reaction to raw, land meat. Ursula said it had done wonders for her and might do the same for him, one of the many debts he owed her.

Shep caught up to Ursula. "Urlibird, how are you doing, really?"

"Better now that folk like that are no longer in the world." Ursula jutted her chin at the scrolling text relaying the details of the Architect of Sorrows's death. "Now, if only they could reach the rest of them."

Ursula's face became shadowed, her eyes smoldering orange. Shep touched her shoulder. "Why did you take off so fast last time?"

"It doesn't matter anymore." A manic light replaced the shadows. "Not when there's so much work to be done."

Work? That did not sound like the Urlibird Shep knew. "When was the last time you went for a run?" he asked.

"I've been trying something different. Come with me."

Ursula and Shep caught a routed transport to the seaport district. Shep gazed out the transport widows at the ever-wakeful city, and it's spindly, impossibly tall buildings that hid the sky and horizon.

After Jhee and the *denyes*—his co-spouses—left Tranquility Bridge's abbey, Shep had stayed a few more days. He availed himself of the peace and solitude of their garden. He slipped his Folk skin and ran the bluffs with Dari, his therapeutic shark hound companion. With Jhee not around, he even did some cliff diving. When the time came to leave, instead of taking the barge to the capital, he hopped a steamer where he worked as a member of the crew. It had reminded him of the months he spent out to sea as pre-jubilant, learning the diving trade. He had left the Far Reaches a scrawny kid with corrective lenses and came back a stout diver and one of the best swimmers in the whole district.

Fight. Protect. Survive. The old berserker mantra kept going through Shep's head. It had a clear, simplicity to it—clarity he sorely missed. Shep turned over this evening's events from Ursula to his anger at Jhee again and again. One thing he did know was the absolute last thing he wanted to do now was talk. A good run might clear his head. He had not had one in a while, and neither had Dari. Even that did not feel like it would quell the storm raging within him. This place did not afford him the space and privacy to go all out as he might have in the Reaches.

This city did not move right. Shep barely felt connected to the waves and the sea here. Perhaps it was that they were so far inland. How could Jhee and the others not notice? Whatever the cause, Shep just felt so boxed in. Is that what was affecting Ursula? Many accepted into the Skin Slipper program had come from the Empire's outer rim islands like the Reaches. Ursula was one of the few inland berserkers he knew. Maybe it was just some aspect of their berserker nature, which would never be at ease amongst the ordinary folk?

When was the last time Shep felt at ease on this strange isle? He did not have to think long to come up with an answer: the retreat. While Jhee and the *denyes* had stayed in Galleon City, Shep went ahead to get their home ready. At least, that was the excuse he gave. What he had done besides that was seek treatment because of his losing control at the abbey. He stayed on a few extra days at the abbey, then sought counseling meant to get his berserker instincts under control. No matter how it happened, Shep could not allow another incident like that.

Ursula led them to the docks. His fur raised at all the random toughs milling about. Some paced. Some toked smoke root. Others sat still and tensed watching the others with shifty, watchful gazes. His hackles rose. Berserkers. A foghorn sounded in the distance. The gathered berserkers snapped to attention.

The shadow of a ship loomed large over the dock crowd. A gangplank lowered for man and a woman to disembark. They assessed and sorted the group.

The couple led the selected folk, Shep and Ursula among them, up the gangway to the deck. The transport ship carried them beyond the harbor to one of the most extensive mobile gyms and obstacle courses Shep had ever seen. Shep fingered his facial scar as he inventoried the set-up: grab bars, rope swings, wheel runs, climbing walls. He whistled.

Ursula smiled. "Better, right?"

"Amazing. What's the hitch?"

"I did some work for the owners, and they let me use the place whenever I want. I can even bring a friend. Tonight, that friend is you."

A little while later, Shep and Ursula sparred. The freighter pair pointed at and consulted about various folk using the equipment. They came to a stop in front of Shep and Ursula. "Skin?"

"Maye," Ursula answered.

They gave Shep a once over, pausing on his scarred face. "What about you, gorgeous?"

Shep fixed them with his good eye. They were asking the easiest skin they slipped into, their base skin. "Orcinus," Shep answered.

The orcinus or the whale crusher was a hulking black sea mammal covered with white splotches. The man did a double-take. A smile widened across the woman's face.

"Excellent," she said. "Don't get many heavy-class. We'll find something for you."

"Best reinforce the equipment first," the man said.

While Shep grabbed a swig of water, he saw them slip a few notes to a solidly-built Water Folk with straw-colored hair and missing a chunk from one ear.

Some time later, the transport ship returned to bring everyone to the docks. Berserkers slunk off into the night. After the blare of the foghorn signaled their hosts' departure, Shep, Ursula, and a few stragglers lingered, wondering what to do next.

"What'd I tell ya?" Ursula said.

Shep stroked his scar, ashamed he had enjoyed hitting the heavy bag so much. "I needed that."

Someone bumped into Shep nearly, knocking him off his feet.

"Out of the way, pup shark," the half-eared Water Folk growled.

"You bumped into me," Shep said. He felt a twinge of anger at the use of "pup shark." A name that hit too close to home.

The man gripped his gym bag strap and puffed out his chest. "Oh, really. Are you looking for an apology?"

Shep shook his head. "Just forget it."

Shep turned back to Ursula. A hand grabbed his shoulder and roughly spun him around.

"Nobody turns their back on Hammad the Hammerhead."

"Hey, gul, sorry. It's all good," Shep said though he felt the faint stirrings of annoyance. He had just reached equilibrium again after his recent upsets. He held up his hands.

"What if I say it's not?"

Hammad the Hammerhead poked his finger in Shep's chest.

"Tell you what, gul. Why don't you let me and my friend buy you a drink?" Ursula said.

Hammad hesitated then fixed a mean expression on his face. "Hammad the Hammerhead buys his own drinks."

The remaining berserkers had gathered around them. Clearly, Hammad was spoiling for a fight. Shep wasn't about to give it to him. He must keep his violent impulses in check. Besides, he already imagined having to explain himself to Jhee and Kanto after having brawled like some stripling.

"Come on, Ursula. Let's leave."

Shep patted Ursula's shoulder, and they began to walk away.

"Nobody walks away from Hammad the Hammerhead."

Shep's senses narrowed to the sound of Hammad's gym bag dropping and a shoe squeak. Shep and Ursula dodged in opposite directions. The slow, clumsy haymaker punch missed them by leagues. When his fist failed to connect, Hammad caught himself before faceplanting. The brute glared from Shep to Ursula, picking his target. A menacing mask settling in on Hammad the Hammerhead's face informed Shep he had made his choice. From the narrowed eyes when his gaze settled on Shep, Shep had a fraction of a second's warning before The Hammerhead lunged at him with a yell. Shep brushed aside the charging brute.

The Hammerhead's face reddened at being denied again. "What sort of berserker are you? You run like a coward. Fight. Protect. Survive."

Shep sighed and squared up his fighting stance. "I'm not running now."

The Hammerhead grinned. He matched Shep's stance, and they circled each other. Hammad the Hammerhead went right into a series of hooks and jabs, likely the set up for a decisive body blow or uppercut.

Shep had a moment to react when he caught the telltale signs of the wind-up. He hopped back. The miss overextended Hammad again. Shep caught the vulnerable arm in a lock, which brought the Hammerhead to his knees. As the Hammerhead struggled to free himself, Shep made fast his hold.

"Stop struggling, or you'll break it," Shep said.

Hammad made a groan of impotent fury. His eyes smoldered orange rage at Shep.

"Raise your chin," Shep said. Hammad complied. "Higher."

Hammad raised his chin higher. Shep drew back and knocked the man out cold. The berserker crowd cheered and jeered. Folk bore him and Ursula off to a bar. After several rounds, silence fell over the bar. Hammad the Hammerhead filled the bar doorway. The patron's parted as he lumbered toward Shep. Shep rose. They stood just an arm's reach apart.

The Hammerhead grinned. "That was magnificent! Get this man another drink. On me. Hammad the Hammerhead buys the drinks."

Shep reacted with dumbfounded paralysis as the man crushed him in a hug then ruffled Shep's hair. They spent the next hours drinking themselves stupid. By the time he and Ursula stumbled out of the bar with Hammad in tow, the three had taken to singing sea shanties at the top of their lungs.

Their singing and camaraderie caught the attention of two uniformed imperators on patrol. Hammad the Hammerhead took loud exception to this and did what he did best, started a fight.

~

The Man or The Beast

Some friend of Hammad's showed up and spoke to the imperators' wallets. Both parties to the transaction had taken it in stride. "See you in a few days," Hammad said once they were released.

The sleepy friend, a woman, approached their gang of three. "Is it too much to ask at least one long-tide go by where I don't have to come out here?"

Hammad grinned.

The woman rubbed her eyes and looked at Shep. "Who might you be?"

Hammad answered, "This is Hammad the Hammerhead's new chum."

The woman fluttered her eye color in frustration and offered Shep a credential card. "Counselor Medea, caseworker from veteran's outreach. Here's my c-card. If you keep hanging out with him, you will need it. Now, I'm going back to the center to get some sleep."

Shep tucked away her card. "May I ride back with you?"

Counselor Medea sighed. "Fine."

In the meantime, Ursula had slipped away again. Shep paced in the transport car, surprised he, Ursula, and Hammad had not ended up in jail. At last, he sat down.

"How'd someone as even-keeled as you hook up with the Hammerhead?" the counselor asked.

"A fight," Shep answered.

"Of course."

"You work at the veteran's center? I live near there. I kept meaning to go."

"Why haven't you?"

"Those places never helped me."

"What did?"

"I used to love diving.," Shep said. "I was a great diver."

"What happened?" Counselor Medea asked.

"I had to stop. My wife became deathly afraid of the water. We couldn't dive together anymore. When I went out on my own, I'd return to find her pale as a morning mist, waiting up for me. She didn't used to be that way. I remember when we were younger, how much she loved the water, even until secondary school. The whirlpool of fate stole her joy of the sea from her. 'What a thing to see, a Water Folk who hates the sea.' I poured my efforts into being a great husband."

Then it was as if a dam within Shep had burst and expressed his frustration about the night and the move to the capital. The counselor nodded along and interjected supportive or clarifying comments. Eventually, she yawned.

"Excuse me. We'd be more comfortable at the center." Counselor Medea dropped into a mumble, "Padded chairs, fresh-brewed kolal. A chance for me to review your case files during decent hours."

The counselor scribbled something down on a bio-film sheet, then handed it to him.

"What's this?" Shep asked.

"A veteran's retreat. Gardens. Sea views. Great diving. Other berserkers to talk to. You just get some quiet time with other folk who might know what you're going through."

"I just came from a monastery like that."

"Where I can sense you felt calm and at peace."

"I did. It didn't stop me from going into a frenzy, anyway."

"It happens from time to time. What you have to decide is if you will let that possibility rule your life forever? Decide which you want to be more: the man or the beast. Then find a way to reconcile that choice. This is my stop. Please, I encourage you, stop by the center."

Shep refused to meet her gaze because he knew how unlikely that was to happen.

"Right, not helpful," continued Counselor Medea. "How about this? Exercise with your dog or therapeutic companion at the section nearer the center. Join the center's pet walkers' group. Maybe you'll even be tempted to go in."

Shep nodded, though confused how she knew he had a canine companion.

"Dog hairs," she said.

Shep almost laughed out loud. One would think after all these years with Jhee, he would recognize that trick by now.

"Who knows? Maybe we'll run into each other some time?" Counselor Medea said and exited the transport.

The light from the first dawning of the lesser sun had just illuminated the world when Shep carefully slipped into the house via the kennels. He crept up the backstair making as little noise as possible.

Jhee would know he hadn't joined her in her chambers. Hopefully, no one would know he hadn't slept in his rooms either. Shep checked the hour and winced, as much from his bruises as the time. He had a barber's appointment with Kanto soon. Shep had to find a way out of it. If Kanto saw him like this, the young spouse would run straight to Jhee.

Last night's events still fresh in his mind, Shep removed his shoes. Generalized anger at nothing and everything still had him in its grip, and he was not sure if he was ready to talk with Jhee yet. It had been so much easier to express himself to a virtual stranger. The time at the gym with other berserkers had done him good, too. He had needed to hit something to let off steam.

Shep had just reached his door when her chamber door opened. He pressed against the wall out of sight. Kanto emerged, followed by Jhee.

"Everything will be fine," Jhee said.

"Thank you for letting me stay," Kanto said. They embraced a long time then touched escae.

Shep's dander rose until he realized he had his excuse, his pretext. He revealed himself.

"Denme, morning," Kanto said with a warm smile. Shep puffed up his chest. Kanto and Jhee's smiles faded.

"Shep, I know what this looks like," Jhee said.

Shep growled then slipped into his room. He slammed the door, pressed his ear against it, and listened.

"He doesn't think we…" Kanto began.

"I'm unsure," Jhee answered. "I'll talk to him later and explain the situation. Let's give him some re-centering time for the moment."

Aim achieved. A twinge in Shep's side reminded him of what state he was in. Shep showered and performed field healing on his bruises until they had mostly faded and were no longer tender. As long as Kanto, or especially Jhee, did not get too close for the next day or so, they'd be unnoticeable.

3

~

The Invitation

Lunch the next day dragged by in awkward silence. Jhee monitored Shep for signs of violence. Her arm sigil tingled with the residuals of his anger, but it remained at the same intensity as it had since the previous night. Even when he had seemingly caught Jhee and Kanto being unfaithful, the sensation had not increased, although the sigil had been less of a barometer of his mental state lately.

The day schedule was the chosen mechanism by which their household operated. Other cohorts had their arrangements, this one was theirs. From breakfast to breakfast, each day of the long-tide belonged to one of Jhee's spouses except the last, which was an open day. On the designated spouse's day, Jhee spent time exclusively with that spouse unless otherwise agreed or an emergency occurred. Jhee and the day's spouse decided upon their activities together, though she usually deferred to their favorites. They became her primary consort, and the others, especially in romantic terms, became friends. The last was where the misunderstanding had come in. There was leeway, but it had to be mutually agreed upon, or else it was considered a violation of trust. Their family decided Jhee would not be a snipping thistle crab hopping bed to bed throughout the night.

Shep had yet to let her explain. Jhee stuck close to Kanto's side just in case. It served multiple purposes. One, to be there in case the young man still needed someone to talk to; two, to selfishly use him as an emotional buffer between her and Shep; three, a precaution if Shep instigated a delayed quarrel with him.

The door chimes rang. A moment later, their housekeeper, Irina, informed them an imperial messenger had arrived. Kanto bounded to a standing position and adjusted his dressing gown. He shook his head at both Jhee and Shep's appearance. With barely contained excitement, Kanto shooed them out to the entryway.

The messenger's livery was of the finest make. He dipped his head and held out a silver tray bearing a bio-film invitation which had been expertly folded into a flower shape.

Once Jhee had taken the invitation into her palm, and her credential ring lit in response verifying its authenticity, the messenger spoke, "Sirs, my Lady. On behalf of the dual thrones of Emperor and Empress of the Blessed and Glorious isles of the Empire of Narhiya, you are invited to attend the Imperial Electors at their Summer Sojourn held at the imperial resort on Sovereign's Isle in two long-tides."

"An invitation to the imperial resort," Kanto said.

The messenger raised his head and waited. Drench. Jhee glanced at Kanto's excited expression and Shep's annoyed one. She had little choice. The invitation was now or never. Marital difficulties would not be accepted as a reason to refuse an invitation to the Imperial Sojourn.

After Jhee touched her credential ring to the message's response plate, Jhee unfolded the invitation and went through the formality of reading it in full. The messenger bowed, then took his leave.

"It's so exciting, isn't it?" asked Kanto.

"Thrilling," Shep replied.

"I've got to get to work on new outfits for us. We'll need a whole new long-tides worth of clothes. I'll need to hire assistants; there's no way I'll be able to design and finish a new holiday ensemble for us in time. These are such problems to have."

"We'll leave it to your expert judgment."

Kanto clapped his hands together in happiness, then summoned retainers. Jhee watched Shep to gauge how he viewed the matter. He shrugged. She supposed that was an improvement from his breakfast demeanor.

"Of course you will," Kanto said. "Color schemes, patterns. Oh my. I just happened to have received bolts of custom fabric back from the textile shop. You both need to give me your opinion on it. I designed a new house insignia and colors based on the combined motif of our houses. I think it's quite clever if I do say so myself. Also, we'll need to do some briefings so you can have a rundown of the players before we get there. No need to start an Imperial incident."

"I need to work on my lesson plans," Jhee announced. At least, Kanto was looking forward to this. She would have to have another instructor fill in for her. Usually, it would not be a problem this late in the academy year, but she had signed up to teach some courses in the extended season.

"Dari and I will go for a walk," Shep said.

"Let me take your measurements before either of you go anywhere," Kanto said. "Then, we'll have to do fittings."

"Perhaps later," Shep said over his shoulder. He grabbed the leash and headed for the kennels. Kanto waved him off.

While Kanto measured Jhee, she worked through her lesson plans on her conch. The house buzzed with excitement.

A delayed message from Mirrei arrived. It glitched and warbled.

"Sorry… Tried several times to get through." The skies behind her were dark, gray, and overcast. Half the message lost itself to the storm. "I really think I'm doing some good here. Miss you muchly."

The message cut off. Kanto hummed a bright tune now as he measured Jhee. Jhee glanced out the windows of their home to the clear skies and near-constant lack of storm clouds. The capital really was like its own little bubble. She smiled.

Kanto and Mirrei had found their paths. Jhee gazed down the hallway to the kennel. Shep, however, seemed more adrift than ever, and she did not know what she could do to reach him.

Shep had been keeping his own counsel more and more as of late. They used to be able to talk. Maybe not about everything but more than this. Was it being cooped up at the capital that was doing it? Or the visits from Ursula? His time in the service, in the berserkers, was catching up to him in a way it never had before. She had thought he had adjusted well, but maybe that was because they were just so far away from society in the Far Reaches. Here they were in a large city, one of the busiest in the empire. This many people living on top of each other may have been too much for him.

"I think I have what I need for now," Kanto said, in buoyant waters, after the message from Mirrei. "If you hurry, you can catch up to him."

"Thank you," Jhee said.

Kanto shook his head, already furiously at work in his sketchpad. "So much to do. So much to do."

Jhee walked up the mahogany steps to her room. The house was brilliantly appointed because of Kanto's excellent eye. She paused briefly at what they had intended to be Mirrei's room. All of her belongings sat still neatly wrapped. Jhee was not sure if she should have them unpacked and put out. It seemed like wasted effort if she would have to send them along elsewhere. Mirrei had still yet to mention if she had wanted a divorce. Somehow their calls always ended before it reached that point. Jhee, though, preferred to prepare herself for the inevitable.

She dressed and caught up to Shep and Dari at the park. Jhee spread her hands in askance. Shep offered his hand. Jhee took it, and they touched escae while Dari looked on, tongue lolling in seeming approval.

"You are wind and waves, my lady of the Isles," Shep said.

~

Departure

The intervening long-tides between the invitation and the departure date for the sojourn rushed by on rip currents. So fast, Jhee still found herself working on lesson plans and presentation materials the day they were set to leave.

"Jhee, what are you doing? We're going to be late," Shep said.

"A few more minutes," Jhee said. "I have to finish this lesson plan."

Along with her lesson plan, Jhee had spent a lot of time studying Saheli's last sermon. True, it had influence from the fell text, but it did not account for the whole of the formulations. They were innovative. She verged on calling them revolutionary. Jhee's experiments with her siren module and templarite dust were at a critical stage. After her experience in the mines of Galleon City, she deduced her module used templarite in some fashion. It reacted similarly to the synchronator regarding the mist. If she could have had just a few minutes to try out some fabrications...

Then there was the stack of case consults she had to sort through. She still saw those Albatross files. She opened up the file packet for another quick peek. Perhaps, something new would jump out at her that didn't the last time.

Shep blocked her conch screen with his hand. "You know how Kanto gets. We were supposed to be ready for his final inspection by now."

"He's worse than our training inspector. I have to get this done."

"You should have managed your time better." Shep shook his head and put on his sashes. He tugged at them while frowning. "I'm not sure I like these color choices. Don't you think they are a bit brash?"

Kanto gave a rhythmic knock before breezing in from the adjoining room without leave to enter. "It is a perfectly good complementary color palette. I already toned them down. If you think they are too much, wait until you see some of the flamboyant colors of the other houses."

Kanto stopped dead when he saw Jhee was still in her dressing gown. Jhee swore under her breath and braced for the admonishment she knew was coming and deservedly so.

"You're not even dressed?" Kanto turned on Shep. "Why isn't she ready? You said you would see to it."

"You know how she can be. One more lesson plan," Shep answered.

"That's what she does. Always one more experiment, one more derivation, one more puzzle. We keep her grounded, so the other things don't slide."

"I'm right here," Jhee said.

"Good, so you are hearing the tongue-lashing my denme is getting, which rightly should be yours. Now finish up quickly."

Kanto flounced down in the chair next to her, looking profoundly piqued and bored.

"I can't with you hovering over me. This will go much faster if you just go get Shep ready."

"Shep is ready. We're both ready. Everyone is ready except you. After you get dressed, I still need to touch up your hair and trim your nails."

"I have to get this done. Go on ahead without me."

"We will do nothing of the sort. The resort is close to Emperor's Isle. Two males can't wander about there, let alone arrive at a court function without their denbe. Without notice of intent papers, we'll be stopped every fifty feet or worse detained if you aren't with us. It would serve you right if the two of us were added to the imperial companion collection."

"Oh, all right."

Shep gave her a smug smile. Jhee typed with one hand or narrated into her conch as Kanto and Shep helped her dress. Eventually, she handed her free hand to Kanto so he could begin manicuring her fingernail claws.

Now and then, Jhee forgot and attempted to adjust or scroll something with her "free" hand. He refused to let go. Once he had finished trimming and painting the first hand, Kanto switched to the other. He slapped the back of her finished hand every time she attempted to lift it off the table. Now, she had no hands to use to finish. Shep chuckled before he left to oversee the servants and their luggage. Eventually, she sat there with both hands flat on the table. A firm flick from Kanto greeted any attempt to move.

Jhee waited quietly, watching her lesson plan's sample cypher derive. The conch had been left at an odd angle, so she had to strain her neck to monitor its progress. She leaned over and painstakingly used her nose to move her conch into a better viewing position while her nails dried.

Kanto wrinkled up his snout. "Really, denbe?"

Jhee grinned. "I couldn't see it."

They burst out laughing. Shep returned to the room. He saw them sitting there with Jhee's freshly trimmed and lacquered hands clasped in Kanto's. Shep shook his head then exited. Jhee and Kanto burst out laughing again.

"I heard from Mirrei again," Kanto said.

Jhee sat back and smiled. "Me too."

"She wants to set up a remote meeting for after we return." Kanto looked smug. "She tries to hide it, but I think she misses us."

"I think she does, too."

"I never doubted it for a moment."

Jhee raised an eyebrow.

"Maybe for a moment. I haven't told her about the work I've been doing at the center. I wanted it to be a surprise. When she calls again, I'll tell her all about it."

"She'll be thrilled."

"I know. I told her I was proud of her. We're in a good place right now, I think."

"Let her know what an inspiration she's been to you and your philanthropy work."

"Good influence on me? Hey, I started it all back at the abbey. If it weren't for me, she would still be lying abed like some wasting whelk."

"You know, *dende*, one of the many things I admire about you is how humble you are."

"I know." Kanto stood. "Now, hurry, so we won't be late."

Jhee's conch beeped to indicate her derivation had finished. The fabrication station beckoned Jhee. She almost grabbed her tools and started working immediately but remembered at the last moment about her freshly manicured hands. She held them delicately as if covered in goo or slime and stepped away from the fabrication station. Far be it from her to ruin Kanto's gorgeous work!

Shep entered the room again. "Yav-yav, everyone. The transport will be here any minute," he bellowed in his military voice.

He grabbed her conch and walked out with it. What could she do but follow? Her hands held up, Kanto somehow put a coat on her without so much as brushing her nails.

The amphibious transport arrived at their manse promptly at mid-dusk, the time after the elder sun had set. Realizing she had forgotten her tabard, Jhee turned to retrieve it. Shep intercepted her and escorted her into the transport.

They spent the transport ride to the pier politely nodding as Kanto tried to brief them on the power players while interspersing a lot of court gossip. She should have learned her lesson about paying attention to these, but it was so dull.

Jhee and Shep made eye contact. He gave a slight smile, knowing exactly where her thoughts must have been. He knew her so well.

"Are you two even listening to me?" Kanto asked.

"The vizier from Graydale hates crustaceans," Shep said.

"No. He is in a feud with the Cetaceans over a broken shipping lane contract."

"Right. Right."

"I won't be able to do all the talking there." Kanto frowned and clutched at his robes. "If either Shep or I so much as make eye contact with the wrong woman...."

Jhee touched Kanto and Shep's hands. She recalled now why she detested these imperial functions so much. The Imperial grounds were like stepping back centuries in time. Yet, Kanto enjoyed the opportunity to mix with the Imperial family. "You know I won't let anything happen to either of you."

Jhee's arm sigil warmed. Shep had, also, straightened up while watching the assembled nobility.

"What is it, Dawn Wolf?" Jhee asked using Shep's outside name, a social name for use outside the home in mixed company; now become quite old-fashioned.

With a shrug, Shep sank back into the cushions. "I don't know. Just thought I saw someone I know from the gym."

"It's not impossible," Kanto said. "Imperial consorts have some odd pastimes."

Shep worked his jaw. "I didn't say it was them."

A tingle from the sigil grafted to Jhee's arm and bound to the brand on Shep's neck indicated his distress. Jhee rubbed each husband's nearest arm in turn to ease the growing tensions. "It could be just someone who looks like them."

"Perhaps you're right," Shep said.

Kanto took a breath. "Please, esteemed spouses, I know the gossip seems a bother, but take heed to these trifles anyway. Wars spring from less."

"All right, denye," Shep said.

"Now, the scuttlebutt in Graydale..."

Graydale, also known as Greater Dale, was the largest of the Dale island group, another group of rim islands like the Reaches where Jhee and her household had grown up. And like the Reaches, it supplied numerous Folk to the war effort. Her thoughts returned to the sea dog who suspected her neighbor was a war criminal. First Ursula, then the sea dog, it must be catching.

The transport pulled up to the pier. Jhee and her husbands joined the other dignitaries lined up to board the Imperial yacht to the Imperial Isles.

~

A World Apart

A dedicated group of Imperial porters greeted each retinue upon their arrival on Sovereign's Isle. A taupe-colored woman porter whose arm bore a band with Jhee's house colors and crest gave Jhee a slight bow.

"Welcome to Sovereign's Isle, my Lady Justicar. I am Pela. It will be my team's pleasure to serve you during your stay."

The woman made a discreet gesture, and her team of porters spirited away their luggage. Meanwhile, Pela escorted Jhee and her husbands to a covered beach skimmer equipped with iced mango punch. They sipped punch as Pela narrated the island's history and pointed out various land-marks. The tart punch with a hint of citrus tasted almost the same as Jhee remembered. One sip transported Jhee back to summers at Hillside with grandmamere and gram-gram. By the time Jhee's household arrived at their quarters, porters had almost completed furnishing their rooms and unpacking according to the detailed instructions Kanto had sent ahead of them.

"Allow me to show you to the hall of alcoves so you can make your devotions," Pela said before Jhee could ask to be shown to their shrines.

The hall of alcoves contained many and sundry variegations and representations of nearly every Maker, great and small, Jhee might name.

"How many Makers do you worship here?"

"It's hard to say, my Lady Justicar. Hundreds, perhaps. It depends on who currently occupies the isle. I believe you'll want to visit the First Makers architraves, then I'll allow you to pick which variant of Futou, Lashae, and Pascoe to commemorate."

"You have more than one shrine to them?"

"Dozens for each."

Jhee performed her First Makers' devotions at the pillars and basins under the enormous architraves. She gave offerings of the four elements to the trio of sky, earth, and sea, plus the Unknown Maker. The eyes of more than her ancestors watched her. The more of this sojourn she saw, the more of a backwater rustic she felt. Mechanist devotions were much more personal, and she would perform those in private later.

The rest of their first day at the sojourn saw them attending a series of lavish receptions. Lengthy feast tables bore fare of every description from any isle one might name: Laruscan pork, Dalesian watercress, aged Valerian cheeses, rare Chalumet wines.

Similarly, the guests hailed from every corner of the empire. They brushed metaphorical fins with Findari, commonly known as Water Nomads, nobles, and teal-eyed, blue-black complexioned imperials. The dark skin-tone implied high-born ruling elites while teal eyes meant they had Fire Folk ancestry or had resided in the Scorched Lands long enough for their eyes to change.

The clothing ranged from simple wraps and pullovers to glittering dresses with elaborate embroidery. And then, headwear. The headdresses ran the gamut from scarves and jeweled turbans to hats with outrageous fascinators or brims so wide even Jhee's mentor, Jeja of Marpele, known for her impressive hats, might weep at the sight of them.

Jhee and Shep went about trying to mask their astonishment, while Kanto introduced them to all the right people. As the junior spouse, he could not have pride of place on her arm, but somehow still managed to call the tune.

"We should suspend the schedule while here and let Futou guide our play," Kanto said, and they agreed.

While Jhee and Shep may have been the veterans, this was Kanto's battlefield. Shep held back half a step and let Kanto walk by Jhee's side. It was his night, but he knew it would make a better impression if she walked in with the gorgeous, decked out Kanto. Shep would present as a protector spouse, but Kanto was the showpiece with his impeccable grooming and flawless body lines. His steps were graceful and lithe. He never overtook Jhee at any point. He never spoke to anyone except without her presenting him to them and speaking first. Kanto gave her subtle nudges as to who and when to introduce him to someone, a slight tug in the direction he wanted to go or a gentle touch to her elbow. He led her through the political maze, with no one being the wiser. She made occasional eye contact with Shep to check in on him.

By the next day of the sojourn, fun and games, Kanto had secured them a weirs match with the Vizier of Finance and the official in charge of trade.

After a rousing game, the vizier asked, "Now, Justicar, what is this I hear about you having one of the lowest overturn rates in the circuit?"

Jhee inclined her head, and they clasped forearms. "Not much to say about it other than that. That was in my field work days. Now, I'm strictly an instructor and consultant for the Justicar Annex."

Kanto took Jhee's arm. "Denbe is being modest. She also had one of the lowest requests for appeal."

"Indeed?" the Vizier asked.

"Yes, Vizier."

"Is that terribly hard?"

Jhee answered, "It can be. A lot of reviews are triggered by unsatisfied litigants. I usually did my best to explain to my litigants the full extent of my ruling and also mete out a fair punishment."

"I'm inclined to think a criminal never views their punishment as fair."

"Not in the main. However, it is rare for a criminal to commit their crimes out of a wholly criminal mindset. Many crimes are done by people at their limit or desperate, justified or not. The crime is their way of trying to fix an imbalance in their lives."

"Denbe is being too modest," Kanto said.

"Tell her about the opening," the trade official urged.

"Oh, yes. I have it on good authority one of the chief reviewers of the judicial archives will be stepping down soon. She will need to be replaced. The Chief Justicar will be putting in an appearance at the sojourn, I'm sure. You might want to talk to her when she arrives."

"We've never been introduced."

"I'll introduce you. She's currently in the process of screening nominees and considering replacements. With your record and reputation, I'm sure you would be a logical successor."

"Thank you, Vizier. I look forward to the meeting."

"Care for another match, Justicar?"

"I suppose I could let you embarrass me again. You are one fierce player."

Kanto beamed at Jhee as they walked back from the weirs field. He took her arm. "See, this has already been a productive trip. Aren't you glad we came?"

"Perhaps."

"We are at the Imperial Sojourn, teeming with a surprising number of eligible companions. Not a bad place to catch the imperial eye."

"I thought we settled this before, Jhee."

"I meant for me."

Kanto slapped Jhee's arm. "Being one of what—ten, twenty spouses—would be an improvement in either of our situations, how? I can barely deal with being a second, let alone a tenth. This is not to be squandered so."

"I stand corrected."

"Duly so."

"What if I'm not speaking of improving your situation, but one of companionship, solely for your benefit?"

"Companionship isn't a complaint I have at the moment. Only a desire to feel more fulfilled and serve the community, which my work at the youth center helps."

Jhee spared a thought for Shep, who had mostly chosen to closet himself in their rooms. Kanto pecked Jhee on the cheek. They went on a walk, which took them back to the pier where the Imperial yacht had appeared again, dropping off another round of attendees.

4

———————

~

Breath of the Past

That evening their household dined together in the great hall on a feast of halibut and sea urchin, all poached in a lovely butter sauce with a hint of tarragon. Jhee and Shep ate it with great relish.

"Such compliments to the chef," he said.

"Yes, yes," Kanto and Jhee agreed—Jhee, if only because Shep had found something to enjoy during this trip. Whatever haze he had been in appeared to have lifted.

The doors of the great hall opened with great fanfare, and a bustle of people arrived.

"As I live and breathe," said a statuesque Water Folk woman who shared Shep's chestnut coloring. The recent arrival, attired in a billowing sun cape and summer lenses, breezed into the dining hall and made straight for their table.

Shep stopped mid-chew. "No," he said, "no."

Jhee choked on her sea urchin. "It can't be."

"Ah, brother dear." The woman passed off her lenses to a companion and held out her hands to Jhee and Shep. "Don't be like that, kin. Give us a kiss."

Shep stood and clasped forearms with her. She kissed him on each cheek. Jhee expelled a slow breath and rose.

"Sharlet," Jhee said.

"Sister-in-law, lovely to see you, too. I see you've been taking excellent care of my dear brother. How are you, though?"

Jhee gave Sharlet a half-hearted clasp because she was sure the Imperial family would disapprove of her stabbing another guest.

"I'm well. What of yourself?"

"Well, see for yourself. I'm simply marvelous, and it's great to see how far the three of us have come. Who would have thought two divers' kids from Briny Town and a smuggling, monogamist's spawn would wind up at an Imperial Sojourn? Who would have thought events would turn out this way when we were younger?"

"Indeed."

"All right you suckerfish, where's my drink?" A retinue of sycophantic assistants hustled off to do Sharlet's bidding. Her eyes zeroed in on Kanto. "And who might I ask is this fine drink of water here?"

"I'm Bright Harmony," Kanto said.

"My second," Jhee said.

"Really?" Sharlet laughed uproariously and continued on for some moments.

"You are truly Shep's sister?" Kanto asked.

"Guilty as charged. Oh, look at you. I see sister-in-law's taste in men has improved. Oh, Makers my, whatever possessed you to throw in with these two?"

"It's purely physical I assure you," Kanto said.

"Is it now? Gorgeous and with such a glorious sense of humor, too. Well, I'll be having a salon later. You are, of course, invited. You can even drag these two along if you wish. Though, I don't recommend it." She leaned in and whispered, "Bad blood. Maybe one of us will tell you about it one day."

Jhee clenched her jaw and contemplated how quickly she could be at the woman with her nail pike.

Sharlet addressed Shep, "Brother, you going to let your wife do all the talking for you?"

Shep sat.

"Bright Harmony, pleasure to meet you, and remember, my invitation still stands if you wish."

Kanto gave a polite bow as Sharlet and her entourage left to make the rounds; Jhee and Shep didn't bother. Kanto took his seat. "May I ask?"

"No, you may not," Jhee snapped, then mitigated her tone. "Apologies, not just now. Perhaps when we are back at our rooms, and I'll be at my leisure to rage and yell with full abandon."

Kanto cocked his head at her and brightened his golden eyes. "That bad? Look alive, Jhee, isn't that the Chief Justicar over there?"

At Kanto's urging, they met the Chief Justicar as she shook hands and received people, but Jhee was in no mood for politicking at the moment. However, Jhee straightened her posture and tucked her hands into her robes.

"Ah, Justicar, you're the one in charge of the Far Reaches?"

"Just so, Chief Justicar."

"Please, call me Elver. Exemplary work out there. You truly brought law and order to District Sixteen. The number of complaints I had on your predecessor. It was a nightmare over at review. You, however, were a breath of fresh air."

"Thank you, Elver. If you will excuse us."

"Yes, yes, of course. Have your social secretary contact mine, and maybe we can play some weirs while we're here. I've been eager to ask you about some of your cases."

Jhee made a curt response. As Kanto bowed and smoothed things over, she took her leave.

"You must excuse, denbe," Kanto said. "Dinner didn't agree with her."

"Of course. You better run and take care of her. Have her contact me."

"I will do that, Chief Justicar."

Jhee and Shep quickened their pace. Kanto scrambled to rejoin their side. Shep outpaced both, leaving Jhee to decide if she should speed up to catch him or slow down to insure they didn't lose Kanto. Jhee commandeered a spot between the orchestra and the azaleas. If either husband wanted to join her, they were perfectly welcome. Kanto did so immediately. Not long after, Shep reappeared with a drink for each of them. Kanto excused himself, and Shep replaced him at her side.

Jhee took the fluted glass from him. "That wasn't so bad, was it?"

"He makes it look so easy," Shep said and gestured his glass at Kanto, who had begun to enchant the gathering.

"But this is for us. He knows what needs to be done and who needs to be flattered. A lesson you think we would have learned after all these years."

They both dropped into silence. "Our solution was to hide once we came home."

"I know, but that's no longer an option. This is our new home. That crumbling pile of stones is just barely above water."

"Me too," he whispered. "We had pleasant times there, though."

"And just about as many bad," Jhee said wryly. "I have to admit, while I don't like everything here, it is growing on me."

Shep took a drink. "Not me."

As Kanto kept his charm offensive circulating among the guests, Sharlet never seemed far behind. Jhee set down her drink when Sharlet snuck up behind Kanto and wheedled her way into conversation with him. Once Sharlet pulled out her conch, Jhee's curiosity propelled her across the room with Shep in tow.

"That's clearly you. That's Star Mirror's mamere," Kanto was saying. By "Star Mirror," Kanto meant Mirrei. That was her name for mixed company. "Denbe, denme, Miss Sharlet was showing me images from your old swim team days."

Jhee flushed while Shep tugged at his collar.

"This smart-looking young lady with the clipboard and cap, trying to fade into the background, has to be my esteemed wife. Is this slick slim swim boy the infamous Rennie Crag Hall?"

"Guess again," Sharlet said. "If you like those, I have some even better ones to show you. Guess who this scrawny male with the gigantic head and lenses nearly the size of his face is?"

"Shep, I mean, denme?" Kanto took the hand viewer from Sharlet. He scrolled a few more images along. By the end, Kanto was practically in hysterics. "Well, I'll be Futou's fiddledrum."

Shep's skin had reddened, and his eyes widened from all the attention. Jhee brought up images of Shep from her academy days. Jhee handed Kanto her conch.

"Ah, that's more like it. Hm, no scar. This is how I imagined he looked when younger. You had one drench of a bloom, denme," Kanto said. "You bulked up quickly."

The corners of Shep's mouth drooped. "Courtesy of the M-Prot exercise regimen."

Kanto handed Jhee back the hand viewer. "I'm sorry."

With a desire to steer the conversation away from the Medical Protectorate, Jhee brought the topic back to their swim team days, "Shep showed up the rich jerk, beat the bullies, became captain of the swim team, and won the girl of his dreams."

Jhee finished the recitation with a smile.

"You," Kanto stated.

Sharlet answered first, "Mai."

Jhee tucked away her conch and sought to put a positive frame on it. "Her family did not approve. I used to cover for them so they could date."

In a way, Shep besting Rennie Crag Hall and getting together with Miramar had felt like her victory as well. A mirthless chuckle escaped Shep. Any hope of a pleasant close to conversation left with the tide.

"That's the way it went," Shep said. "Families like theirs undulated over who got to be at the crest or the trough. What remained steady, though, was that families like mine were always beneath theirs. We didn't get to go to Imperial Sojourns unless we were delivering the catch."

～

An Odd Couple

Was this truly the path Jhee wanted to travel? Jhee sat stoic as Sharlet received guests and circumambulated the room. How had Kanto convinced them to attend?

"If you want to know what she's up to, you need to monitor her. What she does. Who she talks to. The salon makes a perfect cover for her to conduct business," Kanto had said.

Sharlet kissed cheeks with a blue-black furred high Imperial. "Welcome, gentlefolk, distinguished guests."

"I'm sure you will love the treat I have in store for you," the High Imperial said.

"I'm sure," Sharlet said. Her voice oozed that false note Jhee despised.

Jhee's attention went to the two large Fire Folk companions at the Imperial's elbows. Their eyes scanned the room but showed nary an expression. They held themselves stiff but ready.

Shep's instant focus on them told Jhee most of all and confirmed her suspicions they had served. He examined them extra hard. His nostrils flared.

"Berserkers," Jhee said.

Shep gave a curt nod.

Berserker Fire Folk. Jhee's back went straight and rigid. Only one regiment of berserkers had ever been Fire Folk. What was Sharlet up to?

Later, Jhee and her husbands walked into one room of the gallery. The High Imperial's pets waited in the center naked.

The High Imperial leaned in and whispered something to them before she handed them a small vial of reddish liquid: bioplasm. But from what creature?

"Whenever you feel ready or comfortable," the royal said.

The male of the couple knocked back the infusion then started huffing and puffing. The woman took hers. She joined him in the huffing and puffing.

The pair pumped their arms. They went into a series of strong exhales and stomps until they started to sweat. The crowd had gone uncomfortably silent. The pair worked their arms and jumped up and down.

Both Jhee and Shep had gone still. Jhee stroked the sigil on her arm.

At last, the manfolk's eyes went red. Other features changed. Shep tensed when the womanfolk's eye turned red also. They were forcing themselves to skin slip.

For most in the Outer Reaches, it was a gradual process, one adapted a little as they went about their business. On occasion, someone did not look quite the same: sleeker fur, finger webbing, bigger or larger ears, mostly slight changes. Then the next time one saw them, they were back to normal. Jhee had heard inlanders could do it too, but it was much rarer.

However, the only way most went into a full skin slip was traumatic, sudden immersion into an extreme environment. Unless one underwent the berserker procedure. For a creature other than their base skin, animal shifters usually required a fresh infusion of bioplasm from the target animal.

Jhee waited for the berserker pairs' limbs to twist and shift into some sea creature's shape. Folk in the Far Reaches sometimes did this as a parlor feat at parties back home. Not everyone could go the full way, especially if sharing one bioplasm infusion. Shep had been one of the talented few that could. Given how matters turned out, would that he couldn't.

Instead of the pair's limbs changing shape, their esca did. The Fire Folk's distinctive teardrop-shaped mark transformed into the star shape associated with Water Folk's esca. Their furred skin likewise changed from the Fire Folk's signature stripes to solid brownish in color. Their hands had become less claw-like, and their size had decreased by about a factor of two.

Jhee and her husbands gasped. The attendees, as well, once they realized what they saw before them were two Water Folk where once were two Fire Folk, down to the eyes going from teal to gold.

Applause broke out. Shep sat there with a snarl and Jhee with her mouth agape. Even Kanto frowned. Jhee stroked the arm sigil as much to calm herself as Shep.

This technique or condition those from the Far Reaches had was not a party gimmick. Transformations such as this had serious consequences. This was a mockery. They took it seriously, and what they certainly did not do was mimic the Other Folk. Other Folk's composition was too similar to Water Folk, which is the reason one did not shift into them. It might wind up being permanent. Despite what Water Folk thought of the Fire and Other Folk, this proved they weren't such a unique sort as the propaganda would have many believe.

Attendees had approached the berserker pair to fawn and fondle them. Kanto sensing his household members' distress, began subtly maneuvering their group towards the door. Sharlet headed their way only to be intercepted. The High Imperial caught up to them all at the same time.

The High Imperial addressed their hostess. "What did you think of my little entertainment?"

Sharlet, whose smile remained plastered on her face though the corners of her mouth twitched, replied, "Quite illuminating, high born."

"Excuse me," Shep grumbled.

Shep cut through the crowd unceremoniously and left. Kanto replaced Shep at Jhee's side and prevented her from following by grabbing her arm. For Jhee to leave the conversation in such a manner too, without basic pleasantries, was a social misstep bordering on an insult.

"Sorry, did you think that was dreadfully gauche of me?" the High Imperial asked.

It was an abomination, Jhee wanted to say.

"I'm given to understand that many of the folk from your region have similar abilities."

"Yes," Sharlet answered, "many say it is a side effect of being so close to the vagaries of the open seas."

"Sounds probable. It is remarkable, though, that some good could come out of those atrocities. The Medical Protectorate research appeared to have perfected the process in the berserkers."

"Apparently so." Jhee drained her glass and tried to keep her expression blank.

"The trick I found is not to trigger them like the berserkers via combat and violence, but with basic excitement and adrenaline. Hence, all the arm-waving and huffery and puffery."

A man bearing an island senate badge approached and asked leave to join the conversation with a slight bow. After they acknowledged him with a nod, he spoke, "Indeed, it seems to be quite effective. Your companions had me completely fooled. I thought we were being invaded. It appears those freaks over at the Medical Protectorate did something right for all their dreadful experiments. I hear the Medical Protectorate were on the verge of taking it even farther."

"How much farther can there be?"

"Total mimicry. Not simply general characteristics of the Other Folk, but the specific features of a specific individual. There's also mimicking plants and objects. I heard their first experiments were quite... messy. Folk losing coherence and degenerating permanently into puddles."

"Sounds dreadful."

"But you have to admit the intelligence applications would be enormous. You were in the intelligence pool, my lady Justicar. Wouldn't you agree?"

Jhee swirled her drink. "I can see the benefits. The berserker program was not without its drawbacks. I'd say it'd be much simpler to meet such aims with more mundane means such as disguise."

"Or arcana perhaps. Eh there, Professor of Arcane Forensics?"

Jhee chose her words with care and tried to sound casual, "There are some glamors which allow the manipulation of appearance. You also have to take voice and mannerisms into account. However, without close study of the subject, the effect is uncanny like bad prosthetics. The illusion can often be shattered under fast movement or the constant challenge of, say, heavy rains."

"Ah, but therein lies a situation in which physical mimicry of the sort we are discussing proves its worth."

"You have me there, Senator."

Another person, a duchess of some sort, said, "I'd prefer plants and objects. I, for one, find the prospect of someone else running around out there with my face downright disturbing."

"Unless, of course, they could take your place in commerce meetings," the senator responded. "Am I right, Duchess?"

"How right you are, you scoundrel. Though a potted plant could replace most of the folk in those and it wouldn't make much of a difference."

The High Imperial gestured with her glass toward where Shep had left, "I fear my little demonstration did not go over as well with everyone."

"Not at all, your highness," Sharlet said. "There are still some residuals which he has trouble dealing with from the service. He merely needed some air."

"Oh, my word, forgive me. Your brother was part of one of their programs, was he?"

"Yes, he was."

"I did not mean to offend. I simply wanted to show off the talents of my consorts. Forgive me."

"It's not for me to tell your highness what she can or cannot do."

"Marvelous, perhaps you can have him demonstrate his transformation technique for us sometime."

Jhee's jaw clenched. A few choice responses for Sharlet and the High Imperial took shape in her head. Her posture tensed, and she opened her mouth.

~

Hedge Maze Timeout

"Perhaps," Kanto said before Jhee or Sharlet answered. Right after agreeing to that, perhaps Jhee would sail a raft out to the breakers by the Rock of Woe and go for a swim. Even joking about being alone in those waters made her break out in a cold sweat and quickened her breathing.

Kanto tightened his grip on Jhee's arm. It was enough to make Jhee reconsider her actions.

"High born," Sharlet said, "isn't that the Earl of Marsh, conversing with your companions?"

The High Imperial set her drink down on a passing server's tray. "My word, I need to rescue them before that lecher gets too handsy."

As soon as possible, Jhee and Kanto excused themselves. They found Shep on a balcony. Before they could say anything, Sharlet joined them.

"I'm sorry, kin," Sharlet said. "Not only was that display offensive, but it was also tacky in the extreme, and I would not have allowed it if I had known."

Shep regarded his sister with his brighter, unscarred eye.

"Kin, you still can't be upset about that? I did what I had to do to protect the family. Your drenched hormones brought us to the verge of ruin. Someone had to be pragmatic."

Jhee itched to go for the utensils, fireball her, or maybe just cut off her air. "I suppose your special appointment helped. Where was your protective instinct when the lottery came up? Perhaps you should have protected Shep instead. Then maybe we wouldn't be so upset. You could have protected your family without abandoning him."

Sharlet raised an eyebrow. "By throwing in with you?"

"I won, didn't I?" Jhee said.

"Of course, you did." Sharlet smiled and addressed Shep, "You know it wasn't just my call. I was only a pre-jubilant, not much older than yourselves. Mamere and papere had the final say. Please, don't be this way, brother. For all we know, it's just you and I left. We should make amends."

Shep continued to fix Sharlet with his eye and remained silent. She wrinkled her nose.

"Well, if you are going to continue to be so unreasonable, I'm going to find better company until you decide to act civilized."

"Hence why we haven't seen you in ten years," Jhee said.

"I've been around. I didn't hear my conch chime either."

"Ah, Lady Sharlet, there you are," the island senator called. He had tracked them down and now stood at the threshold of the balcony. "Sorry to disturb, but we need to finish our conversation, sooner rather than later."

"Of course." Sharlet raised the corners of her mouth in a not-quite smile. "Ta for now, and do look after yourselves."

Once they were alone again, Jhee placed her arms around Shep and rubbed his ears with her thumbs. She traced her gaze along the scar running down his face through one eye. Then Jhee frowned and faced out over the balcony. The eye's light was dimmer because of a dagger's damage, her dagger's damage. She wanted to wrap her arms around him longer to comfort him. Yet, the venue and the party made it impossible.

"Let's go find Kanto," Jhee said.

They found Kanto inside commanding the attention of some younger party-goers. They pried him away to sit down for another quick course of drinks and food. Jhee chose a neutral conversation topic, Kanto's work at the youth center.

"Is volunteer work not paying off like you hoped?" Jhee asked when the topic made Kanto wistful.

"To see children develop a passion for music every bit as deep and abiding as House Kenyatta used to be known for. To see the passion for music developing in those youthful faces matches the ecstasy of performance. On the other hand, having to work around the education council's rules and regulations is quite a pain. It would be nice to take a hand in getting the regulations cleaned up."

"Fancy being a Vizier, do you?" Shep asked with a hint of sarcasm.

Jhee brushed it aside, "Aren't you happy at the youth center, dende?"

"The children are brilliant," Kanto said, "the bureaucracy though... So much of my frustration is chronic and systemic to the institutions themselves."

Shep sighed. "Vizier Kanto to the rescue."

"If only. In most cases, you need to be a veteran. Or an imperial lickspittle to even be considered."

Jhee nodded. "True. A history of military service increases one's odds of becoming a vizier by almost forty percent."

"You, in the service?" Shep scoffed.

This time Kanto could not help but notice Shep's mockery. Jhee glowered at Shep's uncharacteristic rudeness to Kanto.

"It appears it might also improve my chances of being taken seriously one hundred percent. I require refreshments," Kanto said, bowed, and returned to the salon.

"You know what Shep, let's get you a timeout. Look out there. You see that? They have a lovely hedge maze. I think I would very much like to see it in person."

Shep nodded in recognition of the escape she offered him. A chance to get away from the crowds and people suited him fine. "It would be my honor."

Shep presented Jhee his arm, and she looped hers through his. A servant directed them to the hedge maze entrance. If it would not have been a social insult, Jhee would have allowed him to stay home. Though, was more time alone truly what was best for him? He did not do well at these events. This was among the reasons he had sought a second. As second, Kanto handled all the balls and social events required at court and the capital. The invitation to this retreat, though, had specifically named Shep and Jhee, as some form of recognition for their military service.

"Sheepdog and Sniffer, you dog-eared bastards."

Shep and Jhee paused at the threshold. A giant walrus of a male lumbered towards them, supporting his weight with a cane.

"Captain Odo?" Shep asked.

"Yep, I see you got my invitation."

"It was you who invited us."

"Least I could do once I heard you had taken up residence in that Maker-forlorn city. Sniffer, how are you doing?"

"Captain Odo, you old bag of blubber," Jhee exclaimed.

Odo shambled closer and pulled them into a crushing embrace.

"So, we have you to thank for trapping us here?"

"You don't think I want to suffer through this torture alone. I figured I'd share my misery with others. Is that young bull gadflying about yours?"

"Yes, Bright Harmony," Jhee said.

"My second," Shep said.

"Har!" Odo said. "That pretty boy is living with you two curmudgeons. Now, I've seen it all. Going to the maze, eh? Allow me to give you the tour."

"Unnecessary, old friend."

"Nonsense. This way. None of this queuing business. Sure way to get lost." Odo took off in a manner that made it clear he expected them to follow. And surprisingly fast. Jhee and Shep had to hustle to catch up to him. "I presume you've heard about this tribunal nonsense."

"Which tribunal?"

"Which? Have you been under the rocks? Ah, yes, I forgot who it was I was speaking to. The jelly-hearted politicos have decided to open up a tribunal into the Medical Protectorate's atrocities."

"We're aware," Jhee answered, "but there are multiple. Which do you mean?"

"The House of Knives."

Jhee and Shep stopped dead calm.

"Exactly my reaction, too. No one needs to go poking about those old wounds. Come on now. This maze isn't getting any easier."

They followed Odo through a secondary entrance to the maze. They eventually found their way to a dead end.

"I thought you said you knew how to get through without getting us lost," Shep said.

"He's not lost," Jhee said. "We're exactly where he means us to be."

"Sniffing out the truth as always," Odo said, his voice serious and low, "ever the precocious Justicar."

Shep bristled up his fur and stood at Jhee's side. "Explain yourself, cap."

"Calm your seas, Sheepdog. I wanted to make sure we lost our tails, so we had privacy for our chat."

"I can provide an additional guard against eavesdropping," Jhee said.

"No, that would only draw attention to us. They are at least as good at detecting as you."

"You mentioned the tribunal and old wounds."

The captain wrinkled his mouth. "Ursula's gone missing."

"Not surprised," Shep said. "She's had more trouble adjusting than the rest of us."

"True, but recently," Captain Odo began then shook his head, "she had been doing better. Then I saw her a long-moon ago."

"So did we."

"She was paranoid, raving about the tribunal. She said she saw death, and it had her face. I'm worried about her."

"You're the one with imperial clout. Why ask us?" Shep asked.

"The situation is delicate."

"You never told your wife about Ursula," Jhee stated.

"I was a dutiful boy. I told the Princess Regent all about it. She took no action but set a condition I was never to see Ursula again. If my Imperial wife learns I've met with her twice, let alone once, I fear it will be worse for Ursula than me. I'm worried, though. This last time I saw Ursula, it was different. I'm afraid she may have done something to herself. Track her down and get her help if you can."

"We'll do this for you, cap. And for Ursula and the others," Shep said.

"We will see what we can do, Captain. Where was the last place you saw her?"

"Packer's Pier One. Thank you. Best get back before we're missed."

Jhee's mind had already begun to turn over the puzzles. Death had her face. She had been witness to some of Ursula's episodes, and she had said nothing like that before. The three of them returned to the party in silence, and the captain went his separate way. Jhee's arm sigil remained inert. She watched Shep but could not get a good gauge on his mood in the dark. He had put on his stone face. Jhee suspected she had as well.

5

———————

~

Old Wounds

By the time they saw Kanto again, he stood amongst a group of youthful
men indeed decked out in color schemes fathoms more daring than his.
Kanto raised his glass to his spouses when he saw them. Jhee hailed Kanto
back before taking a walk about with Shep.

"If something's happened to Ursula," Shep said, "That means I'm the last
of my berserker gang. We should've done more to help her when she came
to us."

Jhee glanced about to see if they were being watched. She stroked his ear
with her thumb. He rubbed his head against her hand a moment before they
continued to stroll the gardens. The skies here were clear, with barely a hint
of lightning or the Storm Wall's ever-present glow. Imperial artificers likely
had much to do with that. The arcana that infused it still reached her. One
would have to leave the isles and probably travel all the way to the Scorched
Lands before that would ever not be the case. Or ascend the Grand Tether to
the Stars.

Jhee and Shep stopped on a footbridge, which offered an unobstructed
view down the river channel to where the Tether touched the ground on
Tether Island. The thin granite line bisected the horizon view. A lightning
flash every few minutes illuminated it towards the top where it disappeared
into the clouds. The Tether led directly to Equilibrium Point Station at the
heart of the Three Worlds' orbit around each other, remnants of the Proto-

types' tech. As a feat of mortal design, only the Storm Wall had even come close to matching it.

The wall had been Jhee's hope that horrors like the Medical Protectorate and what happened to Shep and the berserkers would never happen again. She stepped closer to Shep and laid her hand on his shoulder. The Fire Folk may have been stymied, but their off-world counterparts, the Other Folk, were as belligerent as ever.

Later that night, after Jhee and her husbands had retired for the evening, Shep knocked upon her door. Shep regarded her with more intensity and passion than he had in a long-month. They fell into each other's arms. Too soon, Shep sank back into an unreachable silence. He flinched when Jhee reached out to him. Then he rose and paced the floor. She sighed.

"It's fine, Shep," Jhee said.

Shep grabbed a dressing robe and shoved his arms into the sleeves. "No, it's not."

He sat on the edge of the sleeping pallet and rested his head in his hands. At last, he laid back down. Jhee traced one of the scars that left a line through his graying fur and brushed one of the smooth patches where scar tissue had prevented hair from regrowing. Overall, Shep's body hair was coarser and more unruly than Kanto's. Whereas the latter was all slim and sleek, everything about Shep took up space: from his bushier, curlier hair to his wider frame and features.

"I've yet to see those pictures of you in the lenses or any of the ones before secondary school," Jhee teased.

"That's because I thought I'd destroyed them all. I hated the way I looked then," Shep said. His rhythmic breathing hitched, then continued. "Kanto is smooth. No scars. I've seen him bathe. Not a blemish anywhere on him except for his gentleman's scar. I was never that beautiful, even at his age. Noblewomen are judged by the quality of the things they keep around them. He's a much more suitable choice to be on your arm than me. For your introduction to court society. I don't think he's ever known a hardship."

"His hardships don't leave scars on the outside."

"Like some of ours. You should afford yourself of his company more often. You spend half your supposed days off with me. Give him both Mirrei's days. You have my permission. Virility was one of the criteria I selected him on."

"You think I care about any of that," Jhee said. "All I ever wanted was you, and you, me, and Mai, the whole of the Far Reaches, suffered years for it."

Much as the tides, Reach feuds ebbed and flowed. It seemed terribly fitting that the fight, which had once been Jhee's and Miramar's and had spilled over to their families, became theirs again in due course. Jhee did not know who she intended to hurt more with the marriage: Miramar, her family, or the Reaches.

The rules would have to change. As Jhee had reached accommodation with Kanto and Mirrei, the relationship between her and Shep had become unmoored. As she had found roles in her life for the younger spouses, Shep had lost some of his. While it had been as he intended, he was not ready for how it would feel.

Jhee had suspected this might happen. She had resisted becoming attached to her younger spouses. Shep, though, had been driven to find a second husband for her: one more suited for high society, one with all the graces he lacked and who would provide her what she needed to survive the political battlefield of the capital.

Now, Jhee must do the same for him. To survive here, Shep had to know he was still essential to her and had not trained his replacements. She had taken it for granted no topic was off-limits between them, even Miramar. She owed him some small peace of his own in exchange. He sacrificed the actuality of his singular and central role in her life. In exchange, she offered the illusion nothing had changed.

"New rule," Jhee said. "When we are together, we don't talk about them. This is our time. Do you remember how we met?"

Shep sat up. "I think I was bringing in the family nets."

Jhee snuggled up behind him and draped herself on him. "You'd been diving. You emerged from the sea like a sea king of old must have. It must have been cold that day as you had turned more seal than otter. Miramar and I were both instantly smitten."

"I'm not sure if I've ever deserved your devotion." Shep closed his eyes then turned away. "I took a fathership test, Jhee. I needed to know about Mirrei, even if you didn't. She's not. I would have put a stop to this marriage otherwise. You were right to have suspected, though."

As if Jhee had been burnt, she snatched herself away from Shep. The relief was bittersweet as it confirmed what Jhee had never wanted to know: he had had an affair with Miramar. The three of them—Jhee, Miramar, and Shep—were once the best of friends and inseparable until Shep and Jhee eloped in her academy days. Miramar was Mirrei's mother and the woman whose ghost hung over Jhee and Shep's marriage for almost a full jubilee. She had needed the sliver of deniability. Now, it was gone. Jhee left the bed and slipped on a casual robe.

Shep grabbed her hand. "Jhee?"

Jhee tugged her hand loose. Before she left, Jhee asked without turning around, "Congratulations, you've succeeded in pushing me away. One more question: Mirrei's crush was only one way?"

"Yes."

She recited cyphers and statutes in her head to maintain her composure. The First Makers' Design guided her steps to a quiet place in the gardens where her Imperial shadow's presence wouldn't be too noticeable. She pulled out her conch and pored over charts and derivations while small sobs shook her body.

~

A Search for Equilibrium

Once Jhee had poured out enough tears, she petitioned her Maker within for equilibrium. She returned to the main building and endeavored to find a nice quiet study. A lengthy reading session would recalibrate her. As Jhee reached an enormous set of ebony doors, they pushed open. An imperial lady with saffron eyes and a lithe, sinuousness which reminded Jhee of a water snake swept out nearly leveling Jhee in the process. The imperial paused to raise an eyebrow at Jhee then turned her back on Jhee with a grand sweep of her skirts and haughty, dismissive wave.

Through the open doors, Jhee's search bore fruit when she spied an enormous library. Shelves bulged from floor to ceiling with bio-films and bound seaweed paper tomes. She touched the palms of her hands together at angles before she entered and ran her fingertips over one gorgeous volume bound in burgundy sharkskin, *Imperial Births and Lineages, Volume Twelve*. She let her fingers linger on the pitted, rough pores of the material.

A cup rattled with small items behind her. "Care for a game?" a feminine voice asked.

Jhee gasped and whirled toward the corner from where the offer had come. A dark-skinned, feminine hand holding a dicing cup poked out from an overstuffed chair in the corner.

The woman shook the cup again. Jhee approached cautiously and respectfully. The woman's robes were fine, yet studiously devoid of any insignia or identifiable pattern or crests Jhee could attribute to any house. "All pardons, I thought I was alone."

"No pardons necessary. Please, sit."

Jhee took the chair opposite the woman at a *gammancala* game set. Even with the lack of identifiers, the woman's demeanor carried the force of rank, though, from military service or Imperial blood, Jhee could not fathom. Her dark, blue-black skin suggested the latter.

The woman poured them tea from a nearby tea service. Jhee slipped the insulated sleeve over her cup, then turned it three times before picking it up in both hands. "All honors...."

"Lady Amani." The lady turned her cup twice. The number of turns indicated rank based on the degree of removal from the Imperial line. Jhee did not believe for a moment that this woman was only one step closer to the succession than her. Nevertheless, she had to abide by it. Jhee certainly was in no position to challenge the assertion. She was sure to learn the truth fast enough if Jhee crossed the woman's line. The ones who wanted to blur the class lines were often the most dangerous when crossed. Lady Amani picked up her cup, "Honors to you as well, Justicar."

In accordance with high etiquette, Jhee drank a moment after Lady Amani.

The game board had already been set for two. "I hope I didn't interrupt, my lady."

"A habit. My playing companions are limited. I've had to play both sides of the board lately. It's an excellent way to keep oneself sharp. Though I always welcome a new player. Keeps things fresh."

Jhee chose not to mention the woman she had seen stalk out of here. "Just so."

They diced for a while in high spirits. Once they switched to playing a two-person trick-taking card game, Jhee's Maker within answered her petition. The gears began to grind in Jhee's head about how to find Ursula. Perhaps the pier was not the best place to start the search for Ursula. She might want to start with the sailor who had come to see her. Also, there was that hardwood disc Ursula dropped. Jhee had no time to dwell on old betrayals. Her old friends required her assistance in the here and now.

Lady Amani won the first play due to Jhee's distraction. Jhee recovered and won the next two tricks. The game eventually ended with a draw, the preferable outcome to Jhee winning until she knew what kind of noble Lady Amani was. With her mind focused on the Ursula matter, Jhee might miss any warning signs for poor sportsmanship.

Communications on Sovereign's Isle were limited and heavily monitored. Jhee understood that before she accepted as it only made sense. The Regent might intercept a direct search for Ursula while here. It was the sort of pragmatic action Captain Odo's wife, the Regent, would take to keep him honest. With her composure regained and renewed purpose, Jhee excused herself.

~

To Play With the Courtiers

Kanto touched his credential ring to the verification stone. "I accept. I would also be honored to play with the courtiers' orchestra."

"A servant will contact you about accommodating whatever instrumentation you may require."

Once the messenger left, Jhee gave Kanto a playful clap. "Seems as though you made quite an impression. An invitation to the imperial spouses' luncheon and to play with the courtiers' orchestra in the petite hall!"

He bowed slightly. Then a look of panic spread over his face. "By the First Makers, I need to practice. I also need to brush up on my notation reading. And do I bring my own lute? It would surely be too plain beside what the Imperial courtiers would have. Should I use one of theirs? Then I would have to acquaint myself with the idiosyncrasies and peculiarities of a new instrument on such short notice. What if they give me one from the Imperial collection? What if I drop it or snap a string? Some of those instruments are hundreds, thousands of years old."

Kanto bolted to the next suite and spent the rest of the evening going through outfits and examining his instruments. Once he had finished with that, he practiced on his lute for most of the evening. He swore as he messed up notes over and over.

"Calm yourself, dear one. It's the anxiety. You are putting too much pressure on yourself."

"I know. Gah. I'm just so nervous. I want to make a wonderful impression. This is it, Jhee. The Imperial family. It doesn't get more upper class than this. Aside from an audience with the Grand Sovereigns themselves. If that were to happen, I am liable to pass out and die."

"Stand up," Jhee said.

"I have to practice."

"I said, 'stand up.' Obey your denbe."

Kanto sighed and reluctantly got to his feet. Jhee dropped into a wide motion meditation stance. "I don't have time for this."

"Yes, you do. What you need to do is meditate. Clear and center first. Then you can go back to practicing."

Jhee guided Kanto through motion meditation sequences for several minutes. "Now, try again."

Kanto sat down and picked up his lute. Beautiful, dulcet tones flowed from it as he played along with a piece he had never tried before. He finished the piece to great applause from Jhee.

"Thank you. It was the first time I tried that piece."

"See. Clear and center. Now what you also need to do is rest, so you are fully refreshed for your performance."

"By the Maker's plan, you are right. If I don't get enough sleep, I'll show up with puffy eyes. What sort of impression would that make?"

"One, I'm more than sure your make up skills could turn around."

"Thank you, Jhee."

"No 'thank you' required. It's an honest assessment of your skills."

"No, I mean for everything." Kanto came over and put his arms around her waist. "I dreamed of being at the imperial palace, meeting the Regent Sovereigns when I was young. Now, because of you, I just about realized that dream."

Jhee's face felt warm. "You would have found a way."

"No, nobody but you could have done that for me. We did it together. This is why I never regretted marrying you. Even when you were acting like a complete saphead."

"Thank you for putting up with me while I came to understand your worth."

Kanto grinned. "I'm flipping priceless and don't you forget it."

"Wouldn't even dream of it. Never crossed my mind. Not in a millennium."

"You know what, Jhee? You are too."

"I'm glad you can see that despite how I acted."

Jhee worked with Kanto up until a messenger collected him for practice and staging. At the petite hall, Jhee was seated in the section reserved for performers' guests and imperial benefactors. Shep was nowhere to be found. Eventually, the seat to one side of her was taken by a flamboyant yet dignified older male. A slender male with statelier, single-colored robes and sandy hair took the other seat beside her.

When Kanto played, Jhee perched on the edge of her seat, almost as anxious about his performance as he was. She restrained herself from clapping like a ninny once his group finished. Jhee caught his eye, and they shared a smile.

"Talented companion. Yours?" the sandy-haired male asked.

Jhee nodded, though she bristled at the notion of Kanto as property. Then a feeling of hypocrisy set in. Before Jhee could dwell on it, she spotted Shep's sister Sharlet talking to the same island senator who had collected her after the appalling slipping demonstration at her salon. The sandy-haired male continued to make small talk while Jhee watched Sharlet and the senator speak.

～

The Return to "Normal"

The rest of the sojourn proceeded without event, though Jhee and Shep kept their distance from each other. Kanto was the star of the show. At least, he had enjoyed himself. He remained ecstatic after they left the sojourn. Jhee tried to match his enthusiasm. She and Shep grudgingly acknowledged each other when they had to.

Kanto checked their messages. There was a message from Mirrei. "Hi, kin. I know you are at the Imperial Sojourn, but I just wanted to say 'hi' and 'I miss you.'"

Normally, Jhee would have been ecstatic, but Mirrei's face, the spitting image of Miramar, at the moment was only salt in the wound. "I'll be in my study," Jhee said. She went to her study and closed the door. She took a finger quill and began to list every data point she had for Ursula.

At Captain Odo's suggestion and her own common sense, she delayed her search for Ursula until they left. Upon their return to the normal world, Jhee threw herself into the search. She spent her first night home locked in her study, contacting folk via conch.

Jhee tapped the data shell Ursula had dropped against her esca. She weighed the invasion of privacy against its evidentiary value. Before it came to that, Jhee had other less invasive means to find Ursula. She used her credentials to access the Justicar code base and check the death records. None of the local morgues or body disposal facilities had a record of anyone matching Ursula's description, nor did the veterans' last repose societies and services. A dread notion within her released. Though, they just could not have found the body yet.

Next, she checked with local hospitals, mental institutions, and veteran care facilities to see if they admitted anyone with Ursula's features. Last, she checked the major imperators' branches for anyone arrested who might fit her description. All came up empty.

Ursula might still be alive. She was resourceful and had a small military pension-provided residence, which came as part of their separation benefits. Checking that out would be the first item on tomorrow's agenda.

Jhee had fallen asleep in her study and encountered Shep on her way to her rooms.

"Come with me to exercise Dari?" Shep asked.

The morning run was usually his alone time, except for Bax and Dari. Despite their estrangement, Jhee felt honored. The run was Shep and Bax's exclusive routine with Dari because the pair and Dari had bonded in a way Jhee would never know, a way she and Shep used to be. They had started the routine when the pair went ahead to set up their house while Jhee and the younger spouses stayed at the villa of an old schoolmate on the outskirts of Galleon City.

Shep and Jhee walked arm-in-arm to the area of the park where many did their morning exercises. She participated in one of the devotions-in-motion gatherings. He removed Dari's leash and let the shark dog run about and play with the other hounds.

Jhee picked up a stick and played fetch and retrieve with Dari. The shark hound served as a cautionary tale of where Shep could end up if he neglected his health. Dari ran into the distance and dutifully brought back the stick. Her tongue lolled out in expectation of praise. Jhee knelt and ruffled Dari's fur. "Good girl. Good girl."

As Jhee fought off the shark hound's rough tongue, she noticed Shep scanning the park.

"What is it?" Jhee asked.

Shep shrugged. "One of the other hound owners who normally exercises their dog around this time isn't here."

"Schedules change from time to time."

"True, we've only been here a few moons. Yet, every day like clockwork, she was there. It's unusual is all."

"Is there some other reason you're worried?"

"I think she ganged."

"Another berserker? Are you sure?"

"No. I'm not sure," Shep snapped. He contemplated the ground. "They, we, have a look, one you can recognize on others. You've seen it. A way they carry themselves. Also, some things she said. I couldn't put a finger on it. Sometimes you just know. What with Ursula missing…."

Jhee took a breath. "Do you want me to ask around while I look for Ursula?"

"No. No. I don't suppose we should. She was practically a stranger, after all."

Jhee hurled the fetch stick so hard she nearly wrenched her shoulder, and Dari ran after it again. Shep continued to search the faces of everyone who passed them by in the park. Jhee didn't want to name what she was feeling.

Eventually, Jhee and Shep put Dari back on the leash and stopped at one of the beverage carts for kolal and pastries. She thought through her plan to locate Ursula because it kept her mind off other matters. Jhee had a cinnamon-raisin twist while Shep ate a peach tart. Dari panted at them expectantly.

"None for you, old girl. You're on a strict diet."

Jhee and Shep found a bench nearby on which to sit and watch the suns rise higher. Off in the distance, the shadowy outline of the Grand Tether split the skyline. The sinking feeling Jhee got when Shep mentioned the hound-walking woman had taken her by surprise. It reminded her of the dread she carried after finding out Miramar and Shep had corresponded after their marriage.

"Mai told me, you know?" Jhee said, unable to state her feelings more directly than that. "When the situation was at its worst, she threw it in my face. To be honest, though, I shouldn't have been surprised. You cheated on her with me."

"The woman with the hound is just a friend, a counselor from the veteran services center on the other side of the park," Shep said, having discerned the source of Jhee's anxiety. "She works with gangers. I thought maybe, Ursula, us, too."

Jhee gave a nod. She and Shep brainstormed all the places they would expect to find Ursula.

"Where would Ursula go if she were feeling agitated?"

"Many of us like calm places full of greenery; parks; gardens. It's the flip side of our conditioning. How they calmed us down."

"I remember." They held hands, and he ran a thumb over her knuckles. "We'll start with other parks. You should stay here."

"But, I can help."

Only the top floors of the veteran's service center could be seen when Jhee gazed in that direction. She had attended a counseling session as she promised she would, one single session. Shep, though appeared to have kept his word better than she had on that score. Jhee talked to Shep about everything. Where did she go to talk about him or the self-doubts she did not want to burden him with?

Jhee brushed Shep's facial scar with her thumb. "I have no defenses when it comes to you. You'll be more of a distraction than anything if you come along. You blind me in a way nothing else does."

"Please, Jhee," Shep said.

"I will take Bax. I'll let you know when I return."

6

―――――――

~

The Search Begins

Jhee summoned Bax, and they called a transport around. "Bax, are you familiar with those Shep talks to while he is out with Dari?"

"Aye, Justicar."

"Are you familiar with the hound owner? The one who he is concerned about?"

"Aye, Justicar. I may have seen them speaking in passing."

"Did you see her speak with anyone else?"

"A few other hound owners. As I said, Justicar, I only saw her in passing."

"Was she there on the regular like Shep says?"

Bax fidgeted. "Aye, Justicar."

Ursula missing and also Shep's acquaintance: one definitely a berserker and the other allegedly, or at the very least, berserker adjacent. Jhee worked over in her mind what it might mean. Coincidence perhaps? She needed to keep her Maker's eye open and not let a preconceived notion blind her.

Jhee decided against visiting Ursula's last knowns and old hangouts, flashing a picture of her. If Ursula were just lying low, that would be the quickest way to ensure she'd go to ground. Then they might never find her.

Jhee and Bax spent the better part of the day checking parks and gardens, including several zoological ones near areas Ursula had been known to frequent. After a while, Jhee's knees and feet ached fiercely. Some park, preserve, or another occupied every patch of this Maker-forlorn city. That did not even count the numerous private courtyards. Jhee pinched the bridge of her nose.

Perhaps they should have started closer to home with their own park. But Jhee had needed distance from Shep.

Jhee and Bax made more inquiries, which also came up empty. Perhaps she should not have been so quick to prevent Shep from joining them. She had meant what she said about him being a distraction. Her feelings were in flux between the confirmation of the affair with Miramar and the knowledge of this dog walking friend of his.

"Did you follow him that night?" Jhee asked Bax. "Do you know where Shep went that night he took off after Ursula?"

"Aye, Justicar. You came home from date night alone, and you seemed sore worried."

"And?"

Bax fidgeted some more. "Begging your pardon, Justicar, but I'm asking your leave to keep that between me and Mr. Shep."

While Bax was Jhee's head servant and trusted adviser, he also claimed to be a distant relative of Shep's. Bax came into her employ after she saved him from being mutilated by the previous Justicar of her home district. He pledged his lifelong service to her because he owed her a life debt, as he put it. Even if Bax's claim of kinship to Shep was dubious, he became almost as loyal to Shep as to her. Because of Shep's bond and caring for Dari, Bax behaved almost as an uncle to Shep, too. Did where Shep go that night involve Dari? That might be the only topic that could split Bax's loyalty this way. Jhee respected the old man enough not to force him to betray Shep's confidence, yet.

Bax and Jhee went to Ursula's apartment. He rubbed his chin and grunted approval at the lock. Though she had no doubt Bax could have gained them entry without it, Jhee produced the key Odo had given her. This was not her jurisdiction, and she had less latitude, though Captain Odo had given her an open, notarized writ for emergency use only. Jhee chose not to question Odo about why he had the key, but she would revisit the matter with him later. She suspected a stronger connection between the captain and Ursula than he let on. Until it became immediately relevant to her preliminary inquiries, she would let him keep his own counsel. Jhee had been doing that a lot lately. Perhaps she should start demanding more candor from the men in her life.

"Perhaps we can enlist some other members of you and Mr. Shep's old unit to help track her down?"

"Shep, the captain, and Ursula are the only ones left. The other problem is, Bax, Ursula was the unit's scout and tracker. If it was someone else who had gone missing, she's who I might send to find them. Which means if she doesn't want to be found, we'll need Lethys Luck to find her."

"Then, we best give libation to Lethys and the Rum Toad at every shrine we come across. Couldn't hurt."

She chuckled. It was as fine an idea as any she had.

Jhee had not been sure of what she expected to see on the other side of the door. The neat and cleanly kept apartment was not it. Between what the captain said and their knowledge of Ursula's condition, she had expected a mess; empty or half-empty liquor bottles; trash. This is not the apartment of someone unable to take care of themselves. This almost made no sense.

"You're probably right." Jhee touched her palms together at angles in a minor act of blessing.

Jhee walked through the apartment. A cleaning or home care service might have done it. But a closer inspection showed the neat, well-maintained folds and alignments of military discipline. Ursula still kept the apartment to the nines, regimented like during their service. The order, the discipline must have been what Ursula needed most once she returned home. Shep had been the same. The lack of structure sometimes drove him inward.

At last, Jhee discovered a bound picture of Ursula and Odo, a recent one. She picked it up and felt a bulge in the back of it. Removing the frame's back exposed an envelope. Jhee read the contents. These were intelligence credentials, signed by Captain Odo, which designated Ursula as a confidential informant or asset.

Saw her only occasionally, my snout, Jhee thought.

~

An Empty Plate

Jhee and Bax returned home from their day's adventures empty-handed, disappointed, and with more ambivalence toward Shep than ever. She had done what she could and found neither hide nor hair of Ursula, let alone some random hound-walking woman counselor. Shep and Kanto laid out pots and utensils in the kitchen together. She paused to observe how they got on without her influence. She was also loathed to break the mood with her lack of progress.

"You can't cook in that," Shep declared.

"What's wrong with what I'm wearing?" Kanto asked.

"Your sleeves. No sleeves or narrow sleeves are best for cooking unless you plan on catching them on fire or trailing them through grease and sauce. Once you change, the first thing I'm going to teach you is called a reduction."

"Why did we set up Mirrei's chemistry lab in the kitchen?" Kanto asked.

Shep sighed. "It's not a chemistry lab. It's molecular gastronomy equipment. Some sort of fancy way of cooking she was just getting into. I meant it as a surprise, but now I think I might want to learn it myself."

"Oh, I've seen and heard some of what they can do with their dishes. A chemistry lab, as I said. It is kind of ingenious. You'll be able to make creations like those with these kitchen stations?"

"Maybe. Though, seems like an awful lot of trouble. A good sous vide. A nice sauce and done is my usual go-to."

"But molecular gastronomy makes it the pinnacle of high art. It takes the dining experience to another level."

Shep slapped down a skillet on one of the burners. "The pinnacle of the dining experience is having a good, tasty meal. Everything that doesn't contribute to that is a waste and a distraction from that. Food preparation, the serving of a good plate, meals are about the people. Giving them great tastes to nourish their bodies as well as their senses."

"I'd argue that last part is what molecular gastronomy is trying to do. Feast the senses as well as the appetite. But this is your area of expertise, and you know better."

"Nice to see you agree," Jhee said and pulled up a stool at the kitchen island. Two empty place settings waited there: one for her and one for the Lost Makers. An empty place for the Lost and Unknown Makers was an old outland tradition. They could have fed an army in their kitchen. They had each put their imprimatur on the house. All she had wanted was a study and an arcane workshop, preferably connected. For safety reasons, they had convinced her to put her workshop, which housed her more volatile experiments at a remove from the house.

Jhee admired the impressive, state-of-the-art kitchen Shep had designed. Each member of the household got to put their stamp on the house. Shep and Mirrei planned out the kitchen. The kitchen was Shep and Mirrei's passion project. Shep and Kanto largely designed the landscaping and hardscaping except for the plants and gardens. She and Mirrei had masterminded those: herb gardens, hot houses, and even an algae pond. Kanto and Mirrei had planned many of the connective and social aspects of the house's functions. Music systems, redundant power arrays, extra tethered and ether connectivity. Jhee and Shep worked on the physical security. Ever the cautious ones, they put in a panic room and a few secret hiding spots. She, Mirrei, and to a lesser extent, Kanto had overseen the learning areas like the studies and entertainment rooms. A winding practice space and a small place, which could be a mini-lecture hall. A workshop or craft room or studio for each of their interests. Kanto, herself, and Shep had overseen the layout of the exercise room.

Shep turned to Jhee, expectant. She shook her head. While Kanto left to change his robes, Shep plated some pasta and set it on the table in front of her.

"Bax and I checked every park, garden, and bush from one end of the city to the other. I checked her apartment, with the morgues, etc. Nothing. Not a trace of her."

Shep's expression fell. Jhee chose to hide her disappointment. Ursula was Jhee's friend, too, maybe not like she was to Shep. Jhee still had the folk from her old intelligence unit that she would drop everything for in a minute. Jhee had been the liaison officer to Shep's berserker gang; the closest she had been allowed to get to their unit due to the conflict of interest it presented. Jhee had, however, used what influence she could, where she could on their behalf. The shaky ethics of it had been justified, she told herself. At the time, they were still fighting the machinations of Houses Mitsu and Crag Hall. They tried to make conditions worse for him, and she countered to ease his burdens.

"Well, you did your best," Kanto said upon his return. "You did do your best, didn't you?"

Jhee nodded, even though she was not sure.

"Now, what is it you think you can teach me about good food, denme, that I don't already know?"

"You know about good food and good wine because you've read about them or seen them in a publication," Shep replied, "or you've seen them on a list somewhere. I want to teach you both why they are good, and that inexpensive ingredients can sometimes be just as good."

"They taught me to enjoy good food at finishing school."

"Correction: they taught you to pretend to like good food. I'm going to teach you how to truly appreciate it."

Kanto touched Jhee and Shep's hands. "Who knows? Maybe your friend will turn up safe and sound, and this worry will have all been for nothing?"

Jhee smiled. She might have been won over by Kanto's optimism if she and Shep had not exchanged looks. Neither of them said it, but they were sure Ursula was dead or worse.

$\sim$

The Commission Files

The search for Ursula fell by the wayside as Jhee resumed her duties. While she was working at the legal clinic, she received a visit from the academy dean.

"I'm sure some of you are aware of the ongoing tribunal about the Flower Wars and the abuses of the Medical Protectorate," the dean said. Xe straightened the burgundy sleeves of hir dean's robe. "The clinic has been asked to catalog some findings, help identify victims, and perhaps triage many of the cases to determine if they should be included in the tribunal. This will be the prelude to the establishment of a reconciliation commission to address some wrongs the Empire did to its citizens and others."

"Wrongs done? The empire has done nothing but protect and defend its citizens. These people should be grateful."

The comments were greeted with furious knocks on the tables. Several of the students shook their heads. Jhee folded her arms.

"My Lady Justicar, I wanted to ask you and your clinic if you would be interested in spearheading our efforts, as a veteran yourself."

The Knock Brigade now regarded her with a touch of admiration. "I'll do what I can, Dean."

"Thank you. Who knows, Justicar? Do a good enough job, and they might appoint you to the tribunal or reconciliation commission."

After the dean left, Jhee pulled out the case files xe had left behind.

"You served, Justicar?" one student asked.

"Yes," Jhee replied.

"Where?"

"Wherever the empire needed me."

Another student spoke, "But you were an influential noble, so you got kept off the front lines?"

"Did you kill any barbarians?" another student asked.

Jhee shut her eyes to block out the images, but that only made it worse. She sneered, then marshaled herself to stillness. "Never ask a veteran that. I was in the intelligence pool, which, as has been aptly noted by some, kept me off the front lines. We pushed paper and deciphered messages."

"I heard the intelligence pool was full of spies," a fourth student remarked.

Jhee sighed. "It was full of those wealthy and powerful enough to get themselves out of combat—in case they could not find some other way to manipulate the lottery. We should get back to the task at hand. We're going to go through each of these case files."

The e-tech gul arrived, and they spent the day setting up students with limited access to the judicial archives. Jhee watched them eagerly work while she found it hard to open the case files. On the occasion she did, she saw all the acts she had done in service of the Empire.

The tribunal had been mainly convened due to public outcry from the families of the victims after they found out the truth of how they died. During the decommissioning of one of the old Medical Protectorate buildings, a mass grave was found. The island facility had been due to be sunk. Instead, some enterprising person had bought the property, which was little more than a bit of island and dirt poking out of the ground and planned on turning it into cheap, refugee housing.

Until they discovered the macabre remains on the site.

Soldiers and knights who had been reported killed in battle or, as was the standard explanation, lost at sea, LAS.

Jhee shuddered. She thought about her two older sisters. She thought about the hardships she and those like Shep had to endure. The popular consciousness dubbed the main Medical Protectorate facility, the House of

Sorrows. Those experimented on there had another name for it: The House of Knives.

Her disappointment in the Storm Wall resurfaced. Would it never end? Would the Empire always betray them? In the end, what did it matter? Those skin-scrapers would find some new ways to steal their blood, sweat, and tears. And then come up with some new way to do it all again.

Jhee rested her head in her hands and thought about Ursula out there. The Empire had used her as a chew toy and spit her out. When had Jhee last checked in with veteran services? The Empire had managed to get proper care for their physical wounds right at least. The veteran services division, though, had fallen woefully short on services for the wounds that mainly showed on the inside. The closest they came was the therapeutic companion program Shep and Dari participated in—even that, though, had its own peculiar drawbacks.

Ursula and the tribunal still weighed on Jhee's mind as she returned home. Shep and Dari relaxed in the study while Kanto played his lute for them. She sat down on the arm of Shep's overstuffed chair. She rubbed his shoulders as they appreciated Kanto's lovely playing. This is what it was all about: their family.

Jhee pulled out her conch and made herself comfortable in her armchair beside Shep's. The four, Shep, Jhee, Kanto, and Dari, sat wordlessly together. No strife. No worries. It occurred to Jhee this was what she and Shep had fought so hard for. The person beside you is who you fought for. Did this make it all worth it?

Jhee closed her eyes and allowed Kanto's playing to transport her to another place and time of youthful optimism and vast, empty homes where sadness appeared to be a part of the walls themselves, a House of Sorrows all its own.

Shep and Miramar: it was like a wisp fancy. Jhee was enamored of both of them and the idea of them. She could go home to a cold, humorless, empty, dark house where her parents did nothing but cry all day, or she could hang out with them: two young, carefree lovers living their fullest lives. The oppressive atmosphere of Hillside only worsened once she went away to the academy. She hated coming back there.

Jhee opened her eyes when Dari began to whine. The shark dog had gone on point.

The door chimes tinkled. They had dismissed the servants for the evening, so Jhee took it upon herself to answer the door.

Ursula waited on their doorstep, wide-eyed and in deplorable condition.

"Shep!" Jhee called.

Shep and Dari bounded into the entryway. He stopped short.

Ursula clutched them. "Thank the Makers! I didn't know where else to go. Sniffer, Sheepdog, you have to help me. Death is after me."

With that, Ursula collapsed. Jhee and Shep caught Ursula, punctuated by more whining from Dari.

~

The Gray Lady of the Deeps

Jhee and Shep had Kanto make ready the secret room for Ursula. Meanwhile, Shep tended their fallen friend and kept her comfortable as she lay unconscious. While Shep strove to diagnose her condition, Jhee took charge of Ursula's clothing.

"Sheepdog," Ursula said in a hoarse whisper.

Shep used a wet cloth to wipe the woman's brow and gave her a sip of water. She gulped at the glass. "Easy, Urlibird. You're dehydrated and malnourished."

Ursula fell back on the bed. "Thank you."

"Now, Urli, tell us what's going on, if you're up to it," Jhee said.

Ursula nodded. "I saw the Unmaker. In the guise of the White and Gray Lady of the Deeps, except she had my face."

"What does that mean, Urli?"

"The Unmaker is coming for me, coming for us all."

"Yes, we all die."

Ursula shook her head, then fell back on the pillows in frustration.

Jhee tried again, "What are you trying to tell us?"

"Jhee, enough," Shep said. "Let her be."

Ursula lapsed back into a fitful unconsciousness. Jhee pulled Shep aside. "Do you have any idea what she means?"

"Outside my depths."

"When she's stronger, perhaps I'll use inspiration on her."

"No, you won't." Shep looked apologetic when Jhee pursed her lips. "*Our friend* needs time to heal. Her system may not be able to handle anything so invasive."

Jhee tucked her hands into her sleeves. "Do you think it was the news about the HOK?"

"Could be. Why did they have to go poking into that? Why couldn't they just let it lie? We'd made our peace with it."

Jhee pressed her hands together inside her robes. "Ursula hadn't. I didn't tell you this, but Ursula came to me a few years ago. She wanted to know how to convene a tribunal. I gave her the names of a few contacts. I didn't think much of it at the time."

"And you never told me?"

"I figured it was just Urlibird being flighty. She seemed desperate for someone to listen."

Shep tugged on his arm hairs. "Of course, of course. Do you think Ursula is one of the anonymous plaintiffs?'

"Would that track with what you know of her?"

"Yeah. Do you think someone would be willing to kill her over it?"

"You tell me, Shep."

"Maybe. None of us wanted to revisit it. Many of us told her to let it lie. It's one of the reasons we drifted apart. Maybe I should have listened."

"Could any of those who wanted it that way have wanted it badly enough to silence her permanently? That could explain why she thought the Unmaker was coming for her."

"It could."

Jhee tapped a finger against her nose. "But why would she say it had her face?"

"Either way, we should tell Odo we found her. He would want to know."

"I think we should hold off for the moment."

"Why, Jhee? Surely, you don't think Cap's in on this?"

Jhee showed Shep the image she found of Ursula and Odo she found. "The captain is not telling us the whole truth at the very least. It might be best if no one but us knows she's alive and where she is for now."

"I'll defer to your wisdom."

"I think we should examine her clothes. Perhaps we can figure out where she's been all this time."

Kanto held out his hands for the bundle. He wrinkled his nose once he got a good whiff. After he recovered, he turned out the pockets, patted the garb down, and checked the hems.

The lining of Ursula's overcoat bore fruit. Kanto held up a slim, leather-bound journal. "Jhee, this leather is expensive and well-maintained. I thought you said she was broke and practically homeless."

"She was." Jhee took the journal from him and undid the clasp. It was a volume full of illegible cacography. It did not resemble the basis of any arcane cypher, though it did have the characteristics of a traditional cipher. "Maybe this was why Death was after her?"

With a little more thought, it reminded Jhee of finger sequencing mazes. Though not one Jhee had ever seen, and there was no starting sequence, a must if you were to figure out the movements required to solve a watchwork puzzle. The journal also contained identification belonging to Ursula, but an address that matched none from her public records. What sort of dual life was Ursula leading?

"I'll cook her some healing broth," Shep said, "and see if I can follow along with one of Mirrei's healing draught recipes."

"Good. Good."

"Death had her face."

Jhee tapped her snout some more. She might check out the new address at first-sun tomorrow. A return to her legal clinic might also be in order. The tribunal files were sensitive enough no one was allowed off-site access, not even the low-level data being worked on by the legal clinic students. She would examine the tribunal records and see if there was a clue contained there. If Ursula was one of the anonymous plaintiffs bringing the suit, she needed to know who would have the most interest in keeping Ursula quiet.

Jhee waited with Ursula while Shep concocted a healing draught. The data shell Jhee found some time ago rested in Jhee's pocket. She brought it out and considered again if she should read it. After a moment, Jhee realized Ursula had regained consciousness again. Her eyes fixed on the data shell.

"Urli, you planted this on me, didn't you? May I have your permission to look at it?"

Upon seeing the data shell, Ursula set her jaw, and the sharp shades of anger infused her eye color. "I don't care. It's no use to me anymore. I never want to see that again."

"May I look at it?"

"Do what you want."

"I'll need the access code."

"I don't have it."

7

———————

~

The Face in the Mirror

The tribunal files remained as inscrutable and disturbing as before. Dozens and dozens of folk like Shep and his unit gave their accounts. Jhee tried to focus on the puzzle, the mechanics of the matter. This was about getting to the truth and not about her family or their grief. No. She shook her head. Her sisters were heroes killed in combat. They had not met this fate. She could not afford to think anything else and be distracted.

Eventually, Jhee closed her eyes and rested her head in her hands. She needed a break. The cafeteria would be closed. Instead, she prowled the halls for a food dispensary. When she eventually found one, she stared through the banks of heavily processed treats and snacks. Jhee sighed. The noodle nook on the corner might be the better option. A nice sit and some kolal or spiced zoba tea might allow her to focus better.

The fine hairs on the back of Jhee's neck stood up.

She stilled herself and glanced in the reflective surface of the dispensary's front. Nothing behind her. She turned her head one direction. Nothing but shadows. She turned her head the other. Only shadows there, too. She relaxed. Then one shadow moved.

Jhee stepped back in alarm. So did the shadow. Jhee dropped into a stance. The shadow mimicked her. She prepared a cypher. The shadow matched her movements. Exactly. Then Jhee noticed the background behind the shadow matched what she had seen as she came down the hall.

Jhee realized with a chuckle she was looking at a mirror. She approached it and had another laugh at herself. Hands reached out of the mirror and grabbed her shoulders.

Jhee jerked awake, still at her desk in the clinic with the tribunal files arrayed on the desktop before her. The siren module in her neck ached something fierce from the odd way she had slept.

With deliberate slowness, Jhee pored over the tribunal files. Case after case after case, a pattern emerged. Not about misreported deaths, but about the address where many of the pension drafts were being sent. Seven of the sixteen families received their death benefits drafts at the same address. They may have signed the pensions over to a settlement service in exchange for a lump sum; except when Jhee performed an address lookup, the address resolved to the middle of the East Harbor.

Next, Jhee researched the families and crosschecked who they claimed as their qualifying veteran. The trail led away from the parties to the main suit, to an unrelated group of service folk. According to services records, half of the veterans had no family on file. Half those whose deaths the tribunal sought to answer had no family on file. Then who were the folk pushing for the reconciliation council?

It may have been extreme expunging. Some deep cover operatives had their records erased during their assignments. Or the complementary process where they had created a series of deep assembled identities that could be used in a pinch. What if those identities had been put to a different use by the Medical Protectorate? False identities created for experimentation victims. Perhaps not volunteers or criminals but everyday folk kidnapped and sold to Medical Protectorate like the refugees trafficked at Tranquility Bridge.

Jhee laid a finger aside her nose. Her mind went back to the Imperial Sojourn and the two companions who could skin slip into Other Folk. The questionable veterans may have been killed or died in the Scorched Lands in one of the Empire's numerous deep infiltration operations. The chosen operatives would live out their lives reporting back to the Empire from deep within the heart of the Other Folk's territories. For that matter, were these folk even dead?

The bodies were real enough, but those could have been swapped for others no one would miss.

What was Jhee going to do with this information? This was a matter of Imperial Security, and that meant the Abyssal Constabulary might be involved. If she told anyone else about this, even an official such as she could be made to disappear. Jhee scrolled through the records. *Stop now.* She did not have to keep looking into this. *Let it go. Protect your family.* They mattered most. Right?

Right. Jhee gathered her papers and packed to leave. She would let this rest. A montage of all the damage her selfishness had caused in the past replayed in her mind. Recently, she had almost made that mistake again twice. There would not be a third—not if she could help it. She would not go down the path of the puzzle, the game, at all costs again. Family is what was important. Family is what mattered. It had taken her so many years to rebuild her family, Jhee would not risk it now.

Jhee tucked her valise under her arm and walked out of the clinic and back to the loving embrace of her family. The family plus one ate their dinner of halibut.

"What was it like being in the service?" Kanto asked. "Growing up in the Reaches, I remember the posters of those proud, resolute folk in their bespoke uniforms. Noble-looking folk with bright eyes, bold stances posed above messages to join the military for a chance to prove your quality. Not only that, but it was also your duty and obligation as a citizen of the Empire."

"And I knew folk who joined because it meant they got to kill 'barbarians,'" Shep said.

Ursula pushed some food around her plate. "For every two military recruiters who candidly wanted to ensure I knew what I was getting into, there was one who only cared about the recruitment bonus. They promised easy assignments in exotic locales."

Shep smiled and nodded. "Instead you got stationed on some polluted, hardscrabble atoll or in a Scorch hole with spider-mice the size of dogs. Do you remember that one Lockjaw shot with the forty-cal? I think he just pissed it off. You should have seen it, an entire squad fleeing from one spider-mouse."

"Um, yes."

Jhee laughed while holding what she had uncovered close to her heart. Ursula kept poking at her halibut with her nail pike. This was a much more stable if taciturn Ursula than Jhee was used to seeing. Despite how she turned up on their doorstep, the wasted away aspect of her appearance had gone as well as the pall that had hung heavy on her.

After dinner, Jhee pored over the Albatross dossiers again with an eye toward different irregularities, safer irregularities. Having once seen the pattern, she could not help but notice it anyway. How could she not be horrified by what she had found?

"Denme," Kanto said.

Jhee reacted with a startled, "Hm?"

"Everyone's retiring."

"Yes. Yes. Help Ursula up to her room if you would."

"What about you?"

"I have work to finish up for the evening. Keep her company. I'll be up soon to say good night."

In her study, Jhee stared at the Albatross dossiers. Something must be done. *But not by you.*

Jhee left the study. Kanto and Ursula were still enjoying drinks in the sitting room.

"Miss Ursula, why don't you have brands like Shep?"

Ursula lifted her pant leg. "A brand? I do. Right here. Ain't she a beaut? Says I'm property of the empire."

"Shep has that, but he has an extra one on his neck."

"Couldn't tell you anything about it, son."

~

The Youth Center

Jhee wandered the capital streets, allowing the Path Maker and the First Makers' Design to guide her steps. The impulse to visit Kanto seized her. She hailed a transport, then did not hop out until in front of Kanto's youth center.

The youth center's neighborhood was not all that different from the area near the free clinic she supported in Galleon City. It was the same in most cities and towns. The poor gathered where they were allowed, where the affluent seldom frequented. Noisy transport hubs, dumps, and industrial areas housed those who had no options or resources to find alternatives. Anywhere else until the more well off in a search for bargains arrived to push them out by driving up costs. Then the cycle began anew elsewhere. In these areas, the poor always remained because the risks still outweighed the bargain.

Inside the youth center, a volunteer pointed Jhee to Kanto's location. Kanto's bright citrine and amethyst trimmed robes contrasted with the dingy classroom and similar but dirtied colors of the children's toys. Muddled light beamed in from frosted windows covered with rusty security grating and in need of a good cleaning. Jhee took a moment to watch him with the children.

Despite being in an environment Jhee was sure he would not be caught dead in as little as a year before, Kanto appeared the happiest she'd ever seen him. He and the children bounced along to the beat of the radio as it played one of those songs she had been hearing everywhere. A presentation board behind him bore musical notations and the lyrics. She puzzled out that it was one of the other songs she had heard many of her students enjoying. That was an excellent teaching technique she sometimes used herself: relate one's lessons to a cultural touchstone that would be of interest to the children.

Many of the children and Kanto sang along. Jhee never recalled hearing him do more than hum. At the chorus, all the children joined in, and he performed some trendy dance move. Had she ever seen him dancing in such a common fashion? Jhee knew him to be a gifted dancer, but all she had ever seen him perform were the formal tunes of courts and the partner dances.

Kanto smiled when he saw her. Jhee gyrated along with her head at least, but she knew it looked awkward and offbeat. The song ended, and Kanto turned off the broadcast receiver.

"See what I mean about the timing and rhythm patterns?" Kanto asked his students. "It's very similar to those played by our ancestors of thousands of years ago, or even the First Ones. Folk are wired for music. Some beats may be universal and have a similar energizing effect on folk today as they did back then. Now, get out your toy flutes, and we'll try to play it ourselves. I'll be back in one moment."

Kanto touched Jhee's waist and gave her a quick muzz on the cheek. "You're a natural," Jhee said.

"I learned by watching the best. My, this is a pleasant surprise."

"I haven't been here since you first started and wanted to see you work."

"I'm glad. Though, your anonymous donations have been much appreciated."

"Anonymous donations?"

"Don't be coy. I'm privy to the household finances now. Both you *and Shep* have been giving the center money. I also suspect he's the one who's responsible for the long guard who make sure I get to and from here safely."

"That's me."

"Then he must be behind the toughs across the street who keep the area around the building clear."

"Sorry," Jhee said. "We know you wanted to do this all by yourself."

"I'm not complaining exactly. My ego is less important than helping these kids. I'll be finished in an hour or so. Stay, and we can go home together?"

"Agreed."

The children acted moths to Kanto's charisma. They crowded him and leaned in as he demonstrated techniques on the harp. He sat one child on his knee and had them blow into a horn. The noise was loud and Maker shaming. The children covered their ears and giggled.

Few by few, parents or siblings arrived to collect the children. A few of the older children went home on their own. Kanto and the other volunteer waited with the last child. They kept a positive face for her but gave each other frowns. Jhee waited with the little girl while Kanto and the volunteer locked up. The four waited together on the front steps some more. It was practically last-sun when a little girl, dirty and barely older than the one they waited with, arrived.

"Baba's sick... I'm sorry. I'm sorry." The older girl repeated it over and over while she smoothed out the younger child's coat and escorted her down the steps. The task barely kept her embarrassed tears at bay.

Jhee watched and pursed her lips as the two children hurried down the street. "Shouldn't we walk them home?"

"It will only make it worse for them. Their baba's sick from drink and doesn't like them being here," Kanto said and held up his conch. A blinking, red dot on a city grid moved away from the center's marker. "Here's us. Here's where they live. We'll wait until they reach it. There is not much else we can do about what comes after. The classes are their time to be happy, to be kids."

Jhee watched the dot without breathing. Once the dot reached its destination, she breathed again. She sighed but could not help but think of what would happen after. Kanto presented Jhee with his arm, and they headed for home.

Kanto remained quiet during the ride, not full of his usual gossip and details on scandals. Jhee missed the chatter a bit. More than once, it had turned out to be useful, and she had to admit having lived with too much silence over the years. Information she had been too obstinate to realize until he had patiently proved it to her. Had he matured, or had she mellowed? She instructed the transport to leave them at the foot of their driveway. She savored a few more minutes like this with him, such a marked difference from where they were before. Even more, his excitement for life had grown on her.

They reached the main door. When Jhee placed her hand on the ornate handle, Kanto touched her wrist. She waited for him to speak.

"I want to join the services," he said.

Jhee closed her eyes and gripped the handle tighter.

"Nothing?" Kanto asked. "You're not going to try to talk me out of it?"

"Do you want me to?"

"Yes. No. I don't know."

"If this is because what Shep said at the resort... You don't have to serve."

Kanto sighed. "I know. You and Shep, both did. I feel as though I should be giving back more. What you two went through, so Mirrei and I can have options."

"Exactly. We did so others like you and she didn't have to." Jhee cut herself off. "I know you don't think I fought hard enough for Mirrei."

"I was wrong. That's not why I'm doing this."

Jhee laid her hand on Kanto's cheek. "I want to respect your choices and treat you as though you know your own minds. If I don't fight you on this, please know it's not like it was before. I value you and your place in our family. More than that, I respect you. I can't speak for how Shep will react, though. If your mind is not already made up, and even if it is, if you have questions, I'll do my best to answer them without trying to push you one way or another."

"Thank you, Jhee."

Jhee and Kanto touched escae.

The Turquoise Typhoon I

A curious quiet greeted Jhee upon her arrival home a few days later. She set down her valise in the entryway. No music played as was Kanto's wont about now or other acknowledgment came from her husbands.

Shep entered the foyer from the sitting room, wild-eyed. He hustled to her. "Turn around. Leave. Quickly," he whispered.

"Is that her?" an older woman's voice called from whence Shep had come. "Tell her to get her tail in here."

Jhee matched Shep's grimace at the sound of the voice: the Lady Kaydence, Kanto's grandmamere. Would Jhee be able to run for it?

"Well, get in here. I know you're out there."

Jhee inched around the foyer door. Kanto sat in his favorite spot, head down, hands folded in his lap. He glanced at Jhee, seeking some form of mercy or relief.

"Get us a drink, yes?" Lady Kaydence directed him.

"Straightaway, grandmere."

Kanto ran off. Lady Kaydence smiled after him. A moment later, her smile dropped. She whipped her turquoise hover chair—which matched the color of her robes—around to face Jhee without so much as bumping the end table. Jhee took a step back.

"Lady Kaydence," Jhee said, "to what do we owe this lovely, but unexpected visit?"

"Clam it. Did you think I wouldn't find out?"

"Find out?"

"About that one trying to join the military."

"Lady Kaydence," Jhee said, "both Shep and I have spoken with Kanto at length. This is something he wants to do."

"Fix. This," Lady Kaydence finished sweetly.

When Kanto returned with an iced melon drink, they gossiped and made small talk. Shep used playing host as a reason to leave every so often. Over Lady Kaydence's drink, Jhee received stares so cold they should have frosted the rim of her glass. When the lady said, "fix this," she meant it.

"Your idiot cousins are still idiots," Lady Kaydence said. "I swear you are the only one of this generation of Kenyattas worth your salt."

"What of my sisters?" Kanto asked.

"Your sire's children are fine. Last I heard, they are making plans to relocate to the inner isles, too. Like everyone else."

"I shall have to look them up."

Lady Kaydence frowned, then sighed. "Enough of that. I'm sure it hasn't been nonstop parties and fashion. What else have you been doing to keep yourself busy?"

"I've been volunteering my time at a youth center. I give underprivileged children music lessons. You should see how eager and precocious they are. They are quite adorable children."

"I bet they are. What of children of your own? I'm not getting any younger. I want some grand-grands to dandle on my knee or more accurately give hover rides to. These taffies won't eat themselves."

Kanto sipped his highball and glanced at Jhee demurely. A sudden rush of guilt made Jhee face away. She wanted nothing more than to make a hasty exit again.

"I'm on a breeding cycle with Shep," Jhee blurted out. "It's just taking longer than expected. Once it resolves in children or not, Kanto and I will discuss the matter further."

"Also, still a second, I see," Lady Kaydence said. "You told me you'd be denme by the time you reached the capital."

Kanto wiggled his shoulders defensively. "It's proved to be more difficult than I imagined. Jhee and Shep are very close. He deserves his position. Besides, at the Imperial functions, I am given pride of place on her arm. You should have been at the imperial resort with us, grandmere."

"At my age, I've got no cause to be running around an island resort with a bunch of backstabbing phonies. Could you see me and this thing on the weirs courts?"

"Nonsense, grandmere. You were kicking my tail for years after you got that thing."

"That's because you let me win."

"No one lets you do anything."

"You better remember that."

"The Imperial Sojourn was everything I hoped. I think I glimpsed both the Regents. We attended the private opera. A select group and I were asked to perform at a private event where they attended. They must have been practically within arms' reach."

"You were quite the highlight," Jhee said. "How many lords and ladies asked you to tutor them or their relations?"

"Too many to count. I'm still considering it. I have some time left in between the center and my charity work. I could fancy being an Imperial tutor."

Kanto's expression clouded over for a moment from the specter of the abbey and the vizier in residence. The vizier had been an imperial tutor once and had abused her position.

"I always knew our isle was too small for you," Lady Kaydence said.

After Kanto set down his drinking glass, he stiffened his spine, "Grandmere, I know why you're really here."

Lady Kaydence glared at Jhee, then whipped back around to Kanto. "You mean this nonsense about you joining the services? Of all the dunderheaded, misguided notions. These two were supposed to be pampering and taking care of you, not letting you sit vigil over dying women or go haring off to die."

"Grandmamere," Kanto said, "it's peacetime."

"Save it. That only shows how naïve you are. There are plenty of places for you to wind up stationed even in peacetime: a barbarian breach here, an uprising there. The Shield can't save you from those."

"Please, Lady Kaydence," Jhee began.

Jhee lost her thought process when the grand dame rounded on her again. "As for you. I agreed to this match for you to lavish affection on him and keep him in the style to which he was accustomed. Not for you to fill his head with jingoistic nonsense."

"Grandmere, they didn't. They have been nothing but frank and candid with me." Jhee placed a supportive hand on Kanto's shoulder. Shep moved in behind them. Kanto took courage from a glance at them before he faced down his grandmamere. "It's my decision."

Lady Kaydence sneered at them in turn. She zoomed her chair right up to them. As Lady Kaydence fixed each of them with a glance, Jhee swallowed. Kanto clutched her hand.

Lady Kaydence scoffed and held out her arms. "You impudent, young pup."

Jhee, Kanto, and Shep relaxed. Kanto went to his grandmamere's arms in relief. "Thank you, grandmere."

"I couldn't be prouder of you."

Kanto blushed. Lady Kaydence pulled a paper-wrapped lace root melon taffy from a compartment in her hover chair.

"Grandmere, I'm too old—"

"Ah." Lady Kaydence held the taffy closer, and Kanto took it. She patted his cheek. Lady Kaydence dabbed her eyes. "Now, Jhee, you best show me around this manse of yours, so I can acquaint myself while I'm here."

"I can do it, grandmere."

Lady Kaydence held up a hand. "You've played host enough for the moment. It's your denbe's turn. However, if you want to have a quick tea in my quarters before I retire, that would be acceptable. Only the two of us like old."

With a smile and taffy proudly consumed, Kanto set about having the servants clear their drink service. "Yes, grandmere."

~

The Turquoise Typhoon II

With envy, Jhee regarded Shep when he excused himself and made his escape. Jhee led Lady Kaydence down the hall. Their townhouse had been outfitted with access ramps in anticipation of accommodating Mirrei's mobility chair. They served just as well for the grand dame's use. A twinge of regret over Mirrei made her pause.

Lady Kaydence did not allow it to last long. "Do you think you can dissuade him with Imperial music lessons? I raised him more determined than that. It's times like these I regret it. And, another thing, if I wanted him saddled with another dying woman, I would have kept him at home with me. He needs someone to caretake him for a change."

"Kanto is grown and fully capable of making his own decisions."

"Which is why you have to be extra devious about making him think the decision is his. He can see through most common ruses."

"To what end?"

"To keep him safe. I presume you have contacts, misfile his documentation. Do anything and everything to delay him until he comes to his senses. Barring that, exercise every influence to not have his service interfered with like your first husband's. I figured after your go around with the Mitsus and the Crag Halls, you'd have built up a healthy contingency of favors and leverage points. You don't want history to repeat itself."

Jhee clasped her wrists behind her back. "Trust me, I have no intentions of letting anything like that happen again."

"I should think not. With my dowry and those you gained from other families over the years, you'll have one and a half, maybe even two full shares of M-corp preferred company stock—if the nightmare with the Mitsu estate is ever sorted out. Enough to make you an elector at the very least. If you don't now, you definitely will once I pass and all mine pass to him and by extension you. He can't inherit my seat, and I don't trust any of the other heirs with it."

"That's none of your business."

"Don't be so naïve, girl. If I could find out, you are drenched sure these Imperials will, eventually. They'll be courting you soon if they already haven't. With the way the succession fights are going, one vote more or less could make all the difference."

By "M-corp," Lady Kaydence meant MANTEL. The MANTEL corporation held nearly all the mineral, land, and natural resource rights in the Empire. Its charter expressly forced the passing of shares and, by extension, voting rights through the female line. As a male, even if Kanto possessed shares, he couldn't be seated on the MANTEL board or participate in the mineral rights exchange council.

"I will protect my grandson and won't have him treated as a tile like they did to Shep. You think all is forgiven now that you've moved to the capital. If anything, your parting act as the district's Justicar cemented the old grudges for those who wound up on the wrong side of the Spectral Armada fiasco. Even my own Kaisonia was never so petty, and believe me she could be petty, to Kanto's detriment."

"Which is why it's so important I don't undermine him or his decision."

Lady Kaydence sighed. "I was never so disappointed in her as I was when he was born."

Jhee gripped her wrists harder.

"Don't mistake me. Her behavior…. I hadn't truly seen her for who she was until then. I was so grateful to still have her I'd spoiled her. We Kenyattas are a proud lot. I hadn't realized how much I had taught her to be cruel and undervalue family. It's a hard lesson when you thought you raised one kind of child, and she shows you she's another. You do what you can to raise them the best you know how. You may even think you've done a good job."

The Kenyattas were one of the families who lost the most the day the ferry sank. Jhee reached out hesitantly to Lady Kaydence's shoulder. "I'm sure you did your best. That was a tough time for everyone."

"You don't have to flutter foot around it, Jhee. My heirs were a bunch of morons and trenchers, and now most of them are dead. I've made my peace with it and tried to do better with Kanto. Your sister, may the Makers and Waves keep her, is the only reason I didn't lose Kaisonia."

"Is that why you threw your support behind me?"

"I was neutral."

Dubbed the Turquoise Typhoon, by those who had the misfortune to stand in her way, even if she had not thrown her full support behind Jhee, it was enough that she had stayed out of it.

"How long do you have?"

"By all rights, I should be under the waves already. Does he know?"

"I have not told him, but I think he understood what you were up too."

"Of course, he did. He's my grandson. He's quite clever, you know. Don't let the appearances fool you. I wish I had told him that more."

"I think he knows."

"What of you, dear? I had hoped to have some little squirts to spoil with taffy by now."

"It's complicated."

"Uncomplicate it. You're not a hermit, Jhee. Don't wait until you're like me to realize it. Now, you best show me to my room."

Jhee brought the grand dame to her suite, where Kanto awaited them with a freshly set tea service.

"Everything arranged to your liking, grandmere. The tea will be prepared momentarily."

"Such a good grand prawn. Now, let's catch up. You are excused, Jhee."

Lady Kaydence piloted her chair into her suite. Jhee kissed Kanto on the cheek. Jhee had already reached the hallway when she realized she had just been dismissed in her own house. Kanto caught up to her.

Kanto gave a quick glance at the door to the grandmamere's suite. "Whatever she asked you to do, don't do it."

Jhee glanced around. Now she was keeping secrets in her own house. "I hadn't planned on it."

"Did you get lost?" Lady Kaydence called. "This tea sits too long, the flavor will be even bitterer than I."

They touched escae, Makers' marks, briefly. "Coming, grandmamere."

Some time later, Kanto entered into the kitchen where Jhee was constructing a sandwich. Kanto entered and plopped down at the kitchen island opposite Jhee's sandwich fabrication station.

"Grandmamere has finally gone to bed," he declared.

"Blessed be the Makers." Jhee bisected her sandwich and pushed half toward him. "How did it go?"

"I held my ground." Kanto munched into the sandwich. "Wow, this is good."

Jhee may not have been able to plate a meal like Shep, but no one made better sandwiches. She savored a bite of the sea salt mixing with the dressing. "I meant what I said. It's your decision, and I'll respect it. But I'll answer any questions you have."

"What was it like for you?"

"My two eldest sisters had secretly joined the navy. I later joined too. I wanted to do my duty…. They went to give me my seaworthiness test, and I froze. The incident was quietly scuttled because of my status. I was excused from normal naval service and sent to the intelligence pool because I could artifice. Most importantly, it still was considered the navy. For the daughter of a prominent family to join the army, just wouldn't do. No one was the wiser. My family got to save face. I never told anyone that. I'm not even sure if Shep knows the details."

"There were rumors in the Reaches."

"I know. Spread by the Crag Halls with help from the Mitsus."

"The two sides of Mirrei's family. I'm understanding more and more why you and she chose to marry to end the feud."

"The Crag Halls had to save face once I broke the marriage contract and eloped with Shep. In primary school, our youth cohort declared, we would be different. We would put all the old family squabbles out to sea. Generational feuds? Anchors of the past. Instead, we elevated feuding to a level where you would have to look up from Equilibrium Point Station to see it. Don't feel as though you have to compete with us."

8

———————

~

Dinner Guests

"So, Sheepdog here goes charging in, screaming and waving his arms like a madman," Odo said. "It turned out to be a bunch of pre-jubilants on a fishing expedition. They take one look at him, drop their things, then turn tail and run. He picks up their equipment and proceeds to spend the rest of the day diving. He caught enough sea meat to keep us fed until our supplies arrived."

Jhee sipped her wine, and Shep even smiled. *Those teenagers never knew how close they came to death,* Jhee thought.

Kanto laughed, "Sheepdog? Sniffer?"

"Ah, those were the days," Odo said. "Sheepdog, here, is the one who always did his best to keep us together and looked after."

"That explains 'Sheepdog.' That's precisely what he does with us, too. Why do you call denbe 'Sniffer?'"

"Because she was allergic to everything but the truth which she was relentless in sniffing out."

Shep grunted.

"Sheepdog's better than his original name, Cooky," Captain Odo said.

Kanto barely contained his laughter. "Cooky?"

Shep's nail pike clattered onto his plate. "Lot of units called the gul who prepared the food Cooky. But it got confusing if more than one unit was stationed together."

575

The captain fished out an image from his inner pocket. "This is our unit, the Dawn Wolves."

Kanto practically snatched the framed and bound image from Captain Odo's hands. "Dawn Wolves? You chose your married name from your war unit, denme?"

"I'd resolved not to choose a married name at all in those days," Shep said. "I was a modern man, and veiled names were a relic."

"So, you and denbe were married when you served? I thought married men were excluded from the lottery?"

"I didn't serve because of the lottery."

"You volunteered?"

Shep's mouth twitched. "No."

Kanto took the hint and asked, "When was this taken?"

"Right around our discharge," Captain Odo answered.

"Shep still doesn't have his scar."

Shep had begun to tug on his arm hairs. "The scar happened after I left the service."

"I always assumed you got your scar in the military. Did you get into a street fight?"

"We can talk about that later," Jhee said. She stroked the command sigil, as much out of reflex as to calm Shep. "What say we have a game of tiles?"

"Excellent suggestion, Sniffer."

Servants cleared away the dinner plates and glasses. The four of them retired to the parlor.

"Overrun… Sniffer," Kanto teased.

"That's Puzzler to you," Jhee said.

After the quick game, Jhee broke out her best brandy. Odo pulled out a cigar case. "May I?"

Jhee looked to Kanto, who answered, "This once. Only because you are our honored guest."

"Bah, naw, you've been such a gracious host. I'll go outside. Sniffer, Sheepdog, care to join me?"

"Go," Kanto said. "Reminiscence with your friend. I'll square everything away."

They retired to the rear veranda attached to Jhee's study. Odo produced the cigar case again. He took out a tightly rolled smoke root cigar and drew it under his nose. He offered one to Jhee and Shep, but they declined.

Odo clipped the cigar end, then used a finger flint to spark the end with fire drawing. "One of the few the missus lets me do. How are we doing with the investigation?"

Shep opened his mouth, but Jhee interrupted him.

"I'm sorry, Captain," Jhee said. "We looked everywhere. If she is still alive, she doesn't want to be found."

Odo took a long draw on his cigar. The tip glowed an intense orange, matching his eyes then ashed over. A white wisp of smoke floated away on the breeze. "Drenched shame. She was the best of us Wolves. She deserves better than to be chewed up and spit out like leaf mash."

"We all did," Shep said.

Odo nodded. "True. True. I only wish there was something we could have done for her. In your search for Ursula, you didn't happen to come across an old attaché case, did you?"

"No, why?"

"It contained some sentimental items of mine. Old photos, mementos, and keepsakes from our time in the service. I gave them to Ursula to see if it would snap her out of it."

"Keepsakes and mementos? I didn't find anything like that, but then again, I wasn't looking for them. What's really in the case, captain?"

Odo grimaced. "No fooling you, is there, Sniffer? They're of a rather explicit nature. I wrote Ursula off and on over the years. The life of a secondary spouse is a lonely one. I wrote to her. She wrote to me. We saw each other in person only occasionally, I swear. If the contents of our correspondence should become public and the missus were to see them or learn about them…. Well, I don't think you want me moving in with you."

Jhee stared at the captain. "I'll take another look, but still no promises. This is it, though. From here out, no more lies."

"I swear. Thank you, Sheepdog, Sniffer."

Jhee wanted to believe him, but her Maker within urged caution. "What else do I need to know?"

"Ursula may have been pregnant."

"Yours?"

"Presumably."

They returned to the parlor. Kanto sat on the couch, streaming the day's testimony from the tribunal. The three, Shep, Jhee, and Odo, perched on the edge of their chairs. A bold and brash vizier in the finest of suits and groomed to the quads occupied a driftwood bench before the balustrade and assembled judges.

Shep sneered. "So, that's her, is it? The one who signaled it all; the one who signed off on all the experiments?"

"Yes," Odo hissed. "The butcher of Haddondeep. The Architect of Sorrows."

The sigil on Jhee's arm burned with Shep's hatred. Jhee kept her own counsel. The vizier presented about how Jhee expected her to look, every bit the arrogant bureaucrat who thought nothing of ruining lives. They were all just numbers on a screen. But for a few quirks of the Divine mechanism, could that have been Jhee on another Path? One who did not see people as folk but as resources to be used and discarded like Shep and the Dawn Wolves.

Jhee would never know the full extent of what the Dawn Wolves went through. She had only been a liaison. The Dawn Wolves were specialized in abyssal missions and infiltration. She had used her family's clout to track down the Dawn Wolves and get herself embedded with them in violation of service rules. Though Jhee had been one of the few field trained artificers at the time, so they had had little choice. Jhee and Shep were discreet and kept their relationship under wraps, a habit hard to break once they returned to civilian life. They were always mindful of public displays of affections, even beyond what propriety had demanded of an official such as herself.

Even now, there was a distance between Jhee and Shep, one she could not always attribute to their service. The open affection Jhee could express for Kanto had become a relief. The distance went beyond their war service and kept coming back to one woman, Miramar. The distance was born of the knowledge Jhee always tried to hide and hated to admit: Shep may have loved Miramar more than her. When Shep lost the lottery, Jhee, not Miramar, had done everything she could to stop him from being sent to the front lines and track him down once he had disappeared into the bottomless trench of bureaucracy. Shep had been grateful, but gratefulness is not love. Shep's affair with Miramar had simply driven it home.

"Odo?" Ursula said.

Captain Odo's face brightened. "Suli."

"I thought I'd never see you again."

"Me too. I thought the regent..." Captain Odo swept her up in his arms. "Suli."

"I had to show myself when I heard your voice."

Odo cast a dark glance Jhee and Shep's way. "You were here this whole time?"

"Don't be angry. Our friends only did as I bade. Come, my love, whisk me away from here."

Jhee approached Ursula in the hidden room as the now chipper woman packed her what few belongings she had.

"You're leaving?" Jhee asked.

"Why yes, you've been such true friends. But now I think it's time I get out and face the world again."

Jhee held out the data shell. "Don't forget this."

"Oh, that. It's nothing, a bit of file work from a troublesome client. Do me a favor and throw it away."

After Ursula and the Captain left, Jhee and Shep had a quick discussion.

"Pregnant?" Shep mused.

"Did you see any signs of breaching or pouching when you examined her?"

He shook his head. "No obvious ones."

Shep paused. His eyes worked back and forth, weighing if he should add more. He shook his head again.

"The captain said 'might.' Perhaps she wasn't. Perhaps she only thought she was. Perhaps she…"

"…lied," Shep finished. "To get Cap to leave the Regent."

"Perhaps." Jhee rolled the data shell Ursula had left behind between her fingers. "That doesn't seem like her, though."

"Nothing seems like her these past long-tides."

Jhee tried to reconcile all the different facets she had seen of Ursula since Jhee served as their unit's liaison: from the manic one determined to mete out justice via tribunal, to the self-possessed one checking in on them. Next came the beaten down, broken one and then back to a more stable if mercurial one who just left.

Shep stretched in his chair. "Time—desperation—changes folk."

"Perhaps." Captain Odo had acted strange, as well, and lied to them several times. Was Ursula trying to keep the data shell away from him?

"Jhee, I can see the gears grinding in your head. What are you thinking?"

"Nothing concrete. Only nascent doubts."

~

The Passing of the Storm

"Explain this, Justicar," the man with an island senate badge said.

Jhee took a moment to focus on the parchment the senator had thrown on her desk at the legal clinic. He had been at the Imperial Sojourn and spent time talking to Sharlet, Shep's sister. She knew she should have recused herself. Nothing connected to Sharlet ever turned out to her good.

Jhee sighed. "It's a criminal referral. What's to explain?"

"What's to explain? It's against me, you backwater twit. You're calling me a murderer."

"Our legal clinic only made a referral. I suggest you engage a legal team and consult them and the Inquesters' division."

"Withdraw this accusation you piece of swamp trash, or so help me, I'll see you sent back to whatever marsh spawned you. You don't know who you're dealing with." He leaned in. "I have imperial favor."

The island senator left with a smug smile. It turned out the senator had been the benefits director administrator for the scam she uncovered. He had been on the verge of being discovered by a lower-level official who either blackmailed him or threatened to expose the whole scheme. They found the lower-level official murdered, and the senator was suspected of killing him to keep him quiet.

The data shell Ursula left behind had some information about the Albatross dossiers, as well. Ursula may have stumbled onto it in a similar manner as Jhee, just from the opposite angle. Ursula wound up at the veteran services center hunting for answers but dead-ended in their fake identities. She had also uncovered another three missing minor officials Jhee had not.

Another three missing low-level officials... Jhee checked the public records and judicial archives on them; no liens against their homes; no public judgments against them. All of them, however, disappeared under mysterious circumstances. She dug around a bit to finesse her way into uncovering their Imperial identification codes. She would not be able to read the code itself, but she could transmit it and have records requests run on it. She accessed the birthing records, nothing too unusual, born and raised at the central facility on Princess Isle. Many nobles and rich had been. They had the best Academy prep program. They guaranteed their graduates would pass the civil services exam, which would make them eligible for public office. Once Jhee had come to accept the truth of the Divine Mechanism, she had developed a skepticism of coincidence. Sometimes it did hold, but on a case such as this, in a time such as this, it strained credulity.

Nevis might have better results. Jhee left a copy of her findings at the adjunct office for her colleague and headed home. Jhee stared at the cold, dark multistory townhouse. It was beginning to have the feel of Hillside back home, a house of deep loneliness and mourning.

Jhee steeled herself and trudged up the steps. She juggled her conch, valise, and keys, as she left a message for Nevis, "I left some files for you at the adjunct office. Would you run background checks or check the deep records on those folk, please?"

The automatic lights turned on when Jhee stepped into the sitting room. A sob followed right after. Kanto sat in his favorite spot, holding a dispatch.

"Kanto, what is it? Why are you sitting in the dark?"

He gazed at her, his golden eyes swollen and dull. "Grandmere... she's— she's.... Grandmamere has passed. She knew it might come to this. So, she sent me away. In her opinion, I had spent enough time caring for an ailing woman. She wanted me to be happy."

Jhee knelt and took the dispatch from him. She read it briefly. They touched escae. They held each other a long moment. Their gaze met. Kanto pressed his mouth against her firmly and urgently. She thought about pushing him away. Instead, she pushed the thought of houses of mourning and denying him out of her mind.

~

Of Rules and Regrets

Shep crept up the backstair, mindful of the creaky boards. He had to think up an excuse to miss his barber's appointment with Kanto. When he heard movement from Jhee's chambers, he found the shadows and concealed himself. Kanto emerged from the door, putting on his robes. He turned back and kissed Jhee. They embraced for a long while.

Kanto grasped her and nuzzled her neck, seemingly intent on pushing her back into her chambers. She pushed him away and put a finger to his lips. "No. Tomorrow."

"Tomorrow," he repeated. "I'm not sure if I can wait that long."

Kanto scooped up his dropped robes. He turned to regard her with longing before quietly slipping into his room. Jhee smiled. Once his door closed, her smile faded.

Jhee leaned against the jamb of her rooms. "I shouldn't have done that," she whispered.

Shep shifted his position and stepped from the shadows. Doubt left her face at the sight of him. They caught each other's eye. She jutted her chin defiantly in the air. As if she had already not been inconsiderate enough, she had taken Kanto to bed on his night. He clenched his jaw. Pain lanced through it. He flinched.

Shep's dander rose. This time there was no misunderstanding what had happened. He had signaled shark—raised a false alarm—and the Makers had implemented his design. Jhee showed him her back with a crisp turn before closing her door to him. Shep expelled a breath. She had not seen how he looked.

A knock upon his door came a few minutes later. "Shep," Jhee called.

She knocked again and louder when he did not answer. She kept knocking. Shep cracked the door and peered at her.

"We must talk," she said. "I debated letting this lie, but I feel I owe you an explanation if not an apology."

"We'll discuss your infidelity later," Shep said and closed the door before she could say more.

Shep tried not to work himself up too much as he showered and enacted healing on himself. Now, he no longer wanted to skip his barber appointment. He marched down to Kanto's workshop and waited in the barber's chair, eager for the young man to arrive. This was a clear challenge to his household status. He and Kanto would discuss this violation of the rules.

After a few moments sitting, Shep's eyes felt heavy. He awoke when Kanto entered and went over to the mortar and pestle with barely a glance at him. He poured in his soaps and tonics. Clink-clink-clink went the pestle against the bowl. Shep's head pounded. The sound of the pestle striking the bowl got louder and faster. Shep's annoyance grew with it. Despite how he had spent the evening, he was still spoiling for a fight. Shep left the chair and loomed over the upstart. Kanto slammed the pestle against the bowl. Shep tensed. Kanto picked both mortar and pestle up and dashed them against the wall. He hunched over the countertop. Sobs shook his slim frame.

"Kanto?" All thoughts of putting the young pup in his place fled. Shep gently put an arm around his shoulders.

"Grandmamere wanted grand-grands, you know? I wanted to give them to her. I wanted them for myself. I always imagined what it would be like to be in a house full of happy children with their screams and their laughter. I want a house full of children. Yours. Mine. It doesn't matter. This big empty house needs children. As many as we can stand. When you and Jhee are off your breeding cycle, no matter what the outcome, I want Jhee and me to have children of our own. I want to be a father, Shep, not a sire. I wanted to ask you before I bring it up to Jhee."

Shep pulled the young man in against him. Birthing cycle? Jhee and Shep were never on a birthing cycle. They had decided against it long ago. It seems she had lied to him too. "Whatever you wish, denye, my brother groom. We'll discuss it with her together."

Shep cradled the young man and just let him cry. So last night had not been some random tryst to spite him. The young man's grandmamere had died. The Lady Kaydence had died, the last full-blooded matriarch of House Kenyatta. Kanto was the last of the primary birthline of his family, a harsh reality for the proud line of song and music makers. Of course, the younger man wanted children, preferably ones not sired. Kanto could not inherit the bulk of the Kenyatta estate as a male. All anchor holds and proprietary cyphers had to pass on to a female. The deal Shep and Jhee had made with Lady Kaydence was that it would be Jhee until such time as they produced a female heir from her and Kanto. Even so, until that heir came of age, Jhee would have control over the inheritance.

Eventually, Kanto pulled away. "Sorry. I must look a fright. You certainly do. Come. Sit. Let me have a moment to whip up some new lather and pull out the clippers. I can't have my denme looking like a leviathan chewed him up and spit him out now, can I? I'll have you looking like the most distinguished gentleman of gentlemen in no time."

Kanto patted the barber chair. Shep waited patiently. He soon came over with soap and a cape. He secured the cape around Shep. He hummed as he applied the lather. Every so often, Kanto choked back a sob or the melody caught in his throat. He shaved Shep quickly and expertly.

"I'm sorry about last night," Kanto whispered. "I crossed a line. Thank you for understanding. It won't happen again."

All that remained was to straighten matters out with Jhee. Her lies had to stop.

~

Sealed and Dated

"Are we going to talk about last night?" Shep asked.

Jhee sipped her tea, then folded her hands in her robes. "Not if I can help it."

"So, you are just going to run away from it?"

"What do you want from me, Shep? You're the one who shut the door in *my* face. Why are you shutting me out?"

"The irony of that coming from you."

"What is that supposed to mean?"

"Nothing, Jhee. Nothing."

"Don't do that. This is precisely what I'm talking about. You are shutting down on me, and I don't know how to reach you anymore."

"Too busy with other things."

"Is this about Kanto? Are you feeling threatened? It was your idea to marry him."

"I know, I know." Shep threw up his hands.

"I'm trying, Shep. All I want is a peaceful house, calm and order."

Jhee trailed off to watch Shep pace, unsure of how else to continue.

Shep halted and spun on his heel to face her. "Is that why you don't want children? I spoke with Kanto. He's of the notion we're on a breeding cycle. There's only one place he could have gotten that idea. Although, by my reckon, you and I had decided on exactly the opposite."

"I panicked. Since we've settled in the capital, he speaks about children more and more. It's been so long since that was an option. Even after we fully accepted him into the household, it's remained an unspoken matter between you and me."

"You claim you're denying him on my account?"

Jhee pursed her lips. The new spouses had shaken up their household for both good and ill. The increase in household numbers multiplied the emotional complexities of every household decision and interpersonal conversation. "Not wholly. I don't have an honest answer to give him."

"Jhee, don't deny him on my account. Kanto's young. He's fit with an excellent pedigree. The anchors he carries inside are different. And he wants to give you children so your line can continue."

Jhee rubbed the bridge of her nose. She thought back to the Far Reaches when they used to cliff dive as youngsters. In those days, even though she was a weak swimmer, she took the leap as fearless as anyone. Shep's eyes turned a more muted shade before he dropped into his easy chair beside hers.

Shep said, "The M-Prot experiments' effect may not be solely on my potency. We don't know the extent of what Medical Protectorate did to me. We don't know if what they did could affect our children."

"We don't know the extent of what they did to either of us. More than that, though, I like what we have. It's safe, comfortable."

Shep held his hand out to the side in the distance between their chairs. She reached over and took it. "You're scared. Don't you think I am too?"

"Are we parent material? What kind of mamere would I be? I'm careless and preoccupied. I let important issues slide because I don't realize how much they matter to others. Think about my recent behavior. Will I disappoint our children the way I disappointed you?"

"Will I lose my temper or shut down like I did with you?" Shep and Jhee interlocked fingers. "It wasn't all you. I don't know where I fit anymore, Jhee. New house with plenty of servants to do whatever we need done. You don't need me to help you out with cases or security. Then there are the more personal matters."

"I'll always have a place for you in my heart."

"I'm not sure if that's enough anymore. Do you know where I was last night?"

Jhee swept her gaze over him quickly. He had showered and shaved. There was the faint yellowing of old bruises. "A street fight?"

"Close. I found an unsavory all-night gym filled with unsavory gym rats where I sparred and beat the Trench out of the heavy bag. It felt so good, so simple to just hit something again. For all that happened to me during my service, it had a visceral simplicity to it. Fight. Protect. Survive. You're not the only one who longs for order, discipline, something to make sense of it all."

Jhee grunted. "Maybe you should take up arcana and teaching, and I'll do the hitting things."

"To calm the chaos with violence. To find the obvious with the arcane."

"Pastimes, causes," Jhee declared. "We should find you more productive interests outside the home. It may do you some good. Kanto has his volunteer work. What about you? Are there subjects or causes you are passionate about now? The city is the hub of so many paths. Maybe you can find a charity or center which needs help. Maybe something with veterans. The local service center always needs help. Maybe you can see what you can do there."

"Maybe." Shep touched his hand to his chin and nodded. "I have some morning exercise buddies from there."

"It's been just us for so long, and now we're in such a lively place where you can meet all manner of new people."

"Jhee," Shep said, his tone more somber. "Consider what to do about Mirrei's days. We don't know when or if she's coming back. Give them to him. At least for the while. He needs your support more than I do right now."

"Are you sure?"

"I need time to figure out how to just 'be' with our new status quo."

Jhee rose and placed her hands on Shep's shoulders. "About last night. I'll try to do better. Nay. Scratch that. I will do better, by you and by Kanto. I've been a poor denbe of this household. Keeping our house together can't solely be you two's responsibility. I must stop shirking my part of the burden."

"A household sit-down is in order, Jhee. We need to either redefine or recommit to the household rules."

"Mirrei wants a remote meeting. We'll do it then."

"Those of us here need to consult sooner. Especially given his desire for children and to join the service. You can't keep lying to him. There was no excuse for it. You should have told him how you felt all along. Together, the three of us will discuss our options. The death of his grandmamere has hit him hard. We'll need to hammer this out, especially if he is also still intent on serving. A front-line assignment may be out of the question. It will affect his service options if he wants to go the parent route."

"You are as always right, dear one. We need to clear the air. How about tomorrow night? I'll leave work early. Pick us up some crescent pies."

"From Bartir's. Extra garlic. Extra anchovies."

"Deal: sealed and dated." Jhee and Shep stood up. "About Mai."

"Jhee, don't."

When Jhee risked those cliff dives, she only did so because those she loved and trusted, Miramar and Shep, awaited her below. "I understand. On some level, I do. You weren't the only one Miramar tried to seduce. I assumed she had come to me after you had ended matters."

"That fits with her operating mode." Shep refused to face her. "You've spoken about a Maker within that guides you. What's inside me doesn't feel like that. It's an Unmaker. I have an animal within. It's a struggle to ignore its guidance."

Jhee touched her esca to Shep's. She left him alone in the sitting room.

9

———————

~

A Reminder of Briny Town

Jhee locked her office for the day. "Bax, what are you doing here?"

"Begging your pardon, Justicar. I found out more about your friend, Miss Ursula."

"Couldn't this have waited until I got home?"

Bax looked this way and that. He continued to squeeze and mangle his hat. "Nay, Justicar. I think you should follow me. These folk don't stay put long."

Jhee took her valise under her arm and headed out with Bax. He brought them to a seedy area down by the docks. Jhee immediately felt out of place in her professor's robe, carrying a valise. Bax led her to a darkened booth in a corner where an old, grizzled woman in a sea captain's hat sat. She looked up at them with one squinty eye when they approached. Jhee and Bax slipped surreptitiously into the booth with her.

"This is the one I told you about," Bax said. "She can help."

The captain sniffed and flared her nostrils as if trying to get a definite scent of Jhee. Between that and the way she moved her head, Jhee knew instantly she was a berserker. "The one you were looking for has been in here a few times. Asking questions just like you. One day she shows up with another fancy woman in tow, pretty much like yourself. They get into a huge argument, and your friend pulls out a weapon. The other woman just laughs at her. Probably cause your friend's hand was shaking so bad. Looks as though she had the shifty shakes. I've seen it plenty of times. We berserkers sometimes need a little something to take the edge off. What's more, a skin brother of mine's gone missing, too."

Gears of thought engaged within Jhee. A third missing berserker, if indeed Shep's lost hound lady was one too. They left the bar and headed for the transport lane. The more the gears turned, the less this felt like a coincidence.

"I've left it be for long enough, Bax. Where did Shep and Ursula go? And what can you tell me about Shep's walking Dari along with this *friend* of his?"

Bax opened his mouth to speak, but no words passed his lips. He carried a look of thoughtfulness.

"Spit it out, Bax. This is not just a jealous wife's probing. A friend of ours is troubled and might pose a danger to herself and others. If Shep put the two women in contact… If you know something, say it."

Bax's gaze darted this way and that as if he wanted a means to escape the transport. "Shep did not always go to the park. There's a place nearby, a bar, where the hound owners, the ones who gang at least, go. They also went there that night."

"Direct me there."

"Justicar."

"At once, Bax."

"Aye, Justicar, but you might not want to go dressed like that."

Jhee regarded her blue and topaz robes of rank, house, and occupation. "I see what you mean."

She removed her over robes and sashes down to an outfit more resembling her teaching garb. She switched to a basic suit and left her sashes and top robes home. Old Jhee might have thought of that sooner. It was so easy to let the details slide here. Her comfortable teaching job had dulled her instincts. She patted down the robes until she found one of Kanto's surprise pockets of essentials. This robe contained some makeup for disguise and a little emergency kit for field injuries, complete with the inclusion of a few gauzes and poison neutralizer draughts. The last, no doubt a suggestion from Mirrei.

"Will this suffice?"

"Aye, Justicar, it will do."

Jhee stepped inside the seedy bar. The establishment was indeed the tough and tumble place Bax implied. She took in the patched holes in the walls along with chairs and tables held together mostly by prayers. It was still early in the day, and she surveyed the patrons who would be here so early. Many had the ruddy complexions of hard drinkers. One gul had already passed out in the corner. Bax seated himself a few stools down and disguised clearing any obstructions to his sleeve knife by taking out his pipe and tapping out the old pack.

"Hey, sister, what can I get for ya?" the barwoman asked when Jhee approached.

"Ale. Whatever you have on tap."

"Right up."

The barkeep placed the ale in front of Jhee. She gave Jhee a once over as if wondering what threat Jhee might pose. "First time? Definitely not a regular."

"I'm just here to have a drink and check the place out."

"I get it. You're a few hours early. Action doesn't really get going until long after last-sun and not here. You won't find any participants here yet either. All that happens elsewhere. You'll be informed."

"I like to assess things myself."

"Eager. I like it. I think I'll put my shell on you. You have a dangerous, shrewd look to ya."

Shep had found some kind of peace here. What would Shep be doing in a place like this? What did it offer that she had missed? It reminded her of some areas in Briny Town back home. She pursed her lips. It had been so many years, she had almost forgotten. Shep came from Briny Town. A place such as this might feel like home.

Jhee tipped the barwoman and left. Bax slipped out soon after. "What now, Justicar?"

"Keep up what you've been doing and keep an eye on this place."

"Aye, Justicar."

While waiting for a transport, she called her colleague Nevis. They met at the cramped Justicar Annex in at the imperator's station. Nevis was the official Justicar for the capital district, largely a legacy appointment. Both their positions were. Their jobs focused on teaching and consulting with the local imperators' division.

"Did you look into those names?" Jhee asked.

Nevis took her by the arm. "I did. They're dead."

"Dead? All of them?"

"Yes. Also, several had complained to friends about having their homes and transports broken into and a dead toad or frog left behind. Justicar, what's this about? You may have stumbled onto something here. Running the check triggered the algorithm. They have been auto-flagged for follow-up by the system. It's an active case now. I can't share anything with you about it anymore. Since my search triggered it, I'm going to be questioned."

"Is there anything else you can tell me?"

"They were all beaten to death. That's it. Now, don't contact me about this until it is all over. I'll keep your name out of it if I can."

"Thank you. I'd appreciate it."

Jhee thought about what she had learned. All beaten to death like her homeless vets. Again, the Divine Plan made her skeptical of coincidence. She must play this smart. She convinced Nevis to give her a copy of her records on the data shell Jhee provided.

Jhee contacted Inquester Paij from Galleon City. She was not sure if her local imperator department and Justicar contacts needed this kind of heat.

"Well, if it isn't my favorite, way too reasonable and noble Justicar."

Jhee cleared her throat. Abusing her contacts and friendships this way for any but the direst of circumstances still did not sit well with her. For all she knew, this could be nothing. "May I ask you to do something for me?"

"Ask, and I'll decide if I'll actually do it."

"Would you run background checks or check the records on the following people, please?"

"That it? Couldn't you have done that yourself?"

"They may be flagged. Perhaps do it over lunch at the Stingray Club."

"Oh," the inquester's tone took on a serious note. "Understood."

Another Slip

Another day passed, enough time for Jhee's household to coordinate schedules for the family meeting about children. Rather, Kanto had coordinated by trailing Shep and Jhee and keeping after each one until they agreed. She pulled out her conch to send ahead her order for crescent pie from Bartir's and found an urgent message from Inquester Paij. Jhee closed and locked her office for the day, as usual.

"Learned a lot over lunch at the gentlewoman's club. Let's chat. I'll come to you."

Whatever Paij had learned at the Stingray Club must have too sensitive to send via ether. Inquester Paij met her at the capital's natural history aquarium. The woman with her short hair and short robes worn over ankle-length pants looked more at home here than Jhee did. Paij regarded her with a bemused half-smile. Despite the need for discretion, they indulged a friendly forearm clasp between the preserved lesser drake skeleton and a prehistoric leviathan skull. Paij had been instrumental in the fight to save Mirrei's life and talked Jhee down from a few actions she might have regretted in Galleon City.

They purchased some roasted nuts and strolled along the pier with its selection of ocean-side exhibits. Jhee kept her gaze focused in the distance. The pier passed over breakers, which reminded her too much of Wailing Point back home. *Storm Child, Storm Child, not today,* Jhee recited in her head. A mantra her grandmamere had taught her for when the seas got too rough. The Storm Child and the shell drake were said to be the cause of all roughs seas and ill weather.

Paij passed Jhee the bag of roast nuts. Jhee slipped a data shell in it.

"I can't leave you alone for a moment, can I? The second I turn my back, you couldn't help but poke the Ink again," Paij said.

The Ink: Inkerton Enforcement Solutions or Event Solutions or whatever MANTEL needed them to be. Also known as IES or the Squids, they were the enforcement and long arm of MANTEL. Both had many ties to the imperial family. Jhee was shocked, but not surprised. She hadn't meant to tangle with them again so soon.

"I see." Paij noted her reaction. She attached the data shell to a port on the Sensor Suit she wore under her robe. While Jhee had her siren module, Inquester Paij, Galleon City's finest, sported experimental Sensor Suit technology, a thin mesh garment with recording, remote device access, and defensive capabilities. They continued their walk. "They certainly do turn up like scum on water, don't they?"

At the end of the pier, Paij handed over the bag of nuts and the data shell.

"It was good to see you anyway, Inquester," Jhee said.

"Likewise, Justicar. You still owe me a visit to your noble estates. Maybe we'll get together with the misters sometime for dinner."

"Misters? Dinner? Oh Trench, not again."

The crescent pie and the family meeting. She had forgotten all about them. Jhee winced and palmed her esca. She gave the inquester's forearm a farewell clasp, grabbed the bag, and hurried home. She stepped into the sitting room from the foyer with only her valise and the bag of nuts. Kanto and Shep met her with keeled expressions on their faces.

Kanto strode up to her with an accusing frown. "Why would you lie about being on a breeding cycle? I had to learn you weren't from Shep. Were you ever going to tell me?"

"I expected us to find a new situation for you before it became an issue."

"And after? Once you knew I intended to stay? Or when grandmere asked you? Or how about the night I learned grandmamere passed?"

Jhee laid her hand on his upper arm. "Kanto, I'm sorry."

The young man shook it off. "I thought we were past this, Jhee."

Kanto turned and went upstairs. A moment later, a door slammed. Jhee glared at Shep.

"He had a right to know. He is my denye, and I won't keep those sorts of secrets from him," he said and folded his arms.

"If I actually thought that was why you told him, then I'd consider this punishment fairly meted. But it wasn't a noble or principled act."

"If you were here, maybe you could have told him yourself, pleaded your case, mitigated the damage. But you weren't. Like always. What was it this time?"

"I think I stumbled onto something. It may have to do with Ursula."

The self-righteousness slipped from Shep's affect. He unfolded his arms. "What did you find out?"

They brought the data shell she received from Paij to her study. As they reviewed the data, Jhee realized she had been given dozens, perhaps even hundreds of death records and redacted Medical Protectorate files. It would take forever to sort through without explicitly knowing how to narrow her search. If only Mirrei were here with her algorithmic expertise!

"So empty holds, yet again," Shep said. "This is what you stood us up for?"

"My contact wouldn't have given me useless data. There must be something here. I'm just not seeing it yet."

Shep scoffed. "This was a waste of time. Figure it out on your own, Jhee, like you do everything else."

"Wait, Shep, don't go." Jhee followed Shep as he retrieved his overcoat from the coat closet. "Where are you going?"

"To the gym. To look for Urli on my own. I don't know yet. Don't wait up for me."

Shep slammed the door after himself. Jhee stared at the front door glass for a long while. A loud bang outside made her jump. Had Shep returned already? By the time she flung open the door, no one was there. A folded note lay on the mat. A plain, hand-written message read, "We didn't do this. The chamber targets all war criminals regardless of side or division. Your victims had ties to Medical Protectorate only. The chamber wouldn't be that specific." It was signed by "The Star Chamber." Jhee scrambled to seal the note in an airtight container. Before Jhee found one, the letter flashed and consumed itself without a trace of smoke or ash.

Jhee went to the coat closet to hang up her cloak. Her foot hit Shep's gym bag, which remained at the bottom of the cloakroom.

～

The Proctor

Jhee spent the night sitting in her comfy chair in the sitting room, waiting for Shep to come home. In between bouts of worry, she examined the records her contact had provided her via Inquester Paij. With the watchdog systems active, she would have to be extra careful and oblique about accessing the files of the victims she had identified. Perhaps Bax knew someone who could help. She wished Mirrei were here for more reasons than one—the least of which was her know-how of systems' code. Another of the many fascinating facts she had found out about the woman now that her pretense had ended.

After promising to be better, Jhee had screwed up again. Jhee sighed. She was disappointed in herself. She was failing her family, and she did not know how to stop herself. Her household was imploding, and she did not know how to stop it. In fact, it was her failings causing it. Why had she truly lied to Kanto? Why had she kept lying? All she wanted was an orderly house. Was that too much to ask? She liked it calm and peaceful.

She thought about the first of her siblings her family lost, Gascal and Gabi, for the first time in years. When they died, she was so young. She barely had any memory of them. Then there were her older sisters, Gwyn and Gloriana. Both were war heroes, lost at sea, in separate incidents. And last she thought of Ghele, the first hero of her family. Jhee had another sister, but no one had seen her since shortly after her parents' memorial. She just took off one day and left Jhee to be raised by their aging grandmamere.

Jhee was never meant to inherit one house, let alone three. She was meant to be an academic. Now Jhee was the sole bearer of the fabrications and schematics of three lines. She had a responsibility to make sure all those works did not die out. Familial duty had not always driven her. Though by the time it came to negotiate Kanto's marriage contract with Lady Kaydence, Jhee had learned if she did not take on the burden, then many of the Outer Reaches' family legacies might die out—a sentiment the Lady shared.

"Even in death, Kaisonia declared contempt for him via her will. She didn't just leave the special holdings to her nearest female relative, she left everything to her nearest female relative, which luckily for him turned out to be me. I think she still held out for a daughter. I, however, intend to leave everything I can to him and his wife—should he choose to marry. The rules of inheritance prevent him from inheriting either of our anchor holds. Those will have to go to one or more of the idiots. Which are unfortunately the bulk of our estates. Unless he's married, he's screwed. Convince me the woman he should marry is you."

Jhee had understood more than Kanto realized about how it was to grow up practically parentless—with a demanding grandmamere, who wanted nothing more than to fill the void they left behind, but who had her own burdens. Jhee had used that understanding to ingratiate herself to the Turquoise Typhoon long enough to put her marriage offer over the top.

The litany of Jhee's departed family members ran through her head again.

Mamere, drowned; Babere, drowned. Gloriana and Gwyn killed in action or lost at sea, presumed dead. Gascal lost to fever; Gabi kidnapped by barbarians. Gamaje just disappeared one day; Ghele killed rescuing Jhee and other children from a capsized vessel. Had that been what compelled Gloriana and Gwyn to be so ethered up about joining the service, living up to that heroic legacy? Her family gained a measure of love and respect throughout the Reaches despite their crazy grandmamere and criminal past because her sister had died saving so many. If Jhee could swim, could she have saved her? If she could swim, would Ghele have taken one less dive and had the energy to save herself?

Jhee shook her head. No, her first duty was to the husbands who cared for her. She needed to fix this, whatever it was. She did not know if there were any way for her to make amends. Shep had been right. Life had been so much simpler in the outer isles.

Jhee stalked to the closet and threw on her cloak. She looked off into the distance. She saw the nearby veteran services center. It was as good a place as any for her to go.

When she arrived, Jhee sat there with a lump in her stomach. She had dealt with her service in her own way. She was just about to turn around to leave when a voice asked, "May we help you?"

Jhee faced the person who addressed her. It was a woman in a simple proctor's uniform. "It's late. I can come back when you're fully staffed."

"We are always open for our service members. Are you a service member?"

"No, not really. Intelligence pool."

"Some of the intelligence pool were right in the thick of it too, right beside our shock troops."

"Not me."

"Well, why don't you come inside, and we'll talk about it anyway? I mean, you are already here. And I was looking for company on my rounds."

The proctor made a gesture that invited Jhee further into the building. Jhee bit her lip, then crossed the next threshold. She and the proctor journeyed farther into the building. "I'm sorry to impose," Jhee said.

"No imposition. Are you a religious woman?"

"Somewhat. Mechanist. I believe in the First Makers and the Divine Plan."

"It is not a requirement for our help. Simply idle curiosity. We can speak before the shrines or the night gardens if you prefer. Wherever you would be most comfortable."

"The sea gardens," Jhee said, then thought about her sisters. "No, the shrine hall."

"As you wish."

The proctor led her to the shrine hall. Jhee had come empty-handed before the First Makers and would give of herself. She breathed on the ever-burning candle of the Sky Pillar, gave the sweat of her brow to the moss-covered Earth pillar. For the Unknown Maker's hollow, she clasped her hands briefly to honor this Maker but not draw Their notice. To her surprise, the shrine hall housed a Mechanist metronome. Jhee activated it before speaking with the Proctor.

"People are like mechanisms," the proctor said. "Even the most well-constructed ones need maintenance from time to time."

That sounded like something Jhee might have said. "I know that intellectually but rarely put it into practice."

"If you were to speak with a counselor here, do you have an idea what sort might appeal to you?"

"None of those flitty, flowery, wisp whisperer types."

The proctor gave her a credential card for one of the veteran's outreach counselors: Medea. "You're under no obligation to talk to her. The counselor keeps odd hours. I don't think the woman sleeps. She may be available now."

They found the counselor's sparse but inviting office empty. A framed image of the counselor holding up a giant, freshly caught tuna sat on the neatly arranged desk. In the background was the berserker bar. Was this Shep's counselor friend?

"When was the last time you saw her?" Jhee asked.

"I'm not sure. Days."

Jhee tapped her nose. "Is that unusual?"

"Not really. As I said, her hours are eccentric. Shall I leave a note?"

"That won't be necessary."

At the veteran's center entrance, she hesitated again.

"Was there something else?" the proctor asked.

"Thank you. For everything. For taking the time. I hope to visit more in the future."

The proctor inclined her head.

~

The Storm's Wish

In the intervening days, Kanto refused to talk to Jhee. She tried a few ruses to corner him so they could speak. He was not even the least bit interested. She staked out his room, yet he seemed to always somehow slip by her. Shep and Bax often ran interference for him, providing a crucial distraction at just the right time.

Perhaps it was all for the good. Jhee had no idea what she would say to him. She had been lying to him for years. He had every right to be as upset with her as she was with Shep. She was not even sure why she had done it— not beyond what she had tried to explain to him that first night.

Jhee thought about going to the volunteer center. Somehow that felt like a violation to confront him somewhere that meant so much to him, and he could not rightly walk out of it. It was a refuge, and he deserved a safe space.

She spent a lot of her time at home in the sitting room, waiting for the door. Shep also magically avoided her too. Bax's hand in all this rather perturbed her, but she could not fault him. He had served them for many years, and he could not help but have conflicted loyalties about the matter.

Shep had been understandably distant and secretive. When she could get him to talk to her and tell her where he was going, he always said the gym. Yet his gym bag was usually there all night. She had no right to complain, but still, she wondered. Where was he going? Why would he lie about it? What did it mean? Then there was the case. All those missing men and women, murdered, beaten to death. After having a dead frog left on their transports, at their homes, or place of work. It was definitely a mystery for her to ponder. Before she could finish considering these questions, the front door opened.

Jhee was sitting in the study reading when Kanto stepped into the room.

She looked up from her conch. He stood, posture straight and proud, hair trimmed short and neat, in a naval cadet uniform. Jhee blinked. She slowly put down her conch. They never broke eye contact as she went to his side.

"I thought you should know," he said.

Jhee took Kanto's hand. "Are you sure?"

"Yes."

"Then fine."

The tension drained out of his stance.

"Don't get too excited," Kanto said. "I joined the auxiliaries' spirit corps. After some basic training, it's off to the adjunct services and administration division."

Jhee expelled a relieved breath. "Logistics. Quartermasters."

"Apparently, between my marital status, who I'm married to, and a youthful incident which resulted in my both having an injury and criminal record, I got parked in the bureaucracy. There will be some weekend training so we can better understand what the troops go through."

"I'm positive you'll do well wherever you end up, and know that I respected your wishes and didn't interfere."

"The Turquoise Typhoon had the last laugh. Grandmere had me black-listed from service. I wouldn't have put it past grandmamere to have a hand in this. She's still getting her way, even from beneath the waves."

"If you want, I can undo whatever she's done."

"Don't. I think I'll honor her last wish. Only because I found another way to be of service. She wanted to die knowing I was relatively safe. I'll let her have it. Assuming it was her design intent, not yours."

"I played no part in it. I swear."

"You do understand why I have to ask, though?"

"Yes."

"You lied to me for years. There was nothing I think I wanted so much as to be a father or a sire doubly if it was for you and Shep."

"You rarely said anything."

"I was trying not to make trouble. I wanted to learn as my denbe and denme saw fit, especially given your ambivalence about keeping me on as a spouse. I had assumed childbearing was why you had married me. Certainly not to dive and fish for you."

"I convinced myself I was doing everyone a favor. I suppose I was only doing myself one."

"Do you even know why?"

Jhee shook her head. "It had been only Shep and me for so long. I had resigned myself to a life without children so long ago. It simply wasn't an option. It wasn't who I was or compatible with the choices I had made. Then you came along, and Mirrei, I panicked. I'm sorry."

Kanto put his soft top in his hand. "And now?"

"When I saw you at the center with those children, I imagined what it would be like if they were ours."

"And?"

"I didn't dislike the idea."

Kanto cocked his head at her.

"I liked the idea. I saw you and thought you deserved to be a father. And if I was the mother, it wouldn't be a terrible thing."

Kanto furrowed his brow. "It's progress, I suppose. Grandmere gave me everything I needed to have my gentleman's surgery reversed years ago. If I chose, I could have decided the matter for you. If we are to have children, I don't want you to do so to make me happy. I don't want you to even consider it if it's not what will make you happy. Our children, if we have them, deserve parents who both love them. No ambivalence. Don't answer now. Think on it. I don't want us to live a lie. I don't want our children growing up with a mother who resents them. Agree, if and only if, the answer is an enthusiastic 'yes.'"

"That I can promise. We'll schedule another sit down with Shep. During the day, before the remote meeting with Mirrei. This time I swear I'll be there."

Kanto and Jhee touched their esca together.

"Nice uniform," Jhee said.

Kanto raised his eyebrows. "Are you trying to flirt with me, dear wife?"

"Am I succeeding?"

"Whose day is this?"

"Mirrei's. Before my error caused our present turn, Shep and I agreed until such time as she decides to come back, or we all agree otherwise, they'll be yours. If you want them."

"I do."

"When do you have to report back?"

"I think I can squeeze in some time for my dear wife."

Kanto giggled. Jhee joined him. She had a vague thought in the back of her mind about Shep until Kanto swept her up in his arms and carried her to her room.

As they lay cuddling in each other's arm later, they talked. Kanto traced his fingers along her arm sigil and tattoos, coming to rest on the command sigil.

"Jhee, how did Shep get his scar? Does it have anything to with your arm decor? I thought a sigil like yours was how they controlled all berserkers. That's not how to shut down any berserker. It's how to shut down Shep."

"I gave him the scar. I awoke one night to his hands around my throat. He was in a berserker fugue. It was like he did not even see me. I didn't want to bring this up previously for fear it would seem I was attempting to distract from my behavior."

"Would he pose a danger to our children?"

"I don't believe he would. Nothing like that has ever happened since."

10

───────

∼

The Suit

Jhee used the digi-tip on her fingernail claws to write out the derivation for determining the angle and direction of blood splatter. Behind her in the lecture hall, rustling and whispering announced her students' arrival. However, as she continued to write, it grew louder instead of quieted when the more outspoken students settled. At last, she turned around. Many of the students had their conchs out. They glanced from her to their screens in wild-eyed disbelief.

Jhee narrowed her eyes, trying to get a read of the room. Her conch buzzed in her valise. A news alert displayed about the death of the island senator her legal clinic had referred to the Empire for prosecution.

Jhee sighed, sometimes it could not be helped. "All right, students, let's return to forensic cyphers."

The next day students remained abuzz. Her conch buzzed again. Senator vindicated. Within a day of his suicide, the prosecution uncovered shocking new evidence that exonerated him. Island Senator cleared of all charges. The prosecutor's office could not be reached for comment.

Jhee finished her lecture, then read the details of the story as she returned to her office. The senator's family released a statement against her.

"The Justicar who targeted my husband was reckless and had a vendetta. She railroaded him, accused him of a murder he didn't commit, and he killed himself. If anyone needs to be investigated and locked up, it's her for incompetence, malpractice, and malicious prosecution. Someone needs to stop her before she destroys more poor innocent folk. Our family is hereby announcing our intent to sue her for everything she's worth."

Jhee plopped down in her office chair. She received a notice of appeal. One of the people she sentenced in one of her earliest cases was challenging her ruling. She sighed. That was fine. It happened from time to time. It was expected.

What distressed her most was being wrong about the Senator's case. She always did her due diligence. Even then, mistakes can happen. She read through the news stories trying to find out what she can about this exonerating evidence. Finding none, she called up Nevis, her judicial colleague.

"We can't be speaking."

"I know. I just wanted to know. What was this additional evidence?"

"I can't tell you that."

"Please. If I am responsible for an innocent man's death, I want to know. I want to make sure it never happens again."

Nevis lowered her voice, "A surprise new witness came forward, and it turns out he had an alibi."

"What witness? Why didn't they come forward before?"

"An Imperial one. It turns out he was having an affair with an imperial concubine."

"We investigated that possibility."

"Apparently not good enough. Even though he was exonerated, his career was over, and he had an imperial target inked on his back. That's why he must have thought the only way out was to kill himself. Unfortunately, his alibi didn't come forward until they saw his death on the news. He must have been trying to protect them. I'm disconnecting now. Lose my number for the foreseeable future."

Nevis hung up. An imperial alibi made sense, Jhee supposed. But given the severity of the charges facing the man, one would think he would have mentioned having an alibi sooner. Jhee puzzled over it all the way home. Once there, she pulled out the case file and went over every piece of evidence again. She could not see where she went wrong.

The senator had been the mastermind of a benefits scam. He was about to be exposed and had killed an underling who had found out. Or so she had thought. Jhee thought they had invented soldiers so they could defraud the victims' relief funds. The soldiers Jhee thought were fake turned out to be real.

There had been reliable witnesses. With this new alibi, the senator would have had to be in two places at once. Jhee remembered how smug the senator had been when he barged into her office. *"I have imperial favor."* His alibi may have been concocted, but she could not gainsay an imperial without substantial evidence.

Jhee awoke to Kanto gently taking the conch from her hand. She looked around, a little confused.

"You shouldn't be reading that."

"I know. His family intends to sue."

"You'll beat them. Nobody knows the law better than you. Nobody."

"I used to think so. Maybe I erred. I've been so distracted lately. Was there something I missed? He was an abusive ass. I had wanted nothing more than for him to be guilty. Did I get ahead of the evidence? Did I lead the evidence instead of letting the evidence lead me?"

"I don't know, Jhee. That doesn't sound like you at all."

"Ms. Hethyr," she said.

"From the abbey case?"

"Yes. It's like Ms. Hethyr. When I saw the bruises on Mr. Zane, a part of me shut down. I fixated on her. I got tunnel vision. It almost compromised the case and cost folk their lives. Was that what this was all over again?"

"But in that case, the guilty party received justice."

"Perhaps. I wished I could have found a more civilized solution to that. I still hear the screams and the snarls sometimes."

"The abbey killer was a brute and a beast, and the world is well rid of them."

"Was that my call to make? I love the law. I live for the law as much as I do my family, and the law says capital cases must be handled by the full judiciary. It can't be frontier justice. It can't be like it was in the Far Reaches with families bumping off troublesome and meddlesome people as they saw fit."

"I know how much you admire the law. But it's not perfect. How many murders did the abbey killer get away with? Or the well-to-do families in our home district? All because they could pay the right people or choose the right victims. You care about more than the law. You care about folk."

Her conch blinked again. She took it from Kanto. Another notice of appeal. She sighed.

Over the next few days, Jhee received a dozen more notices of appeal. Then on the long-tide, the golden seal of the Justicar council appeared in her inbox. She opened the message and braced herself. Because of the recent events, the Justicar council had no option but to initiate a judicial audit. Her credentials were suspended until further notice. She sat in her office, staring at the note.

Soon came a knock at the door.

"Come in." The dean walked in, unable to meet her eyes. "Dean," Jhee acknowledged.

"I presume you have caught the dispatches," xe said.

"Everyone has by now. I suppose I should expect a visit from investigative services."

"At least. We've received notice of your suspended credentials. I've been asked to encourage you to take a leave of absence. I've also been asked by the board of trustees to scale back the legal clinic. At least for the time being."

"My classes and lesson plans? The legal clinic?"

The dean tugged at hir sleeves. "Another professor will handle it."

"But the tribunal cases."

"Will be turned back over to the imperial commission. It's only temporary. At least until we get this whole situation sorted out."

Jhee wanted to grab the dean and shake hir. "The Academy's support overwhelms me, truly."

"The Academy can't afford the liability, especially with the incident involving the senator being done under the auspices of our legal clinic. You would do the same."

After Jhee snatched up her valise, she smirked. "You're correct, I would. I'm not sure if that makes it right, though."

Jhee stalked out.

~

Another Invitation

Jhee accompanied Kanto as he reported for his first day at the quartermaster's office. She could not help but run her hand through the short, spiky hairstyle he now sported.

While the receptionist connected Kanto with his mentor, Jhee said, "I would have never thought to see you on this path back in the Reaches."

"Back in the reaches, I may never have taken it."

"I always misjudged you, didn't I?"

"And I, you. It happens. We were both feeling each other out. We might never have moved passed that stage if we had stayed in the isles. I would have been too scared to step a foot out of place. I couldn't stand the Far Reaches when I was there, but I do miss it. A little. Still, leaving the Reaches allowed me and Mirrei to live our Make."

"Once we left the Reaches, is when everyone became in danger."

"Danger is sometimes the Maker geld needed to find one's path."

An efficient and well-groomed post-jubilant arrived to collect Kanto, "I'll be your onboarding guide your first week or so. There's some paperwork for you to sign at the service registrar before we can proceed."

Kanto turned to Jhee before he left. "Live your Make, denbe. Always."

To return to the townhouse now, meant Jhee had the place all to herself. She might rather wrestle a spine shark or throw herself off a bridge. The morbid thought stopped her cold. Jhee refused to have another house she inhabited turn into a mausoleum. She treated herself to a shopping trip in the market district where she sourced parts for her roster of Mechanist devotional fabrications. Most of her purchases, Jhee sent along to the townhouse.

She still carried a few finds as the transport passed by the veteran's services center.

"Let me off here," she said.

Inside she found an open discussion session about to start. She kept to herself for most of it. At the end, she re-encountered the proctor. Jhee discussed her mental and legal and career woes with her obliquely. Afterward, she enjoyed watching the breeze play through the sea roses of the garden, then performed Maker devotions at the shrine hall.

The proctor caught her on the way out. "Pleasant news. I just spotted Counselor Medea. We can head over and schedule you an appointment. Perhaps you will feel more comfortable opening up to her."

Jhee's curiosity piqued, she followed the proctor to meet the oft mentioned counselor. She was a simply dressed woman, very much like Jhee with eyes more auburn in hue.

The proctor had barely finished the introductions before the counselor shoved a digital slate in her hands. "Here. Fill this out to confirm your eligibility. You can do it in my office."

The counselor ushered Jhee into her office. Her ordinary looks came as a surprising relief to Jhee. Though her curt, brusque manner was unexpected. As Jhee finished the form under the woman's watchful gaze, Jhee second-guessed this course more and more. She handed over the completed slate, convinced this wasn't going to work.

"Wait here while I talk to scheduling," the counselor said.

To ease her anxiety while she waited, Jhee analyzed the office. Jhee found the address of a slaughterhouse in the counselor's open contacts book on her desk. Jhee recognized Ursula's maye trail mark on a slip of parchment. Ursula's inquiries into the Albatross dossiers had dead-ended here. Why? With Counselor Medea still talking to the scheduling department, Jhee slipped out her conch and captured several images. She slipped away before the counselor returned.

When Jhee returned home, a transport, bearing the Imperial dual wave insignia of the Sea Throne on the doors and identifying tags, had parked in her semi-circular driveway. An Imperial messenger waited on her doorstep.

"Is it for me?" Jhee asked. "I'll receive it."

"Unfortunately, my Lady Justicar, it's for another. I have been instructed to deliver it to him directly."

Jhee quirked an eyebrow. "Which gentleman are you awaiting?"

The Imperial messenger inclined his head slightly. "Begging your pardon, my lady. I am not at liberty."

"I could refuse to receive you."

"You could, my lady."

"So, you are just going to remain there tail dusting my porch until the correct one arrives?"

The messenger's mouth twitched with amusement. "If it pleases, my lady."

Jhee had problems enough without slighting an Imperial messenger, or more dangerously for her, whomever he acted on behalf of. "Best come inside then."

She allowed the Imperial messenger entry into her home and seated him on the servants' bench in the foyer.

The door opened, and Shep entered. He spared Jhee a cool acknowledgment before noting the Imperial messenger. The messenger gave a respectful head dip but made no attempt to present his message to Shep. Shep grunted and went upstairs.

Soon after, Kanto arrived.

"Sir." The messenger rose and held out a black lacquer invitation tray bearing a bio-film invitation folded into a bear. "On behalf of the Gathering of Companions, you are hereby invited to the Imperial spouses' luncheon. The luncheon shall be held tomorrow at the Saltwater Bay Yacht Club. You are further invited should you wish it to play with the courtiers' orchestra. Should you accept, an instrument will be provided for you."

~

The Luncheon

Kanto sat down on one chaise with a carefully chosen selection of delicacies arranged artfully on his plate. His choice of chaise had been calculated. Not too close to the higher born, but near the excellent lighting of the windows. As the first mover of his rank, his peers had adjusted and positioned themselves near him. When no one showed any reluctance to do so, he breathed a sigh of relief. He always had harbored a secret fear of making a subtle political gaffe and not knowing about it until it was too late. It had been the risk of moving first in this unfamiliar environment. This one had worked out to his benefit.

He hoped he projected an air of confidence and self-assuredness. He had talked a strong gale to Jhee and Shep about how much savvier he was than them. While it was true, amongst this crowd, he was every bit the provincial from the shallows, at least in terms of politics. The Outer Reaches had been closer to the deep sea in real terms. In the social and political terms, it was the shallowest of child's wading pools. This was the deep political waters, and here he swam with the sharks, barracudas, shell drakes, and leviathans.

The crowd was a mix of male and female, thankfully. Kanto should have expected as much off the Imperial Isles. Travel and mobility were heavily gender-restricted there so that people were not sneaking about with the Imperial consorts and concubines. Not so much here on the capital isle. A few faces from the sojourn had returned. He examined the rank and clothing of each individual. He had to be strategic about who he spoke to and when.

Foremost, Kanto must approach no one of lower rank than him. They had to be made to come to him, but only after being invited via social cues or introduction through a peer of his rank. The same applied to him when speaking to those of higher status. His safest shores for his first social landings were his peers.

Kanto noted the number of pips on people's various insignia and the specific shades of color on their robes and sashes. Most of them did not wear robes exclusively. Once they had moved to the capital, Kanto had adopted the style of the capital of combining lighter and shorter robes with slacks or suits, and he had encouraged Jhee and Shep to do the same. He wanted to keep some of their home styles, but not so much they looked backward.

As others made the same social assessments Kanto had, they clumped into their peer groups. Not quite talking yet, but feeling each other out and positioning themselves. None of the high Imperials had arrived yet. A calculated move, no doubt, to give the lesser families time to sort themselves out.

Kanto sampled one of the delicacies, a crab puff made with rare truffle and fresh arctic sea crab. Even here in the capital, getting fresh sea crab at this time of year was a tremendous expense with the seaways as congested as they were by all the immigration. The crab had to be flash-frozen, likely by an artificer and flown in. Only a handful of isles were in precisely the right climate zone to grow truffles, isles that could only be found in a few latitudes. Less now that the wall had radically changed the ecosystems of some.

The pastry on the crab puff practically melted in his mouth. He wished the rest of his household were here to enjoy it with him. Shep would point out some nuance of cooking techniques while tasting it with admiration. Jhee would politely scarf it down and maybe note some obscure fact about sea crabs or truffle location. Mirrei would try it for the experience, then likely move back on to simpler fare.

Kanto tried more of the delicacies. He bit into something tart and moving, Dundarian lampreys. He kept his face implacable, then discretely spit it out into a napkin. That was a delicacy he never needed to try again.

"Well done," the sandy-hair male on the chaise beside him said. Kanto sized up his robes and insignia, a peer maybe slightly above Kanto's rank. It might not have been polite of him to say he noticed, but it was still a compliment coming from someone who, by all rights, did not have to speak to him at all. They exchanged quick gestures to signal introductions were fine. "Aiaku of Taelos."

"Aiaku" was likely a public name, Kanto gave his in kind, "Bright Harmony of the Far Reaches."

"Grabbing the sea worms was probably the only misstep I've seen you make. Most of us have been around long enough to know to avoid them.

They are served at all these functions because they are the favorite of the former Emperor's niece and her spouse. When I saw you take them, I wondered if you would actually eat them."

"Lesson learned. However, knowing what to expect should I ever meet the niece and spouse, I'll be less likely to embarrass myself if called upon to eat them."

"True." Aiaku scooped up the sea worms and ate them down with a pleasant smile. "You didn't embarrass yourself at all."

Kanto re-examined the robes, stately, single-colored. His assessment of rank had been spot on, but he was also sure that was Aiaku's way of outing himself as someone of higher rank. Could it be a trap or test? If Aiaku were higher rank, he had signaled they could speak. The only shame came if Aiaku ranked beneath him. Anyone pretending a higher rank than they were would likely be severely dealt with. "A relief for which I am truly grateful."

"Pardon the ruse. You won't tell anyone, will you?"

"Of course not, your…" Kanto paused at a loss for how to address Aiaku without knowing his true rank.

"Aiaku. We're peers, remember?"

"Of course, Aiaku."

A group of four men muscled into the solar, amongst them twins. They made a shark-shot for where Kanto and Aiaku sat. These men wore their rank proudly and brashly.

"Move," one man, a boulder with a head, ordered Aiaku. An *azunate*, hyper-male, build if ever there was one.

Aiaku took his time leaving while Kanto rose to follow.

The slimmer, lead male, no less imposing in his bearing for merely being traditional-sized, pointed at Kanto. "No. You stay. Sit."

The azunate male moved between Aiaku and Kanto. Kanto retook his seat politely. The lead male openly leered at him while the rest pretended as if he weren't there. The four gossiped but made no attempt to include Kanto.

"Zaria's been in a mood," one twin said. "She's split her time the past long-tide between my barge and my brother's."

Kanto put on his best disaffected air. Not metaphorical brother-grooms, but literal ones. Even more scandalous and disgusting, identical twins. The only rationale he could come up with for that made him blush. The Imperials were a breed apart. Aiaku hovered in the background with an anxious look on his face. He talked to a few attendees, then slipped away.

With Aiaku's departure, Kanto's hope for a dignified out dissipated, too. He cast his gaze about. There was no graceful way for him to exit their company. The slimmer lead male, whose outside or veiled name was Zazu, had moved closer to Kanto. Kanto weighed the clumsy gambit versus the wilting weed routine to affect an escape.

When Zazu thought the time was right, he slipped an arm on the chair back behind Kanto's shoulders. Zazu's eyes turned a sultrier molten gold. "You're new."

The wilting weed routine would make Kanto's predicament worse. The twins and the boulder had formed a circle around them to block Kanto from getting away. This spawn of piranha would swarm on any weakness.

"I was at the sojourn," Kanto responded.

Zazu gently rubbed his lip as he talked to Kanto, "We're having an exclusive mixer in our wing later. By invitation only. You should come."

Over Zazu's shoulder, a dark-skinned, teal-eyed High Imperial woman shook her head and mouthed 'no.' An unnecessary warning. Kanto gleaned what their parties might entail and why only certain folk merited invites.

Zazu moved closer. Kanto allowed the saucer he held to slip. The uneaten lampreys wriggled everywhere.

"I'm sorry. How clumsy of me. Allow me to fetch a servant."

Zazu recoiled. "I hate these drench creatures."

Kanto extricated himself from the circle just as Aiaku returned with several friends in tow.

"There you are, Bright Harmony." Aiaku slipped his arm in Kanto's and guided him away, "I have some friends I wish you to meet."

The azunate boulder of a man blocked their path. Zazu reached for them, but a walking stick batted aside hand.

"Go prey on someone else, Zazu," Captain Odo said. Zazu turned, ready to assert his authority against whoever had dared challenge him. Captain Odo loomed over him and raised an eyebrow. The smugness left Zazu's face. "Yes?"

Zazu tried to smile while also gritting his teeth. "Consort Regent."

"Pups."

Zazu's eyes flashed with red. "The Regent isn't Empress yet, Odo. She's practically cut you loose, anyway. The clock's ticking on you, regardless."

Zazu, the azunate boulder, and the twins slunk away. Captain Odo followed, to be sure.

"Zaria's pets," one of Aiaku's male friends said. "Zaria keeps them caged up like prison inmates. I think this is the only time she lets them leave Emperor's Isle. It's a wonder they don't know how to act in polite society and act so predatory on the few grounds where they are allowed to hunt."

"These used to be such nice gatherings," another member of the group said. "They used to serve so many functions. We used to mingle and catch up. Entertain and feel out prospective companions and *denyes*. Upon occasion, conduct business. Thanks to the likes of them, most of the decent companions never attend anymore."

A very sporty male sipped some lemonade, "I guess I lucked out with the Duke. He's gentle, generous, and doesn't have a wandering eye."

"Also, isn't he well into his third jubilee?"

"That just makes him very practiced."

The gathering also held a smattering of part-Fire Folk and part-Findari folk. Findari were sometimes called the Water Nomads. It was rare to find them this far inland. His cousins used to tell stories in the Reaches of how Water Nomads died if they were separated from their ships for more than a long-moon.

"Scoping all the Fin and Fire folk," one of Aiaku's friends said. "The imperials will bed anything."

The green-eyed Lady who warned Kanto away from the mixer invitation joined their group. "Better that than inbreeding."

Blue-black skin but green-eyed with a water drop-shaped esca: she was part Fire Folk.

"It was an observation, not an accusation, my dear."

Captain Odo returned. Aiaku pulled him and Kanto aside.

"Thank you, Captain Odo," Kanto said.

"Yes, thank you, Consort Regent," Aaiku agreed.

"'Aiaku.' Slumming it again, are we? Dress like a plebe. Get treated like a plebe." Captain Odo faced Kanto. He appeared to have several questions but settled on, "Bright Harmony, would you like me to see you back to your denbe?"

Kanto sized up Aiaku and his friends. He had yet to make any allies, and this seemed as good a group as any. "No, thank you, Captain."

The captain whispered to him on the way out, "Those were Zaria's toys. Just like that poor cad Sniffer accused of murder. I hope you know what you're doing in these shark-infested waters."

Me, too, Kanto thought.

11

———————

∼

The Bloody Shirt

A brilliant, vermilion-spotted butterflyfish splashed the surface of the carp pond to retrieve the treat Jhee had thrown in. Kanto had insisted they install the pond and a water feature during the landscaping. Jhee and Shep had decided on their new home before he signed the marriage contracts. A fact Kanto never tired of lamenting, as he would have shown them the absolute perfect house for them. To make up for it, they had to let him furnish their townhouse and put his stamp on the renovations, construction, and decor.

Jhee spooned more flakes into the pond before she returned to the townhouse porch to watch the mid sunrise. The pond was a pleasant touch, and she was glad both Mirrei and Kanto had insisted on it. She was perfectly fine to view the fish from the comfort of her porch. Without her teaching job, she had plenty of time on her hands to contemplate and think about her choices, time to appreciate blessings she did not before. Shep had not come home yet. He still refused to speak to her.

While Jhee contemplated the dawn, furious barking traveled from the kennels. When it did not calm down after a moment, she went to investigate. She crept into the enclosures only to discover a shirtless Shep treating and tenderly probing bruises. At her approach, he turned. He snatched up a shirt and hastily threw it on.

"Shep?"

He started for the door to the house. She intercepted him. He refused to face her. "Please, move," he said.

609

"Please, talk to me. Shep, please, look at me."

He faced her. She saw where his scarred eye now was also bruised. The corner of his mouth was swollen and still had a trace of blood. The end of claw marks peeked out from his partially opened shirt. His fists had abrasions. His fingernail claws were discolored. One was broken and another missing entirely.

Jhee brought her hand to his damaged eye. "You're hurt. Let me."

He backed away. "Don't. Leave it be."

"But."

"I said leave it, Jhee."

"Shep, what's going on? Where were you?"

"The gym."

"Without your gym equipment? You've left it home every night since the first."

"Do you ever stop detecting even for one moment?"

"You stay out to all hours. You lie about it, and now I find you like this. What am I supposed to think? What's going on with you? Tell me what's going on."

"I told you I'm working through some stuff. The least of which is why you would lie to both Kanto and me for so long. You don't think you know me anymore. Well, I don't think I know you either. Now would you just back off and give me some time to get myself sorted out. Kanto needed to find his new equilibrium. Mirrei needed to find hers. Leave me alone to find mine."

"Except you're not. Shep, I need you to get yourself sorted because I stumbled on to something. Our household may need you at your best soon. Get counseling. Maybe go somewhere to find yourself like Mirrei did. Or else, I'll need you to find somewhere else to stay until you do."

Shep turned before he left. "I recognize this Jhee. This is the Jhee that showed up right after our newlyweds' holiday. The Jhee who treated me as much as her cold, deep secret as Mai did."

He pushed passed her up the stairs and into the house. Jhee walked over to where Shep had been when she came in. She found a torn and bloody shirt. She picked it up and examined it. Without testing, she could not be certain, but she didn't think the blood traces were his. A crystal kalacha poked out from beneath the torn cloth.

Jhee held the shirt, uncertain of if she wanted to know more. She needed to trust him. Yet, somehow, she couldn't with his recent secretiveness and bursts of anger. His reactions during the tribunal broadcasts had been full of hatred, hatred so fierce it had burned her through their sigil bond. That meant nothing. Her ire had been no less scalding.

～

Before the Bench

"You may be wondering why we asked you here," Justice One said.

"I presume it has something to do with the claims against me."

"In the course of going over your record, we noticed some irregularities," Justice Two said.

"A matter I'm sure can be quickly resolved. I'm a very fastidious and thorough record keeper."

"We know, which is why these anomalies concern us," Justice Three said.

"We noticed some gaps in your record of the case at Tranquility Bridge," Justice One said.

"Also, your account of the death of the retired official Bathsheba of Toho strikes us as odd."

"Lady Bathsheba died in an unfortunate accident while wandering around the cloister during a storm."

"An accident? Are you sure that's the account you want to go with?" Justice Two asked. "That's almost verbatim what this report says. Allow us to read what you wrote, 'Lady Bathsheba died in an unfortunate accident while wandering around the cloister. She ventured out too soon, having thought the storm ended and took a wrong turn in the waning storm and wandered into the courtyard where one of the visiting actors had their pet bullhound housed. The frightened creature on edge because of the storm mauled her to death.' You fined the actor for improper housing and failure to secure a dangerous animal, suspended due to financial hardship."

"I believe I also noted that the abbey, the only other party with clear standing, concurred and accepted the punishment. Did they file a challenge?"

"No. It did not strike you as odd, the vizier would go wandering about in a storm, especially after," Judge one paused and looked through the file, "not one, but two, attempts on her life?"

"Justice, the vizier had been doing her best to aid me in my inquiries. She even helped save my poor dear husband when he got lost in the abbey then trapped in its torture chamber."

"And the anomalous deaths which made you stop there? Still unsolved?" Justice Three said.

"Not unsolved. I'm sure you should also see there the account of the suicide of the individual I believe to be responsible."

Justice Two chewed on her finger quill. "Ah yes, the suicides. They certainly do seem to proliferate around you and your family."

Jhee shoved her hand in her robes and calmed herself with finger cyphering exercises. "I suspect there may have been an emotional relationship between the wrongdoer and the vizier, which may have led to a falling out or an excess of grief on the vizier's part."

"With you?"

Jhee adjusted her tabard. "Most certainly not, your honors."

"So, not an unfortunate accident then, but suicide?"

"I could not say for sure and why upset any family with the speculation?"

"A first for you, Sixteen," Justice One said. "Normally, you don't seem to mind what waterfalls you chase or waves you make."

The Justice had addressed her by her district number instead of name. Not a wonderful sign.

"I've found my recent marriages have adjusted my priorities," Jhee responded.

"Speaking of your recent marriages. I might like to inquire about your recent adventures in Galleon City, working with Investigator Paij. A private company accused you of stealing their intellectual property. One of your spouses was arrested for disorderly conduct and trespassing. You were arrested for vandalizing the city jail. Your funds were used to bail out agitators engaged in acts of violence against the empire."

"As you know, justices, many riots and protests were happening at that time."

"And you and your household decided to join in?" Justice Two asked.

"It was largely a misunderstanding. I'm sure you justices understand when enormous events happen, it's sometimes impossible not to get swept up in them."

"There were also some troubling allegations of how you handled a legal matter regarding your anchor spouse at the Tranquility Bridge abbey. Play the recording."

Jhee's hand twitched upon recognizing the voice of one the abbey's deacons, Sister Elkanah. She gave the worst possible account of Shep's raw meat-induced frenzy in the refectory, the dining hall. The bitter, disgraced cleric also framed Jhee's resolution of the matter as nepotistic in the extreme.

The three justices gathered their records and rose.

"You are free to leave, for now, Sixteen. Don't go far."

~

A Music Lesson

A servant escorted Kanto to the imperial conservatory. He sat on the bench and waited for his prospective student to arrive. After a few moments, Kanto set up for some pieces. He needed to assess the prospective students' skill levels. That would determine if these lessons would be teaching sessions or just an indulgence for the lessons' sponsor. As he was setting up, the door to the conservatory opened. Aiaku wheeled in a young male in a mobility chair.

"Aiaku. What are you doing here?"

"We were just taking in the lovely weather."

"We?"

"There's someone I want you to meet." Aiaku turned around the young male in the mobility chair. A large patch of hair was missing over a curious depression in his skull. Aiaku reached over and wiped some saliva off his chin. "This is Aeolus, my brother-groom. Aeolus, this is the friend I've been telling you about, Bright Harmony."

Kanto squatted down and looked askance at Aiaku before touching Aeolus's arm. "Hello, Aeolus. I'm Bright Harmony. I'm very pleased to meet you."

The relief showed in Aiaku's posture. Kanto spent the rest of the afternoon with Aiaku and Aeolus, sketching and playing for the pair.

"I'm guessing that noble never was interested in hiring me as a music tutor for their children," Kanto said.

"Pardon the deception. It was necessary with the current state of imperial infighting."

"All right, then why am I here?"

"Aeolus. A procurer plucked he and I off the straits to play in the water fountains during Imperial Sojourns," Aiaku said. "Aeolus and I were commoners. We came up together. We didn't have to worry about each other and had each other's back. Once I gained Imperial favor, I'd convinced my denbe to take him on as well. No minor feat as she could have married two high-borns instead. She loved us that much."

"May I ask what happened to him?"

"Aeolus attended one of the Zariinae cohort's exclusive events. The rest, we're not supposed to talk about. I've been hearing about your denbe in dispatches."

"You invited me to the luncheon."

"I recognized your denbe from the sojourn and the senator from other events. When I saw the Justicar on the viewer, I knew Zaria would come after her. A lesson for you, young Bright Harmony. Don't touch Zaria's toys, ever. Even when she's done with them. I wanted direct interaction with your household before I decided if I should entangle myself in the matter."

"What was your verdict?"

"You're folk worth helping." Aiaku held out a hand to Kanto. Kanto thought about it a moment, then took it. Aiaku rose and kissed him tenderly on the cheek. He smiled. "May I introduce you to my denbe? In case the seas turn for the worse, she can see that you are protected."

"Only if my family approves."

Aiaku nodded. "I think that's enough for the day. Zaria won't come at your denbe alone or directly. Just keep an eye on the shadows behind all these officials looming overhead."

~

The Sailor Reappears

"Do you remember me from a few tides back? Outside your office, at the school. I went there first. They said you was at home. I saw where you was asking around about your friend, the one who reckon I speak with you."

"Do you have information on her?"

"Well, I'm not sure see. It's just… I have another friend. He's missing too. I think he was like her." The woman leaned in and lowered her voice, "You know, a berserker."

"Oh, I see."

"I'm sore worried. I was hoping that you could, you know, help me find him. What with that tribunal being blasted on every screen, he hasn't been himself lately. We walked by a display, playing it this one time. He upped and smashed it. I won't honest with you before. It weren't me what suspected the neighbor, it were him. He had me give report, 'cuz he had a reputation with the Imps, and they'd just dismiss him."

"What's your friend's name?"

"Hammad… the Hammerhead."

Jhee raised an eyebrow but let it go. "Where was your friend last seen?"

"The warehouse club over on Packer's Pier."

"Okay, I'll look into it."

The woman bobbed her head up and down excitedly. She held out her hand. They clasped forearms, and the woman gave a good firm shake. "Oh, thank you, Magistrate. All the Makers' blessings to you. Thank you. Thank you."

Packer's Pier again. The cryptic message Jhee found with Ursula's trail marker in the counselor's office contained today's date and an address for a slaughterhouse near the docks there. Jhee rounded up Bax and Dari to accompany her. A quick change and confirmation from Odo later, Jhee found herself back at Packer's Pier One. As berserkers, surely this place with its ever-present blood smell would be some sort of trigger. What were her dear friends into?

Their arrival there coincided with a few others. A trickle of various Folk, from Fire to Water and all others in between, arrived. She had worn a sea coat and cap to make herself less obtrusive, but she needn't have bothered. Their class likewise was a social cross-section. They chatted in excited but hushed tones. There were high society types and motorcycle toughs; farmers, divers, and fisherfolk. She also noted the stance, swagger, and tattoos of military veterans. Bruised and scarred common folk commingled with the smooth and unblemished elites.

Dari whined and pulled on the leash. "She's got the scent of something, Justicar," Bax said.

"Check it out, quickly," Jhee said. "I'm going to give this a few more minutes, then pack it in."

"Aye, Justicar." Bax barely got the confirmation out before Dari nearly yanked him off his feet to follow the scent.

Jhee entered the building. It was a large converted abattoir with a cage in the center. She smelled the blood instantly, years of caked-on decayed foulness which would never go away and had soaked into the very pores of the metal and polyorganic materials used to construct the building. She wrinkled her nose. The overwhelming urge to pull out a napkin and cover her mouth and nose seized her, but she resisted.

The part glamor, part gutter crowd flowed in around the cage. A man in simple diving skirt and shirt used his conch to amplify or transmit his voice so it echoed throughout the building.

"Next up, we have two prime specimens of fighting power. One hails from the Far Isles. The other from Graydale. Give your best battle stomp for the vicious Daggerfin and the terrifying Seacrawler."

Two combatants waited by the cage steps. The announcer quickly exited. Folk whom Jhee presumed to be the combatants' match attendants sprayed a red-brown substance in their mouths. Their demeanor changed.

The Daggerfin braced and shook her head. Her back arched. She stepped into the cage, and the cage guard quickly locked it. Each combatant went into the jumping and flexing Jhee associated with berserker slipping. The Daggerfin's body hairs became thicker and wirier. Her golden eyes had begun a dangerous smolder matched only by her opponent's. They huffed, puffed, and flared their nostrils. The Daggerfin and her opponent circled each other in the ring warily. The Seacrawler made a dash at the Daggerfin, who backed off. They feinted at each other a moment, growling and posturing. They burst into a flurry of action. The two combatants tore at each other. It had none of the technical assessment or counters and strikes of traditional martial arts or fisticuffs; no carefully orchestrated feints or testing for weaknesses; no timing and setup. This was raw animal savagery.

The flurry of rage quieted. One combatant, hard to tell who, given how much blood they were covered in, staggered to her feet. She spit out blood. It was the Daggerfin. Her opponent lay barely moving on the ground.

The smell of the fresh blood had commingled with the old. Jhee felt a shift in the crowd's mood. They chanted, cheered, and stamped their feet. It was not the random enthusiasm of a typical sporting event. This was a synchronized effort to shift their mental state. One which might lead to a frenzy. From among them, she picked out the telltale signs of blood arousal. Glittering eyes sought any sign of movement or hesitation. Tongues licked lips. And there was the odd, eager snorts and chuffs. She imagined somewhere in there the stamping of feet or pawing the ground from those who had already slipped their Water Folk skin.

Many of the attendees had to be berserkers themselves. Jhee spared a moment to think of her safety should a mass fervor overtake them. Could her siren module affect this many? She had found one berserker hard enough to deal with, let alone a room full.

That had extenuating circumstances. She had not wanted to hurt Shep, and on some level, Shep had not wanted to hurt her. Still, though, Shep bore the scar across his eye to this day from where she had been forced to cut him.

The chanting and stomping continued while the two combatants were let out. The announcer counter chanted and eased the crowd down to a less fevered pitch. Attendants hosed off the ring. A layer of fabric was stripped from the ring. A bloodstain remained, but not a slippery one which posed a hazard.

The announcer named the next two combatants, and another furious match of clawing and biting ensued. *Ursula, what had you gotten yourself into?* Jhee thought. She shook her head. Is this what their old friend had come to? Jhee had seen enough.

Jhee caught her breath outside the building after the match for a bit. She savored the smell of air that did not reek of rage, bodies, and blood. Why would berserkers willingly do this? Why would they risk being a danger to themselves and those around them like this? She saw how hard Shep struggled not to let the fervor overtake him. Jhee could not fathom it.

For all they had been through, for all their experiences in the war together, this was an aspect of Shep's life she could never understand. She had hoped his work with the veteran's service center and being around other berserkers would help him cope better. For a while, it had, but now he was just as distant and keeled as he was when his service was first up. They got through it together once. They would again. Jhee had faith in Shep. She must. She wanted him to be around for himself and for their family. Jhee wished for him to have the solace and peace of children. Jhee may have looked at it the wrong way all along. Had he not brought in Kanto as a signal she should have children, but about a desire of his own for them?

The revelation knocked Jhee back on her heels. She had resisted Kanto's advances partially because she had still held the hope of her and Shep having children of their own. Then she had convinced herself she wanted to be respectful of Shep and wondered how he would feel if she had children with Kanto. She had thought to spare his feelings. Had she gotten it wrong all this time?

Ursula's bruises made sense now if this was the kind of activity she had been into. If Ursula was engaged in such a brutal pastime, it lent credence to the notion of her pregnancy not being real, unless there was more to this. More had to be going on here. Perhaps Ursula had left Jhee another trail marker. Jhee pulled out a smoke root and lit it as she casually scouted the area around the slaughterhouse.

A noise around the corner drew Jhee to investigate. Jhee tossed her smoke root and ground it under her heel. At the building's dockside, she saw folk in cages being loaded onto a freighter. More human trafficking?

A cloth with strong-salts clamped over her mouth.

"More meat for the beasties," a voice said.

12

____

～

Fog and Frenzy

Snarling awoke Jhee. A gag and muzzle had been fitted around her head. She glanced about her quickly. Above her, the moons shone. Earthen walls met her grasping hands. She was in some kind of pit.

The snarling changed timbre. Jhee caught the sight of reddened eyes. She engaged her siren module in animal mode, but it would do her no good if she could not give commands. She felt about her head for some means to release her silencer.

The growling was almost on Jhee. The creature leaped at Jhee. She abandoned her attempts to undo her gag and muzzle. She scrambled up the enclosure's side. The memory of the abbey and the mauling in its gated courtyard, fresh in her mind, fueled her climb to just short of the edge of the pit.

A snarl preceded the beast's bite. The teeth grazed her calf but gained a fast hold to her hem. Her mind was too chaotic to artifice. She reached out via Earth drawing, her weakest element, to the soil. Manipulation of the fine soil eluded her, and she could not get a purchase on the edge of the pit. She gambled on a blind boost with a jet of air.

Her hand breached the top of the pit. She sank her fingernail claws into the dirt. She scrabbled and clambered against the wall of the hole. Clods of dirt fell down. She used her other hand to push herself just up over the edge. The rapidly crumbling side resisted her. A cascade of dirt slipped into the pit. Jhee fought valiantly not go with it. She clawed more and more at the edge of the cavity. Any attempt at artifice abandoned in a desperate bid to escape the pit and make sure her purchase on the edge. Her footing slipped. She started to slide down into the hole, the snarling, biting animal still prizing at her robe.

Jhee became calm and gave her mind over to the First Makers' design.

A hand grabbed Jhee's wrist. Then another one caught her other wrist just as she slid back down into the pit with the monster. Her Maker within gifted her an ounce more fight. She climbed up the crumbling pit side as someone helped haul her up from the edge. At last, she lay face down on the earth.

Blessed are the Makers, she prayed to them silently.

"Justicar, are you okay?" Bax said.

Jhee nodded.

"We have to move. We have to get out of here now. Frenzies catch on like wildfire. Their blood is up, and they will be coming for you with the way you're bleeding."

The berserker from the pit had gotten her a good bite on the ankle. Bax tied up her wounds and removed her gag.

"Can you walk, Justicar?"

"I'll drench well walk out of here," Jhee said and hopped to her feet. The frenzied howls of the berserkers echoed closer than before. If she risked a field healing, they might overtake them. She threw her arm over Bax's shoulder, and they limped away as fast as they could.

They made a good clip, but Jhee's ankle cried out in agony with every step. She was slowing them down. "We have to stop," she said.

"Justicar, we can't. They're gaining on us."

"We must." Jhee dug deep inside of herself and fixed the divine clockwork in her mind. She found her cog in the giant machine and focused inward on her disturbance and imbalance not allowing the device to work as it willed. She turned, wound, and cranked the Divine Mechanism until the pain in her ankle subsided. She flexed her foot, then tested her weight on her ankle. Still sore, but bearable. "It'll have to do. Quickly."

If they had any chance to get away, she needed to slow down their pursuers. A light, low-clinging mist had rolled in from the sea. This far inland, it only carried a trace of the Storm Wall's power. However, she might use it to her advantage.

Her experiments with the templarite dust and her siren module flooded back to her. She fished around her robes for the small packet of templarite powder she kept in her devotion pouch—a minor sacrilege that may now save their lives.

Jhee tossed the dust into the air and used wind and water, drawing to seed the mist with the particulates. She activated the area effect mode of her siren module. A robust exhale dispersed her siren module's silver cloud of inspiration into the fog. With the templarite dust suspended in it, the fog amplified the effect instead of diffused it.

Jolts fed back through the Divine Mechanism, letting her know her compulsion effect found targets: a squad's worth of berserkers, at least. "Flee back the way you came," she commanded.

Her yell reverberated on the winds. The berserker unit fled. They traveled far enough away she felt their connection snap. However, yelping and howling had gained on them. How had it worn off so soon?

Jhee and Bax double-timed it. The cries and howls were almost on them. They echoed from every tree and shadow in the fog.

"Run," Jhee said and picked up her pace. It seemed an unnecessary instruction, but she had gone beyond reason in the now. Bax had already taken off at his top speed.

Jhee retained some clarity of my mind lest they lose their way in the fog. She reached out to the air and water vapor to divine a path through it. The mist reacted as a wild, alive creature in her mental grasp. Even if Far Reach lore said inland fog did not have enough breath of the deeps to capture the dead, this mist did not want to be handled.

With her will joined to the fog, Jhee gained an accurate reading on the number and proximity of their pursuers. Twenty. Thirty. Makers' Mercy, at least a platoon's worth howled for their blood. Far too many for her siren module, even with a templarite boost.

This mist now fought her as if it had a will of its own. She switched to narrow targeting with her siren module and commandeered two new berserkers. Berserkers were more susceptible to siren modules than regular folk, by design. She would also not have to worry about the three-use limit of effectiveness with them. Though, this fog, this drenchable mist, muffled her control. Jhee's hold over those she captured remained fuzzy and tenuous. The fog, the mist, something about it dampened her commands.

The berserkers were closing fast. At their frenzy enhanced speed, they would overtake Bax and Jhee soon. She thought she sensed a narrow corridor through their ranks. "This way."

Jhee veered suddenly towards the clear path she sensed. Bax followed her. His labored breathed sounded thunderously loud in the disconcerting fog. His breathing was ragged. The older man was having trouble keeping up. She heard him grunt. He was no longer at her side. She turned to see him tumble to a stop. She ran to help him.

"No, Justicar, run," he said.

"No! You don't get to leave my service until I say so."

"We will answer for our crimes before the First Makers together then, Justicar."

"Let it be an answer given loudly then." Jhee readied to form artifices, windings, and sequences. At this stage of frenzy, she'd only be able to direct a cell's worth, but she could set them to fight the others. If she took complete control of one, she could have them defend her and Bax while she cyphered and drew. To do that, she would also have to wait until one was practically on top of them. She conveyed the plan to Bax.

"As good as any," he said.

A single guttural howl cut through the snarls, a piercing cry which silenced all the others. Then another. A dark shape jumped into the clearing with them. Jhee prepared to unleash her cypher.

Dari stood before them. She turned back towards the fog. She gave a mighty howl. Then another commanding and louder. She growled way back in her throat when the other howls did not instantly cease. Dari charged off into the fog. The cries from the fog cut themselves off. Jhee heard a few whimpers and yelps, then only silence.

Jhee waited. At last, she tentatively reached out to the fog. Most of the berserkers had gone or were rapidly retreating.

Dari staggered out of the fog and collapsed before them. Her form slowly returned to her folk state, a state Dari had not been able to achieve in years. Bax leaned over her and cried. Jhee used her cyphering skills to listen for the inner workings of Dari's system. She lived, but barely.

Jhee pulled together wisps of whatever arcane reserves she had left in her. Dari's condition was rapidly deteriorating. "Bax."

He continued to cry.

"Bax! I need you. She needs you."

Bax looked up at her. "Do whatever you must, Justicar."

"Roll her onto her back. Gently."

Jhee placed her hand over Dari's heart while touching Bax's chest. She began a prayer to the First Makers and found a strength within from the father-daughter bond Bax and Dari shared. She found the interconnection where their two parts of the divine clockworks intersected and put them together, one turning the other to make the great machine move. Bax slumped over, and Dari opened her eyes.

~

The Diving Boy

"Do you want to talk about your relapse at the abbey?" Counselor Medea asked.

The sanctuary boasted a dormitory made from a converted farmhouse. Counselor Medea kept a small office on the first-floor front. Shep tried to remain seated but reverted to pacing every few minutes.

Shep retook his seat and shrugged. "I'm embarrassed by it if that's what you mean."

"That was the first time you relapsed in how long?"

"Years."

"Tell me what else was going on at the time."

"Jhee had finally needed my help with an investigation again. I had sweet-talked the abbey's mortician into letting me re-examine the bodies of some residents who had died suspiciously. No small feat. The female clergy distrusted males. I felt like more than staff again. It seemed like all I did lately was babysit the new spouses, even more so once we arrived at the abbey. The sheltered, male novitiates were being preyed upon. We wanted to keep Mirrei, and especially Kanto, safe."

Shep tugged at the hairs on his arm. Discomfort in the brand on his neck made him adjust his collar.

"Kanto," Shep said. "His help only made things worse. Then there were his efforts to undermine me."

"Yet you put up with it," Counselor Medea said.

"Our household needs Kanto. I'm beneath her. Kanto's fit and rich, a husband more befitting her rank. He belongs at court amongst royalty, on Imperial Sojourns, amongst polite society. He is not a geyser who can blow at any moment. If I lose myself at court like I did at the abbey, she will be shamed, ruined."

"Didn't you tell me you were fed raw land meat?"

"Normally, I'm fine. I don't have such an extreme reaction."

"Is it possible you may have already been close to crisis? A lot's happened in a short time. Were you troubled or stressed already by the recent upheaval to life?"

"I didn't mention the worst part. How good it felt to let go. There's also a more critical concern. Kanto has been pushing harder for children. What if I lose control around them? I want to make sure my family is safe around me."

"You admitted except for the refectory incident you felt calm and at peace there. Here at the sanctuary, you're unlikely to encounter anyone trying to sabotage your recovery and reintegration into society."

"I wouldn't be so sure about that," Shep said. An acute itching flared in his neck brand. "Gah!"

Shep leaped up.

Counselor Medea eyed him with caution. "What is it?" she asked.

"Jhee!"

The enthused, sharp cries of berserkers in a frenzy reverberated throughout the sanctuary's dormitory. He fought back the red haze that threatened to cloud his vision. The man or the beast? The sensation in his neck usually meant Jhee had found herself in danger again. The sigil had a range of many meters, but much less than the distance from the sanctuary to the capital.

~

The Kniver

The stables Jhee and Bax holed up in with Dari smelled of animal manure. Hay crackled with their every move. It sounded loud as thunder as they listened for the berserker gang. The kennels were next to the stables, and both were a respectable distance from the lake. The animals housed there already been worked into a lather by the heavy berserker presence in the air.

She eyed the lake warily for berserkers lurking in its depths. Despite the wide berth they gave it on the way in, her heart had still raced by the time they reached the stables. Wherever the berserkers had gone, it did not appear to be the lake. Thank the First Makers for small favors.

Bax sat vigil by Dari's side. Jhee's leg had mostly healed. She used a branch to give herself more support. She would refrain from any further healing on it, so she could save all her energy for Dari.

Just as first dawn lightened the skies, they heard voices. Normal Folk voices.

"Over here! Those were pack tactics. They had to be hunting," a voice yelled.

Jhee struggled to her feet. "In here."

"Hello?" The stable doors opened, revealing a woman in clinical dress. It was Counselor Medea from the veteran's service center.

"Counselor Medea?" Jhee asked.

"Yes. Have we met?"

"At the veteran's service center? A few nights back."

"I don't believe so." Counselor Medea eyed Jhee and Bax's bedraggled appearance. "Do you require assistance?"

"Over here, our friend."

The woman examined Jhee's clothing. "You're Dawn Wolf's wife, the Justicar. What are you doing here?"

"Tracking down some missing folk, berserkers. You know my husband? How?"

"We walk hounds together in the park."

"I was under the impression you were missing."

"Who gave you that idea?"

Shep ran into view. "Did you find them?"

He stopped dead when he saw them. His gaze took in Bax, then Jhee, and finally the now Folk Dari.

Bax clutched at Shep's arm. "Mr. Shep, help her."

Shep stood transfixed, but Counselor Medea stepped forward. Bax placed himself between her and Dari.

"Your friend is a full-skin shifter or berserker?" Counselor Medea asked.

"Yes," Jhee said. "She lost her way."

"How long had she been stuck?"

"Years," Jhee said. "Since I was a jubilant."

"Years. That may predate the berserker program. Remarkable. May I examine her? I might be able to help anyway."

"Bax?"

Bax stepped aside allowed them access. He held his hat and worried the brim in his hands.

Counselor Medea touched Dari's skin, and her hand came away covered in sweat. "How long has she been unconscious?" she asked.

"Ever since we escaped the berserkers, ma'am," Bax answered.

Medea shook her head. "Not good. No other injuries I see. Her high temperature indicates this may be a healing sleep, which is good. Some shifters I've treated have experienced this. Her vitals are otherwise strong. No tremors or twitches indicative of deep brain damage. Has she said anything or indicated any other cognitive activity?"

"I think she came out of it once or twice."

"Good. Good."

The sigil on Jhee's arm had grown hotter as Medea worked on Dari. When she sought Shep, she saw him by the door arms folded an intense glare fixed on Medea's life-saving efforts. Their gazes met.

Shep moved to Jhee's side and pointed at the inflamed brand on his neck. "What about you?"

Jhee grimaced. "I'll manage."

Shep worked his jaw, then said, "Jhee, how did this happen? What the Trench are you doing here?"

"One moment I was on the pier, the next I woke up here in a pit with a berserker."

"In a pit with a berserker, where?" Counselor Medea asked.

Jhee shrugged. "The other side of the lake."

"Hm, Hammad," Counselor Medea said.

"Jhee, you're here. He isn't," Shep said. "Does his state require a doctor… or mortician?"

Jhee grimaced, but a found a grudging logic to his premise. "Doctor. Bax and Dari found me before it came to more."

"Is he still there?"

"He may have got out."

"I've done everything I can for your friend," Counselor Medea said. "You two talk. I'll go check on him."

Shep motioned with his head for them to move to a barn stall away from Bax and Dari.

"We had kept Hammad calm. He was getting better until you arrived and set him off. What are you doing here, Jhee? This is a berserkers' sanctuary."

"Shep, the question is, what are you doing here? This is not the gym."

"Look who's worried about secret-keeping now?"

"I never lied to you. Not to you. Not in all the sundances we've been together. You, on the other hand…"

Shep snarled. He bared his fangs but otherwise kept his cool. "You told me to go find myself. I needed time without you. You always do this. Always the puzzle, no matter who gets hurt. Dari had decided to live out her days as a shark hound. Now, she may die."

"It wasn't my choice. I was tossed in a pit here by some folk in this sanctuary while investigating a lead in the case of our missing friend, or have you forgotten about her? If you had told me about this place, I could have been further along."

"Did it occur to you I might not have wanted you to know?"

"That precise thought has crossed my mind, but this is about more than us right now. It's about Ursula and Odo. I would not have disrupted your meditations, and I would have found out what I needed to know quickly and moved on. Instead, I had to go sneaking about and learn about things from the servants. I would have done my best to respect your privacy."

"Fish rot. Jhee, you can never let a mystery go, or crime go unpunished. Well, for some crimes, there is no justice, except one. You understood that back at the abbey. What has changed now? Where did this sudden attack of conscience come from?"

"It was never sudden. In war, it's different. Don't you know how much I agonized over the abbey? Or Galleon City? Don't you know how much I wished I had found another solution in both those cases? I carry it with me every day. Shep, what is it you would have me do? You don't want me inquiring into your affairs. Yet there is still a job that needs doing. I've followed other paths to give you your space. But this is an aspect of myself I can't change. I have to follow where the evidence leads me. I did not mean to intrude or put myself in harm's way."

"Jhee, I'm trying. I really am. But the whole situation with Ursula and Odo has me thinking. Maybe you and our family would be better off without me. I'm a mess. What good am I to my friends and my family? My job is to care for this family, and you are not letting me do it. I can't protect you if you don't trust me."

"How am I supposed to trust you after what you told me?"

"I don't know."

"I don't know either. I don't know how to be a good official and denbe who keeps her nose clean and doesn't keel people off."

"And I don't know how to be some dutiful house pet or kept man. The capital moves wrong. I don't know if I'll ever get used to it."

"Me either. What I know is we can't keep doing this. Shep, you can't fly off the handle every time I get into a minor scrape."

Shep rubbed his knuckles up and down his forearm. "And you need to do a better job of keeping me informed when you are about to go and do something stupid."

"The problem is I don't always know they're stupid at the time."

"I do."

"Do you want me to be the Jhee you know or a cowed, incurious academic?"

"I'd never wish that on you. We have to find Hammad before he hurts himself or someone else."

"Too late for that."

"Let me see." Shep bent down to examine Jhee's leg. Shep grunted his approval.

"I'm sorry I lied."

"I'm sorry I did, too. This isn't about that anymore. I need time, Jhee. I just need time."

Counselor Medea knocked on the entrance to the stall, "Hammad's gone."

"Take it. I also have some questions for your Counselor here."

"I'm at your disposal," Counselor Medea said.

"Is this your service record? And do you recognize this?"

Jhee showed them an image of an amphibian stabbed with a needle talon.

"Not long ago, Ursula said she found one on her doorstep. I offered to hide her for a few days."

"A stabbed amphibian?" Shep asked. "When berserkers leave this for someone, it's like an obituary. If it's stabbed with a regiment pin or crystal kalacha, it's to honor the fallen."

"If it's stabbed with a needle talon like this one?"

Counselor Medea answered, "It let the weak—meat—know they had been targeted."

"Who cares about a stabbed toad out here?" Shep asked.

"A former member of the Medical Protectorate does. Ursula didn't receive the stabbed amphibian. You did."

Counselor Medea went wide-eyed. "The warning frog was Ursula's. It's just sometimes I let her stay with me."

"Ursula found out you had once been a member of the Medical Protectorate. She confronted you at the rough and tumble bar, threatened to expose you."

"No, you have this all wrong. Let me explain." Counselor Medea's whole body sagged. Shep's eyes narrowed and turned burnt umber. "I wanted to tell you. I didn't know how you'd react."

"There's nothing to explain," Shep yelled. "You were a kniver."

"I wasn't. Not truly."

Jhee interposed herself between Medea and Shep. "When Ursula confronted you, she threatened to expose or kill you unless you paid her?"

"With what money? All I have is my Counselor's stipend and a Protectorate pension I refuse to touch. I can't even afford my own place to stay. I agreed to work night rounds at the center, so they let me stay there. As for exposure, the center knew. For center patients, it's my policy to disclose that to them during our intake meeting. For other referrals, the less we knew about each other, the better.

"Yes, I worked *briefly* for the Medical Protectorate, and it's haunted me ever since. Ever since I left their service, I've dedicated my skills to helping its victims. I try to use everything I learned there to help the people I once harmed. I tried to help Ursula. I was her backup. I wasn't the one she confronted. She'd tracked down another of the architects."

"In that case, you can't stay here," Jhee said. "Come with us. I want to take you into protective custody."

"I think I'm safer here. You've experienced the berserkers' defensive capacity."

"If that's the case, what were you doing when I visited your office not three days ago at the veteran's service center?"

Counselor Medea appeared shocked. "Three days ago? I've been here since Ursula came for me. You can ask anyone staying at the sanctuary. I stayed on after she left. She said I'd be safe here and not to leave until she came back. There was something she had to go bring back. That's the last contact I had with anyone until Hammad, and then Dawn Wolf sought sanctuary."

Jhee pursed her lips. She wasn't entirely sure if she trusted the woman. It could be some half-drowned attempt at protecting patient confidentiality. Or, Jhee thought back to the imperial sojourn and the talk of mimicry.

Counselor Medea suddenly looked about her uneasily. "Maybe I would be safer with you."

13

———

~

The Sandwich and the Nondescript Constable

Counselor Medea agreed to be taken into Jhee's custody while Shep stayed behind with Dari until she was fit to travel. They put her up in the room where they had also kept Ursula. Barely a long-tide had passed before her legal team contacted her to discuss the full extent of the professional and financial peril facing her. While they conferenced, a priority message arrived on her conch from one of her old intelligence contacts. After she read it, she put her legal team on hold. Jhee cleared and centered then walked into the kitchen to make some tea and a sandwich before she had to leave.

The construction of a sandwich was not unlike the process of formulating a cypher. It required a particular order to the faculties. Jhee inhaled the sage and coriander aroma of the artisan bread Shep bought yesterday. The one made with just a hint of spinach and hard cheese and some herbs and spices. Less than a half a loaf remained, and it had just begun to go stale and harden. It was good for sandwiches for a day or so before one either had to drown it in soup or make croutons with it.

She laid out the package of slow-roasted, thinly sliced to perfection maye slices. Once Jhee unwrapped the inner sleeve, she took a deep whiff of the hearty scent containing just a hint of the sea and garlic. Shep and Kanto loved the imported brands. She, however, was a sucker for domestic like she used to have as a child. Jhee took out a butcher knife and sliced off two thick slices of bread. She piled it high with meat, eating almost as much as she put on the bread. She topped it off with mild, white cheese. A few leaves of *kato* and a slice of water cuke and tomato together with a little sea salt and pepper, then a smathering of emulsified egg and oil became the finishing touches. She grabbed a nice cup of tea, then retired to the study with her magnificent creation.

Jhee sat in her comfy chair and made herself as comfortable as possible. She took a bite of her sandwich, then closed her eyes and savored the delicious blending of flavors. She chewed delicately and allowed each morsel to dance on her tongue, taking the time to appreciate the flavors as Shep had taught her. Jhee swallowed the bite, then took a sip of tea. She sighed in contentment.

Jhee closed the message on her conch, which had prompted her to fix a sandwich and make herself comfortable. Her intelligence contact had sent her a warning that constables were on their way to interview her. After she allowed herself another moment of peace, she resumed her conference with her legal team. Their usefulness during her imminent interview would be limited. Both her advocate and her solicitor stared at her with astonishment when she took them off hold.

"Justicar, I don't think you realize how serious this is," her advocate said.

"With your prolific case history, case files," her solicitor said, "the fines and appeals fees you're looking at are considerable."

They must not have received the notice yet. Jhee took another sip of tea. "This could bankrupt us."

"Yes. Even if the review board finds in your favor."

"Jhee?" Kanto stood in the doorway of her study. "Is that true?"

She laid her finger against her nose. "Possibly. Yes. Don't worry. I have some contingency funds and assets I can move around."

"And grandmamere's resources too. Don't forget those. I have a small trust she left me."

Jhee gave Kanto a reassuring smile. "See? That predicament has a finite solution."

"Justicar?" her solicitor queried.

Jhee bit into her delicious sandwich again. She daubed the corners of her mouth with her linen napkin. "I need to consider this. I'm afraid bankruptcy's about to be the least of my worries. I'll contact you again afterward, if I'm able."

"Afterward? Justicar, wait."

Jhee muted her legal team again. She took a few more bites of her sandwich. "Magnificent. Great, great sandwich."

The doorbell chimed, and Irina, their housekeeper, answered it.

Her advocate's conch chimed. While the advocate addressed the incoming message, her expression slipped from puzzled to grim. "I'm disconnecting now to call legates. You might want to—"

A stunned looking Irina cleared her throat. With a flustered bunching of her apron, she announced, "S-someone here to see you, Justicar."

Someone. No name. The uncharacteristic informality spoke of the woman's fear. Irina knew.

"Show them in," Jhee said.

The housekeeper kept her gaze averted as a nondescript imperial constable stepped into the study. Irina made her escape as quick as she could.

Jhee's solicitor finished the advocate's sentence for her, "… arrange for a special advocate. Justicar, we'll make arrangements and petition the Justicar's League for a legate with detention experience. They'll be at special intake before you are."

"Begging your pardon, my lady Justicar," the soft-spoken constable said. "I've been asked to escort you to etiquette review by the Style Council."

Kanto stifled a gasp. "I'll contact the Kenyattas' legates."

Jhee enjoyed another bite of her sandwich before handing Kanto her conch. "Will I need my advocate?" Jhee asked.

"I am afraid so, my lady," the constable replied. "Your good folk here can have them meet you at the inquiry office. I second the suggestion you engage the services of a special advocate."

Jhee nodded. "Do I have time to finish my sandwich?"

"If you'd like. I'm here alone as a courtesy. My force is right outside."

"Thank you." Jhee savored every bite of her sandwich as Kanto frantically made calls. She smacked her lips once she reached the end of her meal and had drained the last of the tea from her cup. She stood and accompanied the Imperial constable to the door. "May I ask what this is about?"

"It will be explained down at the offices."

Kanto helped Jhee slip on her cloak. He was practically in tears. "Legates will meet you there. I can't get hold of Shep. They can't do this, can they?"

Jhee held his face and leaned her head against his. "Shep will be home soon. I hate to interrupt Bax, but he should know how to contact him, if he's not."

"Tell me you'll be all right. Tell me you'll be back."

"I'll clear this up and be home in no time."

Kanto broke out in tears. Jhee took a deep, steady breath to prevent herself from joining him. She straightened her posture and touched her esca to his.

"My lady Justicar," the nondescript constable said.

"Yes. Wait for Shep, he'll know what to do. Comfort and occupy yourself with some reading, perhaps something you picked up while we were at the abbey."

"The Tales of Lady Cheiropthys and the Black Book."

"Precisely."

Kanto smiled and daubed his eyes. "Come back. Promise me you'll come back home to us."

Jhee faced the nondescript constable. "Shall we?"

The constable held the door for Jhee with a hint of sympathy. A group of black-clad guards surrounded the pair outside. They held back any action until she was out of sight of her front door. Once hidden from view though, they gagged her, threw the bag over her head, and forced her into their transport. Many who left with the Abyssal constabulary never returned.

The Interview I

The Abyssal Imperators' transport drove for some time. Her rank afforded her the courtesy of being seated on the bench instead of tossed on the floor like a sack of tubers. Eventually, they reached their destination, and she was escorted roughly and firmly, but not violently, down some stairs. Most of her outer clothing was stripped. After she was seated and secured to a chair, her hood was removed.

One plain table, a harsh bank of glow orbs, and a two-way mirror occupied the bare room. Cold metal pressed against the scar on the back of Jhee's neck.

A jolt of white-hot pain shot through Jhee's head. Jhee choked on her gag. The device left her dazed and drooling.

Jhee wondered if her special advocate was making any headway. She supposed if they weren't, she would already be under interrogation by now. The door opened, and a little old woman in a simple robe thrown over her skirt suit breezed in.

Perfume light and flowery accompanied the prim, grandmotherly woman. She carried a gray digital slate. She aligned it neatly on the table and set up a padded folding stool for herself. "No, no. This is much too impersonal."

The woman removed Jhee's gag. She moved aside the table, then arranged the tablet primly on her lap. She sat facing Jhee with the barest hint of a smile on her face. The woman checked the time, then folded her white-gloved hands. Aside from checking the time every so often, she did nothing else.

"Has my special advocate arrived?"

The woman touched a gloved finger to her lips for silence. The door opened. Another woman came in and whispered in her ear and left. She rechecked the time, then turned to Jhee with a pleasant smile. "I am Fire. Shall we begin? Look up here."

The woman pointed to her esca. The Makers' Mark began to shimmer and waver, but that was impossible!

"Confess," she said.

"To what? What am I being accused of?"

The woman held up one finger. "Confess."

"Please, tell me what I am being accused of."

The woman held up two fingers. "Confess."

"Please, I don't know what this is about."

The woman held up three fingers. She shook her head and tsked. With a quick gesture, a tongue of flame struck Jhee across the cheek.

Fire, as she called herself, must have flammable liquid on her. How else could she have created flames? Fire drawing could generate heat and sometimes sparks but not conjure flames. She tapped a few keys on the tablet. She turned it around to show Jhee. It was an official portrait of the vizier, Bathsheba of Toho and Wilobeia.

"An unfortunate accident." Another tongue of flame, hotter and more searing than the last, struck Jhee's cheek. Jhee pressed her mouth shut. The woman raised a hand to the glass behind her.

Again, the door opened. A beaten, bruised young man was ushered in and deposited in the chair opposite Jhee. She recognized him as the infirmarian from Tranquility Bridge Abbey.

"I shouldn't have helped you. I only did because I wanted you and that pretty male gone. You ruined everything. You killed my lady. Before you arrived with your household dripping in silks and finery, she looked out for me. Gave me fine colognes and fancy gifts. Now, look at me." The infirmarian sneered at Jhee, then spit a bit of blood and phlegm in her face. "That's her. She's the one. It was her. She killed Lady B."

The woman adjusted her shoulders after the infirmarian was led away. Jhee tried to engage her siren module. Nothing happened.

"Now you see your lies and denials will do you no good. Please, don't try any other tricks. Your command module has been disabled. Now, shall we begin again? Do you feel the heat upon your skin?"

The woman held Jhee's gaze. Jhee's hands grew warm. Warmth became searing pain. They began to smoke.

"Do you smell your flesh burning?" The smell of burnt flesh, her flesh, filled Jhee's nostrils. Jhee cried out. "Look at your hands."

Reluctantly, Jhee did as instructed. Her hands were unharmed. The man used her slate to show Jhee her face which was likewise unburnt.

"Each time you lie or refuse to answer, the flames will get hotter."

Physical pain Jhee might disassociate from. This, however, was in her mind. What could she do against that? She prayed her advocate arrived before the flames became too hot.

～

To Channel the Rage

"Do something, Captain," Shep said as he stalked their sitting room. A discolored streak marked his path. He had also plucked a bald patch on his arm.

"I'm trying. I've had to move carefully. With that Senator incident, you are drenched near radioactive. They are saying I put her up to it because he was my political and romantic rival."

"That's absurd."

"Don't worry, Sheepdog, aside from this little snag, your political fortunes are poised to rise. Until now, it seemed things only kept getting better for the two of you. You'll get this sorted like you always do and come out the better of it."

"I wish I could share your optimism, Cap."

"It's not optimism. It's observation. You two are practically a charmed pair. Even beyond the politics, you've survived the war and, more importantly, the peace intact." The captain gestured at Shep's eye with his cane. "More or less. The berserker process isn't ravaging your body like mine. While you do have that young pup in the stir, there's still a tenderness, an affection to how you and Sniffer regard each other."

"Don't be fooled Captain, we've had our crests and troughs but nothing on level with this. No matter how things are between us or worse they might yet become, I'd never wish this on her. I think I might give anything just to have her here with us safe."

"You still enjoy being around Sniffer, and Sniffer still enjoys being around you. I wish I still felt that way about the Regent. Do you know how often I see the Regent Sheepdog? Once a month. I used to lament that, but now even a short visit is hard for us to last through without spitting bile at each other." The captain rolled his cane agitatedly between his hands. "At the start, she only had a handful of other spouses. Now she's surrounded by young pups. She sucked them up like kreel to consolidate her power. The last time I saw her, she said I repulsed her. She felt nothing for me, yet she wouldn't let me go. All I wanted was a little happiness and affection. Ursula made me happy, and that vindictive, jealous bitch wouldn't even let me have that."

Shep paused to wonder if he could ever come to hate Jhee that much.

A loud pained grunt accompanied the captain lifting himself from the chair with the help of his cane. "There's one cardinal rule of being an imperial spouse: no bastards. You are allowed to do as you please as long as you don't violate it. The imperials though, they can have all they wish with their concubines.

"But no, not me. I'm a fourth spouse, not even a favored one at that. I barely even see my wife. Once I used to curse that, but now count it as a blessing. Yet, I followed the rules no matter how hard it was or what it cost me. All Ursula had to do was not get pregnant. That's all she had to do. My wife would look the other way as long as there were no children. Ursula had begun to insist. She wouldn't let it go.

"When Ursula got pregnant, I figured that was it. I had had enough and wanted out. Like a dutiful consort, I went to the Regent. I told her I didn't want an allowance or alimony. I only wanted a divorce, a quiet one. No scandal—I would sign anything she wanted. I was still naïve enough to think she might have been happy for me. She agreed. She was very pleasant. All smiles. That should have been my first hint. All I had to do was one thing: make a simple delivery for her. One little thing, and she would grant me what I wanted."

"Captain, I remember how smitten you two were, but I'm not sure if this is the time."

Captain Odo rolled his cane from hand to hand and chewed on his lip. "What if she did this, Sheepdog?"

Shep spun to face his old captain. "Who?"

"The Princess Regent. What if she mistook my contact with the two of you?"

The moment slowed. Shep's vision became a field of red. The captain's voice turned garbled. Shep's pulse pounded furious in his ears. A berserker fury was coming over him.

Shep locked his focus on a point on the wall beyond the captain. He filled his lungs with a deep breath of air. Then another. He took a wide stance and locked his arms. He dared not move or switch his focus.

Find your stillness. Focus in.

Shep chanted the phrase to himself over and over. He took more calming breaths. Another voice just beyond his ken joined in with a down-chant.

The captain's voice came back to the fore, "That's it. Easy now, Shep. Ease it down, soldier."

A frantic Kanto burst into the room, waving the favor list, also known as a book of boons. "Useless. As far as I can tell, none of these individuals have enough clout to help."

The interruption allowed Shep to calm himself even more. That was a fair assessment if the person who had called for Jhee's detention was the Princess Regent.

The captain grabbed his coat and hat. "I'll keep trying, Sheepdog. Plead my case to the Regent herself if I have to."

Captain Odo left.

"Should we contact Mirrei?" Kanto asked. "Maybe she's gained more influential contacts in her travels."

Shep let the tension drain from his body. He must hold himself together for his family. "Jhee wouldn't want her dragged into this."

"Does your friend have any ideas who might have done this?"

Shep considered lying, but lies helped get them into this mess. "The Princess Regent."

Kanto emitted a noise part gasp, part sob, and dropped into Jhee's chair, the spirit knocked from him.

Rage flared in Shep again. That was Jhee's chair. Jhee was coming back, and Kanto had no right.

Stay locked on their goal, retrieving Jhee relatively unharmed.

Jhee had been in custody for nearly two days, still within the window of when most detentions ended without tragedy. At three days or more, the likelihood of the detainee's safe return dropped drastically. If Jhee were here, she might quote an exact percentage. Not knowing the odds, Shep accounted a poor trade for not having Jhee safe at home.

They were running out of options. At this point, Shep would make a Dismantler's deal to see Jhee freed. The last folk he would ever want to approach popped into his mind. On the one hand, he had his sisters and on the other Jhee's mentor. Shep went through his and Jhee's contact lists.

~

The Interview II

The younger, slimmer woman leaned in to Jhee ear and whispered, "Where is the case?"

"What case?"

"Lies will not be tolerated." The woman grabbed Jhee's little finger. Jhee heard the pop first. Then the searing pain kicked. It mirrored itself across her other digits though only the one finger had been touched. She bit down to prevent crying out. "Drawing or cyphering will not be tolerated either. First, I break them. Breaks can be healed. Bones reset. You're out of the arcane circle temporarily. If your lack of cooperation continues, next, I find a more permanent way to take them away. Lose your hands, and you're out of the arcane circle. You may still be able to perform some incantations. Lose your tongue, too, though, and that's it for you, really."

Jhee focused in to distract herself from the pain. This pain was real. The Ladies' Auxiliary, also known as the Style Council, worked for several deep Empire interests such as the Abyssal Constabulary, various other clandestine police forces, and the Invokers, clerics assigned to investigate heresy. The Ladies worked in groups of four, each trained with a different elemental drawing method, to extract information from prisoners. An evaluation with them was euphemistically called an interview, but by any other name, it was torture. Time in their custody had broken many. Fire had reviewed her first with a mixture of real and phantom flames. Water and Wind had visited but had not interviewed her yet. The thin, wisp of a woman breaking her fingers was Earth.

"I've been authorized to make you an offer. My client just wants the case. You met with Ursula after she stole it. Tell me where to find it and you'll be released without delay."

Two slow, ponderous knocks on the room's window interrupted them. The woman looked at the window, then back at Jhee.

"Pardon me a moment."

The woman left. Jhee's finger throbbed, and her heart raced. She stared at the reflective window, hoping to see some sign of what lay beyond. She struggled and jiggered her chair around a bit. Jhee yelped as the motion set off a firestorm of pain in her broken finger. The door to the interrogation room opened. She flinched and let out an involuntary whimper.

Black-clad guards rushed in. They gagged Jhee, threw a bag over her head, and rushed her out. They were not cruel or overly rough, only unconcerned with her comfort. She flinched and yelled whenever one contacted her finger. They put her in a transport and drove.

The transport stopped. Jhee could not hear any city sounds. It had to be some place remote. They forced her from the transport and made her walk some ways. Was this it? No one was too high for them to make disappear. Still, she hoped her rank had at least afforded her the courtesy of her family having a body to bury if nothing else.

Jhee's hood was removed. She blinked against the dawning pinkish rays of first-sun. This made a more pleasant final sight than the inside of a hood. Gascal. Gabi. Ghele. Gram-gram. Gwyn. Gloriana. Mamere. Babere. Gamaje. Grandmamere.

How much of the story about Miramar's death had Mirrei invented? *"... she turned in time to see the towering wave bearing down on her. Defiantly, she faced it as it crashed upon our dock. That was the last I saw of her."*

Miramar. Mirrei. Kanto. Shep. Jhee took a deep breath and steeled herself.

"Jhee! First Makers' pride," Shep said. He rushed over and threw his arms around her. She winced. He drew back.

As Jhee's eyes acclimated to the light, she thought she had never seen anything as beautiful as Shep's face, scars and all. One guard removed her restraints and pushed her towards Shep. They turned away, presumably headed back to their transport. Once Jhee heard the transport's engine noise recede, Jhee cradled her hand and sagged against Shep.

"Let me see," he said. He gingerly took her hand. "We'll get you fixed right up. You're with us. You're safe."

"Thank the Makers, Sniffer," Odo said. "We thought we had lost you there."

Shep and Odo transported her home. She sat on the couch while Shep got his field kit. Kanto hovered over her. She was not sure how long she had been gone, but she could tell he had spent every moment awake and worried.

"I'm fine," she said. "This is nothing. I've had broken bones and burns before."

"Don't, Jhee. I'm fine." Kanto stopped his pacing and put on a brave face. "The Style Council *reviewed* both a cousin and childhood friend once. It's neither here nor there. Tea. I'll get you some nice hot tea. I think we might have a bit of Tranquility Bridge Gold left."

Odo sat across from her on the sitting couch. His face stern and the set of his jaw angry.

"Thank you, Captain," Jhee said.

His face softened. He hung his head. "It wasn't me, Sniffer. They laughed at me when I tried."

Jhee tried to picture the imperial family tree and where the Captain's wife was on it. It just made her head throb. She collapsed back against the cushions of the chair.

"Go. Enough. We can discuss it later." Shep, who had returned with the kit, gave Odo a stern look. At about the same time, Kanto came in with a cup of hot tea.

"I used the waver instead of the kettle. I hope you don't mind." Jhee reached to take the cup. The pain reminded her about her hand. "Allow me."

Kanto tipped the cup to Jhee's lips gently with a practiced hand. He neither tipped the container too much nor took it away before she had finished her sip. It was among the most delicious drinks she ever tasted. She sipped a few more times. She let him know with a simple nod she had had enough. How many times had he had to do this with his mother?

"Thank you," Jhee mumbled.

"You are welcome, dear wife. You sit right there and let denme fix you up." Jhee's eyes and body felt heavy, and the pain in her hand had subsided. She felt a dull burn inside her. Her burn wounds tingled. No doubt, the effect of the Tranquility Bridge's blend's proven healing benefits. It had never made her feel sleepy, though. "A mild sedative," he said as if in answer to her unspoken question.

Shep took her hand. "I have to reset it. I won't lie. This will hurt, even through whatever he's given you. Ready?"

Jhee nodded. Before she had finished the motion, Shep grabbed her hand and gave her little finger sharp pull. She roared with pain. Her hand burned then tingled. In her head, a warm feeling set in.

"See you later, Sniffer," the Captain said.

Jhee barely registered the main door closing. Each husband placed one of her arms over their shoulders and gently lifted her from the couch. Kanto trilled something sweet and melodic as they went up the stairs.

Jhee laid down in her warm, familiar, comfy bed. Shep and Kanto nestled in beside her. Kanto sang to her, every bit living up to his outside name, Bright Harmony.

"Rest. We have you."

Jhee tried to smile and drifted to sleep. The world could turn without her for tonight. Everything could wait until tomorrow. For now, she was home and loved.

~

A Return to Form

With Jhee returned, fury replaced fear. Shep and Kanto's thoughts had turned to vengeance. Kanto then engaged in what he did best: scheming.

"They tortured her, Shep. I want someone to bleed."

Shep did too; in his own way. What would Kanto know about vengeance and blood? It was an armchair boast at best. Worse, Kanto's machinations would take tides, moons, or Makers forbid, years to be realized. Shep wanted someone to bleed now. He did not much care who or what. Though he would prefer the real culprit, their household knew neither the culprit nor the deliverer.

Kanto did not know how to make someone bleed, but Shep did. Shep entered from the top stage left, a catwalk high and to the left of the cage. Across the slaughterhouse, on an opposite catwalk, he saw his opponent. They both descended the steps. The crowd chanted and cheered. Those closest to the catwalk chanted his name rhythmically. Dawn Wolf. Dawn Wolf. He felt the fury beginning to take hold, as the chanting put him into a deep state of trance.

At the door to the cage, a group of fighters, men and women, clapped and stamped in a slower rhythm.

"Oost. Oost. Oost."

A berserker chant meant to hype Shep up and unleash the beast within.

Already Shep could feel it inside him. That thing, that dark animal instinct, the doctors had awakened inside him. The part of him which gave lie to the fact that they had ever been civilized. Inside, no matter what, it always waited. It was there, present in them all.

The Fire Folk understood the veneer of civility to be a guise torn through like paper. They fought with a ferocity which had so caught the Water Folk off guard, it scared them into experimenting on their own people. What Shep had learned in the war, was what the Fire Folk knew, and the Water Folk forgot: the killer instinct the ordinary Folk had suppressed. Underneath the skin, underneath the surface, they were all the same. The Fire Folk fought without fear, without pretense. Some called them barbarians. The truth of it was, they all were. From the loftiest of Sky Folk to the lowest of Earth Folk delvers: they were all one.

Blessed were the Makers who had made them all the same within. Drowned be the Takers who had convinced them all to fight each other over differences of the false skin. The true skin, the true division, was that of the gang. They were all one: One waters.

Shep had never told Jhee of his sympathies, never corrected her. She thought she understood what was going on with him. He let her have the illusion. One day, though, he would try to make her see. She was already coming around. She had learned all on her own to stop calling them barbarians. The two of them would soon break through to Kanto. Mirrei was already there. And from them on to the world. One waters indivisible. Reconcile or die.

In the cage, someone would bleed. Those who hurt Jhee had better pray he never found out who they were.

"Oost. Oost. Oost."

Those fighters nearest the ring kept up the chant. Shep stamped and clapped along with them to get himself hyped. He shook his head and howled at the sky. Medea waited nearby to tend the fighters' wounds. Hammad, his trainer and match attendant, came over. Shep bared his teeth. The match attendant hit him with the bioplasm spray. He roared at the taste of fresh blood. He saw red. His trainer flung open the cage door. Shep barreled through it. He and his opponent collided in the center.

14

~

The Raid

At Jhee's insistence, the household had resolved to have the child discussion again. On the designated day, she awoke, sweating, to the memories of pain and the smell of burning once more. When she was unable to return to sleep, Jhee planted herself in the sitting room with reading materials and schematics. She would not leave for wrack or ruin. Upon Kanto's arrival, he set up his harp opposite her. All they required now was Shep's presence.

Jhee quietly read in front of the fireplace while Kanto saluted her on the harp. The interview memories went to sleep in a corner of her mind. She marked off an article about tandem cyphering and the use of the pair bond in arcana. It involved blood-based arcana. She unmarked it. Shep and Jhee never indulged in blood-based arcana. The involvement of bioplasm made it a risky proposition with Shep's condition.

Kanto gave a flourish with the harp. Jhee raised her attention from her conch to give him appreciation. Kanto smiled in acceptance.

Jhee marked the blood-arcana article again. Kanto might work as a subject. His suitability and willingness to take part in a broader range of experiments had her eager and curious. She scoured her archives for techniques she had previously dismissed. There were promising articles with respect to arcana based on blood. Though, they had other aspects that made her uncomfortable using them. Among them, their close association with the Pillarist Doombringers. She'd discuss the matter with Kanto anyway.

Another article discussed Pillarist healers or Soothbringers' work treating mental trauma with arcana. Jhee marked it. The description sounded like the reverse of what the Ladies' Auxiliary had done to Jhee. No matter what, Jhee had always been able to rely on her mind. If she learned the Pillarists' methods, she might be able to protect herself better.

Kanto began another selection on the harp. It was not as good as his lute playing, but still quite expert. He said he needed to keep up his skills on several instruments. Besides his other talents, he was a bit of a virtuoso. He had been raised to be a concubine or courtesan. When she learned all that entailed and all the skills they were expected to know, Jhee gained a newfound respect for him and them. It rivaled what she had to know as a Justicar and artificer. No wonder Kanto had nothing left to give arcane practice. She had tried to get him a proper tutor or inquire about courses at the academy once they arrived, but he was more interested in his charity work, and they mutually agreed to continue with the private, casual instruction she provided.

So much they did in their lives had been about managing Shep's condition. To converse about less weighty topics, to not have to cross-check every cypher against his triggers, sometimes came as a relief. Jhee continued to vet arcana articles.

No sooner had Jhee returned to her reading, than she received an incoming chime from Nevis, her Justicar colleague.

"I need to lose your number, but you are perfectly free to find mine," Jhee answered.

"You should come down here."

Jhee sobered at her no-nonsense tone. "Why? What's happened?"

"The corruption patrol raided a slaughterhouse on the docks. Some underground fighting society. I recognized one fighter they brought in."

Jhee thought about the bruises and the blood and the late nights where Shep did not come home at all. "Shep. Is there anything you can do?"

"They're still processing the arrested. It's big. They swept up many people. Important people. I think they intend to make an example of some to prove they are tough on corruption. Lots of scrutiny on this one. I can move him to the back of the line. If you get here with an advocate fast enough, you might be able to take him home with a minimum of scandal."

When Jhee hung up the phone, Kanto stared at her with concern. "Shep's been arrested. I don't know all the details."

Kanto stood. "Come on then."

"You don't have to go."

Kanto pfted. "It seems like every time I let a member of this family out of my sight, you get yourselves in trouble."

"As I recall, we had to come after you too."

Kanto helped her into her cloak. "Precisely. I let me out of your sight and found trouble. Besides, I know how to get folks out of jail without tearing it up. This family is three out of four on arrests. You may need someone who has not been arrested doing the talking for you."

"Without an arrest? Didn't you say something about an incident when you were young, which derailed your military enrollment?"

"Fine, a recent criminal arrest record then."

The Transmission

Shep hung up his cloak and went into the sitting room. Jhee and Kanto swept in after him. Kanto checked their missed messages. "Hi, kin. Guess you're not home. *Sas drej*. Terrible connection. Try again later."

Jhee noted the edge of sadness and disappointment in Mirrei's voice.

"Drenchit, the remote meeting with Mirrei," Kanto said. "Shep, what were you thinking?"

"May I have a few moments alone with Shep?" Jhee asked.

Kanto glared at Shep, sniffed, and then walked away. "I'll go call her back and explain to her why we weren't here."

Jhee sat down in her easy chair with a sigh. Shep grunted with pain as he took a seat in his. "Why would you take part in such a barbaric event?"

"I don't know."

"Fish flakes. You asked for space. I gave it to you. Now, I'm asking you to let me know what's going on with you."

"I don't know!"

Jhee set her lips and folded her hands. She took a deep breath. "Do you want a divorce?"

"No. I'm committed to our family."

"Are you having an affair?"

"Oh, by the Makers, Jhee. How can you even think that?"

"Then what?"

"I'm angry. I'm just so drenched angry. All the time. I don't know why."

"You don't know? Perhaps it's all the blood-sporting and immersing yourself in a world of violence and blood. Do you think that might be it?"

Shep shook his head. "I miss simple. We, all of it, used to be so simple. We were at risk in the abbey, and I couldn't even hold my weapon. Mirrei got sick, and I couldn't do anything. They came for you, Jhee, and I was powerless. All because of what the Medical Protectorate did. As berserkers, we were unstoppable. I wanted to feel that way again, Jhee. The elation, the feeling of power, that nothing could stop me or stand in my way."

Jhee held her hand out to the side. He took it. "Is there anything we can do?"

"In that ring, I had a small part of it again. Fight. Protect. Survive. The taste of my opponent's blood in my mouth felt so good. There is nothing else like it. I thought I had dealt with it. I thought I let it go after all these years. But you never forget. You never let it go. The one beneath the skin is always there, waiting. Do you ever miss it, Jhee?"

"What I experienced wasn't like what they did to you. I can't explain it. Inspiration. It's never been like that even before they enhanced it. I've felt the need to change my skin on occasion. Sometimes it's been so strong, a siren call, that's almost impossible to resist. The ability to cast helps, the mediations required to discipline the mind for artificing. I release the urge and feed it to the Divine Mechanism. I channel it there and let the First Makers do with it as they will."

"I wish I could do that."

"So, what do we do now? I've pulled what favors I can, but I'm burning through them quickly. We are low on money and influence. I can't keep bailing you out. I need you to find some other way to deal with this. We'll help you however we can. If you'll let us."

Kanto cleared his throat. "Sorry, to interrupt, denbe, denme. Mirrei left another message. I think you better watch it."

This transmission was clearer than the last but still cut out every few words. That only made the Imperial endowments seal on the letter Mirrei held up clearer. "You see this letter… 'Recent allegations against you… Recently come to our attention your involvement in certain activities.' They are calling me a terrorist. They're threatening to pull our funding."

~

The Dog and Pony Procession

Soon after, Jhee received an informal invitation to the Fancy Foam Equestrian and Canine Showcase to be held at the Temple Downs Race Track. *Lovely*, she thought. The informal invitation meant her attendance was optional, but that wasn't her only consideration in whether to attend.

"Are you sure you are up for this, Jhee?" Kanto asked.

"This is important to you."

"You're important to me." Kanto leaned in and whispered, "Drench this literal dog and pony parade and drench the Imperials, too if even one of them had anything to do with what happened to you."

Jhee and Kanto strolled arm-in-arm along the manicured paddock. The musky manure smell mingled with the sweet-sharpness of pollinating flowers. Proud dog and horse owners displayed their prize-winning pets both of the four- and two-legged variety. She was glad she dosed up on allergy medication.

"Technically, IES/MANTEL had me tortured."

"And they are nothing, if not wholly or partially owned, and in collusion with the Imperial family. How can you be so glib?"

Jhee gave Kanto a look down her nose. At this point, Jhee cared little about keeping knowledge of them secret. She was already on their radar. Silence and secrecy only helped them, not her. If MANTEL was the imperial families' arm, Inkerton Enforcement Services, with its hired security and labor forces, was the sword it wielded.

He sighed. "I'm sorry, it's not for me to say how you process such a traumatic experience. I'm just worried they'll come after you again."

"Isn't that why it's even more important we attend this farce? To show whoever ordered my interrogation, I am not intimidated."

Kanto gave a quick, approving nod at Jhee's correct assessment of the politics of the matter. "I saw a glimmer of the woman everyone in the Far Reaches cursed when you confronted Shep's sister at the sojourn. You know we have to hit back and hit back hard. I wasn't the only one humoring their spouse, was I?"

"I avoid politics because I know that side of me is there. It's *my* berserker essence."

Kanto shuddered. "This might backfire and provoke them. It was hard enough to get you back. It frightens and angers me to think we're at the same event as someone who would do that to you. I do suppose it's what Imperials would do. They would condemn you to a pit and then smile in your face about it later."

"Then, I leave it up to your skills to make us allies even more important than they are, and another reason we needed to attend."

"Is that all?"

"You've repeatedly expressed your faith in me, Kanto. This is my chance to express my faith in you. This is one reason we chose you to join our family above all others. You've studied all the players and what makes them tick. In this, you are the teacher and I, the student."

Kanto squared his shoulders. "Let's rile the Storm Child. We'll have to separate for maximum coverage."

"All right, who do I claver with first?"

Kanto scanned the imperial pairs. He motioned his head at the woman in the center of a cluster of red and gray uniformed men and women. "Her. The Pike branch. They are powerful, though a bit of the pariahs. Because of being highly suspected of piracy. They are heavily into military contracts and have serious military preoccupation despite most of them never serving. They publicly fought against IES outsourcing. She has served though and donates to many vet causes. Tough, no-nonsense."

"After her, who else?"

"The Wrasses. Less powerful, fascinated by all things arcane. The man in the flannel, multicolored robes off to the side, not the eldest or the inheritor but has the genuine power. If you fall into your normal arcane technobabble, he will eat it right up."

"I thought you liked my technobabble."

"He'll love it even more."

"Where will you be? In case I need help or more pointers."

"With the Mandelbrots, also known as the collectors. They like to collect unique and best in class artists, both as friends and spouses."

"And that is indeed you, dear husband. A rare beauty and talent."

Kanto raised his eyebrow. "You haven't seen anything yet. Watch me work."

Kanto sashayed away. Jhee smiled to herself and headed for the Pike matriarch. She paused a few feet from where they had gathered and took a breath. She and the matron spoke for some time. Jhee's eyebrows had drench near developed a permanent, persistent arch by the time they were done. Even those who must have been used to it still seemed taken aback at some of the outlandish and inappropriate things the woman had to say. Clearly, she had been a sailor.

"And when you mount that gorgeous sea stallion of yours tonight, give him a good one for me."

She finally released Jhee to seek other conversational prey. Jhee turned her attention to the Wrasses.

"Justicar, care for a game?" a voice called.

Jhee had not gotten halfway across the room before the voice hailed her. Lady Amani, the woman she had met in the study at the Imperial Sojourn, lounged at a gaming table with several others. She shook the dicing cup at Jhee.

Into the gathering swept the ostentatious imperial who had alibied the now dead senator. The case had discredited Jhee and set much of her current nightmare in motion. This was also the saffron eyed woman who plowed by her outside the library where Jhee had gamed with Lady Amani. The imperial, swaddled in a cream and ebony gilt-edged, crystal-inlaid wrap, bore a lightning-hot elegance, enticing if you were the type who reached out to flames; terrifying if you weren't. She zeroed in on Jhee and struck a path towards her.

Jhee abandoned her pursuit of the Wrasses and diverted to the gaming area. She made the proper gestures and bows to the women seated around the table. "My ladies."

"We were just doing some friendly wagering. Care to join?" Lady Amani asked.

"Don't mind if I do," the saffron-eyed woman answered.

"The invitation wasn't for you, Lady Zaria," Lady Amani said.

Zaria ran her tongue along the inside of her mouth.

"I believe they are serving cocktails in the turf lounge," one of the assembled ladies said.

She and several nobles hastened from the gaming area. Other lords and ladies kept playing but slyly adjusted their positions to listen in.

Lady Zaria gave a tiny fake chuckle, "As you like. See what continuing to play only with plebes nets you."

"Perhaps later," Amani said.

The two stared each other down until some signal passed between them. Lady Zaria glided from the gaming area.

Jhee thought it might be best if she left, as well. "It is most gracious of you to invite me, but I'm not much for gambling."

"Nonsense. Sit down," Lady Amani said. The high ladies rearranged themselves so that Jhee could have a seat. "This one here is simply vicious, she can be on my team."

The cards were dealt, and they began to play.

"My dear Justicar, it has been a while since the sojourn. How are you faring?" Amani asked.

"Quite well, my lady."

"Excellent. Excellent. None the worse from your interview?"

"Interview?" Jhee asked, then set her lips in a thin line once it dawned on her what the Lady had meant. "My interview, yes. It was quite unexpected. I was not quite prepared."

"Yet, you appear to have acquitted yourself well enough?"

"True. Not an experience I'd like to repeat."

"An understandable sentiment. I believe it's to you, Lady Danio."

"The stakes are a tad higher than I care to lose tonight. And with that ladies, Justicar, I shall excuse myself from the table."

Lady Danio gave the other lady the eye. "Me too. You have cleaned us out."

The third lady seemed oblivious. They played a few more rounds. Despite saying she wanted to leave, Lady Danio stuck around a few more hands. She eventually gave the other lady the eye too. She at last finally got it. "Swell playing, Justicar. You've quite cleaned us out."

Only Jhee and Amani remained at the table. "Hmm, well, with all other players eliminated, we can no longer play on the same team."

"No, we can't, my lady."

"Still, it would be a shame to stop the game now. How about we resume our match from the other night? Allow me a chance to avenge my defeat."

"I really must—"

"I insist." Jhee switched to the opposite side of the table to Amani. "Now, we have a clearer view of where the other sits. I was most saddened to hear about your interview."

"I would think such a thing would be beneath your notice. My affairs hardly rate attention from someone as powerful as yourself."

"Quite the contrary. Everyone's taken notice of your prominent role in that suicide business. In fact, I think quite highly of you and take note of much of what you do. I fear you do not fully appreciate the effect your actions have. I trust you understand now?"

"Indeed, my lady."

Amani rolled the dice and moved her pieces. "Your move."

Jhee's hands twitched. Thinking back on their meeting at the resort, the lady had addressed her as Justicar. Yet, Jhee had borne no sashes of office and never introduced herself as a Justicar to Lady Amani. Was Amani admitting to being the one who called for her interrogation? She knew much about it, regardless. Was this a warning or a challenge?

"Fold," Jhee said.

"Conceding so soon? I thought for sure you had a few more rounds in you. I was so looking forward to playing longer."

"My family needs me."

"Ah, family. Do you know where my family stands in line to the throne outside of the elective succession?"

"Rather high."

"Such imprecision and coming from you no less. Though, it is technically correct. Did I hear correctly that you stymied IES?"

"I would hardly say I stymied them. We disagreed over the ownership of a piece of medical technology. Which I thought we had resolved amicably."

"Still, you can never be too careful, especially when it comes to Imperial interests."

"I'll keep that in mind."

"Please do. Now, you may run along to your family. I'll be around if you feel the need to keep playing."

Jhee looked at the Wrasses. Amani knew why she was here and what she intended. Neither they nor the Pikes would be powerful enough to stop her. If Amani was as powerful as Jhee suspected, almost no one here was powerful enough to oppose her outside of the current immediate family of the sitting Emperor and Empress.

Jhee still had to risk it. No individual branch, perhaps. Maybe some form of collective effort on her behalf. All the families were still Imperial electors to the Imperial succession council. It could not hurt to have more allies among them.

~

To Hold Back the Sea

Jhee marched up to the Wrasses and dazzled them with technobabble as if her life depended on it, which it did. As Kanto predicted, they gushed out over cyphering and all matters arcane, even arcane forensics. Although by the end, Jhee had gently rebuffed a few offers of marriage. They did not do much halfway. She was sure they were joking, which she rather enjoyed. Most of these imperial families did not have a sense of humor. She supposed the risk of being murdered by your relations or taken away for reeducation at any moment made you act in strange ways.

Jhee handed the patriarch her credential card. "Have your wonderful niece and nephew call me, and I'll happily answer any questions they have about cyphering training."

"Well met, Justicar, well met. Here, have your man there chime us up to discuss tutoring my youngest as well? You take care. Take care of yourself now."

The patriarch's expression was concerned yet sincere. He had guessed Jhee's purpose here as well. Jhee took the personal credential card. Later she would have their servants arrange the exchange of their more formal credential cards, but this was a direct line without having to go through all the proprieties of a formal meeting. Two down, all to go.

Jhee sought out Kanto. As said, he was still with the Mandelbrot set. They were inspecting a pair of Pomeros puppies. Jhee joined them as they went down the rows of fancy dog breeds. She touched Kanto's shoulder.

"Hello everyone," Kanto said and looped his arm through Jhee's, "this is my dear wife, the esteemed Justicar of District Sixteen and renowned author of 'Dispatches from Arrow Point.'"

"Hello there, my Lady Justicar we were just discussing these magnificent animals with your man here."

"Denbe, these are my friends the Mandelbrots and Aiaku."

"Pleased to meet you, my lords and ladies."

"You as well, Justicar," Aiaku, the sandy-haired man, said.

"We met at the sojourn while Bright Harmony performed."

"Indeed we did. Small seas."

Jhee relaxed for a moment with Kanto, the Mandelbrots, and his apparent friend. Despite the stakes, Jhee's anxiety eased. She had one assurance with this crowd she usually never had: none of them viewed Jhee with an eye to trade up the way most secondaries spouses did when she was invited to functions. They had or were already married to Imperials. They could get no political or wealth gain from a simple government official with fairly distant, almost nonexistent claim to the elective succession. Every noble family had some claim. However, the most powerful families made sure the most distant were kept distant and ineligible. On the other hand, they did like to have companions. If the way many of them eyed her and Kanto was any indication, they were still sizing up their eligibility for that purpose.

Kanto whispered in Jhee's ear, "Aiaku is from Taelos."

"The ones who tried to hold back the sea."

Kanto inclined his head. "Their male population was decimated trying to stop the wall. I think he's on our side."

The young man raised his glass at Jhee and Kanto. Jhee did likewise. It seems her actions against the Storm wall had gained her one admirer instead of an enemy.

Kanto adjusted Jhee's collar. "So, how did it go?"

"I charmed the robes off both the Pikes and the Wrasses."

"Then why do you look like you just ate Dundarian lampreys washed down with a gallon of bitter beer?"

Jhee held Kanto's hand. "Please. We'll discuss it later."

Kanto pulled his hand loose, and his eyes flashed with anger. "Who?"

"Let's just enjoy the rest of the event."

"Point them out."

"It will do no good. They are too powerful."

Kanto scanned the crowd and soon gave a knowing nod. "I see. No one is too powerful. We'll just have to be slower and clandestine. And sweeten the offer of friendship. We already have something powerful to barter: my tenth share of M-corp preferred."

"You'd really give up your noble title?"

"So long as one of us has one or the shares to maintain one, it's all that matters."

"Please, no. I think I got us a truce. Can we please not push it?"

"You think? But you are not sure?"

"No."

"Was it someone you came into direct conflict with?"

"Direct contact, not direct conflict. It didn't seem personal."

Kanto sighed. "We still need to keep to the original plan. The worst thing we can do is being seen to roll over. If we can't do anything about the head of the drake, then we need to strike the tail."

"What do you mean?"

"Find whoever set you up and make an example of them. With no direct quarrel between you, it means they used a lesser branch or slab to do their dirty work."

"Won't that just escalate?"

"Perhaps, but the person who did this is savvy enough to know if you don't retaliate, it will be open season on you. Even if they do nothing, a lesser branch could take you out for their own reasons. It's probably why they so easily agreed to a truce. They will have used a cutout they don't mind losing. Now, this is important. How did they seem to react to your being here?"

"Impressed."

"Good. I think that means they expect you to eliminate the problem for them. They may have been testing you."

"Kanto, can't we just please let this go."

"No, Jhee, unfortunately not. Now think, could this person be the myste-rious imperial Counselor Medea was talking about?"

"Almost certainly so."

"So, that means that to orchestrate the attack on your career, they needed someone privy to your confidences. Someone you would trust. They needed to know something about your movements. And your temperament. They needed to know the senator would set you off. Your prolific and high-profile investigative work would provide some insight, but not all. They needed more to go on, on how to get to you. If our family was in a worse place, I'd say all three of your cohort would be the obvious suspects."

Jhee raised an eyebrow. "Including you?"

"Yes, if we weren't on such excellent terms. Grandmamere said, 'always start with the spouses.' The overly ambitious ones, while obvious, often want to protect their position first and foremost. The ones to watch out for are the ones who feel slighted or harbor unspoken, minor grievances. Those fester and lead to rash action. They often want acknowledgment and to avenge their injury more than they want power. Our cohort is also small enough that we can address most issues before they can fester."

"Someone with a sense of grievance which would make them reckless." The Senator's family or his imperial lover, Lady Zaria, Jhee thought. They fit the bill perfectly. But she did not think it would be a smart idea to be seen to target the people she was in a public feud with and who had a case brought against her. All the reasons Kanto said why they should retaliate made sense. However, if she did, she was committing herself to politics and giving up on the law. She might get herself reinstated, but she would still no longer be considered credible. Her reputation as a Justicar would be tarnished. She needed for the board of Justicars to vindicate her. If she went after her accusers, even obliquely, it subverted the system.

Jhee tipped the peach cocktail to her lips. She watched Kanto work the event. This time they had gone after her. A risk she could live with. Next time, they might go after Shep, Kanto, or Mirrei. Jhee squeezed her eyes shut. She must keep them safe. No matter what it cost her. Preserve life first. Preserve her family first.

Jhee pulled Kanto aside, "If an occasion arises for you to save yourself, take it. If you find a situation that allows you to protect yourself, agree. Use your tenth share if you must. All I ask is for you to help Mirrei if you can."

～

The Flame and The Rod

When Lady Zaria headed for Jhee this time, Jhee had no obvious exit. She stood her ground at the clubhouse bar.

"Ah, Justicar, what an unexpected surprise." The woman narrowed blazing saffron eyes at Jhee. "And in such health, no less. I would have thought you would have been indisposed for longer."

"Well, you know what they say? Hard to cage a goldfish."

"Indeed. I trust you found the experience edifying."

"No doubt. Very educational. It certainly has focused my sights."

"It was impressive that a minor noble such as yourself could have managed such a brief stay."

"I find I am often underestimated." Jhee's boast was a leaky boat with nothing to keep it afloat. She still did not know how or why she had been released. Or targeted.

"We shall see. Won't we?" The woman picked up a flute of champagne from a passing waiter. "Well, how about a toast? Cheers, a drink to your continued good health?"

"And to yours, my lady."

They each drank. Although Jhee did not think the woman would be so obvious as to poison her, she was glad she had taken her poison neutralizer for today.

"Ah, Lady Zaria," Odo said. He hobbled over and took a glass of champagne himself. "Justicar. What are we drinking to?"

Captain Odo had denied credit for her release. One of her torturers promised freedom in exchange for knowledge about a case Ursula was supposed to have stolen. Had Jhee inadvertently provided them with the information they wanted?

"Our continued good health," Jhee said.

"Splendid. Splendid. Do you mind if I steal my old friend here, Lady Zaria?"

"I was just about to move on. Well, until we meet again, Justicar. And make no mistake, we will meet again." The woman inclined her head to Captain Odo. "Consort Regent."

Jhee let out a deep breath once she had gone.

"Making friends, I see, Sniffer."

"Just putting her on notice."

"About your brief vacation. You think it was her?"

"Most likely. Who else could ignore your request?"

Odo upended his champagne glass. "That was foul business. I'm sorry you had to go through it."

"The one who should be sorry is the person who set me up."

Odo cast his gaze about. "Sniffer, call it off."

"What?"

"This entire thing. The investigation into Ursula. The veteran care center. Everything."

"Ursula is gone, Captain. Our friend. Your lover."

"Would you keep your voice down?"

"Don't you want to know why?"

"I know why!" he said then cut himself off. "Someplace private, now, Sniffer."

The captain ushered her to some hedges between the paddock and clubhouse.

The captain continued once they were out of full view, "I'm sorry about what happened to her. I'm sorry about what happened to you, Sniffer. I'm sorry I ever learned about that drenched brief. You should have just told them where it was. It's over, Sniffer. Just let it be."

Odo shuffled away. The Earth drawer with the Ladies' Auxiliary had asked her where to find the case. They knew Ursula had met with her. Jhee's heart constricted. The captain, it had to be the captain. He had informed on her. But why?

Jhee took off after him. "What was in that case?"

"Leave it alone, Sniffer."

"It's you. You spawn of the trench. This is all on you. Ursula. My imprisonment."

"Please, Jhee. No one was supposed to get hurt. Not you. Not her. I didn't know what was in the case. Not until after it and Ursula went missing."

Jhee turned her back on the Captain, "I'm not interested unless you plan on going on record."

Odo snatched Jhee's arm and spun her back around, "You know I can't, Sniffer."

"I'm not interested in more lies or excuses from you, Captain. You may be willing to let the matter drop and forget about Ursula, but I'm not. She tried to mark the trail for me, but I was too full of myself to notice."

Odo's fingers bit into Jhee's arm. "You don't understand. I can't let this go any further."

With fire drawing, Jhee generated a burst of bright sparks in her hand. She averted her face. She tossed the dazzling cluster over her shoulder at the captain. He cursed and released his grip. Jhee sprinted for the paddock. Shep appeared in the exit.

"Jhee? Cap?" Shep asked. "What's going on here?"

Jhee whirled back around. Captain Odo stood, hands trembling. His walking stick poised to strike Jhee down. Odo lowered his cane.

"Jhee, are you all right? I thought you were in danger."

"I'm fine," Jhee said and began herding Shep back towards the crowds. "We'll discuss it at home. If you're here, who's looking after Medea?"

"Bax. Medea suggested I keep watch over you, and she was right. I smell burnt hair. Cap, were you attacking Jhee? Why?"

"Sheepdog, I can explain."

Jhee faced Odo. "No, you won't. We're leaving. Don't contact us again."

"Would someone tell me what's going," Shep demanded. Her arm sigil began to tingle. He refused to be moved. "I'm not going anywhere until I know why were you throwing fire and the captain is singed and looks as guilty as a Trench trawler?"

Jhee closed her eyes and whispered, "It was him."

With a roar, Shep charged Odo. Odo rolled his head from side to side, and his form took on the features of a giant walrus. They went at each other tooth and claw. Once Shep had gained enough of Odo bioplasm, he too became more walrus-like.

Jhee touched the sigil, now burning her arm and engaged her siren module. The timing was key. Incapacitate either combatant before the other, and the deactivated berserker would be defenseless against the active.

Shep was the younger and more combat-trained of the two. He quickly overtook the older man. Jhee knew what she must do, yet an ambivalence, a hesitation, paralyzed her. The captain had her tortured. Her fingers twitched, and her skin tingled in remembrance of her encounters with Fire and Earth.

"Yield!" Jhee yelled, the shutdown signal embedded in the command word. Simultaneously, she dug her nails into her arm sigil. Both berserkers dropped. They shifted back into a more Water Folk form. By now, a crowd had gathered. A few gasps went out. The Imperial guards rushed in and seized Shep.

"Let him go." Odo got to his feet. The Imperial Guard stared at Odo and took in his state of dress. "Nothing to see here, folks. Just a little rough-housing between old friends that got out of hand."

"Any assault—"

"I said, 'let him go.' There was no assault. I just asked him to demonstrate a few wrestling holds. Old and as clumsy as I am, I botched it and fell directly on my tail. No harm done."

The Imperial Guard looked at the captain's bloody and torn clothing.

"Are you refusing an order of a Consort Regent, *Lieutenant*?" Odo asked. "Or is it now corporal of the nursery squad?"

The guard lieutenant gestured. The Imperial Guard released Shep. "My apologies, Consort Regent. Sir, allow us to call a transport so that your friend might take his leave immediately?"

"No need. I'll see to it myself. You are dismissed."

The bulk of the Imperial Guard left. However, two guards remained at the periphery of the crowd even once Shep and Odo began to walk away. Odo clapped Shep on the back to seem chummy. They walked out of Jhee's earshot. Odo seemed understandably agitated and animated. Eventually, he and Shep seemed to calm down.

Shep stalked over. "Let's go."

"Thank you, but never do something that rash again."

"What?"

"You're lucky he covered for you."

"He's lucky I didn't kill him."

"Keep your voice down." Shep looked at her bewildered. Between his obliviousness of the peril and the captain's actions, she refused to hold back anymore. "You almost got yourself arrested on imperial grounds where they'd be able to hold you, put you in a hole, and do whatever they want to you!"

Shep's expression melted into a horrified one. Her equilibrium evaporated. Jhee buried her face in her hands and cried. He crushed her in his arms.

"I'm sorry, Jhee. I didn't think."

Jhee sagged against Shep too exhausted to reply. They collected Kanto and went home.

15

———

~

The Dawn Wolves Reunited

Shep gazed up at the ship docked at Packer's Pier. He had watched from the shadow of a nearby boathouse half an hour for Odo's informant to show before taking a closer look. The gangplank had been left down. He made his way on deck.

Where the Trench was the informant Odo promised? Was this wise? Why meet here? Shep had received a cryptic message from Odo to meet his contact here if he wanted to know who else played a part in Jhee's detention. After a few minutes poking about the wheelhouse and looking through the navigation maps, he was convinced this contact wasn't going to show. He had been sent on a wild wisp chase. Another negative tally to put on on the Captain's balance sheet.

A whiff of cologne made Shep pause.

"Sheepdog?"

Shep came about at the sound of Odo's voice. Whatever else had deteriorated about the captain, his light step had remained.

The captain hobbled forward. "I'm glad you contacted me. I didn't know when I might hear from you or Sniffer again."

"I thought I was meeting an informant. I may not have come otherwise."

"I'm glad you did. About the way we left things…"

"Thank you for calling off the Imperial Guard."

"It was the least I could do."

"You're right. It was."

"Please, let me explain."

Shep pushed past the captain onto the main deck. "I don't want to hear your explanations. I only want to hear who put you up to it."

"It wasn't like that. None of this was supposed to happen."

Find your stillness. Focus in. The time had begun to slow, and the captain's voice recede. Shep muttered counter chants to keep the rage in check while the captain uttered excuses.

"I even went further afield in my affection: a male. The chance of bastards virtually nil and a fellow imperial who could look after himself. I thought he would be safe. *He* was. His other lovers weren't, neither were their children. But me? Wifey never went after me. Never me. She wanted to make sure me and everyone else got the message loud and clear: hers. She made Zaria look like the founder of the Open Seas Movement. I was good for a while. I dutifully stayed on the island and waited for her to show up every few months to insult me and wave her newest conquest in my face. Then Ursula showed up, and it was like the years in between had never happened. She needed my help. I knew if Her Imperial Terror got one whiff of it, it was over."

Shep paced about the deck. He took one calming breath after another. "So, you set Jhee up?"

"I figured the Regent would assume the same thing everyone else did. I was right. The more she thought I cared, the more she wouldn't be able to resist. She knew there was someone before she came along. Someone I served with. The Regent could be quite charming when she wanted something. When she wants you, she pulls out every stop, sweeps you right away like the riptide. Sniffer came to my bunk one time. Did you know that, Sheepdog?"

Shep snarled. "Liar."

"It's true. She found messages between you and Miramar. Jhee would have never looked twice at me if you hadn't betrayed her. I was a nice shoulder to cry on, safe, comforting. I sent her away. One of the few times I ever did the right thing in my life. You remember what I was like in those days. Heart-stopping, virile. Handsome. Too handsome.

"Now, look at me, Sheepdog. Being a berserker did this to me. I'm losing coherence. I may revert completely, lose myself to my berserker skin and turn into a walrus permanently or some Unmaker's hybrid. It was all supposed to be so simple: steal the contents of the case and use it to barter our freedom from the Regent. The Regent had plans of her own, which involved Ursula being killed after we made the delivery. Luckily or unluckily for us, we had to take a peek to see what was in it. After we did, Ursula refused to make the drop and disappeared with the case. That's when I approached you. I needed to find her before the Regent did."

The red began to come over Shep's vision again. He counted and breathed. He moved toward the railing of the deck. That way, he might be able to leap off instead of attack.

"Look, Sheepdog, don't go all red-eyed on me again. I hadn't meant for Sniffer to be taken. Ursula disappeared again right after we left your place. Soon, I got a call. They said they had her and let me speak to her. They would let her go in exchange for the case. I told them I didn't have it. They didn't believe me. I pointed them at the only other person I knew she had been in contact with. I had no idea who they were or who might have sent them until the Abyssal constables grabbed Sniffer."

Shep gripped the railing and bared his teeth. "Because you showed a callous disregard for Jhee's life."

"If it were a choice between Sniffer and Ursula, you would have done the same."

"I would have made them kill me first."

"I'm not you. I'm done sacrificing what I want. It's cost me my youth, my vitality, and my essence. I'd be drenched if it would cost me Suli, too. The one person in this Sphere who still loved me and always did."

Shep tilted his head up to contemplate the thin clouds covering the moons. "You're wrong, Cap. She wasn't the only one who still loved you. I would have laid down my life for you, for any of the Dawn Wolves. Now, only for Jhee."

"So it appears you have chosen. The tribunal, M-Prot's abuses being dredged up, capsized everything."

Deep breaths, one after another, brought Shep clarity, but he did not trust himself to speak.

"Here we are, Sheepdog, the last of The Dawn Wolves. Many were rejects, buried in the deepest hole someone could find. One only wound up there if you were toxic or keeled someone off royally. The only way out: Medical Protectorate. Some voluntarily. Most because they were disposable. It turns out I was, too. I was only supposed to be your minder, not a berserker. But I know I couldn't let my squad do something I wouldn't. How did we get here, Sheepdog? Years ago, I never would have dreamed of turning my claws on you."

Shep glanced at the captain, hunched over his cane, eyes greened by melancholy. "Me neither."

Pity for the Captain came over Shep. Gone was the scheming imperial who had used him and Jhee. Now all he saw was a broken man clutching at anything that might put him back together. Shep stroked the eye scar Jhee had given him. What a hypocrite he was.

"Do you know who gave the order?" Shep asked.

"I was telling the truth when I said I thought it was the Regent. Now, I'm not so sure anymore." Captain Odo refused to meet Shep's gaze. "Please, Sheepdog, let's go for a drink like old."

"Where is Ursula now?"

"I don't know."

"So, Jhee's pain, betraying us," Shep said. "It was all for nothing. You lured me here to talk. You talked, I listened. We're done."

"What do you mean I lured you here? You asked me to meet you here."

~

The Two Theas

With her Justicial authority under review and her teaching credentials suspended, Jhee had all the time in the world now to work on her experiments and derivations. She had tried to relax with net weaving. But after the first few days around the house, she had been bored out of her senses.

After a few more days, Jhee wandered about the townhouse, so empty with only her and Kanto. Memories of doing the same growing up at Hillside while her two parents sat in darkened rooms isolated in their grief overwhelmed her. She needed something else to occupy her time. She fished out her old design for a room-scale orrery, the ultimate Mechanist devotion.

One day, as Kanto was heading out to the center, he stopped by her workshop. "We could easily hire someone to put that together for you."

Jhee climbed down off the ladder, where she had been taking synchronance measurements of the planned orrery space. "That's not the point. The point is to design and construct it yourself as a sign of devotion and adherence to Mechanist principles. Some Makers want you to do pilgrimages or missionary work. The Prime Maker wants Mechanists to construct a series of devices. I must draft the plans and source the parts myself, or else what have I learned about first principles. I've made the compass, astrolabe, sextant, and I'm almost done with the chronometer. I even constructed a few small scale telluriums without all the heavenly bodies. All that remains is a more or less full-sized orrery."

"All right. Enjoy your day."

"Off to the center? How is the fast track to joining an art or education council coming?"

"Slowly. Volunteer work only counts ten percent. Not that joining the council is why I'm doing it."

An idea struck Jhee's fancy. "Mind if I come with?"

"I would be delighted," he said.

Kanto split his time between the youth center now and work and training at the spirit corps auxiliary. He switched to homemade lunches. Instead of the usual transport, Kanto had taken to cycling to work. He had full access to their finances. Even though Kanto had not said so, she was certain he had done so because he knew the financial strain using a transport service was. They each had bicycles, even Mirrei, a gift from Shep. At the sight of the cycles, Jhee couldn't help but feel wistful. Shep still kept strange hours and still came home bruised. She was uncertain what she could do about that.

It had been some time since Jhee had ridden one of these cycle contraptions, but she got the hang of it again after a few hundred meters. She and Kanto cycled to the center together. As they secured their cycles, Kanto smiled at her fondly.

"I had wondered how long it would take for puttering around the house all day would get to you. Shep, Mirrei, and I all had a bet."

"The servants' pool included an over/under? Who won?"

Kanto harrumphed. "Mirrei. She claimed to have used some complex mathematical derivation based on how many current experiments you were running, but I think she pulled the number out of the ether."

Jhee laughed. "Ether way sounds plausible to me."

"Aw, Jhee, that was terrible. I don't see a future in comedy for you." They secured their cycles. Kanto removed his helmet and did a quick touch up of his hair, then offered the mirror to her. "One thing I can say is this haircut isn't prone to helmet head."

Jhee touched hers up. As she handed the mirror back, she ran her fingers through his short coif. Not only his hair had changed, but his stance. He had taken on the more rigid, disciplined stance of someone with training. "I don't know. I kind of like it."

"Guess what happened at the aux?"

"What?"

"You're supposed to guess."

"Work at the auxiliaries is going well." Jhee looked him over. His sketch notebook had seen a lot of recent use. It was too soon for him to be planning next season's household wardrobe. "You got a promotion or additional responsibilities. Something to do with your practiced eye and keen fashion sense."

"Almost spot on. We got the contract to redesign the navy's uniforms. I've been asked to lead a team to come up with some concept sketches. I'm in charge of one group. If they choose our designs, we'll be put in charge."

Jhee hugged Kanto. "Congratulations! You earned it."

He turned away sheepishly. "I haven't been picked yet. Just promise me, no fishiness. I want to know I can do this on my own."

Jhee gave a wry look. She was not sure if she had enough influence left to arrange her way out of a parking fine. "Of course. I wouldn't dream of it."

She and Kanto walked inside hand-in-hand. While Kanto went about his regular duties, Jhee spent most of her time completing paperwork and viewing the center's orientation and training. Towards the end of the day, she could finally assist Kanto during his lessons.

She found Kanto, and they had a late lunch in the break room. They sat and ate together quietly and contentedly. Kanto's lunch bag contained a leftover sandwich and second piece of fruit. As they ate, the quiet girl from the other day wandered over. She said nothing.

"Hello, Almathea, how are you and Ms. Muffin today?" he asked. The girl hid her face in the doll. "This is my wife. Do you remember her from the other day?"

The girl nodded.

"Pleased to meet you. Almathea, what a lovely name. My name is Galatheia. My close friends call me Jhee. Do you know why they call me Jhee?"

Almathea shook her head.

"It's a tradition where we're from to give children a forename tied to their house name. I was the youngest of seven whose name all started with a 'G.' Even my parents had a hard time keeping track of our names, so they gave us shorter ones. For the longest time, I thought my name was g-seven."

Kanto chuckled. "I never knew that. Almathea here has one of the sweetest singing voices I've ever heard. Don't you, Almathea?

The girl nodded again.

"Would you like to say hello?"

"Hello," the girl said in a tiny, hushed voice.

"And hello to you, too," Jhee said.

Kanto smacked his forehead. "Oh, would you look at that? Looks like I brought way too much lunch again. Jhee, would you like some?"

"No, thank you. I think I brought too much myself. I couldn't possibly eat any more."

"What about you, Almathea? I've got all this extra food it would be a shame for it to go to waste. You think Ms. Muffin might like some for later?"

The girl nodded slowly. She shyly and embarrassedly took the apple and sandwich from Kanto. Almathea looked both ways before squirreling the food away inside her doll. She gave a brief smile, then ran off.

Jhee gave a bittersweet smile.

"For her sister," Kanto said. "We're only allowed to give them a single breakfast and lunch. The sister can't stay here because their father insists she work."

Jhee remembered the older girl who had come to pick Almathea up. "What kind of work could a child that young possibly perform that's legal?"

"Selling lottery tickets. There's a chance and entertainment exception. She helps sell lottery tickets to the tourists and the dockworkers from her father's cart. The tourists especially are more likely to buy them from children."

Kanto pulled out a pocket full. "She's a prolific seller and rather good at it."

"Those are Imperial lottery tickets. Do they know children are being asked to sell those? That can't be legal."

"Jhee, don't make trouble for them. Her sister is practically the only means of support for their entire family. She does it so Almathea can spend the day here."

Jhee hung her head sufficiently chastened. "I'm sorry. Old habits."

"You're allowed. I want to help them all so much, too."

Jhee and Kanto finished up their day at the center and waited with Almathea for her sister to show up and collect her. They hopped on their cycles once the two girls made it home.

"I know you asked me to leave it alone," Jhee said, "but I can't stop thinking about them. I can't use my influence to help you, but maybe I can help them."

"How so?"

"Junior academy scholarships come with room and board. With her older sister's math skills and the younger's singing, they may each qualify for one."

"I'm not sure if their father would accept."

"Certain scholarships also come with a stipend which as their guardian he would be in charge of administering. He's already willing to make a living off the backs of his daughters. It should more than calm his objections."

Kanto thought about it and nodded. "I know of someone who can get them the supplies they need for free."

On their way home from the center, Kanto said, "Jhee, I wanted to run something else by you."

They cycled along. "Sure, what?"

"While at the aux, I saw a pilot program they have for the vets. I want your help to set up a mentorship program between the kids and the veterans, a summer program."

"That sounds like a marvelous idea. The veteran service center already has an agreement with both the nearby kennel and stables. Perhaps we can have the veterans help teach the children how to ride and care for the animals, and train the service animals, too."

"Exactly the thing I had in mind," he said. "Thank you, Jhee."

16

Guard Captain Petra

Imperial Guard Captain Petra rounded the corner of the building. The Consort Regent had given her the slip again. She held up her conch and read her tracking devices' signals. After she traced them to the water's edge, she presumed the trackers she had planted lived at the bottom of the harbor. The Consort had gotten wise to those, too. Petra did not envy returning to her superiors yet again with another report of how Lord Odo, a barely mobile blob, had gotten away from her again.

Petra could not express her utter contempt for the Imperial spouses and concubines enough. Shaking their Imperial protection details was a lark for them or a rite of passage; for Petra, it meant life or death or an etiquette training timeout with the Style Council and Ministry of Manners. It was a game to them. She had sworn to die for the Imperial family. Dying in their service meant a pension for her family and imperial honors. Dying in review or etiquette training would see her stripped of rank and her family left with nothing. She was already on notice for losing track of him at the Imperial Sojourn and for the incident at the Fancy Foam Equestrian and Canine Showcase. One more incident and she would have to perform atonement or take the black, polar protection detail.

Guard Captain Petra gave a sigh of relief when she received a signal from one of the backup trackers, the only one not with these. It was almost a game figuring out how to plant them without being found by the target. This one was a tracer she had slipped into his food. It stayed in the bloodstream for a few hours, usually the length of his daily excursions to see his mistress. And more recently, the Justicar.

Petra had not been present for when that report hit the Princess Regent. She swore she had felt the palace quake. The Princess Regent had taken it about as badly as the woman's husband seemed to. It was always something with these neglected spouses. The Justicar was a modestly attractive woman, but every much Lord Odo's type, commanding, no-nonsense, and with just enough power to make the Regent take notice. Petra had been in charge of all the pedigree checks and backgrounds on the entire household.

If Lord Odo confined his activities to commoners, they would all be the better for it. A simple bit of poison or knifework saw those dealt with. Instead, Lord Odo liked to push to see what he could get away with. The palace nearly erupted into a civil war that time Lord Odo tired of nobles and took up with another Regent.

Eliminating nobles took elaborate planning and permission. The paperwork and bureaucracy and negotiation involved meant it sometimes took years. If that was Lord Odo's plan to protect his paramours, it usually failed. Once he had moved on, the Princess Regent, having gone through the trouble of gaining the permissions often had them eliminated for spite. The Justicar had proved more resourceful than his usual lovers.

Petra was rapidly approaching the tracer's location. On top of having to deal with the Princess Regent, there were all the angry spouses, both imperial and otherwise. The Imperials were always seeking ways to advance their position. No one had yet unseated the Regent's current senior spouse, though many had tried. Lord Odo's place was square in the middle—not much to be gained or lost taking him on. The senior spouse's guards practically lived like nobles themselves off of their tips. Petra admitted the monetary tips from the other Imperial spouses had more than covered two of her children's Imperial academy fees. She almost had enough to put her youngest twins through until secondary.

Perhaps the Justicar's spouse did not think what Lord Odo had offered for his silence was enough. Which had happened oft enough, too. Most spousal objections were monetary. They saw Imperial, and they pictured wealth and influence, regardless of which branch had taken up with their spouse. They imagined themselves set for life.

The spouses of the lovers often did well for themselves too. They had various sweetheart deals and arrangements with the Imperial harem. Occasionally, they were jealous, but mostly they objected to the fees being too low. Especially if one of the blood had come after them. Petra assumed something similar had taken place between Lord Odo and the Justicar's husband. Likely a monetary dispute as he had either been present or at least knew of the meetings between the lord and the Justicar.

Petra had read the report on Shepard, a berserker who had served with the Consort Regent. He had been keeling off the well to do for years. One would think his time as a Medical Protectorate plaything would have taught him better, the only fate comparable to an interview with the Style Council. Petra needed to monitor him. She had doubled the guards. His background as a berserker made him very dangerous. The standard imperial detail would not be enough, which was why Petra was even more keeled at Lord Odo. Her approval for extra guards had come in, and if the incident at the dog show was any sign, even the lord's background as a berserker was not enough protection. The other man was the better fighter.

Petra, at last, arrived within a few meters of the tracers. They were at the fighting society's slaughterhouse where the Justicar's husband had recently been arrested. Petra sighed and called for backup. This could not end well.

Petra surveyed the slaughterhouse. She wished she could stride in and grab the lord by the ear. But that was another part of the game: Petra had to remain hidden to at least give the spouses the illusion of privacy. She muffled the light and sound of her conch as she grew closer. She would not feel right until she had eyes on him.

The slaughterhouse was exposed and open. Petra made her way to the center of the slaughterhouse where the cage was. Two figures were in it. One knelt on his knees over the other, who was not moving. Petra rushed the cage and threw open the door. The Justicar's husband knelt over the beaten dead body of Lord Odo. Visions of Petra's modest home, two husbands, her two other children already in the academy, and of the twins' scholarships— they were going to sit for the boards—flashed through her mind. She would end up in review at the Women's Auxiliary for this. Petra dropped to her knees and wept.

~

JHEE'S CONCH chimed with Shep's sequence. She answered. "What's wrong?"

"It's not your husband, Justicar," a voice Jhee didn't recognize said. "He's in trouble. You better get down to Imperator's headquarters with advocates of the highest order. Your lover's dead. Shep was found bruised and covered in his blood."

"My lover? Who is this?"

"No one of consequence anymore. I'm getting my family to safety. You should do the same with yours."

The conch clicked. Jhee removed a digitally sanitized conch from its hiding place in the book *The Harvest Home Tales*. She messaged Kanto on her way to the imperator's station.

~

Worth Knowing

"I hear your denbe is going after IES," Aiaku said and grabbed a glass of champagne from a passing waiter. "It's a bit of a risk. Do you know how many imperials have their hands in that pie?"

Kanto sipped at his champagne and took a gander around at the attendees at the garden party. "I imagine quite a few. Still, they keep coming for us, and well, we need to reach some accommodation with them. It's not our first encounter with them."

"And it won't be your last," Aiaku stated. "How close is your denbe to the elective succession? Why is she doing this? As far as I can tell, she is so far outside the line of Imperial succession, she would have to eliminate most of the court to even be considered."

The garden party was being held at some ghastly ultramodern mansion on a folk-made jetty built to prevent erosion. Rounded, marble lawn fountains clashed with the angular polyglass and chrome house. Whatever decorator had approved this travesty should have been banished. The affair's attendees were many of the same crowd as the sojourn and Fancy Foam Showcase. While it was better if Jhee were here with him, Kanto understood why she had passed.

"My denbe is a woman of principle," Kanto said. "A rare thing around here, it seems. She will do anything to protect us."

Aiaku nodded. "Rare indeed. It's good you're here. You can't be seen to be backing down. What with your denbe's visit to etiquette school, I wasn't sure if you'd be here. How is she doing? How are you holding up?"

"We're doing fine. The attendees are acting differently than I expected. Why are they acting so solicitous? I'd think they'd be scared to associate with her. Or me."

"Quite the contrary. Someone important wanted your denbe taught etiquette, and yet here you are. More importantly, she found a way for that not to happen. In which case, you might be someone good to know."

Kanto still could not believe that Captain Odo had a hand in Jhee's detention. He had eaten their food and enjoyed their hospitality. Then betrayed denbe and denme in the worst way imaginable. Captain Odo was an imperial. Kanto should never have let his guard down. Being around Jhee and Shep had blocked his nose for these matters.

"Any consensus on who?" Kanto asked, hoping to tease out what Aiaku might know.

"You haven't already worked that out?" Aiaku asked.

Kanto chose to play coy. "We have our suspicions and made our moves. It helps to know who else we might have to look out for."

From what Kanto understood, the Captain had pointed the finger at Jhee but not ordered the detention. If he or a Regent had ordered Jhee schooled, Jhee would still be detained. If Captain Odo and the Regent were unlikely to have freed Jhee, that begged the question who got her released. All Kanto and Shep knew was they had received a call where to pick up Jhee shortly after Kanto had made a pass through the vizier's favor book.

Aiaku passed off his empty champagne glass to another member of the wait staff. "The obvious money is on Zaria. She had practically cut the senator loose when he was arrested. Doesn't mean she wanted him dead, at least until she chose. Least of all because of some upstart Justicar from the shoals."

"What of Lady Amani?"

Aiaku lost a step. "She is powerful enough, true. I think there is another player at work."

"Such as?"

Aiaku picked up a crab puff and popped it in his mouth. "Can't expect me to do all the legwork for you."

"Of course not. And what of you, Aiaku? Are you here because you think my household is worth knowing?"

"I'm here because I thought we were friends."

By Kanto's research into those listed on the vizier's books, none of them were powerful enough to challenge Zaria either. Kanto gave 'Aiaku' another examination. His robes and sashes still denoted him as Kanto's peer even though he knew that to be a lie. Maybe a name or two on the vizier's list similarly hid their true rank.

"I suppose we are," Kanto said. "Still, I wouldn't mind knowing more about what you are getting out of all this."

"Aeolus. You remind me so much of him like he was before. He was so handsome, and he had the voice of a siren. We thought he would be the next Nishadahl. We gave him the best instructors and music tutors from all over the empire. Your skills in music and performance are a rare light in this world. I don't like to see such lights snuffed."

"You sound like a Mandelbrot."

"Perhaps."

The crowd at the garden party had begun to murmur. Kanto watched the assembled lord and ladies, concubines, and consorts for clues as to what had happened. The last time it had been a fight between the captain and Shep.

A notable amount of the servants of those who distrusted conchs had arrived to whisper into their employers' ears. Those with conchs had made surreptitious moves to check theirs. Kanto chanced a quick glance at his, as did Aiaku. The assembly's attention slowly turned Kanto's way. A plainly stated message from Jhee advised him to exit the event quickly and quietly. She'd have a transport pick him up dockside near the water taxis.

"Bold move," Aiaku said with a touch of admiration, "eliminating the Princess Regent's consort. And risky. And so publicly no less. The question everyone's wondering: now is your denbe crazy or so sure of herself she feels she can get away with such a very disruptive play? Now they're calculating if it's recklessness or a demonstration of power. I pray it's the latter."

"It's better for them to wonder." Kanto noted the Imperial Guard positioning themselves near the exits. "A bold enough move to back Zaria off?"

"I'd say there is an excellent chance. She can be petty, but not stupid. If it is recklessness, then it's in her best interest to let the Princess Regent do the hard work of finishing your denbe off. If it's not, it means your denbe may be more powerful than she expected, and she should call it even."

Kanto picked up his drink and began to casually stroll around the fountain, looking for other viable exits. There might be a way out through the stables. "That alone would be worth it."

"Which side of your building did you arrange for your transport to pick you up? You wouldn't show up with this news about to break without an exit plan."

Kanto eyed Aiaku skeptically.

"You can trust me."

"North," Kanto said. The water taxi pick-up was actually to the northeast, yet easily reachable from the north side should he need to give Aiaku the slip. This way should Aiaku prove to be false, his exit route would still be protected. If Aiaku were leading him into a trap, there was not much he could do about it now. As they moved, Kanto assessed what had happened. Odo, the Princess Regent's consort, had been killed in a way that made everyone suspect Jhee. Not good. Aiaku had laid it out pretty accurately. It was reckless on Jhee's part. Maybe her imprisonment had upset her more than she let on. He wouldn't put it past her. But she did not act this rashly or angrily. Something else had to have happened. True, they had stumbled upon someone from the vizier's list or a contact powerful enough to get Jhee released from etiquette school, but undoubtedly not powerful enough to provide cover for an Imperial assassination. Jhee would not put them at risk that way.

Kanto's suspicions there was an exit through the stables proved correct. Rather than a route through the stables, Aiaku brought him through the kitchens. A small door and docks waited for fresh sea meat delivery from smaller fishing vessels. "Here, this should provide you with easy access to wherever your transport actually is. Keep along the waterline, and you can reach any side of the building relatively undetected."

"Thank you, Aiaku."

"This is the most fun and excitement I've had in some time. Hopefully, Zaria takes the hint and whoever else she's working with too."

Whoever else she's working with is the genuine threat.

Two-Way Glass

"You should talk to your advocate or solicitor about this, not me," Nevis, Jhee's Justicar colleague, said.

Nevis and Jhee met at the drinking establishment down the street from the Justicar's Annex. They faced away from each other while seated on the perpendicular sides of the bar's corner.

"I'm talking to you," Jhee replied.

"I can't do anything about this. It's a capital case. Imperial security. A royal assassination. This may even rise to the level of treason. I can't go anywhere near this. Unless you want me to wind up in the same black hole you were in."

Jhee flinched, and her hand twitched. Nevis's posture relaxed.

"Sorry. That was uncalled for, but this case and you are toxic. I didn't believe this situation could become even more radioactive than it was before."

"May I at least see him?"

"Imperial Intelligence has him. They're making plans to transfer him to State for," Nevis lowered her voice, "special detention."

"If that happens, I may never see him again. It has to be now."

"Then I advise you to tap one of your other contacts. My hands are rightly and thoroughly tied."

"May I at least know what he is being charged with?"

"For the moment, Imperial assassination. Even if Shep wasn't, Jhee, that's not the only thing."

"What else could there be? What else are you going to charge him with?"

"Jhee, maybe you should back off this one. You've lost your job, you've been detained, and now your husband's in jail."

"Please, tell me."

"The lord consort was beaten to death. They found his blood all over Shep. And Shep looked like he had just been in a mighty fight."

"There must be a mistake."

"No mistake. There's more. The Consort Regent wasn't the only one."

"Wasn't the only one what?"

"Those names you asked me to run."

"The ones who all turned out to be dead?"

"They were all beaten to death."

"Surely, you can't suspect Shep?"

"His berserker bioplasm was found all over the scene."

Jhee touched a hand to her mouth. "Please, I have to see him."

Nevis looked about her. "I can take you to where he's being detained, but that is about as close as I can get you."

"Thank you." Jhee looked at Shep through the two-way glass. Shep sat in a medical gown as they had taken his clothes for evidence. He stared at the wall. "Has he said anything?"

"No. This is bad. The Consort Regent had no defensive wounds, so we suspect he knew his attacker. Shep was found by the Imperial Guard kneeling over the body and covered in the Consort Regent's blood."

"The Imperial Guard. They could have been bribed. What of his protection detail? Where were they? I want to question them."

"LAS or fleeing with their families. At the time, he was only assigned one bodyguard, and he had apparently given her the slip. No one's seen her after she called it in."

"Has it occurred to you they might be the guilty party? Or else why would they disappear?"

Nevis pursed her lips. The expression confirmed what Jhee's worry had caused her to ignore. Involved or not, the Imperial bodyguard expected a Style Council interrogation. "Nevertheless, I have to wait for Imperial Intelligence. They will take over this case. If you have any favors left, I suggest you use them now."

Shep could not have done this. He couldn't. Even after Odo's hand in her imprisonment and torture, he and Shep were still friends. Shep was all about protecting those he loved. That used to be Odo at one time. True, he had lost his temper at the Fancy Foam Showcase, but he had had time to calm down since then.

Yet Shep had been so angry lately. Jhee's gaze lingered on the scar across Shep's eye. Her hand went to her neck. His unyielding dedication to those dear to him had not always held true. Once she had to resort to the knife she kept in the bed stand. He let go but still came after her. It wasn't until she slashed his eye had she been able to talk him out of it.

Shep had been so repentant. Until then, he had been reluctant to get help. He had insisted he was fine and did not need any help. He could handle it on his own. It was after that they had a Fire Folk artificer who owed her a debt outfit them with the control sigil set.

Her hackles raised at the sight of Shep, disheveled and bloody. "Help me, Jhee. I swear it was an accident. It had to be. I just woke up covered in blood beside the Captain's body."

Shep stared at the two-way mirror. He knew Jhee was there. Between the link created between them by the control sigil set implanted in them and his sensitization so she could use arcana on him, he might always know when she was near. Jhee stroked the sigil to calm him. She still could not find the right levers to push to get his protection protocols turned over to her command. The Empire might still have need of their weapon. A looming threat all the berserkers faced: they could be recalled by The Empire to duty at any moment. So could she, for that matter. If the berserkers were imperial property, so was the siren module tied to her central nervous system.

While a siren module did not give the handler complete control over a berserker, it allowed a handler to shut them down. It was an off switch rather than a remote control. Berserkers were at their "best" undirected—a countermeasure to the use of diviners and prognosticators. It kept the Fire Folk and Water Folk diviners and prognosticators from uncovering their true intent.

"May I talk to him?" Jhee asked.

"I'm not even supposed to be letting you see him. You better let your legal team handle this."

"You and I both know once they take him into custody, the chance of that happening will be next to nothing."

"May I suggest you need to concentrate on your own woes and the rest of your household? Given the history between you and all the recent events."

"They'll think he was acting on my orders. My entire family could be charged with crimes against the thrones."

Jhee must think more practically now. Pragmatism required she view Shep as a starfish arm, to be used as a sacrificial limb. The best path, the pragmatic path, forward was to divest herself of him to broker peace with Lady Amani and the Princess Regent. Whether they wanted vengeance or for her to back off, letting him take the fall would be a sign of her good faith and perhaps her only way to salvage her name, reputations, and fortunes and keep Kanto and Mirrei safe. The law had let her down, and so had Shep. She would have to cut him loose. Spending resources to protecting Shep had been a costly mistake.

And yet, the thought of doing so left Jhee's stomach feeling sour. She needed to return to first principles.

~

First Principles

"And that's pretty much the way it happened." Jeja of Marpele, Jhee's mentor and the woman who sparked her love of the law, concluded her talk to the small bookstore gathering.

"Except for the big hats," Jhee yelled out.

Jeja and her aforementioned wide feather-topped hat turned Jhee's way. Her mentor smiled. "Quite right, my dear. Your descriptions failed to capture the scale and grandeur of my hats, which at one point shaded an entire battalion. Distinguished members of the Southern Stars Reading Club. May I present to you the renowned author of 'Dispatches from Arrow Point' herself."

Jhee walked forward to take Jeja's outstretched hand. They embraced. Those assembled applauded. While the indefatigable Jeja autographed copies of her memoirs, Jhee waited patiently. Now and again, someone asked Jhee to sign a copy, too, as she featured in them. Even less frequently,

Jhee was presented with one of her own "Dispatches from Arrow Point" novels to sign.

At last, Jeja and Jhee found a nook in the bookstore to talk in private. "I expected to hear from you much sooner than this. Especially once that cad you married messaged me. I'm glad to be able to see you again. Know I pulled out my favor books as soon as I heard."

"That may have made all the difference with my release." Jhee's fingers twitched, and the memory of the flames made her face tick. Not all of the fire had been real, but she still remembered the searing sensation and cooked flesh smell.

"I hope so." Jeja squeezed her hand and slid a hot cup of kolal and cinnamon roll in front of her. The sweet, delightful scents overwhelmed the remembered ones. "Sorry to bring that up. I also heard about whats-his-name's arrest. I assume that's why you're here."

"Partially."

"While I've never been his biggest supporter, I'll do whatever I can to help. What do you need from me?"

"Tethering. Should I help him?"

"Remember, first principles. Motive? Why would he have supposedly murdered the Consort Regent? I don't believe this nonsense about romantic rivalry."

"My detainment. The Consort Regent was involved."

Jeja's eyes widened, and she swallowed hard. "That would certainly do it. While I don't doubt he might kill for you, I doubt he would risk this sort of peril to you or your family."

Jhee pushed away the half-eaten pastry. "He hasn't been himself lately. Fights. Violence. He joined some underground berserker fighting society."

Jeja polished of the cinnamon roll for Jhee. "He has some sense, if not a lot. He contacted me after all, knowing how I feel about him."

"I'm tired of this, Jeja. I also have two other spouses to consider."

"Dear, I say this with love: get your head out of your Trench and stop the self-pity. *Justicar*, your duty is to your constituents. He's one of your constituents. If he came to you as a stranger and asked for help, what would you do?"

Jhee hated Sharlet for years over the decision to feed Shep to the political leviathans of the Reaches. Was this the choice Sharlet had to make? Cut Shep loose or see her entire family dragged down as well? Yet, should Shep receive a lesser measure of justice than she would afford anyone else because he disappointed her?

The gears began to turn in Jhee's head.

This had to be a setup, Jhee thought. It just had to be. Shep would never beat someone to death, least of all the Captain. Jhee understood traditional law enforcement's logic, flawed as it was. They knew Shep killed the Consort Regent because he killed the others. And they knew he killed the others because he killed the Consort Regent. If Jhee found evidence to break the link between the two, then it would surely exonerate Shep of the other. Since she would be allowed nowhere near Odo's case, she had to start with the others.

Shep's bioplasm being at any of the crime scenes could easily be explained away. From attendee and fight staff to any constable present for the raid, anyone could have gotten a sample after one of his bare-knuckle brawls.

Jeja grinned. "There she is. That's the woman I know."

17

~

Dead End Trail

Jhee took out her notes on the case so far. She needed to go back to the beginning. All these other matters had been distractions. These attacks on her family and her career had been designed to keep her away from something. She needed to go back to square one, Ursula. They had not seen hide nor hair of her since she left with Odo from the townhouse ahead of the Abyssal constables. Ursula had led a double life, not just as the down-on-her luck soldier, but as a spy. What was she investigating that led to this entire mess?

The key must be in the attaché case Odo asked her to deliver. If the killer had found it, he or she wouldn't be out to get Jhee. They must think she had it or knew where it is. Why else would they turn her life upside down like this? Then the question remained where Ursula would hide something like that. Jhee and Bax had turned Ursula's life inside out. They had even found her secret apartment. Or had they?

Ursula was a soldier and thought like a soldier. Where would a soldier hide things?

Jhee palmed her esca. Of course. The answer had been staring her in the face the whole time. The last time she had seen Ursula before this entire fiasco started, Ursula had just been her usual obsessed self. But what if...? What if she was hiding something? Jhee and Ursula had fallen out of touch long ago. Jhee's home would have been the last place they would have looked. It had not even occurred to Jhee until now.

Jhee should not go alone. She went to Bax and Dari's room, where Bax

677

was keeping vigil over Dari. She knocked gently and was given leave to enter. "I'm sorry to intrude."

"What do you need, Justicar?"

"Shep has been arrested for murder. Several murders. They say he killed his friend, the Consort Regent."

"Imperial assassination. The whole house is at stake." Bax drew a shaky breath that caught in his throat. "What do you need from me?"

"Backup and your thief's mindset. I have an idea of where to look for something that may exonerate him, or if it doesn't, gives me the leverage I need to flush out the actual killer."

"Give me a moment." Bax touched Dari's hair, then kissed her on the forehead. "I'd forgotten how beautiful she was. Justicar, did Mr. Shep do it?"

"I wish I could be sure."

"She'd want us to help him no matter what."

Jhee nodded. She and Bax went to her academy office. "She was standing somewhere over here when I came into the room. I came in, she stood up suddenly, and drew me away from the area."

Bax walked over to the trophy case. This was the same mirrored case where Jhee had had an encounter with her mist mimic the other night. The dream still had her shaken. It felt so real. He scanned it. "Aye, here," Bax said.

Bax pointed at damaged plaster next to the trophy case. One of Ursula's trail markers had been carved into it. Jhee pulled out the hardwood disc. She compared it to the marker on the wall then to the image she captured of the marker left in the counselor's office. Three markers Ursula had left at least. Three points made a data set.

With them together, Jhee saw the elements of a rough cypher in the symbols indicating direction and sequence. She reeled back through her conch's image history. At last, she found her record of cacography from Ursula's leather-bound notebook.

The three markers formed the starting sequence. She unlocked the coordinates to a walking trail near the lakebed. The leather-bound book was an investigator's logbook that contained a series of coordinates. From there, each marker they found allowed Jhee to progress further. They followed markers and coordinates through unused walking trails throughout the capital to a mostly ignored section of shoreline.

"Aye, here," Bax said. He pointed at a slab amongst a series of rock formations. It bore the final trail marker.

Jhee and Bax pushed aside the slab. Instead of a case, they found Ursula's twisted and broken body. Jhee clasped her palms together at angles for the First Makers' blessing and touched her hands to her esca.

May Ursula be remade magnificent.

Jhee took out her conch and called the imperators immediately. She had found Ursula's body, but there was no sign of the attaché case. She had thought for sure it would be there. If it wasn't there and the killer didn't have it, where was it?

At the imperator station, Jhee sat pondering. Shep remained in custody. Odo and Ursula both dead. That left Shep as the last of the Dawn Wolves, a berserker orcinus alone without pod or gang. With decent proof or reasonable cause to doubt he killed the Consort Regent, she could free him. Jhee convinced Nevis to meet her at a nearby, busy lunch counter while Bax kept watch outside.

"Did the coroner's report come back in on my friend?" Jhee asked. The way the patrons, she, and Nevis were packed in amongst the bustling meal crowd reminded Jhee of sardines in a packet.

Nevis kept her eyes forward and trained on her conch as she spoke, "Broken neck, multiple fractures of the fifth and sixth cervical vertebrae. Consistent with a slip and fall and with her blood alcohol level, I would agree."

"A slip and fall? Then who stuffed her in the hiding hole?"

Nevis shrugged. "They estimate she's been dead between ten and twelve days."

"Ten to twelve days. That's impossible. Ursula was at our townhouse, not a long-tide ago."

"I'm just telling you what the report said."

"Ridiculous. Let me see that."

Nevis yanked her conch out of Jhee's reach, then gave her a light touch on the forearm. "Take a break. Go home and get some rest. You will need it. I suspect the Imperial Intelligence will want to question you soon. And this time, I bet they are going make sure they can hold you for much longer this time."

Without Shep here to examine the body or access to the autopsy images, Jhee was reliant on the local constabulary who it seems were incompetent or part of the obfuscation. Ursula did not slip and fall, and she certainly did not put herself under that slab. Jhee thought about it more. Some environmental factors may have been at work, which confused the time of death. She accompanied Bax back to Dari's bedside.

The last person her household had seen Ursula with had been the Captain. Could he have killed her? If he found out Ursula lied about being pregnant, perhaps. That made a better motive for Shep to have attacked the Captain than any the imperators had furnished—after the Captain's betrayal and if, and only if, Shep learned Odo killed Ursula. Then and only then would Jhee believe Shep had murdered the captain. That was a ridiculous number of qualifiers.

The question remained, where was the attaché case, the one the Captain had lied about saying they contained love letters and mementos? Jhee had thought for sure she would find it on the shoreline. Ursula wasn't just a soldier, she had been their scout. What if it had been a ploy? Ursula knew someone was after her. She was laying a false trail. But from where to where?

The point farthest away from Jhee. If Jhee was the false trail, she represented the point farthest away from the genuine one: the captain himself. Jhee got Kanto to do some digging in the records. "Look for anything tied to Captain Odo."

Kanto's face went slack with concentration, and she heard furious typing. "Here. Try this address. Marina Place. Apartment sixteen-oh-three."

Jhee gave a wry laugh. The apartment above Ursula's. Rather than under her nose, the solution had been above it. Hidden in the closet, she found the attaché case in a lockbox with Ursula's trail marker scratched on it.

The case contained a series of dossiers on everyone who had worked on the berserker project from janitor to division head. Jhee also found a black sharkskin bound diary, the companion to the Triptych of the Creed, and a copy of *Imperial Births and Lineages, Volume Ten.*

"The Eclipse Chest, or effects and paperwork collection Lot Number Fifty-one. Lot Number Fifty-one was a strongbox containing various papers, relics, and a dode-captych, twelve-part arcane manual, gifted to the abbey."

The Triptych of the Creed was a partial cyphering manual all the clerics had tried to read at the abbey. So much in this investigation kept coming back to that one: the accursed abyssal bible of arcana, the merry little band of smugglers and traffickers. What she wouldn't have given for another sip of that black orchid tea. Why couldn't that have been the item from the abbey that still plagued her?

Jhee tapped a finger aside her nose. While this was all interesting, she had come no closer to breaking the causal link between the cases. Her Maker within pinched her. They were trying to link her beating victims to Shep. Did she still have a copy of her clinic files?

Jhee pulled up her consultation copies. She pored over the trace evidence found. The victims had traces of their attacker's bioplasm on them, which were sent off for bio-typing. Jhee switched to the bio-typing reports. These grouping factors did not match Shep's. How could someone have called these a match?

This time Jhee marched proudly into the Justicar's Annex. She placed her conch with the consultation files on Nevis's desk.

"Nevis, here have a look at this."

Nevis sighed. Her brow furrowed, and she shook her head. "This is hardly conclusive. Records on your conch cannot be taken at face value."

"I'm not asking you to do so. But if these reports are correct, it means yours have been tampered with. Please, check the access logs."

"Fine." Nevis's dubious expression turned to a scowl. "There are some anomalies here, but I don't think it's enough to clear him."

"Is it enough to see him free of special detention?"

"That depends on your legal team."

~

A Dismantler in the Making

The confirmation notice from the flower service arrived. Once Shep had been released to Jhee's custody, she had bought her legal team the biggest floral arrangement she could find. She planned to throw them an enormous celebration if her household came out the other side of this mostly intact.

Counselor Medea and Kanto met Jhee and Shep as they arrived home. Kanto regarded Shep with coolness and uncharacteristic silence.

"Welcome home," Counselor Medea said and fidgeted. The four of them stood about trying to figure out where to look and what to say until Medea broke the silence again, "Dari's doing better. Would you like to see her?"

Shep nodded. He and Counselor Medea left the foyer. Jhee and Kanto had a long hug. He guided her into the study, where they seated themselves in their favorite spots. "What's the situation? Is he released pending trial?"

Jhee rubbed the bridge of her nose. "He's been cleared for now. They found someone had tampered with the test results. There's also some question about the witness accounts as they put him in multiple places at once."

"So, he was set up? Zaria again?"

"Very likely."

Counselor Medea appeared in the sitting room doorway and cleared her throat. She held one of the valises she brought with her from the sanctuary clutched to her chest. "Excuse me, may I speak with you privately?"

Kanto frowned. Jhee motioned for him to stay and got to her feet.

"Let's go to my study," Jhee said.

In the study, Counselor Medea cast her gaze about them.

"Forgive me for not sharing these with you before now." Counselor Medea squared her shoulders then pressed the valise into Jhee's hands. "I managed to get these files for Ursula before I was forced to go underground. They contain personnel records for many of the scientists and doctors at the Medical Protectorate. I thought the duplicate and dummy files were for a benefits' scam, just as you did. Veterans double-dipping, claiming full benefits while working on the side. It turned out to be more than that."

Jhee flipped through the records Medea provided. This was precisely what she had discovered before. Soldiers with no or practically non-existent histories kept showing up to claim veteran's benefits. Jhee dug out Paij's data shell and the one Ursula slipped her.

Counselor Medea straightened a stack of records that had threatened to topple. "I've got dozens and dozens of records of veterans drawing a pension while also being on the IES payroll. Maybe even hundreds. You know what this means? Someone might actually bring down IES once and for all."

Now that Jhee could cross-check the files, the calibrations and alignments of the Divine Mechanism began to lay bear this puzzle's solution to her. This solution linked IES with the Medical Protectorate's abuses. "We'll need witnesses. If we can track some of these veterans down and get them to testify, we could hurl IES on the Unmaker's discard pile."

"Exactly what I was thinking."

The idea of being Inkerton Enforcement Services' Dismantler sent a secret thrill through her. Their involvement in the Galleon City mess, from worker and refugee exploitation, throwing her into a hole to be interrogated, to last but not least, their role in nearly getting Mirrei killed, had her itching to take them apart. Doing anything about their handlers at MANTEL would take more patience and planning.

Medea stared at Jhee a moment, then leaned in and kissed her. Jhee pulled away. Medea's eyes pinked with embarrassment. "I'm sorry. I thought—"

Kanto burst into the room excitedly. "It's time," he said.

"Time? For what?" Jhee asked and put distance between her, Medea, and the stack of bio-parchments.

Kanto folded his arms and glared at them. "The remote meeting."

Jhee touched the heel of her hand to her esca. "Oh! I had completely forgotten."

"So, I gathered. I'll expect you promptly." Kanto gave Medea a contemptuous glare. "Family only."

He jaunted off.

"Remote meeting?" Medea asked.

"My youngest," Jhee said. "She's traveling somewhere remote. She can't always check in. Would you mind continuing to work without me for a while?"

"Not at all. Nothing is more important than family. And yours is quite lovely."

Jhee nodded. "I think I'd do just about anything for them."

"Family is indeed a treasure. About my forward behavior…"

"Never mind. Go to bed, and we'll get an early start on tracking these people down in the morning."

"You do not understand how lucky you are. Now, go tell them how much you love them."

"Thank you."

Jhee pushed away from the table and joined Kanto in the sitting room. Shep arrived shortly thereafter. Kanto flipped on the wall viewer. A generic message said there was no signal and to please wait 'while we connect your other party.' They waited a few minutes, then Mirrei's image popped on screen.

"Hey, kin." Mirrei excitedly waved her hands at them. The background behind her was dark and storm ridden. "Finally."

"Mirrei, it's so good to see you," Jhee said.

"You'll have to speak a little louder. It's hard to hear where I am."

"I said, 'It's good to see you.'"

"You too. Keeping things calm and boring as always, I hear."

"You know us," Kanto said. Her image showed artifacts. The screen blipped in and out and sometimes doubled and dropped frames. Kanto banged on the receiver a few times as if that might do something. "This darn thing."

"What was that?" Mirrei asked.

"I said, 'we missed you.'"

"Me too. Denme, how are you doing? You keeping out of trouble?"

Jhee and Kanto shot Shep a look. "Never," he said.

"What about you, denye?"

"Somebody has to," Kanto said.

"Good, good," Mirrei yelled.

"How's the work going?"

"Awesome. I think we've helped hundreds, thousands even. Finally, I'm glad I got you all here. I wanted to let you know." Her image cut out again, then popped back in. "The clinic. Continue on. Rim isles."

The background behind Mirrei had gotten worse. Water spotted the lens. The background bobbed up and down as larger waves rocked the boat. The image dropped out and in.

"Star, what was that again?" Kanto shouted. "I told her to install a signal booster, first thing. But does she ever listen to me? No."

"They'll be taking the clinic to Far Surdale. With retrofits. Polar."

"When are you coming home?"

Mirrei waved excitedly at the camera and blew them kisses. The image dropped out, but they still had audio, "I have to go now. Looks like we've encountered a squall. These tropical storms are the worst. That's all for now. Bye-e. Love you muchlies."

"Wait!" Kanto yelled when the call dropped. "Did either of you catch what did she said about the polar regions? Does that mean she's not coming home?"

"I'm not sure. It was garbled."

"Has she said anything to you? Asked for divorce parchments?"

"I don't know. In the confusion, I'm not sure if I sent them or if I did, if she received them. There's been so much going on. Pestering her about divorce was the least of our problems."

"But?" Kanto started.

"She's safe and relatively protected where she is," Shep said.

Jhee nodded. "He's right. If she's halfway around the world on a floating clinic, it's probably the best place for her. She's out of harm's way, and it will be hard for any of the blowback we are experiencing to hit her there."

Kanto sighed. "I get what you're saying."

Jhee and Shep both put their arms around Kanto. Shep covered Jhee's hand with his. "We miss her too."

"I know, I know. Well, I had just thought. I had hoped. Well, you know."

When Mirrei decided to go off with the Boundless Healers Alliance, Kanto had hoped it was only temporary. He had expected her to spend a few months out on the rough seas without their luxuries and come running back to them. To be honest, Jhee had hoped so too. Apparently, Mirrei had a different arrangement with the Maker of Paths. "If helping people permanently is what she wants to do, then we should celebrate it and not hold her back. We've always known this was a possibility."

"But the ice caps? I didn't make her any clothes warm enough for that region."

"She'll find a way. But that doesn't mean you still can't. I trust you could whip up a polar jacket and footwear combination, which would make her the envy of every seal and walrus for thousands of miles around."

"You bet I could."

Jhee laid her head against Kanto's. Shep met her gaze and smiled.

A faint shuffle came from the doorway. Medea stood hesitantly outside of the sitting room. "I'm sorry to interrupt, but I think I found something."

"No interruption," Jhee said. She dabbed at her eyes. She had not expected to take the news so hard. Jhee had known, she had known for some time. She had thought she had prepared for this. Still, the reality of not knowing when or if they might even see Mirrei again had hit her harder than she expected.

Jhee would leave whether to divorce in Mirrei's hands. She would respect Mirrei's wishes either way. If she needed it, Jhee might give her a generous settlement. Jhee had made sure not to entangle those funds and properties she received as Mirrei's dowry too closely with her own for just such an occasion. It should not take much to sign them back over to her so she could found a house of her own. Even if the homes and most of the lands were underwater, the sea rights and mineral shares were still worth much.

If Jhee was being honest with herself, she felt a bit of relief. She had speculated about Shep's affair with Miramar, Mirrei's mother, for many years. It had been another matter to have it confirmed. It helped that she did not have to look at Mirrei day after day and wonder. Or be reminded of Miramar and her family's treachery.

"We should really get back to work," Medea said.

"Why don't I help you go through these?" Kanto offered. "More company and hands to make the work go faster."

Kanto placed his chair between Jhee and Medea and grabbed a file folder. Eventually, Shep joined them.

"I found another one," Kanto said. He tagged and flagged another case record. "How many does that make?"

"Almost two hundred," Jhee sighed.

"Two hundred? That almost the size of a whole civilian auxiliary."

"IES had its tentacles in a lot of lairs, and there are many veterans who'd allow their identities to be used, eager to keep working and making a difference."

Jhee hazarded a glance at Shep. He appeared to be studiously avoiding looking at her. That was fine. He was allowed. They would have to hash this out eventually, though.

Jhee picked up the conch to contact Nevis, her friend at the local Justicar's office. She'd have her run down these names, and then maybe they could get some answers. Was this too reckless? If she was on the verge of bringing IES down, they had to proceed carefully. She was not about to risk her family.

The puzzle was important. They knew this was something Jhee had to do. They supported her no matter what, and she must honor that. To move against IES, she must be absolutely certain their evidence held water.

There was another precaution Jhee should take. She composed a simple note to Mirrei, slipped in with the divorce parchments, and prayed it reached her. "Don't come home," it read.

18

———————

~

Protect the Matriarch

"It surprises me you and the Justicar don't have children," Medea said.

Medea made her play and set down her tile. An excellent move, Shep thought. She must have been going for a reverse snake snare.

"You know, with our careers and her duties. It was never in the Mundane Design. Shep countered with a contrasting tile, which would force her to divert.

"Still, a virile man should see his bloodline propagated."

"Ha." It escaped without him meaning it too. Virile—something, if he were honest, he had not been in many years. Not that he couldn't, it was just that it was not consistent. Even when it was, the remotest thought of passing on whatever this was inside him on to a child made him want to vomit his guts out.

"Even with that strapping young pup in the picture?" Medea placed a tile. Suddenly his stronghold was threatened.

"He's rich and fit, and his lineage can bring her legitimacy mine can't. I handpicked him myself. Jhee's line will have strong offspring." Shep had to bring in a Lancer to cover, a play he had not wanted to make so soon. He had thought to solve the heirs problem by bringing in Kanto. Jhee, as always, had her own ideas. His shame had known no bounds when Jhee came home with Mirrei in tow, a proxy inheritor should she have no heirs. What Mirrei became after that was a constant reminder of all the ways Shep had failed his family.

687

"You could have gone with a more traditional sire arrangement. Why did you get her a second husband?"

"I didn't want her to be alone."

"Alone?"

"After I killed myself."

Medea used her tile to execute a handmaiden gambit. "What of yours?"

"What of my what?"

"Your family line."

"The Stargazers were the lowest rungs of nobility who still lived on the wrong side of the channel in Briny Town. My family got our title from rescuing someone important from drowning." Shep placed his tile. Medea immediately set down her handmaiden to neutralize his Lancer again. She was as cutthroat a player as Mirrei. Mirrei always thought he held back when playing her. She had consistently underestimated her skill. "My sisters have heirs more than covered."

"Your family line will be carried on by your sister. Jhee's will carry on through her and Kanto. Then it appears you've served your purpose."

Shep surveyed the board. Her tiles were in no position to breach. He placed a tile to set up for a matriarch formation. "I have other uses."

"How many resources has Jhee had to spend? How many times has Jhee had to bail you out? It appears you've been more of a drain than a help."

"Jhee knows my worth."

"Does she? I know your worth too. You were one of the best fighters in that cage. I wanted to thank you for not telling her."

"Jhee has a lot on her mind right now."

"I think I located another med divisioner."

Shep gripped the tile he held so tightly his knuckles went white. "Where?"

"Are you sure you want to do this? You don't have to be the one."

"You are convinced someone from IES, one of them killed Ursula."

"Yes. I think they might come after your wife. Protect your family."

"This is at least something I can do. End this before anyone else in my family gets hurt."

"One fell swoop. Cut off the head of the drake." Medea placed a tile. "Breach."

"What?" Shep examined the board. His stronghold appeared fine. Then he saw the contrasting tile. Medea had slipped her Lancer through the side to neutralize his matriarch. A risky move as she had to leave a clear path through her own stronghold and leave her matriarch undefended. He could have seized on it if he hadn't been so focused on protecting his position and gone in for the kill. He even had a tile in perfect position for it.

"Your matriarch fell because you weren't paying attention and did not do what needed to be done to protect her. Are you in?"

"Yes."

Shep had been so scared that night he went to Jhee. He had just found out he had lost the lottery. Not only would he be drafted, but his family also did not have the resources to keep him out of the thick of the fighting. He had confessed to her his cowardice and how much he had not wanted to die. One was not supposed to admit that. The war with the Other Folk was stupid and pointless. Yet, everyone was supposed to march off and die with a smile on their face for Imperials who thought you beneath their notice. Armchair tough guls who saw them as pieces on a board just like these tiles.

He had confessed his love to Jhee. They had spent the night in each other's arms. The next day, she summoned a parish priestess and had them married. It had been such an edifying reversal: Jhee tongue-tied and flustered by him. In those days, if he looked at her for longer than two seconds, she'd blush and look away. He enjoyed that it wasn't him for a change. It might have gone to his head. He had taken that adoration and used it.

Shep had been a weakling and a coward. It was only fitting when they put him in a berserker unit and subjected him to experiments, which ensured he knew no fear and would not run away again. Then there was Jhee coming to his rescue like she always did. Yet, time and time again, he failed her. Shep could not give her children. He could not advance her career. He could not prevent her detainment and torture.

Shep swore and banged the table. The tiles flew up and the air. Many scattered and fell to the ground.

"You were distracted," Medea said. "Your mind was on other things. I took advantage of that. I'm sorry."

Shep sighed. He started gathering up the tiles. "No apologies. I'm usually a much better sportsman than this. It's not like it's the first time I lost."

"Still, it can't do much for your state of mind right now. You were making tyro mistakes. You were too focused on protecting your position. Several times you had a clear shot at my matriarch. You could have ended the game there and saved your entire stronghold. You lost sight of the bigger picture. Save the stronghold. Protect the matriarch."

Shep harrumphed. He had lost sight of the larger image. Perhaps he had at that. Fight. Protect. Survive. "I've already screwed this up once before. Jeopardized my house. Made things worse for her."

"This time, you've got me to help."

~

The Geas

Jhee sat and looked over the records Medea had brought her again. Then she pulled out the files she had consulted on with the imperators and compared them. Her missing persons were homicide victims. Only two had not been killed, Medea and Hammad. They had survived because they fled to the berserker sanctuary. On the other side, though, were those involved with the Albatross files. Everyone who stumbled upon them or was mentioned in them had died or gone missing. It appears someone was tying up loose ends.

Was this like the Eclipse Chest, she wondered? At the abbey, the search for it and its content turned out to be a wild wisp chase. The ill-fated attempt to use the arcane knowledge it possessed had resulted in a cascade of unfortunate events, which led to the deaths of three novices and the previous abbess. Most of that had been from the vizier covering up her tracks.

Perhaps it was the same here. Jhee had gotten to Counselor Medea before the killer could. Who else was left? Jhee brought out Ursula's data shell and her copies of the Albatross files. One by one, she compiled the credentials of those who had signed off on various stages of the identity swaps and benefits approval. Within Ursula's records, which included some Jhee had not found, she uncovered the island senator, the Vizier of Finance, and another name she recognized: Sharlet Stargazer. Jhee wrinkled her mouth.

Sharlet had been involved in this all along. Why should that have surprised her? Over the years, Jhee had murderous thoughts about Shep's sister more times than she could count, yet she deserved better than to be beaten to death by a squad of berserk killers.

Jhee must have faith in the law.

At the end of the Making, though, the berserker squad was the only justice many of these villains would ever see. Jhee could not think about that now. She had skirted the law before and look at how that had turned out and all the unintended consequences that had befallen her. Sharlet and everyone involved in every facet of these schemes had to be brought to the judgment bench.

Jhee left the townhouse and shark-shot to Sharlet's office.

"Why, sister-in-law, what an unexpected surprise."

"Clam it, Sharlet. Tell me about Project Albatross."

"I'm sure I don't know what you are talking about."

"Scores of former Medical Protectorate workers, all given false identities supplied by you."

"Sister-in-law, I don't really think you want to do this."

"Enough, Sharlet. I'm tired. Your fellow schemers have had me arrested, interrogated. I've seen your brother accused of being a sequential murderer. Two of my oldest friends are dead. All because of something you've had a hand in. I'm tired of all these games. Your brother's life and that of his family may be at stake. If you care for him as you claim and you want to make up for what has passed between us, come clean about this now."

"You don't understand. I can't," Sharlet said. Jhee rolled up her sleeves and performed a winding designed to get to the truth. "No. Please. Don't."

"I'm getting the truth out of you one way or the other." Jhee waved her hands and seized the handles of one of the great gears of the Divine Mechanism. This was one of the most compulsive weapons in her magical arsenal, reserved only for Justicars and only to be used under the most extreme of circumstances. She was one of only a handful to whom it had been taught. Not even the Invokers were allowed to use it.

Jhee reached out through the Divine Mechanism and found the connection between her and Sharlet. Jhee examined it and brought order to it and went to the pathways that would unlock the truth from the woman's own lips.

"Tell me about Project Albatross," Jhee ordered.

Sharlet opened her mouth to speak. She made a choking noise and grasped at her throat. Jhee leaned into her cypher and felt resistance. Another force worked against her. The more she tried to loosen Sharlet's tongue, the more the counter force tightened. Sharlet started turning purple and clawing at her throat. With her other hand, Sharlet had grabbed a letter opener. The woman's hand shook as she pointed the letter opener at her throat. Jhee released the cypher and grabbed Sharlet's wrist.

Sharlet dropped the letter opener, coughing and gulping for air. Jhee rendered her aid. Sharlet shoved her away, then flung the letter opener away. "If ever there were a time for you to once listen to me in your whole stubborn life, it's now. No, quite literally, I can't," she rasped.

"An Imperial Silence Geas."

"Worse, an Imperial Compulsion Geas. I can't speak about it even if I wanted to. Anyone tries to force the information out of me, and it triggers a suicide protocol."

"You agreed to that?"

"I didn't have much choice."

Jhee grabbed Sharlet's upper arm. "Fine. I'm taking you into custody."

"What for? You have no proof. It will all just get swept under the rug of Imperial security. Do what I did. Just take the money and agree to keep your mouth shut."

"This explains your sudden rise to the surface."

"There was nothing I could do for Shep. I could, however, try to claw our family out of the trench he had cast it into, though. I figured what harm could it do? The Mitsus, your family, my family all agreed."

"No one asked me."

"Of course, we didn't. You thought we would? You were so snout over flippers for my brother you wouldn't have agreed."

"I wouldn't. You're right."

Sharlet pursed her lips. "We cut that anchor loose because he almost took our family down with him. You should follow my lead and do so, too. Sooner rather than later. He'll only drag you down with him. I always liked you, sister-in-law."

"It didn't feel that way when you and the likes of Kaisonia were taunting me on the fields of play or insulting my clothes."

"Youngsters can be cruel, especially when they're trying to fit in. The unlikely heiress and the diving boy from the wrong side of the channel. Sounds like something from one of your stories. The noble, good-hearted Shep? Or the womanizer with an island-sized chip on his shoulder? Shep had something to prove. He would live in one of those enormous mansions. He would be lusted after by those girls who treated him like a servant. Puberty hit, and he filled out. Shep, the diving boy from the wrong side of the channel, almost did it, too, until he became a proxy in a feud between two powerful families."

$\sim$

The Hunt

Far Reach lore said the restless dead turned into wisps or mist wights and became part of a region's fog. Folk's essences belonged under the waves with the ancestors and the First Ones, or in the Spheres with the Makers. To be trapped as part of the fog, bound to the land of the living unable to pass on or help and only able to mislead, must be the worst fate imaginable. One might prefer Unmaking or the Discard Pile.

Mist, the last breaths of the dead, had rolled in. Shep and his gang did not mind. It would be their ally. They smelled their prey's fear on the fog. They heard his heavy, ragged breathing and tasted the sour, rancid brume of his fear. The ground sent tiny tremors of his panicked flight. It would do him no good. The gang was faster. They gained on him.

They hunted together as one unit: a gang of hes, shes, and even a few xes led by their anchors, Medea and the Hammerhead. Protect the stronghold. Save the matriarch. He remembered now. They must do this.

Fight. Protect. Survive. They had to eliminate the threat, the threat to his she and all his future pups. Protect the matriarch. Protect his she. He did not matter. All that mattered was the survival of his gang, his pod.

Their prey faltered. An excited howl went up from the Hammerhead. Soon they would be their prey. Soon they would eliminate the threat. Through his red-eyed vision, the whole of the fog had become blood-red mist. Only a dark, amorphous shape in the center that represented their prey stood out. Shep stopped and took a good sniff of the air and the ground.

This felt right, more right than anything had felt in ages. Fight. Protect. Survive. This is what he was meant to do. This is what he had denied himself for so long. Shep had tried to be the man for so long. He had tried to deny how good it felt to dive, to hunt, to kill. No more. Kill the man and let the beast be reborn.

In the back of Shep's mind, he had the vague idea of his life as a man or the older she, Dari, whom he had lived with, who had killed the woman and let the beast take over. He had spent many years staring into her eyes, wondering why she had made that choice. He had understood it on some level, but not like he had now. He had stared into Dari's shark hound eyes. The eyes always had a glimmer of something more than he saw in other hounds' eyes. It was why all the other dogs gave her deference. They knew she was different, something more, something they must fear and obey.

Their prey fell, and the Hammerhead was on him. The scent of blood filled the air, driving all other thoughts from his mind. A howl escaped him. Fight. Protect. Survive. He rushed forward to join in on the kill. Another berserker cut across his path.

Shep looked down at the victim, and a faint flicker of recognition flitted through him. They weren't just chasing some dock rat of the two-legged variety. He had seen this man before at the sojourn: the vizier of finance.

With the delay, an image of the Lady of the Isles appeared before Shep. Her face seemed familiar, a remnant of the man's memories. The vision faded away.

Shep sought to rush forward again to join the rest of the gang. The image appeared before him again. Not his gang. A false gang.

The she, the anchor, she was barking howling insistently that he join the fray. An itch, a tingle in his neck brand brought him to a halt. He shook his head, a man's head, a Water Folk head.

Water Folk. Folk. Beings capable of operating by more than their base skin's needs. Shep peered down at his hands. Hands, not talons. They had claws and paw-like attributes, but they were still hands. He stared at the surrounding berserkers. They stood upright as he did. His companions were Water Folk, not sea wolves or whale crushers. They never were wholly wild animals. They never were. That was the lie. They were Water Folk. They could choose.

Other members of the gang had stopped. They regarded each other and him. They had realized what he had. This was not real. Their false inner essence as mere animals never was real. It was a suggestion the doctor had put in their heads to get them to act like killers triggered by the smell and taste of blood.

Shep realized the deed had been done. Their prey lay dead and unmoving on the ground. His throat ripped out, the stink of death rising from him. Which one of them had done the deed, Shep did not know. He was splattered with the man's blood. Yet others were drenched in it.

The she-anchor came over. "You did it. You saved the pod and protected the matriarch."

Shep and Medea returned to the mansion. They cleaned themselves off in the stable amidst the snorts and whinnies of the animals housed there. They knew there were predators in their midst. As she changed her clothes, he glimpsed her soft, sleek skin and the pale underbelly with two primary teats, four smaller ones. Teats which might someday nurse a full litter. He thought about his she and the young pup with whom she mated more frequently than she did with him. She constantly smelled of his stink. Shep took the all too familiar side path up to his room. Medea had followed. Something stirred inside him, which hadn't in a long time. He moved up behind Medea. The she turned to face him and smiled. He brought her down on the bed.

All Cried Out

While Jhee puttered about her orrery space, she pondered the implications of an all-out war with IES and eventually MANTEL. She found herself headed to Shep's room, as this affected him too, she wanted his input. Kanto might readily agree, but Shep had become more and more of a closed-door to her. She could no longer assume he would just back her up.

Jhee knocked and heard a grunt of acknowledgment. She opened the door to Shep's room and strode in. She found Shep and Medea locked in an embrace, naked. Jhee gasped.

Shep glanced her way. His expression bore surprise as if he had just awoken from a spell. "Jhee!"

Jhee quickly turned around and pulled the door shut behind her. Shep scrambled to follow. Kanto stepped out into the hallway. The entrance to Shep's room flung open, and he came out half-naked, Medea in tow. Kanto's mouth dropped open. Jhee hitched up her robes and ran for the stairs.

"Jhee, wait!"

Tears of humiliation stung her eyes. Shep seized her arm. A blur struck him. He and Kanto crashed into the wall. They fell into a heap on the floor. Kanto scrabbled to the top. He gripped Shep's shoulders and slammed him repeatedly against the ground. Shep did not resist.

"Kanto, enough," Jhee uttered.

The younger husband continued to wale on her older husband. Beyond them, Medea only watched, her clothing clutched to her body in some half-drowned attempt at modesty. Jhee leaned hard into the siren module. "Kanto, stop!"

Kanto sprang to his feet without taking his eyes off of Shep. He came to Jhee's side and held her. She took a step towards Shep. He still lay on the floor. Her gaze went from him to Medea. "Get out! Both of you!"

Jhee squared her shoulders. She straightened her posture, strode passed them into her room, and slammed the door. Inside, she collapsed against the door. She put her entire essence into a soul-yell and slid to the floor, cried out.

19

Unerasable

Jhee stood at the top of the stairs when Shep came by a few days later to pick up some belongings. Bax, Kanto, and the servants kept him in the foyer. He gave them a list of items, and they retrieved them for him. She felt nothing when she looked at him. Not anger, not contempt. Nothing. She had tried so many years. So many years balancing his feelings with her duties. So many years wanting him to look at her with even a fraction of the desire he had shown for Miramar.

She had believed once that Shep would come to love her the way she always wanted. What she had to admit was that she was more adept at lying to herself than he was to her.

Shep approached the bottom of the steps. "Please, Jhee, may we talk in private?"

Kanto blocked his path. "She has nothing to say to you, *denme*."

Shep grabbed him by the robes. The servants unsheathed short knives. Bax brandished his blade at him. "Mr. Shep, please."

Shep released Kanto. He smoothed out his robes. Jhee descended the stairs. She stopped a step or two above him and waved away the servants.

"I suggest you engage a solicitor," Jhee said. "No divorce because I can't deal with another scandal right now. But I'm withdrawing my financial support."

Kanto took Jhee's hand. "We're starting procedures to have your name taken off the marriage charter."

"To be replaced with yours, I suppose," Shep snapped.

"Why not? You've done nothing but shame us since we got here. I've done everything, given everything, to save our family. You've done everything you can to ruin it."

"Why not, indeed? Looks like you are getting what you always wanted."

"You think this is what I want? I admired you. I used to lament the fact that I was not more like you. You're a coward. You have no honor." Kanto stepped closer to Shep. "Don't be another problem she has to manage. You broke her heart, and for that alone, I will never forgive you."

Shep redirected his attention to Jhee. "Jhee, please, if we could just talk."

"I'm done talking to you," Jhee said. "Done. I can't do this anymore. I can't go through this anymore. If you want someone other than me, I release you from your obligation to pretend otherwise. You're allowed to keep my name, but you will get nothing else from me. I have nothing left for you. I'll hold you to the same rules as other noble spouses. Take concubines and whores as you wish, but no bastards."

Kanto returned to her side and placed an arm around her shoulders.

"Now, the servants will oversee the rest of your visit. Kanto, see he takes nothing that is not rightfully his."

"Please, Jhee," Shep said.

Jhee stormed up the stairs.

Once in the comfort of her room, Jhee took out her schematics and parts tables. She arranged them carefully and precisely on her desk. After ensuring each was properly aligned with the corners and in proper relation to each other, she took out a finger quill and a blank sheet of bio-film. She wanted the visceral feel, which could only come from working the derivations out by hand. The precise designs and specifications could be relied upon unlike much in this world. The derivations were challenging but straightforward and elegant. Unlike people.

A rhythmic knock came at her door.

"Enter," she said.

Kanto came in and sat in the chair beside her worktable. He covered her hand. "He's gone."

Jhee wiped a tear from her eye and patted his hand, then went back to her derivations. "Thank you for seeing to it."

"It's the least I can do."

Kanto paused and looked about the room.

"Was there anything else?" Jhee asked.

"No, I suppose not."

Jhee continued with her derivations. Kanto picked up the lute he kept there and played. His sketchbook sat on the bedside table now, and he had moved a few of his toiletries into her bathroom. With Shep's ouster and Mirrei unlikely to return, she felt little point in separate rooms anymore to maintain household unity. She turned her chair to listen to him. It was just vibrations of a string projected through a resonance chamber. Yet, the music it produced was so divine, like the First Makers' Design.

This all had to be the First Makers' Design. Jhee had to believe that. But what lesson did they want her to learn? What device were they trying to construct from the ruins of her life? She must have some greater role to play in Their Design. Had she been too prideful of her intellect? Had she been too lustful of Kanto's beauty?

Kanto finished his pieces. Jhee would have applauded except for the tears running down her cheeks. It was impolite of her, she knew. He wanted to please so much. She should have shown her appreciation, yet she couldn't. "I'm sorry," she said.

Kanto kissed her. They made love slowly and tenderly on the rug in a tangle of half removed robes. He nuzzled her chin afterward.

"And so, the line continues," he said. Her bloodline. Besides him moving into her suite, they had dispensed with all pregnancy precautions. "You loved him while he loved only Miramar. I love you while you still love him."

Jhee opened her mouth to deny it.

"Please, Jhee. Our family has had enough lies. At least respect me enough to admit it. Never lie to me again, and I'll never lie to you."

"I swear."

"I swear, too."

"May I sensitize you so we can practice artificing together?"

"If that is your wish."

"We need to work on a common code. I must look into blood rites and rituals. I always avoided them before for fear of triggering..." Jhee trailed off.

"It's all right, you can say his name. No lies, remember. I know it will take time. I am devoted to you, Jhee, our house, our family. You don't have to pretend you don't still feel anything for him. He's been an enormous part of your life since long before I got here."

Jhee wrapped her arms about him and held him close. "Thank you. Thank you for everything. Your strength, your courage."

"Jhee, I know you said you're not worried Shep would be a danger to our children... With his erratic behavior.... What if I am?"

She took his hands in hers. Kanto had that right. Yet Jhee had no answer to his fears. He nestled against her.

"I don't expect you to forget about him overnight. You can't erase him from your thoughts or your heart so quickly, and I wouldn't want you to."

Can't erase? Jhee thought about Kanto's complaint he could not erase the copy of the judicial archives she put on his conch at the abbey. She sat up suddenly. "Kanto, may I see your conch?"

He raised up on his elbow. "What is it?"

"The copy of the judicial archives. Is it still on there?"

"Yes, unfortunately. It says I don't have permission to delete it, and it's encrypted, so I can't even see what's in it taking all the space."

Kanto handed her the conch. She kissed him. "Brilliant. Thank you."

"If that's the thanks I will get, I should let you borrow my conch more often."

Jhee used her old access credential and opened the judicial archives. It was out of date and was not connected to the primary system, so her old credentials still worked. The hack they had done had preserved it and kept in roughly the shape it was when they set it up at that night on the yacht. She did not need the latest codes and records, all she needed was basic access.

～

Of Uniform Design

"What is it, Jhee? What have you figured out?" Kanto asked.

"Medea," Jhee said.

Kanto wrinkled his snout. "That viper. I can't believe what they did after all you've done for them."

Jhee shook her head. "I can't think about that right now. I think I know what the mastermind behind all this is after."

"Seriously? You are thinking about the case at a time like this."

"I can't help it. I can't explain it. Everything that's happened to us. I feel it's all connected."

"And you have to see it through. It's in your nature." Kanto sighed, hopped to his feet, and helped her up. "Come on then. Let's help you figure out this puzzle. Left side of the closet."

Jhee cocked her head at him quizzically.

"I know you, Jhee. You should find something sufficiently functional and stealthy there." He went over to the wardrobe and brought out black garments. "Sufficiently stealthy and functional. Whatever you propose to do probably is not best done in full daylight. So, I whipped these up, complete with my handy hidden pockets. Form-fitting with an ear towards minimizing sound. These are yours. This one is mine."

"Yours?"

"I always fancied going along with you on one of your ill-advised nighttime sleuthing jaunts. I knew though that others were more suited for it, like Bax and he who will not be named. You always had a tendency to rush out there unprepared. Well, this time, I intend to make sure that does not happen. I'm the only backup you have right now. Bax's out of commission, and denme's not here. I'm not letting you go anywhere alone right now."

Jhee opened her mouth to protest, then shut it. "Yes. Yes. Of course. Although I prefer social engineering. We won't be needing the night suits."

"Dang, I'd been looking forward to putting all my lessons with Bax to excellent use, at last."

The social engineering Jhee had in mind involved Captain Odo's almost forgotten writ and bluffing their way past the archive company's security. Their search for the right company would be made more complicated by the fact some had gone out of business since the archives first started. Jhee sat and thought it through. "We need to check older company records. We needed an older archive service, one likely to have gone out of business and that either sold or warehoused their assets."

"Doesn't that also mean there is a chance they destroyed them? A merged company is what you want. We need to look for one where the aim of the sale was to get their hands on the struggling companies' assets.... Like the uniform archives."

"The what?"

"The record of the old uniform designs. I have access to those records. Legal bureaucracy. They kept a record of the old designs along with some old personnel files. We had to get them unsealed because they had stored them along with the operational data. They weren't very good about curating their data. There was an old company that had archives of many of the records. Personnel records, etc. One of the old archival companies which had a record of the old uniform design reqs also had hard copies of other data."

"Kanto, that's brilliant."

"I know."

While Kanto changed, Jhee noted the hard archives building's location. She tapped the underside of her desk to reveal the compartment where she had stowed the open writ Odo had given her, along with the key to Ursula's apartment. The captain had said it was good only once, the likely consequence if its notarization came from a stolen seal. The moment she used it, it was burnt, and they would catch on to what he had done. She had to make it count.

~

The Hard Archives

As the guard at the hard archives building processed Jhee's writ, sweat began to make her scalp itch. She recited statutes in her head to keep herself calm. She glanced at Kanto to see how he was faring. He had dressed in the tans of a low-level civil servant. With his hair mussed, he affected the harried demeanor of a junior official quite well.

"All set, Justicar Rasbora. Sign in," the guard said.

Jhee tapped her credential card to the register.

"Your assistant too."

"Ah, of course," Kanto said.

Kanto strode confidently forward and tapped his credential card to the register.

"All set," the guard replied.

The guard waved them by. Jhee queried Kanto via her expression. "Mirrei's wild side had its advantages."

Jhee and Kanto made their way to the records room. She went over to the shelves and started pulling out boxes.

"Now, Jhee, what exactly are we looking for?"

"Hard storage. Cards, acrylics, crystals, etc. from approximately the time of the Flower Wars. Anything that would not be automatically updated along with the central systems. I think main records were tampered with."

"A-ha, I get it," Kanto said and rushed over to a nearby shelf. "Anything connected would be automatically updated with the false information. Hard storage wouldn't as it's kept offline specifically, so should something happen to the primary system, there is an independent record. A backup."

"The question is, though, I'm not sure when the change was made or how many redundant copies of hard storage they keep. I don't know what their turnover regimen for hard storage is. Eventually, the altered data will make it into the hard records. If the alteration is relatively recent, we might get to the hard storage before it's replaced."

"Understood."

Jhee and Kanto tore through storage boxes. They could not conduct a systematic search of each of the archives, because she was not sure how long it would be before they were found out. Jhee and Kanto proceeded through the archives box by box. At last, Jhee found what she wanted. "Kanto, I think I got it. We must check these out and get them to an old crystal reader. We can't view them here."

"There's an old crystal reader at home. It used to belong to grandmamere. I use it to listen to recordings of Grand Mere singing." Kanto paused.

Jhee squeezed Kanto shoulder. "All right, let's go."

After they arrived home, Kanto said, "I'll go get the crystal reader."

"Good. I'll work on wiring it to the viewer."

Jhee examined the face associated with bioprint via the crystal reader. It wasn't the real surgeon general who committed suicide and whose likeness had been splattered all over the tribunal coverage as the Architect of Sorrows. This face belonged to the women they knew as Counselor Medea.

They had found the original bioplasmic records of the actual Architect of Sorrows, the head of the Medical Protectorate. The bioprint confirmations of her remains had to have been faked.

Jhee heard a sound behind her. She turned Medea stood there bearing the provenance and dodecaptych from the Eclipse Chest. "Hello, Medea. Or should I call you the Haddondeep's Butcher?"

"Oh, so you figured it out, did you?"

"It took a while, but yes."

"As one of my former participants, I rather prefer you call me Architect."

"Never again."

Jhee flipped on the light. Medea replaced the dodecaptych in the Eclipse Chest but kept the provenance. Jhee jutted her chin at the Eclipse Chest beside Medea.

"Is that what all this fuss has been about?" Jhee asked. "Is that what you detonated my life over?"

Medea sat down in the chair opposite Jhee and stared at the uncleared game of tiles on the kolal table. "It was you or me. Simple choice."

"What in that chest is worth all this?"

"Proof pointing to the location of the last remaining record of my identity and heritage."

"And that is?"

"Vivyan-Rin Shodan."

Jhee gripped the armrests. "The butcher of Haddondeep."

20

———————

～

The Last Scion

"The butcher of Haddondeep," Jhee repeated.

Medea folded her hands, then started resetting the tile board. "The last scion of Haddondeep. The residents of Haddondeep killed themselves."

"Would you prefer the Doctor of Death?"

"Actually, I think I would. I rather like that one. It includes the title to which I am more than entitled. I fancy I feel about Doctor the way you feel about Justicar."

"You and I are nothing alike," Jhee said.

"Aren't we? If only in our taste in men?"

Jhee cleared and centered and did not rise to the bait. "So, you didn't commit suicide?"

"Afraid not."

"And the poor unfortunate they found in your cell?"

Medea rotated the tile board, deciding which color to play, blue or green. "No one of consequence. Are the rest of the Eclipse Chest's content still here?"

"What are my chances of living if I were to reveal that?"

"I don't want to kill you. I've done my best to avoid it, though you have given me cause."

"Sorry to disappoint you," Jhee said.

"Not at all. I understand you and what drives you. I spent time under your roof with you and your family. Such a lovely family. I envy you, you know that?"

"Is that why you seduced Shep?"

"I would have preferred to have seduced you. Go right to the source. You're something of a frigid bitch, you know that? No offense."

"None taken."

Having decided on green, Medea doled out the tiles. "It's a compliment. I am myself. Shep was already vulnerable and close to crisis. Add in some pheromones, and all it took was a nudge. In the throes of passion, though, your name was on his lips. He's so wracked with guilt. Now, Kanto, his attraction to powerful, older women is fascinating, if obvious. I'm sure with time, I might have swayed him, too. Even your do-gooding junior wife if she were here. You are all so predictable. It was quite disappointing. I would have thought you had better taste. Speaking of tastes, that blood of Shep's. Had you and he really never sensitized him?"

"Enough!" Jhee said. She placed her hand in the center of the tile board. "What will it take to get you to back off? You want Shep. You can have him with my blessing."

Medea lifted Jhee's hand from the board, then laid her first tile right-center. A standard opener. Jhee capped it with her blue tile.

"Hmm, feeling me out, are you? Try this."

Medea put a green tile at parallel to Jhee's. This did not just limit Jhee's moves, but hers. A more likely move would have been to cap so she could work towards a stronghold. Jhee placed her tile to block Medea's in.

"Going for early aggression. Don't get too far ahead of yourself."

Medea's counter tile placement blocked her in. Jhee swore. She needed to keep her head in the game. Jhee went back to Medea's original tile and placed to expand.

"Good. Good. Now, you're thinking more clearly. Shep wanted nothing more than to protect you."

Medea placed a tile to lure Jhee in. Jhee opted to continue expansion and said, "Protection is his instinct. You and the doctors saw to that."

"Quite the contrary. The berserkers were shock troops. Their tendency to coordinate and work in packs was born of some instinct within the Water Folk nature. It was almost uncanny really how they could position themselves across immense distances with little overt communication. Pack is less appropriate. Makes us sound like Earth Folk. Perhaps more accurate is a flock, a swarm, or school."

As if to illustrate her point, Medea placed a tile in formation. She had enveloped Jhee's expansion line.

"Would you like to ask me questions? I'm sure you must have many."

"How far are you from the succession?"

"Closer than you, further than the likes of Zaria and Adama. The Princess Regent is in her own league. Why? Are you looking to move up? For now, those three are playing nice with each other. When they go at it for real, you could use some protection. I can make that happen. But to do so, I need everything from that chest."

"What for? A cyphering manual can't be worth all this," Jhee said.

"No, no, no, the Eclipse Chest contains several items far more valuable than arcane polyptychs. One of those compendiums contains a family tree and other pseudo journal entries made by one of Thaedra's pupils while she mused on formulas. It gives insight into a certain love child."

"The Halfmoon Cove Compact. You didn't want the dodecaptych or the Eclipse Chest. You wanted the chest's provenance."

Medea smiled. "I see you know your history."

"I know my law. It set an obscure legal precedent about inheritance. Half the claimants for the Sea Throne invalidated."

"Just so. What's revealed through those relics could upend the succession hierarchy amongst other things."

Jhee kept one eye on the board and the other on Medea, who had almost forgotten they were playing. "More importantly, it could redistribute the Imperial company shares in MANTEL. With the proper resources and stock interests, one branch could acquire a plurality of electors. Blood order succession can be neutralized. A major bargaining stone no matter where you are on the chain."

"Even without a chance at the Sea Throne, one could become a sovereign appointer."

"No Empress Vivyan-Rin, then?"

Medea folded her arms. "No, that's just how I secured Zaria's help. I have use for all the knowledge in the Eclipse Chest. I'm a simple woman with simple pleasures, much like yourself. This whole tribunal business has forced me to amend my activities. All I want is to be left to do my work in peace."

"The veteran's center and berserker 'wellness' sanctuary."

"Among other interests."

"You've been recruiting new candidates via the veteran's center and street fights. You're trying to start another Haddondeep research facility."

"Biotech is such a fascinating field. My fellow imperials were content to profit off my work so far as no one knew. They didn't care what I was doing as long as their shell investments went up. The hypocrisy. They were war profiteers charging exorbitant fees for substandard equipment and transport. My work improved the fortunes of our warriors."

"By turning them into mindless killers."

"By giving them a chance against the stronger, faster Fire Folk warriors. Our troops weren't prepared to face them. The previous dynasty should account themselves lucky they could escape with their lives after losing all the Sacred Monuments to the Fire Folk. Barbarians, indeed. Their dismissal and condescension of the Fire Folk's capabilities made them send our soldiers out there unprepared. Medical Protectorate was tasked with finding some way to turn the tide. The upper echelons didn't care how. We gave them a fighting chance.

"The Sky Folk can fly. Fly. Luckily for us, they crack like eggs. It's only by the Makers' graces have the ground pounders proved so inept at interplanetary travel, or no doubt they would have defeated us too. Between their toughness and their shielding, the Earth Folk shrug off enormous amounts of damage. The Storm Folk can full shift and are the most powerful artificers I've ever seen. What can we do? Hold our breath and hide under the water? Our grace is our navy; fortunately, the Fire Folk navy is utter trash."

Storm Folk? There was no consensus on if the term referred to the Fire Folk or the Water Nomads, also known as the Makers' Failed Prototypes. The consensus, though, was whoever they were all Folk acquired their ability to skin slip from them.

"With our standard military options dwindling, we had to be more creative and go farther and farther afield for soldiers. When the throne had to step into your feud in the Reaches, we discovered the treasure trove of Folk who inhabited the Rim island groupings. We barely noticed those from the Rim—a snobbery which saw us looking primarily among the populace on the main isles. Short-sightedness on our parts, as your region seemed to be teeming with the perfect candidates for our experiments. Your isles were a treasure trove of those with slipping and arcane abilities. Probably the result of your more frequent interaction with the open sea and interbreeding with other kinds who also have extraordinary aptitude in those areas. It's a shame really that our prejudice has prevented us from studying those whose abilities stretch the boundaries of physical, mental, and mystical limits."

Jhee tapped her nose and positioned another tile. "The berserker program started with full-slippers like Shep."

Minor changes came over all Folk, all the time. A great change total and complete had been reserved for the few, like Shep and Dari, until the Medical Protectorate intervened. Jhee always felt Shep's losing the lottery was no accident of chance, and his subsequent assignment to Medical Protectorate no retaliatory act of a capricious family. Both Jhee had attributed to family politics. What if it was more? A deliberate harvest of those from Rim island groupings such as the Reaches?

"Poor, guilt-ridden creature," Medea said. "Are you looking to me to absolve you? No such luck. Shep and those like him had been beneath our notice until your families' silly games brought them to our attention. Your feud put the Far Reaches on the board, and once on the board, you all became game pieces."

"Parley."

Medea squinted at Jhee, then studied the board. While she had ranted, Jhee had continued her aggressive expansion. Jhee had foregone reinforcing a stronghold to go straight for her opponent, as had Medea. Jhee could breach in two if Medea chose not to divert her.

~

No Parley

Medea's mouth twitched. "Clever. No parley. Let's just see how this plays out."

The woman placed a tile on Jhee's flank. If Jhee did not forcibly divert to address it, she would forfeit her lead tile and be in no position to breach. It had been the downside of such an aggressive approach.

Medea regained her composure. "The downside to such an aggressive approach. I should have been more subtle, wooed you, lured you in more. I must admit I underestimated you. It was a mistake to go after your family. The side effect of dealing with the high born—their family members are disposable. I had expected you to cut Shep loose sooner. I also hadn't counted on the Consort Regent to be such a romantic. He used his own beloved mistress as a tile. I had thought she was another of his side pieces. I didn't realize he had actual feelings for Ursula. It was an unexpected bonus that he brought you in. You played the game well."

Jhee sneered and moved another tile towards Medea's makeshift stronghold. "Breach in two. Parley."

"Not yet. You impressed me. You struck a blow for every bookish nerd against the Zaria's and Princess Regents of the world who think we are beneath their notice and who view our fascination with learning as banal. Overwhelm in three."

Jhee examined the tile board. Medea had lured out and isolated her tiles. If she made a move to breach with any of them, she left the others vulnerable. Jhee placed a tile to consolidate. They might break through and have them reinforce each other.

"Diversion forfeit." Because Jhee had failed to close in for the breach, Medea got to claim one of her tiles as her own. Medea picked up one of Jhee's blue tiles and replaced it with a green. "Looks as though you are running out of moves and tiles. Perhaps you should realize this is not a negotiation. Play. It's the only way out. You can't disengage. You can't detach. No negotiation. Those are the laws, and you always follow the law."

Jhee continued with the consolidation play and lost two more tiles. The only pieces she had left was a rough spearhead formation, which in no way threatened Medea's measly one tile stronghold.

"See, it's not always the size and strength of one's fortifications that count or the ability to aggressively take the fight to the enemy. Sometimes, it's simply the willingness to die on the smallest of hills. Fight for such small stakes that it confuses your opponent. Sad, lonely little Justicar. Always the one left waiting behind on the shore."

Roaring and the sounds of struggle carried from upstairs. Medea smiled and placed the lute pick on the table.

"I suspect that's your oldest husband reclaiming his rightful place as your First. Or maybe it's your Second confirming his Naming Rights status. It doesn't really matter to me. A shame, really. Both beautiful and talented in their own ways. I wonder how much it matters to you?"

Jhee rose.

"Sit down, please," Medea said. Her voice bore no hint of anger or it being a command, but Jhee complied. "Jhee, I need that Chest. I'm prepared to be generous."

"I don't want or need your blood money."

"Don't you? Defending yourself against all those lawsuits must have taken a toll. I know funding them was."

"So, the litigants were all cut-outs, proxies, funded by you?"

"Guilty as charged. You know a little something about that, don't you? Just ask the Mitsus." Medea held up a lute pick, one of Kanto's favorites. "This might make for an interesting Lancer. What I am offering isn't money. I'm offering to return your loved ones to you in more or less the condition I found them. Now that we have completed the preliminary round, how about we move on to the final?"

Jhee kept her face still as she picked up her conch and tried to contact Kanto. Kanto's distinctive chime for her communications emanated from Medea's pocket. She pulled out Kanto's conch and answered it. "Kanto can't answer right now. I've got him under lock and key."

Medea disconnected.

"How?" Jhee asked.

"The same way I got in here."

Jhee tucked away her conch and left her hands within her sleeves. Instead of practicing finger cyphers, she prepared a stunning grasp cypher. "Shep."

"Partially. You should have changed the security codes. Shep was more than eager for a little payback on your poor, untrained weekend warrior. Can you imagine the gall of Shep to be jealous? He brought him in, practically forced him on you, then complains he's felt shut out. No one enjoys being cast aside. Imagine what he might do once he finds out the junior spouse is in the early stages of pouching. You didn't waste time, did you?"

A rustle behind Jhee caused her to turn with her cypher at the ready. The Gray Lady of the Deeps stood there bearing Jhee's face. Jhee hesitated. A blow struck Jhee across the head. She slumped over, scattering the tiles.

~

The Needle Talon

Jhee awoke strapped to a med table. She struggled.

"Please, don't bother," Medea said.

Jhee turned her head what little her restraints allowed. Medea sat on a stool beside the med table. Shep stood beside her, eyes half-focused, staring off into space. He had taken on more of the appearance of a sea wolf with its sleeker shark-like form rather than an orcinus like he did when he was in the middle of a full berserker rage.

"Shep?"

"He can't hear you now. I have him in standby. That is unless you activate your authority chords. Then you may get through to him."

"Shep, please."

Medea picked up her conch and tapped it a few times. "I'm finding the deep encryptions on his berserker conditioning hard to crack. They've been rewritten. I can get him to act in a limited fashion for a certain amount of time. Somehow, he keeps resisting. You must have buried an override deep within his psyche with your siren module. It activated whenever we tried to take complete control of him, then broke our hold over the others. Perhaps, if I can unlock your siren song…" Medea seized Jhee's arm, turning it, so her sigil was in full view. "All right now. Here we go. Berserkers are imprinted to obey and protect the Architect via pheromone coding and conditioning. It seems you found a means to disrupt it. Is this how you did it? Why the sigil when you have a siren module?"

"He's immune to my module. A security precaution because we were married." What game was Medea playing? She knew why. Did she want Jhee to confess to treason? Perhaps, if Jhee kept her talking, she might find a way out of this, or Shep might break free from his berserker fugue. "The knowledge on how to make my module work on him was classified. To reveal it would be to betray the Empire. It would be treason to share it with anyone else. If I wanted to talk him down, I needed to use another means."

"You opted for a foreign Arcano-tech implant. Such loyalty to the empire. You wouldn't have to tell me. I could reprogram your siren module for you. I wanted you for the berserkers. Intelligence wanted you, too. In the end, we compromised. That Fire Folk device in your arm now makes me want you all the more. I have so many ideas how I want to play with it and you. What I need are exemplars from someone with the original, unencrypted copy of the siren code and uncorrupted bioplasm from a berserker who isn't losing coherence. Which I could get by merely dissecting you. Or, we can avoid making a mess of your flesh. Just tell me what I want to know, and you can all walk out of here."

"In exchange for my silence."

"That would be a necessary part of our arrangement. I've seen from your case files you have used inspiration to get a confession out of several witnesses as recent as a few moons ago. Why isn't your module failing? Why isn't he degenerating? I also have these."

Medea showed Jhee her conch.

"Your original Medical Protectorate records. Before you had them expunged. What is it you don't want people to know, I wonder? It can't be the siren module. Those were small fish as far as state secrets went. Why are you two fine?" Jhee looked defiantly at Medea. Medea tilted her head to one side, "As expected. Asset Sheepdog, there are three wheels in the sky. The third wheel controls the yaw."

Shep's head rose, and he blinked. Jhee struggled. That had to be a code phrase to deactivate standby mode.

"This spy has vital documents hidden within her somewhere," Medea said. "Help me find them. Hold her down."

Shep pinned Jhee to the med table. Medea took out a long wicked sharp looking piece of biometal, a talon needle. Jhee's eyes grew wide. As Medea pierced Jhee's side with it, Jhee screamed. Medea withdrew the talon needle from Jhee's flank and glanced at Shep for a reaction.

"Use your command codes. Tell him to release you," Medea said.

Jhee's side burned. Her breathing was heavy. She huffed and puffed to calm herself. Medea pierced her side again. Jhee screamed again.

"Don't scream. Command, Magistrate. You sees, I be knowed all about you, the secret thirteenth member of their gang. All the berserker regiments had 'em like. They'd have given you the command codes and whatnot to shut down any of the berserkers in your unit or call 'em to ya aid. I know this hurts. Now, cry out to him for help."

Jhee only had a moment to register an oddness to the way Medea spoke, before the woman stabbed her again. Jhee felt the spittle flecking her mouth. Her chest heaved. "I don't have them," she yelled.

Medea cocked her head at her. "I don't have time for these games. You were their intelligence liaison. Of course, you had them. I take no pleasure in this. Not like some did. I find it all rather vile."

Jhee squeezed her eyes shut. "Conflict of interest."

"I need those codes if me and or those like me are ever to be free of this thing, this whatever it is they did to us."

"They wouldn't give me his codes because we were married. Yes, I could pull strings to get myself assigned to his unit. But they drew the line at giving me everyone's code except his. They gave that code to someone else."

"I don't believe you."

"It's true. Captain had his shutdown code. He was the only other person in the unit with the clearance. The regular troops weren't supposed to know, or else they might do exactly what you are doing now. It was too big a risk if they found out."

Medea looked confused. Jhee might have been breaking through. She looked at Shep. He had cocked his head and stared at her. "Shep, please. I know you don't want to hurt me."

Medea snapped out of it. She placed a gag over Jhee's face. "If what you say is true, then you are of no use to me, and this has just been a waste of time. She lied to me. She must have known you would not have the codes. So why did she—"

Shep fell upon Medea before she finished securing the gag. The two squared off. Medea changed into an ocean lynx with its feline snout but webbed, taloned almost Folk-like hands. Unlike a normal skin slip, Medea's form melted and undulated in a way that made the bile rise in Jhee's throat. Medea's face melded into a facsimile of Ursula's then the sea dog sailor's before settling into its feline appearance. They went at it tooth and claw.

Medea, a berserker.

The thought drifted through Jhee's mind. Medea? The way Medea spoke clicked into place, a sea dog accent. Jhee rocked her head to dislodge the gag. Pain lanced through her stab wounds. She took heavy, panicked breaths to cope with the pain. With gritted teeth, Jhee engaged her siren module.

"Yield!" Jhee yelled the shutdown command, imbuing it with every dram of power that remained in her.

"Medea" dropped. Shep's claw caught her across the belly. Shep's focus snapped in Jhee's direction. He growled, but his brow furrowed. "Medea" lay dead on the ground. A victorious Shep stumbled over to Jhee and rubbed his head against her and lapped at her wounds. Jhee winced. His eyes changed first, then the rest of him.

"Pity," Medea's voice came over an intercom seemingly from every corner of the room. "She was one of my favorites, you know? When the shifting process started breaking down for her, it granted her a certain elasticity, the ability to mold and shape her form in remarkable ways. I have new favorites to play with now."

A hissing emanated from the vents and gas filled the room.

~

Hammers and Bars

Shep awoke slumped against metal bars. He pulled himself upright and looked around. The floor swung underneath his feet as he rose. He saw a familiar hulking form standing on a nearby platform.

"Hammad. I suppose I have you to thank for this cage?"

"The work isn't done. There's still more of them out there," Hammad the Hammerhead answered.

"This was a setup, from the moment they paid you to pick a fight with me."

"You got it backward, *Dawn Wolf*. The payment flowed up to Hammad the Hammerhead, not down." Hammad slapped his chest with his palm. "Those recruiters worked for the Hammerhead. It was my gym, my training facilities, my slaughterhouse. I started this because something needed to be done about those bastards. The Counselor and the Hammerhead needed the strongest, Toril's finest. Someone had to do something, or else those bastards would get away with it again. I helped turned those like Ursula around, gave them purpose, like the Counselor did with me.

"Who wants reconciliation? Meat. Another excuse for them to get away with it. I wanted blood. They needed to pay the ultimate geld, their lives to Toril. The Empire owes us blood, their blood."

Shep tensed at the mention of Toril the War Maker, a controversial Maker many berserkers worshiped. They weren't supposed to because he had been stricken from the Maker canon. That hadn't stopped them. When he stayed on at the abbey on Torilsisle, even he took the rare opportunity to perform devotions to the chiseled-out effigies that remained there.

"Warriors fight in the arena. Meat is brought to the slaughterhouse. Are you a warrior, Dawn Wolf, skin brother, or meat?"

"Open this cage, and you'll see which I am."

"Your brand and sigil are an invisible leash. Free yourself. Leave their world behind, stay with us. Complete the work. Makers make it so, for the War Maker."

"My family needs me."

"Do they? They can join, too. More geld for the Merry Maker. All they have to do is accept the gift and gain the ability to full slip. And survive the ring. We will welcome them with outstretched limbs."

Hammad the Hammerhead flexed his now clawed hands and slipped partially into his shark form. Shep resisted his desire to snarl and bare fangs. He stared Hammad down as the man, not the beast. Hammad pushed his cage away from the platform to hang over a pool.

"Meat it is," Hammad said and activated the crane controls on the platform behind him.

Once Shep's cage lurched to a stop, he climbed to his feet again. Another occupied cage hung across from his.

21

The Moon Pool

Jhee awoke she was not sure how much later in a strange room.

"Good. Good. You're awake now. Pardon the violence. I was unsure of how else to get you here."

Two transparent enclosures hung suspended above a gigantic pool of water. Someone moved inside each. Jhee squinted to clear her vision. Shep and Kanto waited, restrained in an enclosure. Jhee yelled, but a gag muffled any sound. She struggled and found she was likewise secured to a high-backed chair. A strap across her forehead prevented her from turning her head either to the left or the right.

Jhee tried her hands against her bonds. She could not see her hands and thus could not correctly work a silent cast. She had not done it frequently herself. Her mentor had taught it to her for situations where you found your-self in a jam.

Jeja had taught her a few other things. Don't use artificing as a crutch. Her restraints were entirely secure. Had she been awake when they secured her, she might have been able to use Jeja's old stage tricks to ensure the bonds had been loose.

Medea walked over behind her and tightened the straps. "Excuse me. It appears someone has loosened these. We can't have that now."

She sat in a chair diagonally from Jhee just inside her range of vision but left a clear sight line to the enclosures. She pulled out a conch. "Let's see here. Galatheia-Jaide Gombessa. Jhee to her friends and intimates. May I call you Jhee? After having slept under your roof and partaken of you and your husband's hospitality, I feel I've earned."

Jhee struggled against her restraints.

"I'll take that as a 'yes.' Youngest and only known surviving daughter of House Gombessa. Infamous pirates and squelch-runners turned right-side up. Long before your time. Money can buy you a nice pedigree, as you earlier surmised. Your treatises on the legal ramifications of magical experimentation, brilliant. You have a fascinating mind, Jhee. Much like my own. How I would love to crack open that skull and unravel its secrets. What sort of person volunteers not to join Medical Protectorate, but to be a subject? I suspect that had something to do with Shep. You ran chasing after him into the infantry like the seastruck jubilant you were. After all this, was it worth it? The berserker procedure is breaking down in most of the subjects. Those implanted with siren modules aren't faring much better. All except you two. Maybe it's your support network. Maybe it's those illicit Fire Folk implants. I will enjoy cutting you open to find out.

"You failed the water and ocean fitness proficiencies. The Mitsus got hold of it and spread the rumor you failed deliberately because you were a coward. Miramar knew the truth, yet didn't speak up. Did it hurt to have her help her family use that knowledge against you? That she stayed silent as it spread throughout the Far Reaches you were a coward? The friend you trusted, the one who knew you better than anyone else, and the friend you betrayed."

Jhee yelled and tried to scream despite her gag. Perhaps she had always hated Miramar. Perhaps that made it so easy to ruin her after she had seduced Shep. Beautiful, popular Mai. Hunky, athletic Shep. Plain, but rich Jhee. In contests between them, Miramar won. She always won. It hurt no one believed that even for a moment Jhee had seduced Shep. Not this time, though. And Miramar couldn't stand it.

That night Shep arrived at the Academy was like a fantasy come true. So much of a fantasy, Jhee never stopped to question why then. What had changed with Shep? The clues were there. Jhee should have figured it out.

Shep had taken off Jhee's lenses, let down her hair. It was slow with none of the previous awkwardness of the night Jhee's sister died. He whispered against her skin repeatedly how beautiful she was, how he had always wanted her secretly for years. Jhee did the same. She poured out the unrequited feelings she had for him. They awoke before dawn and went in search of an officiant to marry them. She found out when they returned to her family and declared how much they were in love, Shep had lost the lottery.

"Tell me, Jhee, did it feel good to bankrupt those who tried to take advantage of your family in their time of need? Don't answer just yet. I will allow you to prove it. I'm proposing another game.

"Oh, sorry about all the precautions. We can't have you artificing your way out of this. This is to be a pure contest of wills and desires. Shep seems to think you have cast him aside, and he has no value to you anymore. Meanwhile, Kanto believes he has now claimed the foremost spousal position for himself. How about it, Jhee? Are they right? If given the choice between them, who would you pick? Mind you, you only get to choose one."

Medea set out the tile board again.

"Now, let's try this again, shall we. I'll control Shep, and you'll control Kanto. I was impressed with the efficiency with which you ran your household. It was a frequent tactic when I was growing up to pit the spouses against each other as much as it was the various branches. It minimized the number of spouses looking to trade up, especially when you were a consort confined to the isles. Confinement to the isles minimized the chances of base-born bastards, but it also put your consorts within easy reach of other Imperials. Zaria made an art of it. Her pack of consorts was especially good at convincing spouses to seek her favor. You were confined to the isles without very much anywhere else to go. Their parties were much anticipated. Perhaps, too much. They lured many an Imperial consort and concubine into a compromising position which she would then use to pressure them to provide information on their fellow cohorts or spouses."

〜

The Perfect Play

Medea undid the restraints on one of Jhee's hands. "You will need a hand free to play. I'm not an artificer myself. I've studied it as a theoretical matter. While there are some single-handed casts, I will risk it. It says here your particular specialties are Wind and Fire. At the berserker sanctuary, even though you had full use of both hands, it didn't help you much."

Jhee struggled.

"The rules are simple: each husband pleads his case, and you decide which one to release. The first move is mine."

Medea moved her piece forward, and Kanto's cage lowered towards the moon pool. Jhee countered. Kanto's pen rose, but then Shep's dropped a foot towards the water.

"Careful now, Jhee. We don't want orcinus fricassee. Have you learned your lesson? Or are you still just as blinded by love as you were then? Maybe you might be fonder of seal chowder."

Jhee made her next move. Kanto dropped a few feet.

"Very sloppy, Jhee. Concentrate or else they both die," Medea said.

Jhee swore, but the gag made it only come out as an angry muffle. She squeezed her eyes shut. She needed to concentrate. There had to be a way out of this. It appeared Medea had thought of everything. If she played too aggressively, Kanto would die. If she played too defensively, Shep would. If she didn't play at all or didn't beat Medea, they both died.

She made her move, and Kanto's enclosure got further away from the hazard. Shep's cage dropped precipitously closer. He placed his head against the glass. "Save Kanto, Jhee. I'm ready for this all to be over."

You don't get to decide that for any of us.

Jhee screamed silently at him. With all the wreckage and broken lives they left in their path, she would not have his death on her conscience, as well. He did not get to walk away. None of them did.

Jhee examined the board. Her pieces were scattered all over. She had not formed a cohesive strategy. Jhee had played solely to keep their cages above water. She had played to not lose instead of win. The board reflected that reality.

Medea had been brilliant, cunning indeed. She knew Jhee's inherent curiosity would keep her engaged. She would want to uncover the secret as much as Medea would.

"You're like me, Jhee, you will see the game through to the end no matter what. We are both driven by knowledge. We both have to know. It's a curse, really. I have to push the limits of science to know what it's capable of. Just like you have to push the limits of the law. There is another way out of this, Jhee. You could kill me, then have to face another judicial review. Given all that has happened, they would probably excuse your conduct. However, you'd never be able to practice law again. Killing a court official and an heir elective: I can't think of an even more blatant way to flout the law. Your career would be even more over than it is now. There would be no chance you ever get your credentials back. Ever."

If Medea died, there would be no proof of her crimes, like Jhee had thought with the vizier. Medea would be a martyr. She had made a mistake with the vizier. But it had been the only play she could make, yet to this day, she still regretted it, and it had come back to bite her. Had there been another way out of that? Or had her outrage at what the vizier had done, kidnapping Kanto and perhaps more egregiously outsmarting her, blinded her? Had her decision to kill the vizier been a just one or a vengeful one? The revelation of the copy of her records on Kanto's conch proved had she left the vizier alive, she might have been able to bring her to justice. All she had needed to do was be patient and have faith in the First Makers' Design. But she had acted as if she were above the law. She took the law into her own hands and look what it had wrought.

Medea was right. Jhee and Medea had much in common. She was every bit as arrogant as Medea. It was always about the game, the puzzle, and when the vizier beat Jhee at it, she could not cope and accept the loss gracefully. If Jhee had, there was a slim chance she could have brought the vizier to justice someday. The right way. In the meantime, though, how many other youthful men would have fallen into her clutches? The vizier had vowed not to stop, and Jhee had believed her. Could the vizier have gotten another puppet abbess installed? Another bureaucrat disdainful of men and refugees who viewed them as vermin no better than crab-rats? Who would look the other way? Or worse, see the vizier as performing a valuable service? View it as justified because, what were they, just men and refugees? A burden on society better off eliminated.

"Of course, if you'd rather not play against me, you can slip the skin with this and get out of those bindings." Medea held out a vial of bioplasm. She placed it on the edge of the table, within reach of Jhee's free hand. "I've been working on a new serum."

Jhee surveyed the scene of Medea's game. All the pieces were positioned precisely as Medea wanted. No matter what Jhee did, Medea would win. She would have her proof Jhee was no better than her. What was it Medea had said? Accept her as her master, accept her teaching. She viewed herself as another Thaedra. She wanted another disciple. Not one like the vizier or the berserkers, but one in her own image, who thought as she thought, did as she did. One who understood that science and knowledge came first. People were just a means to an end. They were all secondary to the law or to science or to whatever other philosophy or academic pursuit. Knowledge first.

The vizier: pleasure first.

The Imperium: power first.

The vicar: identity first.

Medea: science first.

Herself: the law first.

Something else always came first, except for what truly mattered. Jhee had lost sight of why the law had mattered to her. On her isles, growing up, the lords had acted as a law unto themselves. They had ground the common folk in their gears. There was no fairness, only arbitrary whims, as if on the sea and subject to the moods of the Storm Child. Jhee had hated that. She had wanted circumstances to be better. To be fair. So that those with little power like Shep's family would not be subject to the whims of the rich and powerful. Her family had power by the time she had been born, but they had come up almost by accident. In the meantime, other families had fallen. It was all subject to the whirlpool of fate. The law, on the other hand, the law, like the Divine Mechanism, was governed by knowable rules. You could learn them and manipulate them. You could bind them to your will to bring order out of chaos. Jhee had naïvely thought at the time it was so egalitarian. Everyone was protected by the law or could use arcana to better themselves. Unfortunately, it did not work that way. Some gatekeepers controlled it all.

Folk were always only pieces in someone else's game. Jhee was no different. On the cosmic scale, what was the Divine Design then? A cosmic game in which Jhee was just another piece. Like a tile, it was arbitrary which one became the matriarch based on which moves the player made. Initially, no piece was more important than the others.

Jhee struggled, and her chair moved. Medea looked over at her. "Jhee, what are you doing?"

She jumped her chair a few more inches backward. It teetered but did not fall.

"Jhee, stop!" Shep called.

Jhee hopped her chair once more. She fancied trying to smile as her chair tipped over the edge, and she hit the icy water.

~

Storm Child, Storm Child, Today

When you know it's the end, think of pleasant events, of what you most wanted to see, of all the loved ones you miss, and let them take you away.

Frigid water enfolded Jhee in a long-awaited embrace. Her Maker within guided her back in time to the day her sister, Ghele, died. Jhee could not swim. She had never learned how. Ghele had barely finished the proficiencies, but that had not stopped her from jumping in to save Jhee and others.

Jhee's mind went into a panic. There was nothing she could do tied as she was to a chair and with only one hand but not the arm free. Even if she could clear and center, she had little control over water. Everything beneath her fell away. Down and ever down, she sank.

That was what disconcerted Jhee most about water. A body could seldom tell where they were. Up could be down, and down could be up. One never knew unless they reached the bottom. A person could sink forever. To her, that always represented the greatest horror of the Unmaker's Trench, to fall forever.

Jhee tried to hold her breath. Eventually, her lungs burned.

What Jhee needed to do now was not panic and think through calmly and rationally what was happening to her. Still, Jhee tried to keep her mouth shut, to keep the water out. She had felt dizzy. Her lungs screamed for mercy. Her flesh burned as her body changed and reconfigured itself to the watery environment. There were limits, though. She could become a seal or an otter or some other sea mammal. Their lung capacity was limited too. Even if she had not gone into the water with only her Water Folk skin's lungful, what she could not become was a fish. Shifting did not allow you to change your skin that much. That was a change that went way beyond the skin to the essence. It always worked with what you were.

Her chair struck the bottom with her attached. She had gone in the water as a Water Folk with only a lungful of air. Despite the changes to her body, she must surface or else run out of oxygen. Her body reconfigured itself to a skin more extreme, a maye then a shark. Closer. Her fuel reserves were running low, not just from lack of air, but the rapid shifting. But tied to the chair she could not pass enough water over her gills.

Emissary. Until all are one.

The sigil on her arm, her esca, and the siren module at the base of her skull throbbed.

At last, she could not take it anymore. She opened her mouth, and the water forced its way into her lungs. She closed her eyes and let go.

~

Beneath the Waves

Far Reach lore said the restless dead turned into wisps or mist wights and became part of the region's fog. Many times since the tour boat accident, Jhee had dreamed her family and the sea folk beckoned her from beneath the waves.

Jhee was underwater again. She felt the eye of the drake upon her, bathing her in light.

Jhee sank under the ocean again, drowning. She couldn't touch the bottom. The waves battered her about. Now and then, they slammed her against hard, sharp rocks. The wind forced from her lungs by the impact. Her limbs were so heavy. She could not fight anymore. Mouth clamped shut, lungs burning, she contemplated the briny depths below. As she let go, an enormous, brilliant, scaly eye opened, bathing her in light. She opened her mouth to scream. Ocean poured in. A hand grabbed her collar.

She had visions of the deep, of being welcomed by Gwyn and Gloriana and her parents. Gascal and Gabi were there too. They all welcomed her.

Stay beneath the waves with us.

Gascal and Gabi knocked an air bladder about with their snouts while Gwyn, Gloriana, and Ghele swam around a warm volcanic vent. Every one of them appeared as mayes, but her Maker within recognized their essence. They frolicked and batted about an air bladder in the waves as the Sea Kings and Queens of old they were. Her family had not drowned. They had been remade magnificent and taken their rightful place beneath the waves.

Stay with us. Stay and play forever. We are not dead.

Yes, Jhee thought. They had not died; they were only awaiting her arrival. Her kin and skinfolk waited for her to shed the skin of land and take on the true form of her spirit and theirs, the maye. None of them were dead, only where they belonged under the waves with the sea children. It was where she belonged too, where she could stay if she so chose. Disappointment that Miramar was not there cast a pall over the scene, though she thought she might have glimpsed some of her old friend's drowned kin. Jhee had hoped that somehow in the Makers' Sphere, they had sealed the breach between their families, their two pods joined as they should have been in life.

An ethereal, billowing woman appeared, gliding towards her. At first, Jhee thought it to be the White and Gray Lady of the Deeps come to bear her to the Trench. As if in answer to her silent wish, the figure became Miramar.

Miramar greeted her bright and shining like the Lady of the Isles Jhee sometimes fancied herself to be. Turtles and sea folk, the Lady of the Isles spectral companions, surrounded them. Miramar seized her and headed for the surface. No, they should head down to be with her family. If Miramar sought to take Jhee away from her family, she was the Lady of the Deeps. Jhee struggled until her limbs widened into maye wings.

Miramar released her. Jhee strained to swim toward her family, but they receded farther and farther away. She heard their muffled voices calling her name.

"Stay with us, Jhee."

Seaweed wrapped itself around Jhee's limbs and prevented her from following. The more she struggled, the more it bound her. Her form had become as heavy and solid as quick cement, holding her where she was, preventing her from joining her family and friends in the depths. Jhee belonged with them now.

The voices calling Jhee's name had become clearer. Though they still sounded far away. They, however, came not from below. They came from beside and above her. The First Makers calling her to the Spheres and the sea in the sky, perhaps.

Jhee came to in a shallow canvas hammock with water running past her. Life-giving oxygen made its way over her gills, deep into her core. Her gills gradually returned to lungs.

"Jhee! You're going to be fine."

Jhee's lungs suddenly ached and felt heavy. She gagged. Water forced its way past her lips. Her lungs seized. They spasmed to rid themselves of excess water. She coughed, and more seawater forced its way out of her. Jhee wanted to tell the voice to go away. She had found her true home. She wanted to stay beneath the waves. Instead, her current skin rejected the water.

"She's Folk again. Bring the oxygen." Her head pounded. Jhee reluctantly opened her eyes. A paramedic leaned over her. A bright light swept across her vision. She squeezed her eyes shut. "Good, we've got pupillary response."

"Jhee! blessed be the Makers!" the words, this skin's name, sounded so strange to be coming through the air instead of the water. The words were spoken by her family above the waves: Shep, Kanto, Mirrei.

Jhee shook her head. She tried to tell them to let her go back. All she managed was a series of gagging coughs. The arms of her family above the waves enfolded her. Kanto rocked her back and forth. Shep and Mirrei wrapped their arms around them both. Jhee stared out through the haze.

"Don't talk. Go back to sleep if you need to," Shep said.

Imperators led Medea by her gathering. Her hands were secured behind her. She smiled with relief when she saw Jhee awake. "You won, Jhee.

Drench it all if you didn't win. You're a worthy adversary. I underestimated you again. I won't next time. Be warned. I never lose twice."

Medea's grin grew impossibly wide. The imperators carted her off.

"Don't you ever do something so foolish again, denbe," Mirrei said.

"Star," Jhee began, but it unraveled into a cough as the air and foam tickled her tonsils. "Dreaming?"

"No, I tried to tell you during the remote meeting. I was coming home. I tried to reach you again, and there was no answer. Looks like you all were having quite the adventure without me. You can tell me all about it at the hospital. The irony I'd be the one looking after you."

The paramedics placed Jhee on a gurney and transported her away.

22

~

A Fish Tale

At the hospital over the next few days, Jhee's throat remained so raw she could barely speak. Mirrei turned the tale of how she found them on the Medical Protectorate's deep-sea platform into a performance using traditional academy cyphers combined with ones learned in her travels.

Mirrei narrated as she used light and shadow to re-enact coming home to find the empty house. Bax informed her of some of what had happened. She had found Kanto's discarded conch and notebook. She knew something had to be wrong then. The youthful spouse went nowhere without one or both.

"I tried contacting folks via conch to let them know I had arrived. My conch was inundated with messages and alerts once I got in range. It died, but not before I had caught up with some of what had happened. I tried the townhouse first and found the tracking program on Kanto's conch. I remember from Galleon City he threatened to put a tracker on me if I didn't report in more. It only stood to reason after everything he'd put a tracker on one or all of you. I opened it up, and sure enough, he had multiple trackers going."

The young woman waved a hand. Several pinpoints of light faded in. She mimed throwing away the extras lights.

"I picked the signals I thought would likely be you, and on the off chance followed it. Turns out I was right. A friend of his called while I was tracking you down, an Alexi, Aiaki, or someone. I told them I suspected you were in trouble. By the time I got here, the Imps had also arrived. I'd never seen a law enforcement response like it. This gul got the Imps here so fast including gyros, I didn't even know what was up. The tracker, though, was pointing out to sea."

A bird-like shadow flew into Mirrei's mystical frame over sailing ships.

"The Imps gyro'd me to some Findari ships near the tracker location. I had made friends with the Water Nomads during my healing work. They gave me passage back inland. I contacted them before they headed back out. I used the tracker to trace you to the rig in the middle of the ocean. The Findari refused to take their ships too close. According to them, and I concur, it was a foul accursed place, the House of Knives. The perimeter was guarded by lesser drakes, likely berserkers, and patrol boats. So, a small dive team and I went in alone in a small submersible."

With a gesture, Mirrei reconfigured the shadows into fish and whales approaching a rock formation.

"They still spotted us. The Findari engaged them in underwater combat while I went on ahead. I reached the moon pool not long after your chair hit the water and sank. I grabbed the chair and tried to swim up with you. But we started to get dragged down until the fascist lady helped. Though, I didn't know who she was. You had adapted some, but as we pulled you up, you full skin slipped into an otter and escaped your bonds. Then you became a maye and tried to swim for the depths. We barely caught you and got you back on the rig. Once we were back on the rig, Shep and Kanto called out just as the fascist lady tried to brain me. I punched her out and freed my brother grooms. Shep and I kept you watered until the paramedics arrived, while Kanto made sure she didn't get away. We almost lost you, Jhee."

Mirrei ended with a maye silhouette turning into a woman's silhouette.

"Fascist lady got you out of the water," Kanto said, "but Shep and Mirrei, they saved your life, Jhee. Though, if it hadn't been for him, your life wouldn't have been in danger in the first place."

Jhee stared at Shep and tried to feel grateful. All she felt was anger and loss. Shep refused to meet their gaze.

"Never forgive you," Kanto mouthed at him.

As grateful as Jhee was to Mirrei, a sliver of disappointment undercut it. Miramar had not appeared to welcome her. There had been no posthumous reconciliation. In her oxygen-deprived state, she had mistaken Mirrei for her mother, Miramar.

The doctor came in. "You should all go. The patient needs her rest. Come back tomorrow."

Kanto and Mirrei kept her company the next few days as she recovered. She developed a mild case of pneumonia and had to remain in the hospital. She did not see Shep. However, when she awoke in the morning, she always had the sense that someone had been there, a trace of musky cologne. She, also, sometimes found a shark's tooth or shell carved with the Lady of the Isles' likeness.

A small cask of Tranquility Gold healing wine arrived from the abbey with a note from their new permanent abbess: Umeala.

"The prioress has taken the name Umeala, and she wanted you to have this as a token of thanks for all the help you've given her with the refugees."

"Aw, wasn't that sweet of her?"

At last, Jhee was released. Mirrei and Kanto wheeled her out to the waiting transport. She thought she glimpsed Shep, but when she looked again, there was no one there. She must have been mistaken.

~

An Enthusiastic "Yes"

Jhee rested on the porch and watched Kanto and Mirrei play with the butter-flyfish in the carp pond and water feature. A dispatch from the estate of the Lady Kaydence, the Turquoise Typhoon and Kanto's formidable grand-mamere, had arrived recently. Jhee reread it.

I had my doubts about you, Jhee, but you've done well enough by him I feel confident enough to leave the most important part of my legacy aside from him: a full share of MANTEL preferred stock. Use it and him wisely.

Jhee's attention returned to the younger spouses. How different and more vibrant Mirrei appeared because the skin underneath her fur had taken on a deeper, more golden color. She had the deeper blush of health to her, whereas before, she often looked deathly pale. Together with her sun-lightened brown fur, she glowed like a star. She had also filled out enjoyably. Mirrei had acquired much healthier proportions, which no longer filled Jhee with the compulsive desire to feed her. She had all but abandoned the robes in favor of loose pullover shirt and wide-legged pants. Necklaces and bracelets of shells and beads hung in layers from her neck and wrists. Her hair had gotten long. She now sported several braids adorned with beads and shells and a feather or two. Kanto had given her a critical eye at first but had kept his own counsel about it.

The three of them sat on the porch, taking in the mid-dusk sunset. They had ordered food from a restaurant yet again. Although Jhee made an impressive sandwich and Mirrei had learned how to cook a host of more straightforward provincial dishes, none of them was an adept cook. They tried together last week to put some molecular gastronomy equipment to use. After the fire service left, they had to dine at a local eatery while the house aired out. No one said it, but without Shep, they would soon have to decide whether to hire a cook and cooking staff.

Jhee and Mirrei went through a series of finger casting exercises. Mirrei demonstrated some unorthodox methods she had learned on her journeys.

Jhee favored her stiff fingers, the ones the Ladies Auxiliary had broken. She had regained most of her physical dexterity, and the wounds had been healed in short order. The psychological sensation, though, lingered.

Kanto paid them little to no mind. He perched on the steps of the porch, conch balanced on one knee and his sketchbook on the other. He bobbed his head up and down and chewed on his finger quill.

"I've got it," he said. "Look at this. Tell me what you think."

He displayed his sketchbook to them, which contained a series of new robe designs. Kanto projected images from his conch, copies of those Mirrei had taken during her journey. He pointed to the various robes and the elements from the images that had influenced the design.

"Inspired by your travels," he said. "I wanted to incorporate your new style."

"Drej," Mirrei said. Drej was slang she had picked up on her voyage. "I love it."

She and Kanto hugged.

"It's so good to have my denye back."

"It's good to be back."

Jhee touched them both. "What made you come home? We had thought you would continue to the arctic. My note, it said for you not to come back."

"Correction. It said: *don't come home.*"

Jhee laughed uproariously. "I guess I gave myself away."

"Yeah, you did."

"You staked much on one word."

"Besides, I missed my family," Mirrei said and shrugged. "That floating clinic was very uncomfortable. I'm not crazy. Why would I continue if the choice is between going to the frozen southland with nothing but snow-mist bears and waddle birds or coming to stay with my family in a fabulous townhouse? I know which one I'd pick. If it's a choice between you guls and the waddle birds and the snow-mist bears, I'd choose you guls every time."

"Thank you. I think," Jhee said. "Does this mean I should tear up the divorce papers?"

Mirrei's smile faded. "Not quite yet, not until I come clean about all the lies I've told you."

A glimpse of movement in the tree line caught Jhee's eye. She saw a quick image of glowing eyes in the darkness. A bird flew out of the underbrush. The tree branches shook for a bit, then went still.

Kanto's hackles raised. "Do you want me to get Bax?"

"No," Jhee said. "Let Bax and Dari enjoy their time together."

Kanto stood up. "I'll deal with it myself."

"Leave him be," Mirrei said. "He's not harming anyone. You know what? Let's just go inside."

"He can't keep doing this." Kanto turned to the trees. "If you want to see us, you need to horn up and do it to our face. We have a front door. Use it. Coward."

In the sitting room, Mirrei told sea stories in the proud tradition of the Reaches to lighten the mood. "In the proud tradition of the Reaches" meant gargantuan-sized embellishment and color. Despite Mirrei's efforts, they slipped back into picking at their food listlessly.

"If this is going to be the new way of things," Mirrei said, "we need to reach a new understanding."

Jhee glared at Mirrei, then expelled a slow breath. The youthful woman was right. "I'll leave it to you and Kanto to manage. My days are free now. I'm fine with only one day completely to myself, however else you want to balance it with your various activities."

"I think I might want to volunteer at the nearby veteran's center. Don't want to horn in on Kanto's work."

"No, seriously. More help equals more geld for the Merry Maker. I could see you with a little children's health clinic across the way."

"The youth center's your path. I think I want to do a little something different. Veterans and refugees. A series of nursing or teaching schools for the Fire Folk, though there aren't as many Fire Folk here. I think I definitely want to do something more about those state schools. If you have the proof of wrongdoing by IES, I say we go for it."

"Have you spoken to the Academy about reinstating your teaching credentials?" Kanto asked.

"Not yet," Jhee answered.

"Why not? You love to teach. You love to learn. Bouncing all your ideas and exchanging notes with all those students and other colleagues. I couldn't have thought of a more natural environment for you."

"I think I need more time."

"Well, you can't just sit around the house all day. That's not the woman I married," Mirrei said.

Jhee nodded. "I'll think about it."

"Promise?"

"Promise. Now, tell me about you. I saw some recurring faces in those images. Any special face I need to note?"

"Perhaps. We'll see after I've been home a little longer and the lack of close quarters has given the ardor a chance to cool."

Kanto gave Mirrei a droll look. "You are lucky you came home when you did. We were five seconds away from turning your room into a nursery."

Mirrei's face lit up. "Really?"

Kanto gave a smug smile. "Really. We're still considering options right now. We wanted to discuss it with you first."

"I'm in. Whatever you want me to do. I can be Auntie Mirrei. I can be co-mother Mirrei. Dame Mirrei."

"I think I want to pouch. I want your name on the birth charter with ours, though. But you have to teach me how to put on one of those shadow shows first."

Mirrei left her seat and threw her arms around them. "I'm so happy for you."

"For us." Jhee held them tight. As excited as she was about children, her thoughts went to Shep somewhere outside, stalking the grounds trying to get her notice.

"Us," Mirrei amended.

A New Make

Jhee and Mirrei watched from the front row as Kanto and his team unveiled his new uniform designs to the public. A Kanto with a very swollen belly pouch came forward to take a bow with his team. Jhee and Mirrei stood and cheered when each of them came forward to take a bow.

Kanto walked them through the showcase for each design.

"A new Make for a new age," the solemn, theatrical voice-over said. "These new suits and uniforms feature the latest in concealment science with light- and sound-absorbing materials. Made of lightweight, self-wicking fabric, the marine models sport the latest in waterproofing technologies for conditions on the open seas where excess water can mean life and death. The polar editions are designed to insulate and capture body heat to prevent hypothermia. They are rated for temperatures as extreme as fifty degrees below. These desert skins can withstand and keep the troops relatively cool at some of the most extreme heat conditions. The tropical model also features some marine model waterproofing and features an antimicrobial lining specially designed to resist mildew and rot."

Kanto further regaled them with why his team had made individual design choices and the various cutting techniques they used to make the uniforms easy to mass produce with minimal waste, yet still maintaining maximum functionality.

"Now, these are my personal contributions and the ones I'm most proud of: the dress uniforms. Because when they are parading around for us civvies, they must look top line. Nothing says that while they are keeping us safe, they can't also look good."

"Amazing," Mirrei said. "My denye helped make all these. Who would have thought it?"

"You did amazing work," Jhee said. "I'm sorry I ever doubted you."

Kanto smiled and blushed. "No worries."

The three of them walked hand in hand through the exhibit.

"Ah, Justicar," an authoritative voice said.

"Chief Justicar," Jhee said. "Justicar no longer. I am merely a regular citizen now."

"Hm? I was given to believe you were reinstated."

"Not that I know of."

"Odd. I viewed the registers this morning, and your name was clearly listed. Perhaps it was an error."

"Must be."

"Have you tried recently? Why not check now?"

Jhee pulled out her conch and tried to access the judicial archives. The "Welcome Back Justicar" screen displayed as if she had never left. "Well, quench me in the quiet."

"You see. Right as rain. Now, if your lovely household doesn't mind, I'd like to speak to you a bit about a new training program we are starting at the Academy."

Jhee and Chief Justicar Elver walked on further. "How can I be of service, Chief Justicar?"

"Allow me to first apologize about that business with the review. We had to do our due diligence, what with the seriousness of the allegations against you and your family."

Jhee put on her official-at-court face. It no longer felt as natural as it once did. It had been so long since she had to don it. "Of course, Chief Justicar."

The Chief Justicar lowered her voice, "Given the way this 'Medea' business turned out, you were definitely in the right of matters at Tranquility Bridge. This upcoming trial will be a disaster."

Jhee could not believe what she was hearing. Was the Chief Justicar praising her for the killing of Lady Bathsheba? She set her mouth in a thin line. She clenched her teeth together, knowing she was only mere moments away from telling the Chief Justicar exactly what she could do with her credentials.

"Our extra thanks for the discreet way you handled the abbey matter. We had not understood the choice until we received your full record. You were right to be concerned about the scandal and give the vizier a choice. We see now that offering her a choice was the only proper action to take under the circumstances."

"Choice?"

"Of a messy trial or quiet suicide. It was best for everybody. We got to avoid an imperial scandal, and the abbey could keep her Imperial pension. When that member of the Imperial family came to me and explained to me the situation, I realized it was the only course you could have taken. The debt of gratitude we owe you."

"The Imperial Family?"

"Yes, and your mentor, the honorable Jeja Marpele. They both backed up your full account entirely and said that you had been sworn to secrecy. You had asked her advice. How you simply wanted to spare the Empire a messy trial. For which, you have my eternal thanks and that of the entire judiciary. Between the mistaken prisoner and the many Imperials implicated, this Architect trial has already been a profound embarrassment to law enforcement and threatened to tear the entire palace apart. Again, my gratitude; however, if you ever tamper with judicial records again, there will be no more second chances and no quarter."

The capital's lone Justicar save herself, Nevis, approached Jhee after Jhee and the Chief Justicar finished their chat. Her colleague briefly flashed a six-pointed Star Chamber emblem pinned to the inside of her robe. "Delicate work with Vivyan-Rin. How would you like a chance at calling all the Architects to account? She was only one, the Architect of Knives. We believe scientists on both sides were secretly in contact and working together. They seem intent on taking up where the Doombringer nihilists left off. Think about it. Get back to me."

Nevis slipped away, leaving Jhee with her consternation. At the far edge of the crowd, she saw Shep clearly, as did Kanto and Mirrei. They quickly came over to her and took her arms. Shep raised his hand in a tentative greeting.

"We've got to talk to him some time," Mirrei said.

"No," Kanto said.

"Why is there forgiveness for me but not for him? Was what we both did really so different?"

Jhee turned her attention to Mirrei.

"Of course, we know why you would want to forgive him," Kanto retorted.

"Hey, keep it nice, would you? I'm on your side, remember. I had a foolish crush. It's long over now. We still need to have a serious talk, Jhee, about him and about me. I'm all about our family now. And until we divorce him, so is he. We have to decide one way or the other because this right here is not working. If you don't want him around, cut him off. If not, we need to come up with a better arrangement than this nightmare."

〜

A Wanderer Returns

Jhee, Kanto, and Mirrei gathered in the sitting room, going over the backgrounds of prospective birthing helpers for the baby. Kanto examined swatches and furniture for the nursery. Jhee projected one profile for a pair of caregivers in front of Mirrei.

"How about these two?"

Mirrei gestured through their background, then threw out their file. "No."

"What was wrong with those two?"

"Nothing if you are a fan of human trafficking." Jhee stared at her with consternation. "See here. Doublefire Caregivers has a history of ethical and labor violations as well as hiring and exploiting refugees and undocumented Fire Folk."

"I hadn't realized that. Are all the employment and birthing helper agencies corrupt?"

"Not entirely. Be more careful about which agencies you are getting the nannies from. Look, really look into their backgrounds."

"I thought I was."

"Let me see this list. No. No. No. You have to be better at checking out the agencies they come from."

"Is there a list?"

"Yes. The Blue Waters Foundation and the Forging Forgiveness Project put out a list of ethical labor agencies, including nanny services. They rate various employment agencies on their human rights record."

"See. Therefore I left it to you," Kanto said.

"I can't save every starfish. I can only ensure our servants are sourced from a reputable and ethical agency."

Mirrei winked. Jhee could not have believed how much she had changed and grown in such a brief time. She must admit it was very attractive. Mirrei had also filled out nicely, her figure now more on the traditional side than dainty. She no longer felt as if you might break her if you held her too close. Jhee leaned over and gave her a kiss. Kanto cleared his throat.

"What do you guls think of this layout?" He placed his conch flat for them to see. "I'm thinking one of these two color schemes."

"We want the crib over here so we can get the positive energy from the western wind and waves."

Jhee browsed at the layout and moved the crib. "No, we want the crib over here so we can watch the water feature and the sunrises while we are nursing."

"You are both wrong. We want the crib precisely where I put it, or else everyone who goes into or out of the room will trip over it and wake up the pouchlings. You want to nurse while looking at the sun or getting positive vibes? Move the drench nursing chair. What's wrong with you two? I thought you two were supposed to be the practical ones?"

"What about these two?" Mirrei brought up another caregiver profile.

Kanto grimaced. "Blessed Makers, what are they wearing?"

"We are not hiring them for their sense of fashion."

"You're not. I suppose I could put a detailed outfit list for them to follow."

"Are you telling me you don't already have a series of drej baby jumpers already planned?"

Kanto plopped his sketchbook on the table and opened it to pages of baby onesies. "Plenty. I'd be constructing them now if you two would let me."

The alarm on all their conchs went off. "Nutrient up."

Kanto sighed and made a face. "Do I have to?"

"Yes," Mirrei said. "We put you on a strict dietetic regimen with a strict supplement schedule."

"I forgot once. Once."

"You forgot 'once' a day for two tides and nearly passed out."

Jhee pulled out the chart. And looked at the nutrient schedule. "Your turn."

"Done." Mirrei leaped to her feet. "You've got two choices. Kelp or seaweed?"

"I'm just on bed rest. I'm not an invalid. I can make my own snacks," Kanto said. Mirrei folded her arms. "Kelp."

"One nutrient blend and kelp salad coming up."

Jhee pulled out the pill organizer and lined up the proper dose of prenatal vitamins for her and Kanto to take. "It will be over soon. The appointment's all made at the breaching center. They have a lovely water breaching room where you can pass on the sac to Mirrei."

"Then she gets to be the one everyone's hovering over."

"I remember there was a time you would have relished being the center of my attention."

"I still do."

The water chimes sounded. They heard the servants go to answer it. A moment later, Mirrei came to the door of the room, bearing Kanto's snacks. She seemed dazed.

"Who was at the door?"

Mirrei looked at the floor. "Don't be mad."

The sitting room door opened wider. Shep stepped inside. He gave a sheepish smile.

Kanto rose from his chair. "What is he doing here?"

"Kanto, no." Jhee made him sit down. "You can't have any stress right now."

Shep tugged at his arm hairs. "You look well. I expect you will breach soon."

"What do you want?" Jhee asked.

Shep eyes were wet with tears. "I want to come home, Jhee."

23

———————

~

A Case Argued

"You've got some nerve." Kanto tried to rise from his chair again. Jhee stopped him.

Jhee stalked over to the door and forced Shep out into the foyer. Mirrei went inside with the snacks and closed the door.

"Is this your home now? Or just a place for you to breeze into between bouts of getting your head bashed in and rutting with deviants?"

"I deserved that."

"First Makers' blood, you did. Do you need money?"

"Your allowance has been more than generous."

"Then what?"

"I miss my family, Jhee."

"Or do you just have nowhere to go with no one else willing to take your raggedy tail in?"

"I've been staying at the veteran's hostel at first. Then Sharlet's been letting me stay with her and her family. I've been going to counseling."

"Good for you." Jhee turned away, then turned back. "I begged you to confide in me. I begged you to get counseling. You threw your family away for a fight and a fling with a woman who turned out to be a psychopath. If she hadn't, would you even be here right now?"

"She meant nothing to me. I know I messed up, Jhee. I'm sorry."

"Sorry? You're sorry. Fine. Apology accepted. I'll double your allowance. So long as you never come here again."

"I don't want more money. I want my family back."

"You don't deserve your family back."

"What a world this would be if we all got what we deserved."

Jhee yelled in frustration. She stalked to the veranda entrance. He followed and placed a hand on her shoulder.

"Why?" she whispered.

"I don't know why."

"Bilge and cockle drivel. Was she that irresistible? Did you love her?"

"I love *you*, Jhee."

"What do you want me to do with that? Loving me wasn't enough to keep you faithful. Loving me is never enough. Loving me, raising me, wasn't enough to keep mamere and babere from drowning themselves. And it wasn't enough to make Jay stay around once they were gone."

"She meant nothing to me."

"Then, why? I have a way to get the truth out of you." Jhee rolled up her sleeves. She formed the gesture for the first sequence of a compulsion cypher. "They haven't geased you. I'll have the truth out of you one way or the other. You know I can."

Shep dropped his hands to his sides. "To know if I could. It was precisely because she meant nothing to me. I would know, and then I could walk away. It was after the raid, I felt pumped, on top of the world. I wanted nothing more than to be with you, but you were with Kanto *again*."

"So, this is my fault?"

"It's our fault. She was like a viper in my ear. It's no secret our sex life has been less than satisfying for years. When I met Kanto, I thought I had found the perfect solution for everybody. It turned out to be the perfect solution for everyone but me."

"I didn't want a second husband. I was fine with our marriage as it was."

"Were you, Jhee? Could you have been once we got to court and the Imperials' intrigues and scrutiny abounded? A place full of the conniving who all wanted to know about the status of your house."

"I would have dealt with it."

"You would have done what you've always done, sublimate your needs to mine or your duty. No matter what you wanted."

"You brought him in. Insisted."

"And you did what you usually did, your duty. Until you didn't. I'm not sure if I thought it all the way through how it would truly make me feel. When I got jealous, I thought I could plow through it. At first, you were so standoffish to him. I thought it would be a few months, maybe a year. You constantly announced your commitment to offloading him once we reached the capital. I thought that would be it. You'd have your needs met, and we might get children out of it. Then once we got to the capital, it would just be the two of us again, possibly plus pristine children. Except it wasn't. It backfired. You grew fond of him, of both of them. You came in with Mirrei in tow, and then it became clear neither one was going away."

When Jhee refused to do her duty, she nearly broke the Far Reaches. Her duty had been to marry a Crag Hall heir; instead, she eloped with Shep.

"You should have said something," Jhee whispered.

"What? I owed you, Jhee. You don't think I know that. You saved my life. Gave me a loving home. I should have been grateful. You deserved to have your needs met."

"'What a world this would be if we all got what we deserved?'" Jhee quoted. "This whole arrangement was your idea."

"I know. It wasn't supposed to be like this. I wasn't supposed to be here!"

"What?"

"I chose him because I didn't want you to be alone after I…"

"After you what? Left me?" Jhee finished. Shep's deflated posture and inability to meet her eyes seemed to confirm the assumption. Then she looked closer at his trembling hands. Memories from when he first brought Kanto around came to the fore. In preparation for their relocation to the capital, he had given away many of his war souvenirs and keepsakes from his sisters. He had been preparing to leave her, but not by walking out. "After you killed yourself."

"Yes," he sobbed.

Emotion seized up Jhee's throat. She rocked back on her heels. Despite her near-obsessive inability to let a mystery go, to forgo the chance to solve a puzzle, if Shep had gone through with killing himself, she would have failed to solve the one puzzle that meant the most to her. He had needed her, and she had been so absorbed in her job and her duty she almost missed it before it was too late. Had she been too quick to lay the blame solely at his feet? "You—How—"

"Throw myself into the sea for one last dive."

Drowning. Like Jhee's parents who had filled their pockets with rocks and swam out to Wailing Point. Like Ghele. Like Gwyn and Gloriana. Jhee wanted to flee, then spun back to face him. "The sea," she whispered.

"I know. You understand the lure of the Storm Child and the ones beneath the waves. I've seen you gaze over the vast waters of the sea folk's domain. I've known what was in your mind. To be one with the sea, to rejoin your family under the ocean. I tried more than once. I adapted. Gills. That's when I realized how extreme the changes were, what they did to me could bring about. Ursula talked me back from the brink."

~

The Unlikely Heiress and The Diving Boy

Jhee reeled, grasping at the veranda's balustrade for equilibrium. She scraped her hands against the gritty stone. The painful abrasions and the solidity of the material grounded her.

Shep took her hands and performed a minor arcane field dressing.

"When I met with the Captain the night he died, he was so bitter, resentful. He railed against his wife, his situation. He was a Consort Regent, and he hated the woman he married. I remember how much he had adored her in the beginning. He thought he would be fine with it. In the end, he resented her. They were full of nothing but venom for each other. She found him disgusting, and he found her vile. I didn't want that for us, Jhee. I wasn't sure how to stop it."

Jhee pulled her hands away. "And you thought Medea would fix us, is that it?"

"Not us, me maybe. I don't know. She tricked me. I came home from the raid that night. She had filled my ears with venom before that. How I was a burden, unneeded surplus. I had no role in the family anymore. I had been replaced by a younger, more handsome man. Then afterward, she was full of compliments. But it was what I wanted to hear. How useful and great I was. I alone had protected my family."

"Lobster drivel. I want to believe you. I might believe you if you hadn't already betrayed me with Miramar. What was your excuse then?"

"I was dumb, cocky, seastruck. I had gone to Mai, where I proposed and confessed my love. She laughed in my face. When I lost the lottery, I had thought it might change things. She rebuffed me again. You think I would have learned. Years later, when you and I seemed to have some semblance of happiness, Mai visited me. Some part of me still loved her then. I thought she realized she felt the same. It turned out what she cared about was that she lost. To you. When I realized that, it killed whatever feelings I had left over for her."

Miramar's mention snapped Jhee back into hostility. She clapped her hands slowly. "Are you done? You've had your say. Now what?"

"Please, Jhee."

The sting in her hands paled compared to the one in her heart. "Was Mirrei's crush only one way?"

"I already told you so, Jhee."

"Once a cheater. Always a cheater. I don't think I can ever trust you again."

"You can. I love you, Jhee. You believe you know about secret longing. For as long as you have loved me, I've loved you longer."

"A love so deep and abiding when Mai crooked her finger, you went running right back to her bed."

"Do you remember what you were like back then, Jhee? Once we came back from our newlyweds' holiday, you changed. You started treating me as she had, like a drench servant, a dirty little secret to be hidden away. If I wanted to be treated like that, I might as well have stayed with her. That's what she offered at first. She had to marry Crag Hall, but that was no reason for us to stop our relationship. She'd set me up some place nice and come visit me when she could. Sound familiar? I was her grimy secret, too. The hugs and the smiles and affections went away the moment we got anywhere near her family or anyone who 'mattered.' I think I was five minutes away from being sneaked in the servants' entrance when her parents weren't looking. Her family may have had lower social status than yours, but they were ambitious. Their daughter, the pride of their family, would not marry some diver boy who still stunk of the Brine. When her family refused suit, I knew it was only a matter of time before I lost her. My losing the lottery wasn't the whirlpool of fate. It was the Mitsus getting rid of an unwanted suitor."

"You two deserved each other."

"No, you two deserved each other. You're right. Miramar was passionate and funny and all about living life to its fullest. But she wasn't you. It could get fatiguing, keeping up with the Mai show. She was always on."

"Don't I know it." Jhee faced out into the night and focused on the water feature. "Once we returned from our holiday, several people almost gleefully informed me you'd been conscripted. After proudly declaring our marriage, I was berated for my stupidity at being taken in by an ambitious schemer who had only married me to get himself out of military service. In my insecurity, I believed them."

Shep moved close enough she felt his warmth behind her. "On some level, they were right. My plan was to hop a smuggler's boat out of the isles. I hadn't gone to the academy to woo you, but to say goodbye. Though, I may have had some vague notion of you coming with me. When I gazed longingly at your home, my sisters thought it was envy. It was you. I always wondered about the pretty girl who took a stick and chased away the bullies with me and then needed someone to sit with her while the search team looked for her family."

Some youths from the Bracken family had decided to filch the catch a puny boy had been set to watch. Jhee had come upon the outnumbered boy trying to fend them off. Later, after the ferry accident, when everyone else was preoccupied, he made sure she wasn't alone. She used to think him a mute until he started appearing every time she and Miramar turned around during their early adventures.

Jhee faced Shep with a sharp turn then touched his jaw lightly. "You were Pip Shark, the gangly kid with the dirty skin always shadowing me and Mai?"

"Long after the rescue parties had stopped, I went out to the site of the wreck. I dove and dove until I recovered a turtle-shell locket. It was your sister's, and you used to wear it when she let you. I left it on your window."

"That was you?" Jhee's words hitched as she remembered finding the locket and presenting it to her parents. The only other trace of Ghele they found was a shoe. Having the necklace for Ghele's memorial had brought her family such peace. She clasped Shep's forearm for support without thinking.

Shep steadied her, then placed his hands on her shoulders. "They didn't start calling me Pip Shark, Patchy the Pip Shark actually, until after that. Because of those dives, I caught pneumonia and reef rash. I was sickly, a runt, for a while, barely able to help my family, a burden. Then my glandular bloom happened. Our first meeting was you chasing away my bullies with a stick. Yes, we met while I was bringing in the family nets, right before those bullies jumped me. The story you like to tell of our first meeting with me laying bounty at your feet wasn't. That was a carefully staged meet to get your attention.

"You never noticed me until I filled out. I mooned over you for years as the skinny diver boy with the temporary skin condition. Then I got sleek and thought you'd notice me. You didn't. She did. I tried to wait for you. Finally, I got tired. Miramar was as fun as she was unapologetic in her interest. It felt nice to be the one pursued for a switch. When I won that swim meet, my social currency went up. When I dated Miramar, my social currency went up. At last you noticed, but by then, we were Miramar and Shep. I became as much a prize for her as she was for me. If we broke up, that went away."

"I noticed. Mai noticed you too. I decided to step aside. I thought I was being noble. The last thing I wanted to do was quarrel with my friend over a boy. She usually won anyway. She wanted it more. Miramar always wanted it more. No matter what it was. It meant more to her, and with her demanding family, why not step aside and allow her something she clearly wanted more than I did? My ambivalence made me doubt if I'd be a satisfying partner or show you the affection you'd want. No, she would make the better romantic partner for you in every measure, so why risk our friendship."

"Did it ever occur to you to get my input? Or declare an interest and let me decide?"

"You would have never chosen me over her unless you had no other choice."

"How do you know? You never asked. Jhee, I didn't think you cared until a jealous Miramar is accusing me of flirting with you and exploiting your crush."

"I thought I had hidden it. I didn't want the situation to be awkward."

Shep roared with laughter. "It was nothing but awkward!"

A mixture of laughter and sobs overtook Jhee.

"Thank you," she whispered once the reaction passed.

"We can't keep doing this." While Jhee had raised her voice, she tempered her tone with humility and compassion, "I have nothing more to give you. I've got two spouses, a brace of pouchlings on the way, and a new judicial division to set up. Shep, I can't manage you too."

"It doesn't have to be permanent," Shep said. "I'm asking for a chance to earn my way back as a member of this family. Besides counseling, I've been taking child-rearing courses and household management and jealousy exercises. I've looked into trust breach services and infidelity reconciliation. I've been doing the work. Jhee, I screwed up. I know you've been looking into caregivers. Well, I've been working on getting a caregiver certificate—from a reputable and ethical agency, of course. I'll work part-time and maintain the same living situation. I'll stay with Sharlet for now. And if at some point—after I've earned it, if you let me, if you want me too, I'll move back in. Whatever it is you need me to do. I'll do it."

"Of course. Sharlet always lands on her feet, doesn't she?" Jhee shook her head, then continued, "It's not my decision alone. You didn't just hurt me or breach my trust. We are a family unit. I'll discuss it with Mirrei and Kanto. It's them you need to convince. I'll abide by whatever they decide. Plead your case to them, not me, but after the breach. Kanto can't have any stress right now."

Jhee withdrew inside with as much dignity as she could muster. In the foyer, she fled to her bedchamber. Her door creaked, and she realized Shep had followed. He waited beyond the threshold. As she went to close the door, he blocked her with a firm, gentle hand on the main paneling. Shep brought his hand down to cover hers and stroked the back of her hand.

"Don't. I barely remember a time when I wasn't in love with you. My feelings for you unmoor me in a way nothing else does. You know it, and that's why I can't have you around."

Jhee freed her hand and sought to close the door by pushing higher on the edge. Shep rubbed his head against her hand. Despite herself, she brushed her knuckle along his facial scar.

"Love unmoors us all, my Lady," Shep said and cupped her face. They kissed. He pressed against her, letting her feel his desire.

This was the Shep she hated, the one she never got enough of, the one to whom she was always vulnerable. Jhee wanted to push him away and scream for him to leave the bedchamber. The action though between her mind and the execution, turned into them removing each other's robes.

She dreamed of that night, of them meeting alone. Of him telling her, she was the one he truly loved, of them making love, and finding a priest the next morning.

Jhee awoke before Shep did and went to work on her orrery. A minor noble and divers' son not far removed from Briny Town had married the plain daughter of a wealthy family never meant to inherit. This had been the opposite of how Jhee thought this would work out so many years ago. Kanto would be her First and the career man, while Shep would be the stay-at-home caregiver. Mirrei was a world traveler, bolder than them all, while Jhee nested.

~

New Rules

Shep awoke to an empty bed. Mirrei's day. He had to leave soon. With a slow sweep, he took in the extra room details. It showed the younger spouses' influence everywhere, now. From lacy window treatments to lilacs, the room contained little flourishes and decorative touches Jhee never considered. Whatever room she designated as hers had always been laid out functionally and pragmatically. A little chair next to her desk held Kanto's lute. The two Findari green and gold polyglass mosaics and a seashell doll were likely Mirrei's contribution.

After morning push-ups and sit-ups, Shep meditated for a few minutes. He had stopped frequenting the berserker gyms and the arena. His calm had to come from other means. He had so much work to do on himself and on regaining the household's trust. There was still also stamping out the last of Medea and Hammad's operation. Even if Shep had wanted to with Hammad gone and Medea in jail, the entire operation was in disarray.

The thought of Hammad still out there wound Shep up, so he meditated again before he slipped from Jhee's room.

Kanto caught Shep sneaking out. "Let's tame that mane of yours."

Shep helped Kanto down to the salon where two green blended concoctions awaited with a note from Mirrei, which read, "Pick one."

With a disgusted face, Kanto downed one bottle. He pushed the other toward Shep. "Breakfast with me."

Once Shep choked it down, he asked, "What is this we're eating?"

"Mirrei's green drinks. Don't ask for more specifics than that. I've got some maye steaks we can throw on the grill once Mirrei goes to work." Kanto paused, then straightened his posture. "So, she's taken you back in?"

"Subject to your and Mirrei's approval."

"You brought me in as a second for when your tail screws up. I'm fulfilling my role. Guess what? You screwed up imperially. You and I need to work something out."

"I know I need to do right by her and by you. Is there anything I do to make up for what I did?"

"Yes." Kanto moved into his space. He raised his gaze to Shep and stood there in challenge. "Unbreak her heart."

"I wish I could."

Kanto lowered himself and his swollen belly into the barber's chair. "You coward."

Shep rested his hands on the countertop and hung his head. "That I am. I never claimed to be otherwise. When I mocked you being a soldier, I had no right. I jeered those principled refusers—those who objected to serving—as loudly as anyone; meanwhile, I prayed I'd never have to join."

The young man rubbed his hand over his pouch in a circle. "Medea tried to get to me too while you were in custody. 'Surely, it must have occurred to you, Bright Harmony, that maybe, you had not won her over. She was simply biding her time until your grandmamere died. That, of course, was the deal she made with your grandmere. Marry you and become her heir. Now that she has inherited, she can return to her original plan of seeing you married off to another.'"

"I don't know what else I can say."

"Shep, the pouchlings are moving. Do you want to feel?" Kanto asked.

Shep's breath caught. "May I?"

Kanto placed Shep's hand on his breach pouch. The pouchlings undulated under Shep's hand like a wave. A fresh life wave on waters made indivisible. A smile twitched on Shep's lips.

"Do you feel that?" Kanto asked.

"I do," Shep said, tears welling up in him.

"It's not just the movement. It's the fear that comes with the knowledge you're ushering another of the Makers' creations into the world. That they're depending on you."

"Yes," Shep said, unable to hold back the tears.

"You feel that, too, don't you? The protective instinct?"

"Yes."

"The certainty you'd destroy anyone who dared harm them?"

Shep nodded. "Fight. Protect. Survive. But more than anything, protect."

Kanto removed Shep's hand from his breach pouch. "These pouchlings matter more than any of us. I won't let Jhee's weakness for you jeopardize them. Hurt this family again, there will be no reprieves or pleading your case to her. There won't even be a body. Do we understand each other?"

"If I hurt this family again, I'll do it myself," Shep paused, then added, "denme."

"Denye," Kanto replied.

Kanto held out his hands to Shep. They clasped forearms, then lightly touched their foreheads together enough for their esca to brush. Then Kanto seated him for a shave and haircut.

~

After the breach and once they were certain Mirrei's pouching had taken, Jhee allowed Shep to return and speak with the rest of the household. Shep made his case plain. Mirrei and Kanto did likewise. They were civil, and Jhee contented herself to a limited role as scribe and arbiter.

Shep would be taken off the marriage charter. His name would not be on the birth charter either. They would revisit the issue if they had more children. He had no legal standing regarding the children. Not co-father, sire, or father of record. They would be allowed to call him uncle. In the case of any calamity befalling Jhee, Kanto, and Mirrei, only then would Shep be named guardian. Shep did not like it at first, but he thought it was fair and more than he deserved. She wrote up the new agreement which their advocates made official later. They still brought in another nanny to complete the pair.

24

———

~

A Friendly Game

They received an Imperial lunch invite from Kanto's friend Aiaku. It had a handwritten note. "Not one of those luncheons. Please, come. Whole family welcome."

The invite named them all. Jhee wanted to refuse anyway. She had had enough of the Imperials, their invites, and their intrigues.

"He did save our lives," Kanto said in the transport on the way to the yacht.

Aiaku had mobilized an amphibious rescue operation for them at the House of Knives when Mirrei told him Kanto was in trouble. Her husbands may not have escaped Medea's clutches without it. That counted for much with Jhee. What she feared was the hidden cost attached.

"To which he will expect no end of gratitude," Jhee replied.

"He's not like that."

"We'll see." Jhee patted Kanto's hand at his sad face. "If you say it, I take you at your word. I trust you. If he is your friend, he is my friend."

"Given how you treat your friends, Jhee. Perhaps it's best if you treat him like he's a royal."

Once the Imperial yacht docked, Kanto's friend Aiaku greeted them along with the same porter from the Summer Sojourn.

Aiaku held out his hands to Kanto, and they clasped forearms. "I'm glad you accepted."

"How could I not, Lord Aiaku?"

"Please, call me Aiaku-xan."

While this still meant they were on an external name basis, "xan" was a diminutive which denoted friendship and informality. Aiaku greeted the rest of their family in a similar, warm manner. They walked slowly and leisurely from the dock to the atrium, a suitably covered place for them to dine more or less privately.

"As you wish, Aiaku-xan. I hear we have you to thank for our timely rescue."

"Think nothing of it. I account you, Kanto, as a good and true friend of mine."

"Is that to which we owe some of our other wonderful fortunes?" Jhee asked.

"Not entirely." They reached the atrium doors. Aiaku paused with his hands on the handles. "My denbe would like to meet you both."

Kanto gave a sad smile. "Our family needs us. My situation has changed. I have other responsibilities now."

"I gathered." Aiaku inclined his head towards Mirrei's swollen belly pouch and smiled. "Please, I would still like our *denbes* to meet."

Jhee nodded to Kanto.

"All right," he whispered.

Aiaku pushed open the doors. A male in a mobility-assistance chair sat beside a stuffed high-back chair. Jhee heard the rattling of a dice cup. A moment later, a dark, smooth-skinned hand appeared from behind the high-backed chair and slammed it on the table to reveal the results of the throw.

"Amazing, you win again, Aeolus." Lady Amani peered from behind the chair at the newcomers. She raised the dicing cup and shook it. "Would you care for a game, Justicar?"

Jhee stopped dead in her tracks. Lady Amani set aside the cup and approached her. Jhee regained her wits and made a traditional bow. "High lady."

Lady Amani gave Jhee the polite acknowledgment of an equal. Jhee stayed in the bow, dumbfounded. "It's customary for you to rise now."

"Of course," Jhee stammered. "High Lady."

"Amani. And I may call you Jhee?"

"Yes. Yes."

"This must be your lovely family. Star Mirror, Bright Harmony, and Dawn Wolf. Did I get it right?"

"Yes."

"Aiaku, have the servants get the Justicar's household some refreshments. They must be tired after their lengthy journey. I have things I wish to discuss with the Justicar."

"Yes, dear wife."

Aiaku escorted Jhee's household to the table. Amani had already started walking. Jhee hurried to catch up.

"Have you seen the hedge maze yet?" Amani asked.

"Not in full light."

"Then that shall be our first stop." Amani slipped her arm in Jhee's. They entered the hedge maze. "I will show you right to my favorite spot. At various times, one or the other of the Imperial branch's job is to see to the upkeep or make their own additions to the maze. This one was my contribution. Do you like it?"

"It's very lovely."

"Do you know what I love so much about it? One feature of this part of the hedge maze is a charm against eavesdropping."

"I hadn't known that."

"Now, you do. Mauled to death by a wild animal. I imagine with delight it was a rather painful way to go. Please, tell me she suffered."

"High Lady?"

"You're supposed to be calling me Amani. You have my sincerest gratitude. Lady Bathsheba was a rabid dog who needed to be put down. I see you are too polite to take such pleasure in such things. I had tried to see the deed done myself, but my hands were tied. We shall speak no more of it. Now that I know who had protected her, I can openly express my thanks. I tried to declare my support at the Fancy Foam Showcase. It wasn't until much later I learned you thought I was declaring myself the architect of your misery, not your ally. Didn't you wonder how you got released so quickly?"

"Yes, but I thought perhaps my mentor or the captain...." Jhee trailed off thinking about Captain Odo and Ursula. The Captain had outright said he hadn't.

"I thought I was wrong about backing you when you capitulated. Nice to know I wasn't. I know value when I see it. I must thank your man and Aiaku for helping me realize my mistake. Finding out who saved Bathsheba from me was a delightful bonus. As you learned, her support had a long tail. It needed to be to protect her from me. Also, don't worry about Zaria and her brutes. Without the Architect to back her up, you seem more than capable of dealing with her. She'll slink off. I'll take care of it if you want me to, but it will be best if you do so yourself."

Jhee glanced back towards the atrium and Aeolus, the man in the mobility chair. "Lady Bathsheba's handiwork?"

"Because she supplied exotic mood adjusters, Lady Bathsheba could always finagle an invitation to events, especially those teeming with younger spouses. While there, she socialized with the imperials and indulged in her favorite pastime, corrupting youths. We're not sure what she gave him. Something to calm his nerves? Something to make him play better? It took days to find Aeolus. After so long, there was only so much even the best healers could do."

"Amani, I don't know what to say."

"Thank you would be a start."

"Thank you." Jhee thought about it a moment, then added, "I don't know how I can repay you."

"Consider this a gift. Also, the offer Aiaku extended to your husband does not just apply to him. I could see a place for you here. I'm much more selective than others. My spouses number only two: Aeolus and Aiaku."

"I am honored, truly."

"Ah, 'no' then. I get it. However, would you be willing to be my partner for cards and gammancala? I would like to continue where our last game left off. I'm willing to stipulate that you folded in error. If you would be amenable, I would like to extend an offer to join my dicing club. We meet twice a week on different imperial isles."

"That would be acceptable."

"Lovely. Now let's return to the atrium and get some of those refreshments I promised. You fancy mango punch if I remember correctly. No Dundarian sea worms, thank the Makers. I ate them as a gag once, and everyone became convinced they were my favorite dish. I have them put out now as a prank to see who is actually foolish enough to eat them."

Jhee and Amani returned to the atrium and ate lunch with their spouses. Afterward, Amani and Jhee retired to play cards. "Jhee, where do you stand on the wall?"

"Nowhere anymore."

Amani took a long sip of punch and dealt their cards. "It's an unworkable mess. Those of us who oppose it must play the long game. The wall folks may have won for now, but we have planted the seeds which will grow. It starts with reaching out to them and the Fire Folk, knowing them, knowing what they want. For when the day comes to reconcile with them."

"You're a One Waters reformist?" Jhee said, wondering if she should have stated it so bluntly. Jhee picked up her cards and arranged her hand.

"Nothing so extreme." Amani looked at her cards, "But, perhaps with the little shakeup your little discovery caused, we might make a little forward progress."

"Instead of fifty serious candidates for the throne," Jhee said after she drew a card, "you are one of thirty, forty."

Lady Amani discarded. "Likely twenty-five or even twenty when it's all said and done. And lest you think me thoroughly altruistic, I did a thorough audit of your holdings before making my household offer."

"Why give the provenance back to the Halfmoons of Haddondeep? Why not use it yourself?"

"To blackmail Zaria? I've poked that bear enough for now." Amani laid down her cards, having made her trick. "They need my support. She and the Princess Regent leave me alone as long as I don't interfere or make a play for the throne myself."

Jhee made her matches as well. "But the Halfmoons are now back in the eligibility for the Sea Throne. How does that help you?"

Lady Amani smiled and took another sip of punch. "The Halfmoons have nowhere near enough support to be genuine contenders. They are just another vote."

This hand Jhee dealt. "Voters who owe you a debt of gratitude."

Amani arched an eyebrow and discarded a card.

Jhee surveyed her hand. It was workable at best. "Like me."

"No." Lady Amani laid her hand on Jhee's wrist when she reached for another playing card. "You owe me nothing. I still feel it is I who owe you."

Jhee nodded.

Amani returned to a more relaxed posture. "The Princess Regent doesn't quite have the electors needed to win the vote. Any scandal can derail her negotiations or cost her the votes she needs to ascend to the throne proper. Had she kept her temper in check, perhaps she would have won you over."

"I've heard she's quite charming when she wants to be."

"She is." Lady Amani took another sip of mango punch and studied Jhee. "From the runt of the litter to the inheritor of three, or is it four houses."

Jhee gazed up at the Maker Sphere. "I'd trade each to have my brothers and sisters back."

"Just so. All military?"

"Only two," Jhee replied.

"I must have been misinformed. Thank you and your family for your sacrifices on behalf of the Empire, regardless."

A cog clicked into place in Jhee's mind. Her mouth dropped open once she puzzled out with whom she had been dicing and playing cards. "Amani? General Amaneri Adama Arie. Amani, the ever-victorious."

"If only."

"Gwyn, one of my sisters, served with you on the Blue Sword. She was there when you…"

"Mutinied."

"Saved the ship and its crew from a captain who had lost her nerve mid-battle. Gwyn admired you greatly."

~

Next Move

Mirrei blocked the sitting room's closed double-doors. "Now, remember, you said you would keep an open mind?" she said.

Jhee, Kanto, and Shep passed looks between each other as they waited in the foyer to be allowed back into the sitting room.

"Just let us see it already," Jhee said.

"Okay," Mirrei said. She threw wide the sitting room doors and stepped aside.

Their full household, Jhee, Kanto, Mirrei, and Shep, surveyed the new arrangement of chairs and furniture in the sitting room. Mirrei waited, lips parted for them to speak. Irina placed a fluffed throw pillow on the relocated couch. Off to the side, Bax stood cap in hand while Dari supported herself with a standing roller.

Kanto entered the rearranged sitting room first. He inspected every relocated bit of furniture and new addition with much ceremony. Findari wall hangings replaced several military souvenirs. Cords and plugs had been secured or concealed. His performing seat had been positioned in between Shep and Jhee's two cushioned chairs with hers now facing the fireplace while Shep's remained off to the side. At last, he walked to the rocker chair that occupied the performing seat's former location.

"No," Kanto declared.

"You said you'd keep an open mind," Mirrei cried.

"I did," Kanto said.

Jhee and Shep gazed Sphere-ward. She sighed, knowing this just meant longer before she might be able to sit down for a relaxing read and some tea. Kanto strode to the performance seat and started dragging it. They rushed forward to stop him.

"You shouldn't be moving furniture so soon after pouching," Shep said.

"Neither should Mirrei, but you didn't stop her," Kanto replied.

Mirrei rubbed her stomach, now swollen even more by the nearly due birthing sac. "Correction: Bax and Irina moved the furniture. Dari and I supervised."

Speaking of the servants and other vital parts of their home, Bax, Dari, and Irina had hustled from the sitting room, closing the door behind them.

"There," Kanto declared again. While they had been distracted, he had swapped Shep's chair for the performing seat. The cushioned chairs faced the fireplace. Now, though, each husband's designated seat flanked hers.

Mirrei nodded, then Shep, and finally, Jhee. They guided Mirrei to the rocker. Everyone else took their seats engaged in their favorite relaxing activities: Jhee reading, Kanto playing, Mirrei embroidering, and Shep watching cooking videos. Once everyone was settled and comfortable, Jhee sent for tea.

After tea, Jhee retired to her study. She shut the door, leaving her spouses to entertain each other. She went over to the corner and pulled out a gaming table. On it, she had replicated the tile board as it had been in her showdown with Medea. Jhee had examined the crime scene images and had a simulation of the scenario Medea had enacted recreated in exacting detail. She had ended the game on her turn by taking herself off the game board. Deep inside, though, she wondered. One more move, and it had meant death for one or other of her husbands.

Sharlet had sacrificed Shep. Kaisonia had discarded Kanto.

Jhee seated herself at the tile board, where she lifted the piece she had been holding. The game had ended on her turn because she had chosen not to choose. If she hadn't, could she have sacrificed one of her husbands as their families had? She stared at the board and contemplated her next move. She held the piece over the board.

The End: Book 3

Please, consider leaving an honest review on the bookseller's website, Goodreads, or BookBub so others can discover Justicar Jhee—and tell all your friends to download a copy as well.

ACKNOWLEDGMENTS

Adam C., Anne K., Elizabeth Frenette, Joe H., Melissa V., Michael S., Molly K., Tina P., Val A.

JOIN THE SWIFTNESSE COMMUNITY

~

Join the Swiftnesse Readers' Club to get a free copy of **Justicar Jhee and the Spectral Armada**, receive special offers, and hear about future books!
swiftnesse.com/spectral/

EXCERPT: JUSTICAR JHEE BOOK 4

Please enjoy this excerpt from Justicar Jhee Book 4…

Death sails the high seas… Only Justicar Jhee, the Empire's foremost magic-wielding sleuth, can stop it making landfall.

Justicar Jhee and her spouses continue to cope with the capital and its challenges to their unconventional family. When a body is discovered in the ruins of her wife's ancestral manor, they must return to their home district to confront ghosts of the past.

Chapter 1

The jailer beside Jhee signaled to the one in the booth. She tipped her hat, and then the gate in front of Jhee slid open.

"Sign in, please."

Jhee tapped her credentials against the visitor's log.

"All personal effects and minor items in the box, please." Jhee emptied her pockets, even those Kanto hid in the robe linings, and put them in the box. An instant manifest was generated that she had to sign off on. "Here's your claim ticket. You get them back at the end of the visit."

Another jailer gave her a quick pat down and sweep with a detection wand, then nodded to the other to show she didn't have any deadly items secretly hidden on her person. She wondered if Kanto's signature pockets would have gotten by them.

"You are an artificer, yes?" the warden asked.

"Yes," Jhee said.

"I'm not legally allowed to bind you, but I must ask that you refrain from any aggressive actions which might resemble cyphering or drawing. I'd also like you to wear this tag. It will change color in the presence of arcana. The guards are under strict instructions should any cyphering happen, both you and the prisoner will be subdued immediately. No exceptions. Do you understand these terms as I have given them to you?"

"Yes."

"Do you agree to abide by them?"

"I do."

"Good. Thank you for doing this, Justicar."

"I don't understand. She asked for me?"

"Ayup, that she did. You understand the position the throne is in. We would like to avoid a long drawn out messy trial. She offered to confess only if you were the one she could allocute to. Otherwise, she threatened to summon an army of advocates and solicitors which would have the crown tied up in courts and tribunals for years to come. She also threatened to name and shame the Imperial family. I've been asked to reiterate how much the Prince Regent prefers to avoid that and would take it as a personal favor if you could get her to confess."

If choosing the successor to the previous Empress had turned into a chill, bitter war, the Emperor's succession had been a hot and bloody one. A boy barely beyond his first jubilee had emerged as the winner.

The fallout from the IES and Medical Protectorate experiments still had yet to settle throughout the Blessed Isles. A great number of Imperials had died suddenly or took sudden retirements. Not everyone's involvement in IES business had come to light, but enough had that the rest ran scared. Jhee had half expected some mishap to have befallen Lady Vivyan-Rin Shodan before this. The heightened security was as much to keep her safe as to protect the public from her. Vivyan-Rin still must have some leverage.

Jhee entered the gray visitors' room. Vivyan-Rin was already there, shackled to the table. Vivyan-Rin wore the traditional prisoner's wrap robe. She leaned back and crossed her legs when the jailers shut the door behind Jhee. Jhee pulled out the chair opposite her and sat down.

"I'm glad you came. You should see the food. Nothing like even the simplest dish Shep could whip up. How is he doing, by the way? Has he swam his way back into the house or your bed yet?"

"What do you want?"

"I just wanted to see you again. How's your head feeling?"

Jhee regarded her with an ice-hard expression.

"You full slipped with a siren module in your head. We specifically screened against that when choosing siren module candidates. Wouldn't want it tearing its way through their brain and spinal column if they shifted. I'm so glad that didn't happen to you or that your head didn't explode back in Galleon City."

Jhee fought not to touch the surgery scar for her siren module. She had long since surmised the danger a templarite chain reaction might cause. The effect of an ill-advised skin slip, on the other hand. "I asked what you wanted."

"There is no need to be so unpleasant. How is your family? I meant it before when I said you had a lovely family. In another life, I could have seen myself with a family like that."

"They say you've offered to confess."

"Yes, that. They seemed keen on it." Vivyan-Rin held up her mangled hand. "They even had some very polite ladies ask me nicely."

Jhee swallowed. She felt a twinge in her fingers.

"But I don't want to talk about that. I saw you on the viewers the other day. read about you, too. I hear you will be a proud mama soon."

Jhee adjusted her robes and blanked her face to not give anything away.

"Don't be like that. It's so boring here. They won't let me near anything remotely sciencey. I guess they are afraid of what I can do with a little knowledge and ingenuity. And you know what? They're right."

Vivyan-Rin leaned forward and her eyes went dark umber. Jhee fixed Vivyan-Rin with a frigid stare while assessing the rooms' exits and objects either might use as weapons. The jailers faced them. One's hand hovered over a giant red button.

The madwoman tone faded from Vivyan-Rin's eyes. She grinned, leaned back, and held up her hands again. "As if I could artifice. I was never fantastic at cyphering or drawing in the first place. It's the practitioners like you who give us an awful name. They think we are all some mini goddess of arcana. Most of us can barely generate a spark. But then there are those like you. You have a thirst for it. Like I do for science."

"I understand the fear of magic. I understand why people distrust it. Yet, so far, the Empire's worst abuses were often done without it."

"Too true, Jhee. Too true. But if you believe it is Their design for us to know all and master all, you must also concede that I am also a part of it. My lack of conscience, a counter action, a correction to those who would never dare. I am the balancer of the equation."

Vivyan-Rin had been a brush with evil such as she had never experienced before in her entire career. Jhee recited statutes and cyphers in her head lest she forget herself. Her hands she kept still. Her normal habit of doing finger cyphering exercises might see the jailers rush the interview room.

"If you want to confess, confess. Why ask me here?" Jhee asked.

Vivyan-Rin feigned hurt. "I thought we had gotten close. That we understood each other. You should have killed me, Jhee."

"You belonged to the law."

"Drivel. Do you know why you couldn't? Because although you refused to admit it, we're the same. You had wanted to see the game play out. You wanted to know just like I did how the game would turn out. Which one of us would prevail. Who's will and wits and were stronger. Given the option of whether or not to play, you will always choose play. You will want to see it out to the bitter end. Even now you are still wondering how it would have turned out if we weren't interrupted. You can lie to yourself, and you can lie to everyone else, but you can't lie to me. I see through you."

"We're done here."

"Hardly, Jhee. We've only just begun."

"You murdered a pregnant woman."

"A pregnant woman, yes. Not the children inside her."

Jhee's lurched forward. "What?"

The jailers tapped on the glass. Jhee smoothed her robes.

"I figured that would get your attention," Vivyan-Rin said. "The Regent was always so short sighted in romantic matters. Two of my creations had bred. Most of you opted not to, or the procedures left you fallow. The Regent was fixed to wage war. She had determined to kill Ursula no matter what. Ursula went to her friendly, sympathetic counselor and confessed her fear for herself and her unbreached children. I hid her and took care of her. I made sure she and her offspring were safe until she gave birth. Of course, I had to protect the fruits of my experiments."

"Where are they?"

"I'll tell you, eventually. You just have to keep coming to visit me. Have them bring a recorder. I'm ready to give my confession now."

Jhee paused before fulfilling the request. "The face shifter mentioned something about my M-Prot records being expunged? I never did that."

"In due time. Now, you sit right down there and listen to me and take down everything I say."

Jhee sent for a recording device and a finger quill. "Shall we begin?"

Vivyan-Rin smiled. "It started back in the years before the Flower Wars."

More Coming Soon

*Thank you for reading this Book 4 excerpt! If you would like to read more, consider joining the **Swiftnesse Patreon community** – a tiered rewards program for avid readers and superfans. There you can get exclusive flash fiction and early access to scenes from my upcoming novels.*

ALSO BY TREVOL SWIFT

Justicar Jhee and the Cursed Abbey

Justicar Jhee and the Hole in The World

Justicar Jhee and the House of Sorrows

ABOUT THE AUTHOR

TREVOL SWIFT is a sometimes-sassy author of fantasy who grew up in Connecticut. She graduated from WIT with a BS in Computer Engineering Technology and now lives in Eastern Massachusetts. In her spare time Trevol enjoys gaming of all styles, cosplay, reading, writing and dancing. She also likes to relax by getting creative, with drawing and storytelling among her favorite pastimes.

Follow her on BookBub to get notifications of new book releases and sales:
    bookbub.com/authors/trevol-swift

You can also contact Trevol Swift at:

Website: swiftnesse.com

facebook.com/swiftnesse

pinterest.com/swiftnesse

twitter.com/Swiftnesse

instagram.com/swiftnesseauthor

www.ingramcontent.com/pod-product-compliance
Lightning Source LLC
Chambersburg PA
CBHW032152180726
48284CB00001B/8